A STUDY IN ASHES

Emma Jane Holloway

DEL REY • NEW YORK

2013 Del Rey Mass Market Original

Copyright © 2013 by Naomi Lester

Published in the United States by Del Rey, an imprint of The Random House Publishing Group, a division of Random House LLC, a Penguin Random House Company, New York.

DEL REY and the HOUSE colophon are registered trademarks of Random House LLC.

ISBN 978-0-345-53720-1
eISBN 978-0-345-54567-1

Printed in the United States of America

www.delreybooks.com

9 8 7 6 5 4 3 2

Del Rey mass market edition: January 2014

Praise for A STUDY IN SILKS

"This book has just about everything: magic, machines, mystery, mayhem, and all the danger one expects when people's loves and fears collide. I can't wait to return to the world of Evelina Cooper!"
—KEVIN HEARNE

"As Sherlock Holmes's niece, investigating murder while navigating the complicated shoals of Society—and romance—in an alternate Victorian England, Evelina Cooper is a charming addition to the canon."
—JACQUELINE CAREY

"Holloway takes us for quite a ride, as her plot snakes through an alternate Victorian England full of intrigue, romance, murder, and tiny sandwiches. Full of both thrills and frills."
—NICOLE PEELER, author of the Jane True series

"A Study in Silks is a charming, adventurous ride with a heroine who is both clever and talented. The brushes with the Sherlock Holmes mythos only add to the fun of this tale, and readers are bound to fall in love with Evelina and the London she inhabits."
—PIP BALLANTINE

"In A Study in Silks, Emma Jane Holloway has created a wonderful reimagining of the Sherlock Holmes mythos set in a late-Victorian Britain ruled by nefarious industrial titans called steam barons. Holloway's clever writing, attention to detail, and sublime characters forge a fascinating world that combines brass-plated steampunk technology with magic. By turns a coming-of-age story, a gas-lamp thriller, and a whimsical magical fantasy, A Study in Silks is the premier novel of an author to watch."
—SUSAN GRIFFITH

"Holloway stuffs her adventure with an abundance of characters and ideas and fills her heroine with talents and graces, all within a fun, brisk narrative."
—Publishers Weekly

By Emma Jane Holloway

A Study in Silks
A Study in Darkness
A Study in Ashes

The Baskerville Affair would never have
unfolded without the encouragement (and brilliance)
of my agent, Sally Harding,
and the patience, conviction, and edit letters
of the indefatigable Anne Groell.
Anne has read these manuscripts through more often than
any human being should ever be asked to
and still answers my emails,
which says everything about her pending sainthood.
Thank you, ladies;
this airship would never have flown without you.

I do, however,
extend apologies to the nineteenth century and
that dog of Arthur Conan Doyle's.

A STUDY IN ASHES

CHAPTER ONE

London, September 16, 1889

LADIES' COLLEGE OF LONDON

7:10 a.m. Monday

"YOU ARE NOT WELCOME HERE," SAID THE MAN IN THE QUIetly understated brown suit. "Forgive my blunt speech, but I cannot make it any more plain. Those of us on the faculty have established policies."

Those of us on the faculty. That meant this man who had interrupted her work was a professor. Evelina Cooper gripped her notebook until her knuckles hurt, wishing it was heavy enough to knock reason into his head. Surely he could see the equipment in this place was infinitely superior to what they had at the Ladies' College. And what harm was there in her using it? She wasn't in anyone's way.

The man waited for her to acknowledge his words—no doubt expecting swift obedience—but Evelina couldn't look at him. A painful knot lodged at the back of her throat, like a stillborn wail of frustration.

"I am happy to assist you in clearing away this equipment," he offered, "and we'll say no more about this incident."

Stubbornness made her stall, and she fiddled with the photograph slipping out from between the pages of her book, tucking it back into place. It was of her uncle Sherlock, his likeness no doubt at home between the ruled pages of formulae and lecture notes. *If someone had tried to toss Sherlock Holmes out of a lab, he would have knocked the offender down.* But young ladies were expected to be meek and mild.

Marginal politeness was a more attainable goal. "Your offer of assistance is kind, sir, and yet I don't understand why I can't use this facility."

"I think you do. None of the sciences are required for a Lady's Certificate of Arts." He swept a hand around the laboratory. "Therefore, all this is unnecessary for students of the female college."

"I protest that logic, sir." It came out stiff with displeasure, but Evelina knew she had lost.

"Miss, be reasonable."

"I am perfectly reasonable, sir, which is why I am astonished by this restriction." Evelina twisted her silver bracelets around, fingers alive with agitation.

Her gaze searched the high-ceilinged room, though there was nothing to find in the gray shadows. The laboratory, with its rows of tables and shelves of gleaming equipment, was empty this early in the morning. Most of the students were still groping for their second cup of tea. And the fact that the door to the lab had been locked hadn't slowed her down for more than half a minute.

He gave her a hard look from under beetling eyebrows. He wasn't one of the creaky old dons of the University of Camelin—not yet, anyhow—but he had perfected the glower. "Perhaps you should consider something in the line of elocution or moral philosophy."

Evelina bit her tongue. *Do my morals appear to need philosophy, sir? Outside of picking the lock, that is?*

The man harrumphed at her silence. "Domestic management, then. Or maybe literature." He pronounced the latter with a curl of the lip.

Evelina looked away before her temper led her down a regrettable path. She had powers this man had no idea about. She could command spirits of earth and tree. She had dabbled in sorcery and tasted death magic. She had nearly bled to death in a Whitechapel gutter and had made enemies and allies of some of the most powerful men in Mayfair—one of whom had bound her magic to his service with the pretty silver bracelets she was forced to wear. And yet she couldn't get a seat in a proper chemistry class.

At last, she let out a sigh. "I am an eager student of languages and literature, but I am here to study science."

"A worthy ambition," said the man. He might have bottled the tone and put it on the shelf next to the other dangerous acids. "But perhaps the practical work is a little beyond your scope."

Bugger that. Evelina's equipment was already set up to begin her exercise. Surely, if she got through it without a mistake, he would see she had a right to be there?

The exercise was of intermediate difficulty, a standard every serious student in the field was expected to know. She reached for the striker and, with a deft movement, lit the gas in the burner. A pale flame sprang to life, and she settled her flask of solution into place. Much depended on getting the exact proportion of alcohol to pure water, and then adding just the right amount of several organic compounds, but she'd measured carefully. "Your kind concerns about my abilities are unfounded, Professor . . . ?" She let the question dangle. The man hadn't given her his name.

But he knew hers. "Miss Cooper," he snapped, "turn down that flame at once!"

Months of frustration made her balk. She stiffened her posture and stood her ground. "I am here to study science. Therefore, I require access to equipment and materials."

More specifically, she was there to learn the connection between science and magic. Evelina's mother had been gentry, the younger sister of Sherlock and Mycroft Holmes, but Evelina's father had been a commoner and a carrier of magic. She'd yearned all her life to make sense of these two opposing legacies, because surely everything was ruled by the same natural laws. If she understood those, there was much she might understand about herself.

But first she had to learn the basics, which was why she had wanted a higher education. Of any place, a university should have been eager to throw open the doors to new ideas, but all she'd met so far was a wall of cold displeasure.

Never mind telling them about her magic—they still hadn't seen past the fact that she wore petticoats.

There was a tense moment of silence as the gas hissed and bubbles formed at the base of the liquid. The solution heated quickly, but not fast enough to calm her mounting temper. She could hear Professor No-name's quick, irritated breathing as he hovered uncertainly at her elbow—flummoxed by her insubordination but too outraged to back away.

She felt her stomach coil into an aching knot. Her fingers crushed the heavy, dark fabric of her skirts until she forced them to uncurl and pick up a glass wand, ready to stir her concoction. She kept her features deliberately bland, hoping that as long as she reined in her mood, she would have the upper hand. *That always works for Uncle Sherlock.*

Finally, No-name spoke. "I will say this one last time. Students of the Ladies' College of London are not permitted to use the Sir Henry John Bickerton Laboratory for the Advancement of Chemical Science."

"But are we not part of the university, along with the other colleges?" Evelina asked tightly. "I believe our tuition flows to the greater institution." Except that the students resident at the Ladies' College experienced shorter academic terms, had access to fewer courses, and were only granted an LCA rather than a proper bachelor's degree.

"The young men will someday attain positions of economic importance, whereas women will not. Squandering resources where they will never amount to anything is simply poor management."

Evelina couldn't stop herself from making a derisive huff as she measured out grains of crystalized aether onto a scale. The lime-green sand pattered into the steel pan. "Perhaps a sound understanding of the volatile properties of sodium bicarbonate will assist me in perfecting my muffins, Professor . . ." She let the name dangle once more, this time more rudely.

"Professor Bickerton. And this is my laboratory, young lady."

That surprised her enough that she spun to face him, spilling grains of aether onto the tabletop. *This dead squib is the mighty Bickerton?* If he'd made assumptions about her, she'd done the same to him. She smoothed her skirts with her free hand, a little flustered. The man held one of the most important faculty chairs at Camelin. "Sir!"

He adopted a lecturing stance, his hands clasped behind his back. "And I note you are attempting the reconstitution of crystalized aether into liquid form. What industries require liquid aether, Miss Cooper?"

Her brain stalled for a moment, then lurched forward awkwardly, like a poorly maintained engine. "Aeronautics, primarily. Also weapons manufacturing, cartography and exploration, and some forms of advanced telegraphy."

"You neglected to mention submersibles and a few branches of agriculture. Do you plan a career in any of these fields, Miss Cooper?"

"No, sir." She felt her cheeks heat.

"As I thought," he said with a twist of his mustached lip. "And what is the most salient point about liquid aether in the laboratory, Miss Cooper?"

She answered quickly, eager to redeem herself. "Aether is stable, which is why it has replaced hydrogen as the fuel of choice for dirigibles. But it will ignite if exposed to a steady, high heat. Ergo, one must be careful to regulate temperature to avoid combustion."

"Indeed. And the fact that your solution is at a rolling boil demonstrates your inability to translate theory into safe practice." He chose that moment to make a grab for the jar of salts.

"I would have turned down the heat!" *If you hadn't distracted me!* Already on edge, Evelina jerked at his movement, snatching the open container out of reach. Their hands collided and a thick plume of green salts flew into the air, coating the entire table and plopping into the bubbling solution.

"Bloody hell," she cursed before she could stop herself. Boiling aether equaled an explosion.

She felt Professor Bickerton's grip on her arm and was wheeling around to protest when he pulled her under the heavy oak table. She opened her mouth to complain, but the professor's weight shifted away, and then he was scrabbling at the floor, shutting off the valve that supplied gas to the worktables.

Terror made her entire body clench into a ball. Instinctively, Evelina raised her hands over her face. She squeezed her eyes closed as Professor Bickerton drew her closer, sheltering her with his arm. And then, right above them, the aether dissolved and came to a boil. She knew the moment it happened because the skin of her face went tight, and her ears popped. Then a blast of light turned Evelina's vision red through her eyelids—followed by the crash of glass and the rustling rush of flame. She felt rather than saw the rush of air like a wing sweeping across the laboratory, brushing aside everything in its path.

When Evelina uncoiled moments or years later, she felt deaf and blind, and her entire body was shaking. She scrambled out from under the table, boot heels catching in her skirts. Pages of her notebook fluttered to the floor like glowing feathers. With a pang, she thought of her photograph, but there was no chance it had survived.

Green flames licked across the work surface above, but her apparatus had been the only equipment in the path of destruction. In truth, the scene wasn't as bad as she'd expected, and that helped tame her panic. She stopped, gathering her wits and looking around for the heavy copper-sided fire extinguisher. The air was choking, the smoke heavy with the minty scent of aether distillate.

There! She lunged toward where the extinguisher sat at the front of the room. It was heavy, three gallons of liquid in a solid metal canister, but she heaved it onto a nearby table and depressed the plunger. Inside, a vial of sulfuric acid broke and mixed with sodium bicarbonate to create a carbon dioxide propellant that pressurized the water. Evelina aimed the hose at the flaming table, nearly catching Professor Bickerton as he rose.

She saw his eyes widen, his finger point. Her eyes followed the direction of the gesture and suddenly understood his wordless yelp of dismay. The flames were slithering around the fallen jar of aether salts where she had dropped it, and the container was open and still half full. If a generous pinch had done this much damage, what would twenty times that do?

Her throat closed as if a giant fist had clenched around it. She aimed the spray of water in the direction of the jar, hoping to at least stem the tide of destruction. The hose jumped in her hand, alive with pressure, but it wasn't enough. With a hungry green flame, the fire licked toward the jar, dancing along the worktable like an evil spirit. Somewhere outside the room, a bell was clanging. They were no longer the only ones aware of this catastrophe.

Her eyes met the professor's and she saw his face turn chalk-white. He dove for the door and she took her cue, dropping the hose and leaping toward the exit. They nearly collided.

"Run!" Evelina cried, and she pushed the man ahead of her. Cold certainty said they wouldn't make it out in time.

She turned at the last moment to summon her magic. She needed power, and she needed it fast; there was no time to summon a deva or weave a spell. That meant the more dangerous option of grabbing the fear-fueled energy already inside her and using sorcery.

She shuddered as the dark side of her power reared up, savage and ready to fight. It whispered of hunger, sliding through her with the deadly ease of a serpent—but it held the strength she needed. Evelina was backing away, aware that Professor Bickerton was almost through the door and yelling at her in confusion. He would have no idea what she was about to do, and with luck would never figure it out.

She raised her hands just as the contents of the jar ignited, sending shards and fire and crystalized aether in every direction. The shield of her power surged into place in time to deflect the shower of glass. Force jolted the shield, numbing her arms with the blow. She stumbled, falling to one knee, and braced for what came next, sending a fresh wave of magic surging forward. It wavered as it encountered the resistance of the bracelets, but steadied a second later; the barrier held. She reeled, giddy with the sensation.

Then the aether exploded in earnest, the airborne crystals

finding flame. Glass shattered throughout the room, the combustion crushing beakers and retorts, flasks and tubes, and a bank of locked cases filled with myriad substances in stoppered vials. The glass doors of the chemical stores burst in spinning shards, seeming to splash like water through the smoking air. Then the eruption of chemicals met a storm of fire, and the hammer of expanding gasses smashed into Evelina's protective shield and hurled her through the air.

She landed outside the laboratory door, her back smacking against the hard ground. A wave of sick dizziness rose up, making her head spin as a blast of heat raked over her skin. She rolled over, her hands over her head as the ground shuddered with an explosion. Hands grabbed her, hauling her to her feet and dragging her across the lawn. Her shoulder joints protested as she tripped on her hems and went down, slamming her palms into the ground. Her relentless rescuer heaved her back into a forward stagger.

"No, no, please, let me sit down," she murmured, but she couldn't hear her own voice. The blast had done something to her ears.

A fit of coughing took Evelina, her eyes and nose streaming from the fog of chemical stink. She fished for her pocket handkerchief, dimly aware that it was Professor Bickerton at her side. She was glad he was all right—even if his face was a peculiar shade of outraged purple as he shouted at her.

And then she began to understand part of what he was saying, because he was repeating it over and over again. "You foolish girl!" He was so angry, he was spewing saliva.

Evelina stopped, the will to move her feet deserting her. The incident hadn't been entirely her fault, but she could tell he was going to make it sound that way. She shut her eyes, exhausted. It was abundantly clear that she shouldn't have defied the man—and yet even now she recoiled at the idea of meekly abandoning her equipment and crawling away.

"I will see you expelled!" Bickerton finished with a roar loud enough to penetrate her stunned hearing.

Expelled! Her eyes snapped open. She clutched at her bracelets, knowing they bound her to this place for her own safety—because the alternatives for a magic user like her weren't good.

"You cannot!" she protested.

"Take note and learn, Miss Cooper." Then he turned on his heel and went to speak to the horde of men arriving to deal with the disaster.

Expulsion? What will Keating say? What will he do to me?

Jasper Keating, the man they called the Gold King, had soldered the bracelets around her wrist—a mark of his patronage and her prison. Wherever she went, the bracelets signaled her presence to Keating's minions, making her easy to find. They also delivered a painful shock if she strayed out of bounds. She was his property as surely as if she were in chains.

He was one of the steam barons, the foremost businessmen in the Empire with interests in everything from coal to war machines. He'd learned of her magic when she'd bargained away her freedom for the life of the man she loved. And now that he knew her secret, freedom was out of the question; magic users were under an automatic sentence of death.

He'd allowed her to attend the university as long as she never left the grounds. The arrangement was generous, given that the alternatives for someone with magical Blood were execution or a short, brutal future as a laboratory rat. And now—at least as far as public opinion went—she'd shown that his generosity was misplaced. Her patron did not like being in the wrong.

Another small explosion went off inside the burning building, letting out a cloud of stink and sparks. Evelina sank to the ground with a noise halfway between a groan and curse. *Mr. Keating is going to be very displeased indeed.*

CHAPTER TWO

TWO DAYS LATER, EVELINA LEFT THE LADIES' COLLEGE AND crossed the University of Camelin grounds toward the New Hall, which looked as if it was at least three hundred years old. Plane trees lined the narrow, cobbled road, their wide leaves giving a dry rustle in the light breeze. Though the air was cool, the afternoon sun and the rising slope of the path made her warm, and she paused to catch her breath.

She had been here nearly a year. The weather brought back the previous autumn, when Keating had first forced her into his service. The job had taken her into the slums of Whitechapel, but it had also reunited her with her childhood sweetheart, Nick. She turned her face up to the sunlight, feeling its warmth even as her chest tightened with grief. After so many years of coming together and parting over and over, Nick had finally become her lover.

She remembered him as a boy, brown-skinned and fleet among the horse-wagons, teasing her as he took the last of Gran Cooper's thick brown bread. He'd make her chase him for it, her shorter legs struggling to keep up, but he'd always surrendered it in the end. She remembered him performing in the ring of Ploughman's Paramount Circus, daring impossible feats with his flashing knives. And she remembered him as he was when he left her, promises to return warm upon his lips. He was an outlaw and finally, after so long, her lover: Captain Niccolo, pirate, last seen on the *Red Jack* as it careened in flames to earth.

That battle that had changed everything. She'd traded her freedom to save Nick's airship from Keating's guns, but her sacrifice had come to nothing. Nick was dead, she was a prisoner, and the last year had been the loneliest of her life. Though it would have ruined her in the eyes of Society, a child would have left her at least something of the man she loved—but even that comfort had been denied her.

And alone, she would go to face the consequences of the laboratory accident. Grief clawed its way up Evelina's throat. She squeezed her eyes tight to hold back tears. *If I give in and cry, I might not stop.* She bit her lips together, refusing to let them tremble. It was a battle she quickly lost. Tears leaked from under her eyelashes, and she hurriedly wiped them away. The last thing she wanted was to stand before her judges red-eyed and sniffling.

This won't do. She had to go on; Nick himself would demand no less. Despondent, she began walking again, the soft soles of her boots scuffing on the cobbles. She blinked away the last wetness from her eyes and looked around, hoping no one had seen her moment of weakness.

To her right were the mellow stone arches of Fullman College, to her left Usher College with Witherton House and its regal gardens behind. Gowned faculty clustered around the buildings like crows, but this close to the heart of the university they were an almost exclusively male flock. The Ladies' College of London was at the bottom of the hill, secure behind high walls. It was part of the university, and not.

Rather like her—and based on Professor Bickerton's harangue after the explosion, soon she wouldn't be part of Camelin at all. If this summons to the vice-chancellor's office unfolded as she suspected it would, her academic career would set before the sun did. *And then what?* Would she go back to working as a spy, or something worse? She couldn't bring that future into focus. Every time she tried, her breath grew short.

Evelina noticed several conversations breaking off as curious faces turned her way. She looked over her shoulder, making sure there was nothing behind her that was attracting attention. That gave her a view of the lower campus, the blackened shell of the laboratory conspicuous against the pastoral green. Sick, cold dread settled in her gut, driving out the warmth of the sun. She tucked in her chin, letting the brim of her hat hide her face as she marched the remaining distance to the entrance of the New Hall. The watching faces followed her as if pulled by a magnetic force. *There goes the silly woman who blew up the laboratory.* As she neared the door, she shuddered, the touch of their gazes an almost palpable pressure along her spine.

Once inside, she mounted the stairs to the offices, her stomach a leaden ball of apprehension. Marie Antoinette could not have felt less doomed as she climbed the scaffold. But Evelina bravely knocked and entered the vice-chancellor's chambers. When the young man who was his secretary rose to show her into the inner sanctum, she followed him with her gloved hands clasped nervously at her waist.

The decor did nothing to lighten the mood; the walls were covered in dark walnut paneling made darker still by age. As she crossed the faded carpet, the smell of old tobacco rose up, tickling her nose. Three men were ranged in a conversational semicircle of oxblood leather chairs. In her anxiety, she had half imagined a judge's bench and uniformed guards, so the informality was a relief.

They rose as she entered. Bickerton was one, and another was old, white-whiskered Sir William Fillipott, the vice-chancellor. The older man bowed, his manners as always impeccable. "Miss Cooper, how gracious of you to join us."

"Sir." She curtsied, long training helping her to fall into the ritual of pleasantries. She'd always got along with Sir William, and hoped that counted for something now.

"You have met Professor Bickerton." The vice-chancellor gave a rueful smile, and then indicated the third member of his party. "And this is young James, our new chair of mathematics. I have asked him to observe and record this meeting."

Sir William patted the mathematician's shoulder with a

fond, fatherly gesture. The man nodded politely to Evelina, adjusting a small clockwork device that inscribed a squiggling code onto a wax cylinder. She had seen the police use similar equipment for taking statements. The brass contraption with its whirling gears was not the latest technology, but it was advanced for Camelin, steeped as it was in tradition.

The young professor had nutmeg-brown hair and a tidy mustache. His lean build and fastidious air reminded Evelina of Uncle Sherlock. She was sure she'd seen his face before, though she could not remember where. On the campus? She didn't think so. Memory itched at her like a healing cut.

Sir William gestured toward another chair, arranged to face the three men. "Please, Miss Cooper, have a seat."

"I'm sure you know why you are here, Miss Cooper," Bickerton began. "What do you think will be the outcome of this interview?" The man gave a hint of a smile, and she didn't like it one little bit.

Evelina sat with all the grace she could muster. When she opened her mouth to speak, her throat was so tight she could barely breathe. She cleared it as delicately as she could and tried again. "I would not presume to anticipate your judgment."

Sir William frowned, both at her and at Bickerton. "Even if no one was seriously injured and even if it was accidental, this was a grave occurrence. Can you please tell me, Miss Cooper, why you were in that laboratory?"

Bickerton snorted, but Evelina was grateful to Sir William for asking. "The Ladies' College does not have as good a facility or equipment. Nor does it offer the same level of instruction in the sciences. What we get are shorter, less demanding classes that do not teach us nearly as well."

The vice-chancellor's bushy white brows shot up. "And so you took it upon yourself to break into our laboratory and help yourself to the men's equipment?"

Bickerton leaned forward. "A criminal act, I might point out."

"Let the girl speak," said Sir William.

"If no one was willing to instruct me at the level I desired, it seemed I must help myself to advance." Even as she said it, Evelina felt her cheeks heat, alarm trickling through her insides. It sounded so high-handed, but solving the problem on her own had been a natural response. "At the time, it did not seem so rash an act."

"Let me assure you, it was extremely rash." Sir William's tone was dry. "I know the destruction of the lab was not your intent, but bad action inevitably leads to bad results. For shame, Miss Cooper—for you clearly *did* intend to flout our rules, and see what came of it."

And yet it really had seemed like a reasonable solution. In the last year and a half, she'd been in too many dire situations, with her life on the line, to bother with rules. Yet somehow that recklessness had trickled down to her everyday conduct. Her goal was to learn everything she could to understand her powers in a scientific light. The lock on the laboratory door had just been another obstacle to overcome and she had conquered it. Such a will to succeed might be heroic, but she had to admit that it hadn't been smart.

"There is no apology that I can make that will be sufficient to the situation," she said, meaning every word. "And yet I do apologize. I am wholeheartedly sorry."

The transcription device whirred and bobbled, writing down her guilt and contrition. The professor operating it watched her with cool, appraising eyes.

"Prettily said, Miss Cooper," Sir William replied, "but Professor Bickerton has requested your expulsion, and he is within his rights to do so."

She drew breath, ready to launch into her defense, but Sir William held up a quelling hand. "However, there are a number of factors that come into play, including the wishes of your patron."

"Does he know?" she asked meekly.

Now she felt her fingers tremble, and she clasped them in her lap. Jasper Keating could buy the University of Camelin a dozen times over, but he could also crush her like a gnat. She couldn't assume anything, least of all his tolerance for failure. The last time she'd worked for him, she'd nearly been killed. If he lost interest in her, he could order her death in an eye blink.

"Mr. Keating is aware of what has happened." Sir William reached behind him and picked up a letter from the desk, unfolding it slowly with the thumb and fingers of one hand. He glanced down at it and let the paper curl shut again, his expression carefully neutral. "He responded in no uncertain terms."

Nerves made her temper grow sharp. She fingered her bracelets, picturing her patron's hard, patrician face. "And?"

"You are a fortunate young woman. He is desirous that you remain here."

She might have been relieved, but the way Sir William said it left room for doubt. She inched forward on her seat. "You said there were a number of factors. What are the others?"

"We must consider the wishes of the governing body of this institution. The chancellor in particular."

At least there had been no mention of magic, which meant Bickerton hadn't figured out how he'd lived through the explosion—and that meant, in turn, she might survive. Still, the situation was bleak. Some would align with Bickerton, and yet others dared not offend the Gold King. He owned too many important men and could easily scuttle university endowments. *And here I am, the cause of discord.* "I assume, then, it will take time before my fate is decided?"

"It will be discussed at the end of the month, during the governing council's usual meeting."

As Sir William spoke, Bickerton looked like he'd swallowed one of his own chemical preparations. "An unnecessary waste of time in my opinion. I say make the decision now."

Part of her agreed. Waiting for judgment would be excruciating. "Is there nothing I can do to redeem myself?"

Sir William frowned, his lined face stern and sad. "It is a question of principle. Mr. Keating has offered a sum in recompense for the damage to our facility, but there is more at stake than mere money. The sovereignty and dignity of our institution is at risk."

Evelina lowered her eyes, staring at her gloves. She'd put on clean ones to come here, but somehow still managed to get a smudge of ink on one finger. She curled her hand closed to hide it. *How am I going to get out of this?*

Sir William leaned forward, his hands on his knees. "My advice to you in this interval is to behave as a lady ought, to study what you are assigned, and not to rearrange the natural boundaries of custom to suit yourself."

Feeling suddenly ill, Evelina slowly sat back in her chair. It was a simple command, and yet unpalatable. She was already confined to the campus. He was taking away the one liberty the university offered—the freedom to learn.

"And you will confine yourself to the precincts of the Ladies' College. You are to remain within its walls."

What? She looked up, meeting Sir William's stern gaze and Bickerton's mocking smirk. "Not leave the college?" Her voice was high and incredulous. "Not even to walk the rest of the campus?"

"It will spare the feelings of the faculty if they know you are not loose upon the grounds," Sir William replied. "Especially since locks are apparently no obstacle to you."

Unless of course I'm trying to escape altogether. But the bracelets took care of that.

"I see," she said faintly. Bloody hell, she would be penned into a tiny area, just the quadrangle and the buildings around it. She lifted her chin, her face numb with dismay. "That is going to make my world a very small one."

"But at least it is still a foothold at Camelin," Sir William said gravely. "Do not slip again, Miss Cooper, lest you fall entirely. The University Council will make its decision in the fullness of time, and how you adapt to these rules will count for much."

"Or perhaps not at all," Bickerton added tightly.

"Professor," Sir William chided, "let penitence do its work."

Evelina bowed her head, her rueful anger an open wound. If it weren't for the bracelets and the threat the Gold King posed to her loved ones, she would have simply walked away. She'd disappeared once; she could do it again. "I will do my best, Sir William. You may rely on that."

"Very well. And now it is time that you retired to meditate upon your actions." Sir William rose, the others following his lead. "James here will escort you to your rooms."

"Miss." The man switched off his device and rose. Then he gave an almost mocking bow and held out his arm.

Evelina felt her eyes widen in shock. Now she remembered where she'd seen the man before. *It's Mr. Juniper!* She had seen him almost a year ago, when she'd been sneaking through the compound where the Blue King kept his war machines hidden. Juniper was the Blue King's man of business, and therefore one of Keating's bitter enemies.

The memory brought a fresh flood of loss, remembering her hand in Nick's as they crept unseen through enemy territory. Her body tensed as she clamped down hard on her emotions. Nick was gone, and she had to focus on the threat in front of her. *Does Juniper recognize me? Does he know it was me who stole the designs for the Blue King's weapons?*

She could feel the three men watching her, and quickly hid her confusion. "Then I will bid you good day, gentlemen," she said with a neat curtsy.

The men bowed—Bickerton with a perfunctory jerk, Sir William with gravity. Steeling herself, she took Mr. Juniper's arm and let him lead her from the room and down the stairs.

Juniper gave a small, cold smile as they left the New Hall. "I see that I am familiar to you, Miss Cooper. No doubt your association with Mr. Keating has acquainted you with many players surrounding the Steam Council."

"Only in a modest way." If he believed that she knew him through Keating, it was far safer than the truth.

He led her along the path with a casual air, as if they were just out for a stroll. In the afternoon sun, his face seemed pale to the point of translucence, blue veins visible beneath the fine skin of his temples. "And so here we are. Academia makes strange bedfellows."

She couldn't argue with that. "How did you come to be here?"

"Ambition," he said, without the least embarrassment. "I have been working on a binomial theorem. Perhaps I shall publish a treatise. A university chair gives me credibility in a way that a steam baron's patronage could not."

It still seemed a strange leap from managing a steam baron's business affairs, especially since the Blue King held sway over the poorest parts of the city. "It seems you are a man of hidden talents."

"We share that quality in common, though your abilities are far more controversial than mine. Oh yes," he said, smiling at her fresh surprise, "I know what those bracelets you wear mean. Most students just think they're prisoners here. You are chained in fact, bound to do Keating's bidding whenever he finally chooses to crook his finger."

Evelina was speechless for a long moment. "How do you know about that?"

Juniper narrowed his eyes. "Think about it. The public version is that you are a ward of sorts to Mr. Keating. No mention of magic is made in the official records. Still, you must know by now that you are watched, and not just by Keating's pet thugs."

"What do you mean?" She tried to pull away, but he grasped her more tightly, keeping her arm linked through his.

"Word of your talents has got out, Miss Cooper. There are those on the Steam Council who know where you are." He stopped walking. They were almost to the gates of the Ladies' College, but still far enough away that no one else was close enough to hear his words. "Both you and Bickerton should have been blown to pieces. How did you do it, Miss Cooper? I've always wanted to know how sorcery works."

Evelina shielded her eyes from the sun, studying his sharp features. He might have been handsome but for an unpleasant glitter in his eyes. "Are you really here for your theorem, or did the Blue King send you?"

His smile made her pulse skip, and not in a good way. "I have my eye on many interests, Miss Cooper. The steam barons are titans, and they will go to war with one another before long."

"I think that is common knowledge."

"Perhaps." He finally released her arm. "In any event, creatures like you and I will be looking to our own survival once it happens."

She almost smiled. "Are we not doing so now?"

"A valid point, Miss Cooper. You are as astute as you are troublesome." A flock of birds flashed across the sun, their wings casting a fluttering shadow. Juniper looked up, seeming almost uneasy. "Nevertheless, I would be very careful to watch my back if I were you."

"I always do." Evelina turned away. Juniper was trying to lay the groundwork for something, with his dark observations and half confidences, and she wasn't having any of it. She began walking again, returning the conversation to safer territory. "But my chief concern at the moment is my education. I have to say the entire college experience has been a severe disappointment."

His bright gaze darted toward her. "How so?"

"I've been to one finishing school already. I did not come here to learn flower arranging and domestic economy."

Juniper laughed softly to himself. "Then allow me to do you a favor, Miss Cooper, in the name of equitable education. Tutors can be arranged, as can a modest amount of scientific equipment. As a member of the faculty, I will gladly provide you with anything that is not poisonous or combustible. For the time being, that should satisfy your needs and those of the administration both." He pulled out a silver case and extracted a calling card. "Make a list of what you need and send it to me. I will do what I can to ease the burden of good behavior."

She took the card from him, still wary. "And why would you do me this favor?"

"Because someday I may need one from you. I am still at the start of my career and building my capital. Do not look for complications where they do not exist." He gave a slight bow. "And here we are at your gate. Good day, Miss Cooper."

"Good day, Mr. Juniper."

"Ah." He gave a slight grin—a real one this time—gesturing toward the card. "I do not use that name here. Arnold Juniper has nothing to do with my career as a professor of mathematics."

Evelina inclined her head. "I stand corrected, sir. It seems a nom de guerre is de rigueur these days."

"As is schoolroom French."

"Touché."

And with a last tip of his tall hat, Mr. Juniper left her there, his tall, slim frame elegant in the mellow sunshine.

At last Evelina turned to enter the gates to the Ladies' College of London. Reluctance seized her, but there was no option but to obey. She shivered as the lock clanged behind her with a sound like the snap of iron jaws. *Here I am, and here I shall stay.* At least, until she discovered a way out. Evelina walked slowly across the quadrangle of the college, disgusted with everything. *Surely I can do better than this.*

Only then did she pause to read Juniper's card: *Professor James Moriarty.* She slipped it into her reticule without another thought. The name meant nothing to her, except that he looked more like a James than an Arnold.

CHAPTER THREE

TOBIAS ROTH SAT AT HIS SISTER'S BEDSIDE. IMOGEN SLEPT AS she always did, still and pale as a marble effigy. *Good God, Im, what happened to you?*

It wasn't a new question, and he had no new answers. Though the space was quiet and dim, there was tension in the air of the sickroom. Tobias likened it to a hunter with a drawn bow—muscles quivering, breath held, gaze sharp on the target. But when would the string release, and where was that arrow going to land?

There was no telling when the wait would end. Imogen had been like this for nearly a year, sunk deep into this artificial sleep. She was lovely to look at, her long, straight hair the gold of a summer wine, or sun on ripe wheat. And yet that beauty was like a photograph, factually accurate but capturing little of the woman who was his sister. It didn't show the flash of Im's eyes as she teased him, or the flight of her fingers as she played the pianoforte. The real woman had been stolen away. Surely magic was involved— otherwise, she would be dead. But why wouldn't she wake? And if she did, what would happen?

Tobias rose, apprehension driving him from his chair. He wasn't even sure what the hunter and his arrow meant in his analogy—bad luck, retribution, fate—but he knew it didn't bode well. He crossed the room to look out over the back garden of Hilliard House. The light was fading, and he was restless with worry that the damned bolt would end his sister's life. He had tried to protect her, to rescue her, and he'd failed. There were fairy tales about maidens struck down by poisoned apples and wicked fairies, but he suspected it was something even darker that had wounded Imogen.

And yet suspicion was useless. The concrete facts in the case could be counted on one hand. Imogen had tried to elope. The sorcerer Dr. Magnus had plucked her from the street and taken her to his black, dragon-prowed airship, the *Wyvern*. Two other ships had pursued Magnus through the skies over London: a pirate vessel named the *Red Jack,* and Keating's ship, the *Helios*. Tobias had led a rescue party from the latter and had got Imogen back. The mission should have been a success.

But it was at that point in the narrative that everything gave way to conjecture, leaving any real evidence far behind—and there was no way to know if what he saw and heard had been true. No one else was there that night except Imogen, and she couldn't help him now.

Tobias's memory of that night was never far, like a hidden stream that flooded the space between conscious thoughts, biding its time until it could drown him in nightmares. It didn't take much to hurl him back to that hell:

Last November aboard the airship <u>*Helios*</u>

FLAME CURLED THROUGH the blackness, unfolding into the night sky like the petals of a fat crimson peony.

The explosion was beautiful, Tobias thought wildly, in the way that a tiger is beautiful right before it makes an hors d'oeuvre of one's head. His gut twisted, but ordinary fear seemed a paltry response to the occasion. The charge had detonated just off their bow, close enough to feel the heat and the slap of air pressure. There were at least two airships intent on blowing the Helios to bits—and he didn't fancy a fiery plunge to the spangled gaslights of London far below.

Another roar shook the deck, deafening passengers and crew. Imogen stumbled into him, her footing lost. Tobias grabbed his sister, as much to support himself as her. He thought he heard the crack of wood, and it couldn't have been more terrifying had it been his own bones. The entire ship was shuddering, propellers useless against the blast.

"That's a bit close!" he barked at the captain, but the man was bawling orders to the gunners and paid him no mind. Tobias had played his part in the fight already, and had gone from mission commander to irrelevant annoyance in the time it had taken to rescue his sister from the enemy and return to the ship.

"Come on." He dragged Imogen closer to the cabins, looking for shelter. But then another strike hit, knocking them both off their feet. Tobias hit the deck, the force of impact shooting up his arm and into his shoulder. Imogen collapsed in a heap beside him. Ignoring the pain, Tobias put his arm around his sister's shoulder, drawing her to a sitting position. They sat huddled in the shelter of a locker, drawing their feet in to stay out of the path of running airmen.

It felt as if they were Hansel and Gretel, hiding from the monsters. The comparison wasn't as far off as he'd have liked. "What did Magnus want with you?" he shouted over the cries of the crew.

Like him, Imogen was tall, fair, and gray-eyed, but she'd gone from slender to frail in these last difficult months. She shook her head. "I don't think he cared about me. I was bait. He counted on a rescue."

Tobias understood. Besides him, someone else had come to save the day—the infamous pirate vessel, the Red Jack. *Captain Niccolo—Nick—had personally delivered Imogen from danger, a noble gesture that might cost him all. He'd put the miraculous navigational device aboard the* Red Jack *within reach of his foes, and now both Magnus and the captain of the* Helios *were intent on taking the pirate ship prize.*

"Tobias!" Imogen gripped his arm, surprisingly strong in her panic.

Tobias tightened his protective hold. "What is it?"

She pointed upward. A net of ropes attached the balloon to the wooden gondola beneath. In the heat of battle, the ropes looked as flimsy as a spiderweb—and they were on fire. Imogen's eyes flared with horror.

Tobias pushed down the panic that crawled up his throat, forcing logic around his thoughts. It was like stuffing an octopus into a teacup. His breath was already coming a little too fast. "The fire is not as bad as it looks."

"Oh?" Imogen's voice steamed with sarcasm.

"Look, there are already men up there putting it out." Or at least they were trying—little ants with little buckets in the vast tangle of rigging. "Warships like this one use aether distillate, which has better lift and is much less explosive than hydrogen. The ship is far safer than you would think."

"I hope you're right," she said grimly, "but at the rate this is going, we don't have much time to talk. You need to know what I learned aboard Magnus's ship before we shower down in gory droplets over Buckingham Palace."

Tobias opened his mouth to reply, but then grabbed her as the Helios *fired on the* Wyvern, *the recoil jolting the deck. Grit and soot crunched between his teeth and his ears sang with the noise of explosion. More airmen stampeded past, their uniforms tarnished with ash and sweat. He saw them hauling out the huge, copper-sided water guns, pointing hoses at the burning rigging, but the wind of the ship's movement was fanning the flames.*

The Wyvern *was turning, gun ports swinging into view. The black ship was hard to see against the starry sweep of the sky, but the red eyes and smoldering jaws of the dragon-shaped figurehead leered like a demon in the dark.*

"Ready harpoons!" the captain bawled, and the gunners scrambled. The flaming projectiles they called hot harpoons could turn a ship into a bonfire in minutes. It meant a ruthless, horrible death for the crew.

And those harpoon guns were only a dozen yards away, the sweating gunners muttering prayers to whatever dark gods they worshipped. A misfire with a harpoon would kill anyone who came too close.

"Let's go," Tobias said, jumping up and pulling his sister toward the cabins. He'd meant to ensure Imogen was safely away from battle as soon as he'd set foot on deck, but there hadn't even been time for that before the cannonades had begun.

She stumbled against him as he ran, gripping her hand too tightly in his fear. He banged through the hatch to the cabin deck, grateful when the door closed and muffled the noise. It wasn't the best place to be if the rigging burned through, but it was safer than being on deck while the harpoons were in play.

The main corridor on the Helios was narrow and claustrophobic. A long, yodeling scream came from the far end where the taciturn surgeon ruled his white-walled domain. Imogen flinched at the noise, making a tiny cry of her own, and Tobias pulled her in the other direction, away from the sound. The amount of blood on the floor said the surgeon already had more than one customer.

Tobias pushed open doors until he found a tiny room at the fore with a table and two chairs. Imogen fell onto the closest seat, clearly exhausted. It was the first moment he'd seen his sister in good light since her rescue. Her hair was falling from its pins in a straggle of wheat-blond wisps. Tears tracked her cheeks, leaving pale stripes through smudges of soot.

Tobias's emotions, bludgeoned into numbness, stirred back to life. If he had possessed the least talent with those harpoons, he would have cheerfully smashed Magnus from the sky.

"I know that look," Imogen said.

"What look?"

"Your older brother look." A smile stirred her features, the merest flicker of her usual self. "But right now, I need you to listen, not to thump the schoolyard bully. You've already done the brave thing by coming to fetch me."

"Your pirate captain saved you," Tobias said, surprised by his own bitterness. Had he needed to play hero that badly? Lord knew he needed redemption, but still . . .

"Nick isn't mine," Imogen said. *"He's in love with my dearest friend. And he might have got to me first, but you brought me back here. Yet none of that matters now. There are more dire matters than our pride."*

Her voice rang whip-sharp in the silence between explosions. Imogen was normally soft-voiced and graceful, the perfect image of femininity. This mood was something new. Frowning, Tobias sat across the small table, close enough that he reached out to touch her cheek. She took his hand, squeezing until her nails bit his skin. Something boomed overhead, and dust fell from the ceiling with a sound like rain on dry leaves.

"Listen," she said, her voice quick and low. *"Magnus has automatons like I've never seen before. They're far more refined. I suppose one might almost say beautiful. One of them was named Serafina."*

Tobias swallowed, his mouth tasting of blood and smoke. *"I know. I saw her once."* The memory of the thing, seemingly alive, still made his flesh creep.

Imogen's expression crumpled, her face growing pink with emotion. *"I shot her to pieces! I killed her."*

Tobias blinked, putting his other hand over hers. *"However realistic she might have looked, she was just a machine."*

Imogen's eyes went wide, the gray irises translucent through her tears. *"She was alive. And quite mad, but that was the least of it. Magnus had altered her in terrible ways. He had Father's old automatons, too. And what Father said about Anna, Tobias . . ."*

It was clear that she would have said more, but a jolt shuddered through the ship, bumping Tobias like a cart hitting a rut. The rigging. It well might have been giving way. He jumped up, throwing open the locker near the wall. This was where parachutes should be stored and, sure enough, there were half a dozen stacked neatly inside. He picked one up, hating to interrupt Imogen but more worried about getting her safely home.

Another roar rocked them where they sat. Tobias grabbed

for the wall, losing his grip on the parachute. Imogen started to fall, and he caught her, her thin body so light he might have crushed her with the gentlest squeeze. He could feel the tension knotting her frame, leaving her quivering like a harp string. As the ship tilted to evade the attack, a glass decanter slid across the table with a rasp. Tobias noted with acute regret that it was empty.

"What's happening?" Imogen demanded in a tiny voice.

Tobias let go of her and rose to peer out the window. The cabin wasn't quite tall enough to stand up straight, so he felt like a creature peering out of its burrow. He had a good view of the starscape, the blackness shrouded by veils of smoke. He squinted in one direction, then shifted to see the other way. Fire. But this time, it wasn't coming from their ship. The hot harpoons had done their work.

Nausea crawled up his throat, but he wiped it from his voice. "The Wyvern's *ablaze. So is the* Red Jack. *We must be winning."*

Guilt clawed him. All those crewmen were burning. He tried to put the image aside, but failed, breaking into a sickly sweat. Truly, he should have been glad the Helios *had the upper hand, but all he felt was a different shade of panic. Before he could close his eyes, he saw crewmen leaping from the* Jack, *so desperate to avoid the flames that they would brave empty air. He hoped to God they had parachutes, too.*

"Nick's ship has been hit?" Imogen said with alarm. She was up in a moment, pushing him out of the way to see out the window. Her hand beat against the window, a single, hopeless gesture followed by a strangled noise from deep in her throat. "But he saved me! Does that mean nothing?"

"It's a pirate ship."

"He still saved me!"

Tobias's hands made fists. Sorrow rose, lashed by anger at the despair in her voice. She was right, there would be no justice. They had their orders. They were to capture the Red Jack—*preferably intact, but lightly toasted would have to do. "Nick has a special navigation tool. Keating wants it for himself, and what Keating wants, he gets. The* Helios *is his ship to order."*

Imogen put both hands to her mouth. "Does Nick stand a chance?"

Tobias looked inside himself and found a wasteland. "No. He's a pirate, and he stole the device from Keating in the first place. If he's caught, he'll be hanged. If he dies tonight, at least he's free." Even as he said it, he hated himself. "He'd like that better, I think."

"Is that why Keating sent you? For the spoils of war?"

When did you get so worldly-wise? *Tobias wondered sadly.* When Father denied you a love match so that he could use your beauty to lure rich suitors? *Suddenly he remembered that Imogen had been eloping when Magnus had grabbed her. She'd dared everything—a bright flame fighting the wind—and lost.*

She pressed her forehead against the glass of the window.

He hardened his heart before he started to weep himself. "Put on one of those parachutes. We need to be ready to evacuate."

But Imogen looked up slowly, the delicate lines of her face in silhouette against the blaze of the Wyvern. *Her features were shadowed in muted sepia and gray, the combination of night and the afterglow of destruction. "Then we don't have much time, and you need to hear this. Magnus had put Anna's soul inside Serafina, and she used that body to try to kill me. She was jealous that I had lived. Tobias, she was still alive."*

The words skimmed past Tobias, refusing to catch hold. Or maybe he shoved them away because they were too awful. "What are you saying?"

Her lips parted to answer.

The next instant, the Wyvern *exploded, a flash of orange flaring outward from the midpoint of the gondola. A tiny part of Tobias's mind—the part that thrived on mechanics and technical theory—decided it was a malfunction of the aether distiller, brought on by excessive heat. A moment later, the enormous black balloon went up in a billow of white-hot fire, scorching what was left of the sleek gondola to ash.*

Imogen's eyes flared wide, meeting his with an expression of astonishment so profound that Tobias looked over his shoulder to see what was the matter. There was nothing, the tiny room exactly as it had been a minute before. Yet as he turned back, she was falling, folding up like a scarf tossed carelessly to the floor. He barely caught her in time to ease her down.

"Imogen?" he cried. "Im, what's the matter?"

She was shuddering, fighting against a force ravaging her body.

Tobias fell to his knees and bent over his sister, pulling off his jacket to cushion her head. "Surgeon!" he bellowed. "Surgeon, come quickly!"

She whimpered, her back bowing as if in some terrible agony. Her fingers clutched at him, her eyes holding his as if his gaze alone was keeping her tethered to her body.

"Stay with me!" he urged. "Imogen, hang on. You know you can. You're strong."

But her eyes slowly closed, the light in them dimming as if someone had turned down the wick inside her. Fear struck deep and true, shredding him to the quick. There was little he counted on anymore, but he counted on Im. She was all that remained of an innocence he'd lost.

"Surgeon!" he bawled, but the man never came.

The ship jolted again, and he knew the rigging was about to give way. He could feel the ship descending and he could only pray they'd reach the ground before they fell. And yet that wasn't the thing he feared most right then.

His hands turned chill and clammy, clumsy as paws as he held his sister, trembling as the battle—barely worth noticing now—raged on outside. "Im?"

Her lips moved, her voice so faint he was sure he'd misheard it. "Im?"

She spoke again, and this time he bent close, putting his ear close to her mouth. "Surely I killed you?"

And then she did not speak again.

CHAPTER FOUR

Visitors to London never fail to be charmed by the many-colored globes of the gaslights illuminating the public streets. Swaths of gold, green, and blue glow along the horizon, an exotic panorama of the modern age. But these delights to the eye serve a practical purpose, each hue indicating which utility supplies their gas. The owners of these companies are therefore known by the colors of their gaslights—the Gold King, the Green Queen, the Blue King, and so forth. It is an altogether quaint custom that goes far to enhance the air of charm and eccentricity already inherent in Londontown.

—*The Serendipitous Armchair:*
A Gentleman's Travelling Companion to London,
2nd edition

Mother Empire is held hostage, bound and weeping, to Industrial Vampires known as the steam barons. GOLD, GREEN, BLUE, or SCARLET, they monopolize railways and manufactories, coal mines and docks. Merchants must pay to sell their wares while the POOR PERISH in the DARK and COLD. Let it be understood that the only recourse to this TYRANNY is WAR.

—Political pamphlet, Baskerville Rebellion, 1889

THE MEMORIES OF THAT NIGHT WERE STILL WITH TOBIAS AS he walked through a dark alley, a peculiar strain of horror plucking at his soul. Anna had been Imogen's twin, and she'd died young. Lord Bancroft, their father, had confessed that he'd attempted to save Anna by allowing Magnus to transfer her soul into an automaton. That she'd survived and tried to kill Imogen . . . but that was where his mind ducked sideways, refusing to engage. Had that truly been what he'd heard Imogen say? If it was, then what was he supposed to do about it? Magnus and all his creations had burned up that night. But then what had Imogen's final words meant? *Surely I killed you.* Had she meant Anna?

A prickling of alarm surged through him, as it always did when he reached this point in his thoughts. Had Anna somehow touched Imogen at the very end? Was that the reason Imogen was ill? This was why Tobias hated magic with a virulent revulsion. It didn't make sense, but then it did. The logic appealed to a dark, hidden part of himself that was more frightening than any fireside tale. And in those terrible moments, he felt strangely like the Grail King—wounded at the heart and never able to heal, even if that healing would cure the whole world.

But really, how can I fight a ghost? And surely family ghosts were the most horrible of all. *It's all nonsense. I was panicked by the battle and only imagined what she said. War plays tricks on the mind.*

The click of his heels on the cobbles was a solid, reassuring sound, and he clung to it like a drowning man clutches a spar of wood. *I am the Gold King's maker. I build engines. I deal in brass and steel, not death magic.*

He kept one hand on the Webley revolver in his pocket. The feel of the grip against his palm comforted him more than he cared to admit. He'd customized the gun with a magnetized action for switching between conventional bullets and an aether discharge—not as impressive as some of the hardware on the underground market, but it fit into the pocket of a dress coat. He'd carried a weapon ever since the battle in the sky, his innate sense of safety going down in flame and ash with the ships. They'd barely made it to the ground before the rigging on the *Helios* turned to ash.

Soldiers referred to their first battle as seeing the elephant. It was more like looking into the mouth of the Inferno. Like everything else from that night, the image of those burning airships lurked forever just behind his eyes.

And there had been no quiet, sane life to return to. London was restless, every night putting new cracks in its facade of civilization. Rumors of rebellion gave even the lowest thief an excuse for anarchy. Even this neighborhood near Bond Street was growing unpredictable.

He turned from the alley into what was little more than a passage between brick warehouses. The lowering shadows kicked his pulse into a higher gear, reminding him he was alone. Stopping in his tracks, he cursed himself for forgetting to bring a lantern of any kind, and then decided he was better off invisible.

Cautiously, Tobias forged ahead, finding just enough ambient light to keep from pitching into the mud. It had rained earlier, but now the sky had cleared and the ground glistened with moisture, a silver track sketched by a faint moon. Tobias took his time, listening to the squish of his boots—his valet was going to quit in high dudgeon any day now—and feeling the cool, wet air on his face.

Then the building to his left gave way to a tall fence, the signal that he'd arrived at his destination. The place was little more than a shack in an unkempt yard, but Tobias knew every inch of it; he'd spent half his time here only a few years ago. Candlelight shone around the circumference of the ill-fitting door, making it easy to find his way inside. The first thing he recognized was the smell—coal smoke, alcohol, rotting upholstery, and a lingering whiff of scorched wool. When he stepped inside, it seemed nothing had changed inside the clubhouse of the Society for the Proliferation of Impertinent Events, better known as SPIE. Still, Tobias took a good look around before taking his hand off the Webley.

"Drink?" asked Mr. Buckingham Penner, who was sitting

in an armchair that appeared to have survived being launched by a trebuchet over enemy lines.

"You know me too well," Tobias replied to the man who had been his best friend ever since knee pants and toffee. The sound of Bucky's voice uncranked the muscles in his back and his breath released in a whoosh.

Bucky poured wine into elegant glasses. He must have brought them with him, because nothing so fine had survived five minutes in the clubhouse. "Do you know the remnants of that giant automated squid are still in the yard? Quite rusted now, but it certainly brings back memories."

That it did—memories replete with friendship and the sweet taste of irresponsible youth. There had been four charter members of SPIE, all full of ideals and devious plans. They'd scattered since, each to his own career. Of any of them, Tobias saw the least of his old companions. He walked forward and took the wine Bucky offered, tempted to drink it off at a swallow. "Those were simpler times."

"Good God, you sound old."

"I feel it."

Bucky didn't argue, but instead applied himself to his own glass with savage determination. He was a big man— he had inherited the physique of his blacksmith grandsire— but it was all fit muscle. He could hold his liquor, but he'd never sought oblivion the way Tobias had. Watching him gulp down the wine made Tobias wonder what was amiss— beyond the obvious, of course. Bucky had been betrothed to Imogen; they had been ready to elope when she had been kidnapped. Needless to say, there would be no wedding now.

"How is she?" Bucky asked, not needing to specify whom.

"Unchanged."

Wisely, Bucky didn't press the subject. He still came to sit at Imogen's bedside when Tobias's mother, Lady Bancroft, was alone in the house. She let him mourn in peace. Lord Bancroft blamed him for luring his daughter away.

"And how is your wife and scion?" Bucky asked.

Tobias blinked. It was easy on days like this—days so

fraught with ghosts—to forget that he was married and had a son. But that said a lot about his marriage. It was all so damned complicated. "In good health."

"I'm delighted to hear it."

Unhappiness made Tobias truculent. He fell into the chair opposite his friend, dangling one leg over the arm. "So, did you ask me here just for old times' sake?"

Bucky refilled their glasses. "Do I need a reason? Maybe I just like to revisit happier times."

But Tobias knew his friend well enough to suspect there was a reason lurking in the wings. He would just have to wait to find out what it was. He looked around at the moldering furniture and the derelict worktable crouching against the wall. "Memories are like the dirty dishes after a party. Best cleaned up and put away."

"You make our past sound like a catalogue of disappointments."

Whether he liked it or not, Tobias's mind drifted back to the last of SPIE's heyday. Back then, he'd almost become the man he'd wanted to be. It had slipped through his fingers, of course, but he'd felt his own potential with all the tingling excitement of thrusting his hand into a magnetic field. That last episode—with the squid and Dr. Magnus promising him the world—had lasted for skull-popping days before collapsing like a deflated dirigible. Before he'd lost Evelina Cooper and sold his soul to the Gold King.

Disappointment? What welled up was closer to grief. Still, Tobias made himself laugh. "Too much has happened. Being here feels a bit like walking on my own grave. There's something dead in this place and I think it's me."

Bucky let his head loll back, sliding in his chair as if speared by the dart of exquisite boredom. "You always were the most maudlin bastard. Did you read *Childe Harold* one too many times?"

"I hate Byron. He whines."

"Imagine the burden of listening to that."

"Very droll." And then he remembered that it was Bucky who had asked him to the clubhouse, and the reason for going there was suddenly clear. *It's Bucky who wants to re-*

member that time. It's been a year and he still pines after Imogen when most men would have drifted away. Guilt raked Tobias, and he wished he'd thought before opening his mouth. Bucky wasn't the kind to make a show of grief, but his emotions burned stronger than those of anyone else Tobias knew. He wouldn't give up on Imogen until the bitter end.

It was too much. Tobias needed light and cheerful noise before melancholy pulled him under. "Shall we get out of here? There's got to be a club with comfortable chairs and a proper fire." Tobias tossed off his wine and rose, promising himself he would talk about Imogen if his friend wanted it—just not here.

With a groan, Bucky followed and before long they were back in the alley, picking their way through the smelly grime between buildings. Tobias fingered his Webley again, feeling only slightly better with company along.

Unfortunately, the ghosts of SPIE trailed after, poking at memories of afternoons building machines, drawing plans, drinking, joking. There had been four members: Tobias, Bucky, Captain Diogenes Smythe, and Michael Edgerton.

"Do you even talk to Smythe anymore?" Tobias asked as they walked side by side.

"I don't," Bucky said evenly. "We fought a duel over your sister, remember? And he's away with his regiment most of the time. I do see Edgerton now and again. We took flying lessons together. We're both qualified to pilot a private dirigible now."

Tobias cast him a sidelong look, suddenly worried. "Edgerton is rather on the wrong side of the law these days."

"Only because his father's ironworks in Sheffield fell afoul of the Scarlet King."

Tobias stepped around a suspicious puddle. "I've heard he's thrown in with the rebels."

"Edgerton's family was ruined, the way yours would have been if you hadn't gone to work for the Gold King." Bucky paused, his broad shoulders tensing. "The way mine well might be. Both my father and I work in the Gold King's

territories, for all he's in Yorkshire and my concerns are in
London."

They were on Bond Street now, walking southeast in the
vague direction of St. James's Park. It was drizzling faintly,
not quite enough to admit that they were getting wet. Passersby walked in twos and threes under the gold-tinted gaslights, but it was nothing like the crowds of even six months
ago. There weren't many women, and fewer still looked respectable. That, more than anything, spoke to public unease.

Tobias considered Bucky's statement, wondering where
this conversation would lead. "Your father's always been on
good terms with the steam barons. He makes firearms and
beer. Everyone loves that."

"But he's come under pressure to double his production,
and he's wondering why the Gold King is ordering so many
shipments of arms. He wants to know if there is any truth to
the rumors of war with Bohemia."

"And you think I know the answer? Is that really why you
asked me here tonight?"

"Not particularly, but I thought I might as well ask the
question." Bucky shrugged, the motion stiff with embarrassment. "You're the Gold King's chief maker. You married his daughter. You would know if something was
coming."

"My esteemed father-in-law doesn't tell me everything."
What was more, Tobias didn't like being lumped together
with the Gold King's camp. It made him feel soiled. "I
haven't heard anything about a foreign war. And why would
we invade Bohemia, anyway?"

Bucky's brow furrowed. "Then the war's to be at home?
My father doesn't fancy making guns to blow up his coun-
trymen. If that's the case, he'll refuse."

"As I said, I don't know everything." Tobias was about to
add that denying the Gold King anything at all was a very
bad idea—but he never got the chance.

A fleet of Steamers careened down the street, the tall back
wheels churning with a skull-splitting rattle. Engines belched

smoke and steam out the high, crooked exhaust pipes, fogging the streets in a foul cloud.

Bucky coughed. "What are they burning in those things? Old libraries?"

"They look like the types," Tobias replied.

Black-masked youths crowded every one of the vehicles, and those who wouldn't fit inside were draped over the roofs and clinging to the doors. They let out a loud, trilling yell as they sped down the street. *A very few years ago, that was me.*

Tobias counted five Steamers and probably thirty young men and women, though it was hard to tell. They had just about reached Piccadilly when the vehicles stopped so abruptly some of the hangers-on lost their grip and flew into the street. The rest dropped off like ticks abandoning a dog, pulling the doors open to let their fellows out. They ran away from the vehicles, leaving the Steamers puffing uselessly in the middle of the street. In a span of seconds, the road was jammed with masked youths.

"Hardly Bond Street quality," Bucky muttered.

He was right. There were plenty of silks and velvets, but none of it matched or fit. Instead, it appeared to have been pilfered from a theater's castoffs. There were broad-brimmed cavalier hats crowned with sweeping feathers, Punchinello's puffy breeches, and ragged uniforms straight from Waterloo. One girl wore a ballerina's spangled costume and thigh-high boots, her hair flying loose in the wind.

One young man leaped into their path, threw back his head, and howled like a wolf. Tobias winced.

"I didn't know lycanthropy was a problem in these parts," Bucky said dryly, unbuttoning his jacket to be fisticuff-ready.

Tobias snorted. "The moon isn't even full. We're clearly dealing with amateurs."

Oblivious to the critique, the howler ceased to bay at the gaslights and lolloped off.

The respite was short-lived. One of the Steamer crowd pulled a cricket bat from the back of his vehicle and swung it experimentally even as he loped toward a draper's shop window. And then he shattered the glass in one mighty swing, roaring with glee as shards flew into the street. He wasn't alone. Bats, sticks, and canes of all kinds appeared and the crashing of windows came from every side, punctuated by the shriek of a constable's whistle.

"Bloody hell!" roared Bucky, surging into the fray. He grabbed the cricket bat out of the man's hand and thumped the vandal over the head.

Tobias was half a step behind, using the butt of the Webley to fend off attackers. Fighting beside Bucky was a bit like guarding the back of a rampaging bear, but it was a role Tobias had played a hundred times back in school. For all his mild manners, Buckingham Penner was a full-steam-ahead kind of fighter with little regard for sneak attacks from behind.

A plump young woman in a black mask was leaning in through the broken window of the draper's shop, dragging bolts of silk into the road and dumping them into the mud. Tobias didn't stop to wonder why—this was just pure mayhem. Disgust surged through him until he could almost taste it at the back of his tongue. He grabbed her by the scruff and shoved her away, letting her get a good look at the Webley. Her mouth made a startled *O* the instant before she fled, one hand holding a purple velvet hat atop her unbound hair.

Distracted, Tobias didn't see the fist coming. He staggered sideways, careening into the bricks of the building. His opponent—a tall man with a scruffy mustache—closed in. Tobias got one foot up in time to thrust him back. There suddenly seemed to be too many people—ordinary people and coppers as well as the attackers. There was no way he could fire the gun without risking an innocent life. And then the man was back, a nasty little knife in one hand. Tobias smashed him in the mustache before he had a chance to use the blade.

Bucky appeared at his elbow, blood running into his eyes from a cut to his scalp. "I think it's time to go."

Tobias wiped his mouth to see his sleeve come away bloody. "Fine. Take me to a party and then insist we leave before I've paid my respects to our host."

Bucky nodded toward the end of the street. "At least one of our hosts is already in handcuffs. Best we go before we join him. I think half the constabulary in London is here."

"That was fast. Think someone tipped them off?" Tobias wondered aloud, surveying the crowd with suspicion. The road was packed curb to curb, but there was nothing festive about the feel. A low, ugly muttering had started. And then something caught his eye. "Damnation."

Bucky turned to follow Tobias's gaze. Another fleet of Steamers was arriving, twice as many as the first lot. Worse, the occupants were firing shotguns at the gaslights as they went, their aim perilously bad.

"Go," Bucky said. Tobias didn't argue.

They turned and dove into the crowd, fighting their way with elbows and fists toward Piccadilly. It was like trying to wade through a flock of panicked sheep. Tobias began to despair of ever getting through—but then he remembered the Steamers.

He hauled on Bucky's arm. "The one at the front. Get in."

"With dozens of coppers around?" Bucky asked incredulously.

"We're leaving. They'll be in favor of two less toffs to worry about." Tobias pushed him toward the Steamer closest to the corner. It was mobbed by the crowd, so it wasn't easy to open the door. Bucky managed, but Tobias gave up, grabbing the roof instead and lowering himself through the open window.

Although he didn't own a Steamer of his own, he'd driven them before. He released the brake, allowing it to roll forward slowly. Bucky leaned his head out the window. "Get out of the way! You with the bowler hat. Step aside, sir, please. Coming through."

He kept up the litany for a block, but eventually gave up. The riot had spread for a mile around. Tobias went with the flow of the mob, grateful for the steel walls around him but unable to turn aside. Progress was excruciatingly slow, especially when he was afraid of crushing someone beneath the wheels. They'd reached the edge of St. James's Park when the Steamer finally ran out of fuel. Tobias put on the brake and they got out.

"Are we any better off?" Tobias asked, taking stock

around them. It was less crowded by the park, but he wasn't any closer to the safety of his bed.

"No one has tried to hit me in the last ten minutes." Bucky's scalp had stopped bleeding, but he looked a fright with blood smeared down his face. "I'll take what I can get."

Worry tugged at Tobias. He wasn't going to be happy until Bucky's wound was properly cleaned and bandaged. They were closest to his house, but it was still far away. However, his father-in-law had property all over London. "Keating Utilities has an office across the park. We can wait out this nonsense there."

"Are you sure that taking refuge on the Gold King's property is the best idea? Someone is bound to set it on fire."

"Since when are you so full of gloom?"

Bucky stopped, exasperation plain on his face. "Tobias, think about it. We don't want to go there."

"Why not?"

"Cast your mind back. SPIE was made up of four young, promising men of excellent education and deep pockets."

"What's that got to do with anything?"

"Think!"

"About what?" Tobias asked with a snarl. "Is this some convoluted point of logic?"

"I thought returning to the clubhouse might refresh your memory, but it seems you found that distasteful."

Tobias's mind ricocheted from one idea to another, not liking any of them. "Am I somehow to blame for something?"

His friend pressed on. "Smythe's regiment has been in chaos since the Scarlet King purchased them for his own private army. Edgerton's ruined. My father is well on his way to disaster. You're the only one still standing and that is due solely to the fact that you bowed down to Keating to keep the wolf from your family's door. The only people who do not loathe the steam barons are the barons themselves, and even they don't like each other."

A stinging mix of anger and shame shuddered down Tobias's spine. He clenched his jaw. "So what are you trying to tell me?"

"The rebellion isn't just talk anymore." Bucky raised his hands, silencing Tobias before he could interrupt. "This is my point. The longer you stand with Jasper Keating, the further away you are from the rest of us."

That stung worse than if Bucky had clipped him on the chin. "I joined his company because he was about to crush my father! Where would my mother and sisters have been then?"

Bucky nodded. "And now your wife is his daughter and your son his grandson. He has you trapped right and proper."

The logic infuriated Tobias, mostly because he'd known it from the start. Anger crackled over his skin, making it feel too tight. "What do you want?"

Bucky's expression wasn't hostile, but it was serious. "Someday I'm going to fight and you won't be at my back."

"Nonsense. I'm your friend. Who I work for doesn't change that."

"If you leave it too long, you won't have a choice anymore. If the Steam Council turns on the people, each of us is going to have to decide where we belong."

"And you're going to play the rebel? You won't even carry a gun," Tobias snapped. "Your father may own an arms factory, but you make toys for a living."

"I don't carry a gun because I'm too good a shot," Bucky said quietly. "But when I fire, I don't miss. I never want to find you in my sights."

"It's not that simple," Tobias shot back, feeling a need for justification.

Bucky shrugged. "No, but the barons are running out of time, and that means we won't have many more chances to talk before everything falls apart."

All at once a flash made them both fall silent. A bright light bloomed from the lake in the middle of the park. "What the bleeding hell is that?" Tobias asked.

Bucky drew in his breath, probably to tell him he was avoiding the subject, but then let it out with a hiss as the glow grew stronger, like a small sun rising over the treetops. "Is that some kind of a dirigible?"

They hurried toward the apparition, anxious to see who

was launching a craft in the middle of the city—on the night of a riot, no less—and why. Anyone with innocent intentions would have gone home and locked their doors.

At first, greenery blocked their view. All that Tobias could see was the netted curve of a balloon surrounded by a glow of light. And then the tip of a propeller came into view. "By God, it *is* some sort of airship," he exclaimed. They started to run to get a better view.

The first thing they encountered was a scatter of horses, carts, and running men—some of them armed—making for the street. That solved the mystery of how the thing had got there—and judging by the size and number of conveyances involved, there had been some assembly required at the last minute. Debris from the construction littered the shore of the lake. A handful of cheaply built rafts still floated on the water, spinning slowly in the current. Tobias tried to picture where the rafts came in, but was immediately distracted by the ship itself.

What rose above the lake was like nothing Tobias had ever seen. A graceful gold balloon suspended an enclosed body coated in brass. The balloon was augmented by ranks of steam-driven propellers heaving against the weight of their burden. Tobias immediately calculated the difficulty of lifting such a machine into the air and the fuel required to do it. Wherever the thing was meant to go, it wasn't far—maybe just a mile or two away.

The general shape of the thing was insectile, made up of three sections with the largest in the aft. Whirling propellers were set on rectangular frames attached to the midsection like wings. The entire body of the ship was studded with lights, making it glimmer in the night sky. Apparently, it was meant to be seen. But most disturbing was a long proboscis-like spike emerging from the prow. Tobias tried to make sense of the shape, and felt a headache coming on.

"What the feckin' hell?" muttered Bucky. "You say it, because I don't want to."

"It's a gigantic brass mosquito," Tobias replied as the thing lifted above the greenery.

"Why?"

The question really did sum it all up. Sadly, there was no good answer, so they increased their speed to race after it. They weren't the only ones. The mob that had followed the police to Bond Street earlier that night now turned like a giant, sluggish tide to flow in the direction of this latest apparition. But unlike the park, the streets were jammed. There was no possibility of the coppers catching up to the ship or the mischief-makers who had sent it into the sky.

Undoubtedly someone *had* tipped off the constabulary about the riots that night. It was the surest way to get them out of the way. How else did one launch a giant bug in the middle of a very public park, save by creating an even bigger distraction down the road?

The mosquito, and everyone else, was heading toward Westminster. The face of Big Ben loomed in the night sky like a gigantic clockwork god. A few tiny police balloons wafted into the air, looking rather like the bubbles in a champagne glass, but there was no hope of catching the intruder. Tobias watched with mounting horror as it powered along, propellers churning, toward the Palace of Westminster—and more specifically, for the Clock Tower.

Tobias and Bucky became tangled in the crowd as it funneled toward the east end of the park. Directly ahead, a carriage had become mired in the midst of the throng and the mare was whinnying in panic at the crush. They were more or less at a standstill.

Bucky dragged Tobias by the arm, pulling up against the side of a white stone building. Silent, they both watched with mute horror as the brass mosquito sailed steadily toward Big Ben. The symbolism of a blood-sucker nagged at Tobias's mind, but nowhere had he seen any indication of who was behind the attack. The anonymity of this action made everything worse.

The clock was chiming eleven, the huge bell bonging with certitude, the elegant hands uplifted against the illuminated face. And for a moment, Tobias thought the weight of majesty would be enough to protect the monument. The mosquito seemed to pause, lights shimmering against the dark sky, suspended by the vibrant voice of the bell.

And then it dove, nose skewering the glass.

"Blood and thunder!" Tobias couldn't hear it break at that distance, but he saw the flash of reflection in the lights of the attacking ship. A collective gasp of dismay went up from the crowd. The proboscis drove in deep, crushing clockwork as if it were tissue paper. Metal flew, arcing into the air, but it was hard to tell what was the clock and what was the ship. Even at that distance, Tobias could tell both were wrecks. The bell made an odd, choking ring and went silent. Then, the crowd's gasp became a roar as what had just happened soaked in.

The light from the Clock Tower winked out. Big Ben was dead, one side burdened by the brass monstrosity that had speared it. Then the ship's lights, too, flickered and went out.

Tobias was growing cold inside, as if he were being drained of blood. Westminster was the heart of the Gold King's territory, the jewel in his crown. Keating was going to be furious right down to the bottom of his spats. "You were wondering about a war?"

"But who did this?" Bucky waved at the spectacle in the sky, for all it was now shrouded in darkness. "Why put the Empire at risk with such a pointless gesture?"

Tobias closed his eyes for a long moment. Bucky was right. The steam barons distrusted one another, and once the balance of power between them tipped, every industry they owned—power, transportation, manufacturing, and even the brothels—would suffer. There would be chaos unless the culprit was found and dealt with in short order. Innocent people would be hurt.

For Tobias, this was bigger than picking sides. This was about protecting everyone he cared for. He handed Bucky the Webley. "You need to get home."

Bucky's brown eyes widened, but he took the gun. "What about you?"

Tobias looked over his shoulder at the clock. As the Gold King's maker, he had permission to poke his nose where he liked in Keating's territories. "I need to get up there and figure out who made that thing."

CHAPTER FIVE

TENSION REIGNS AT THE PALACE

Almost immediately after the attack on our beloved Big Ben, the Empire has suffered another blow. The Prince of Wales has taken to his bed with a sudden and serious illness. Some fear a return of typhoid, which nearly took his life in 1871, but unconfirmed reports claim palace physicians believe this to be a new malady. It is further said that they cannot discern its cause, much less prescribe a cure.

—*The London Prattler*

London, September 19, 1889
LADIES' COLLEGE OF LONDON

5:05p.m. Thursday

"COOPER!"

Evelina looked up from her book, squinting a little. Her mind had drifted to a place far away from the words before her—back to a spring night when Nick had crept through her bedroom window. It should have been night, and it should have been Hilliard House, but with a wrench, she realized none of that was true. Instead, she was sitting in a sunny patch at the south end of the quadrangle, warm enough that she'd shed her wrap. The air smelled dusty, carrying the faint scent of windfalls from the orchard behind Witherton House.

She raised a hand to shelter her eyes from the low angle of the sun and was rewarded with the sight of a familiar form approaching with a newspaper clutched in one pearl-edged glove. The young woman's skirts were patterned with orange and red chrysanthemums, her fitted jacket a burnt umber that nearly matched the shade of her thick hair. The ensemble gave her the air of a harvest sprite.

With a dramatic sigh, Deirdre Livingston flung herself onto the bench beside Evelina and thrust out the newspaper. "I need you, my darling girl."

"Oh, do you?" Evelina unfolded the special edition. It was the *Prattler,* one of the more outspoken of the London papers—not the sort of thing Deirdre would normally read. The first article that caught her eye concerned a cholera outbreak. Clean water was something else the steam barons were trying to charge for, and disease was the inevitable result.

"This is an academic emergency," Deirdre said in a stage whisper, a tiny frown bunching her eyebrows.

Evelina hid a smile. "I thought you'd charmed your way to a passing grade in French literature."

"*Bien sûr.* This is far more urgent. I'm about to go walking with Mr. Edward Pringle, and he's all about Parliament. I need to give the impression that I read more than the fashion papers."

"But you don't."

"You don't know that." Deirdre tried to sound scandalized and almost succeeded.

"Your room is across the hall from mine. I think I would know if you actually read something."

"How?"

"Because you wouldn't be knocking on my door at a quarter to midnight just before each and every exam."

Deirdre snatched the paper and folded it to the article she wanted. "Give a girl a chance, Cooper. We can't all be dedicated to our studies. Some of us are here for husbands."

"I admire the clarity of your focus."

Deirdre held up the paper, pointing to a headline. "Tell me about this."

Evelina read the type held inches from her eyeballs. Then

alarm rippled up her spine and she sat straighter. "Good heavens!"

"Exactly," said Deirdre. "The prince is ill. That's all Edward is going to want to talk about. I need to know what to say."

"The crown prince is the heir to the whole Empire!"

"I knew that much." Deirdre smoothed her skirts, her chocolate silk gloves gliding over the autumn-colored pattern. "Who would the crown go to if he didn't recover?"

It was a good question. Although Victoria and Albert had begun with a houseful of children, their brood had dwindled one by one. Some had been carried off by typhoid, others by the bleeding sickness, and still others by circumstances none could understand. It was almost as if a curse stalked the palace, seizing each of the heirs in turn.

Foreboding chilled Evelina like a sudden breeze. "If the crown prince dies, I'm not sure who would succeed the queen. There are relatives of the royal family still in Germany, but I am not sure who has precedence."

"So what does this mean for the government?" Not that Deirdre actually cared, but Edward Pringle would.

Evelina set the paper aside. For a moment, she was back at the Wollaston Academy for Young Ladies, whispering about boys with Imogen. Memory hit her like strong drink, leaving her dizzy. Wollaston had been a hundred years ago, before the air battle and Keating and losing Nick. It wasn't fair, but she almost resented Deirdre for not being Imogen.

Evelina drew a ragged breath, forcing herself back to the present. She actually liked her classmate very much, and tried to get into the spirit of her matrimonial chase. But during the last year of danger and tragedy, Evelina had lost her light heart. As a result, she tended to remain aloof from the other students, feeling more like a ghost than one of the young, boisterous crowd.

She tried to smile. "Well, Mr. Pringle will say that there is the Steam Council to consider. For the sake of the royal family, it would be better if the heir were someone very capable and charismatic."

Deirdre's face was intent. "Why? Because of those rebels? The Baskertons?"

"Baskervilles," Evelina said automatically. "They're a rebel group who are against the Steam Council."

Deirdre blinked, clearly lost already.

"Think about it this way," said Evelina. "The members of the Steam Council hate each other, but they hate the rebels more."

"And where does the prince come in?"

"My uncle believes that if the queen died and there was no one strong to take over from her, the Steam Council might just push the monarchy aside and take over the government for themselves. The Baskervilles want to stop them."

"So the rebels are actually protecting the queen?"

"That's right." Evelina had met a few of the leaders—including the ringleader they called the Schoolmaster—and she was reasonably sure that both her uncles were involved up to the brims of their top hats.

Deirdre looked grave. "In other words, if the prince dies, it's a bigger problem than just finding another heir. Everyone will start fighting one another."

"Exactly."

Her friend picked up the newspaper and began folding it into the smallest possible square. "Now I understand, and wish I didn't."

Evelina knew all too well what she meant. "I hope that helps to entertain Mr. Pringle."

Deirdre smiled slyly. "At least until we get to more engaging topics."

"You're wicked."

"I do hope so." Deirdre stood, abandoning the newspaper on the bench. "I fancy myself as the wife of a prime minister."

"Good luck." Evelina picked up her book.

"Enjoy your studies." Deirdre sailed off across the lawn, the sunshine caressing the warm tones of her costume.

Evelina managed to read a few paragraphs before the newspaper tempted her away from the slog through Goethe. She reread the article, but it was short on details. The *Bugle* or the *Times* would have been better. But that meant getting down to the main road in front of Camelin where the newspaper boys sold their wares—and with a headline like that, the papers would sell out quickly.

Temptation fluttered through her, bringing a smile to her lips. She was restless and weary of looking at the same walls. Evelina picked up her wrap and slid her book into her coat pocket. The shadows were long and thin, the afternoon classes letting out. She wasn't supposed to leave the Ladies' College, but what harm could there be in getting a newspaper?

She hurried across the lawn toward the college gate. She wasn't sure which of the faculty knew that she was confined to the college, but the fewer people who saw her, the better. Walking with her head down and her hands in her pockets, she avoided the other students crisscrossing the grounds. The scent of the early evening meal—lamb stew by the smell of it—was already wafting through the crisp air.

The gates were ajar, students coming and going in twos and threes. Evelina stepped to the side, waiting for the stream to pass. The path to the main buildings snaked up the hill, but she wanted to go in the other direction. It was a two-minute walk to the street—one she'd done a hundred times. As long as she didn't go more than a dozen steps from the university's front entrance, she obeyed the letter of Keating's orders not to stray from Camelin.

A knot of excitement was building inside her—proof of just how bored she was if buying a paper was a grand adventure. She darted toward the gate, meaning to slide through and away before she was noticed.

Heat flared up her arms, sharp to the point of searing. She jerked to a stop, no more than four steps from the open gates. The heat coalesced into a sharp prickling, as if thousands of hot pins were stabbing her forearms. The bracelets! She jerked up the sleeves of her coat to look at them, but they didn't look any different. Yet what else could it be?

She'd known the bracelets allowed the Yellowbacks to track her, but she'd had no idea they could deliver this kind of pain. Growing stubborn, Evelina took another step forward. The pain intensified until it seemed swords stabbed her through the elbows. She jumped back with a gasp, cradling her arms. Sudden, frantic panic surged up. It was one thing to be forbidden to leave, quite another to be caged. She rushed toward the gate, desperate to hurl herself against the barrier, to break through to safety. Agony blinded her before she gained two strides.

Evelina staggered back, sweat turning chill in the autumn air. She was shaking, sickness rising inside her, but it was hard to say how much was physical shock and how much was anger.

"Miss Cooper?"

Her head snapped up. It was Juniper—Moriarty—standing outside the gate. He had a walking stick in hand as if on his way out for a carefree stroll. He turned and came her way, the sleek malacca cane swinging as he walked. "You look rather peaked."

Her words came out almost as a snarl. "What have you done?"

His eyebrows went up in mock surprise. "Me?"

It had been bad enough being confined to the entire university campus, but now she was stuck in an area one-twentieth the size. As her nausea faded, fury came to the fore. "You might have warned me that the bracelets would keep me locked up inside the Ladies' College!"

He stopped a few feet away, the cane elegantly poised. "Testing our limits, were we?"

"Are you amused?" she snapped.

"Not really. None of this was my doing. I would be far more interested to see what you might accomplish unshackled. But that was the short-term compromise Mr. Keating reached with the chancellor until your ultimate fate has been decided."

She seethed in silence.

"No one told you that your, uh, restraints had been altered?"

"No."

"It did not occur to you that this might be the case?"

Evelina looked away, angry with herself for not anticipating more betrayal. "I just wanted a copy of the *Bugle*."

He made a sympathetic face. "I'll have one delivered."

"Thank you." But she didn't care about the paper now. Her mind was too busy scrambling to grasp the implications of her shrinking prison.

Moriarty cocked his head. "I understand that the restraints are painful?"

"Quite."

"Interesting. They are quite ineffective unless one is born with inherited powers."

That caught her attention enough that she met his eyes—and then she regretted it. There was an avid sharpness to his expression that made her feel like a bug in a jar. "How do they work?" she asked. "They look like plain silver. That accounts for some of the reaction, but not everything."

Though metal and gems often absorbed magic—especially gold—silver and the supernatural were a poor mix. No one knew why. Of course, that was precisely the sort of overlap of science and magic she wanted to research, and Camelin's archive of books on magic had made the Ladies' College her first choice. Little had she known that attending a university was no guarantee of the education she'd desired.

He went on. "I've never examined the mechanism, but both clockwork and magnetism are involved, as well as a rare element that reacts with magical energy to produce a chemical discharge. Only someone with inherited talent will trigger them."

"Do you know how to get them off?" she asked.

"Alas, no. All that I know I've gleaned from the letter your patron wrote to Sir William, and Mr. Keating omitted that detail."

"How unfortunate."

"I concur."

Moriarty took her arm and began slowly leading her toward the residence. Evelina forced herself not to shrink away. Common sense said that he might be as dangerous an ally as he would be a foe, but she wasn't in a position to be choosy.

"I count my blessings that I aligned myself with King Coal and not Keating," he said. "Your patron is too fond of absolute control. It's impractical."

"For me, certainly. It seems to be working for Keating," she snapped, her anger hardening to a clear, sharp focus.

"For now, perhaps, but force is a clumsy weapon. It will fail him in the end."

Moriarty's calm critique amused her even as it made her uneasy. "Why did you involve yourself with the steam barons?"

Moriarty gave a quiet laugh. "Let us just say that I was in need of a position to get a start in the world. The Blue King opened my eyes to a dazzling array of enterprises that I had only guessed at as a well-bred young man of middling fortunes."

"Enterprises?"

"There are men and women in all walks of life who will do one's bidding. If there is a want or desire, they will fill it as long as one provides something they want in return. The Blue King is a master weaver of such webs of reciprocal desires. I studied his methods with great interest."

She wondered what desire the Blue King had seen in Moriarty. Ambition seemed likely, but there was also the hauteur of one convinced of his own intellectual superiority. In fact, he was a bit like her Uncle Sherlock. "You are very frank."

"Only with you, Miss Cooper. You of anyone understand the twin attraction and danger of being close to one of the Steam Council."

"True." And she had been resigned to Keating's chess game until now—but after what just happened, part of her was screaming to dash the board and all its pieces to the floor.

Moriarty gave a thin smile. "Evidently Keating wishes you to remain close."

"So it seems." Evelina clenched her teeth at his quip, but then forced herself to remain polite. "And the Blue King let you go so that you could pursue your academic career?"

"He will recall me if he requires my services." They had

reached the steps of the women's residence. Moriarty stopped, his expression serious. "I assume the reason you wished for a newspaper was that you've heard about the prince's illness?"

Evelina nodded. "We may both be recalled to our respective masters."

"I certainly hope not, Miss Cooper. I would not choose you as an adversary. Despite the circumstances, I have enjoyed our conversations."

She was about to say she had as well, but then she saw that cold glitter in his eyes that she didn't trust. He was trying to win her confidence. That worried her almost as much as the damnable bracelets. "Thank you again, Dr. Moriarty."

"I still await the list of supplies you need for your studies."

"I won't forget."

He gave a slight bow, touching the brim of his hat. "Good afternoon, Miss Cooper. Perhaps we shall yet find a way to be of use to one another."

She fingered the silver about her wrists. "Good afternoon, Dr. Moriarty."

As she turned and mounted the stairs to her room, instinct made her look over her shoulder. The professor was making his way back to the gate of the college, his cane swinging. And yet, she still felt him lurking behind her, as if some part of his intent remained. He reminded her of a desert serpent with most of its coils still hidden in the sand. The head might look small, innocuous even, but beneath the surface there were yards of deadly muscle coiled to strike.

The question was when and where to turn that to her advantage.

CHAPTER SIX

London, September 20, 1889

HILLIARD HOUSE

8:15 p.m. Friday

PENELOPE ROTH—BETTER KNOWN AS POPPY—PAUSED OUT-
side the main drawing room of Hilliard House, feeling hurt
and betrayed by her parents. It was a feeling she experienced quite regularly these days—something her mother
put down to being fifteen years of age, but any girl with an
ounce of true poetic feeling knew better.

Poppy peered inside the room, not quite committing to
the act of stepping over the threshold. The place was
crowded, a surf of voices washing over a small orchestra
playing Haydn. The room was elegant, with a gilt ceiling
and gaslit chandeliers, and white pilasters dividing the walls
into harmonious proportions. There was nowhere to look
without seeing expensive objets d'art, unless there was a
duchess or a cabinet minister standing in the way.

It was the first time since early last November—almost
eleven months ago, now—that her father, Lord Bancroft,
had entertained on this scale. Eleven months of grief, and
he'd done a decent job of wearing a long face and a black
suit. It was what was expected of him and, after all, Imogen
had been his favorite. But eventually his ambitions had got
the better of him. Like a hound scratching at the door, he
wanted back into the games of power, and this gathering of
London's elite was the signal of his readiness.

And Poppy loathed him for it, because he had chosen to

move on. He either didn't see, or refused to see, why his choice was so wrong—and whatever Papa decreed, her mother embraced. There would be no help from either of them.

After all, it wasn't as if Imogen was actually *dead*. She lay upstairs, deep in a sleep that should have seen her starve to death, or corrode in a mass of bedsores, or otherwise dwindle away in some nasty fashion. The nurses were able to administer broth and gruel, but little else. Yet she survived, lovely and remote as a fairy-tale princess in an enchanted tower.

Of course, such phenomena worked better between the covers of a book. Poppy could read her father's silences and frowns. As far as he was concerned, Imogen's besetting sin had been that she simply *would not die* so everyone else could get on with things. Lord Bancroft's pity only extended so far—eleven months, to be precise.

Poppy would not forgive that. She trembled with fury at the tide of brittle laughter tumbling from the drawing room. She loved Imogen fiercely, and she wouldn't give up on her. And perhaps that meant not being at this wretched party at all. Poppy turned, determined to march back to her bedroom and strip off the ridiculous ruffled gown the maid had stuffed her into.

But before she made it three steps, her mother appeared out of thin air. "Penelope, you're late."

She only got "Penelope" when her mother was upset. Poppy turned, cheeks hot with defiance. But Lady Bancroft—her fine brows drawn into a sharp crease—was having none of it.

"My stays are laced too tight," Poppy declared, a little too loudly.

"Hush," her mother whispered, since feminine undergarments were hardly drawing room fare. "That's what you get for refusing to wear your training corset all those years."

"I can't breathe."

"Young ladies are not required to breathe. They are required to be punctual." Lady Bancroft, pale and slender as a reed, gave the impression of a delicate, biddable woman. Poppy had never experienced that side of her. "If I let you return to your room, in an hour I'll find you with your nose in a book."

"No one else will care."

"Your task is to make them care." Lady Bancroft grabbed her elbow, her pale pink gloves nearly matching the lace on Poppy's sleeve. "You will go in there and be charming. If not for your own sake, do it for your father."

That was hardly incentive. "I'm not even out of the school-room yet! I have at least a year before I have to be pleasant to people."

"You need the practice, and there is never a time like the present to begin."

And to Poppy's chagrin, her mother steered her through the door into the crowded drawing room. Poppy pulled her arm away and lifted her chin. If she were doomed to attend the party, she would face it with dignity. They hadn't gone a dozen feet before Poppy was forced to plaster a smile on her face.

"Lady Bancroft," said Jasper Keating, emerging out of the crowd like a ship under full sail. From what Poppy could tell, he was usually a vessel of ill omen.

Keating had thick, waving white hair and amber eyes that reminded her of some monster from a storybook. He bowed over her mother's hand. "You are enchanting as always, Lady Bancroft. I see you've lost none of your touch as London's most elegant hostess."

"You are too kind, Mr. Keating." Lady Bancroft granted him a queenly smile. "And it is so good of you to bless this gathering even after the, uh, incident."

That would be the affair of the bug in the clock. Poppy had endured an entire day of her parents agonizing over whether to cancel the party because no one wanted to make light of what had happened. For her part, Poppy had been forced to stifle the giggles when she saw the cartoons in the *Prattler*. Her father had given her the Glare of Death over the breakfast table.

"If the culprit sees us cowering under our beds, he has won," Keating replied. "Though when the time comes, we will be swift of action and merciless in our wrath."

If his words were chilling, his smile was even worse. Poppy wondered if people called Mr. Keating the Gold King because of the yellow globes of the gaslights his company owned, or because of his sulfur-colored eyes. Or his heaps of money. There were a dizzying number of reasons to be wary of the man.

And he was one more reason to slip out of the drawing room. Poppy began inching away, eager to vanish, but he turned and looked her square in the eye. "And here is Miss Penelope."

Trapped, Poppy managed a proper curtsy, proving that she hadn't ignored all her lessons. "Good evening, Mr. Keating."

He gave her an approving nod. "You will grow into a lovely young lady, I can tell."

"Thank you, sir."

Keating's strange eyes glinted. "Such lovely manners never go amiss."

She nearly snorted. All the young ladies she knew— Imogen, Alice, and Evelina to be specific—had hardly profited by learning to use the right fork. Maybe they would have done better if they'd spit tobacco and sworn like sailors—or at least had a bit more fun before their lives ended up snarled like a yarn ball once the cat was through.

Her mother unfurled a clockwork fan, which opened, stick by stick, in a profusion of tiny sapphires. "And she's the baby of the family. I can't believe it's already time to begin thinking about her Season next year."

Deep inside, Poppy shuddered. The Season meant being presented to the queen—she supposed that could be endured—but then came the marriage mart with all the balls and routs and dancing parties. If the sheer dullness of it all wasn't enough, the first man who made a decent offer to Lord Bancroft could cart her away like a goat from the livestock auction, bleating as she went. So much for her future.

"Is not Alice the very model of a mother?" Lady Bancroft said to Mr. Keating. "She did not come tonight, which is a pity, but little Jeremy caught a sniffle. She could not bear to be away from him."

"Then you have heard more details than I, Lady Bancroft. My daughter clearly favors her mother-in-law for talk of babies."

No doubt. Poppy couldn't imagine writing Jasper Keating about throw-up and nappies. Although Poppy wasn't supposed to understand such things, Alice had obviously been with child when she'd married Tobias, for all she'd been packed off to the country the moment she'd started to show. And sadly, while Tobias and Alice did their best to get along, theirs was a far halloo from a love match. It was too bad, because Poppy adored her sister-in-law.

Besides Alice the fallen angel, I have a sleeping princess for a sister, a knave for a brother, an evil queen for a mother, and Papa thinks he's Signor Machiavelli. How did I end up in this house? Poppy knew everyone complained about one's family, but hers had to be eligible for some sort of prize. Or a scientific study. She wondered if Mr. Darwin was still writing books.

Poppy fidgeted, her attention wandering even further. More people had arrived, filling the room with a seething mass of bare shoulders and stiff white shirts. She recognized many of the faces, although by no means all. It was going to be a miserable crush if too many more people turned up. It was already like standing beside an overperfumed furnace.

Her gaze caught on a tall, dark-haired man with piercing blue eyes standing at the far end of the room. It was William Reading, the Scarlet King, sporting the bright red waistcoat that was his trademark. *He still hasn't figured out that sort of thing went out of fashion years ago.* But that didn't seem to stop his success with the ladies, judging from the flock chirping around him.

The one woman who had never fallen for him was Imogen, but that might have been because her heart had already belonged to Bucky Penner. Then again, it might have just been good taste. The Scarlet King's oily smile reminded Poppy of an advertisement for hair pomade.

Keating leaned close to her, making her jump. "You should go see what Mr. Reading brought with him."

Escape! For an instant, she almost liked the Gold King—although it said how bored she was that seeking out Reading was an enticement. Poppy glanced back at her mother, who nodded—although her eyes still delivered a warning glare. "Don't make a nuisance of yourself."

Apparently the bar had been lowered from being charming to not causing a scandal. "Of course, Mother."

"And don't touch the champagne." Lady Bancroft dismissed her with a flap of the hand.

Poppy slipped through the throng with profound relief. It was clear that Reading had indeed brought something, because the crowd was clotting around him. Only her quick reflexes got her through the mass of people in time to see what the man was holding.

Then curiosity seized her, making her forget even the hideous discomfort of her stays. Whatever Reading had, it was so bright with gold that for an instant she couldn't make it out. She had to look away and then try again, taking in one detail at a time. On his right hand, he wore a glove that extended all the way to his elbow. It seemed to be made of spun ice—though possibly it was just chain mail so fine it rippled like silk and gleamed like polished silver. What sat on it, though, was surely a demon forged of fire.

Awe took her. Poppy chewed her lip as she catalogued every feature. Brass claws dug into the steel glove, shifting uneasily while the thing looked about with bright ruby eyes. It was a smallish eagle, perhaps, though that didn't begin to describe the beautiful ferocity of it. Every bright gold feather was carefully etched to capture nature's texture, and when the bird opened its wings, they fanned and quivered like a living thing. But it was the beak that caught her interest, for it wasn't all gold. Like the claws, it was brass tipped in steel. The thing was clearly meant for hunting.

"Can it fly?" one of the ladies asked.

"Of course," said Reading.

He had one of those low, musical voices meant to read poetry about snowy flesh and bodices. Not that Poppy ever got into her mother's private stock of romantic novels.

"My firebird here contains a miniaturized burner for

aether distillate. He can fly every bit as high as his living cousins, and his logic processor is a step above anything on the commercial market. That's really why I made him. I wanted a means of testing the sort of decision making we'd expect of a raptor. Imagine the possibility for such creatures on the field of battle."

The bird shifted from foot to foot, ruffling its wings back into place. It was clear how Reading controlled the creature, for there was a small box in his other hand with dials and buttons. But the exquisite artistry outweighed the need for illusion. Poppy caught her breath, wanting to ask something just for an excuse to get closer. She'd seen plenty of wondrous inventions, but this was so beautiful it was almost beyond the reach of understanding. Looking at it made her heart ache.

"What sort of decisions?" the same woman asked. She was looking at the Scarlet King with a sly smile, as if there was more to the conversation than met the eye. "Are you asking it to kill pigeons?"

He laughed, holding the bird up a notch. The gesture spoke to his strength, because the thing must have been enormously heavy. "Perhaps to roast them."

The creature opened its beak, and a tongue of flame lashed out with a sound like ripping silk. The crowd leaped back, cries of alarm filling the room. Reading laughed again, clearly enjoying himself. "I said it was a firebird."

The thing spread its huge wings and gave a single flap. Metal feathers whistled through the air as it launched toward the high ceiling. For a moment, all Poppy felt was a fizz of delight that raised the fine hair all down her arms. The firebird sailed in a lazy circle, reflecting the bright lights and sparkle like an orbiting sun. But her pleasure quickly soured to alarm as the thing brushed the crystal droplets of the chandeliers, making them wobble on their chains. And then another blast of flame licked out dangerously close to the drapes.

Poppy suddenly had visions of Hilliard House ablaze. Dark fear snaked under her ribs as she glanced at Reading. What she saw there made her shrink back. His bright blue eyes held an unpleasant spark—this bordered on more than mischief. He was enjoying the crowd's distress.

The firebird swooped over the table where footmen were replenishing the refreshments. They ducked from sheer surprise, one of them dropping a bottle that smashed with a sound like a gunshot. Guests began backing toward the door.

Poppy looked around for her mother, who was open-mouthed with horror. The party was about to become a disaster, but no one was brave enough to tell a steam baron to stop playing with his toys. Like Keating, Reading was too powerful to insult.

Poppy's fingers crushed the ruffles of her skirts, anger curdling her fear. It was unfair and wrong for grown men and women to cower before an idiotic bully. *Blast him anyway!* What could he do to a fifteen-year-old schoolgirl? She wheeled around and stood squarely in his path.

"Sir," she said in her best public-speaking voice, "wouldn't you agree that this is a pleasure best enjoyed out of doors?"

Everyone within earshot went quiet. The firebird flapped lazily over the startled orchestra, finally coming to rest on the column of the harp. The instrument teetered dangerously.

The Scarlet King's smile grew broad as he swept an elaborate bow. "My beautiful young miss, I don't believe we've met."

They had—when he'd been courting Imogen, he'd foisted his presence upon the family far too often—but there was no point in reminding him of the fact. "My name is Poppy, and this is my house. Please don't burn it down."

"Ah," he said with aggravating slowness, his gaze traveling over her in a way that made the blood rush to her cheeks—and not in a pleasant way. "And if I take my firebird outside, will you come along to enjoy it with me?"

Embarrassment corkscrewed her insides. It wasn't the fact that he'd asked, but the way he'd made it sound like another proposition entirely. No one had ever spoken to her like that, not even in jest. And he was *old*—much older than even Tobias. The man had to be twice her age.

"Good God, no!"

His eyes went wide—that had caught him by surprise. *That was stupid, you idiot, now what's he going to do?* It was one thing to be bold, quite another to cause offense. But then Reading burst into laughter, mortifying her even more. It was a fat, loud guffaw that spared her no dignity—not one little scrap. Poppy slunk back a step, quivering, not sure if she was supposed to slap him or run from the room.

But then he stopped as abruptly as he had started. "I apologize, my sweet Miss Roth. That was unconscionably rude of me. You are quite right, my behavior is *hardly* suited to such delicate company. I hope we can still be friends."

Reading reached into his jacket pocket and pulled out a small enamel box. He pressed a spring that flipped it open, revealing neat rows of small pastel candies. "Peppermint?"

Poppy really didn't know what to make of that. What a strange man! Did she refuse the candy out of caution—who wanted to eat anything that had been on his person?—or did she take one to smooth over everyone's feelings?

Rescue came from the most unexpected quarter.

"Are you truly proposing to rob the cradle, William?" Keating said, suddenly appearing at her elbow. He tucked her gloved hand under his arm as if he were to lead her to dinner and pulled her well out of reach of the little enamel box. Under the circumstances, she almost welcomed the gesture.

Reading gave the Gold King an outrageous wink. "Off limits, then, old man?"

Poppy's eyes widened. The two men were supposed to be allies, but she'd never heard anyone speak to the Gold King this way. She looked up from under her lashes, turning icy at the grim set of Keating's mouth.

"Yes, very much off limits."

"And why am I obeying your commands?" Reading sneered.

"Are you drunk?"

The Scarlet King chuckled. "You don't think I'd come to this sort of an affair without lubrication?"

Poppy gasped on behalf of her mother.

Keating squeezed her arm. "Get your bird under control, William. I have any number of chefs who can provide expert advice on plucking and skinning a troublesome rooster."

Reading made a noise like he'd swallowed his own tongue. "I have a few recipes of my own, old man," the Scarlet King said in a low, dangerous voice. "Have a care."

But Keating didn't back down. Poppy looked from one to the other, her interest quivering like the antennae of a butterfly. She'd seen half-wild alley curs circle one another, looking for any weakness worth exploiting. This was the same, only neither man actually moved. *I don't think they are as good friends as everyone thinks.*

She barely dared to breathe, her heart thumping against the bodice of her dress so hard that it surely must have showed. Willing her feet to move, though, didn't seem to work. It was as if her legs belonged to someone else who just wasn't listening to her desperate urge to back away.

Then she saw Reading make a small motion with the hand that held the controls of his mechanical bird. In a lazy flap, the eagle launched from the pillar of the harp and drifted back to the Scarlet King's arm, coming in so close to Keating's head that the older man had to dodge the razor wingtips. Reading lifted his wrist, letting the bird catch the glove in a motion as neat and graceful as a dance move. Keating stood, smoothing his hair, and glared at the firebird.

Scarlet smiled. "You know your problem, Keating? You never let yourself enjoy any of the power you work so hard to get."

"Go sober up," Keating snapped. "You and I have business to conduct together. You don't want an unfortunate incident to poison our accord."

Some of that must have penetrated Reading's skull, because his smirk soured. "Fusty old bastard, aren't you?"

He slouched back a step, a movement out of keeping with his usual military dash. It was as if a mask had slipped, and someone much rougher and hungrier peeped out. Someone Poppy never wanted a good look at. She hated Jasper Keating, but all at once she feared the Scarlet King more. Keating at least seemed to have reasons for the things he did.

Then Keating turned and walked away, as if he knew Reading would leave just because he'd told him to. On one hand, Poppy was disappointed. A real fight would have been much more interesting. On the other, she wasn't sure her mother would have survived any more excitement. The moment Keating moved, Lady Bancroft descended on the Gold King and started apologizing for the upset, as if there should have been a rule about guests leaving their birds at the door.

That left Poppy standing there, facing the Scarlet King. His angry blue eyes met hers, and a chill speared through her. It was almost painful, but it unglued her feet from the floor. She was suddenly able to walk away—so she did. When she glanced back over her shoulder, he was carrying his firebird from the room. Poppy's breath escaped in a relieved *whoosh*.

At least she wasn't bored any longer. If this was a representative sample of her parents' social evenings, graduating from the schoolroom might not be as dull as she'd thought.

CHAPTER SEVEN

OUR NATIONAL MONUMENT BLINDED

Reports on the damage to Big Ben are grim, prompting a public outcry for the blood of the perpetrator who launched an airship through the nation's best-loved timepiece. The Palace issued a statement condemning the act, while Mr. Jasper Keating, in an interview with this correspondent, cautions against responding with passion rather than reason. "My staff are committing all our energies to the solution of this unusual crime," he declares. "There will be no mistakes made because evidence is lacking. The time for passion comes when judgment is handed down. Now is the time for detection."

—*The Bugle*

BIG BEN GETS A POKE IN THE EYE

Critics question the sluggish reaction of both the Palace and the Steam Council to this latest attack on our fair city. Is this going to be another case such as that of the Whitechapel Murders, on which authorities are slow to act and never do convict? If so, the citizens of London had better begin building some very large flyswatters in the event that the carnage has just begun.

—*The London Prattler*

TOBIAS CONCENTRATED ON THE CREASED PAGES OF HIS pocket notebook, scribbling down an idea that had fluttered like some exotic moth into his awareness. He was upstairs in Hilliard House, and he could hear the mutter of the crowd below, but he was avoiding the party until he absolutely had to put in an appearance. None of his friends would be there, and he wasn't in the mood for polite chitchat about the weather. He hadn't been since the air battle.

Plus, his mind was still dwelling on the brass mosquito. It had taken them till late the next day to get the thing down. He'd spent all day today with his head in its workings. So far he hadn't figured out who had made it, but he had learned quite a bit of interest, including the fact that there had been a pilot who had somehow slipped away.

But every maker had a unique signature, just as individual as handwriting or the ridges on one's fingertips. The trick was to recognize it in the way a housing was put together or how a steering problem was resolved. A man's work showed who he was. And there was something about that steering he recognized, though he couldn't recall where he'd seen that design before.

Tobias tapped the end of his pencil against his teeth, the etched brass holder softly clicking. He ran the faces of the other head makers through his mind. He knew most of them from the Steam Council meetings, where the entourage of each baron was expected to stand behind his lord and master's chair. The makers sometimes exchanged sympathetic looks as their bosses droned on and on, and Tobias figured most of them were nice enough blokes. But which one had that kind of talent?

Eyes closed, he leaned back, feeling sleep tug at the edge of his consciousness. The familiarity of the room coaxed him to relax, even though it was the last place he should have felt welcome enough to sleep. He was in his father's study, in his father's chair, and beneath the stuffed tiger's head that hung high on the wall. The spot held so many memories, most of them unpleasant—and yet it felt more like home than his own town house a few streets away. It took time to put down roots, and he hadn't been given a chance. Too much work, too many emergencies—and for a long time, Alice had been at Horne Hill in Devonshire with the baby. They were in London now, but they hadn't completely settled into a habit of familiarity. He and his wife were still strangers living under the same roof.

It would have been worse without Jeremy. In truth, he hadn't expected to feel such instant devotion to a creature only minutes after he had been born. He'd seen the same look on his wife's face, that shock of belonging to a small, red-faced despot. It was the one thing they truly shared.

"What are you doing here?" his father asked from the doorway.

With this additional interruption, the idea he'd been trying to write down fluttered out of his grasp and back into the wilds. Tobias tensed, his mouth going sour with dislike. "Keating made me come."

Lord Bancroft was an imposing man, gray haired but still fit enough to put younger men to shame. He regarded Tobias with a coolness that bordered on amusement. "You missed a spectacular scene involving two steam barons and a fire-breathing bird. The drawing room curtains nearly caught fire, but we're guaranteed to make the society pages in the *Bugle*. I couldn't have planned it better if I'd tried. Too bad everyone's friends again, or there might have been a follow-up piece."

Good God, he doesn't miss a trick. Disgusted, Tobias folded up his notebook, slid the pencil down the spine, and tucked both into his pocket. "Perhaps I should get downstairs."

"Don't let me keep you," his father said with deceptive mildness. "Since I'm your host, convincing a guest to join the party is rather the point."

"And why aren't you with your admiring public?"

"I was looking for you. I heard rumors that my son graced this humble abode. I could scarce credit such a miraculous event." Bancroft's expression was hard. "I imagine you were just trying out my chair for size. After all, someday this will all be yours." He swept his arm around the room.

"I don't want your chair."

"No? It comes with a seat in the House of Lords. Those cushions are even better."

Tobias swore under his breath. "Why are we arguing?"

"I'm not. I'm trying to have a conversation. You don't make it easy."

Tobias sat back in the disputed chair. "About what?"

"It was the Scarlet King kicking up a fuss downstairs. Is he the one poking holes in Big Ben? He seemed to relish provoking your employer."

That was an interesting tidbit, and Tobias filed it away. "I don't know who was behind the attack, and Keating refuses to speculate. He has no desire to rush about with guns blazing and troops scouring the streets."

Lord Bancroft digested that. "Interesting. And wise."

"How so?"

"No point in showing his strength."

"I think it has more to do with the disturbance just before the attack. I was there; the mood on the streets is dangerous. Someone put a crowd of rioters into motion, but the public was eager enough to join in once there was a fight."

"That's my point. He's right to hold back. Whoever did this is trying to draw Keating out, to assess what forces he has at his disposal. They did much the same thing last year with that bomb in Baker Street. It didn't work that time, so now they're going for bigger game."

The bomb had been the Blue King's work, but Tobias doubted King Coal was behind this attack. His maker had been Dr. Magnus, and the sorcerer had burned up last November aboard the *Wyvern*. And as far as Tobias could tell, there was nothing magical about the brass mosquito.

"Speaking of Baker Street," his father mused, "is there any plan of calling Holmes in on this?"

"Not yet. I have an airship the size of a small carriage, and the best clues will be in its engines."

Lord Bancroft, who knew his way around a toolbox, nodded. "If anyone can decipher it, you will."

Tobias was almost startled. "Was that a compliment?"

Lord Bancroft's eyes almost twinkled. "You're an idiot about many things, but I've never doubted your talent with machines."

Before Tobias could reply, he heard the thud of feet pounding up the stairs. Tobias and his father exchanged a look, confusion mirrored between them. No one, gentry or servants, clomped about like farm boys in Hilliard House. It simply wasn't done.

"Who's that?" Tobias asked, his suspicion forgotten—at least for the moment.

"Damned if I know," Bancroft replied.

There was a pause followed by the sound of smashing china. Bancroft spun and was in the hall in seconds, with Tobias right behind him. Bancroft held up his hand for silence. Both men listened, Tobias holding his breath.

Heavy feet thundered on the stairs that led up to the bedrooms. The bedrooms? Alarm tightened his entire body. Closing his hands into fists, Tobias strode quickly toward the sound. "Call the footmen," he told his father. They would all be downstairs with the guests.

Surprisingly, Lord Bancroft turned to obey without argument, and Tobias mounted the steps alone. He'd barely gone a dozen feet before he heard loud, drunken laughter. Shards of white and blue china littered the stairs—the remains of a tall vase that had been one of his mother's favorites. Then Tobias bounded up the stairs two at a time.

He saw at once what was going on. Two young men—tall, mustachioed, sporting types—were reeling from wall to wall. And they were engaged in fisticuffs. One swung at his friend, staggering forward, but the other was too tipsy to dodge away in time. Flesh hit flesh with a resounding crack and both collapsed into the wall, knocking over a delicate étagère holding a collection of ferns. They began to giggle with the sloppy, high-pitched hiccups of the extremely drunk.

Tobias surged forward, grabbing the nearest one by the collar and dragging him toward the stairs. "Steady on!" said the man stumbling beside him. "No way to treat a guest."

"Hospitality has its limits." Tobias heaved him faster, rather enjoying himself.

"Don't you know who we are, laddie?" the man protested.

Tobias growled in reply. The man and his friend were dressed in evening clothes, but both wore a puff of red silk in the breast pocket of their tailcoats. It marked them as men in the service of the Scarlet King. "I don't bloody care."

He heard the feet of the other man behind him, building up momentum like a rusty engine. Tobias sidestepped in plenty of time, releasing his hold on his prisoner. One crashed into the other, and they both tumbled down the steps, narrowly missing the clock and all but landing in the arms of the footmen coming up the staircase. Since footmen were generally hired for their healthy physique, they grabbed the men with ease. The younger of the two looked up, inquiry in his wide brown eyes.

"Do something with those two, will you?" Tobias said wearily.

"Aye, sir," the lad said, heaving his charge upright. "Right away, sir."

"And call one of the maids to clean up. There's a bit of a mess."

Lord Bancroft, standing at the bottom of the steps, looked like he'd swallowed a mouthful of vinegar. He led the footmen and their burdens toward the door, no doubt to put a favorable mask on events, or perhaps to spout a few lines to any roaming newspapermen. The brief moment of father-son cooperation was at an end.

Still twitching with energy, Tobias turned and went back up the stairs, pausing to set the étagère to rights and rescue what plants he could. He scraped dirt back into the pots, covering over the straggling roots of the ferns. It was a servant's job, but he couldn't stand to wait for someone else to repair the damage. A low fury thrummed through him, setting every sense on alert. It wasn't just the broken vase or spilled dirt that set his skin prickling, but the disrespect. The minions of the steam barons seemed to feel the world was theirs—even the private places of their host's family home. And whatever Bucky had said, Tobias never counted himself as one of the steam barons' insufferable hangers-on. Tobias's set had never been angels, but they knew to take their bad behavior to a brothel or a private club.

He'd barely finished the thought when he heard the creak of a floorboard. He rose, turning and flicking dirt from his fingers. Imogen's bedchamber, as always, showed a light under the door. She had always suffered nightmares and, at

Lady Bancroft's orders, her daughter was never left alone in the dark.

The creak came again, and Tobias wheeled around. The sound hadn't come from Imogen's room but from the stairs behind him. William Reading was watching him with his head cocked to one side, his lips in a sly curve, and a large brass bird clutching his wrist.

POPPY WAS GETTING bored again. Guests were crowding back to the party now that the crisis of the firebird was past, and there seemed to be twice as many people as before. The talk was mostly about the attack on Westminster. Poppy had heard all that already in the past few days—even the wilder theories. The rest of the chat was about politics in general. It was a subject she couldn't care less about—or at least never had—but a sense of self-preservation had forced her to pay more attention lately.

As she understood it, there were two main groups of citizens in the Empire. There were the steam barons who made up the Steam Council, and then there was the rest. A few nobles still wielded a lot of power, but everyone up to and including the queen herself had lost ground to the barons. Poppy had learned a lot about that from her own family. Lord Bancroft had done something that displeased Jasper Keating—she'd never learned exactly what—and that hadn't sorted itself out until Tobias married Alice and went to work for Keating Utility. Unfortunately, Tobias had wanted to marry someone else—Imogen's best friend, Evelina Cooper. Her brother hadn't been quite right since.

The problem was that people talked about politics but nobody ever *did* anything—about the barons, or the poor, or the crime, or even how uncomfortable they were in fashionable clothes. People were too busy fussing about what everyone else thought, and her mother was trying to make Poppy just like the rest—a good and dutiful girl. It made her want to kick something over.

She wondered if whoever had driven that ship into the Clock Tower had felt that way. A tiny part of her admired that kind of initiative and, after all, no one had actually been hurt, right?

She'd made it to the food, arranged as a buffet on one side of the room. It was just light fare, meant for grazing rather than as a full meal. That would come later and be served with the proper pomp in the dining room.

Footmen guarded the table, though they occasionally glanced around at the ceiling, presumably looking for flaming birds of prey. Beside them stood a steam samovar that automatically dispensed tea with lemon or milk at the touch of a button. Poppy eyeballed the savories, arranged temptingly on silver platters. Snowy damask linens draped the table, giving it the appearance of an altar. *All hail the temple of luxury.* Too bad her stays were too tight to eat a thing.

And then she spotted a lone figure dressed in black, standing near the end of the table. He must have arrived late, because she hadn't seen him before this, but she knew the man at once—Sherlock Holmes, the detective. It was likely he was there at Keating's request—the Gold King liked to show off those he considered his extended entourage.

Intrigued, she watched him from the corner of her eye. *This* was a man who did things, whether people thanked him for it or not. He didn't let mysteries fester like something nasty left under the table for the dogs, and he didn't give up on people in trouble. When Evelina Cooper had disappeared, he'd kept looking for months until she was found wounded in the East End. Of course, Evelina was his niece.

Just as Imogen was her sister. There was no giving up on people you loved. Still, Poppy felt a rush of trepidation, like something cold trickling down her back. She cast another glance in Holmes's direction. He was tall, thin, and austere looking, all lean angles. Dark hair swept back from a widow's peak; a hooked nose emerged like a blade from sharply marked brows. He looked like a man with no tolerance for trivialities.

If only she wasn't wearing pink frills! It was bad enough being fifteen without looking like a raspberry trifle. *Never mind. There is no time like the present.* That was her motto. Or at least it was now.

Poppy took a gulp of air to stifle the butterflies in her stomach and approached the foremost detective in London. She affected a stroll, refusing to creep or cringe or, worse yet, bound toward him like an eager puppy.

"Mr. Holmes, I presume," she said, trying to sound like her mother.

He turned toward her. His eyes were gray—not the stormy gray of her brother's, or the dove-gray of Imogen's, but the gray she imagined for Antarctic ice. For the merest second, Poppy quailed—but it didn't last. With her, fear seldom did.

"You are Evelina's uncle," she said.

There was no obvious change in the man, but the corner of his mouth quirked, as if some of that ice had thawed. "And you, I believe, are Miss Poppy Roth."

She liked the fact that he used Poppy and not Penelope. That meant he knew something about her. "I am. And I would like to engage your services."

She had half expected him to laugh then, but his face grew utterly serious. "What is the case, Miss Roth?"

Her pulse was pounding, and the wretched stays were stealing her breath. She suddenly realized this was why so many women fainted all the time—they were being strangled by their underthings. "I require someone to look into the circumstances of my sister's illness."

The detective's eyebrows drew together. "I understand that the underlying ailment is of long standing. Since childhood, in fact. I assume you are referring to her condition since her kidnapping."

He would have heard all that from his friend Dr. Watson, who had been consulted on the case. "That's true. She's been sick before but never like this. Dr. Magnus kidnapped her, and she fainted when his ship plummeted from the sky. It stands to reason that there is a connection. The last words she spoke were 'Surely I killed you'—or something to that effect. Tobias couldn't remember exactly."

Holmes gave her a quizzical look. "I haven't heard that last part before now."

"No one has. I don't think Tobias told anyone else. He

can't quite believe that Im would say something like that. She's usually more, um, conciliatory."

"Ah." Holmes lifted a hand, beckoning her to follow him away from the table and into a quieter corner of the room. "That one detail changes things utterly. Tell me everything, Miss Roth, from the beginning."

She tried to decide if he was just humoring her, but the grave expression in his eyes argued against it. Well, there was nothing she could lose by giving him the facts.

"These are the things I know for certain." Poppy forced herself to stand still, for all she wanted to wring her hands or dig her toe into the carpet. The detective's intense gaze was making her nervous. "Imogen eloped that day. She meant to run away with Bucky Penner, but on the way Dr. Magnus kidnapped her and took her to his ship."

"And then your brother took her back to the *Helios,* and the battle followed."

Poppy nodded. She had seen the fight from the upstairs window, her pulse pounding so hard she thought she could taste her own blood. Poppy's voice snagged on the next words. "Imogen should be dead by now. The doctors cannot understand why she still lives."

A silence fell between them, the detective letting her swallow down a wave of pain that threatened tears.

"I understand there was history between Dr. Magnus and your father," Holmes said.

"They were friends," Poppy replied. "But that all stopped around the time I was in leading strings. I don't think they saw each other again until Dr. Magnus came to London a year and a half ago. Tobias knows the whole story. I was too little to remember."

"But Magnus is dead," Holmes mused. "Therefore, he is not a factor. The *Wyvern* was utterly destroyed."

"But I think he *is* a factor. Or at least the consequences of what he did haven't entirely faded away. Do you know about his automatons?"

"Yes." Holmes's face went dark. "Evelina told me."

"Did she tell you that the one named Serafina held the spirit of Imogen's twin?" Poppy shuddered, and she avoided saying the name with an almost superstitious dread. She didn't remember Anna, but her dead sister's face stared out at her from old pictures. She was supposed to be identical to Imogen, but Poppy always knew which twin she was. There was something cold in the eyes and the smile, as if the angels had run out of souls before they got to her.

"No, she didn't," the detective said quietly.

"Evelina might not know. I think Imogen might have found out on the ship." Poppy chewed her lip. "Imogen killed the automaton and then it burned up when the ship went down, so it was destroyed. But then what did Im's last words mean?"

That made his eyes go unfocused, as if he was looking inward. "That is a very, very good question. There was no one else present when she uttered those words?"

"Just Tobias. Something happened to my sister, Mr. Holmes. I need to find out what it was so we can fix it."

Holmes gave her a look that was unexpectedly kind. "You have met Evelina, so you are aware that I have experience enough not to underestimate young ladies. Especially those with promising minds."

Poppy flushed. She'd never actually done all that well at school. She was too easily bored. "Thank you, sir."

"I will do you the honor of being frank," he said. "I am sure your suspicions are based on observation and not fancy, and there is in fact something real amiss with your sister. But I suspect that magic is a factor, and that is not my area of expertise."

Magic was also highly illegal—a prejudice that the Steam Council promoted with all its money and power, mostly because they couldn't buy, sell, or otherwise control it. Most convicted of using magic were burned to death or locked up in a remote laboratory for study. No wonder Holmes didn't want anything to do with it. Who would willingly risk association with anything of the kind?

"I understand," she said softly, her gaze shifting away.

"You misunderstand. You need someone with more ability to assess the situation. Have you heard of Madam Thalassa?"

Poppy's eyes widened, hope reviving just as quickly as it had died. "Who hasn't?"

Holmes gave a slight smile. "Madam and I have an understanding. My methods and hers are universes apart, although we are both highly effective at what we do. Our spheres of interest might not touch upon any point, but we do each other the courtesy of redirecting clients when they stray into the wrong camp. If I ask her to see your sister, she will come."

"And she'll be able to help Imogen?" Poppy said breathlessly.

Holmes held up a hand. "She will know if there is anything to be done. That is as much hope as I can give you."

"Thank you, Mr. Holmes!" For a moment she lost her poise, feeling as if she might weep and grin at once, but then ducked her head, wanting to get this moment right. "I'm so grateful for your time and assistance."

"And now perhaps you can answer a question of mine."

"If I can."

"I understand the Scarlet King was here tonight. Did you see him?"

"I did. He's gone now."

The detective's brows drew together. "What did he do while he was here?"

"He brought a mechanical bird that breathed fire and he offered me a peppermint. Then he argued with Mr. Keating. Why do you ask?"

"Like everyone else, I am curious about the attack on Westminster. I've been watching the possible perpetrators with interest. I do not think that he did it, though."

"No?"

"No, but I do think he knows something." Holmes seemed to catch himself. "You didn't eat the peppermint?"

"No, sir."

"Good. It is not common knowledge, but Reading dabbles in poisons. It's how he got where he is today."

Poppy felt her eyes going wide. "Are you quite certain, Mr. Holmes?"

He gave her a sidelong look. "I don't trifle with such matters."

"Then thank you for the warning."

"My pleasure, Miss Roth," he said gently. "As I said, I have great respect for young ladies. And now, if you will excuse me."

He gave a slight bow, and she curtsied, and as quickly as that the encounter ended. He walked away, disappearing into the crush. She lingered in that spot for a moment, suddenly shaky as she reviewed the conversation. She was so glad she'd mentioned Imogen's final words. That had meant something—but what?

And how was Madam Thalassa ever going to see Imogen? The woman was a renowned medium, but stayed in hiding in fear for her life. How did Holmes even know how to contact her? Poppy's stomach knotted with uncertainty. She'd set something in motion, but was more than a little fearful of its end. If the law caught a psychic medium in the house, every member of the family would feel the Steam Council's wrath. But there was no other way Poppy knew of to help her sister.

Poppy had a sudden, aching need to see Imogen. It struck so deep, she caught her breath. She didn't care what her mother said; it was time to leave the party.

Poppy inched around the edge of the room, her skirts a ridiculous pouf of frills that seemed forever in the way of effective sneaking. Her mother, happily, was sunk deep in conversation with the Duchess of Westlake.

Poppy gained the hallway and began creeping toward the staircase. The spot between her shoulder blades prickled, wary of eyes that might spot her and drag her back into the stifling room.

The moment her feet touched the first tread, she bolted upstairs in a rustle of silk, past the longcase clock on the second-floor landing, and up to their bedrooms.

CHAPTER EIGHT

TOBIAS CROSSED TO READING IN THREE STEPS. HIS TEMPER was still up after tossing out the drunken Scarlets, and heat surged through his blood as he stopped before the man. He was already furious and Reading hadn't even opened his mouth yet.

"It seems your entourage has volunteered to be the entertainment," Tobias said shortly. "I just removed two of your men for brawling in our private quarters."

"I know. I was enjoying a pleasant conversation outside when they came tumbling down your steps. I came up here to apologize for their atrocious manners." Reading sounded almost sincere. "I'm afraid they made rather too merry tonight. Not exactly cutting the dash I expect from my men."

Tobias relaxed a degree, but it was a small one. All he wanted was for the Scarlet King to leave—although he wouldn't have minded a closer look at his mechanical pet. "I accept your apology. Is there anything else?"

Reading nodded. "Is there somewhere we can speak privately?"

Tobias hesitated, his instincts prickling a warning. The man was Keating's ally, but he was still a rival steam baron. That made any exchange complicated. Still, it was better to know what was on the Scarlet King's mind. "My father's study is below."

Reading waved toward the stairs. "Lead on."

Tobias complied, though he didn't like the man walking behind him. It made the skin between his shoulder blades itch. He didn't know Reading well, but he'd heard plenty of gossip. If half of it was true, the Scarlet King's public face—

the smarmy, hedonistic lecher that had courted Imogen—
was only one layer of the man's personality. What lay below
was even less appealing and far more dangerous. Tobias
breathed a sigh of relief when he pushed open the study door
and could turn to face his guest.

"Does that bird really breathe fire?"

Reading grinned. "Would you like a demonstration?"

"Perhaps not in the house. But I am told it is very fine."

"Thank you. It is my intention to make a flock of them as
a weapon against troublesome airships. The *Red Jack* had a
flock of trained ravens that were a damned nuisance. It gave
me the idea."

Tobias remembered seeing Nick's birds—huge black
creatures that could blind a man with their talons. They'd
fought as hard as the men. The grief that always followed
memories of the battle seeped into the room, seeming to
displace the air.

"How is your unfortunate sister?" Reading asked as he
settled his bird on the mantel and peeled off his glove of
silvery mail. "She was an exquisite beauty."

Tobias's shoulders stiffened. "Her condition remains the
same."

The man fell into a chair, a picture of elegant ennui.
"Would it be possible to look in on her?"

"No." Im had obviously loathed Reading. Now she was
utterly helpless. There was no way Tobias would expose her
to the man's roaming gaze now.

"Pity. Such a lovely girl. I had half a mind to marry her."

Tobias allowed himself a sharp smile. "And she had no
reservations about turning you down, as I recall."

"She would have come around. They always do." The
Scarlet King fingered his mustache, a look of irritation
sharpening his features. Tobias remained perfectly still,
though his muscles coiled to pounce. After the fight last
night, and then the Scarlets, he was on something of a roll.
He would have welcomed the excuse to smash the man's
face.

"But never mind all that." Reading pulled out a silver cigarette case, flipping a lever on the side. A tiny metal hand

passed out a cheroot, which Reading took. Then the hand burst into flame long enough to light the tobacco.

Tobias sat, reminding himself that he was there to get information. "What might I do for you, Reading?"

Reading blew a cloud of smoke, and then leaned back and crossed his legs. "I want to know what it would take for you to come work for me."

That was the last thing Tobias had expected to hear. It caught him off guard long enough for the Scarlet King to break into a laugh. "Oh, Mr. Roth, surely you know your own value. We all have makers, but you are the one with the real talent. And you are perfectly situated to give me exactly what I want."

Not in a thousand centuries would I take your coin. But despite himself, Tobias cast a glance at the metal bird. It really was exquisite, and it was no doubt the work of Reading's own maker, a fellow named Hedgely. Was Tobias really the better craftsman? It was all he could do not to get up and examine the thing, just to satisfy his pride.

But he knew better than to fall into that snare. "I am flattered, but surely you realize that such a thing would be impossible, even if I desired it. My wife is Mr. Keating's daughter."

The Scarlet King shrugged. "There is no obstacle that cannot be removed."

Tobias flushed. "I do not regard my wife as an obstacle."

"As you like. I will pay you twice whatever Keating gives you."

"Keating is the devil I know." The Gold King was foul, but he was better than this man. His moral compass was severely twisted, but at least he had one.

Reading's eyes glittered with challenge. "I would have thought you, of anyone, knew better than to trust that old Beelzebub."

"What makes you think I won't turn around and tell Keating that you're wooing me?"

"He'd be surprised if I didn't. This is just business."

Tobias doubted that. Keating was very particular about loyalty. He was also the biggest and most savage dog in the pack of curs that made up the Steam Council. If Tobias had to serve one of them, he preferred it to be the winner. "I'm afraid I'll have to decline."

Reading smiled, showing broad, white teeth. "You're not even curious to know how much I'd be willing to give you?"

"Money isn't everything. I'm curious to know why you're set on challenging the Gold King all of a sudden. I would have expected more subtlety."

"The moment that brass bug hit the clock, Keating's star began to set. Now is the moment to press my advantage." The Scarlet King rose. "Take this rope I'm throwing you, Roth. It may be the only thing that keeps you from sinking."

Tobias stood, refusing to let Reading stand over him. "I'm perfectly content in my position."

"And I want you to stay there. Perhaps I was not being clear. Stay with Keating, but work for me."

"You want me to spy?" Tobias's voice was flat with incredulity.

"Catch up, Mr. Roth. I want to know exactly what Keating's planning."

Tobias's mouth went sour with repugnance. "Get out."

He reached for the Scarlet King's arm, but Reading caught his hand in a grip as strong as an iron grapple. He pushed Tobias away as he might an importunate mutt. Tobias stumbled and caught himself against the desk.

Reading raised his eyebrows, mocking. "I know you are Keating's *intensely loyal* maker, but it is still only proper to show some civility to someone of my station."

Tobias's voice sank to a growl. "Leave, or I will throw you out myself if I have to. In fact, I beg you for the opportunity."

Reading gave a low laugh. "I'd like to see you try. Keating will have your head, at the very least. He's set on being my ally, for all his snarling."

"He won't be your ally for long."

"You mean to tell him about this conversation? Be my guest. What I have to offer him is worth more than any annoyance he might feel about a bit of poaching."

"You're betraying him."

"So will you before the end. That's how these games work."

"I don't play."

Reading let his breath out in a huff. "Then you'd better get the hell off the board."

POPPY SLOWED ON her ascent of the stairs when she heard raised voices. She was on the first landing, and the sound seemed to be coming from her father's study. Alarm sparked through her, making her tense. One of the speakers was certainly her brother—and he sounded furious.

She hesitated a long moment, foot poised on the next tread, wondering what she should do. Tobias could look after himself, but the emotions in the house tonight were running like riptides, invisible and dangerous. A little reluctantly, she stepped into the hall. She should investigate.

Poppy had barely taken three steps when the study door banged open and the Scarlet King swept out, holding his bird under one arm, as if he'd scooped it up in a hurry. He stopped directly in front of her, his blue eyes wide with anger. "Miss."

"Sir?" She couldn't help glancing at the bird, its feet sticking awkwardly into the air. She felt a giggle rising, and she swallowed it down, biting her lips together.

Tobias emerged from the room, his face sharp with tension. "Get the hell away from my sister, Reading."

The Scarlet King bent down, whispering confidentially, "You have a fool for a brother."

"Sometimes," she said, forcing herself not to recoil at the alcoholic tang of Reading's breath. She knew very well the only reason he was talking to her was to annoy Tobias, who was steaming down on them like an express locomotive.

The Scarlet King slowly grinned, restoring his phoenix to a more dignified position. "Impudent little baggage, aren't you?"

Poppy didn't answer, because Tobias was at her side, his features tight. "Go upstairs, Poppy. I'll come find you in a minute."

Reading gave her another look, raising one eyebrow. It was a taunt, daring her to disobey. For once, insurrection didn't tempt her.

"Go." Tobias gave the man a push from behind and, thankfully, Reading went. Tobias followed, no doubt making sure the Scarlet King went all the way to the curb outside.

Poppy shook out her skirts and hovered in the corridor until they were out of sight, and then she slowly mounted the stairs to Imogen's room. What exactly had happened between Tobias and the Scarlet King? No one except Mr. Keating had dared to confront the Scarlet King earlier, and yet Tobias had just shown him out of the house. Stranger still, he'd gone without a fight. *Why does that worry me more than anything else?*

Because villains only left the scene quietly when they had what they'd come for. What had the Scarlet King wanted? Something to do with Tobias? Or was he still lurking in the shadows, waiting for Imogen to wake up? A nasty feeling, a little like the slime that lurked in drainpipes, crawled through Poppy's insides. She broke into a run, taking the last few steps in a bound.

When she reached her sister's bedchamber, Poppy made a circuit of the room, carefully checking to make sure everything was in order. The space was large, really two chambers in one with a sitting room near the door and a large bed in an alcove at the other end. Bed curtains of heavy sky-blue silk were looped to the bedposts, framing Imogen where she lay against the eyelet snow of her pillows.

On the bedside table sat Evelina's gift to her friend—a little clockwork mouse and a bejeweled brass bird, both barely the size of Poppy's hand. That, more than anything else, told her that the Scarlet King hadn't found Imogen's room. Given his penchant for fancy animal toys, he would have picked them up for a look—and Poppy would know if they had been disturbed.

Her shoulders relaxed, letting go of the tense knot at the back of her neck. She sank into the chair beside Imogen's bed, grateful for the soft quiet of the room. She could hear the party below like a distant ocean and she closed her eyes a moment, imagining a safe and distant shore, with water lapping at her feet.

A few minutes later, Tobias joined her. "I guessed you would be with Im. Are you all right?"

"Yes," she said, not quite ready to come back to the here and now. All at once, she was so tired her hair ribbons ached, and a lump of what might become tears lurked at the back of her throat. "Why were you arguing with Mr. Reading?"

Tobias's eyes darted to Imogen. "He asked me to do something I didn't like."

Whatever it was must have been bad, because the turmoil in his expression made Poppy uneasy. "Did you refuse?"

"Of course." Tobias ran a hand through his fair hair. "I was offended that he thought I might agree. He must not think much of me."

She was dying to know what the Scarlet King had asked of her brother, but knew better than to come at the question head on. "Was he angry?"

He gave his head a slight shake. "It wasn't that straightforward."

"You should have punched him in the nose," she said with decision.

That brought a sad, weary smile to his face. Not as good as his old grin, but it was better than nothing.

"Don't ever change," he said. "But do be careful."

She nearly laughed at that—they were mutually exclusive ideas—but nothing in her brother's voice invited banter. Tobias had changed in the last few years. He was like a fire burning low in the grate, more ash than flame.

"I'll be careful," she promised—though she might already have broken that vow by inviting Mr. Holmes into their troubles. "I swear that I'll do the best that I can, circumstances permitting."

"I almost believe you." Tobias put his arm around her, pulling her close.

Poppy hugged him back fiercely, grateful for his unquestioning affection. He never scolded her for saying outrageous things, and never told her how to walk or dress or what she should or shouldn't read. Tobias wasn't a perfect man, but he was the best kind of big brother.

"I had better go downstairs and keep an eye on things," Tobias said, releasing her. "Stay here with Imogen and lock the door when I go."

Poppy nodded, feeling suddenly guilty. She had wanted to escape the party, but not because something had gone wrong. *Be careful what you wish for.*

After Tobias left, the silence in the room was a palpable thing. Poppy drew near the bed, her dress whispering into the candlelight. Imogen's face was utterly serene, dark gold lashes fanning her cheeks. Her hair was plaited into two long, pale braids that trailed to her waist. She truly looked asleep, the smocked bodice of her nightdress rising and falling with her gentle breaths.

The somber atmosphere brought the evening crashing in on Poppy. Wetness coursed down her cheeks, but she paid no attention even when it dripped off her chin. The party had been a mistake, and the Scarlet King had made it all so much worse—but that wasn't why she cried. Poppy wept because Imogen had loved parties, and now she didn't even know there was one going on a few floors below.

Poppy took her sister's hand, the soft cool fingers utterly relaxed. For a moment, she studied the contrast between them—Imogen's pale skin against her own. Poppy's hands were brown, scratched by the cook's cat and raggedy where she'd chewed her nails. For some reason, that made her want to cry even harder.

Where are you, Im? There had to be magic involved, or else her sister would have faded away. But how long could a spell like this last? Another month? Years? Forever? And what would happen when it ended?

Poppy had read plenty of fairy stories and tales of dark enchantment and knew anything was possible. Holmes was right. They needed expert advice. *Imogen* needed it. Poppy drew in a long, shuddering breath. If she could stand up to a steam baron, she wouldn't shy away from what needed to be done.

Come what may, Poppy was going to get help for her sister.

CHAPTER NINE

IMOGEN WOKE—OR AT LEAST THAT'S WHAT IT SEEMED LIKE. It was hard to tell as there was no sequence of night and day to mark the passage of time—just an eternal dull twilight. Had she truly been asleep? Or had her mind just wandered for the blink of an eye?

Disorientation clutched at her as she flailed for some reference—where she was, or when, or how she'd got there. She caught her breath and held it, listening for a footfall or a cough to indicate another living creature. But there was nothing. There never was.

She was still in the study where she'd awakened the first time—though she couldn't begin to say how long ago that had been. She was lying on the sofa, her cheek resting on a cushion she'd propped up against the arm. She'd have odd creases where the wrinkles in the cloth pressed into her face. Or that's what she assumed. The place had no mirrors.

Imogen let her gaze roam around the room, her stomach queasy with anxiety. Instinctively, she drew her knees up, making a protective ball. The air was gray, not quite twilight but dark enough she would have liked to light a lamp—but there were none of those, either.

As a result, the place seemed short of color, the pink and green carpet dingy, the spines of the books on the shelf a murky reddish-brown. It didn't matter that it was too dim to read the books. Even when the room had been bright, the pages had never quite settled down to a readable state, as if the type was playing a game of hide-and-seek upon the page.

Imogen paused, her mind drifting. The room had been bright once. That was right, wasn't it? She remembered the drapes once had been a bright lemon yellow. Or was that green? Just like the type, the room never quite settled down to a predictable form.

It's darker now, and smaller. There was one more book-shelf along the wall, but now it's missing without even a blank spot to show it was there. All at once she was light-headed, as if thinking about the changes was giving her a headache. Since she'd been there, ideas had become will-o'-the-wisps, shining bright and then vanishing before she could quite reel them in. But she wanted to remember—it felt terribly important that she pay attention.

Imogen sat up carefully, clutching her thoughts so hard she ground her teeth. After a shaky moment, she rose to her feet, smoothing down her skirts and combing her hair back with her fingers. All her hairpins had been lost along the way, so she'd plaited her hair into one long braid down her back. Her clothes had suffered, too. At some point she must have opted for comfort, because her bustle, half her petti-coats, and corset were gone. Her dress didn't fit right with-out the undergarments, but there was no one there to witness her fashion faux pas.

Experimentally, she paced the distance from wall to wall. Last time she checked it had been twenty-one strides. She was sure of it. Now there were merely seventeen. *And what happens once there are only ten? Or five? Or none? Or do I simply never sleep again, so nothing can shrink when I'm not looking?* Or maybe she would just forget that she'd ever existed, and wink out like a sparkler on a cake. Imogen made a terrified noise, filling the austere silence with even that tiny whimper. The place suddenly seemed deathly cold. *Why is this happening?*

She couldn't quite remember how she'd got there, or where she'd been before. Someplace else with other people—that much was obvious—but she had the feeling her memories were fading along with the room. There were snatches of conversation, the images of parties and school but not much more. *Why is this happening?* She wanted to know while she still remembered to care.

Imogen pushed aside the drapes to discover there was nothing but a blank wall behind them. An image flickered through her mind of a window there, looking out onto . . .

She couldn't remember. At least, she couldn't remember an exact picture of what had been on the other side of the window glass—but she did remember a feeling. Blind, abject panic that pounded like a fist from her gut through the back of her throat. She'd screamed until her voice had shattered, and then she'd cried hoarsely, moaning like a bereft child.

The notion seemed ridiculous, but her body remembered her horror, as if the vibrations were still rippling through her flesh. *Why can't I see now what I saw then? Where did the window go?* And why hadn't she remembered that before now? New foreboding crept over her, kicking her heart into a higher gear. *You remember because this time you made yourself remember. But there's something in this room trying to make you forget.*

Something, maybe, but she was more certain it was a *someone.* And the reason she was certain was because the notion made her stomach turn to ice. Her body knew the truth. Someone had brought her here to this shrinking room. And the only person who would do that was a bitter enemy.

It all seemed madness, but the chill in her gut said it was true. And unless she wanted to fade and vanish, she had to leave. *And no doubt this is an obvious conclusion you've drawn before.* This time she'd have to get past deciding there was a problem and start doing something about it before she slid back to the beginning all over again. *So find a door and leave, ninny!*

"Would I even remember if there was a way out?" she asked aloud, her voice thick with lack of use. "But surely I've looked for one already."

Imogen paced, rubbing her arms more to keep herself alert than because of any cold. *And now I'm talking to myself. Holy hat ribbons, I'm getting as barmy as Aunt Tabitha.*

"But so what if I've looked for a door? I don't remember doing it. That's almost as good as hope."

She returned to the wall behind the curtains, running her fingers over every inch, but finding only ordinary paint and plaster. And then she began a careful circuit of the room, testing every crack and cranny for hidden switches or evidence of concealed doors. When the walls revealed nothing, she began on the floor, peeling back the carpet and tugging on every board to make sure the fit was tight.

This at least didn't seem silly. She had a vague recollection that her father had a concealed compartment beneath his study floor, full of nasty secrets. There'd been a family row about it not long ago. That made her smile—not about the fight, but the fact that getting active seemed to be doing her memory good.

She hauled the sofa aside, pushed back the tables, and stomped her feet, listening for the sound of a hollow. Nothing. Frustrated, Imogen sat down, biting her thumbnail. What had she been hoping to find, anyhow? A tunnel to China?

And why was she sitting there again, with the room a mess around her? Imogen pondered a moment, recollection of what she had been doing bobbing just out of reach as her stomach grew cold. She was losing. *What? What am I losing?*

Time stilled for a moment as she groped toward her thoughts as if they were the string of an errant kite. *A door! I was looking for a door.* She'd checked the walls and the floor, so she looked up at the ceiling, but it was blank as paper. *Where else is there to look?*

Imogen rose and began taking the books off the shelves. There weren't that many, but she hauled books until her arms began to ache. Almost at once, she realized that they filled up as quickly as she emptied them. Frustrated, she began flinging volumes, shoving them away to land like broken birds on the floor, white pages fluttering as they fell. And then she simply burrowed, thrusting her head between the shelves and sweeping with her arms.

That did the trick. The shelf seemed to grow and widen

until it was a platform broad enough for Imogen to kneel
and then push through a chasm in the wall behind. Ragged
plaster scraped at her arms and ankles, but the hole was
wide enough to crawl through. Imogen stumbled to her feet,
blinking. Had she crawled out of the room, or into something else?

"Out, I think," she murmured, allowing her eyes to adjust
to an even greater darkness. The sharp breeze on her face
told her that she was out of doors. *So I escaped through the
side of the house where I was trapped?* Something about
that didn't seem quite right.

She walked a few steps, feet crunching on fallen pine needles. When she turned around, she could still see the hole—
there was a brighter light beyond—but there was very little
impression of anything but vague shadows around it. "What
a peculiar place."

Hesitant, she took a few more steps away from the hole,
liking the sensation of freedom. Despite her lapses in memory, she was fairly sure she hadn't escaped this far before.
Then again, liberty brought risk.

Tension cramped her neck muscles, making it hard even
to turn her head. She seemed to be in the middle of a clearing. About twenty yards away was the edge of a woods. The
tree trunks were spaced far apart and covered with moss,
some just jagged stumps as if lightning had blasted them
away. Age hung in the air like a scent, as if this place had
seen the birth of the universe.

It was too dark to see the treetops, but something blocked
the stars. The only light shone down on the clearing from a
shrouded moon. Nothing stirred but a chill, sterile wind.
*And yet I don't hear the wind in the leaves. Maybe it's winter
here?*

The detail struck her as odd since she wasn't longing for
a coat, but larger problems loomed, starting with what to do
next. There were no cabs driving by, no helpful signs with
an arrow pointing toward home. But surely there was a path
to somewhere, and unless she wished to remain stuck in the
study, she would have to take a chance.

Really, you're a town girl, a debutante who knows how to

match bonnets to dresses and not much else. You'll lose yourself in the trees and perish.

"Oh, do be quiet," Imogen told herself. Sometimes she really was no help. She took another couple of steps toward the edge of the woods and searched for some sign of a track.

But the farther she got from the room where she'd been, the less she felt that she was alone. She didn't like to fall back on the cliché about feeling eyes follow her every move—and yet there was a sense of tingling pressure that said something slid through the darkness ahead.

"Don't be ridiculous," she said harshly, forcing herself forward until she was right at the edge of the clearing. The air felt odd, as if the pressure changed right on that line between open space and the murky forest. The grass beneath the trees was long and pristine. She didn't see any paths, any sign of footprints. Maybe no deer lived in those woods to make trails. Maybe there was something around the other side of the house. Not, of course, that she could see the corner of the house in the dark. It just looked like an ocean of blackness behind her. *And if it's a house, who lives there?*

Fear crowded around her like a fog, a malevolent intelligence plucking at her braid, her clothes, the skin of her face with a touch that was not fingers—not exactly. And yet, horribly, that tactile quality was real. Imogen shuddered, frozen in place. Part of her revulsion was because the feeling was so familiar. She'd had dreams that made her feel this way—she remembered *those* all too well. The frozen, suffocating horror of being stuck, unable to move while her breath was stolen away. And the ones about wandering away from her body, unable to find her way back. And then there had been the dreams about the Whitechapel murders.

That thought turned her insides to a block of ice. *And the reason I dreamed all that was because Anna was there.* Her dead twin had somehow shared her dreams while she slept, turning them into nights of unspeakable horror.

Anna, whose soul had been preserved by Dr. Magnus and installed in the murderous automaton named Serafina. *And who then tried to kill me.* Except that Imogen had blown her to pieces aboard the *Wyvern.* And even if Serafina had survived that, nothing could have been left of the doll by the time that ship had burned and crashed. But if the body was destroyed, what about the soul? Did killing one automatically do away with the other?

Imogen remembered Nick and Tobias rescuing her. Images were coming back in a flood—the battle, the fire, Tobias trying to make her put on a parachute. And then—everything had gone black. All that she remembered was the horrific sensation of being torn apart. *I thought I had killed her.*

Blood began pounding in her ears, loud beneath those soundless trees. Silent, still, ancient—the place looked cursed. And whatever waited in the forest wasn't anything with a heartbeat. It was far more sinister.

Somehow her sister's shade had dragged her here, and it was waiting for her in the forest.

Before she even knew she was doing it, Imogen backed away—retreating toward the break in the plaster wall between the shrinking study and the trees. Her steps turned to a jog and then she broke into a stumbling lope. She was sure she hadn't walked far from the hole, but now the distance grew, leaving her running and running while the lurking darkness closed in.

Imogen bashed into the wall before she saw it, making herself reel. And then she remembered to crouch down, diving through the hole in a scramble of elbows and knees. She fell onto the carpet of the study amid the litter of books, rolling to an ungainly stop when she hit the divan.

Shaking, Imogen drew her knees under her and gripped the back of the sofa, pulling herself to her feet. Her long skirts tangled around her ankles until, furious, she kicked out at the froth of petticoats and ruffles—now grimy from the outdoors. Her foot connected with one of the books, sending it spinning into the wall with a thump. She bent and grabbed another book, throwing it as hard as she could. It connected with a china vase and sent it crashing to the floor.

"Ugh!" she snarled, the full force of circumstances closing in. She was trapped. Utterly trapped. Anger, dark and thick, began to bubble up—and it wasn't just a red-tinged fury at the present. There was old rage, too. She was resentful at her father, for treating her like an investment to be sold at a premium. Angry at her mother, for letting it happen. Furious that Tobias had bartered his own freedom to Jasper Keating. Hating that she'd lacked the tools to protect herself.

And more than anything, loathing the terror that Anna represented. Anna, who seemed to be indestructible. Stronger. The survivor. *She should be dead. I was the one who lived.*

She picked up another vase and smashed it into the wall. The crash filled her with an unholy satisfaction. She picked up another book—despising the shifting letters on the page—and tore out a fistful of leaves.

She'd never allowed herself this kind of a tantrum before. Destruction, delicious and wanton, soothed the raw heat in her brain. Then she flung the disemboweled book aside and stomped to the drapes, shoving them aside once more. This time—perhaps her perception had been cleared because she was so enraged—the window was there.

Imogen choked on a cry, smacking at the curtains when they tried to fall back and obscure her view. Logic said she'd see the forest. Instead, she saw the inside of a house. *Her* house. Those were the stairs descending from the bedrooms to the second-floor landing—but to see it at this angle made no sense. There was no room where she stood, much less a window—and everything she saw was far too large.

As she slowly realized why the perspective was so wrong, a memory of screaming returned—screaming and pounding on the glass. She'd had this same experience the first time she'd looked out the window.

To see what she saw, she would have to be inside the longcase clock that the sorcerer Dr. Magnus built. It had sat on the landing of Hilliard House, facing the stairs, ever since her family had moved in.

Shock melted her insides to a puddle and she leaned against the cool glass to hold herself up. *Is this where I begin shrieking again?* Reflexively, she sucked in her breath, but a stab of fury made her cough it out again. *Fear doesn't work. Fear doesn't help you fight back. Anger does.*

Rage cleared her head, sharpening her senses and blowing the last fog from her wits. Blood pounded in her ears, deafening her—until it dawned on her that it wasn't her pulse at all. Now that she knew where she was, she realized that thudding heartbeat was the clock's steady tick.

But why in damnation am I in a sorcerer's clock?

She sensed, rather than saw, the change around her. Slowly, she turned to face the room, her face going slack with astonishment. Now, instead of shrinking, the room was simply fading. She could see the pattern of the carpet through the sofa, the bookcase through the wing chair. The study had been an illusion, and no doubt the woods outside had been some sort of construct, too. She'd been tricked.

Because what she saw now was Dr. Magnus's clockwork, the wheels and gears moving in carefully regulated increments. The moment her mind grasped that, the furnishings disappeared altogether. *Now that I see what's real, I can act.* She wasn't going to be fooled by a comfortable sofa or a scary dark woods one second longer.

But for a moment, Imogen yearned for those soft cushions—for now everything was unfamiliar. She tilted her head back, her gaze going up and up. Brass gears the size of waterwheels arched up into shadowy darkness, their polished teeth looking sharp and pitiless as they clicked past. She started as something spun to her left, sending a shiny arm flying to a new position. Another thing clunked and she whirled around, half expecting a gyrating mechanism to smack her in the head. Her breath was coming fast, her pulse—hers, not the clock's—was speeding with alarm. There were springs and cogs and wheels everywhere, all ceaselessly moving, and all looking like they could crush flesh and bone without missing a beat.

She understood none of it—Evelina and Tobias had been the ones crazy for taking things apart. Yet now this was her landscape. She would just have to learn how to navigate it. There would be no sitting out this quadrille.

Anna was somewhere in there, too. Imogen could feel her presence, just as she had throughout a dozen years of nightmares. And her twin had chosen this particular battleground for a reason. *She tried to kill me once. I did my best to kill her.* There was only one way this confrontation would end.

Imogen's mouth went dry, her eyes prickling with hot tears. She wrapped her arms around her middle, as if holding herself in one piece. This was the nightmare of nightmares.

She needed to find her twin and destroy her, once and for all.

CHAPTER TEN

IT HAD BEEN FIVE FRETFUL DAYS SINCE EVELINA HAD DIS-
covered she was penned within the college walls. She'd received no word from either Keating or Sir William. The
only thing that had changed was that she had received a delivery of equipment from Moriarty.

Evelina sat in her rooms, elbows on her worktable and a
scatter of projects on every side. Sunlight touched the silver
bracelets she wore, the buttons down the bodice of her fashionable day dress, and the implements spread out before her.
There was a heavy brass microscope, a gas burner, a leather
case of slides, and enough half-assembled pieces of clockwork to give a horologist fits. The clockwork had been her
own project, but the rest was from the professor. He had sent
the very best.

After indulging her talents in secret for so many years, it
was a luxury to have a private workspace and the time to
sate her curiosity. But that was the problem, wasn't it? She
had all that leisure because the rest of her life had been
taken away—including Nick and Imogen. And being confined had given Evelina too much time to grieve for their
loss. She was starting to feel frayed, like pieces of her were
unraveling and falling away. She either slept too much or
not at all, pacing her rooms until her feet ached.

Some primitive reflex warned her she was in danger of

collapsing altogether. She needed a problem outside of herself to keep her moving forward. So escape was at the top of her list, and Moriarty seemed the best tool she'd found—not a comforting thought. But while she made up her mind about him, she forced herself to concentrate on the unsolvable problem of her friend's illness. Though different, her grief for Imogen was every bit as acute as the wrenching loss of Nick.

She'd sat by Imogen's bedside that November night when the *Helios* had returned victorious, but Evelina had enough magic to know the young woman on the bed was just a shell. Imogen's soul had been ripped away. Could Evelina do anything to put it back?

She asked herself that question plenty of times, but a letter had come from Baker Street yesterday—delivered by one of her uncle Sherlock's pet urchins who'd clearly climbed over the college wall—with news that Poppy Roth had approached the detective with a view to hiring him on the case. But, Holmes went on, magic wasn't his forte. He had promised to turn the problem over to Madam Thalassa, but apparently she was proving hard to find. Since Evelina knew both magic and the Roth family, did she have relevant data to add? Strange but true, Holmes was very nearly asking her opinion.

Her first thought was that he did well to treat Poppy Roth seriously. The girl was a force of nature. Her second was that she was on dangerous ground. It was her magic, and that of the devas at her command, that was keeping Imogen's body alive in hopes that she would recover on her own. Evelina had set the spells in motion the night she'd spent at Imogen's side—it was the best she could do when she had so little time. She'd tried to work from afar since, but navigating the realm of spirit was not her talent. Not even the university's impressive archives—which had special dispensation to maintain a collection on magic and the spirit realm—had been able to help.

The difficulty was that if a true medium—even one as reputable as Madam T—went crashing through Evelina's existing spells, things could go horribly wrong. And yet she

couldn't take those spells away because Imogen would die.
She had to explain all of this to her uncle, but it was hard
when she had to smuggle letters out of the college with all
the cloak-and-dagger drama of an international spy. It would
be a damn sight easier if she could just fix things herself.

Her jaw set, Evelina concentrated on the surface of the
worktable, the grain of it flowing through an archipelago of
chemical stains and the odd crumb from her breakfast. She
would make one more try before she admitted that for all
her vaunted talent, she couldn't help her best friend in the
world. She let her consciousness drift, her vision going soft
as she passed into a blank, rudderless state.

The odds of finding Imogen's spirit were negligible. Without knowing where in all the possible realms of heaven and
earth she had gone, all Evelina had to draw on was the long
friendship that bound them together. That made for a slender thread, but it was far better than nothing. *Imogen?*

There was no response, and Evelina pushed harder, broad-
casting her call through the aether that connected all the
realms together as blood binds the body's organs. She could
feel the tug of the bracelets holding her back. They didn't
stop her magic—their primary purpose was to confine her
physically—but the silver they were made from made it
clumsy, as if she were trying to repair clockwork while
wearing ill-fitting gloves.

Her eyes began to drift closed, her gaze still fixed upon
the table. The pattern of the wood grain melted into metaphor, outward sight changing to a landscape of the mind.
She reached out again, and the sensation was like swim-
ming in thick, warm water, every stroke a satisfying effort
that sped her along. She could feel the ripples stirred by her
power, and summoned more energy, digging deep into her
reserves. She was still recovering from confining the blast
that had destroyed the laboratory. Calling on it again so
soon would drain her, but no matter. If it helped her friend,
she would spare nothing to send those waves to the very
ends of that ocean and beyond.

But wanting too much was her mistake. She'd gathered
some of her power under the tutelage of the sorcerer Dr.

Magnus, and that dark energy was treacherous stuff—all the more so because she'd locked it away so long, afraid of what it stirred in her. But unthinking, she reached for it, ready to put everything on the line.

It bubbled up, sweet and thick as death. Evelina flinched from the contact, her bracelets making her awkward. All it took was for her mastery to slip for one hairbreadth of time and, like a serpent, it turned on her.

Evelina gasped, the sweet ache of the power splitting her in two, as if an ax had riven her breastbone. But what that sharp blade released was delicious, silken fingers delivering equal parts pleasure and pain along every nerve of body and mind. She froze, her body locked in that inhalation of surprise at the same instant her perception flew outward in a sudden burst. In that moment she encompassed so much, too much, but she indeed sensed Imogen, a quivering mote in a vast, unformed Somewhere.

Imogen! Joy rang through Evelina, her vulnerable state making every emotion thunderously acute. She lunged for Imogen, the flicker of Evelina's conscious energy darting out. She needed to touch Imogen, to grab her and pull her home.

But Evelina didn't really know how, and she had lost full control of that wild, serpent strength. The lunge made her lose her inner balance, a sudden slip and fall, her mind frantically twisting to keep the power steady but fumbling it all the same. Imogen's location spun out of mind.

Evelina's head hit the table with a crack. It snapped her back to herself, the wood-grain pattern suddenly stark before her. "Ow!" She pressed a hand to her forehead, her stomach lurching dangerously.

And then the scattered power crashed through the room, animating the scraps of unfinished clockwork strewn across the table. Gears whirred, levers pumped and clicked and chirruped—nothing quite working because nothing was entirely finished. Most of the machines didn't even have springs to wind them yet, but they still flailed in a mockery of life, half-formed creatures born before their time. Only the clock on the mantel chimed a coherent protest, its careful calibration knocked askew by the marauding energy.

Damn and blast. Evelina covered her ears at the racket, sickened by the pulse of uncontrolled power, and then had to jump up to close the valve of the gas burner when it tried to set itself alight. There was a pain behind her eyes that threatened a nosebleed, but trying to dampen the energy would only make it worse. The only way to avoid that was to wait out the maelstrom and hope no one else heard it.

Eventually, slowly, the power dissipated into hiccups of activity, and then finally nothing. She fell back into her chair, covered in perspiration that cooled until she shivered. Fright crackled like static through her body. Falling, whether it was from a tightrope or from the construct of a spell, always left her wide-eyed and prickling.

She was drained and she had failed—and it stung. Bracing her elbows on the table, Evelina pressed her face into her hands, pushing back her emotions. Now all that was left was to get word to Madam Thalassa—if Holmes could find her—and warn her about the protective magic she'd set around Imogen. She hoped the medium could find a way around it. But worse in Evelina's mind was having to admit that she wasn't up to the job of helping her own friend. What kind of a half-trained, ham-fisted magic user was she?

Evelina rose from the worktable, her knees still shaky, and pushed open the window, one of her silver bracelets clattering against the glass. The air was cold, but it would help to clear her head. A dirigible floated above the college rooftops, the fat red balloon as cheerful as a child's toy in the pewter-colored sky. Behind it, the sun struggled against the thick cloud, but it was a losing battle. By nightfall, there would be rain.

Her gaze left the sky as the clock across the common struck three. She'd gone up once to look at the workings inside. They had been unremarkable, but the view of Highgate and Hampstead Heath had reminded her of all the places she was now forbidden to roam. The isolation was worst. It had been nearly a year since she'd been allowed to visit freely with friends or family and she craved contact.

Just as Keating used the bracelets, he used family affection as a weapon. He'd manipulated her into the Whitechapel escapade by threatening her uncle. Now he enforced her obedience the same way. She had to earn time with those she loved through perfect obedience—and no doubt the laboratory incident would weigh against her.

But there were the secret letters. Her gaze fell on the modest Ladies' College library. It was open to the public on Tuesday afternoons—a concession to the township that formed part of the agreement for using the land. A man in a tweed coat was sitting on a bench outside the doors, smoking and thumbing through a book. As the last chime of the clock melted away, he opened his watch, checked it, and rose. He was in his thirties, brown haired, fit, with a mustache and pleasant, open features. Evelina knew him at once: Dr. John Watson. *Twice in one week. Something's up!*

As he stood and tucked the volume into his pocket, a dog she hadn't seen emerged from under the iron bench and trotted at his heels. It was a water spaniel with rusty-brown spots and probably belonged to a patient who was too indisposed to walk it. The dog was perfect camouflage. With the animal in tow, Watson looked every inch a gentleman of the half-rural neighborhood, out for a pleasant stroll to the library. He wasn't as well known as her uncle—in fact, though he was a handsome man, he had a gift for making himself utterly invisible. Nobody, including the Gold King's Yellowbacks, would give him a second glance.

Evelina knew better, excitement mounting inside her. There would be a letter waiting for her in their secret hiding place in the library wall. Gratitude to the dear, loyal doctor burned hot within her, bringing tears to her eyes. Evelina grabbed her coat and nearly ran out of her rooms.

She reached the quadrangle and began hurrying along one of the paths that crisscrossed the green between the buildings. She pulled her coat closer, realizing that she'd forgotten to button it in her haste, and then fumbled for the gloves she knew were stuffed in her coat pockets, barely slowing her pace. Soon frost would extinguish the last of the flowers. Already, the creepers that covered the walls were touched with red.

Hunger nagged at her, reminding Evelina that she'd drained her power. And it wasn't just hunger for food, but for darker things. She shoved it down, cursing Magnus for burdening her with the need. Death in battle had been too good an end for him.

She reached the bench by the library, the cold feeling more like November than September. Nevertheless, she sat down on the wooden seat, scanning the quadrangle. There were people hurrying between buildings, but their heads were down against the wind. No one was looking her way. She twisted around. Behind the ornate black iron frame of the bench, there was a gap in the mortar of the library wall. Between two of the smooth gray stones, she could just make out a corner of paper. She slipped off her glove for a better grip and tugged. The bundle of pages was fat and didn't want to move. Dr. Watson must have wedged it in with force. Swearing under her breath, Evelina turned back to the quadrangle, taking another look around. A knot of students was coming her way. She tugged again, and the paper tore.

The other girls were too close now. Evelina dropped her glove, giving herself an excuse to fumble about for it until they had gone. Then she turned, jammed her fingers into the crack, and pulled out the packet with no regard for skin or the condition of her fingernails. She slipped the pages into her pocket and started back for her rooms in a better mood than she had been in all day.

It lasted until she opened the packet and started to read.

CHAPTER ELEVEN

SHERLOCK HOLMES ENTERED THE DIOGENES CLUB—AN IN-
stitution well known as a haven for misanthropes. Feeling as
he did—nervous, headachy, and with his stomach in a roil—
it was a comforting venue. It was the next best thing to a
desert isle. Members were not permitted to acknowledge one
another, much less talk. After three infractions of this rule,
even an excess of coughing could result in expulsion.

But behind this curmudgeonly facade, the club was the
unofficial headquarters of the wealthier members of the
Baskerville rebellion. That, and a measure of fraternal curiosity, was what had brought him there that day.

Holmes was immediately shown to the Stranger's Room,
the only place visitors and conversation were allowed. The
space was pleasant, with green walls and potted palms lending a vaguely tropical air.

The footman who had shown him in still hovered uncertainly at the door. Holmes gave another peremptory flick of
his fingers, and finally the man bowed and left. As his footsteps faded, the only sound that remained in the club was
the *clop-clop* of horses along the street below. The detective
set his hat and stick aside and subsided into one of the arm-
chairs. The breeze slouching in through the sash windows
was unseasonably cool, carrying the scent of the Thames
the way some men carried a libertine past.

His stomach, already unsettled, raised a protest. *Damnation.* Whatever Watson was dosing him with was only slightly less obnoxious than no medical treatment at all. Holmes stood to close the window, every fiber of his being protesting the motion. He sat down again, this time without his usual grace. A light sweat dewed his forehead, but he didn't permit the moment of weakness to last.

What sort of a pathetic creature are you? Irritation stiffened his posture, and he snapped his cuffs straight. Holmes had his own way of dealing with his chemical habits, and that was simply ignoring any discomfort that arose whenever he chose to lay his syringe aside for a while. Bad habits had to be treated sternly. It was a question of fortitude.

Never mind that he felt like something scraped out from under the shoe of a hackney driver's nag. Maybe Watson's cures weren't such a misbegotten idea after all.

He pulled out his watch, checked the time, and replaced it in the pocket of his waistcoat. His brother, punctual to a fault, would arrive in precisely one minute. Holmes wiped his upper lip, forcing his mind on something—anything— besides his own discomfort. Outside, he watched a flock of police constables—City of Westminster and Scotland Yard both—hurry by. The attack on the Clock Tower had garnered one positive result: London's two police forces might still be incompetent, but at least they were for once united.

The door opened and Mycroft strode in, his size making the floorboards creak. He was every bit as tall as Holmes and built like a bear. With a huff of exasperation, he stopped a dozen feet away and gave Sherlock the full benefit of his ice-gray stare. "Are you in your right mind?"

Holmes leaned back, familiar irritation sparking along his abused nerves. "Do you mean that philosophically or medically? If the latter, I suggest you speak to Watson. He has a better grasp of the diagnostic arts."

Mycroft pulled a chair close and sat near enough that he could keep his voice just above a whisper. "I mean pharmacologically. You look like someone just dug you out of one of the Highgate mausoleums."

Holmes considered a moment, and decided with satisfaction that his horseshoe comparison was more creative. Sadly, Mycroft was prone to favoring the obvious over the poetic. "I assure you I am very much alive."

"I heard Watson moved back in."

"His wife died."

"And he was obliged to clean you up."

"The man needs a hobby."

Mycroft's mouth turned down, the contemptuous frown of the older brother. "Apparently yours involved a syringe. Are you an idiot, with all we have at stake?"

His brother's words stung deep enough to stir the embers of shame. Holmes could come up with excuses for his lapses, from his failure to save the Ripper's victims to his inability to protect Evelina from the Gold King. The last year had left his pride in pieces—but failure was not something he could discuss with Mycroft. Instead, Holmes shrugged a shoulder as if he didn't care. "I don't adjust well to boredom."

"How can you be bored? We're on the cusp of a civil war."

"I have not been as involved as you are."

"You can't be. The Gold King has you under watch."

"So he does." Holmes steepled his fingers, his elbows resting on the arms of the chair. "Everywhere I go I trip over the Gold King's men; it has impacted the efficacy of my work. And I am not the only victim of their influence. Crime used to be a relatively wholesome affair, fueled by anger, avarice, and lust. Now it is all political maneuvering with all the passion of a tuppenny whore. Our criminal class has lost its verve."

Mycroft's frown wavered into amusement. "I would never have put you down as a traditionalist."

"I have a positive nostalgia for an everyday art thief. At least they were stealing something worth having."

"Is rulership of the Empire such a poor prize?"

Holmes fell silent, wondering where to take the conversation. The Diogenes Club and the rebellion shared a founder in Mycroft Holmes—a supreme civil servant who acted as an informational repository in official government affairs. Unofficially, he had designed the shadow government meant to take over when the Baskervilles succeeded. He claimed to have orchestrated the new regime for sport, but Holmes had long doubted that was true. To begin with, his brother was far too invested for someone conducting a recreational exercise. *Could it be that my brother has at last discovered the vice of ambition?*

Even that much thinking made his head hurt worse, so Holmes got straight to the point. "The last I saw of you, you had broken free of Keating's prison and were about to make for Scotland on the *Red Jack*."

Mycroft's gaze slid away. "You're wondering why I came back to London."

"More *how,* given that you are a fugitive."

"There was a discreet inquiry into my activities, and nothing could be proven against me. As you know, I cover my tracks well. In the end, the inquisition looked rather ridiculous."

Holmes couldn't suppress a smile. There was no question of his brother's skill. "And yet, they could have convicted you if they chose. Many have swung based on the slimmest evidence."

"Her Majesty decreed me innocent of wrongdoing."

"And the Steam Council accepted her decree?"

"The royal heels dug in deep. My services are valued. More to the point, Keating has too many other problems to bother with me."

"Are you sure about that?"

"What do I matter, when one of his own has thrown down the gauntlet?"

"The episode with the clock?" Holmes asked.

"Yes. I think everyone agrees that was a deliberate insult. Keating is readying his army. So is the Blue King, and that has long been Keating's greatest fear."

"Do we have eyes on Blue's forces?"

Mycroft sat back. "Not as good as I would like. Blue is suspicious."

"I know." A year ago, King Coal had asked Holmes to find the traitor in his court. Events had interfered and he'd never properly investigated. "Is there a weak link we can exploit?"

"Perhaps his man of business, Juniper. He's a little more enterprising than your average lackey."

"I wonder if he was the one who first initiated the bomb in Baker Street." A chill tingled down Holmes's limbs at the memory. At one point he had almost suspected Mycroft.

"The incident served a purpose." Mycroft rose and pulled the bell for the footman. "It kept the Steam Council unsettled enough that we had time to solidify our advantage before the steam barons came knocking on our door."

"The bomb came within a whisker of killing everyone in the house."

"But it didn't." Mycroft waved a hand. "I found out about it in time to bring everything under control."

Holmes narrowed his eyes, but he was given no chance for a retort. There was a discreet knock at the door, and one of the club's uniformed waiters appeared. As Mycroft ordered refreshments, Holmes's thoughts drifted back over the bomb and its aftermath and finally to his conversation with Mycroft last November.

His brother had wanted him to continue stirring up trouble between the steam barons. It hadn't been necessary—the Steam Council had done a fine job of bickering all on its own—and the rebels had been granted an extra year to gather their forces.

"Are the Baskervilles ready for war?" he asked when the footman left.

"We're more ready than we were."

"Is that why you've returned to London?"

Mycroft returned to his chair, his mood suddenly subdued. "Yes and no. I'm not sure my absence has had a favorable effect where the Schoolmaster is concerned."

"Oh?"

"Edgerton has become close."

Michael Edgerton was a talented inventor and had once run in the same set as Tobias Roth. By all accounts, he was a smart lad. "They are of an age. Friendships are healthy."

Mycroft sat forward, tapping the vast expanse of his waistcoat. "I am the one who has given this rebellion form, elegance, and intelligence. He should be listening to me."

Was that jealousy in his brother's voice? Holmes crossed his legs, intrigued. "The Schoolmaster might be the face of the rebels, but he is no fool. Surely he understands all you've done on his behalf."

"If he is the face, I am the mind."

But never the heart, Holmes thought. It was there that friends like Edgerton were important. Even he needed Watson more than he cared to admit.

Mycroft sank back in his chair. "I intend to visit Sir Charles and ask his opinion about the lad."

"His opinion?" Holmes asked, confused. Sir Charles Baskerville had taken in the Schoolmaster as an infant and raised him as his own.

"There are things the old man knows that no one else does. He raised the boy, after all."

Holmes didn't like the sound of that. *You want to find out his weaknesses. Always easier to play puppet master once you know which strings to pull.* "What do you expect to learn?"

"You don't approve."

"I dislike manipulation."

But Mycroft's thoughts had already galloped ahead. He drummed his fingers on his knee. "Too bad our niece is in Keating's clutches. She is pretty and the right age for our protégé."

And mourning the death of the man she loved. But Mycroft had never paid the least attention to such things. After abating for the last few minutes, Holmes's headache returned with hammer and tongs. "Evelina is closely confined at the Ladies' College. The only way I have been able to communicate with her is through subterfuge. Smuggled letters and the like."

Mycroft tilted his head. "I'm surprised that you have not attempted a jailbreak. That is rather your style."

"I'm conscious of the coming war. Oddly, I've felt somewhat easier knowing that she is protected by Keating's influence."

Mycroft snorted. "Perhaps not for long. I've had word that she blew up a laboratory and is under threat of expulsion."

Shock brought Holmes upright. Evelina had mentioned nothing about this in her last letter. "When? Why am I just hearing about this now? Was she hurt?"

Mycroft ignored the first two questions. "No. Thank the gods no one was actually injured."

The door opened and their refreshments arrived on a steam-powered trolley laden with food. A footman followed with a silver tray of drinks. There seemed to be enough refreshments to stuff half of Westminster.

The smell assaulted Holmes's tender digestion, but Mycroft perked up, rubbing his hands. "Just leave it, my good man."

The footman bowed himself out. Mycroft reached for a decanter of whisky. "Drink?"

But Holmes was still digesting the image of his niece exploding a laboratory. It was the first entertaining thought he'd had in days. And yet the result was serious. Holmes had considered the college an acceptable place for his niece to wait out the coming conflict—but if Keating withdrew his protection from Evelina, something had to be done.

Apprehension jolted his sluggish brain into gear. Double agents, Baskervilles, and Mycroft's ambitions ricocheted through his imagination—but he couldn't wrestle with any of those until he knew Evelina was safe. That meant tackling the Gold King—a dangerous proposition at the best of times, and this was the brink of war. "What does Keating fear, besides the loss of wealth and power?"

Mycroft finished pouring himself a drink and turned to regard Holmes, a glint of amusement in his eyes. "The unexplained and unexplainable."

"Magic?"

"Yes and no." Mycroft waggled his hand side to side. "He is eager enough to get his hands on the type that will make machines run, but dislikes the rest. Witness how eager he is to root out all the herbwives and sorcerers."

A flash of eagerness pushed back Holmes's queasy stomach, and he rose to help himself to the decanter. "How is he on séances?"

"I have no data on that," Mycroft replied with a dubious frown. "What have you got hiding under your hat?"

"The faintest glimmer of an idea. It's time Evelina began earning her keep for Keating."

"Are you serious?"

Holmes gave a short laugh. "Whatever Keating demands, she won't throw any magic users to the lions, you can be sure of that."

"Then what are you plotting?"

"Not much yet. But Keating needs to remember that he values Evelina, and she needs to start leaving the university from time to time."

Mycroft's eyes brightened. "Because if he's used to the idea of her getting out and about . . ."

Holmes raised his glass to Mycroft, for once in perfect accord with his brother. "When the moment is right, it will be a thousand times easier to set her free."

CHAPTER TWELVE

London, September 24, 1889

CAVENDISH SQUARE

7:45 p.m. Tuesday

TOBIAS ARRIVED AT HIS TOWN HOUSE IN CAVENDISH SQUARE just before the supper hour. His ears still rang with the din of the Gold King's workshop, and his mind felt like something dropped from the top of Nelson's Column. As he stepped out of the cab, all he wanted was a drink, a meal, and a good night's sleep. He'd spent the day dissecting the great brass bug—an activity that produced more questions than answers. Exhaustion battled irritation for possession of his soul.

As the cab pulled away, the horse's hooves *clip-clop*ping into the darkness, Tobias loitered in the street, taking deep breaths of the cool air. The park at the center of the square was quiet. All around, the glow of gaslights softly brushed the pillars and pediments of the Georgian town houses. Above, the sky was a deep indigo fading to black. It was one of London's rare peaceful moments.

Somewhat refreshed, he mounted the front steps of his house, the granite stairs lit by the fan light above the door. A twinge of pride buoyed his mood. This was his place, not his father's. It wasn't nearly as grand as Hilliard House, but it was more than enough for any reasonable man. And it had all the modern conveniences—hot water, indoor plumbing, steam heat, and gas lighting on every floor. The endless renovations had been worth the time and cost.

The door opened before he'd mounted the last step. He stepped into the pool of warmth and the butler took his hat and coat. Whitford had come with Tobias from Lord Bancroft's residence, glad of a chance to be the head of a new establishment.

"Please let Mrs. Roth know that I have gone upstairs to dress for dinner," Tobias said. "I'll be down as soon as I can."

"Very good, sir," Whitford intoned.

All butlers intoned, Tobias decided as he mounted the stairs. It must be part of their training, right along with the supercilious eyebrows. Amused, he started down the hallway to his bedroom.

But he hadn't gone far when his feet took a turn toward the nursery, the way they did every night. If there was someone inside with the baby, he would pass by, a busy man with places to go. If no one was there to see, he would enter. He stopped to listen, his hand on the painted china doorknob. There were no voices, no lullabies haunting the air. A sliver of light crept from beneath the wet nurse's door at the end of the hall, so he turned the knob quietly, hoping to steal in without attracting notice.

The door drifted open on silent hinges. A lamp was turned low, shedding just enough light to make out the cradle and its tiny occupant. Tobias crept closer, feeling gigantic and awkward in the pastel sea of tiny blankets and knitted toys. Savoring the private moment, he peered into the cradle at the chubby, perfect face of his son. As always, a wash of confused, almost painful amazement flooded over him. He had done nothing to deserve a blessing like this—rather the reverse—but he would damned well make himself worthy of the innocent child who'd been entrusted to his care.

Jeremy had his amazingly small fingers dug into the knitted coverlet, as if determined to keep what was his. Tobias rather liked that sign of tenacity. In this world, and with Keating and Bancroft for grandfathers, he would need all the stubborn spirit he could muster if he was to find his own way. *But he has one thing I never did. He has a father who will fight for him.*

Tobias reached down, his fingertips just brushing the baby's blanket. Jeremy scrunched his eyes tight, a tiny frown making him look alarmingly like Lord Bancroft. But Tobias let his hand linger there, needing to feel the warmth of the little body. Perhaps it was to remind himself that good things could still happen—ones that he could see and touch. Someday he would teach Jeremy all the necessary skills men required, like how to skip stones and swing a cricket bat, and especially how to find his way around a toolbox. One of the few good memories Tobias had of his own father was repairing an old steam-driven water pump together. It was hard to connect that memory of his sire with the Lord Bancroft he knew now, but at least he had it.

A soft footfall made him look up. Alice was on the other side of the cradle, the lamplight turning her fox-red hair into a burning halo. She was lovely, with a heart-shaped face and wide blue eyes, but there was a peppery streak to her character that could surprise the unwary. None of that showed now, though, as she looked down at her child.

"Enjoying a private moment?" She said it with a touch of amusement.

"Just some man-to-man time."

"Too bad he's asleep," she murmured, adjusting one corner of the blanket. "His Royal Stickiness loves to see you."

Tobias gave a rueful smile, though he was still in mourning for his favorite waistcoat. "How was he today?"

"I think he's over his sniffles."

Tobias nodded, more relieved than he cared to show. He could see it in Alice as well, a softening in the angle of her mouth. The year since their marriage had been a process of discovering such signs. He'd learned her limits and boundaries, what she liked in her tea and the fact that she saved the gossip page of the newspaper until last.

He'd known none of that beforehand. For him, the union had been an act of duty, and at first he hadn't always been kind. They were still more strangers than not, but things had become much better. They'd both made an effort to forge something worthwhile, and he was more than grateful for her willingness to try—especially at moments like this, with the lamplight gilding the graceful lines of her profile.

He leaned across the cradle, catching her hand and pulling her closer. Alice was small and as dainty as a sprite, but she rose up on her toes to lean forward. His height made up the distance, and he brushed his lips against hers. Beneath the bridge of their bodies, Jeremy slept the profound sleep of infants.

She was warm and delicious, tasting of sherry and possibilities. He kissed her again for good measure, and she caught his lip with her teeth, nipping lightly. A rush of interest blew away the last of his fatigue. As she heated beneath his touch, her scent grew stronger—a perfume of sandalwood and jasmine and the softness of female skin. He began to calculate how long it would take to get her out of all those elaborate clothes.

"Alice," he said softly. He finally released her.

"Papa has arrived."

Damnation. He had entirely forgotten that the Gold King would be there tonight.

She lifted her gaze. There was an element of apology there, and not a little worry. She loved her father, but she knew him far too well. He was only a comfortable guest when it suited him.

Seeing that apprehension, Tobias's first instinct was to reach across and smooth away her frown. But Keating's presence seeped through the floor, souring his stomach. He dropped his hand with a silent oath and went to make himself ready. A man was lord of his castle until his father-in-law and employer came to dine.

When Tobias finally went downstairs, the Gold King was in the drawing room, a glass of whisky in one hand and a silver-framed photograph of Alice and Jeremy in the other. He set it down on the mantelpiece as Tobias entered.

"How went the work today?" Keating asked. A speculative glint passed through his golden eyes as he took a sip of the whisky. He might have been there on a social visit, but he was no doubt far more interested in whatever Tobias had learned about the brass bug.

"The work goes slowly." Tobias had washed and changed, but didn't feel refreshed. Keating's presence made it impossible to relax.

"Have you found any clues as to who made the craft?"

Whitford entered with a drink on a tray, and Tobias accepted it gratefully. "I'm not sure. All makers have a signature—a way of approaching things that marks a work as theirs. But an effort was made to disguise that here. Many of the parts are salvaged from other ships."

"But surely something stands out?"

"The steering system is clearly drawn from the one used by underground postal carts."

Keating set down his glass, his expression incredulous. "From the underground? Are you telling me that the Black Kingdom attacked the clock?"

Even the notion made Tobias stiffen. The Black Kingdom was one of the enduring mysteries of the age. No one—not even Keating—knew who ruled it or exactly what powers it controlled, only that it claimed everything under the streets as its territory.

Tobias shook his head, fighting off a frisson of superstitious dread. "No, no one has ever seen any machines created by those that dwell underground. The steering system originally came from the Scarlet King's foundries and was adopted by several others. Green uses it on the carts that run the post from one part of London to the other on the underground rail lines."

And they paid for the privilege of using Black's tunnels. The postal system was exclusively Green's enterprise, as were most of the counting houses, law offices, and many of the banks. "Of course," Tobias concluded, "that's not enough evidence to prove who built the ship."

Keating grunted his agreement, albeit reluctantly. "I want to see progress."

Tobias bit his tongue, calling on long training as a diplomat's son. "Of course, sir. I'll return to the problem first thing tomorrow."

Alice arrived to herd them to the table. The dining room was a modest size but showed off her taste. The colors had been chosen for a sense of light and air, and the ornate plaster of the ceiling had been painted a plain white. Alice herself was the brightest thing there, the deep green of her dress like the first leaves against the snow.

They sat, the soup was served, and they began to eat with the determination of people obliged to be polite to one another. Normally, dinnertime conversation between husband and wife was pleasant and of late had become comfortable. But tonight, Keating's impatience hung like a pall in the room.

Alice cast a glance at her father, speculation in her wide blue eyes. "How goes the development of the battery-powered generators?"

Keating cast his daughter a cool glance. "You have a good memory. It's been a year since I worked on them."

"I have an interest in that project."

Tobias looked up from breaking apart his dinner roll. This was the first he'd heard of it. "How so?"

Her face took on a sharpness that said she was engaged by the topic. "Small generators have so many uses, especially in rural settings, or where people cannot afford a constant power supply. It could ease a great deal of hardship if the poor could pay for only the fire or warmth they needed as opposed to an ongoing charge."

"And what about revenue?" Keating said, his tone slick with contempt.

Tobias set down his butter knife. "There are many who can only pay now and again." The cost of power was an ongoing grievance against the Steam Council. It wasn't hard to see why the rebels had gained a foothold.

Keating flicked a hand, consigning the subject to the dustbin. "Unpredictability is the enemy of sound business. Besides, I have more pressing affairs, as do you." He turned to his daughter. "Raising Jeremy must fill up your days. I'm sure you don't have time to ponder what goes on in your old father's factories."

She flushed at the rebuke. "I will never grow weary of hearing what you do, Papa."

The next course arrived, and Tobias exchanged a look

with Alice, whose heightened color said she was fuming. He raised an eyebrow, doing his best to take the sting out of the moment. She rewarded him with a small, tight smile.

And then she tried again. "So what are you engaged with, Father?"

Keating dusted salt over his potatoes. "There are always a number of projects in hand."

"It seems odd for me not to know each and every one," Alice said with the slightest suggestion of an edge. "There was a time I think I was as informed as your foremen."

But she was no longer part of Keating's plans. By marrying and producing an heir, she had served her function. Unfortunately, Alice refused to accept her irrelevance. Tobias wondered if the meal would ever end. He cast a sidelong glance at his father-in-law, who was chewing as if his dinner had done something to offend him.

"When Jeremy is old enough, why don't you bring him to the London factory for a tour? You can see it then," Keating said.

"I'll look forward to it," she said, her eyes downcast as she abandoned her plate.

Tobias guessed what she was thinking. She would only need to wait a decade or so to see the business she could have run as capably as any man. Whether they meant it or not, parents had the power to wound as no others could.

Frustration burned and he set down his cutlery before he was tempted to use it on his guest. If so many people hadn't been counting on Tobias to keep Jasper Keating on good terms, he would have slammed the man's face into his veal roulade. Restraining himself took a special kind of fortitude.

He turned to Keating, a smile fixed on his lips. "Would you like to try the pinot?"

"Please," said the Gold King, pushing his glass forward.

The servants were out of the room, so Tobias poured, his mind churning with useless resentment. Keating lifted the glass to his lips, his nostrils flaring as he tasted the wine.

Tobias watched the man the way he would a deadly spider. Others might have daydreamed of poison in the wine, or a knife to the throat, but Tobias just wanted his household to be left in peace.

Unfortunately, the price for such freedom would be far more complicated than simple murder.

CHAPTER THIRTEEN

HEAT WAS A PALPABLE FORCE INSIDE THE BUILDING, SO thick it might have been sliced and shipped for shillings a pound. Sweat trickled between Tobias's shoulder blades, adding an extra layer of irritation to his foul mood. He'd been hard at work investigating the brass bug, but this was the third time he'd been called away. Nothing was working right.

He was in his shirtsleeves, his coat and vest tossed over a reasonably clean crate. All around him, the vast warehouse pulsed with the noise of engines, a rusty light shimmering from the coal-powered furnaces. Workers swarmed like jungle insects, hands and minds busy with one project or another, turning plans into prototypes. Tobias had designed most of the machines there, but every unit built was for the greater glory of Keating Industries. Here, the Gold King ruled all.

Sadly, Tobias's latest invention wasn't about to be ruled by anyone. At eight feet in height, it stared down at him with that insouciance peculiar to malfunctioning machines. *Go on, make me work,* it seemed to say. *I have all the time in the world to watch you try.*

Tobias wasn't impressed. *Bloody fart bucket.* By now there had to be enough steam inside to send it rocketing to Mars. Why wouldn't it run?

"We checked the pressure, guv," said the man standing beside him, whose name was McColl. "And there's not a leak anywhere. I looked myself, every inch."

Tobias nodded, hearing but not bothering to waste mental capacity on speech. He was rechecking his math and re-imagining his diagrams, comparing them to the monstrosity a dozen feet away. Keating had asked for weaponized ground transport, and this was it—a steam-driven engine surrounded in armor plating. Or rather, it was a steel and brass dome on wheels, somewhat taller than it was wide, with enormous gunports on the roof. It had an extra knob on top, giving it the appearance of a huge covered dish. However, the knob was the greatest feature of the thing, because it allowed the contraption to fly. Then again, it could also explode the entire warehouse.

"Have you checked the aether distillers?" he asked McColl. The man mopped his shining brow with a sleeve. "I had a look at 'em, guv, but I'm no expert."

Tobias's neck went rigid, and his temple throbbed—but he kept his tone civil. Decent workmen were in high demand all over London, and McColl was better than most. "If they're not calibrated, they can drain power from the main engines. That could explain why nothing else will work."

"All I know is that they were green and bubbly."

Despite himself, Tobias's tone went sharp. Bubbles meant the distiller was growing volatile. "How bubbly?"

"Like a good stout sir, with a bit of froth on top."

Tobias's heart lurched. There was no time even to curse. "Gloves!"

McColl stripped his own off, handing them over. Tobias lunged toward the machine, pulling them on as he went. "Turn off the engines!" he roared. "Power it down!"

He vaulted from the ground to the lip above the wheels, then clambered up the dome, using the overlapping plates as hand- and footholds. When he got to the smaller half-sphere on top of the dome, he balanced precariously, digging the edges of his fine leather boots against the housing, and attacked the wing nuts holding the faceplate. The gloves were clumsy, so he grabbed the fingers in his teeth, tasting the heavy oil-soaked leather as he pulled off the right one so he could work more quickly. But as he feared, the metal was scorching hot. The thing was overheating. *Faster, faster!*

The principle of the distillation device was simple: it took ordinary air, separated out the aether, and then concentrated it into a liquid form that could be stored. When needed, the aether could be converted back to gas to fill a balloon, providing greater—and much safer—lifting power than hydrogen. Tobias's domed invention was equipped with storage canisters and a tightly folded balloon. In the event a rapid escape was needed, the balloon would inflate and an interior cage would separate from the rest of the machine, floating the operator and key equipment to safety. Because the distiller itself was on board, there was no danger of running out of fuel.

But ironically, that safety feature was about to combust them all. He burned his fingers for a few twists and then snatched up the glove again, using it like a pad between his skin and the nuts. When he finally freed the cover, he tossed it aside. The thing clanged and skidded across the floor. Tobias could hear McColl working below, hopefully shutting down the boiler.

Tobias caught his breath. Behind the brass cover of the distiller was a glass plate, and behind that a double helix of clear tubing. Inside was the bright lime-green fluid that was distilled aether, snaking in a continuous journey that spiraled up and back through the tube. But rather than the clear jewel-like serpent Tobias should have seen, it churned with agitation. Tobias had a moment of mild surprise—not that it was about to explode, which was obvious, but that it was such a stellar example of improper installation that he wished he could show it to the apprentice mechanics.

The housing began to make a loud ticking sound, the temperature inside obviously out of hand. Visions of flames and flying roof tiles crowded his brain. Maybe a crater where the street used to be. Surely it wouldn't be that bad, but he was on top of the thing and didn't fancy ending up as bits of gooey muck on the walls. Tobias jammed his fingers into the glove again and dug down inside the workings, feeling for the hose that was supposed to take in fresh air and release excess heat outside the glass housing. Even if McColl shut down the steam engine, it would take too long for everything to cool to a safe level.

Tobias felt his feet slipping and gripped the dome hard with his left hand. He could feel the hose he wanted, twisted uselessly under some pipes instead of venting like it was supposed to. All he had to do was hitch himself up and lean a little farther in. He did, dangling a moment, but he got hold of the tube. It was a special material, a combination of rubber hardened to withstand extreme temperatures and a finely knitted steel, so flexible it crumpled like cloth. It burned him right through his glove, and experience had taught him to beware the scalding steam trapped inside.

Then McColl slammed a gear, jolting everything. Tobias had a good grip with his hands, but his feet flew free. That jerked the hose, and all the pressure that should have been loosed for the last hour shot out—and so did he. Tobias sailed backward, shrieking as steam knifed out just inches from his skin.

He landed hard, but years of riding lessons had taught him to fall. He rolled to a stop, gagging with pain. For a moment, the world rotated, reminding him of an era when he'd spent most days drunk, and for an instant he wanted desperately to go back there.

The sound of feet skidding to a halt jerked him back to the present. McColl was leaning over him. "Guv? You all right, guv?"

An eerie silence hung over the place. Every other pair of hands had stopped moving, all attention on him. Tobias sucked air between his teeth with a hiss. It felt like his body wasn't sure where to begin hurting, but he couldn't exactly start moaning. He wasn't just the spoiled son of an aristocrat, he was the Gold King's head maker, and there was an example to be set.

He cleared his throat. "What's the green light at the top doing?"

"It's gone out, or just about."

"Good."

"What's it mean?"

Tobias sat up, and that sent his gut rolling like a wind-tossed airship. "We don't die today."

McColl looked happy about that, then twisted around when the door to the offices slammed. Keating was marching toward them, the silence growing so profound as the workers quieted their tools that Tobias could hear the soles of his employer's shoes scuff the floor.

"What happened to you?" Keating demanded.

Tobias looked down at his arm, which seemed to be hurting worse than the rest of him. There was a strip of flesh between the gauntlet of the glove and his shirtsleeve, and it was lobster red from the blast of steam. "Damnation."

"Get up," Keating ordered. "I take it the transport is not working yet?"

McColl had already faded into the sea of workbenches and mechanical monsters. Tobias found his feet, though quickly discovered moving his arm hurt like blazes. "The new unit needs adjustment."

Keating grunted. "So do you. Better get some ice on that. Let's go someplace where we can talk."

They went through the door to Tobias's work space, which was a separate room with an adjacent office attached. Long tables covered with disassembled parts lined the walls of the main room, evidence of his interrupted work.

They went into his office. It was utilitarian, with plain white walls, sturdy oak furnishings, and a small window that looked onto a featureless back alley. Tobias didn't care about the lack of a view. Keating had workplaces all over the city, but Tobias preferred the simple, workmanlike utility of this one.

They sat down at the small, square table and waited while the young doctor who worked on site iced and bandaged Tobias's arm. It hurt somewhere beyond reason, and Tobias gratefully accepted the glass of whisky Keating poured for him. Now that the crisis was over, he felt an odd agitation, as if he wanted a fight. He'd got off lightly, but was still furious at having to take such a risk. And of course it was his right arm, which would hamper him for days.

"How long do you think it will take to get the transport working?" Keating asked as the doctor left.

"It will take a day or two of tinkering and we can test it again."

"We need to get it into production as soon as possible." Keating paced the room, circling it like one of those exotic fighting fishes that constantly prowled the confines of its tank.

Tobias tried to watch him but then gave up, since every blink seemed to jostle his throbbing burn. Wearily, he wondered how many of the transports would roll out of Keating's factories. Tobias had designed half the weapons, but Keating hid the finished product from everyone but a handful of warehouse workers. No one knew just how strong the Gold army might be, and Keating liked it that way. "Is there a time constraint that I should be aware of?" Tobias asked.

"Yes," Keating said conversationally. "There's going to be a war. Surely you've noticed?"

"You sound like my father."

Keating's look was dryly amused. "Lord Bancroft and I see eye to eye on very little, but I think we agree on this point. The natives are restless. Why do you think Reading was on edge at your father's party?"

Because he was working up his nerve to ask me to play traitor. But mentioning that now would only open the door to a conversation Tobias didn't have the energy for that day. Not with his arm throbbing and the Gold King already spoiling for a fight. "He was drunk."

"He's up to something. Most of the time he knows far better than to draw attention to himself. Or to challenge me—especially when we have agreed to an alliance."

But the bargain Keating offered was enough to make anyone wary. The Gold King wanted Scarlet's fleet of dirigibles, but he had little patience for the man himself—and Keating tended to dispose of things he couldn't use. "What are you going to do about him?"

"I'll bring him around," Keating said shortly. "Can you tell me anything new about the abomination?"

That was Keating's way of referring to the bug. Undoubtedly, there was something about saying "the sanctity of my territory was destroyed by a giant brass mosquito" that irked the Gold King past endurance.

"You don't think Reading had anything to do with it?" Tobias asked.

Keating's look was impatient. "Of course I've thought it. Everyone has after that disreputable performance at your father's party. It's the one reason I think it's unlikely. He's not subtle enough to do something that obvious."

Spoken like a steam baron. "Who else?"

"If I've learned anything from Holmes, it's the value of evidence. What have you found since last night? Anything besides that steering system? You've had a week."

Tobias was tempted to say something unwise. A week wasn't a long time when it came to the amount of work involved in disassembling a machine of that size and complexity. Not when every bolt had to be examined for clues. But Tobias rose, a little dizzy from the pain, and motioned for Keating to lead the way toward the workroom. "Whoever manufactured this machine used parts from other ships. Finding out where it was made will be a challenge."

Keating moved to center of the room and gave the ring of worktables an imperious glare. "You told me that already, and it's not particularly helpful information."

Tobias crossed to the nearest heap of parts, running one hand over the smooth brass. "I have men researching where the donor ships might have been located. I'm hoping we'll find a wrecking yard in one city with the right combination of old ships." Of course, given that air travel was relatively new, he wasn't even sure such a selection of salvage existed. He'd asked the Merchant Brotherhood of the Air for help, but so far they'd been coy.

Keating swore. "There is nothing? Nothing at all you can provide?"

"I've mentioned the steering system." He pointed to another table, where a steel cube bristled with copper wires. "The logic sorter is interesting. It is different enough that I'm concentrating my efforts there."

"Good. Spend more time on it."

"And what about the transport?" Tobias waved his good hand in the direction of the main workshop.

"Keep on it. We need it faster." The Gold King leaned against one of the tables. "Understand this. The air battle over London stirred public resentment. The *Red Jack* was a popular icon, the captain something of a romantic hero. The man in the street has a soft spot for rogues."

Nick. Tobias hadn't known the man well, but he had saved Imogen. The thought left a guilty, bitter feeling that had Tobias reaching for his whisky glass. If Nick had been a popular hero, he'd paid for that status with his life.

"And that battle was not the only cause of resentment," Keating continued angrily, crossing back into Tobias's office long enough to return with his bottle of whisky and a second glass. "Who knew Dr. Magnus's theater was so popular? The Steam Council was blamed for the fact that his automaton ballet was destroyed, and for the fact that the Whitechapel Murderer was never caught."

"At least he's stopped killing," Tobias offered.

Keating huffed. "None too soon. Rebel sentiment has grown in the last year, and I intend to be ready to defend myself. I defy you to find a member of the Steam Council who is not."

That was no more than he'd guessed, but Tobias still felt a frisson of unease. He sat silent for a moment, considering. Keating was surely holding something back. "Have you heard anything further about the Baskerville affair?"

Keating gave him a hard look. "Why do you ask?"

"I saw another mention of them in the papers." He wasn't sure where the name came from, exactly, although he'd heard there was a small estate somewhere in Devonshire belonging to a Baskerville family. For some reason the word had become a rallying cry for dissidents, especially those of good birth. "You know, the usual blather about how, if only the aristocracy banded together, everything would go back to the good old days."

"When dukes were dukes and peasants were footstools," Keating growled, pacing back into Tobias's line of sight. "Everyone is quick to take what the Steam Council provides, but no one wants to pay the price for what we offer."

That was a bit like saying nobody appreciated the excitement of being raided by Vikings, but Tobias kept his mouth shut.

"Do you know what the latest ploy is? The latest insult against me?" Keating asked conversationally. "Psychical societies."

"Palm readers and the like?" Tobias instantly regretted his incredulous tone. But really—what could they do to someone like Jasper Keating? Illusion was always permitted for entertainment purposes—mostly because no one believed those tricks were real. The moment true magic was suspected, there would be an arrest and trial.

"It's not as innocent as you might think. These societies claim they're investigating rumors of witchcraft. All based in science, of course. Except they're bringing in celebrated practitioners to educate them." Keating finally sat, running a hand over the perfect wave of his white hair. "This came in the mail this morning. If that's not sedition, I don't know what is."

He pulled a piece of paper from his waistcoat pocket, unfolded it, and thrust it out. Tobias took it. It was a sheet of ordinary writing paper, but the words upon it were cut from a newspaper and glued into a single sentence. Tobias read it, and then reread it: *Bite me and I will sting you in the fullness of time. The spirits so decree.*

Sting. Time. It was a clever reference to the brass bug. His first impulse was to snicker, but he got that under control before he spoke. "This is a threat. There's nothing psychic about it."

Keating gave him a withering look. "I know that much. But I gave this to Holmes immediately, along with the envelope it came in. He had an answer within the hour. The newspaper these words were cut from was printed on the same date as a meeting of a prominent parapsychological society. And what's more, that meeting was at the same hotel on the same night as the last whispering of Baskerville activity."

"Baskervilles? You are quite serious?"

"You heard me. Holmes confirmed it."

"And none of this has to do with the actual Baskerville family in Devonshire?"

"No," Keating said, annoyed. "We've investigated them a dozen times. Sir Charles is as prosaic as they come, and his adopted son is no more than an idler. We're speaking of the political movement."

"And you think the political Baskervilles are in league with tea-leaf readers?" Tobias asked, trying to keep the disbelief out of his voice. "They must be desperate."

Keating shrugged. "You know what they say about strange bedfellows."

Personally, Tobias loathed magic—deeply—but there were many prominent men who did not. Nevertheless, true rebels would choose bombs and bullets for an attack, not a deck of tarot cards. "This has to be nothing more than a political statement. How great a threat is it?"

Keating refilled their glasses. "You've heard of Madam Thalassa, haven't you?"

"I've seen notices for her performances. She talks to the dead, I believe?"

"So she claims. She's been in hiding since she caught our attention, but now she's frequenting these psychical salons." Keating took a sip of his drink, his expression between derision and anger. "Salons that are in the same time and place as my sworn enemies. She spoke at the one connected to the Baskervilles. Apparently the spirits predicted my assassination within the year."

Whisky caught in Tobias's throat. "Good of them to inform you."

"There are too many questions here. Too many coincidences." Keating set down his glass, his voice a sudden frost. "Holmes suggested I look in on a society run by one Miss Barnes, a spinster nurse. She has requested Madam

Thalassa's presence at her next gathering. Word has it that she will come."

There was a long pause. "And?" It didn't sound like Holmes to give anyone up to Keating, but Tobias wasn't going to raise the point. The detective was up to something.

"I want the medium taken prisoner."

The room went perfectly quiet, Tobias's own breath the loudest thing. His arm throbbed, nausea hovering at the back of his throat. "You do?" he asked stupidly, distracted by a fresh wave of pain.

"Whether or not she had a role in the abomination's attack on Westminster, I don't allow disrespect to go unpunished. One way or the other, I mean to see her dead."

Tobias felt as much as heard the rage in Keating's tone. It was neither hot nor cold, but something else, like the potential disaster he'd seen in the bubbling green distiller. It was an explosive force under pressure and just looking for a way out. An edge of fear pulled details into sharp focus and Tobias could see every fold in the white linen wrapping his arm, every crease and shadow on the pasted letter before him. *Madam Thalassa is just an old, angry woman, but he doesn't see anything but the fact that she won't bow down.* "How do you mean to find her?"

"Evelina Cooper."

Involuntarily, Tobias clenched his fist, and then gasped as the gesture pulled at his burn. Keating laughed long and low.

Tobias chose to let the threat fall unacknowledged. "Why Evelina?"

"Why not? She's my prisoner at my disposal. She understands magic."

My prisoner. Tobias shifted on the hard chair. *Bastard.*

His own feelings for Evelina were a snarl. He had loved her. The question was whether he still did. He'd never seen a single sign of Evelina's magic, and never tasted it on her lips. Bloody hell, he'd wanted to *marry* her. But learning she was one of the Blood had turned his stomach. Unfortunately, even that couldn't completely purge her from his system. A person didn't just stop loving as if a switch had flipped.

"But she is at college, isn't she?"

"Indeed. She just blew up the laboratory."

"She what?" Tobias's lungs froze with panic. "Was she hurt?"

"No, it seems she needs a bit of excitement to keep her occupied."

Tobias's mouth had gone dry. "Why would she hunt down one of her own kind?"

"Because Evelina is mine to do with as I please." Keating narrowed his eyes. "And I please to make her your responsibility."

"Mine?" Tobias jolted upright, but this time didn't even notice the pain. "What do you mean?"

Keating shrugged. "From now on, you will be the one to look in on her. Chaperone her if needed, deliver my orders, and make sure that she does what she's told. If I tell her to hunt, you'll make it happen."

Confusion turned his thoughts to soup. Clearly Evelina was getting dragged into a larger game, and so was he. Somehow this medium and Holmes were involved as well, and the only reason Keating seemed to be oblivious to it was that he was distracted by so many other threats.

Or maybe the Gold King was just changing the rules. Not so long ago, Keating was threatening dismemberment if Tobias ever looked at Evelina again. Now he was throwing them together. "Are you sure I am the best choice for this?"

"Why not?" His amber eyes were predatory as they searched Tobias's face. "Because now that you have taken my daughter to wife, Evelina Cooper means nothing to you anymore. Or am I mistaken on that point?"

"Of course not," Tobias replied, bleaching the syllables of any meaning. That didn't stop the maelstrom inside him, since his indifference was an utter lie. He had never stopped wanting Evelina, even when he had driven her away. *Why open this wound? Why fetter me to a woman I can't have? Why try to smash what little accord Alice and I have built?*

Because, even if he wasn't sure that he loved Alice, she deserved the best of whatever he had to give.

"There is a war coming," Keating said. "I need to know who plans on obeying my orders."

"You're testing my obedience?" Tobias snarled, forgetting his mask.

Keating pushed the whisky bottle in Tobias's direction, his smile that of a man who's just checked the king. "What other reason is there for anything in this world? Take it from me, boy, what hold you have over other people is the only currency that really buys anything."

CHAPTER FOURTEEN

See enclosed report. I'm terribly sorry. I wanted you to know before you heard elsewhere. S.

London, September 25, 1889

LADIES' COLLEGE OF LONDON

3:55p.m. Wednesday

EVELINA HAD READ THE NOTE SHE'D PULLED FROM THE LI-brary wall several times already. She had been expecting something else—a request for information, or an opinion about something from the magical realm. Sometimes it was a question Holmes wanted her to slide into a conversation she had with Keating, never letting on who wanted the answer. She'd become her uncle's direct line to the Steam Council—or at least one of them—since she'd become the Gold King's prisoner. Keating liked dropping ominous bits of news, presumably to keep her afraid. Anything credible she passed on via the library wall. Playing informant gave her a sense of purpose beyond her life as a caged pet.

But this time the note was different. Her uncle didn't pep-per his letters—or any other communication—with expres-sions of emotion, so if he said he was terribly sorry, it had to be awful. Evelina had left the report folded shut since she had pried it from its hiding place yesterday, terrified of what it might contain. This morning, she had imprisoned the un-read thing underneath a heavy book about scientific weights and measures.

Now hours had passed and shadows crept from the edges of the room, eating into the pool of light cast by the gaslit chandelier. A few wall sconces joined the combat against the gloom, but it felt as if the air itself was growing gray with the gathering dusk. It mirrored Evelina's burgeoning sense of unease.

So she forced herself to get to work, focusing hard on the tasks she had set for herself. Moriarty had sent her the assignments the male students had to complete, as well as the supplies to work through them herself. It was the first real help she'd had since arriving there.

Briskly she gathered the chemicals, cleared the worktable, and began to measure and pour. All she had to do was perform the steps, observe, and take notes—it was as simple as following a recipe. Except that every time she read the instructions she was supposed to follow, her mind darted back to the folded paper her uncle had sent, the unread set of words imposed over the others like a ghost determined to haunt her. She was going to accomplish nothing until she knew what it said.

With a curse, she fished the tightly creased scrap of paper out from under its imprisoning tome and fumbled it open. She stood as she smoothed it out on the table, as if towering above the words gave her power over their message. The report was a single handwritten page, marked up as if an editor had gone at it with a pencil. It was the draft of a story to be printed in a newspaper; her uncle had contacts at the *Prattler,* so it probably came from there.

REMAINS OF PIRATE SHIP
LOCATED AT LAST

After months of speculation as to the final fate of the pirate vessel the *Red Jack,* sources report the charred remnants of an airship matching the size and configuration of the notorious craft have been found on a farmer's property due south of London at the Willington crossroads, along with the bodies of the crew.

> Londoners will not soon forget the air battle last
> November, when the rebel pirates met their end. Nor
> will the populace soon forget the supplies the brave
> outlaws ran through the barricades of the Steam
> Council, enabling those who cannot afford the heat
> and light due to the cupidity of the so-called steam
> barons . . .

"Cupidity" had been struck out and "greed" written above, and then the rest was barely readable, crossed out and reworded in a cramped handwriting Evelina couldn't decipher. That part wasn't important to her anyway. What did matter was the fact that Nick had been captain of that ship. Imogen hadn't been the only one struck down that day. *Oh, Nick.*

She'd offered Jasper Keating access to her magical talents in return for the *Red Jack*'s safety. He'd intervened too late to save the ship, but had taken her captive anyway. The devil's bargain she'd made with the Gold King might have been worth it if only Nick had lived. But the article confirmed one more time that he hadn't.

Shaken, she braced her elbows on the table and leaned her forehead on her clenched fists. She feared the sorrow pounding through her, hollowing out what little courage she had left.

She'd searched for Nick at first, hunting for him in the spirit realms as she had hunted Imogen, but there had never been a sign. Admittedly, Nick's magic was tied to the air the way hers was tied to earth and woodland. They were opposites, two halves of a magnet, and sometimes that made them blind to each other. But still . . . no, there was no reason to think he lived. Not after that crash. Not after those cold words in some reporter's scrawl.

The pain of loss came in hot, salty tears tracking over her cheeks. Until now, until this fresh slice, Nick's absence had grown familiar, thumbed through like a diary written end to end with the story of her guilt. Evelina had asked him to help in Imogen's rescue, and he'd done it at the cost of his own life. It was her fault he'd been there at the battle. Yes, she had tried to save him, but she'd failed. She made a strange, gasping sound, and started to sob silently, clenching her teeth so she didn't make any noise. She didn't want anyone passing by her rooms to hear.

If only. Her life had been a string of *if only*s, but the real question was *what now*? She had been numb and then furious at her fate. The anger had risen like a fever, but like a fever it had eventually broken. It had to, or she would have burned to death in the fires of her own outrage.

She had felt empty ever since. Most days she could keep the chasm inside hidden even from herself—but not after news like this.

The shuddering stopped, and Evelina wiped her eyes with the heels of her hands. Mechanically, she rose and went to her bedchamber to wash her face. The room was pleasant, but had little that marked it hers. The only familiar object was the black leather train case her Grandmamma Holmes had given her, sitting on her dresser.

She poured water into the basin and splashed her face, her bracelets clinking against the china washbasin. Normally she avoided the mirror, but she couldn't help catching a glimpse of herself in the oval glass that hung above the washstand. *Why are you here, when Imogen and Nick are gone?* There was no good answer to that. She wasn't even sure it was true. Her dark hair was neatly pulled back, her features as they had always been—but today she seemed a stranger, as if somehow she'd walked into the wrong life.

The disorientation was nothing new. She'd felt it often since arriving at the college, as if this was all someone else's nightmare. Maybe too much had happened. Maybe she spent too much time alone. Or maybe it was that everything she'd hoped to find here had been a false promise. Perhaps Deirdre, simply looking for a husband, had the right of it— except that there would never be anyone else for Evelina. All she could do was endure.

She pulled a towel from the hook beside the washstand

and dried her face, scrubbing until her cheeks lost their bloodless hue. Then she went back to work.

This time the words on the page behaved themselves, and she began making progress. She measured and mixed carefully, her mind as carefully calm and light-footed as someone venturing across a fresh-frozen pond. This was the same experiment that had blown up the laboratory— Moriarty was taking a risk by giving her the materials for it—and she refused to contemplate anything except what was right before her nose. She turned on her small gas burner and picked up a beaker with a pair of long-handled tongs.

A noise outside the door made Evelina jump, and the beaker in her hand wavered. A drop of liquid spilled from the lip, splashing to the burner below. She shied away just in time to avoid a rush of bright green flame that fountained upward.

She barely had time to suck in a breath before the flame vanished, the destabilized aether distillate consumed in a flash. Evelina's hand shook slightly as she placed the beaker back on the table and turned down the flame. Only then did she have the nerve to look upward and see yet another nasty scorch mark on the ceiling, joining the other two she'd already made so far since setting up her own equipment.

"Bugger," she said quietly, and then hastened to open the window before the matron detected the odor of her handiwork. The quadrangle lay steeped in semidarkness. As predicted, the skies had opened up. The brown stone buildings had assumed a dour air, as if they disapproved of the sensibly dressed young females hurrying through the pelting rain.

Then the noise came again, and what remained of her concentration scattered. At first she'd thought it was another student crashing about—give a girl a hockey stick, and bid the walls farewell—but it was someone knocking on the door. *Damn and blast on toast with cheese.* The last thing she wanted was to face a visitor. Irritably, she went to answer the door.

"Who is it?" she asked, half expecting the matron. The stern-faced woman checked on her daily, no doubt to make sure she didn't perish from a nasty chemical accident.

The Clock Tower blearily announced five o'clock, its bongs sounding forlorn through the steady patter of the downpour. Evelina opened the door, heard the familiar creak of the hinges, and stopped cold. For a moment, her mind lagged behind her senses, failing to process obvious data.

"Tobias," she said stupidly. "Why are you here?"

The look in his gray eyes was impossible to read. He'd always been tall and fair, handsome as a fallen angel. That was still true, but there was no denying he had changed. The lines of his face were sharper, the set of his mouth devoid of any laughter. Tobias Roth looked like a man who rarely slept.

"Are you that shocked to see me?" he said, his voice flat.

"Frankly, yes." The last time they'd been alone together, all kinds of disaster had followed.

"Then we are of a single mind. I'm astonished to find myself here." He took off his hat. "The matron knows of my presence. You needn't worry about being thrown out for entertaining unauthorized visitors."

He clearly expected an invitation into her rooms, but Evelina balked. Once Tobias had been her best friend's dashing brother, and she had loved him with the innocent fervor of a schoolgirl. Then he had been the man she'd wanted to marry, and he had all but proposed. Now he was a husband and father, and he had no business standing on her threshold.

A thread of anger, and anguish, tightened her throat. "You didn't answer my question. Why are you here?"

The corners of his mouth twitched down. "It wasn't my idea. Keating sent me."

That made her fall back a step. He took the opportunity to push past, the folds of his coat swirling behind him. Evelina smelled the rain and a waft of his cologne. Once that alone might have made her weak, but she'd learned the hard way it never paid to be too soft when it came to Tobias. The man had a way of obliterating her good judgment.

But that wasn't her only worry. "Is there news of Imogen?"

"Nothing new. Nothing new with anyone."

He was still using that flat tone, and it raked her already raw nerves. She was still teetering on the edge of weeping, and that was the last thing she wanted. Not in front of Tobias. "Then to what do I owe the honor?" she asked dryly. "I thought it was Keating's wish that we stayed apart. I seem to recall you marrying his daughter."

"That's old history."

The offhand remark smarted. "You must be close to your first wedding anniversary."

Tobias didn't reply. Instead, he stood uneasily in the middle of the room, looking around at the bookshelves and stuffed furniture.

"Things have changed." Tobias set his tall hat on the table. It looked elegantly out of place beside the explosion of her books and papers. "I'll be the one checking on you from now on. Once a week."

Evelina's face went numb with surprise. She'd thought things couldn't get worse. "What? Every week?"

His brow furrowed. "For pity's sake, I'm not a leper."

No, you're a knife to the heart. "It's always been Keating, or his man of business. Why you?"

Tobias gave a short, sharp laugh. "Don't you wish to visit with me?"

A protest hovered on her lips, and she teetered between honesty and good manners. Honesty won. "Is this some kind of test? Are you here to shake my virtuous resolve, Mr. Roth?"

Is that even possible anymore? Too much had been stripped away from her. She wasn't even sure she had that kind of feeling left in the ruins of her heart. And yet, while she'd adored Nick for as long as she could remember, she had once pined for Tobias, too. There was a time when they had both held a piece of her soul, and to her confusion she had learned that it was entirely possible to love more than one person.

But in the end, it became all too clear that Tobias couldn't love whom he chose, and now he was more entangled than ever. And after the feast of Nick's passion, she would never go back. She would have all of a man, without reserve, or nothing at all.

Tobias was regarding her sadly. "You were never the one at fault, Evelina. That was always me."

Evelina gave him a long, careful look. His clothes were still fine, but there was something untidy about him. It wasn't the disarray of a drunkard or a mad genius. He looked as if he simply didn't care anymore. As if something inside him had broken.

"Don't be daft," she said more tartly than she intended, and turned to fuss with the books on her desk. "We never did more than kiss."

"Only that? I rather thought we meant something to each other once."

Evelina froze, her back to him. She gripped a heavy book, longing to throw it. "Of course! Yes!"

"I'm happy to hear it."

Anger speared through her—at him, at Keating, at herself for rising to the bait. She didn't want this, and Tobias didn't know enough to leave her in peace. She felt her fingers clench hard, nails digging into the book's fat spine. "I surrender. What do you want me to say?"

She abandoned the volume and turned. They ended up mere feet apart, squared off like opponents in the ring. Gradually, a silence fell over the room, the only sound the rain pattering outside, a door closing down the hall. Evelina could feel the space between them like a physical pressure, hot and prickling on the skin.

"Say nothing." Tobias's face was bland but when he spoke, his voice held an entire palette of emotion. "I'm forced to be your jailor. I'm supposed to ensure you are behaving yourself. That is all."

And at that moment she knew that this visit was his punishment, not hers. Keating was well aware that it hurt Tobias to see her. How much her magic appalled him. She sucked in her breath, feeling it catch under her heart. It would destroy Tobias if he thought she understood—and worse yet if they acted on any lingering feelings. They knew that from the last time they'd slipped. *Never again.*

Evelina felt as if she were falling. She was already choking on the ocean of grief in the room and it seemed unfair that she had to find strength to face more. But there was no choice—people in shackles didn't get to walk away. And just because Tobias couldn't be her lover, that didn't mean she dismissed his pain.

Mustering her courage, she drew herself up, raising her chin at a teasing angle. "I'm going to write and complain. Even a prisoner has rights."

His eyebrows rose. "Rights?"

"You're like a bad omen. Whenever you and I meet, things go wrong. The least Keating could do is protect me from that."

One corner of his mouth quirked. "You can't blame me for everything. It smells like something exploded in here."

"You knocked and startled me."

"And caused an explosion?"

"I spilled my solution into the flame. It *was* your fault."

"That's logic fit for a madhouse."

"Don't be cruel." She held up her wrists to show the silver cuff on each arm. "If I've gone half insane, consider my circumstances."

His chin tucked in, a gesture of surprise, and then he grasped her right forearm for a better look. Silence held them for a moment. Until Keating had taken her prisoner, Tobias had never known about her magic—indeed, he loathed anything that smacked of the supernatural. She braced herself for recrimination and distaste, but it didn't come.

"Keating told me about these." He turned the bracelets over. They appeared solid, their only markings a tiny bit of flowing script that read: Her Majesty's Scientific Laboratories.

"Did he tell you how they work?" she asked.

He shook his head. "Only that the cuffs keep you within

the boundary of the college. Keating's men can track you if you wander off."

She shuddered. "I would never make it that far. They deliver a horrid shock if I try to leave. It's as if a thousand darning needles are amputating my arms at the elbows."

Evelina felt a bloody satisfaction at the horrified look on his face. But beneath her triumph was a twisting mass of hurt and shame. She'd been trapped and caged, and it galled her.

"That's monstrous," he said softly.

She didn't know how to reply to the pity in his voice. But then she saw his bandage, and it gave her something else to focus on. "You're hurt." She reached out, touching the wound linen that peeked from beneath his sleeve.

"Just a steam burn," he said. "Nothing at all. Nothing like the rest of our wounds." And he put his hand over hers, fingers gently wrapping hers in familiar warmth.

Oh, no. She put her other palm against the gray wool of his coat, jewels of rain still caught on the soft weave. His chest moved, alive and warm, and loneliness swamped her. But this time she knew enough to pull away. That loneliness was her ache for someone else. Someone who not only loved her magic, but had his own. "I made this bargain."

"For the sake of Captain Niccolo," Tobias said in a tight voice.

There was nothing she could say. "Yes."

There was a long silence, then Tobias sighed, something extinguished in his eyes. "I'm sorry. Believe that I want you to be happy."

Evelina felt her chin tremble and ducked her head. If she cried, Tobias would hold her, and right then they were both sad enough to need the warmth of it. But it wouldn't lead anywhere either of them could go. She cleared her throat, pulling her pride to her like a child clutches a blanket. "Are you happy?"

He hesitated, but then his mouth quirked. "Sometimes."

"I'm glad." She felt the energy between them shift, moving away from the most dangerous ground. She relaxed an infinitesimal degree. "And at least I get the education I always wanted."

"Is it everything you thought?"

His question caught her off guard. "No."

Tobias stood patiently, waiting for more.

"I don't know," she finally said. "I've been through too much to content myself with the predigested nonsense they consider suitable for females."

A smile tugged at his lips. "I understand there was an incident. Were you making a statement?"

She sighed. "For the record, the demise of the laboratory was not premeditated."

"Keating hopes you'll find a way to put magic into machines. It would put him miles ahead of the rest of the Steam Council."

She already knew how to do that, but wasn't about to put that kind of advantage into the Gold King's hands. "He may wait for a long time. That secret's been lost for centuries, and if they never teach me anything here, it will be lost a while longer."

"He'll grow impatient. He wants the technology for his airships."

He wanted a ship of wonders, like the *Red Jack* had been. Evelina wondered what had become of Nick's air spirit. "Breakthroughs of that nature don't come on command."

"I know." Tobias swallowed, as if choking back words he couldn't afford to say. His eyes met hers, gray and bleak. "I know and I'm sorry, Evelina. I wish there was something I could do."

"I didn't ask you to do anything," she said softly. "You've too much at stake in this." He was every bit as trapped as she was. "Perhaps you should go," she added softly.

He looked away, misery plain on his handsome features. "Keating has another assignment for you."

She closed her eyes, fear rising like an evil mist. The last assignment had left her bleeding to death in a Whitechapel alley. "What does he want?"

"You're to investigate an amateur parapsychological society."

"Amateurs?" Evelina's eyes snapped open. "Are you quite serious?"

Tobias looked apologetic. "A séance, to be more precise."

"Table rapping?" Her brow furrowed, not sure whether to be alarmed or insulted.

"You sound chagrined." A hint of amusement lurked in the corners of his mouth, making him look almost himself.

"I feel a bit like a thoroughbred asked to pull a pony cart."

"Sadly, that's the assignment."

"Will it get me out of the college? Bracelets notwithstanding?"

"I'll make sure of it."

"Then I am utterly at your disposal."

"I'm glad to hear it." Tobias dug in a pocket, pulling out a leather notebook that had worn through on the corners. It would be the one he used for his work, and it gave her an odd feeling to think her business was mixed in there. He flipped it open to a dog-eared page. "They're called the Parapsychological Institute. It's quite fashionable at the moment."

Now Evelina was curious. "If they're a bunch of dabblers, why does Keating care? They can't possess actual magic. Table rapping is all wires and hidden springs."

"Keating believes it's a cover for rebel sympathizers, and your uncle Sherlock confirmed it. You know, Baskervilles hiding under the bed."

Uncle Sherlock? "Are you certain?" Her uncle's involvement complicated everything.

Tobias shrugged, his expression haunted. Whatever was going on, he was caught in the middle. "The word is that the society is hiding Madam Thalassa. Keating wants to find her. He thinks it's time for an arrest and execution on either political or paranormal grounds. He doesn't much care which."

Evelina's jaw dropped. "And you want me to find out if she's actually there?" *What about Imogen?*

"I'm informing you of what Keating wants." And Tobias's expression told her precisely what the Gold King had in mind. "You can get close to these people in a way others can't."

Evelina lost the power of speech. *You mean I can win their confidence and betray them.* Her heart was in her throat. *No bloody way!*

And she saw the jaws of Keating's trap close. She had no choice but to become Tobias's enemy.

CHAPTER FIFTEEN

NICK'S LIPS CRACKED IN THE HEAT, SORE AND SWOLLEN with thirst and unspent curses. A kerchief tied over his face, he sweated in the scorching murk, one more shackled prisoner laboring among hundreds. He was used to hiding, to seeking anonymity, but this was oblivion. Ash veiled the air in a false dusk, motes swirling like souls lost in the updrafts of hell. On every side flames roared, the furnaces like hungry devils demanding fuel for their red-hot bellies. For the prisoners shoveling coke and pig iron, those furnaces might as well have been sucking down their souls.

There were bigger and better steel plants in the Scarlet King's territories, some with machines that did the work of dozens. Here, though, in the place Nick only knew as Manufactory Three, mortal labor was cheaper than any machine. Incarceration was a death sentence—eventually. The heat alone killed many of the men, sweating them day after day until their bodies gave in.

Ironic that Nick found his way into this fire pit right after surviving a fall from his flaming airship. He had gone overboard locked in a death struggle with a sorcerer, their fight over the metal cube that housed the air spirit named Athena. Without a parachute, Nick should have been smashed to pulp, but Athena had used her power over the winds to cushion the fall.

But that had just been the start of their troubles. He'd known they were vulnerable once they'd reached the earth, and the moment he'd heard the soldiers coming, he'd hastily buried the metal cube, even though Athena loathed being in the earth. Just in time, too, because the soldiers had taken him prisoner and Athena would no doubt have gone for scrap. Beneath the stranglehold of the steam barons, any kind of metal had value. The only good thing was that his captors had arrested him simply as a vagrant. They had no idea that he was the fearsome Captain Niccolo, or things would have gone much worse. At least he wasn't trapped in a cell. Unfortunately, bound with iron chains and surrounded by every kind of metal, his air magic failed him utterly. He was as helpless as Athena trapped beneath the dirt. The only strength he had was in his bones and brawn.

In fact, his job that day was to move the raw materials from the mountainous supply in the yard to a giant clay-lined vessel suspended between two huge legs. The smelter consumed its meals faster than Nick and the other prisoners could feed it—fifteen tons at a load. Sometimes they hauled bars of the pig iron made from ore and scrap. Steam-powered trolleys moved enormous bins of the stuff right up to the furnace, where men shoveled fuel like imps serving their demon god. But the bins had to be filled, and that was done with muscle and sweat—a job that broke bones and spirits as swiftly as a fire ate kindling. The one boon of the job was that the yard was a few degrees cooler than the furnace shed, and on the days he loaded iron, Nick got to see the open sky.

Today a heap of scrap sat in the yard—carriage wheels and railway ties, old generators and coal grates. Some was the detritus from industry, some the remains from domestic use. Nick even saw a tiny wagon made of tin—a child's toy painted in bright colors. His crew had been assigned the task of throwing the scrap into the bins to be melted down.

It was a job they did at least once a week. Whether one was in the city or a country village, metal was hard to come by—and these furnaces were the reason. Old materials could make new machines, and so the steam barons' men scoured town and hamlet for anything they could take. After all, there was no profit in the townsfolk building something for themselves.

Nick bent, picked up an old wheel, and heaved it into the bin, his sweat-soaked shirt clinging to his skin. They had given him gloves, but those had quickly worn through, and he could feel flakes of rust clinging to his fingertips like bloody sand. Next, he grabbed a cast iron pot just like the one Gran Cooper—the fortune-teller who had all but raised him—used to hang over the fire for soups and stews. He slung it over the side of the bin and heard it fall with a hollow crash. The men never talked as they worked, the roar of the machines around them making conversation impossible.

Even after work stopped for the day, they had little to say. Half the men there were deaf, blind, or struggling to pull air into their scorched lungs. Anger here was a dull thing, crushing resentment more than a lancing fury. Fury took strength, and theirs was all spent under whip and short rations.

Nick found an old coffee mill, the paint chipped away from its iron sides. This he lifted more slowly, using his legs because it was heavy and awkward to hold—and even so, he could barely shift it. He didn't notice the guard speaking until the man rammed the butt of his rifle into his shoulder. The wheel barked his shin as he lurched forward, catching himself just in time to keep from falling against the waist-high rim of the bin. He dropped the corner of the mill, barely missing his foot. Anger flared as he turned, hands closing into fists, but he banked his temper at once, self-preservation smothering his reaction. The guards at Manufactory Three never hesitated to put those rifles to use.

Keeler, the man standing next to Nick, wasn't as quick. He slammed into the bin, his feet leaving the ground as momentum took him over the edge. Nick grabbed the back of the man's sweaty shirt and hauled him to safety. Keeler landed with a grunt and shuffled around to face the guard, not even acknowledging Nick's help. A dull, mute acceptance drained the expression from Keeler's eyes, like a horse beaten too often to fight the bit. Nick understood all too well—Keeler had begun to spit up blood at night. He wouldn't see another springtime.

Another guard joined the first, and Keeler, Nick, and another prisoner were shackled, one linked to the next. The iron chains rattled, a counterpoint to the clank and rattle of the scrap in the bins.

"This way," the guard said sullenly, prodding three of them toward the furnace.

There was no explanation, and that was worrisome. "What's going on?" Nick asked, but all he got was a rap to the head with the rifle barrel.

So Nick followed, shackles clanking, glad of the chance to rest his aching back and shoulders. Though he'd been fit and healthy when he'd arrived, nine months of hard labor had pushed his body to its limits. He could feel every joint as he moved.

A steam whistle sounded as they walked toward the furnace, signifying that a batch of steel was ready to pour. The bulbous vessel swiveled on its enormous legs and vomited a shimmering river of molten steel. It had a strange if terrible beauty, like the birth of dragons. Even from where Nick stood many yards away, a hot wind found him, stinging against his skin and driving the moisture from his eyes and nose.

But not even the hellish winds slowed the guards. They turned the prisoners to the right, leading them along a path that ran to the outside of the shed, past the place where they lined up for rations of bread and stew and past the infirmary that was little more than a quiet place to die.

Their journey finished at a low building of brown, sooty brick. Now Nick could see something unusual was afoot. More guards stood at attention outside. A fleet of Steamers sat on the pavement outside the building, drivers polishing the steam-powered vehicles from steering wheel to the upright exhaust pipe that reminded Nick of a squirrel's tail. Every one gleamed with gold accents and lush velvet seats.

The place had visitors, and they were wealthy. Now very curious, Nick allowed himself to be herded inside.

Beyond a small reception area was the domain of Commander Rose, despot of the prison factory. He was one of the Scarlet King's right-hand men and as such an important figure in the Empire.

As the prisoners shuffled into the room, more guards joined them, forming a tight wedge. Nick was in the middle, behind Keeler, and he strained to see past the man's shoulder to catch a glimpse of what awaited them. Nick's gaze found Rose at once. The man was tall and spare, distinguished without ever having laid claim to good looks. He wore the uniform of the Scarlet King's men—a quasi-military jacket with a red waistcoat beneath.

As they came in, Rose sat down at a long mahogany table, inviting his guests to join him. Soon, a half dozen men flanked him, all facing the prisoners. With a pang, Nick saw that several wore the crisp uniform of the Merchant Brotherhood of the Air, dress swords rattling as they shifted on the leather-covered seats. He imagined the clean, crisp wind clinging to the airmen's hair and clothes and ached for it.

The three prisoners were brought to a halt, the muzzle of a rifle to each of their heads. Nick stood, feet braced a little apart. Keeler slumped to one side; a bearlike man named Ambling loomed on the other. In the clean white room with its shining brass lamps and scrubbed wooden floor, the prisoners seemed a species apart, a smelly offshoot of the human race due to be extinguished as a bad job best forgotten.

Rose looked from one of them to the other, a thin, disapproving crease forming between his brows. Then he turned to address his guards. "Is this the best you could do?"

"These were doing shoveling, sir," replied the one who had fetched Nick. "Strong 'uns."

"Nimble?" Rose looked doubtfully at Ambling. "I need someone who can climb. Someone who won't matter if he falls."

The guard helpfully pointed to Nick.

"Whatever it is, I'll do it," Keeler broke in. "It truly doesn't matter if I fall."

But no one paid him any heed. Prisoners were regarded as no more than the insubstantial dead.

"Why is he here?" Rose pointed to Ambling.

"Public drunkard," the guard replied.

"And him?" Rose pointed at Keeler.

"Second-story man." That meant he was a thief who specialized in sneaking in my lady's window to pilfer her jewels.

"And him?" Rose pointed to Nick.

"A vagrant. Probably a thief, too. Found wandering the road with no excuse for being there."

As usual, Nick held his tongue, since piracy and magic were both guaranteed to see a man swing. And since Dr. Magnus—he of the sorcery and all-black wardrobe—had broken free of their midair death struggle and was now a grease spot south of London, there was no one to give Nick away.

"A second-story man would have the best chance at this," Rose decided. "But keep the vagrant here as backup. The drunkard can go."

Ambling was led away, back to the scrap heap. Nick and Keeler stayed put.

Rose steepled his fingers. "I'm prepared to grant clemency to the man who successfully completes this mission."

Nick and Keeler shared a glance. Nick noticed he didn't say "freedom," and "clemency" was too vague for his liking. Still, he listened.

"We require someone to assist in the retrieval of a rather valuable piece of equipment."

"Where is it?" Keeler asked.

This time Rose acknowledged him. "The Church of St. Margaret and St. Anne."

Nick had been brought to Manufactory Three, along with a few dozen other prisoners, in the windowless boxcar of a train. He wasn't sure where in England he was, but the name of the church was vaguely familiar. However, as he'd grown up in a circus that traveled all over the country, that didn't mean much.

Rose went on. "The equipment was part of a personal

flight device that these gentlemen came to demonstrate today. Unfortunately, the church got in the way."

"It crashed," said one of the merchant airmen flatly. "There is no point in mincing words. It crashed and what we need is on the steeple. Someone has to go up and get it, but there are too many obstructions on the roof to reach it safely from the air."

"How heavy is the equipment?" Nick asked. That would make a difference.

The airman gave a quick, approving nod. "Barely a pound. It's part of the pilot's harness. It will have to be cut free."

"Captain, we can't give a prisoner a knife," Rose snapped.

The airman snorted. "We will unless we want him to chew through the strapping."

"Is the pilot alive?" Keeler wanted to know.

"That depends on what happened with the propeller," the captain replied. "We can't tell. The roofline is too irregular."

Rose chopped the air with one hand. "The equipment is the priority. The Scarlet King does not wish his maker's work to fall into enemy hands. There is a war on, you know."

Nick and Keeler exchanged a startled glance. It was the first either of them had heard of it. *What side are these men on?* Nick wondered. The Scarlet King's, obviously, but what did that mean? That was the difficulty with politics in the Empire—there were too many choices for an obvious answer. And that led to an equally interesting question.

Who is the enemy?

CHAPTER SIXTEEN

THE WINDOWS UPSTAIRS GAVE A VIEW OF THE DISTANT church. The airmen argued for Nick's presence as they all trooped up the stairs to watch Keeler's progress. Accordingly, Nick climbed the steps, the heavy chains around wrist and ankle clanking loudly in the stairwell. Guards marched before and behind, muttering that there was more valuable work to do. Nevertheless, Rose agreed with the airmen. If Keeler failed, the next man up would need to know where the first had gone wrong. It was good logic, but it would have been better if Nick had not lost his spyglass in the wreck of the *Red Jack*. It was hard to see much at this distance beyond the building itself.

The Church of St. Margaret and St. Anne was an unusual design—at least as far as Nick had seen. The roof was in two parts. The front had the usual tall steeple, and the back of the building was a long rectangle with a steep peak and the usual buttresses, gargoyles, and other medieval fancy. But someone along the way had liked the first steeple so much they'd added more points. They weren't true spires, but were tall, slender points needling into the clouds. One sat at each corner of the rectangle and halfway down the long side, creating a cluster of obstacles that meant the roof was impossible to access from the air.

A Steamer eventually appeared near the church and men piled out, Keeler still in chains. The clutch of men disappeared inside the building, presumably to use the stairs to access the roof. Twenty minutes later, Keeler was a small black dot inching up the side of a steeple toward a patch of something Nick couldn't make out. He squinted, irritated by the fact that he couldn't quite see what Keeler was doing. Plus, the tickle of a rifle muzzle caressing his ear was more than tiresome. Backbreaking labor was preferable to the constant tease of a quick death. But then again, no one was asking Nick's opinion.

The room where they stood wasn't much to look at— empty except for oak cabinets containing the paper records for Manufactory Three. There was enough room to stand by the row of windows, the workings of the plant strewn several stories below. Nick had never seen this view of the place and studied the layout carefully, keeping his features a blank. His pulse quickened as he noticed the slash of turned earth on the west side, where a new building was going up. The fence was down there, but extra watchtowers had been raised. Was that an opportunity for escape?

And then he heard a collective intake of breath. His gaze slid back to the dot on the rooftop, his own chest wrenching tight. The dot was moving downward with excruciating slowness. Nick shifted slightly, wanting a better angle, and felt the rifle jab him in the neck.

"Stand still," the guard ordered.

Nick clenched his teeth, swatting his own anger aside. Keeler had got himself in trouble trying to reach something that had wedged between the slope of the roof and the base of the southeast tower. Keeler was approaching the join of roof and tower from below, but the angle was too steep and he kept sliding down. After every attempt, he would dangle precariously over the sheer drop to the paving stones below, kicking until he found the strength to pull himself up. Keeler was sick and couldn't keep that up for long. Ignoring the guard, Nick leaned forward, as if a few inches would make a difference to his ability to see.

"He should have gone down from the ridge," Nick muttered. "He could have used a rope." But then Keeler was a second-story man, used to nipping up drainpipes and trellises to pry open house windows. *Dark Mother protect him!*

"You've some experience with heights?" the airman standing near him asked. They were all subdued, and Nick guessed why. That was their friend who had crashed on the

church roof. "Not everyone can stand being near a high balcony, to say nothing of being up there with the birds."

Nick's vision fuzzed with memory, blocking Keeler from
sight. Nick had grown up as part of Ploughman's Paramount
Circus, ropewalking almost as soon as he learned to run. "I
have some. Not as much as you, I'm sure." That was a lie,
but Nick preferred to be careful.

The man met Nick's eyes, ignoring the shackles. "Ever
been on a flying ship?"

Nick choked on a sudden longing for open air, for the feel
of a cloud kissing his skin. That was where his magic lived,
the very stuff that called his Blood. His answer came out
clipped, almost hostile. "Yes, but it seems a long time ago
now."

The rifle poked him again, and Nick's fist clenched. The
chains clanked, the cold metal speaking his anger. And then
someone cried out. Nick's attention was instantly back on
the spire. He sprang toward the window, stumbling in the
chains. He grabbed the window frame to break his fall, but
it wasn't his own fall that he cared about. "Damn it to hell!"

Keeler was already plunging to his death.

WITHIN THE HOUR, Nick had traded his place by the window
for a view from the church roof. The assignment remained
the same: to untangle their precious equipment from the
harness of the airman who by now was surely dead.

He'd asked for a rope, along with a small pocket knife.
The fact that no one had agreed to a safety line for Keeler
spoke volumes about just how expendable the prisoners
were. Ropes and prisoners were a bad mix, to say nothing of
blades. However, it was clear the airmen didn't have the patience for a third attempt, and that forced a change of rules.
Nick was to keep trying until he got the prize—but he got
his equipment and now he stood by the door to the rooftop.

"Don't think you're going to try anything," growled his
guard. "I'm right here, and there's a man at the door on
t'other side."

Nick simply nodded and held out his wrists. They'd had to remove the iron shackles from his feet to climb the narrow, winding steps that led all the way up there. Grudgingly, the guard produced a heavy key and rattled the locks, exposing Nick's chafed wrists to the blessed air. As the irons fell away with a clatter, Nick immediately felt a hundred pounds lighter, his perception as sharp as if a blindfold had been stripped away. He felt the first stirrings of his magic, weak from long exposure to the iron chains but still alive.

"Don't get any ideas," the guard warned. "There's nowhere to go."

He was right about that much. The roof doors were simply small access points for maintenance. There was little place to stand beyond the opening. The roof sloped on the right down to a narrow gutter, and over that edge, somewhere below, was what remained of Keeler. Nick decided right then he wasn't going to look down.

On the left was a sharp rise to the ridge. The spine of the roof was decorated with a long line of wrought metal decoration turned to verdigris. The roof itself was overlapping sheets of lead and copper that reflected back the warmth of the sun. Nick surveyed the roof dubiously. No wonder Keeler had trouble climbing—the slick metal offered few footholds, especially at that angle.

"Only a lizard would keep its grip up here," the guard mumbled. So far he hadn't put one booted foot outside the stairwell.

"I'm fine with heights," Nick replied.

The guard's only reply was the rattle of the rifle. *Fool,* thought Nick. With so many obstacles on the roof, it would be almost impossible to get a clean shot—unless the guard ventured onto the roof himself and, from the pallor of the man's face, that wasn't going to happen. Nick turned his attention to the task at hand, and threw the loop of his rope toward the metal filigree on the roof ridge above. On the third try, it caught.

Nick knew better than to trust his weight to the metalwork, but it might catch him if he slipped. Until the *Jack* had gone down, he had scoffed at things like safety lines, but that last fall had taught him caution. There had been too much time on the way down to think. So, hand over hand, he began the careful ascent of the roof, placing each foot firmly as he went. The wind ruffled the long tangle of his hair, carrying the clean scent of pine and meadow. For that moment, balanced between flight and falling, Nick was a prisoner no more.

As he reached the roofline, he could see for miles. Closest to them was the ruin of a monastery, the high arches supporting only half a roof. A little farther along there were pleasant houses with chickens scratching around the doors and gardens arranged in tidy rows. He saw the silver arc of a river, rolling fields, and a tousled blanket of trees. He spied a ribbon of railway tracks heading south, with crows circling above them in search of anything good to eat. Best of all, the sky opened up all around him—wide-open freedom that he'd lacked for almost a year. And there was birdsong—few had ventured near the great furnaces, but here they chattered with abandon.

Yes, that's the place!

You don't say?

Huge worms! The good ones!

I like a good worm. Better than grubs any day.

Birds weren't always profound, but at least they were cheerful. He balanced at the peak, unhooking the rope and lightly gripping the curling metalwork. He closed his eyes for a moment, tasting the breeze. He knew there were guards in the staircases and at the foot of the walls. Although airships couldn't maneuver easily near the forest of spires along the roof, there was a small zephyr-class vessel patrolling the sky, watching his every move. Nevertheless, he could feel the potential magic in the air.

Athena. A pang of loss hit him so hard he thought his chest might cave in. He'd kept her safe, but where he'd buried her was a mystery now. He would have to find out where the ship had gone down and retrace his journey—though now he knew better than to travel the roads alone.

And where was he now? He guessed north of London, but not so far as Sheffield. They were in the Scarlet King's territory, and his lands tended toward the northwest. And there were train tracks just over there. There would be a train, and a journey south, and then life again. He would find his crew and get Athena back, and then he would find a ship.

And Evelina. In a wave of dangerous vertigo, the memory of the nights he'd spent with her hit him like a broadside of twenty-pound shot. Nick's eyes snapped open. In a few seconds, his imagination had carried him into a future he had no idea how to reach. But the details didn't matter. Fate had given him a chance, and he wasn't going to waste it— because once he had his deva and his ship and his woman, he was going to have his revenge.

He savored that thought a moment, letting it melt on his tongue like a sweet. He wasn't a political man, but the Scarlet King had thrown down the gauntlet when he'd clapped Nick in chains. No one did that to the Indomitable Niccolo and lived to tell the tale.

But first things first. What was so important that men were being sacrificed to get it off this roof? He inched along, drawing parallel to the point where the airman had slid to a stop behind the tower. The man was half hidden in a tangle of propeller and harness, arms and legs sprawled like a carelessly tossed doll.

With one end of the rope wound around his waist, Nick worked his way down the roof, keeping the line tight. He took his time, not letting his sense of newfound freedom make him reckless. When he reached the twisted wreck of the personal flight device, he realized it had been a kind of winged propeller, held on by a shoulder harness and powered by a small engine that strapped about the waist. Nick was no maker, but experience told him winds would have been a problem. A strong gust had probably pushed the airman into the spires, fouling him between roof and tower. *Dark Mother of Basilisks.* The force of the whirling blades had cut the airman nearly in two.

Nick turned away a moment, appalled. Then he pulled out the pocket knife and began sawing through the straps of the harness. The leather gave way easily, and soon Nick was able to push the propeller assembly aside. It slithered off the roof, barely catching on the gutters before falling to the ground. A lone, ragged cheer wafted up. Someone was pleased that Nick was making progress.

Now that he could get close to the body, Nick began searching for whatever devices he could find. He hadn't been given much detail to work with and he wished Striker, his second in command, was there to help. The man knew machines. *Gods, what I'd give for one of his aether guns about now.*

Nick ran his hand over the airman's bloody uniform, feeling the cold stickiness of gore. As he began to turn the body, bone and entrails showed through where the propeller had struck. The only thing that had kept the body in one piece was the engine strapped to the small of his back. It had been destroyed, but the steel casing had stopped the whirling blade. As Nick lifted the man's shoulder, he thought he saw what the men surrounding the church wanted back. There was an octagon of black metal at the front of the man's harness. Nick could just grasp it from edge to edge with one hand if he stretched his fingers wide. Brass rings secured it to the harness, and he quickly sliced through the straps holding it in place. Nick let the body sag back to the roof and examined the box. The cover was hinged at the bottom and latched at the top, and he quickly opened it. The inside of the cover was a mirror, and the face of the device was a map. Nick frowned at it, unsure at first what he was looking at. Then he flipped it around and viewed it as the airman would have seen it, reflected in the mirror as he opened the case midflight. It was a map of England with a compass in one corner. Useful enough, but what made it unique was a series of red arrows, all swiveled to point at a single location on the map. The river he could see was the Severn. London was but a few hours away by rail. Somehow this device knew exactly where he was.

Nick stared for a long moment. The map was painted on glass, and in the strong sunlight he could see the gears turning behind it, moving as he changed the angle of his body. Some of the workings at least had to be magnetic, but the nuances escaped him. Nevertheless, he could see why the device was important. It made independent flight a thousand times safer. As long as a soldier could read a basic map, he could find his destination.

Nick stuffed the device inside his coat. He knew he was raising the stakes by taking it, but he couldn't simply hand it back to the enemy. Then he sat on his haunches a moment, staring at the face of the young airman. He was painfully young, with the farm-fresh good looks that only came from a lifetime of early rising and milk warm from the cow. No doubt there would be a family wanting to bury him. It was the only thing they could do now for their young man. The thought of it made Nick cold inside.

He cut away the heavy motor and threw it to the ground as well. It landed with a crash in the middle of Keeler's bloodstain. At least his fellow prisoner's body had been hauled away. Then Nick ran the rope through what was left of the harness and rolled the body off the edge, bracing his own back against the tower and letting the rope out bit by bit. The airman's body drifted to the ground quickly, but not so fast that it suffered further damage. Then, when the men on the ground swarmed the dead, Nick scrambled to the roof ridge, all but forgotten—at least until the guards discovered the device was missing.

The two roof exits were guarded, and so was the perimeter of the grounds, but Nick had ideas. The main steeple housed the church bells; intricately cut openings all around the spire let out the call of the hours that Nick could hear all the way to the furnaces of Manufactory Three. The only problem was that the opening was nearly seven feet above the roofline.

He looked around for the zephyr making its lazy loop around the top of the church. It was approaching the north end of its patrol, and Nick had about thirty seconds to grab the bottom of the opening and haul himself inside before the lookout would spot him. He wasn't sure the men on the ground could see where he stood, but they were attending to their fallen comrade.

Nick grabbed the stone edge of the opening and heaved himself up. The one good thing about the brutish work he'd been doing was that he was strong through the arms and shoulders. In mere moments he had hauled himself inside. Below his feet were rows of bells attached to vast iron wheels, each one of the huge things ready to swing in a circle the moment the peal was rung. The sound alone would be enough to crack an intruder's skull. His stomach in his throat, Nick dropped to the narrow walkway and edged between them. On the far side, there was a ladder down to the platform where the bell ringers normally stood. He paused a moment, listening, the cool air inside the tower whispering against the metal of the bells.

Outside, songbirds were rejoicing. A fat bee zigzagged in one window and out another, oblivious to Nick's problems. It calmed his nerves. Song, flight, air, the freedom of rooftops—he was in his element. Nick took a breath, summoning his power. Then he began to walk, swift and silent. Where he stepped, no tracks appeared in the fine layer of dust.

Down the ladder, and then to another staircase. It corkscrewed down in pie-shaped slices of stone, the tower black but for a few tiny windows. Nick stayed close to the wall, going carefully until light from the floor below crept up to meet him. But there were voices along with that light. He stopped to listen.

"What do you mean, gone?" It was Rose's voice, muffled by a closed door. He must have come inside to wait in comfort rather than stand out in the cool wind like everyone else.

"The prisoner took the compass, sir. I told you he was a thief." That was Nick's least favorite guard.

"Damn his eyes." A door just around the curve of the stairs opened. Nick could hear the creak of hinges and saw the splash of brighter sunlight across the stone floor. "Did you send for reinforcements?"

"More airmen are already here. They've been guarding the site since the crash."

"Good. Tell them to shoot to kill."

Nick swallowed. He'd expected no less, but the words still

made his shoulders hunch. Then he heard the scuff of boots and something blocked the light.

"Don't go upstairs, you dolt," Rose snapped. "Look in the yard. That's where he'll be going."

The boots scuffed again, and the light came back. A moment later, he heard boots clumping down the stairs ahead of him. Rose sighed, and the door slammed shut, leaving Nick alone again. He remained utterly still while his heart thundered and his mind raced. If he was going to get out of this place, it wasn't going to be by these stairs. He went down the last few steps that led to Rose's door, then paused, thinking of the pocket knife. If it hadn't been a church, he might have taken a chance and turned the knob—but instead, he moved past.

The next door opened into a room that might have been used by the choir, because it held a row of black robes on hooks. Nick grabbed one, pulling it over his filthy clothes. From there, he found the choir loft and, at the other end of that, a stairway to the main floor. But he wasn't sure that was a victory, for by then the entire church was crawling with airmen and guards.

Nick's insides turned to ash, a chill sweat trickling down his ribs. He was all too conscious of how he looked. A robe couldn't hide his face; his scruffy beard and lank hair only emphasized his dark features. He'd never known his parents, but everyone said he had the look of a Gypsy. In a place like this, he stood out like a wolf among sheep.

He didn't relish going underground—not so soon after finally feeling fresh air—but his best chance was to get to the crypt. He'd seen the monastery from the rooftop. He knew little about history, but he was almost certain the Benedictine monks kept to themselves rather than mixing with the world. That gave him an idea.

He started down the aisle, walking a measured pace with his head down, as if deep in contemplation. He walked silently, keeping his footsteps as light as the shadows and pleading with the darkness to hide him. To his right, niches held the tombs of wealthy merchants and celebrated knights, faithful dogs at their feet and marble ruffs framing pale faces, their hands folded in eternal prayer. To his left, pillars screened the aisle from the pews, their delicate fluting giving the illusion of a divide. High above, the pillars burst into fan vaults, like the exotic palms from a South Seas island enchanted into stone. Dead ahead, there was a double door. In two other large churches he knew, that spot led down to the crypt. Nick prayed this one held true to form. If nothing else, it was a reasonable place to hide.

But a pair of guards was coming directly toward him, one the same man who had removed his chains. Nick's hands instinctively fisted, as if refusing to be shackled again. As the guard lifted his eyes, Nick turned to his right, drawing farther into the shadows beside a sleeping crusader. Every muscle tensed as the guards walked right behind him, their feet loud in the vaulted hush. And then they stopped.

Nick was already in motion, hurtling toward the double doors. He was close now, only a dozen yards away, but he wasn't used to running anymore. He could hear their feet behind him as he banged through the door, desperation making his feet fast on the steps.

"Damnation! There's no light down here," one of them snapped.

Nick stumbled but leapt, landing clear of the steps. He crouched in the moldy, damp silence, hoping for the best. The other guard stopped, fumbling in his clothes. Nick could just see them in the light from the door above—a pair of backlit shapes patting their pockets for matches. He took the opportunity to creep into deeper shadow.

Then the second guard—Nick's special friend—drew out a chemical lantern, shook it, and twisted the shutter open. A lurid green glow surrounded the two men.

"Ugh, smells foul down here," said one. "Like something died."

"It's a crypt, you buffoon," grumbled the other.

"Do you suppose there are rats?"

"Only if they like very old leftovers."

Nick backed away, leaving them to bumble about at the foot of the stairs. They inched forward, looking from side to side at the sarcophagi arranged in haphazard rows across the floor. There were vaulted arches here, too, but they were plain, the only ornament leering faces at the top of the pillars. It was clear from the tight shoulders and stiff walk of the guards that they didn't enjoy hunting through the graves. That was good. Jumpy men made mistakes.

Nick crouched behind a marble tomb, peering around the corner to watch his pursuers. As he had hoped, they were going deeper into the crypt, leaving the safety of the stairs behind. Nick looked around for weapons. There were plenty of stone swords and even a few real ones resting atop the graves, but nothing that looked like a match for a rifle. He was good with knives, but his pen knife was hardly up to the job. So instead Nick found a piece of fallen masonry the size of his fist. This was a back-to-basics moment. Then he rose and glided along the ancient marble floor, quiet as the dust.

He waited until they came to a narrow passage, where one fell behind the other. Nick came up behind the shorter of the two men, clipping him behind the ear with the rock. He dropped like a sack of laundry. By the time the other one turned, Nick had vanished again.

From where he was crouching behind a pillar, he heard the low cursing of the guard. There was a note of fear in the mumbled words that Nick understood all too well. His own fingers were shaking, nerves wound to a screaming pitch of desperation. Nick clutched his weapon, the sharp edges digging into his fingers. He heard the awkward footfall as the guard stepped around his friend, and then hurried back toward the stairs—no doubt going for help.

Nick was up in a flash, and in three steps he was behind his foe. But this time the guard turned, drawing a pistol, not even bothering with the more awkward rifle. In half a second, the muzzle was in Nick's face. "You'll need more than a rock, you bastard."

Nick let his eyes go wide with fear. At the same time, he planted a kick in the man's kneecap, just a little to the side to do maximum damage. The shock of it let Nick sweep the pistol aside and bash the man's temple, knocking him to the ground. The man fell against the edge of a sarcophagus, the force of it sending the weapon spinning away. Nick pounced on the man, grabbing his jacket and slamming him into the stone floor once, twice with all the ferocity of his pent-up fury.

The guard sagged, face slack. Nick's breath was coming in ragged gasps, each inhalation a tearing wheeze that was almost a sob. Slowly, painfully, he made himself let go before he reduced the man's skull to pulp.

Priorities. Nick grabbed the lantern, the pistol, and then searched both men for more weapons and ready cash. To his joy, he found a knife and almost a pound in coin between them. And then he stripped off the ridiculous robe and took the taller man's jacket. He ripped off the prison insignia and dropped it to the floor. Finally, he began hunting for a way out.

Nick found the tunnel to the ruined monastery almost at once, and bolted toward freedom.

CHAPTER SEVENTEEN

September 27, 1889
SOUTHBOUND TRAIN, GREEN LINE

2:20p.m. Friday

NICK PRAYED THAT NO ONE WOULD NOTICE ONE MORE DIRTY, desperate stowaway hiding on the rusting boxcars. He had spent the night lying in wait for a southbound train, but now he was finally near his destination. He was by no means the only one who'd jumped aboard without paying, but he'd kept to himself. Guards wearing the green uniforms of Spicer Industries—the Green Queen's men—came through regularly, swinging batons like they were cricket bats. Two of the unwanted passengers had been tossed to the rails.

Nick had crammed himself between the piles of crates of foodstuffs and the steel walls, smelling the vile mix of ash, grease, and the cloying scent of honey. Somewhere a container had broken, and the rail car was thick with flies. He was desperately hungry, but wouldn't risk giving himself away by breaking into the crates in search of dinner. After all, the trip wouldn't take more than half a day.

At least he had time to think—a good thing when one's life had been blown to pieces, and the retrieval of even one shard was bound to be a complex affair. But there were things he needed first—starting with a good place to hide. For that, London had no equal. He made his move when the train began to slow, making its way into Paddington Station at a rolling wheeze. Nick hit the ground, rolled, and vanished into the crowds. The first thing he wondered as he slipped through the familiar alleys was who among his associates was still there, and whether or not they could be trusted. He'd been gone almost a year, and that was a long time in the game of survival.

Instinct told him to avoid any of his old haunts. The Saracen's Head tavern had already proven to be the target of the Gold King's spies, and any of the rooms he had rented had probably been taken over by others. After a moment's hesitation, he turned east, working his way toward Russell Square. There was a small handful of men he trusted enough to ask for help, but only one he knew who was even better at hiding than himself. Not even Nick knew the Schoolmaster's real name, but they'd shared risks in their short acquaintance. It was a mark of trust that the man had given Nick an address to use in case of emergency. Nick was reluctant to put himself in debt to the rebel, but if this wasn't an emergency, what was? And he had a delivery to make to the man anyway.

It was early afternoon, the sky a deep autumn blue. Nick stayed in the cool shadows, making himself invisible as he worked his way through the streets. A few yellow leaves crunched under his boots—a sound Nick had almost forgotten in the wasteland of the manufactory. But as beautiful as the natural world was, he found his gaze straying to the people passing by—ordinary people chatting, laughing, and sitting in tea room windows eating platefuls of perfectly ordinary food. He'd almost forgotten all that, too. It was one thing to know that he'd lost a year of his life, quite another to feel it in the pit of his gut. The Scarlet King had sliced away a piece of him.

Before, he'd had a ship and crew. He'd had friends— Striker, Digby, and the others. He'd had his ship, and the deva who had taught him to use his power. And—after years of yearning—there had been Evelina. Against all odds, they had finally found a way to be together and then— then loss had burned him away until he was nothing but a husk of ash. He wanted her back—all of them, but especially her. Maybe after that, he would find himself again.

Fury curled inside, speeding his steps toward his destination. He knew the small rooming house was occupied by artists, which meant the rents were cheap and the landlady oblivious to the kind of visitors tramping up her stairs. A good thing, since Nick was too exhausted to scale the wall and climb through the window. In fact, he rather wanted someone to carry him the rest of the way. Not the mode for daring pirates, perhaps, but he'd had a long day.

He went through the tradesman's entrance and trudged up the back stairs to the second floor. The door he wanted stood slightly open, as if a servant hadn't quite pulled it tight. He pushed it open, wondering if the Schoolmaster even still lived there.

The sitting room that came into view was shabby, but bright and pleasant in a disorganized way. Papers, discarded clothes, and a guitar littered the sagging furniture. A huge, threadbare armchair faced the door, and in that chair sat the man Nick had come to see. He was tall and lean, about thirty, and he wore green-tinted eyeglasses that all but hid a pair of shrewd blue eyes.

The Schoolmaster raised his eyes at the squeak of hinges, one hand reaching for the pistol half hidden in a stack of newspapers. Then he froze, his eyebrows lifting in almost comical surprise. "Captain Niccolo? We all thought you were dead!"

Nick stepped inside, pulling the door shut behind him. A flash of his old pride brought a grin to his lips. "They didn't call me the Indomitable Niccolo for nothing."

The Schoolmaster's face crumpled into a grimace. "Oh, come now, you've been saving that line. Gods, man, you look awful." And then he sprang to his feet, grasping Nick in a bear hug that nearly squashed the last breath from his body. The Schoolmaster laughed. "It's good to have you back. Where have you been, you old dog?"

The greeting was so warm, so *normal,* Nick had a momentary urge to weep. After feeling like the dead watching the living all the way there, he was suddenly folded back into the human race. "I've been in Manufactory Three."

The Schoolmaster fell back, stunned. A sober silence rang like a bell through the room. Then he ran a hand through his sandy, curling hair, as if he didn't know what else to do or say. "Gods."

"I made it out," Nick offered.

Coming back to life, the Schoolmaster took Nick's arm, guiding him to a chair angled to the right of his own. Nick obeyed, although he wanted to point out that he needed rather more than a sit-down after months in the Scarlet King's hell.

"No one has lived to tell a soul what goes on there," said the Schoolmaster. "Surely you know that. So how did you get out?" His look turned suspicious. "How *did* you get out?"

Nick understood. The Schoolmaster, as a rebel, had placed a lot of trust in him by giving him this location. There was every chance Nick had bargained for freedom with the Schoolmaster's life. "I swear on everything holy that no one knows I'm here. They didn't even know who I was in that pit of Hades."

"Good." But the Schoolmaster didn't relax.

"Give me a glass of brandy and I'll tell you everything."

The man's lips quirked. "I'll do better than that."

He pulled open the door and yelled down the stairs at the top of his lungs. "Mrs. Pennyfeather!"

There was a long pause, and then a shrill voice floated up from below. "What is it, scamp?"

"Be a love and give us a bit of a spread, will you? Bread, cheese, and meat and maybe a bit of that steak-and-kidney pie? And a jug of ale?"

There was grumbling from the bottom of the stairs, but it concluded—after a bit more boyish wheedling—in assent. Nick listened to the exchange with his eyes closed, the soft cushions of the chair urging him to sleep. Fatigue had him in its undertow, but he forced himself to rally as the School-master returned.

"Don't you have any guards?" Nick asked. "I could have walked right in here and shot you dead."

The Schoolmaster shrugged. "That only makes me more conspicuous. I do my best hiding in plain sight. Besides," he said with a smile, "you mustn't forget there's Mrs. Pennyfeather. Now." The Schoolmaster leaned on the arm of his chair, his chin in one hand. "Do tell. You promised to give me everything."

Nick pulled the device he'd taken from the fallen airman from beneath his coat. "The reason I got away was because I was sent to retrieve this."

He put the device on the small table that sat between their chairs. The Schoolmaster picked it up with obvious curiosity. "Why you?"

"It was on a church roof—an awkward spot nearly impossible to climb. It didn't matter if one of the prisoners fell to his death. In fact, one did. I was luckier."

The Schoolmaster opened the device, and his eyes went wide. "I'm glad you didn't fall, my friend. This is quite the diverting little toy."

The food arrived, and Mrs. Pennyfeather spread it out on the low table that sat before the two men. Then she took one look at Nick and brought back another slice of pie before leaving them in peace.

They ate and talked, Nick doing more of both. It was plain food, but to him it was a delicacy—soft bread, sharp cheese, and ale as richly golden as the sun on the windowpane. And there was more than enough. He ate until his sides hurt and talked until the pitcher of ale was dry.

When he got to the end of his tale, his companion was listening with rapt attention, the device forgotten in his lap. "This explains much," the Schoolmaster said.

"How so?"

"There have been rumors of Scarlet's ambitions. His real strength is in his air fleet and his European allies. The word is he's itching to make a move on the Gold King, for all they're supposed to be friends."

"That's madness. He doesn't have the resources."

"I never said he was smart. His vanity—not to mention his very bad manners—will get him killed. But then sometimes all it takes is one idiot to kick over the first domino, and everything falls."

"And then, war," Nick said, finally putting it all together.

"Indeed. I wondered if it would come when the Steam Council murdered the Gray King. Fortunately, it didn't. We wouldn't have been ready then."

"Are you now?"

"Are we?" The Schoolmaster shrugged. "Let me say simply that we are less unready than we were. Our best hope is if the steam barons destroy each other and then we come in to mop up. But the Gold King at least has figured that out. He'll not be quick to show his hand. That's the only reason he has not torn London apart looking for the culprit who destroyed the Clock Tower."

"I read about that," Nick said, chewing a last slice of bread and butter. "Train stations are a treasure trove for old newspapers. It was all Big Ben, stock prices, and cholera."

"The steam barons have taken to selling water they have to pump. The poor have gone back to some of the old wells. It was only a matter of time before disease broke out."

Nick swore under his breath. Victims of cholera died of dehydration, too weak to escape their own filth. It wasn't a death he'd wish on his worst foe.

"It surprises me that you came here first." There was no judgment in the Schoolmaster's voice, but there was caution. "You're a pirate first and a rebel only a distant second, or so you've always told me. You began by saying you weren't a rebel at all."

Nick dusted the crumbs from his fingers. He decided to skip the fact that he'd had no other place to go. "I was never locked away before. Now I have something precise to hate."

The man nodded, as if he'd heard that story before. "Can I trust you?"

That made Nick blink. "Of course."

The Schoolmaster laughed. "It seems like a strange thing to ask, but I wouldn't believe you unless you had that astonished look on your face. Honest men never anticipate that question. Liars do."

Irritation prickled. "I thought you already trusted me."

"With some things. If you are going to work with us, there are other details you will need to know."

"I want vengeance. All I need is a place to report, and I'll fight."

"That's just it. There is no rebel army in the conventional sense. Our weapons makers are scattered all over the country, and I am the only one who knows where they are. That gives me rather a lot of responsibility when it comes time to rally the troops."

Nick frowned. He liked the Schoolmaster, but wondered if he was as good as the rebel army got. "What about Mycroft Holmes? Wasn't he preparing a shadow government to take over after the dust settles?"

"Yes. He is our liaison to the queen. Oh, don't look so shocked. We count ourselves patriots."

"But . . ."

"But?"

"What military experience do the rebels have? If you're coordinating the makers and their war machines, how much do *you* have?"

The Schoolmaster pulled off his glasses, giving Nick the full power of his blue eyes. All at once Nick felt churlish for doubting him. "About as much airmanship as you had when you became captain of the *Red Jack*. But I know when to stop talking and listen. Like you, I have gathered a seasoned crew."

"I *had* one," Nick said quietly, the hollowness inside telling him that he'd lost too many friends. "I have to go to Cornwall to find out if any of my men are left."

"Cornwall?"

"We were building a ship there. We chose a village along a forsaken bit of coast where no one would bother to look for an enormous steamspinner under construction."

"A steamspinner?" The Schoolmaster was impressed. "That would be a welcome addition to our air forces."

They were in Nick's territory now. "What's your strength?"

"Not enough. The Merchant Brotherhood of the Air has taken umbrage with the Steam Council, but they aren't battleships. We want to attract a few pirates and have dropped the word in one or two taverns, but you captains are hard men to reach these days. The air over London is constantly patrolled, and smugglers are having a hard time bringing in their wares."

"Perhaps I can help with that," Nick said. "Though it may take time."

"If we win, any man fighting for us will be pardoned of his crimes." The Schoolmaster gave him a significant look. "Gentlemen of the airways included. We have Queen Vicky's word on it, and she does love a dashing hero."

Nick heard that with a mix of emotions. The Schoolmaster was right. He was a pirate first. On the other hand, a rebel victory might rewrite his future. War would bring death but there might also be opportunity. And of course, there would be vengeance.

He allowed himself to hope just a little. Just enough to take a leap of faith. "I'm your man," Nick said to the Schoolmaster. "But there is one condition."

"Which is?"

"Before I went to the Manufactory, I kept hearing about a mystery group of aristos calling themselves the Baskervilles. That was the code word you gave me when I took Mycroft Holmes north."

"Ah, you want to know what it means. I should never have used that as a code word. Unfortunately, it became a rallying cry." The Schoolmaster filled their brandy glasses again, his eyes bright with mischief. "I suppose it is only fair to know for whom you fight."

He set the bottle down and held out his hand. "My name is Edmond Baskerville."

"You? You're Baskerville?"

"Indeed. My father is Sir Charles Baskerville, a quiet country gentleman. I, on the other hand, am an infamous sluggard who prefers low taverns and music halls to anything resembling honest work. If it appeared otherwise, I would need more than Mrs. Pennyfeather guarding my door."

Nick was speechless.

The Schoolmaster grinned. "As it is, I've been picked up for questioning more than once because of the name, but as you can see"—he swept a hand around the derelict room—"there was nothing to find."

So this was the famous Baskerville. Nick's doubts came back. The young man was capable, charismatic, even a little ruthless—but he seemed far too civil to lead a country to war. It made Nick wonder what he wasn't seeing.

The Schoolmaster drank off his brandy and pushed his glasses back into place. "I'm leaving London soon. You might as well come with me since your ship is in the south. We can go part of the way together."

"Where are you going?"

The Schoolmaster's voice was suddenly brisk. "I'm calling a council. I'll show them what you found on the body of the Scarlet King's airman. That's an important find. Thanks to you, we've known for a while what weaponry the Blue King commands, and we've had an informant in the Green Queen's ranks. The question is whether or not we can wait for more. It might be time to pull our forces together and prepare for action."

Nick paused, a question working its way to the front of his brandy-addled brain. "Why do you fight? What's this war to you?"

The Schoolmaster froze, his eyes unreadable behind his tinted glasses. Then he smiled, but it was bitter. "The steam barons killed too many people who were close to me."

"You want vengeance, too."

"I want order with at least a teaspoon of social conscience. I want clean, free water so that no one even remembers what cholera does to the body. I want everyone to be able to read. I want everyone to have access to heat and light. What the Steam Council offers is the amoral governance of greed. I'm not a philosopher, but even I can tell that's a bad idea." He gave an apologetic grimace. "And that is enough of my moralizing. Will you leave London with me?"

The abrupt question pushed Nick's weary brain into action. He hadn't made up his mind whether to look for Athena or the crew first, but traveling with the Schoolmaster might answer some other lingering questions about the Baskerville business—such as who else was involved. "Yes, but there is someone I must see first, if she is still in London."

The Schoolmaster's face grew wry. "The fair Miss Cooper? Holmes's niece? Wasn't she the one who went with you to spy out the Blue King's army?"

"Yes." Nick's stomach grew chill. "Has something happened to her?"

"You'll find her at the Ladies' College. Holmes gave me her address in case—well, in case his work prevented him from being able to watch over her. I don't know the details, but I'm told the Gold King has her under his thumb."

"I'll take care of that," Nick growled, impressed by the level of trust the detective placed in the Schoolmaster. "I've always taken care of Evie."

"Indeed? Then far be it from me to interrupt your gallant supervision."

Nick rose, ready to find this college and reclaim his love, but his body had endured enough. He had labored in the manufactory for a year, and had just had his first good meal in all that time. It sat heavy in his belly, reminding him how hungry he had been. And now that he wasn't fleeing for his life, exhaustion and alcohol hit him like a rogue wave. Nick swayed a moment, and then sat down quickly as the room did a stomach-churning spin. He blinked hard, struggling to pull this vision into focus. Before he could stop himself, he broke into a prodigious yawn.

The Schoolmaster looked over the top rim of his tinted glasses, back to his mischievous self. "Before you rush off to save the fair maid, might I suggest a nap? And maybe a bath?"

CHAPTER EIGHTEEN

SO THIS IS WHAT IT FEELS LIKE TO BE A HUNTING DOG, RESTlessly waiting to be unleashed.

Evelina gazed out her bedroom window as she tugged on her gloves. It was night and there was little to see beyond the mullioned glass panes, but she was eager to get out of the college. With Tobias holding that metaphorical leash, she was to attend that night's meeting of the Parapsychological Institute and meet the famous Madam Thalassa. Evelina's instructions were simple. As the tame magic user of the Gold King, she was to find some excuse for the Steam Council to arrest and execute the famous medium.

It was true that the Steam Council's soldiers might have stormed the place without a preliminary investigation, but even the barons were not so bold quite yet. The Parapsychological Institute was made up of rich merchants and minor aristocrats—and while they didn't hold much power individually, together they had the ear of the press. That meant there was an expectation of fair play—or at least decorum—and that meant Keating required a plausible excuse for murder. Ergo, Evelina had to play her part.

Not that she intended to comply for one minute. She couldn't surrender Madam Thalassa to the law when she wanted to enlist her help for Imogen. But then there was Tobias to consider. She had to appear to be carrying out orders unless she wanted him to land in trouble. That was a complication she could have done without—but a complication that Uncle Sherlock no doubt expected her to manage. *I wish I understood what was going on.*

Evelina pinned on her hat. For someone who supposedly held lives and reputations in the balance, she looked ordinary enough. Her skirt, waistcoat, and fitted jacket were all made of dark blue wool. They were practical, well-made garments suited for someone without the luxury of a lady's maid. The only touch of whimsy was a panel of blue floral embroidery at the front of the skirt, giving the impression of a fancy petticoat. The rest was all starch and buttoned-up propriety, the very picture of a female scholar. Evelina picked up her parasol and went into the sitting room to wait for her escort to arrive.

"Good evening," said a voice.

Evelina started, the soles of her gray kid boots actually leaving the floor. "Tobias!"

He rose from the armchair, setting aside the chemistry book Professor Moriarty had loaned her. "I remember this literary treasure from my own university days. Not exactly a thrilling read."

She was still stuck on the fact that he was already there, in her private space. She didn't have a servant to answer the door. "How did you get in?"

He patted the breast pocket of his coat. "With a key. Keating gave it to me today."

Evelina struggled to rein in her temper. These rooms were her world now, the only sanctuary she could expect. The thought that the locks meant nothing shook her more than she cared to admit. "A perquisite of your position as jailor?"

Tobias's smile held a trace of the rake he'd once been. "Evidently."

She gave him a hard look, making sure that he knew he had crossed a line. "That is hardly the act of a gentleman."

Surprise widened his eyes. Whatever he'd expected, it wasn't that. "My apologies. I did not intend to cause offense."

Evelina took a deep breath. Even now, Tobias seemed not

to understand what it was to be utterly vulnerable. He was a lord's son, after all, with a fortune of his own and a title in his future. The best she could hope for was a teaching position, if she was extremely lucky. "Very well. Shall we go?"

Her tone displeased him. His mouth thinned as he fumbled for his pocket watch. "Hold out your hands."

She complied, the silver bracelets gleaming softly in the lamplight. There was a tiny key, no bigger than her smallest fingernail, hanging from Tobias's watch chain. He slid it into a hole in each bracelet, giving it a single turn. At the sound, she felt the dark hunger stir inside her, a sleeping beast twitching its ears. She tried to recall Moriarty's explanation of the bracelets' mechanism, but rational thought was swamped as a rush of power slipped over her skin. It felt like taking that first deep breath after her corset strings were undone for the night.

But while the bracelets clicked, they did not budge. "Aren't you going to take them off?" she asked tightly.

"No. Turning this key will only stop the mechanism for twelve hours. You need to be back inside the college by breakfast to avoid suffering the consequences."

That meant no dash to liberty. Disappointment slashed at her, reminding her that they were on opposite sides. "I wouldn't expect my freedom to be so easily achieved."

He put his watch away, buttoning his coat. The look in his eyes said he was still smarting from her rebuke. "Tell me this, Evelina. How did you manage to keep your abilities a secret from us for all those years?"

"I was wondering when that subject would drift to the surface." Evelina slipped on her coat and they left, locking the door to her rooms. Despite everything, she felt light. It was impossible not to relish the prospect of something different in her relentless routine.

"I never had any sense you possessed magical abilities," he said, his voice flat. "It's just surprising."

Stung, Evelina straightened her spine. Suddenly she didn't feel like participating in an adventure. "I imagine tonight is going to be difficult for you, if you despise magic so much."

He shot her a narrow look. "But not for you."

Her temper slipped. "Oh, for heaven's sake, it's not like I have wings or a tail. The gift came from my father's side, and my Gran Cooper was very strict about how a person used such things."

"Then what about Magnus?" Tobias sounded as if he'd been itching for the argument for a long time.

"He was a sorcerer. That kind of magic is different. My gran's folk magic coaxes spirits to lend the practitioner strength to work a spell. Sorcerers use their own strength, or they steal life from another living being. There's a world of difference."

"But that's a choice." As he led her out the front door, Tobias gripped her arm so hard it hurt. "It's not like you *can't* drain someone of life and use it to work evil. Not if you decided to do it."

Evelina stopped walking to stare at him. They'd passed quickly through the building, meeting no one along the way. Now they stood in the chill night, the smell of rain and dying leaves thick in the air. "Actually, that's not true. A sorcerer has to learn how to do those things."

"You studied with Magnus."

"For a very short time." Enough to infect her with a taste for stolen life, but not enough to learn how to satisfy that craving. Regret and relief clamored inside her, but mostly relief. *Mostly, but not always.*

"And yet even his prize automaton knew how."

Shock coursed through Evelina. "How did you know about Serafina?"

Tobias made a sour face. "I read the diary of the man who built her, but I didn't understand it at the time. Not until Im told me about the soul trapped inside her."

"How . . . ?"

"Magnus left Imogen in Serafina's care. It was Anna."

"Anna?" Imogen's dead twin. Horror slammed into her, stealing her breath. Evelina's lips parted, but she couldn't find her voice. Her mind was too busy linking facts together, rearranging everything she'd believed. *Dear God!* There had been something childlike and endearing about the doll at first. Had that been some echo of Evelina's love for Imogen? *But then she left me bleeding to death. She would have torn me to pieces if she could.*

"I'm sorry," she said softly into the darkness.

"It was a foul business," he muttered. "I hope to God she's at rest now that she's free from Magnus and his damned spells."

"There was nothing left of the *Wyvern* when it went down."

"That was the only good thing to come out of that night." Tobias gave her a narrow look. "You didn't know he'd given her Anna's soul?"

"Not at all!"

"Are you telling me the truth?"

Another sting—and now Evelina was too upset just to swallow it. Her eyes burned, but anger blocked any tears. "Would I lie about something like that?"

"I don't know."

"You used to value my honesty. Have I changed that much?"

His answer came back sharp with resentment. "To be utterly frank, I don't understand why you had anything to do with Magnus, much less why you gave yourself up to Keating. What game are you playing? I try to figure you out, and that stops me every time."

She felt an almost physical jerk at the change in topic. "We talked about this already."

"Tell me again."

A lump clogged her throat, and then melted into rivulets of pain. "I traded myself for the *Red Jack*. It didn't work."

Tobias swore softly. "For Nick?"

"You gave yourself to Keating for your family. I did the same thing."

"And still Nick died."

She nodded, unable to say more. Tobias shook his head, as if he still didn't believe her, and stalked toward the carriage he had waiting a dozen yards away. The set of his shoulders was like a door slammed shut.

She tried to guess the cause of his mood. There was a

sliver of jealousy, but surely some of it was nerves. He didn't like magic, and they were up for an entire night of it. And then there was the simple fact that they were forced to be together. They hadn't learned how to manage that yet.

Evelina followed, recognizing the vehicle as one of the Gold King's black victorias. A pair of gray horses waited patiently in the damp night, flicking their ears as the first raindrops fell. The driver was nearly invisible beneath the thick, dark folds of his caped coat.

Tobias handed Evelina into the vehicle and then joined her on the opposite seat. "I'm sorry," he said.

"I know," she replied, her voice husky. "But I can't talk about Nick anymore."

"It's just that I never knew you loved him."

"Neither did I until it was too late. At least, I didn't realize how much." And she hadn't known that the wild magic that flared whenever they were together could be tamed. Nick had learned to handle his power, and when they'd finally made love, it hadn't been simply with their bodies. Their union had been far more profound.

She had no idea what showed on her face, but Tobias gave her a look that might have been pity or anger, but she couldn't read it. The carriage was picking up speed, and bars of illumination from the streetlamps flashed through the carriage. They were on the border of the Scarlet King's territory, and the red globes turned the gaslight bloody. She turned to the window, looking for some sign of where they were going. She thought she saw the edge of Highgate Cemetery. *It would at least be peaceful there.*

"I should have fought to marry you," Tobias said into the darkness. He spoke so softly, the words were barely audible over the rattle of wheels on the road.

"You didn't love me enough," she answered.

"I should have."

She shrugged. "These things don't always come out the way you expect."

Tobias sank back against the seat cushions. There wasn't anything to say. And so they rode in silence, sitting far enough apart that they never touched, even when the victoria lurched on the uneven roads. The silence began to oppress Evelina, whose mind reeled with everything he'd said about Anna, and about them. She might have tried to speak, but Tobias stared out the window, one hand clenched in his lap. It didn't seem the time to prod at his misery.

After a half hour, they pulled up before a tall, narrow house. They still had to be somewhere at the northern edge of London. As the driver folded down the stairs and helped Evelina descend, she looked around in search of landmarks.

It was too dark to see far, and the meeting place turned out to be an ordinary house on a very ordinary-looking street. A wrought-iron fence surrounded a modest front lawn much like every other lawn in view. The bland neighborhood looked like one of those built in haste when the expanding railways made commuting from the suburbs practical. Evelina felt a pang of disappointment. As far as adventure went, the night was lacking.

The interior was slightly more promising, with an eclectic collection of pictures and shadowboxes crowding the walls. They were shown at once into a parlor done in red velvet. Evelina paused on the threshold, getting a first impression. Five other guests—two men and three women—sat in the ample chairs, guarded by a trio of cats that lounged bonelessly on the empty seats.

Evelina reached out with her senses, questing for magic, but all she felt was mild chaos—and that had more to do with the housekeeping than with the company. With the exception of a square table in the middle of the room, every surface was crammed with pictures, shells, comfit boxes, clocks, bits of lace, and curiosities so that Evelina had little idea what the furniture beneath looked like. If there were any actual psychic vibrations at work, they were buried in the clutter.

Tobias was already making introductions. A wiry woman with upswept gray hair nodded graciously. "I am Emily Barnes."

"Our hostess, I believe," Tobias said with his most winning smile. "I trust our credentials are in order?"

"Yes, that's right. I received your letter of introduction to our little society. Thank you so much for sending it in advance. We have to be careful, as I'm sure you understand. And I'm so delighted you were able to bring your lovely cousin."

Evelina started a little at that, but it made sense. A man could accompany a relation without a chaperone—and cousin sounded far better than prisoner. She tugged the cuffs of her sleeves over the silver bracelets and made her how-do-you-dos.

Miss Barnes pressed her hand warmly. Her fingers were strong, her movements brisk and efficient, and Evelina recalled something Tobias had said about the woman having an interest in nursing. From her age, she would have been among the first wave of gentlewomen who had chosen it as a profession. That made Evelina curious about her.

"Please have a seat," said Miss Barnes. "We'll be starting in a very few minutes." With that, the woman bustled off to do something in another part of the house.

Evelina ventured into the room, glancing at the faces of the others. Their hostess had introduced them all, but she'd already forgotten most of the names. They all looked ordinary, and she was certain none was Madam Thalassa. She sat down gingerly on a settee coated in enough cat hair to knit another kitten.

"It's very lovely of Miss Barnes to let us use her house," said a blond woman with a round, rosy face.

"Yes, it is." Evelina realized that she was rusty at making small talk. Then again, perhaps her sudden awkwardness was that this girl's pretty features reminded her of poor Mary Jane Kelly, who'd met a terrible end in Whitechapel not quite a year ago. She had been bright and friendly, too. "I've not been to one of these meetings before. Can you tell me what happens?"

"Oh, it's different every time," the young woman said enthusiastically. "Sometimes it's a lecture and sometimes it's a practical demonstration."

"And tonight?"

"We're going to try a séance."

"Who will be leading it, Mrs. Phillips?" Tobias asked. An

ambassador's son, he had a knack for remembering names and titles. A black-and-white feline had taken up residence in his lap and was kneading contentedly.

"I shall," said a man, who was sitting in an armchair in the corner, chewing the stem of an unlit pipe. He was weathered as a sea captain, with brown side whiskers grizzling to gray. "I'm stepping into the breach, it's true, but I think I shan't disappoint."

"I'm sorry, sir," said Evelina. "I didn't catch your name."

"Wood. Leonidas Wood."

"Stepping into the breach?" Tobias prompted.

"A confusion of dates," Wood answered. "The planned guest had the wrong night. Shoddy record keeping is the bane of anything run by volunteers."

"For shame," said Mrs. Phillips. "We should be thanking those that donate their time."

Wood huffed and clamped his teeth around the pipe stem with an audible click.

"I'm sure whatever occurs tonight, it will be of great interest," Evelina said with all the diplomacy she could muster.

Tobias caught Evelina's eye. *No Madam Thalassa.* Disappointment swept through her, suspicion hard on its heels. They hadn't bothered with disguises or false names—few would recognize Evelina, and none would know her as Keating's pet practitioner. But had someone known Tobias? Although he had no interest in this type of gathering, the Roth family was well known. Had Miss Barnes left the gathering to warn the guest of honor away?

"There," said their hostess, bustling into the room. "All details sorted. It's time we began."

Everyone rustled to attention. As if on cue, the three cats jumped to the floor and trotted from the room. Tobias brushed at the cat hair clinging to his clothes, but it was a lost cause. Evelina tried not to notice that he'd gone white around the lips. He really wasn't happy about being there. *Poor Tobias. Everyone is afraid of something.*

The next few minutes progressed as Evelina expected.

The eight members in attendance gathered around the square table, pulling their chairs close. The gas was dimmed, drapes drawn, and a single candle placed at the center of the table. Finally, Miss Barnes closed the door and took her seat.

Wood cleared his throat and hitched himself forward. "Now, if everyone would please join hands."

Tobias was sitting to Evelina's right, Mrs. Phillips to her left. The young lady was bright-eyed with interest, but Evelina wasn't expecting much. Even if someone did summon a ghost, they usually didn't have much to say.

She took Mrs. Phillips's dainty hand, and then let Tobias grasp her other. His fingers were long and strong, just as she remembered them. Wood's voice was no more than a distant murmur behind her unsettled thoughts.

Eventually, she drifted back to the matter at hand. It was the usual routine about spirits of the great beyond, were there any loved ones, and so on. She'd seen the show a thousand times as a child with Ploughman's Paramount Circus. The theory was that any spirit desiring to speak with a participant could use the medium as his or her mouthpiece—but whether that was true was beyond Evelina's knowledge. Velda the Glorious—who also charmed snakes—pretended to call the dead, but would pick the pockets of the gullible while they sat with their eyes closed. Evelina's Gran had read cards, but never traded in ghosts.

Tobias's hand was turning cold. A pang of concern caught at her; she thought it was too bad he was worrying over nothing. But then again, the entire room was starting to get chilly—no, downright frozen. Evelina snapped to attention, her own magic suddenly on alert. Wood had stopped talking, but she could still see a faint mist where his breath warmed the air.

Who would have thought? Something is here after all. Evelina reached out with her senses, tentatively touching the energy in the room. There were eight normal, healthy presences there, a few burning more brightly than others. So, some of the society members, including Wood and Miss

Barnes, probably had a drop of the Blood. Nothing about that was worrisome.

But they were not alone. The darkness in her magic stirred. It wasn't just hunger; it was the part of her that sensed danger soonest, and it knew instinctively how to fight.

"There is someone here looking for you, Miss Cooper," Wood said softly. His voice was rounded with a slight lilt, as if he'd come from Cornwall. "The entity says you were looking for her."

Evelina sucked in her breath, a quick, desperate inhalation. There was only one female she'd been looking for. "Imogen?"

Tobias squeezed her hand hard. "What?" His voice was sharp.

The temperature in the room dropped so low that Mrs. Phillips cried out. The flame of the candle at the center of the table suddenly grew until it was twice the height of the wax pillar and thin as a needle. Evelina's heart began to pound at the eerie sight. A primitive instinct inside her wanted to snarl and bare fangs at whatever had invaded the room.

The skin between her shoulder blades crept, as if someone was staring at her back. "It can't be her." And yet— what other roaming spirit would want to speak to her?

"Steady on," said Miss Barnes in the kind of voice meant to quiet hysterical children. "No one moves; no one lets go of the hand on either side."

The candle seemed to be growing dim, a strange dark haze muffling the colors in the room. The crawling sensation over her skin increased, making her shudder. And then it made her think of spiders begging to be brushed away— but that would break the circle.

Mrs. Phillips tugged at her grip, but Evelina just held her more tightly. "No, don't let go."

Tobias's hand was growing clammy, his breath quick. "Im?"

One of the other women was starting to make small, frightened sounds.

"Evelina," said Wood, the voice his, but not his. There was something too soft about it. "Evelina, I need your help. Something has gone very wrong."

An eerie sensation filled the room, almost as if they were inside a bubble about to pop. The scent of iris stole past— Imogen's scent—and for a moment, Evelina believed.

"That has to be her," muttered Tobias. "She always turned to you."

That much was true. Evelina had been her friend's protector, nurse, and confidante. When Imogen had nearly died, it had been Evelina who had literally held body and soul together that long and fearful night. "Imogen? Where are you?"

The iris scent grew stronger. "I'm in—"

The words cut off abruptly, and the sweet perfume turned to the gagging stink of decay.

All at once, it didn't *feel* like her friend, and Evelina stiffened. "Whoever you are, I don't believe you."

Wood gave a short, sharp laugh. "Oh, but it's true. I'm very, very lost in ways you can't begin to imagine."

And then the air began to congeal, stifling with the sweetish stench of rot. One moment, Evelina could breathe normally. The next, it was like trying to inhale jelly. The effect on the company was immediate. Mrs. Phillips gave a shriek, pulling away from the circle. Evelina was too surprised to stop her. Three of the others jumped to their feet, caught in sudden terror. Surprisingly, Tobias was completely steady, his nerve holding up when the danger became real—but it was too late. The circle was shattered, and with it all protection from whatever it was they had summoned.

"That's quite enough!" Miss Barnes barked sharply. "Get thee gone, spirit!"

The brisk command steadied Evelina. She knew instinctively that she was the most powerful magic user in the room. Revealing her own talent was risky, even in a group sympathetic to magic, but letting the entity run rampant was more dangerous still. She rose to her feet, releasing Tobias's hand.

"Evelina!" he cried.

"I'll take care of this," she said with more confidence than she felt. Then she reached for her power, letting it rise in her like light filling a prism. Her limbs tingled, and suddenly she could inhale freely again. "You heard our hostess. You've outstayed your welcome."

"Is that right?" Wood rose to face her across the table. In the murky light, all she could see was the dim white oval of his face. She could have sworn it wasn't the man she had met barely an hour ago. The chin was too pointed, the hair too fair. *Don't let it be her. It can't be her.*

Power snaked at her, a fast, furious strike. Evelina slapped it back without thinking. She'd dueled with Magnus, once in earnest and many more times as his student. Whatever this thing was, it was hardly on the sorcerer's level. It struck again, this time with a hot bolt that singed like flame. Her dark hunger leaped for it, craving the ambient energy, and snatched it from the air before it could even land. She felt the light inside her tinge with shadow as her darker power rose, but she couldn't afford to push that strength aside. Whatever was posing as Imogen was stronger than she'd thought.

"Feeding on scraps?" the thing mocked. "I would have expected more from you, Miss Cooper."

Evelina cupped her hand, summoning witch fire. A cluster of pale flame danced in the air above her hand, throwing bizarre shadows over the company. Someone gasped, "Sorcery!" Evelina ignored it.

"Show yourself," she commanded, throwing compulsion into her voice.

As if in obedience, Wood slumped to his knees. "Evelina!"

The voice was Imogen's. It was so startling, Evelina lost concentration, and the witch fire died abruptly.

"Help me, Evelina!"

"Dear God," Tobias started forward, lurching a few steps before stumbling to a confused halt, obviously unsure of what to do.

"I don't know how to get out of here," Imogen said in a tiny voice.

"Do something!" Tobias roared, his face twisted with fear and disgust.

The air was clearing and the other participants had backed away, though Miss Barnes now stood guardian at the door, making sure no one—and no *thing*—entered or left the room. Evelina circled the table, approaching Wood's crumpled form. She could feel the entity possessing him, tingling and sparking like the static from a coil. Wood held out a hand—a square, male hand that was simultaneously the slim white fingers of her friend. Evelina drifted closer, still unsure, her power coiled like a spring.

"Evelina, help her," said Tobias, pleading now.

"Please, Evelina," whispered the thing that was and was not Imogen.

She only stood a few feet away now, her heart yearning to believe she had finally found her friend. From here, she could get help, find a way to lead Imogen home.

Evelina reached out, inches away from grasping Imogen's hand.

"Watch out!" Imogen cried.

And Wood sprang at her, launching from the floor to pounce like a spider. The voice that snarled should not have come from any human throat. Evelina released her power, slamming him backward. Wood flew through the air, crashing into the back of the red velvet settee. The long, thin candle flame flared into a ball of fire, roaring and then blooming into a bright, miniature sun suspended over the table. Mrs. Phillips screamed.

Then it was Evelina's turn to attack, flinging her power again, this time to trap. But the entity was too quick, corkscrewing out of her grasp like an eel. She almost caught it, tightening the whip of her power like a noose, but it slipped out, gone before she could even get a better look. Then something popped, as if a cork had been pulled from a bottle.

And it was gone. All she was left with was a lingering scent of the grave. The hunter in her howled with hunger and fury at the loss of its prey. Evelina staggered, dizzy with a cramping, desperate need to feed. She'd experienced the hunger before, but never with such ferocity. But then, she'd never starved for lives so long as this.

Evelina grabbed the back of a chair, her mind rendered blank by too many horrific ideas. And then, with a flash of insight, she understood what else the bracelets did. They dulled a sorcerer's requirement for human life, neutralizing the impulse to gather power. Unless she used her magic, she had been able to forget the desire for days at a time. *What would I be like if they came off altogether?*

There wasn't time to think about it. Wood fell to the floor in a dead faint. The ball of flame above the candle went out with a thunderclap, plunging them in darkness. Evelina cried out, finally, suddenly afraid.

After a heartbeat, and then two, Miss Barnes turned up the lights. They all stared at each other in astonishment. Evelina started to shake, hot tears streaking down her face as the hunger died back to a simmering, constant discomfort. But at least now she could think past it enough to function.

"What the bloody hell was that?" said a gentleman in a tweed suit, thick mustaches quivering. "Was that a ghost or a demon?"

Tobias grabbed Evelina by the arm, spinning her around. "What *are* you?"

She met his eyes. They were bleak, as if what he'd seen her do had stripped him of some last shred of comfort. He'd been told she had magic, but clearly seeing it in action was something far more horrific. Her chin started to tremble, presaging yet more tears. "Damn you, Tobias, you asked me to come here. I did what I had to do."

His grip on her tightened until it was painful. "Was that Imogen?"

"No," she said hoarsely. "At least I hope not." She prayed it wasn't, but then a whirlpool of doubt tugged at her, doing its best to drag her under. *That was her voice. She knew the right words to say.* "Sometimes it seemed like her, sometimes not. At the end, she tried to warn me."

"You don't know."

"It sounded as if she was fighting to be heard, but something wouldn't let her speak. Once she called me Miss Cooper. Imogen would never do that. I was always Evelina to her."

"But you don't know anything for certain."

"No," she whispered, tears of frustration stinging her eyes. "But Serafina called me Miss Cooper."

Tobias flinched. "Serafina—Anna—perished on the *Wyvern*."

"Did she?"

"Damnation." He dropped his hand, flexing it as if he wanted to wipe it clean of her magic-infested touch. Then he turned away without another word.

Miss Barnes regarded her steadily. "You have some interesting talents, Miss Cooper."

"But not enough," Evelina said bitterly. "Not enough to do one bit of good."

And then she started to weep in earnest.

CHAPTER NINETEEN

Unknown

IMOGEN CROUCHED BEHIND A CLUSTER OF GEARS, CLUTCHing her knees to her chest in a desperate effort to make herself small. The air was filled with the hot, tangy smell of working metal, and the entire space pulsed with the incessant, relentless ticking of the longcase clock. It vibrated through her feet and rang in her skull, shaking every tooth in her head.

She was out of breath, and her hands and forearms were nicked and bruised from climbing through the bizarre landscape of the clock. Crawling through it was frightening, not to mention a challenge for someone more used to the ladylike arts. She'd had to be quick to avoid the swinging pendulum, and the sudden click of a gear could crush a hand or foot if her attention wavered.

But as bad as that was, being chased was worse. It had begun the moment she'd first felt the tug of Evelina's mind on hers. Her friend's touch had been just that, like a hand on her shoulder, bidding her to turn around and follow. And then a huge, fierce blast had torn her away, as if a giant had backhanded her into the gear works. Anna, she assumed. Her sister never had liked anyone else having friends.

Imogen had learned to hide after that, keeping to the spaces in between protective fortifications of brass and steel. When the blows came, ducking behind a solid object helped. She glanced up at the hands of the clock face, which was mirrored inside the clock as well as out. The hands always matched the chimes, and yet their movement was ut-

terly random. Two o'clock might be followed as easily by
eleven or six as three. Wherever she was, time obeyed different rules.

And today—or tonight, or this morning, because who
could tell?—she'd been able to make at least some contact.
Perhaps because Evelina had touched her, she knew at once
when the séance had begun. The medium's invitation to
visit had been as clear as the peal of a bell. Unfortunately,
she hadn't been the only one to hear. Again, she had come
under fire, but at least now her friends knew she was still
trying to get home.

Imogen raised herself up just enough to see over a giant
spoked wheel of brass. She pressed a hand to her side, feeling the ache of a bruise. As much as it hurt, the pain was
worthwhile because she'd actually witnessed the séance
through the eyes of the medium. She'd seen Tobias and Evelina, and the hope and worry on their faces gave her something to clutch like an amulet. And she needed whatever
luck and strength she could get.

She stretched up another inch. The view offered a narrow
sightline past the thing with the chain and a vial of bubbling
green goo. She had no notion what any of these parts were
called and didn't care. If she got out of here, she was going
to toss every timepiece in the house—whether or not it was
made by a sorcerer—onto a gigantic bonfire. Imogen
squinted and waited, the tick of the clock lapping around her
like waves.

Then she saw something move, a shadow sliding between
the wheeling gears. Her instinct was to catch her breath, but
she stopped herself. Despite the racket of the machinery, she
didn't want even a tiny gasp to give her away.

"I can feel you watching," said the voice from the shadows.

Anna. Imogen knew the timbre and the pitch, the slight
roughness when the words dipped low. She'd heard that
voice in her nightmares before—so like her own, but not.
The voice was a relief in a way. There had been no way to
tell how her sister would appear. She could have shown up
as a monster or a mist or an ostrich or nothing at all. The

dead seemed to have different rules. A sister who had been trapped in an automaton and slashed six women to death had none.

Imogen stayed silent as a mouse. Why had Anna chosen to emerge from the woodwork now? The séance, she supposed. Strangers were interfering in her domain.

"I suppose there are a number of things you're wondering about," Anna went on. "Why I brought you here, for starters."

Because I blew your head off with Captain Niccolo's aether gun and you're very, very upset? Fortunately, while Anna had shared her dreams in the past, she could not read her waking mind.

Her sister continued with a lecturing air. "Last time we met, you saw me as Serafina. I was Dr. Magnus's prize creation. He brought every automaton to life with a piece of his soul, but Serafina got a bigger piece because he wanted to make her—me—something more than the others. And so I learned everything that little nub of soul knew, and that included the secrets of this clock. He made it, you know."

And that knowledge gives you an enormous advantage. Imogen's gaze searched the shadows, trying to see Anna, but there was no movement where she'd been. And with the damned ticking, she could hear no footfalls. As interesting as this all was, she started looking for a way to retreat.

"It's a very special kind of clock." Anna's voice filled with pride, as if she'd made it herself. "The tubes of liquid are aether receptors. They translate the vibrational frequency of thought into a concrete form through a series of selectors that choose precisely which thoughts from all over the aether to record. Those get coded onto cards."

Imogen had always wondered what was on the messages the clock spit out from time to time. Only Lord Bancroft had ever collected and read the ciphered notes.

"And then of course there is the environment within the clock. Magnus built it as a magically protected refuge for when he was out and about in an incorporeal form. It seemed a perfect place for me to hide after Serafina went down with the ship. I didn't know if I'd survive, but Magnus had made me strong."

Imogen swayed where she stood. *And she pulled me right out of my body to go with her.* That was strange enough, but Imogen had even been on a different ship. *She's my twin. I'll always be vulnerable to her.*

She gripped a piece of metal frame, steadying herself. As she turned, she could see the narrow passage between gears led to one of the many sections of the clock that had no floor. There was a dark chasm below where the pendulum swung, and a misstep would be disastrous. Since, in her current state, the clock was huge and she was tiny, it would be the equivalent of falling off a mountain.

But there was a narrow steel bar that ran from this side to the other, and from there a chain, heavy and thick as a ladder, went up to another level. Imogen started inching that way.

"This place can be anything one likes." The pride in Anna's voice curdled to contempt. "I was able to wish you into that salon for almost a year before you found me out. It's easy enough to do if you've lived with a piece of a sorcerer in your soul—and of course you always were *such* a gullible simpleton. You'd believe anything."

Oh, really? The words opened up a wellspring of old resentment. Imogen flinched, dragged back to the thousand battles that had waged between them before both sisters fell sick. Imogen, the quiet shy twin, had survived. Vivacious Anna had not.

And apparently, Anna still resented the fact. "I should have been the one to live, you know."

Imogen reached the beam that went across the deadly gap. She didn't much like heights, and she could feel her heart skitter with apprehension. But the steel bar was a good eighteen inches across. Evelina had walked tightropes. She could do this. But then she looked over her shoulder and saw . . . herself. Her mirror image stood only a few yards away.

Anna was wearing identical clothes, with the very same smudges and tears in the hem. Revulsion reared up inside Imogen, almost masking her fear. "Can't you even get your own dress?"

"But I want to be you." The tone was soggy with mockery.

With a stifled gasp, Imogen began walking across the beam, knowing she was risking too much but needing distance between them. Anna had been a bully as a child and she didn't expect anything different now.

"You're still alive," Anna said matter-of-factly. "I can't take your body until you give it up. The sooner you do, the sooner this ends."

Imogen quickened her pace, nearly breaking into a run. When she got to the other side of the gap, she finally allowed herself to turn. She put one hand on the thick chain that hung down from the upper levels, feeling better with something solid in her hand. "It's an obvious question, but I have to ask: What makes you think I'll give anything up to you?"

"You will. You always do." Anna smiled with lips identical to Imogen's own, but the effect was chilling.

A cold claw of terror struck deep into Imogen, but she refused it. "Bollocks to that, Annie. We're not in the nursery anymore."

"No, we aren't. There's no one here to stop me."

That was all too true. Evelina had tried to reach Imogen twice, and had failed both times. Who else even had a chance? The thought made Imogen quail, but she grabbed at the chain anyhow, fighting down the knot of fear clogging her throat. Nerves made her fumble the chain before she caught it again and started to climb, her shoes poor protection against the heavy links of brass. She struggled up, hand and foot, hand and foot, in a ridiculous scramble that was no escape at all.

Anna stood below, silently watching with flat, gray eyes.

London, September 29, 1889

HILLIARD HOUSE

2:05 p.m. Sunday

POPPY WAS SURE that there was something wrong with the longcase clock on the stairway landing. It was still keeping time, but the tick sounded unwell and it had been making

peculiar creaks and clicks, almost as if there were mice inside. She examined it carefully, peering closely for any
signs of cracks or rust.

She had to stand on tiptoe. The clock, far taller than
Poppy, was made from beautiful rich walnut rubbed to a
shining gloss. The top was arched with finials at the corners, giving it the look of ears. There were seven moving
dials besides the usual clock face, each with its own measurement of time and weather. The Scorpion followed the
Scales across the top of the clock, and the moon phases—
currently in a state of one-eyed wakefulness—cycled below.

Most interesting were the coded messages the clock spit
out from time to time. Poppy had never cracked the cipher,
but she'd heard that Evelina had done it. Her father had con-
cocted it with Dr. Magnus long ago, back when they were
still friends. Poppy supposed that being not only evil but
dead, the doctor wouldn't be coming around to make repairs.

"What are you doing?" Tobias asked blandly.

"I'm looking at the clock."

"Why?"

"It doesn't sound right. Did you ever find out the cipher
for the clock's messages?"

"No, it's Father's."

"But you said once Evelina knew it."

"Then I suppose Holmes does," Tobias said, almost to
himself.

That was an interesting tidbit. Poppy came down off her
toes and then turned to face her brother. He looked like he'd
slept badly, and he had the hectic flush of someone running
on nerves. She forgot about the clock and decided to worry
about him instead.

The bags under his eyes were only the first sign that something was amiss. To everyone's surprise, he'd suggested the
family go to church together. He'd settled down quite a lot
since marrying Alice, but Poppy couldn't ever remember him
initiating a Sunday gathering, much less one involving ser-
mons. But they had gone and now Tobias, Alice, and Jeremy

were there for a meal. Lady Bancroft was delighted, but Poppy was bemused.

"What's wrong with you?" she asked.

He gave an uneasy shrug. "Work."

"Are you still trying to figure out the brass bug?"

"I am," he said so quickly that she knew there was more. "And right now I'm going with Father to see about a logic processor. One of his cronies has an Italian pleasure craft with a processor that might be the same as the brass bug's brain."

"Why does that matter?"

He flashed a smile. "How many personal crafts are there in London, much less Italian ones? It should be fairly easy to trace where it came from."

With that, he sprang down the steps with more energy than she'd seen from him in months. A few moments later, she heard her mother's moan of dismay when she heard the menfolk would be late for the meal. *Oh well, Tobias needs a victory more than he needs a roast of beef.* Mind you, that roast did smell delicious.

Poppy decided there was nothing more that she could do about the clock and drifted downstairs to the drawing rooms. Alice was in the smaller, brighter of the two with Jeremy in her lap. Tobias was there, shrugging into his coat.

Alice gave him an admonishing look. "You shouldn't be working on a Sunday. You need to rest sometime."

He gave her a kiss on the cheek, but it was a real one, not a quick, formal peck. "I'm not working, I'm looking."

She gave a huff. "Which means you won't be fixing, tinkering, or otherwise applying tools to any fabricated surface. I will check your shirt cuffs when you return."

By way of reply, Tobias poked Jeremy in his round tummy. The baby made a squeak and giggled, his fuzz of ruddy hair floating with the movement.

"I'll be back in good time to take you home," Tobias promised his wife.

"You'll be back sooner than that," Alice admonished in a gentle tone. "You mother is holding the meal. We poor ladies will be getting nothing but tiny sandwiches until you return."

"But I have to catch my amateur airman before he flies away for a fortnight."

Alice clutched his arm in mock distress. "Then hurry. We might starve."

"I can't have that. Besides I want some of that sherry trifle. Don't let Poppy eat it all."

"What?" Poppy protested.

Tobias raised his eyebrows, lowering his voice to a stage whisper Poppy could hear perfectly well. "It's the only way Mother lets her drink. It's sad, watching my little sister squeeze out all the cake to get at the liquor."

"Get out of here!" Poppy cried with a stamp of her slipper, which made Jeremy squeal in excitement.

Tobias disappeared with a laugh and a swirl of coattails, and Poppy and Alice were left alone. Jeremy, now wide awake, began a quest to grab the shiny brass buttons on Alice's dress—a task that seemed to also involve much wiggling of feet.

"He's in a fine mood today," Poppy said, squeezing a tiny foot just to see him squirm.

"Tobias played with him for hours this morning," Alice said, struggling to keep hold of her son.

Poppy sat down across from Alice. "Before church? He must have been up early."

Alice gave up and set the baby on the floor. Jeremy was too young to crawl, but engaged in a determined sort of slither. "I'm lucky to have a husband who can keep our son entertained. I can hardly get a proper cup of tea when it's the nurse's day off. Our upstairs maid is a good girl, but not an expert when it comes to babies."

Poppy didn't know what to say to that. She was the youngest and hadn't witnessed child rearing up close. The whole business sounded unforgivably damp. "Good for Tobias."

"He turned out all right." Alice gave a small smile that made Poppy's face heat. "But I do worry about how hard he works. I'm not even sure when he came home last night. Father has him out at all hours."

"Did he say what he was doing?"

"No, he wasn't in the mood to talk this morning. He just played with the baby."

Tobias had always been good with children, but something wasn't right. Poppy chewed her lip. Both Tobias and the clock were ticking wrong, but she didn't have the experience to fix them.

"Look at that!" Alice said excitedly.

Poppy looked down to see Jeremy gather himself onto all fours and lurch forward. She dove just in time to catch him before he tumbled over into the leg of a chair. Jeremy laughed his ear-splitting baby laugh, probably thrilled to see his auntie grubbing on the floor in her Sunday best.

"He's crawling!" Alice exclaimed.

"You'll never keep him contained now," Poppy said, suddenly feeling panicked. Who gave him permission to start growing up already? "Come here, you!"

She picked him up, putting him on her lap without regard for her skirts or her dignity. One hand in his mouth, Jeremy gave her his wide, innocent eyes. For an instant, she wished she could paint because there was so much worth capturing in that gaze. They were the soft gray of her brother's, but with the perfect trust of a child. *So rare and wonderful.*

It was then she realized that she really had grown up.

CHAPTER TWENTY

TWO DAYS OF SLEEPING, EATING, AND SLEEPING AGAIN HAD done much to restore Nick's energy. It was a good thing, because the Ladies' College of London was about as easy to access as the average cloistered nunnery. Not that Nick was in the habit of accosting nuns—it was bad enough being a pirate without diving for obvious clichés. Still, dusk found Nick on the outside looking in—a familiar vantage point for an orphan who never had actually acquired a last name.

The buildings—and hence his Evie—were guarded by a high wall topped in nasty spikes. The gate was something out of a Gothic prison, and some enterprising gardener had removed every bit of vegetation that might have provided access over the wall. If he wanted in, he was going to have to prove his resourcefulness.

Fortunately, this was the sort of thing he was good at. He began a tour of the perimeter, looking for suitable drains to climb. Something underground might have done, too, but one never liked to burst in on the love of one's life smelling of sewers. After all, he had gone to the bother of borrowing some of the Schoolmaster's smart clothes. In fact, he hadn't been allowed out the door until he was inspected and deemed to be in a fit state for wooing. For all his air of mystery and action, Edmond Baskerville had a sentimental streak.

Nick had stopped to inspect a likely looking downspout when a large raven landed at his feet. The size of the black bird was startling enough. The fact that it was wearing a tiny steel helmet had Nick blinking in surprise. He hadn't expected to see his old ally here.

Greetings, Captain Niccolo. You have long been in a place none of the ash rooks dared to fly.

"Fair winds, Gwilliam, Lord Rook." Nick used the bird's formal title. "It has been too long."

The creature spread his impressive wings—larger than the common raven's—and bowed his head. *The seed-pickers and eaters of worms sent word of your flight from the pit of fire. We dared not believe it was true.*

"There is a proverb among the ash rooks that those who cannot soar gather more facts."

If what they saw is not pushed aside by the sight of a tasty bug. The bird cawed at his own joke. *Sparrows are not the most reliable spies. Do you return to the clouds, Captain Niccolo? You fell like rain the night the flying ship burned. Some of my flock still cannot abide the sight of flame. We did not all fly home to roost that night.*

"The ash rooks fought bravely, as always. I mourn for the loss of your comrades."

We are sorry that we could not do more to help.

"I had Athena with me. I was safe enough." Even trapped inside a cube of steel, the deva had the power of flight—enough for two.

You buried her spirit in the cold ground.

"I hid her from the soldiers that took me. I did my best to protect her."

So the seed-pickers say. We honor your intent, if not your methods. Air devas do not belong beneath the soil.

What else could I have done? Annoyance shot through him, confounding his tongue as he searched for a particularly blistering reply. But he never had the chance to make one.

Gwilliam launched himself from the ground with an enormous flap.

"Where is she?" Nick cried. "I can't remember where I was!"

But the bird thundered through the air until he was sailing high above. He drifted over the wall with a rattling croak, and was gone.

"Fine," Nick muttered, backing up enough that he could see the section of wall where the ash rook had disappeared. It had, in fact, lost a few of its spikes. At least the bird had shown him a way over. Nick braced himself, rubbing his hands together to limber his fingers. Here was his way in.

Nick got over the wall, across the grounds, and found the building where—according to the Schoolmaster's notes— Evelina slept. He circled around the outside, waiting for someone to come or go so he could slip through the door behind them. When that didn't happen, he pulled out a set of lock picks he'd taken from the Schoolmaster's rooms and forced the issue.

His Blood gave him a talent for gliding unnoticed through rooms. He made good use of it, ghosting through the halls until he caught the whiff of Evelina's magic. It was a warm, familiar scent drawing him home—and reminding him of the days, and nights, they'd last spent together, tangled in the bed of a Whitechapel brothel. Not the setting he would have chosen for their first such interlude, but now he would ever have a sentimental fondness for Miss Hyacinth's establishment. He paused outside the door, forcing his mind away from that memory and to something far less disruptive to his concentration.

He knocked softly, fingering the lock picks in one hand. The dark-paneled walls of the college pressed down on him, disapproving. The very air of the place reminded him that he was no gentleman. The only way he would have set foot on school grounds was as the gardener's boy. What right did he have to be there?

I have every right. She and I have been inseparable since we were children. But that wasn't true, was it? She'd left the circus to become a lady. *Well, I've loved her longer than anyone else.* And there was no reason for them to be apart ever again. Nick braced his feet a little more squarely and knocked again, refusing to be cowed.

This time the door opened, and Evelina's heart-shaped face appeared. She looked pale, her eyes circled by lack of sleep. She stared at Nick a long moment, her lips parted. Then her hands flew to cover her mouth as if stricken. Nick's chest tightened at her look of obvious shock. Then she fell back a few steps, eyes welling.

This isn't how it should go. She should be happy. He pushed into the room.

"Evie, I'm sorry," he said. "I said I'd come back but . . ."

"You're dead!" The lift of her voice made it a question— or so he thought; the words were almost too muffled by her hands to make out.

He strode forward, taking her wrists and pulling her to him. "Not quite." In fact, he wanted to prove exactly how alive he was. "Just a bit late. I never was good with dates."

She made a noise like an angry cat. "Late? You left last November!"

Tears trembled in her eyes until one at last escaped over the curve of her cheek. Her mouth, always so full and soft, quirked up and down in turns as if she wasn't sure whether to laugh or break his nose. Nick's chest melted in a warm ache. "Sorry."

She felt slight, almost weightless, or maybe that was the strange euphoria filling his brain. He knew her scent, the way her hair curled around the shell of her ears. He knew the way the white flesh of her throat dipped above her collarbone, leaving a hollow that begged to be kissed.

"Bother you, anyway." She pulled her hands away, rushing to the door and closing it. The lock clicked with authority, and she put her palms to the door, as if reinforcing the barrier against the rest of the world. Her shoulders began to shake, and then she sucked in a long, ragged breath. "My heart broke for you, Niccolo. What happened?"

Happiness and regret wrenched hard. Nick inhaled, but there were no words for this. He took her in his arms, turning her around so that she could bury her face in his shoulder. She collapsed against him, nearly boneless.

By the Black Mother. His own eyes stung, and he clenched his teeth hard to hold in the wave of misery he'd banished ever since his ship had crumpled to the earth. There would be time for him to grieve later, when everyone he loved was safe.

"But the *Red Jack* went down," she whispered.

"It did. I made it, though. I'm not sure who else."

She pushed away just enough to look up. Her face was wet, glistening in the gaslight. "I prayed I would die, too."

Nick folded her tight again and kissed the top of her head, at once weary and thoroughly filled with life. He was aware of coming to a resting point, like an arrow finally finding its mark. Waiting for this moment was why he had survived.

"Where were you all this time?" she asked.

In hell, away from this. "In the Scarlet King's prison. I escaped."

Her face turned up again, blue eyes wide as a child's. "How?"

"Let's not talk about it now." He'd already given a recital to the Schoolmaster, and one journey through that ugliness was enough. He wanted to keep this moment clean in his memory. "What about you?"

"Me?" She sounded almost nervous.

Nick eyed the closed door, feeling a twinge of claustrophobia. At least he was on the right side of the locks this time. "What's this I hear about Jasper Keating? I thought we'd got him out of your life."

"Forget him," she brushed her lips against his. "I don't want to talk at all."

He was fine with that, at least for that moment. He dipped his head, catching her mouth with his. She still tasted wild, filled with the rough sweetness of roadside berries—this time salted with tears. The intoxicating softness of her lips pulled him in, melting the anger that had crusted around him after so many months of captivity. She filled him like water finding a desert creek bed.

Instantly, he was little more than primal instinct. He ran his hands down the arch of her spine, feeling the delicate wings of her shoulder blades beneath his palms. Something about her seemed more fragile than he remembered, and a protective heat snagged his breath. As if she felt his emotion, she pulled away enough to wrap her fingers around his and put those petal-soft lips to his fingertips.

And then his power rose, responding to hers. A silver light formed between them, a bright fur of power gloving their hands where skin met skin. He barely had the will to hold his magic back, keeping the leash of it tight—because when their wild magic rose, things could get unpredictable. There was only one way to contain it, and they weren't there quite yet.

And yet he couldn't keep his free hand still. He felt himself growing unpredictable as he traced the round buttons leading up to the prim collar of her gown. Knowing what lay beneath was sheer torture, and after so long without even the sight of a woman, he was about ready to chew those plump little buttons right off. "Evie," he murmured, burying rationality and wondering where the bed was.

"You never did know how to move slowly," she teased, winding her arms around his neck.

"I'll send flowers next time." His gaze searched hers, looking for the invitation to take the next step. But instead of desire in her dark blue eyes, he found fear. His heart all but stopped. "What's wrong?"

"You're going to want me to go with you," she said.

"You're damned right," he said without thinking. It was what they'd promised one another that last night together, tangled in the warm sheets and lost in the novelty of being safe and sure. "I'm going to live up to that promise."

But this time when he took her arm, he felt something odd. His eyes traveled down to where his hand met hers. Beneath the lace cuff of her long sleeve was a band of silver. It was giving off a peculiar trickle of magic. He hadn't felt it before this moment, but that might have been due to the first shock of their reunion having passed. "What is that?"

She held up her other arm and he saw there was one on that wrist, too. "I'm a prisoner here. Jasper Keating knows what I am, and he intends to use me to do whatever skullduggery requires my magical expertise."

Nick dropped her arm from sheer surprise. Even the idea of Evie back in Keating's claws suffocated him—and that had been bad enough before the Gold King knew what she could do. Now she was in unspeakable danger at every tick of the clock, just waiting for Keating's whim to result in imprisonment and—if she was lucky—death. "How the blazes did he find out about your Blood?"

Her expression was unreadable. "I made a deal. He could have me if he withdrew the order to destroy the *Red Jack*." Then she turned away.

Nick fell into a chair, his limbs went utterly numb. *She's here because of me?* "Black Mother of Basilisks, Evie, why?"

"I love you," she said simply.

Damnation. Guilt choked him. He'd wanted those words to come so many times, so many ways, but not like this. He put his head in his hands, black despair warring with an ingrained need to make her safe. Is this what loving him got her? "So we break you out."

"If I cross the boundary of the college, the bracelets let the Yellowbacks know where I am. Plus, they hurt like blazes if I even get close to the wall. I've tried cutting them, and I've tried acid. I can't even smudge their shine. Tobias has a key that deactivates them for twelve hours, but not one that will take them off."

Nick lifted his head, his stomach going sour. This was getting worse and worse. What was the Golden Boy doing in the picture? "Tobias Roth?"

Her face twisted. "Keating made him my jailor."

Bloody hell. Nick leapt to his feet. "I'm going to kill him."

"It's not his fault! He doesn't want it any more than I do." Evelina pushed him back into the chair and leaned over him, putting her hand on his knee. The silver bracelet gleamed softly through the shroud of lace like a veiled accusation. "I want to go. I want to get out, but it's not going to be simple. I have to trick Keating into letting me go."

"How?" A haze of rage filled Nick. He'd expected to grab her and run, barely stopping to pack. But that wasn't going to happen now. He'd escaped his prison, but as long as Evie was trapped, he hadn't escaped the steam barons' chains.

She ducked, turning her face aside. "I'll find a way. Keating's starting to trust me enough to let me outside the walls."

"When?" Nick rose, making her fall back a step. When she didn't answer right away, he grew cold inside, as if he were slowly leaking life while she hesitated. "What's going on, Evie?"

Her eyes darted away from his. "When he wants to use me to track down people like us. Magic users."

"He *what?*"

She read his face, her own going pale with concern. "Don't doubt me, Nick. I won't be his bloodhound. I'll go through the motions, but I won't take the scent."

"And if you're out, can you get away?"

She put her hands on his chest and looked up into his face, her breath soft against his skin. "I haven't figured that part out yet, but with the bracelets turned off, I have a lot more power. Maybe more than I want."

Nick frowned, sensing a new obstacle in his path. "What do you mean?"

"There were things Magnus showed me. Doors I opened that I can't quite shut." Her face tightened. "You said yourself that I was tempted by dark power. Maybe keeping me on a leash is the wisest course."

"You're not Keating's dog."

She looked up, her eyes wide with distress. "I frightened myself. Nick, you don't know what it's like."

He'd been an acrobat and a pirate. He had a pretty good idea. "What happened?"

"It's a long story. I had to fight . . ." She trailed off, visibly recoiling from the memory. "It was something very strong. Something evil. There was a roomful of people and I had to act."

"By the Dark Mother, Evie!" He smoothed his hands down her arms in a gesture of comfort. He was going to get the whole story out of her, but for now she had to tell it in her own way.

She raised a hand, as if to fend off something he couldn't

see. "The power rose like some beast, and it was hungry—stronger and more ferocious than I remembered it. And it was . . ." She looked away. "It was satisfying. That's what scared me. It was even worse than when I was in Whitechapel."

Nick swallowed, the chill in his blood deepening to ice. He knew she had accessed a dark power he barely understood. The line between his kind of magic and a sorcerer's like Magnus was like a thin but very deep crevasse, and she'd stepped over it more than once. But fear—his or hers—wasn't going to help her now.

He returned to the practical problem of her escape. "Keating isn't going to keep you safe from anything, least of all yourself."

Her brows drew together. "And you will?"

And then he understood just how scared she was. Evie was strong, but she had been lost among enemies too often. Now—since this fight she spoke of—she saw her own powers as one of them. He had to remind her that she wasn't alone. "Do you actually feel the need to ask if I'll watch your back? After all we've been through?"

Her eyes were guarded, but he took her hands in his and kissed them each in turn. That made her lips curve into a sweet, wicked bow. "Just my back?"

He grasped her slender waist, pulling her close. "I could be convinced to patrol the other boundaries . . ."

She slid her arms around his neck. She was still tense, the lines of her body saying how deep her anxiety ran, and how much she was counting on him to set her free of it. "Show me exactly what you mean, Captain Niccolo."

This was what he had been waiting for. "My lady." He swept her up in his arms, the wealth of her skirts spilling over his arm like a graceful waterfall. And then he kissed her, drinking in the warm, sweet essence of her lips.

He found the bedchamber more by instinct than by any conscious intent, and set her down as gently as if she were made of spun glass. And that was the limit of his patience. He'd shed his jacket and shoes before Evelina had caught her breath. He stood over the narrow bed, regarding her with anticipation both reverent and filled with shameless greed.

"At the moment, you rather look like a pirate," she said, her voice suddenly shy.

"And yet if I say something about pillaging, I'll sail into turbulence for certain." He slid onto the bed, remembering how much he wanted to undo all those buttons. How long had it been since he'd touched anything so fine?

"I think you almost have a carte blanche at the moment," she whispered as his fingers remembered the art of a lady's garments.

She reached up, her warm, soft hand cupping his face as she kissed him. Then her hands were in his hair, holding him as she took her fill. "The best thing about plundering you is getting plundered in return," he murmured.

He brushed the silk of her throat and almost heard the threads of his self-control snap. He pressed his mouth to the curve where her collarbone flared, and the scent of her skin set him on fire. And yet Nick took his time, making a ritual of removing every article of her dress, appreciating each revelation as it came. If he rushed, he might miss the curl of hair that lay just below her ear, or the way her shoulder sloped when she leaned against the pillow as he tasted her breast.

But as he progressed, her urgency grew. And all at once, her hands were busy, too, helping him unwrap her layer by layer, the satin and lace and steel that was as much a metaphor for Evelina's character as it was the fabric of her clothes.

And then his own shirt disappeared and she was caressing him, hot and needy. He felt the scrape of her nails and teeth, and they thrilled him like the brush of a strong wind. She was all contrasts, soft flesh and sleek bone, sweet perfume and the earthy musk of her desire.

And where they touched, there was the silver fire, binding them closer than any vow. Lights began to wink to life in the corners of the room, blue, and green, and red, as if all the colored gaslights in London had shrunk to bright pinpoints and swirled about the room.

"Devas!" Evelina gasped, but Nick had gone to a place beyond language. The spirits always came when they raised the silver fire, and if they didn't get their fill they would tear the room to pieces. The phenomenon had kept him apart from Evie for years, until they'd figured out what they wanted—which was basically a whole lot more than just two scions of the Blood holding hands. But now he aimed to keep the wild magic flowing until the little beggars exploded.

He had tonight to make sure she remembered they belonged to each other, as no magic on earth was going to tell them what tomorrow would bring.

CHAPTER TWENTY-ONE

London, September 30, 1889

DUQUESNE'S RESTAURANT

1:45 p.m. Monday

LORD BANCROFT EYEBALLED THE SCHOOLMASTER WITH UN-
ease. Duquesne's was a fashionable venue, and the young
man clearly didn't fit with the restaurant's usual clientele. In
fact, he looked like someone's disreputable nephew about to
beg for a loan. "Are you sure it is wise for you to be here?"
Bancroft asked.

It wasn't an unreasonable question. The man was, after
all, one of those planning to upset the Empire's entire political applecart.

The Schoolmaster slid into the chair on the other side of
the small, round table. "Probably not. The maître d'hôtel
looks like he'd prefer to toss me out."

Already caught off guard, Bancroft relaxed beneath the
disarming charm. "You could use a barber."

"Spoken like an experienced father."

Bancroft grimaced. "My son is very different from you.
For one thing, you're early. He's always late."

"Is he?"

Bancroft knew that the smile was a mask. The Schoolmaster was the linchpin of the Baskervilles—charismatic,
ruthless, and with a brilliant mind for strategy. And his coat,
though well brushed, had gone shiny at the cuffs. He obviously didn't waste any of the rebels' money on himself. He
was utterly dedicated to overthrowing the Steam Council.

Tobias, on the other hand, had confined his youthful rebellion to the usual vices. Now he was the perfect employee, shaking in his boots lest Keating strike down one of the family—all the more galling because he'd done it to cover Bancroft's mistakes. *A good man, but where does that get anyone besides an early grave?* Annoyed, Bancroft fidgeted in his chair and then stiffened when he saw Sherlock Holmes drift across the room.

"Are you joining us?" he asked Holmes when it became clear that was exactly what was about to happen.

"I invited him." The Schoolmaster flashed an apologetic grin. "He promised to advise me on the menu."

"I advised him against it altogether," Holmes said dryly, "but he insisted on sampling *la crème brûlée à la vanille* for himself. Youth these days are fascinated by direct experience. None of this business of truth strained through the careful sieves of their advisors. Terribly gauche, don't you think?"

"I think it's unnecessary exposure," Bancroft snapped.

The young man shrugged. "No one here would know me from one of the pot boys. All my friends are in the taverns."

He was probably right. Although most had heard of the Schoolmaster, few had seen his face. Boxing up his temper, Bancroft waved toward the array of food on the table— mostly cheeses, cold meats, a lobster pâté, and warm bread. "Then help yourself. Would you like something more substantial? A roast chicken, perhaps? Or your *crème brûlée*?"

"No, thank you. This is more than enough."

"Some wine?"

The Schoolmaster pulled off his green-tinted glasses, revealing intelligent blue eyes. There were lines around them that said he was a little older than Bancroft had first thought. Those blue eyes studied him shrewdly. "But you don't drink."

"No." Not anymore, and it still cost him something to say it.

"Then I will just have coffee."

"Holmes?" Bancroft eyed the man, who waved away the offer.

Relieved, Bancroft signaled the waiter. He'd sworn off alcohol, but he still craved it. In the meantime, the School-master helped himself, spreading a chunk of bread with a soft white cheese. Bancroft eyed him. His manners were good; whoever the Schoolmaster was, he'd been raised by gentry. "I confess that I expected Mycroft Holmes."

"This is my brother's favorite eatery," Sherlock replied. "But on a Monday he won't make his appearance until half past two precisely. He is a creature of strict habits."

"And after all the support you've given our cause," the Schoolmaster added, "I wish to thank you myself on behalf of the makers. Your generosity is most impressive."

Despite his innate cynicism, Bancroft felt a surge of plea-sure. "There is no need to thank someone for doing what is right."

As Holmes gave a faint cough, the Schoolmaster cocked an eyebrow. "And yet people seem to like it."

Bancroft chuckled. "I concede the point." It was true, he'd given money to the rebel cause—sometimes more than he could afford. Patriotism played a role, but so did ambition. If the rebels overthrew the Steam Council, his political career would be made. He hoped generosity now would pay huge dividends later—and he didn't care if bounders like Sher-lock Holmes called such motives crass. A man had to pro-vide for his future.

Still, there were obstacles. Bancroft shifted uneasily in his chair. "It grieves me to report that you have little to thank me for today. I'm not making much headway with our Chinese contacts."

"Did they give a reason?" the Schoolmaster asked, paus-ing in his demolition of the lobster pâté.

"Not any that made sense to me." It should have been an easy assignment. Like everyone else, the rebels needed fuel to run their armies, whether for engines, cookstoves, or weaponry. The steam barons had the monopoly on domestic sources, so the rebels were forced to buy from abroad. Since the Chinese traders had no ties to the Steam Council, they were an obvious choice—except Bancroft hadn't been able to convince them to do business. "I haven't given up yet."

"Have you had dealings with them before?"

"A few. Or, I should say that an associate of mine did." He shot a warning glance at Holmes, but the man was busying himself with the cheese.

"Who was that?" the Schoolmaster asked.

"Just an importer I once knew." His name had been Harriman, Jasper Keating's cousin. Together, they had stolen a wealth of treasure out from under Keating's nose with the unwilling assistance of some Chinese goldsmiths.

"Fair enough." The Schoolmaster finished the last of the bread and pushed his glasses back on, intense blue eyes vanishing under a murk of green. "But you feel hopeful enough to keep trying?"

Bancroft waived a dismissive hand. "I have nothing to lose by giving it another attempt."

"Excellent. Please let Mr. Mycroft Holmes know how you get on." With that, he rose, adding, "My lord, excuse my unforgivable manners. I apologize for having to leave so soon, but I have pressing matters to attend to."

The detective rose as well, dusting crumbs of cheddar from his fingers.

Bancroft was startled by the abrupt departure, but he had been a diplomat. With a smooth smile, he rose and shook the Schoolmaster's proffered hand. The young man had an understated air of command Bancroft admired. "I do have one question."

The young man paused, his wide mouth curling into a slight smile. "Yes?"

"Did you ever teach school?"

"Ah, no." The smile widened, and the Schoolmaster dropped his voice so that only Bancroft could hear. "I like to think of myself as giving the steam barons a lesson."

"I like it." Bancroft found himself returning that infectious smile. "I hope to give you a better report soon."

"I am in your debt." The Schoolmaster gave a slight bow. "Until later, then, my lord."

Bancroft and Holmes exchanged an icy nod, and then the two men left Bancroft to his coffee. He sat, wondering how best to win the foreign traders to their side. Something in the young man's manner made him want to succeed—and that was the mark of a true leader. So be it. Bancroft had worked for fools; he might as well serve someone who could at least inspire.

Bancroft spooned more sugar into his coffee and stirred, a frown settling over his entire being. The rebels needed coal, and they had money to pay for it, so what was the problem? If the Chinese refused to cooperate, there were a few others he could try, but the steam barons had influence over almost every European concern. There weren't many avenues open unless he changed the game in his favor.

The waiter arrived, a dainty silver dish in one hand. An extravagant pastry perched in the middle of it, the flaky confection layered with dark chocolate and slivers of strawberry floating in custard cream. It looked delicious, but Bancroft was confused. "I didn't order this."

The waiter bowed. "No, my lord. It was sent with the compliments of another diner."

Suspicion made him bristle. Had someone recognized the Schoolmaster? "Who?"

"That person has left, my lord. They did, however, ask me to deliver this note." The waiter produced a small envelope and set it next to the dessert. He bowed again and departed.

Bancroft eyed the pastry and decided to leave it alone. He'd learned long ago not to accept sweets from strangers. Instead, he slid on his gloves—one never knew about poisons—and opened the plain white envelope. Inside was a simple card, stamped with the restaurant's name in heavy black type. Whoever had sent the note must have asked the staff for the stationery. *So why write instead of coming over to speak in person?* There was no happy answer to that question.

Foreboding crept through him as he flipped open the card and read: *I see you have your allegiance, just as we have ours. But your allies do not know you, whilst we do not forget.*

What in the infernal depths? He flipped the card over. There was a Chinese character on the back, drawn in carefully shaded pencil to mimic the strokes of a brush. The shape of it looked vaguely familiar. He had no notion what the symbol meant, but a burst of irritation shot through him, followed quickly by an instinctive fear. With a sharp intake of breath, he dropped the note on the table. Then he glanced around, but no one appeared to be watching. *Perhaps I am being irrational?*

Or perhaps not. Every one of those Chinese craftsmen he and Harriman had hired to steal gold from the Gold King had been a loose end, walking evidence of the crime. Bancroft knew better than to ignore such danger. Consequently, the workers had wound up floating in pieces in the Thames. That had been the final task of the foreman, Han Zuiweng. Later, Bancroft had shot Han himself, for all the brutal bastard had been acting on orders.

He'd almost wiped the entire distasteful episode from his mind. And, in truth, he had no black-and-white reason to revisit it now—except for his own unease. How could approaching the Chinese to do business stir up the past? *No one could have known about what happened.* Or so he fervently hoped.

We do not forget. Disgusted, Bancroft tossed his napkin over the extravagant dessert and rose. Someone was playing games. Surely there could have been no witnesses, for it had all happened underground.

Still, Bancroft couldn't suppress a shudder when it occurred to him that Harriman had died in his jail cell, convicted of theft and forgery. Others involved in the scheme had confessed or fled the country. Only Bancroft had walked away—and only because Tobias had agreed to be Jasper Keating's maker and his son-in-law. Everyone else had paid.

Bancroft stared at the note, then snatched it up and stuffed it into his pocket before he stalked from the restaurant. *We do not forget.* He snorted. No one wrote cryptic notes like that unless they were minutes away from naming their blackmail price. He just wondered what the hell it would be.

HOLMES AND THE Schoolmaster left the restaurant and hurried toward the Thames.

"We need that coal," said the Schoolmaster. The young man's look was expressive, and Holmes felt his worry.

"We do," he agreed, doing his best impression of a seasoned cabinet counselor. "I am willing to bet there will be open warfare within weeks. The potential hangs like a stink in the air."

Especially since the heir to the Empire was critically ill. *The crown prince is the last of all those children that the queen raised around her. What will happen when he is gone?* And when would he be gone? How long did the Baskerville enterprise have before the heir's death forced their hand?

Westminster was near, the crowd in the streets mostly dark suits milling in a self-important bustle. There was scaffolding shrouding the Clock Tower and apparently it would be there for some time. The damage from the mosquito-shaped airship had been significant.

Bloody waste, Holmes thought, although a tiny impertinent voice deep inside had to admit the visual of the bug in the clock had been amusing. Someone out there had a healthy if destructive sense of the absurd.

But any spark of humor evaporated as he saw his brother striding their way. Mycroft wore his bear-with-a-migraine expression.

"You are early," Mycroft said to the Schoolmaster without looking at his watch. Since he was punctual to a fault, there was no need. "And I didn't expect to see you." He shot Sherlock a narrow look, as if wondering what mischief he meant to cause.

"I am precisely on time," the Schoolmaster replied grimly. "I am where I mean to be at this moment."

Mycroft frowned. "But I was going to Duquesne's."

"And I have already been. I spoke with Bancroft already."

The effect of his words was immediate. Mycroft's features flushed, his nostrils flaring as he grabbed the Schoolmaster's elbow, pulling him into the passageway between two buildings. Sherlock darted between them, shoving his brother back against the wall. Mycroft was a big man, and he knew from experience that his brother's fierce grip could hurt.

"Have a care, brother mine," Sherlock said between clenched teeth as he jammed his forearm beneath his brother's chin. "Remember to whom you speak."

But Mycroft was looking right past him to glare at the Schoolmaster. "What do you mean by exposing yourself like that? Now Bancroft knows your face."

The Schoolmaster's cheekbones grew flushed as his temper flared to life. Sherlock had not met the man's mother more than once or twice, but he recognized the stubborn set of the mouth. "I can't let others do all my work. It's not wise."

In other words, he needed first-hand information, not just the facts that Mycroft and his cronies saw fit to share. If that was the only lesson he ever taught the Schoolmaster, Sherlock would have done his job as a friend.

"That's why we're here—I'm here," Mycroft said much more humbly. "To keep you safe."

Sherlock watched the Schoolmaster ruthlessly rein in his mood. "I'm the leader of a rebellion. Safe isn't on the table."

"And what did you just gain by taking that risk?"

"Probably a shred of respectability. Bancroft is a viscount, and Edmond Baskerville is the vaguely eccentric but charming adopted son of a minor baronet. I don't usually lunch in such exalted company."

Mycroft huffed in disgust. "Bancroft is a snake."

Sherlock smiled, finally releasing his brother. Mycroft stepped back and snapped his jacket into place, his gaze trained on Sherlock like twin poignards.

"Snakes eat vermin." The Schoolmaster pointed to the Clock Tower. "We have an infestation."

Sherlock chuckled. "Does that make us a pack of stoats?"

The Schoolmaster grinned. "If I have to be the exterminator in chief, so be it."

Mycroft clasped his hands behind his back, fighting with his scowl. "Just keep in mind Lord Bancroft has a penchant for disaster. He barely escaped Disconnection once. Got on Keating's bad side."

"He seems too crafty for that," the Schoolmaster said.

Mycroft and Sherlock exchanged a look. "There are times that Bancroft is too clever for his own good," said Mycroft. "Every utility was switched off. My informant said Bancroft had to do some impressive backpedaling."

Disconnection was serious. Once that happened, a family was socially dead, plunged into metaphorical as well as literal darkness. Their bank accounts vanished, their credit was ruined. No school, no social club, and no drawing room would accept them. Eventually, they always disappeared, slinking away into obscurity. It was no wonder that anyone who could afford it festooned his house and gardens with every conceivable type of light. Although it was enormously expensive, a bright glow showed just how secure the family was in the steam barons' favor.

"So you see what he risks," Sherlock added. "The gentry who follow the rebels face utter ruin."

"All the more reason to look him in the eye." The Schoolmaster looked away. "When war finally comes, it won't be just my fate in the balance. I need to know who is with me."

Mycroft gave a mordant smile. "A good policy, and while you are about it, always be sure you can see both their hands. When are you leaving for Baskerville Hall?"

Holmes's ears pricked up.

"Very soon." The Schoolmaster sighed. "Very soon I get on a train and face my destiny. I might even splurge and go first class."

"Who will go with you?" Mycroft asked. "As always, I must stay with the queen."

"If you broke your routine, the world would know something was afoot," Sherlock observed.

"And if you left Baker Street," Mycroft shot back, "the world would suspect a crime."

The Schoolmaster looked from one to the other. "I shall travel with Edgerton."

Mycroft looked sour at Edgerton's name but for once didn't argue.

"Perhaps you should go alone," Sherlock suggested. "Whether we win or lose, it might be the last time you are free to travel in private, your face known only to friends and family.

"But be careful. We need you alive more than ever." Mycroft leaned closer, dropping his voice to almost nothing, "Your Highness."

A beat passed between them, the noise of the busy street vanishing behind the thunder of blood in Sherlock's ears. Mycroft had blundered.

"I told you not to call me that." The Schoolmaster's voice grew icy. "Schoolmaster. Baskerville. Never the title."

Mycroft straightened, his own expression frozen. "I'm glad you retain some sense of your peril."

The Schoolmaster laughed, but it wasn't mirthful. "I've been in hiding since I wore nappies. I've met ice cream with a better chance at longevity."

It sounded melodramatic, but Sherlock understood. Alert to the Steam Council's schemes, Prince Albert had secretly placed his youngest son in the care of a loyal subject. It had been a piece of brilliant foresight. Since then, all the prince's brothers and sisters had died one by one, and the eldest was about to go. Many suspected the hand of the steam barons at work, but there had been no shred of evidence to support such an incendiary accusation.

Now the country was on the brink of a civil war, and revealing Prince Edmond's identity would plunge the Empire into chaos. Unfortunately, the rebels consisted of amateur gentlemen and a passel of crazy inventors—not exactly a dream army. It was a wonder the only remaining prince hadn't run screaming to the Antipodes.

"Your Baskervilleness, perhaps?" Sherlock suggested.

At the quip, the Schoolmaster seemed to catch himself. He looked up at Mycroft. "Forgive my ill humor, but I haven't earned the title of prince yet. Until the day I blast the Steam Council from the face of the Empire, I'm nothing but a traitor about to set fire to this land."

Mycroft looked astonished, but Sherlock raised an eyebrow. "Aren't you being rather harsh on yourself?"

The Schoolmaster smiled, but it was bitter. "You told me

history is written by the winner, Mr. Holmes. If I want a happy ending, I'd better get my troops in order."

"Any particular order?" Sherlock asked dryly. "Alphabetical, perhaps?"

Prince Edmond, falling into the spirit, waved an imperious hand. "You know. Pointing at London. Otherwise, they'll fall in the water."

"Very good, sir." Sherlock tipped his hat, including Mycroft in his glance. "You may trust the Holmes brothers to see the proper arrangements are in place."

CHAPTER TWENTY-TWO

London, September 30, 1889

LADIES' COLLEGE OF LONDON

5:30 p.m. Monday

"FORGIVE ME FOR CALLING ON SUCH SHORT NOTICE AND AT an unconscionably late hour of the afternoon," said Miss Emily Barnes, taking a seat in the chair where Nick had been sitting the night before. She was wearing a green and white striped dress that reminded Evelina of a circus tent three seasons out of fashion. "I promise not to stay long. Far be it from me to interfere with a young lady's evening plans."

"That's quite all right," Evelina said, all too aware that the woman's visit would be recorded in the matron's report to Keating. It was just fortunate that she was supposed to be cultivating the leaders of the Parapsychological Institute. "I'm honored that you thought to call. And to bring your friend."

The other woman sat silently. In contrast with Miss Barnes's gaily colored outfit, she was wearing the thick black garb that denoted mourning. A veil hung from her hat brim, shadowing features that might have been attractive in a mature way—but it was hard to tell. She had been introduced as Mrs. Smith, another member of the institute.

Evelina crossed to her worktable, which was doubling as a sideboard at the moment, and began to pour out tea into the college's utilitarian white china cups. Steam rose in lazy clouds, catching the late afternoon light from the windows.

It had been sunny that day, although the autumn beauty had been all but lost on Evelina.

"Our interests are obviously aligned in many ways," said Miss Barnes. "It would be remiss for me not to pursue an acquaintance."

"I'm delighted to hear that."

"I am a firm believer in possibility. A bright young woman who combines such special talents with academic rigor is quite an exciting prospect for our institute."

As flattering as that was, Evelina stifled a yawn while her back was to the woman. She was still reeling and exhausted from the night before. Nick had been gone by the first birdsong, but it was not as if she had been able to rest that day. Agitation had kept her pacing the floor.

First, there had been Nick's miraculous reappearance. That had brought a measureless joy that still fizzed through her. Nick was alive! *Alive and whole and in my arms, if only for one night.*

But then there had been everything that notion brought with it. Last November, during their interlude in Miss Hyacinth's house of pleasure, they had pledged their futures to one another, and both vowed that commitment had not changed. But circumstances now complicated everything.

Evelina paused, the teapot still in her hands. She realized her mind had drifted, and she pulled herself back to the present. She turned back to her guests. "I should start by saying I am terribly sorry for the disturbance the other night."

"It is hardly your fault," said Miss Barnes sensibly. "And it is not as if one has a means of barring the riffraff once the aetheric doors are opened. That kind of disembodied ruffian is the plague of these events."

"Then why does the institute permit séances? After all, isn't your official mandate to debunk all claims of psychic phenomena?"

Miss Barnes made a derisive sound. "We come across charlatans, that is true, and unmasking them is a particular pleasure. But our real search is for bona fide talent. Danger does not preclude the value of the search, and the opportunity for scientific inquiry is too great to pass up because a few bits of china fall victim to a poltergeist."

"But someone might have been hurt."

"But they were not," Miss Barnes said calmly.

Evelina set down the teapot, suddenly weary. To be honest, the séance felt as if it were a lifetime ago. Last night divided her existence into before and after Nick's return. Eventually, they had told each other everything—about Imogen, the battle, and how he'd escaped Manufactory Three. She'd been starving for someone to talk to—and not just anyone, but *Nick,* who understood her as no one else could. Yet the longer they'd talked, the more it was clear there was no quick and simple means to walk away, hand in hand, into the wide, adventure-filled world. Indeed, nothing could happen until she was free and in control of her magic, and he had reclaimed the scattered pieces of his life. When she'd shown him the report about the ruins of the *Red Jack,* they both had wept for his crew. But Nick had rejoiced, too, because it gave him a clue to where, disoriented and running for his life, he had hidden Athena.

And so with reluctance and more kisses, they had parted at the first morning light. Again.

"Miss Cooper?"

Evelina turned, smiled graciously, and deposited one teacup in Miss Barnes's hands and gave another to Mrs. Smith, who stirred enough to accept the refreshment. Then Evelina took her own seat and sipped the hot brew.

"Have you had any experience like that before?" she finally asked, remembering her role as hostess.

"Rarely," said Miss Barnes. "It is just too bad so few were there that night to lend their strength. Normally we number closer to fifty than just eight, but as you heard there was a confusion of dates. An intentional one, I might add. We were cautious of allowing the Gold King's maker into our midst."

Evelina had wondered if the other forty-two members were elsewhere with Madam Thalassa that night, while she and Tobias had been shunted to a smaller decoy meeting. "I see."

"We are all too aware that Jasper Keating is, shall we say, on the warpath. We put him there, with your uncle's help."

She remembered Tobias mentioning Uncle Sherlock, and suddenly had the feeling she was leaving the road for a twisting, rocky path. "Why attract his attention? That could be deadly."

"All for a good cause," Miss Barnes said briskly. "It seems your uncle's interests and ours coincide. At his request, we provided a reason for Keating to let you out of the college on a regular basis, primarily to pave the way for your eventual escape."

Adrenaline bolted through Evelina, and her teacup rattled as she sat forward in her chair. Those brief periods of liberty had already formed a cornerstone for her own plans—and her uncle, as always, had seen the possibilities and manifested them. But that he would take the society into his confidence? "Forgive me for asking, but why would my uncle trust you?"

Miss Barnes cocked an eyebrow. "A good question. He enjoys a cordial relationship with Madam Thalassa, and had already approached her on another matter concerning a Miss Imogen Roth. Which takes us back to the séance. That entity knew you."

Evelina's stomach filled with bone-deep horror at the memory. "Yes."

"It claimed it was your friend, the same Imogen that Mr. Holmes mentioned to Madam Thalassa. What can you tell us about your friend? Who was she to you?"

"Is." For some reason, she cast a glance at Mrs. Smith, but the woman was all but inert. "My friend has been stricken ill. She has been unconscious for some time, and I believe her spirit is wandering."

"And Imogen is Mr. Roth's sister?"

"Yes."

Miss Barnes sipped her tea, clearly thinking. "Is that why you were eager to meet Madam Thalassa when you came to my home?"

"Yes, that was my hope," Evelina said. At least, that was her reason if not Keating's. "I understand Madam has some expertise in this area. I knew my uncle wanted her to consult, and I wanted to warn her about some spells that I already have in place around my friend."

Mrs. Smith stirred slightly at that, as if that had finally caught her interest.

"Spells to keep your friend alive and healthy?" Miss Barnes asked as casually as if requesting a recipe.

"Yes. They shouldn't be disturbed."

"Naturally. I shall make it my business to tell Madam."

Relief made Evelina sink back in her chair. "I would appreciate that greatly."

"I shall tell her word for word."

"There is something else she should know."

"Oh?" Miss Barnes asked, setting her teacup aside.

"I believe there were two entities that night. One was Imogen, the other not."

"Do you know who the other might have been?" For the first time, the woman looked worried.

"Imogen had a twin, Anna, who died very young. Her spirit was the pawn of a sorcerer." Evelina still could barely believe it, and yet what Tobias had told her made perfect sense. "Anna is dangerous, but please understand that I have no proof that entity was her. I want to contact Imogen again, but I've tried alone, and it didn't work. We need to find out the truth, and I don't have Madam's skills."

Miss Barnes looked down at her hands, clearly thinking. "No, you don't. You are powerful, but you are not a medium. And this case has complexities. You could do more harm than good."

Evelina already knew that, but she didn't like the idea of just standing by. "It's been two days since the séance, and I'm worried. What can I do?"

Miss Barnes swallowed. "Anna worries me. Spirits that wander too long begin to turn."

Evelina tensed. "What does that mean?"

"For a soul that's wandered too far, it's a long, painful, and tragic slide into madness. Some say the soul is well on its way to a demonic state."

"They turn into a demon?" Evelina asked, a little incredulous.

"A simplistic, inelegant way of putting it, but essentially correct."

"Miss Barnes, that is utterly . . ." But she was well and truly lost for words. Imogen was at the mercy of such a creature. *But not for long,* Evelina vowed fiercely. She wasn't letting her friend down, if she had to march into the netherworld and drag her back by the hair.

Miss Barnes folded her hands in her lap. "I can see the determination on your lovely face, my dear, but it won't do."

"No?" Evelina's stubborn streak rose.

"My advice is to leave the matter with Madam Thalassa. She has experience with wayward spirits. She will make your friend's case her immediate priority. And this is the point where the society's concerns and those of your uncle intersect. We will convince Keating to let you out of the college, and we will assist your friend. In return, there is something we want from you."

Evelina didn't want to step aside and leave Imogen's care to anyone else—at least not completely—but if Uncle Sherlock was involved, she had to consider what the woman had to say. "I'm listening."

Miss Barnes inclined her head, a bit like a schoolmistress. "I saw what kind of power you used. Once a sorcerer, as the saying goes."

Evelina shook her head. "I am not a sorcerer."

"If you say so. I make an observation about what I saw of your power, nothing more, and you may need that dark strength before this is done."

Now Evelina was worried. "Before what is done?"

The woman lifted her chin, her manner growing sly. "Do you recall the actress Nellie Reynolds?"

"I do." The case had been in the papers about a year and a half ago. The famous actress—the Duchess of Westlake's illegitimate cousin, as it turned out—had been accused of using magic and sent to Her Majesty's Laboratories. Many had thought the verdict unjust.

"She escaped."

"What?" Evelina sat forward. She'd never heard of anyone getting out of the labs. "Really?"

"We've never known precisely where the laboratories were," said Miss Barnes. "Now we do, and we know what's inside."

Curiosity flamed through Evelina, but she sat back, suddenly cautious. "I must say, Miss Barnes, that you are opening up some very dangerous topics. You could be punished for spreading such news, as could I for listening to it."

She wasn't positive that her statement was completely logical, given their talk of séances and demons and evading Jasper Keating, but the woman's manner had changed in the last few seconds, becoming even more authoritative. Every instinct was warning Evelina to be careful—and that wasn't a premonition, just common sense.

But then Mrs. Smith finally came to life and drew back her veil. "Miss Cooper," she said in a rich contralto voice. "Please hear us out."

Evelina's heart lurched. She knew that face. When she spoke, it was barely above a whisper. "Mrs. Reynolds!"

She had been a beauty once, but that had all changed. Her hair was still thick, but it had turned white, and deep lines of pain now traced the angles of her face. Evelina's throat tightened, wondering what other ravages the heavy fabric of the actress's mourning gown disguised.

"The laboratories are in Dartmoor, all but lost in the desolation of the moors," she said. "If one escapes, there is nowhere to run and many, many places to be lost forever. I was lucky. I stumbled onto a private estate and found a sympathetic protector in Sir Charles Baskerville. He hid me on the moors until I could be taken to safety. I slept in the stone huts left by the primitive tribesmen of centuries ago, and his serving man brought me food. It was the only way to hide from the Steam Council's soldiers, who searched every house and barn in the county. I owe him my life, and we all owe him a debt. If he hadn't intervened, everything I know about the place would have perished with me."

For all her trials, Nellie Reynolds had lost none of her

presence. Evelina hung on every word. "Tell me, what happens in those laboratories?"

The actress flinched, and it clearly wasn't for effect. "The scientists employed by the Steam Council are interested in one thing. They want to understand how magic works, and why those of the Blood inherit the ability to use it. And once they find that out, they want to replicate the effect for their own use."

"Especially with machines," added Miss Barnes. "Whoever discovers how to control machines with magic will render all other forms of power irrelevant."

Which was in part why Jasper Keating had Evelina—a magic user with a technological bent—at his beck and call. "So they use the prisoners as experimental subjects?" Evelina asked. "Just like all the old rumors?"

Nellie Reynolds held up a gloved hand, as if warding off the question. "Yes. Dissection, vivisection, augmentation—nothing is beyond them. And it does not matter overmuch if a prisoner has been falsely accused. They found a purpose for me, too."

She lifted her skirt—mildly shocking from the viewpoint of modesty, but what it revealed was far worse. "They cut off my legs and gave me these instead, just to see if they would take."

"Oh, dear God," Evelina blurted out before she could stop herself.

Beginning just above the knees, the woman's legs were a tangle of open wires, cables, and gears. "They left me my feet," she said in a carefully neutral voice. "They preserved enough pathways for the nerves and blood to keep the flesh alive. They wished to study the possibilities for mechanical integration with the human body."

As her stomach rose, Evelina felt herself growing dangerously hot. How many prisoners were there? What happened to the ones who couldn't get away?

She was relieved when Mrs. Reynolds dropped her hems and hid the ghastly sight. "I see," Evelina said, knowing it sounded inane. She didn't understand at all.

"And that was far from all. The scientists at the laboratories went unchecked by law or common decency, and their researches strayed down whatever path imagination decreed. When the quest for the key to magic stalled, they pursued other projects. Some sought to create the perfect soldier, others wished to defy mortality. Still others created monsters for their own sake, and tortured animals out of pure curiosity. There was a hound," she said, pausing long enough to gulp back her emotion. "It was a huge, brindled beast. They attempted to build a clockwork creature within its living flesh. It escaped once, but they dragged it back and locked it away. After that it became utterly savage and unmanageable—no doubt in utter agony. But the poor mad thing showed me the weakness in their security, and I used that knowledge to escape. It did not suffer in vain."

"Why are you telling me this?" Evelina asked, barely able to speak.

"We want to destroy the laboratories," said Miss Barnes in a down-to-business tone. "Your uncle claims it's something of a specialty of yours, and we don't have enough powerful magic users."

"And Madam Thalassa wishes me to help?"

"Yes," said Miss Barnes. "News of Mrs. Reynolds's escape arrived just days before you came to the séance. Madam Thalassa began making plans to follow up the intelligence at once. It seems that the laboratories have magic users as part of their guard. Those who would rather serve than be tortured."

"Collaborators?"

"Yes. However, you have a kind of magic the scientists have not found a means to completely control. You will be an effective weapon for our side. In fact," Mrs. Reynolds said, glancing at the bracelets, "those are the only means they have of even dampening dark magic. I've seen them at work plenty of times. They had to go far beyond just draping sorcerers in silver."

Evelina remembered Moriarty's words. *I've never examined the mechanism, but both clockwork and magnetism are involved, as well as a rare element that reacts with magical energy to produce a chemical discharge.*

Miss Barnes gave a vaguely bloodthirsty smile. "Once you get them off, there's no telling what you might be able to do."

It was true that the dark magic had been stronger at the séance, when Tobias had deactivated the mechanism. Evelina fingered the bracelets, thinking about having the full use of the dark power back. Fear tingled through her as she remembered her hunger rousing a strength and ferocity she'd desperately wanted to indulge. *What if I can't control it once these are off?*

But the labs needed to be stopped, and Imogen needed help. And she had made a promise to Nick. As much as it terrified her, she had to be mistress of her magic, not its thrall. Otherwise, she was crippled. "I would help, but these bracelets keep me here. Can you get them off?"

"If you're willing, we might be able to devise a means of setting you free," said Miss Barnes.

"I'm willing," she said, hoping she hadn't gone utterly mad.

Both Miss Barnes and Mrs. Reynolds stirred, clearly relieved. "Good," said Mrs. Reynolds, rising to her feet. "We'll find some way of getting you to Dartmoor. We're marshalling our forces there."

Evelina's heart started to pound with excitement and trepidation. "Where in Dartmoor are the laboratories?"

It was Miss Barnes who answered. "Near an estate that belongs to the Baskervilles. Sir Charles holds it, but he has an adopted son by the name of Edmond. Quite an engaging young fellow. Very fond of dogs."

CHAPTER TWENTY-THREE

London, October 1, 1889
DUQUESNE'S RESTAURANT

1:55 p.m. Tuesday

"SO AM I TO UNDERSTAND THAT YOU HAVE TAKEN A fifteen-year-old girl for a client?" Dr. John H. Watson asked as he watched his teatime companion demolish each dish of eggs, pies, chops, crab bisque, sandwiches, and tea cakes as rapidly as the white-coated waiters of Duquesne's could bring them to the table.

"Not precisely," Holmes replied. "I merely did young Miss Roth a good turn. She reminds me a little of Evelina. In fact, she wrote to request the cipher of that clock of theirs. You know the one."

"Did you give it to her?"

"Why not? It's their clock. And I have always been of the opinion someone needs to watch Lord Bancroft, even if it is his youngest daughter. She is the last of his children at home, other than her ailing sister. I'd rather Miss Roth knew that she could come to me for assistance."

And with that, the detective began piling his plate full once more. There was a shocking lack of vegetables involved, but Watson had to concede that getting something inside the Great Detective was better than the chemical substitutes that had been swirling through Holmes's bloodstream until a few weeks ago.

Alternating bouts of overwork and idleness had led Watson's old roommate back into the arms of recreational stimulants. The absence of his niece—Holmes behaved himself whenever he assumed his quasi-parental role—had only worsened the problem. The man didn't require a companion, he needed a leash, and perhaps a wrangler. Fortunately, Watson had learned to provide both without Holmes—for all his vaunted powers of cerebration—figuring it out.

"Shall I order more tea?" he asked brightly.

Holmes tossed his napkin aside and surveyed the wreckage of the tea cakes in a way that called to mind Wellington at Waterloo—satisfaction edged in sorrow at the loss of life. "Perhaps a French coffee. Something strong and bitter to temper the sweetness."

The man had to have ironclad digestion equal to one of Brunel's engines. Watson signaled a waiter and placed the order. Holmes picked at the cheese plate.

"Haven't you eaten enough?" Watson asked.

"There is always room for a good cheddar," he said around a toothpick.

"I'm beginning to think you are about to go into hibernation. Where in God's name do you put it all?"

"It is a question of will."

"Keep it up and it will become a question of dyspepsia." But Watson managed a piece of Edam all the same.

"I'm glad you're settling back into Baker Street," Holmes said, turning his attention to the view outside the window. The restaurant was on the upper level and gave a partial view of Westminster Abbey and the Houses of Parliament beyond. The trees mercifully hid the wound in the Clock Tower.

"I am pleased to be back," Watson replied, but stopped there.

Things were the same as before, but different. He *should* have been happy to resume his role as Holmes's caretaker and scribe—and occasional gunman—but the circumstances of his return weighed heavily on him. He had left Baker Street to marry, but he had returned because Mary had died, leaving his own house echoing with recriminations. What good is a doctor who cannot cure his own wife? What good was a husband who hadn't even given her the blessings of a family? Some men wouldn't question such things, but he did. Mary had given him her heart, and he could not help feeling that he had failed.

"You look pensive, my dear Watson." Holmes closed his eyes and sniffed at the steam rising from his coffee cup. "You need to exercise your mental faculties. I had two excellent cases last June, just waiting for your pen. Do you recall that affair in Boscombe Valley? And the beggar with the twisted lip?"

"Is work always your prescription for the blue devils?"

"It is the absence of mental exercise that will trouble me," Holmes decreed.

"So you assume I suffer from an absence of material to beat my brain upon?"

Holmes opened one eye, which glittered with sarcastic mischief. "Perhaps not so much as that. Brain beating has never been your forte."

Watson bridled. He knew he shouldn't, that he was sure to lose, but he simply couldn't help himself. "You speak as if a medical doctor never uses his powers of deduction."

"I do not deny it in the least, my dear fellow. Nevertheless, my observations must range beyond the quantity and quality of what arrives in a patient's bedpan."

The doctor choked on his coffee. "Really, Holmes!"

"Tut, don't be squeamish. I never am. Observe there." Holmes flicked a finger toward the window. "See that man with the embossed portfolio under his arm?"

Irritated, Watson turned. "No doubt you will tell me his blood type and place in the Order of Precedence by the exact shade of his hat lint, I will fall down in awe and admiration, and the overweening self-love that springs from your intellectual superiority will be assuaged. And preferably, it will appear in print so that the world might applaud."

Holmes gave a mild snort. "Ah, Watson, you know me too well. However, it is not hat lint today, but the ribbon pinned on his lapel that interests me."

"It is red. What does that signify?"

Holmes leaned in, lowering his voice. Their table was in the alcove of the window and away from the other diners, but caution was prudent. "The Scarlet King. The man is a government official, and a highly placed one, judging by the cut of his suit. Only someone who can afford a Bond Street tailor will wear such as that. I've seen these ribbons popping up recently and made inquiries. My brother, Mycroft, tells me they're a mark of allegiance to a member of the Steam Council. This one is red, ergo Scarlet."

"Why is that significant?" Watson wanted to know. "Merchants have always painted their doors with the color of whatever steam baron is their patron. The gaslight globes are colored depending upon the utility company that supplies them. Is this any different?"

"It appears that the steam barons are forming political cabals. Steam barons in Parliament—and therefore with the ability to create law—would be allowing the fox free access to the chickens."

"Can the queen or prime minister do anything to stop it?"

Holmes gave one of his lightning smiles, there and gone again in a blink. "I have it on very good authority that Keating Utility holds mortgages on every one of the prime minister's properties. There will be no help from him."

Watson pushed away his coffee cup, no longer interested in food. "And the queen?"

"The Steam Council has a long history, dating back to the 1770s and the colonial rebellion. At first, they were no more than a club of like-minded industrialists. Then they grew ambitious. The first time they proved a real threat was just after the Great Exhibition in 1851. I think seeing their inventions in the Crystal Palace went to their heads, but Prince Albert sorted them out quickly enough that time. The council was sufficiently repressed that it has taken over thirty years to rebuild its influence. Unfortunately, Queen Victoria is not in such a strong position now."

Since the 1850s were before his time, Watson took the history lesson as given—but he wasn't so sure about Holmes's last remark. "Why can't she simply declare them null and void?"

"My dear doctor, they own three-quarters of the aristocracy, lock, stock, and wine cellar. Most, if not all, of the barons have developed secret armies of their own."

"What?" Watson exclaimed in astonishment.

"And furthermore, she has no means to make her objections stick. She is a woman of advancing years, losing her children one by one. Once she is gone, where is the forceful personality who will ensure the council stays meek and mild? Where is the next generation's Albert?"

Gloom descended on the table like one of the thick Thames fogs. Watson made a helpless gesture. "So where is this all to end?"

Holmes raised an eyebrow. "You would raise a hand to help our beleaguered queen?"

"Of course. What truehearted Englishman would not?"

"Your loyalty, as always, is beyond reproach. So, thank God, is your marksmanship."

Statements like that gave Watson a very bad feeling.

"Oh, look," said Holmes blandly. "Here comes my brother."

The timing was a little too pat. Holmes had been expecting this. Mycroft, who was every bit as tall as Sherlock but rather wider, strolled up to the table with an indolent swagger. He made a perfect picture of bureaucratic elegance in gray flannel tails, a top hat, and pristine white linens.

"I would like to point out, Sherlock, that you're *at my table*," Mycroft said with a slight fidget. "I reserve this table from two o'clock on. You know my habits are precise."

"A Mr. Holmes reserves this table," Sherlock replied, with a smugness only a younger brother in the right can muster. "I merely took advantage of the fact that you were being *imprecise*. There are other seats to be had."

"But *this* is the one I sit at."

"You could join us," Holmes suggested.

"I dine alone."

The brothers were intolerable once they got started. "Look here, Holmes," Watson broke in. Both Holmeses looked his way. Watson sighed. "We were done eating in any event."

"That is hardly the point," said Sherlock, rising from the contested spot. "And I was waiting for Mycroft to appear."

"Why?" his brother asked suspiciously.

"To advise you that I am taking Watson with me to Dartmoor."

The doctor pushed away from the table, rising to his feet. "You are?" This was the first he'd heard of it.

"I'll explain everything to him in due course, but I thought you should know."

Mycroft raised an eyebrow. "I suppose medical expertise would come in useful, but the decision about the team wasn't yours to make."

"My piece of the game," Sherlock said firmly, "my rules. Come along, Watson, let us leave my misanthropic sibling to his repast."

"Sherlock," Mycroft replied, irritation leaking into his tone. "We need to have a conversation about this."

"In due course, brother mine. Perhaps when it is all over with." With that, he swept from the restaurant, stopping only long enough to inform the maître d'hôtel that Mr. Mycroft Holmes would be covering their bill.

"I do hate being the youngest," he purred. "My brother never lets me pay."

Being a good servant, the maître d' only bowed.

Watson hurried after Holmes into the fading afternoon. The detective aimed his steps toward the riverbank, where the golden gaslights were already shedding their glow. It was gloomy and growing cold, with a mist already forming over the water.

"I did not follow a word of that exchange," Watson grumbled. "Dartmoor? What, pray tell, is in Dartmoor?"

"A great many wild ponies, from what I hear," said Holmes. He swung his walking stick with a jaunty air. The chaos of the street eddied around them, but he seemed oblivious to it. "The game is a-hoof, Watson."

"We have a case?"

"Indeed. Let me paint for you three facts. One, word has been put about that a dangerous criminal has escaped from the Dartmoor prison, thus giving the excuse for soldiers to roam the countryside without arousing the curiosity of the local population. But it is not a common prisoner they seek.

Second, the local baronet, Sir Charles, well known for his philanthropy, was the one to find the escaped convict roaming the moor. A smart and capable old gentleman, loyal to our queen, he had the good sense to raise the alarm with the right people. Third, he has just been found dead. Word has it that he was murdered."

"There is hardly a case there," said Watson. "My guess is that Sir Charles died because he helped the convict."

"In all probability, you are standing closer to the truth than you know—but as always, facing the wrong way."

"You already know who did it? Where is the entertainment in that?"

Holmes didn't answer, but flagged down a cab. Once they had climbed inside, he resumed. "I need your literary talents, Watson. I need you to spin something out of these events."

"I always do."

"No, I need your invention beforehand." Holmes fiddled with his walking stick impatiently. "Fiction is your purview. Concoct a reason that I will require my niece to join us. Something supernatural that only her talents can unravel."

Watson knew little of magic, but he liked Evelina. Nevertheless, his conscience pricked him. "Isn't that a bit tawdry, Holmes? A man has died. Why use his death as cover for our own purposes?"

"I would not be stretching truth too far if I said more may die unless we can free my niece."

"Why? How can she prevent death?"

Holmes gave him a dark look. "Humor me."

Watson made a gesture of surrender. "Very well, then. A family curse perhaps? A banshee?"

"This is Dartmoor, not Scotland."

"A ghost?"

"Rather dull, don't you think?"

"I don't know," Watson said, growing annoyed. "What do they have there besides ponies? Little shaggy horses don't make terribly convincing monsters. The Dread Pony of Dartmoor, whickering death to carrots across the——"

"No, it doesn't quite work, but you've got the idea. There

are rumors of a savage dog roaming the place. Perhaps you can work with that."

"Tell me the truth. Is this all a plot to get Evelina free?"

The detective made a face. "I require utter secrecy."

"Always."

"This morning I received word from a Miss Emily Barnes, a confidante of the renowned medium Madam Thalassa. Her group is assembling to assist in the dismantling of a laboratory notorious for experimenting on live human subjects without their consent."

"Wait a moment." Watson reached across the cab and grabbed his friend's arm, pulling him close so they would not be overheard. "You're speaking of Her Majesty's Laboratories? No one knows where that is." As soon as he said it, everything fell into place.

Holmes's gray eyes were hard as flint. "One of their charges escaped. I could regale you with word of their atrocities, but let us say for now that Nellie Reynolds is giving the performance of her lifetime."

His shock sharper than the cold river wind, Watson let go of Holmes and reeled back against the seat cushions. His wits scrambled to right themselves. Surely this was treason—and yet Holmes's loyalties were never in question. And then Watson did his mental sums. *Sir Charles?* "Don't the Baskervilles live somewhere in Dartmoor?"

Holmes nodded slowly. "A dreadful coincidence, is it not? The murder victim was Sir Charles Baskerville. He found Nellie Reynolds wandering the moors and contacted Madam Thalassa. His adopted son, Edmond, is the one directly involved with a rebellion against the Steam Council. I have been acquainted with Edmond Baskerville for some years."

Watson's mouth went dry. "What are you proposing?"

"That we catch a killer, of course, and you make a story about the adventure."

"And what are we *really* doing?"

"You are the medical doctor. Is there not an oath to do no harm? Might that promise extend to stopping those who break that oath?"

Watson bowed his head. What Holmes was proposing

was insanely dangerous. But then so was the moral damage of ignoring an abomination like the laboratory on the moor. And he was a widower now. He was free to take risks because there was no one waiting at home—just a lot of empty echoes reminding him that he had failed kind and pretty Mary Morstan when the fever took her. "There is an oath. We all swear to uphold it."

Holmes crossed his long legs. "Then we are going to free my niece and unleash the one thing on the Steam Council that they fear."

"What is that, Holmes?" Watson feared that he already knew the answer.

"Magic. We are going to free the magic users and burn Her Majesty's Laboratories to the heath."

"Magic? You, Holmes?"

"Rebellions are won with logic, but also with passion."

Rebellion! Cold terror trickled through Watson's gut. "Won't that be the next best thing to a declaration of war?"

Holmes gave a smile that was gone in an instant. "I'm afraid that horse has already left the stable—or that pony the moor. No one has admitted it yet, but the war has already begun. And this is the piece of it you and I have agreed to take on."

Watson folded his arms. He'd seen war already, and he hadn't much liked it. "I'm glad we had a good luncheon first."

CHAPTER TWENTY-FOUR

October 2, 1889
SOUTH OF LONDON

1:30 p.m. Wednesday

THE SCHOOLMASTER HURLED AN ACORN AT MICHAEL EDGER-
ton, hitting the back of that morning's *Bugle* with a resounding clatter. The paper dropped and his friend's scowl
appeared over the top.

"Are we bored?" Edgerton asked dryly, shifting his back
against the tree trunk where he was leaning.

It was a lovely morning, if one were a sightseer. Birds
chirped, the sun shone, and the air was filled with the rich
scent of early autumn. Part of the Schoolmaster's prickly
mood was the pain of having to resist the urge for an im-
promptu holiday.

Instead he kicked at a stone, sending it hurtling into a
patch of brambles. "I'm wondering how I plan to rule an
empire when I can't organize one party of people for a train
journey of a few hundred miles. This should not have taken
two days."

He should have gone alone, but one thing led to another,
as happened when there were too many details circling like
noisy seagulls. And, of course, the moment one let people
off a train into the fresh country air, getting them back on
was a challenge.

"You're grumpy when you aren't in charge," Edgerton replied coolly.

"Being in charge is my destiny, or so I'm told." Though

"in charge," he had already discovered, was a complex and fluctuating condition. At the moment, the real monarch was the lure of a magic airship. Despite—or maybe because of—the dim view the authorities took of magic, everyone involved in today's expedition was eager to recover the magic-driven navigation device.

Edgerton folded the newspaper, clearly doing his best not to look aggrieved. "You're the one who suggested stopping here." He waved a hand around. "Wherever here is."

The Schoolmaster sighed, irritated by and appreciating his friend's blunt manner. Much of it, he knew, was just teasing, but it kept him from floating off into dreams of princely greatness in a way nothing else could. "This side trip makes sense. Captain Niccolo was picked up in these woods by patrols. There was no point in having him come back alone and get arrested all over again. Five young gentlemen on a country ramble won't be as tempting a target." Bucky Penner and Captain Smythe were with the air captain, looking for the place where he'd buried his navigation device.

"Especially when they're armed."

"It's a point of conversation during any unwanted encounter."

"I suppose providing a body guard is the least we can do, given the advantage Captain Niccolo represents." Edgerton gave a wry smile. "And I do enjoy watching a pirate rummage through pine cones for a magic box."

"Unfortunately, it's taking rather a long time. We'll miss the next train out."

Edgerton opened his paper again. "Do make up your mind whether a revolutionary species of dirigible is more or less important than making it to Baskerville Hall by tea."

"You're grumpy when you don't have something to do," the Schoolmaster shot back.

"Forgive my disgruntlement. I had a perfectly nice career planned before the Steam Council ruined my father. Now I'm your lackey."

"You're a lackey the way a mastiff is a lap dog." But he

got the point. Edgerton had lost his future, and the rebellion was his only chance at getting it back.

In stark contrast, the Schoolmaster's prospects had always been open to debate. He could ship out to Australia and lose nothing but a chance at a huge *what if.* He'd never known his royal family, except through the stories Sir Charles had told. Contact had been strictly forbidden for everyone's safety— there had never been a birthday gift, a letter, or a secret visit from a bereft mother. Not once. He'd gained in safety but lost any emotional pull to his birth family.

And yet, it was the thousands of lives broken by the Steam Council that made that *what if* a chance worth taking. His friend, as just one instance, had lost more than a career. He'd lost fortune, position, and a father he'd deeply loved, all because the council wanted the Edgerton foundries for its own purposes. And that was a single tale in a litany that went on longer than the *One Thousand and One Nights.* Everyone in the Empire had a story to tell about the oppression of the steam barons. The Schoolmaster didn't consider himself more than usually high-minded, but if he could do something about the problem, it was his moral responsibility to stand up. Sir Charles Baskerville—as much a father as any boy could want—had raised him right.

Sadly, none of that relieved the boredom of watching Edgerton read the paper. "Is there any good news in there?" he asked.

"No. The Exchange reports the domestic market is shaky. There's cholera in the poor districts. Soho is mentioned. Gilbert and Sullivan are fighting again."

"Any news of blockades?"

"None."

"Then there is good news. They don't know we're on the move yet." Their war machines were mostly outside of London, the makers and their workshops hidden from the Steam Council. The drawback was that it would take time for them to assemble and march on the capital. The Schoolmaster had sent word as soon as he was sure war was inevitable, but coordinating their scattered forces would be a challenge. That was where the *Athena* would be key.

The Schoolmaster glanced down the road—more of a dirt track with birch trees arching overhead. They'd been standing guard in case a patrol came by, but the traffic had been nonexistent. It seemed their time would be better spent hastening the search. "I'm going to go check on the captain's progress."

Edgerton was instantly alert. The newspaper vanished into his overcoat, and a slender, three-barreled weapon appeared. It was somewhere between a rifle and a gun and the Schoolmaster had seen it blast through a brick wall.

"We're going for a stroll in the woods, not storming the Tower," the Schoolmaster said with a smile, but he pulled his own weapon nonetheless.

"Part of being a lackey is keeping you alive."

The Schoolmaster huffed. "I'm not helpless."

"You're a target," Edgerton complained, following him into the woods. Their feet crunched on fallen leaves, releasing a sharp scent of loam.

"No one knows who I am."

"You're still a target. It's not who you are—yet. It's what you did. You organized every rogue maker in the Empire."

That was true. The craftsmen had fought the Steam Council first, one forge and workshop at a time, organizing in secret to carry on their trades. And that had been all the rebels had needed as a starting point. Mycroft Holmes and the aristos like Bancroft had come later.

The Schoolmaster pushed a branch out of his path. "Figures I'd be gunned down for illicitly assisting in the repair of a butter churn."

"Let it be known that no matter is too small for the attention of the Baskervilles," Edgerton said mildly.

"Don't quote me at me. And I tried to keep the Baskerville name out of it."

"People need a white knight, so they nominated you. They love you as a hero. They'll like you even better when they find out you're their next king."

They walked a moment in silence, the only sound birdsong and their crunching footfalls. The Schoolmaster broke the silence first. "They want freedom. That's why we'll prevail."

Edgerton smiled brightly. "Plus, you'll look better on a postage stamp than Jasper Keating."

"Maybe I'll clap you in irons."

"You'd never find your way to the royal loo without me."

Probably not. If he did manage to succeed, he was going to need every friend he could get. Running an empire wasn't a one-man show.

They found Bucky Penner and Smythe lounging against a boulder and smoking cigarettes. They were Edgerton's friends from his school days and each had proven his loyalty to the rebel cause over the last year—although neither Smythe nor Penner knew the Schoolmaster was of royal birth. The two were an odd pair, preferring to avoid each other's company unless assigned to the same mission. At the moment, they stood as far apart as they could without appearing ridiculous. Evidently, there had been a duel over a fair maiden at some point in their past, and their friendship had never recovered.

Captain Smythe looked odd out of his cavalry uniform, as if he might as well have been wearing his nightshirt. Penner looked somber, but that apparently was his norm. The Schoolmaster had heard about an ailing lady love—but the man kept his private matters to himself. Still, the Schoolmaster wondered if it was the same woman who was the object of the duel.

The land sloped down to the right, long russet grass waving between patches of gorse and rowan. Captain Niccolo was at the bottom of the valley, digging with his bare hands at the base of a granite boulder. Despite his very ordinary suit of clothes, the man's olive skin and long black hair set him apart from the others. But more than that, he moved with the controlled grace of a hunting cat. No one would have difficulty believing him a pirate. The Schoolmaster was very glad he was on their side.

He stopped beside Penner. "How goes it?"

Penner exhaled a cloud of smoke, looking bemused. "We've

been over at least a mile of road. He says little, frowns at the trees, stops and walks around the rocks, and talks to the birds. It's been fascinating—a bit like dealing with St. Francis turned highwayman."

"Can you tell if there's been progress?"

Penner shrugged a shoulder. "This is the first time he's started to dig."

The Schoolmaster immediately started down the slope, walking sideways to keep from slipping. A squirrel burst from the underbrush, chattering curses as it bolted up a tree.

Niccolo was kneeling in the fallen leaves, pulling handfuls of dirt and debris from a dent in the earth. His hair had fallen around his face, hiding his eyes. The Schoolmaster stopped a few yards away. It was obvious that the captain had found his buried treasure, because he was tenderly pulling something from the ground, every angle of his body proclaiming his relief.

The object wasn't much to look at. There was a crude fabric sling, now filthy, that the captain cast aside. The metal cube within it appeared to be a mess of different metals melted together. Bits of rust splotched the surface, disguising what might have once been gears.

"Is it supposed to look like that?" the Schoolmaster asked, wondering if the device had been destroyed in the crash.

The captain looked up, dark eyes bright with happiness. "Once she was covered in gold and gems, but that was just ornament. Everything that needs to be here is intact." He rose, holding the cube between dirty hands. "This is Athena's Casket."

The Schoolmaster drew near, underwhelmed by its appearance. He had expected something more . . . sparkly. But then, just as he grew close enough to touch the cube, he felt it. There was a drop of the Blood in most of the royal houses. He couldn't work magic, but he could sense a tingling over his face and hands that said it was pouring from that cube. He looked up with a feeling of excitement. "It *is* real."

It was a foolish statement, but Niccolo just smiled. "It will be a long time before she forgives me for putting her in the dirt." And then he stopped, staring at the cube, a frown creasing his brow.

Then he looked up with a pleased expression. "Athena bids you fair greeting."

"Um," the Schoolmaster said, looking at the lump of dirty metal and trying to relate it to the Greek goddess that was its—her—namesake. "Tell her fair greetings from me?"

The captain's eyes narrowed, some new emotion thinning his lips. "She says she sees the Blood in you."

Cold surprise rushed over the Schoolmaster, and he could not hide a flinch. He stared at the lump in the man's hands and could feel the intelligence almost touchably present around it.

"I did not know you carried magic," Captain Niccolo said evenly, keeping his voice low.

"I don't," the Schoolmaster replied tersely. "It's such a small amount that it means nothing."

"Yet it is enough for her to see it."

The Schoolmaster was beginning to dislike this talking cube. "She has good eyesight and possibly a magnifying glass. But I suppose half the population has a drop of the Blood somewhere in their family tree."

The captain nodded. He had brought a leather satchel—or rather, appropriated it from the Schoolmaster's closet—and now he stowed the cube inside and dusted off his hands. "Perhaps someday you will tell me why Athena calls you *vasiliás*."

It was Greek for king. There was a moment of stunned silence on the Schoolmaster's part as he gathered his wits. "Perhaps."

Niccolo gave a low laugh. "I know the word, but I don't pretend to know what it means in your case. Give me a chance at revenge, and I do not care if you are Edmond Baskerville or the queen of Sheba. I will keep your secrets, whatever they are."

"Thank you." There would be a time when he had to reveal himself, but he prayed it wasn't quite yet. He knew how to be Edmond Baskerville. Prince Edmond was—he wasn't quite ready for that.

The captain was watching him, self-contained as ever. "You should know that devas see through to our essence."

"What are you saying?"

"Just that. The land is watching." With that, the captain started up the slope to join the others, taking the incline in long, easy strides.

The Schoolmaster watched him go for a moment before following, now sensing a thousand pixie eyes boring into the back of his head. *The land is watching.* He could well imagine it. He'd grown up on the moors, with their moody, austere personality. *And a king has to answer to the land.*

The Schoolmaster pondered the conversation as they walked back to the roadside inn, where they hired a conveyance back to the train station. He turned Niccolo's words over and over like a tool he couldn't figure out how to use. He'd known about devas all his life—magic clung to the countryside like stubborn brambles. If the spirits could identify him, it was a minor miracle that no woodwife had pointed him out on the street. But he also knew it took more than a drop of the Blood to speak to the nature spirits, and there were hardly any of the old families left. Who besides Captain Niccolo and a handful of unlucky prisoners spoke to the devas anymore? More to the point, who spoke *for* the devas who tended the land?

The notion plunged him into deep thought. But while he was quiet, the others were merry. Even Penner and Smythe set aside their mutual dislike to enjoy Niccolo's success. Victory augured well for the future.

In boisterous spirits, the party reached the train station in good time. The platform was tiny, but there was a tearoom across the way. Penner, Smythe, and the captain went in search of something to eat. The Schoolmaster lingered outside the station, head still spinning with questions.

Suddenly, Edgerton was at his elbow. "I have the afternoon edition of the county paper."

The Schoolmaster looked up, not really caring. "And?"

His friend's face was pained. "I'm sorry. I'm shocked that no one contacted you before this came out, but then you're a hard man to find."

"That's kind of the point of my lifestyle," he said cautiously, wondering what Edgerton had found in the paper. *Did the crown prince die?* He took it, reluctance hitting him the moment his fingers touched the page.

And then he saw the headline. Shock made him fumble the folded sheet, and he had to snap it taught and read the words again. Heat crept up his cheeks in the same instant his whole body went cold.

SIR CHARLES BASKERVILLE FOUND DEAD AT FAMILY HOME

He skimmed the rest of the article, his memory supplying details of place and personalities as he read. Sir Charles had been found dead in the yew walk. The authorities were prepared to claim it was simple heart failure, except for a handful of details—including the look of abject horror on the dead man's face. Sherlock Holmes had been engaged to investigate. *Murder.*

Words caught in his throat, snagged there by sorrow and anger, and it was a full minute before he could get them out. "They found out Nellie Reynolds went to my father for help."

No need to say who "they" were. It was just another of the one thousand and one tales of what the steam barons had done. They'd taken the only family he'd ever really known. And just like that, the rebellion wasn't simply about justice anymore, or ideals, or making sure everyone had a voice. Like the captain, he wanted payback.

My father. Far more than Prince Albert, a man he'd never met.

He slapped the paper back into Edgerton's hands, anger pumping with every beat of his heart. "Cable Mycroft Holmes."

"And tell him what?" His friend's eyes were wide.

I'm going to pound each and every steam baron until there is nothing left but a smear of soot.

"Tell him the hounds are unleashed. This just got personal."

CHAPTER TWENTY-FIVE

"I HEARD SOMEONE IN YOUR ROOMS THREE DAYS AGO," DEIR-dre said archly. "A man's voice. I'm just across the hall, you know, and I'm not old and deaf like Matron."

"You're merely hallucinating," Evelina retorted, although she was seized with a ridiculous urge to grin. Part of her ached to talk about Nick, but that was impossibly danger-ous. Nonetheless, it suddenly made her much more sympa-thetic toward all Deirdre's blather about the young men on campus.

"I am *not* hallucinating!" Deirdre protested, dropping her voice to a whisper. "You were with someone! Or I should say someone arrived and I never heard them leave."

Evelina glanced around. They were walking across the quadrangle from the small college library, their arms loaded with books. Or, Evelina's were. Deirdre as usual had the minimum required for her essay. Fortunately, no one seemed to be interested in their chatter, so Evelina was free to con-tinue baiting her friend. "If someone arrived and never left, then I have an invisible man in my rooms."

"A handsome one, no doubt."

"How can he be invisible *and* handsome?"

"Well, he could look any way you liked if you couldn't actually see him."

Evelina shrugged. "Or perhaps he could change at will. A shape-shifter."

Deirdre rolled her eyes skyward. "Oh, wouldn't that be a lark. I'd never have to make up my mind between tall and fair or dark and mysterious."

"And so much better than invisible. That would be a tripping hazard."

They walked in companionable silence for a moment, and then Deirdre spoke again. "I won't ever tell, you know. Your secret is utterly safe with me."

Evelina didn't doubt it. She'd covered for far too many of Deirdre's escapades to lack ammunition of her own—and she didn't think her friend was the type to tell tales anyhow. "I appreciate your discretion."

Deirdre gave a triumphant smile and put an extra spring in her step. "Ah, then you admit you have something to hide!"

"Not for a moment." Evelina fell silent as Professor Moriarty intersected their path.

"Ladies." He tipped his tall hat. "A word with you, please, Miss Cooper?"

She exchanged glances with Deirdre. The other girl gave a nod and then hurried off, her bustle swaying gracefully as she moved. Evelina noticed Moriarty turn and gaze appreciatively at her retreating form.

When he tore his gaze away, Evelina was waiting patiently. "You're looking well, Professor Moriarty."

"I spent a day or two in the country, which is as good as a month of rest anywhere else." His glance fell on the stack of books in her arms, and then immediately took them from her. "Studious as ever, I see." He cocked his head to read the spines. "You're developing an interest in rare elements."

"This library does not have much," she complained, falling into step beside him as they continued toward her residence.

He gave her a sideways glance, his mouth curled in a half smile. "You are, no doubt, curious about the type contained in the mechanisms of your bracelets."

She flushed. "I am not even sure which one it is."

"No doubt all these heavy tomes will give you a clue." They stopped at the foot of the stairs to her door. He rested the stack of books on the newel post of the handrail, one hand on top to keep them from sliding away. "And your investigation is timely, given the request that just arrived on Sir William's desk. It seems your uncle is asking for your assistance with a murder investigation in the south."

Surprise made Evelina fall back a step. "Murder?"

"So it seems. Sir Charles Baskerville has died. Did you know him?"

She blinked. "Only by name." *He was the one who helped Nellie Reynolds.*

"Yes, the name. It must have been such an inconvenience to have the same moniker as the rebels. Poor old gentleman. From all accounts he was a gem, taking in that foundling boy and raising him like his own." Moriarty's eyes glittered, and she was certain he knew more than he was telling.

But her scrambling wits were too fully occupied to look for more problems. She knew something had to be done to get her to Dartmoor to help with the laboratories, but the murder of Sir Charles? The timing was all too convenient. Or did it just point to the fact that Nellie Reynolds had brought trouble to his door? It could be that the case and her mission were one and the same; any other explanation was too sinister.

"Would you like to go solve a murder, Miss Cooper?" he asked smoothly.

"Of course."

His fingers tapped the stack of library books with a kind of speculative impatience. "It is in my power to convince Sir William to approve your leave from the college."

Evelina regained her composure enough to wonder what he was up to. "I'm sure Professor Bickerton would be delighted to be rid of me for a while."

"No doubt."

"But isn't Mr. Keating's approval the one that counts?"

"Yes and no. He has agreed to your absence, but the university has not. It seems your probationary status complicates matters since there is still the possibility of pressing legal charges. It gives Camelin power."

Evelina looked away, silently cursing.

He narrowed his eyes. "Shall we bargain, Miss Cooper? My influence on your behalf for a future consideration?"

"An unnamed consideration, Professor Moriarty? Do you take me for a fool?"

He stroked his tidy mustache, clearly amused. "I will agree to limitations."

But then Evelina saw a familiar figure striding across the lawn. She held up a hand. "Perhaps this should wait. It appears I have a visitor."

Moriarty followed her gaze. "That is Tobias Roth, is it not? The Gold King's maker and your minder?"

"The same." She wondered what Tobias wanted. After the séance, she wasn't sure he'd ever want to speak to her again.

Moriarty remained glued to his spot as Tobias approached. The two men eyed one another, neither of them friendly. Evelina retrieved her stack of books, and the professor extended his hand. "I don't believe we've met, Mr. Roth. I am James Moriarty, professor of mathematics."

"A pleasure," Tobias said, returning the courtesy without much warmth.

Moriarty made a slight bow in their direction. "I will leave you to your guest, Miss Cooper. We will resume our discussion at a later time."

"As you wish, Professor," she returned.

"I need to talk to you," Tobias said quietly as the man left, and he took Evelina's books.

She leaned close. "Moriarty's other name is Juniper and he works for King Coal."

Tobias's eyes flared with interest. "What's he doing in a university?"

"He really is a math teacher," she said.

"I knew they were all evil." But he made the quip without much verve. He pressed his lips together, clearly worried about something. "We need to go somewhere private."

Evelina led him back to her rooms, imagining Deirdre

peeking out her keyhole to see who came and went. She thought about making a flirtatious fuss over Tobias just to give Deirdre a show, but that would cause too much confusion all around.

And Tobias clearly wasn't in a fun-loving mood. He set down her load of books, frowning at the titles, and quickly got to the point of his visit.

"I need your advice." He took off his hat and gloves, as informal as when they had both lived at Hilliard House.

"On what?"

He sank onto the sofa, his hair golden in the diffuse light that fell through the lace curtains. "You were always my touchstone when it came to making the right choices."

Evelina hovered, afraid to sit down because part of her wanted to retreat. It was true, he'd often come to her as a sounding board, but that had been in a more innocent time. "I'm not sure I can be that for you any longer."

"Please, I need a friend. I've juggled everyone's interests for so long, I can't see past all those flying balls anymore."

The truth in his voice sliced through her. He wasn't here to play games. Evelina sat. "I can listen. I don't know if I can advise."

There was a beat of silence, the only sound the racket of some crows on the roof. "Is it about the séance?" she asked nervously.

"No," he said, almost laughing. "Damn it all, no. That's an entirely different set of horrors. I can't even think about that now."

Evelina wasn't sure whether to be relieved. "Then what is it?"

He let his head drop forward. "Do you know about the bug in Big Ben?"

"Yes."

Elbows on his knees, he rested his forehead in his hands. "I know who made it. I took it apart and looked for clues. It was tricky—I won't go into it all—but the best lead turned out to be an Italian-made logic system. There were only a handful ever sold in the Empire, and I traced this one back through its owners. That told me what I needed to know. What Keating wants to know."

"In other words," said Evelina carefully, "he's asked you to find out who attacked a property on his territory. It's as good as a declaration of war."

Tobias rubbed his eyes, as if what he needed most in the world was sleep. "And the longer he doesn't know who did it, the more foolish he looks. Handing him a mystery like this did far more damage than merely firing a cannon." He lifted his head with a sigh. "So there is every reason in the world to win his favor by giving him the name of the culprit. And anything that keeps Keating content pleases Alice."

She felt a twinge at the woman's name, the ghost of past jealousy. "So why don't you?"

"Because after I do, we've run out of excuses to avoid full-out conflict." Tobias looked at her, his expression raw. "And I will have pulled that trigger. How much blood will be on my conscience then?"

She felt her heart pounding beneath her stays, comprehension unfolding like a deadly flower. But as much as she understood the problem, she had no response.. Lost, she reached over and took his hand instead. "There will be war sooner or later, whatever you do."

He gave a short, sad laugh. "Isn't that always true? But what if a day or a week might make a difference?"

What if it saved a life? He had a son. She had Nick. "What will it cost you to stay quiet?"

He closed his eyes. "Keating might lose the advantage. Those of us entangled in his affairs would suffer if he lost to another member of the Steam Council. It's a choice of delaying in hopes of peace or starting a war we have a better chance of winning."

Her mouth went dry. "Was it one of the council?"

"Of course."

But he clearly wasn't going to tell her who. It was enough that he trusted her this far—even after he'd seen her magic and been terrified by it. "I want to give you a simple answer," she said.

"I wish you could."

She bit her lip. "I can't justify telling you to unleash hell on the Empire. No one can."

His face tightened. "Even if keeping silent costs the lives of those we love?"

"I can't tell you to do that, either." She squeezed his hand tight. "I'm not wise enough to tell you what to do. But I think there will be a war regardless, and you're not the one to blame."

Anguish flashed through his eyes. "But I won't be innocent of it, either. I built too many of Keating's war machines."

And now he was afraid to see them in action. An ache formed in her chest, making it almost impossible to swallow. "We all have our dark magic. This is yours."

He stood quickly and a little unsteadily, pressing one hand to his mouth as he paced the room. "How can I choose when every path leads to someone's destruction?"

Evelina was woefully out of her depth. "My gran said you have to go with your heart when your head fails you."

He stopped pacing, but it was a slow process, as if his spring had wound down.

She wrapped her arms over her stomach. "I don't know what to say."

"It's all right," he said. "I just needed to tell somebody. You're the only one I know who is brave enough to hear it."

A violent rap came at the door, making them both jump. The taut atmosphere in the room snapped with the violence of a breaking wire. Disoriented, Evelina pulled open the door. It was Deirdre.

"Matron is looking for Mr. Roth!" she whispered urgently. "I wanted to warn you."

Evelina wasn't sure what Deirdre had expected to find—or maybe she was. She glanced at Tobias, who had already picked up his hat and gloves, his face a mask of cool reserve. Almost immediately, she heard the matron's heavy tread on the stair.

"Miss Livingston." The older woman's voice rose from the stairs in sepulchral tones. "If you would return to your room, please."

Deirdre vanished with a flutter, and Matron's square bulk filled the doorway. "Mr. Roth, you were asked on a previous occasion to announce your presence to me before visiting Miss Cooper."

Tobias wasn't in the mood. "There was an urgent matter, madam, that superseded formality."

Matron swelled. "Nothing trumps the rules, Mr. Roth. And keep in mind that I know where to find you on this campus." She thrust out an envelope. "A messenger arrived for you, sir."

Tobias took it and ripped it open without ceremony. He read the contents without expression and then stuffed paper and envelope into his pocket. "Thank you, madam."

She sniffed. "I wish that I could say it was my pleasure, but it was not. This is a most shocking breach of protocol."

Ignoring her, he turned to Evelina. "I have to go." He took her hand and gave it a squeeze, the ghost of a smile on his tired face. "As always, you are wise, my dear Miss Cooper. As was your gran."

"I will walk you to the gate, Mr. Roth," said Matron in dire tones.

Tobias wheeled, his annoyance plain, then he seemed to catch himself. Suddenly he was the smooth-talking young gentleman Evelina remembered from her first visits to Hilliard House. He held out his arm. "It will be my pleasure to be escorted, madam."

The masterly switch left Evelina breathless, but the matron accepted his arm with good grace. "I've seen it all before, Mr. Roth. You're not too clever for me."

Evelina wasn't so sure. She waited by her door for them to reach the bottom of the stairs, and then she followed, watching their progress as they disappeared across the lawn. She folded her arms, anxious about what Tobias would do. More than that, she was aching to get free of this place and join Nick. If there was open conflict, she could do nothing while stuck at school.

She heard the scuff of a boot behind her. "Your visitor has left, I take it?" said Professor Moriarty.

Tobias was almost to the gate, and was lifting his hat to a

bevy of giggling students. Her heart ached for him. *What will his decision be?*

"We have a conversation to conclude, Miss Cooper."

She answered without taking her eyes from Tobias's retreating form. "These are my conditions. I won't hurt anyone for you. I won't commit a crime for you. There will never be any romantic favors between us."

"Done. I have others who can provide for all those needs already."

She spun to regard Moriarty. He wore a mask, too, but she could see the eagerness behind it. It made her feel unpleasantly edible. "Just get me out of here."

He gave a short nod. "I can see the paper for your leave is signed, but there is little I can do about the bracelets. Except for this," he held up a tiny glass vial, and then pressed it into her palm. "This is the element the bracelets use. The common name is salt of sorrows."

She held it up to the light. It didn't look like much—just dark gray crumbs that rattled when she shook the vial. "How can a salt be a rare element?"

"The element forms part of the compound. This crystal is what they use in your restraints. I don't know any more than that, but here is where you can begin your researches."

She pocketed the container. "Thank you. Narrowing it down helps."

"Good luck," he said. "If I do not see you again before you leave, know that I will think of you in the days to come."

Her mood, already somber, dipped another degree. "Will you be leaving Camelin soon?"

"Soon." He touched the brim of his hat. "*À bientôt,* Miss Cooper."

As he left, Evelina began to feel the cold seeping through her dress. It was October now, and she would need at least a shawl to venture outside. *Isn't winter supposed to be a bad time for war?* She turned and hurried up the stairs, more than ready to huddle in the solitude of her room.

Except Deirdre was in the hall, waiting for her. "What's going on?"

"You've seen my mystery caller now," Evelina said lightly,

realizing she'd come full circle to their earlier conversation. "Sadly, he only comes on business."

"Business?" Deirdre raised her eyebrows in amusement. "I will do business with him at any time."

Somehow, Evelina managed a laugh. "Once upon a time, I'm sure Mr. Roth would have appreciated that offer."

"Not any longer?" Deirdre asked, clearly disappointed.

"No." Evelina sobered, thinking of the rake with the fallen angel smile he once had been. She would have done anything to give Tobias a little of his younger self back. "None of us are who we used to be anymore."

CHAPTER TWENTY-SIX

TOBIAS POUNDED UP THE STEPS OF THE STEAM MAKERS' Guild Hall, the Gold King's summons crumpled in one hand. He was overtired, jumpy, and in a temper. Irritation prickled like a rash. With all the larger problems in front of him, he didn't appreciate having to dance attendance at the snap of his employer's fingers. It wasn't as if he was sitting about drinking tea all day.

Tobias approached the double doors with a brisk stride, putting on his best public face. Late afternoon sun warmed the stone edifice, giving a grace the place otherwise lacked. The building was a bad imitation of the Roman style, with purposeful pillars and a triangular pediment above the door bearing a frieze of gears and wheels—an anachronism Tobias found ridiculous. Or perhaps pompous was a better word. The Steam Council fancied itself an industrial senate, every member a long-winded Caesar waiting for an empire of his own. *And I hate every one of them.*

"Afternoon," said another of Keating's men, this one exiting the doors at a trot. The man tipped his bowler as he jogged toward the streets. "Himself is in his office. He's waiting for you."

"Thanks," Tobias replied, though he felt far from grateful. Waiting was a bad sign. *Brilliant. Keating's plotting some-*

thing for certain. And despite Evelina's patient counsel, he still wasn't certain what to tell his employer.

Or maybe he was, when he faced the question squarely. Speaking out would be like putting a match to a pile of gunpowder and he simply didn't want to do it. The moment he did, people would die. But Evelina was probably right in that war would come one way or another. Informing Keating now would tip the scales in favor of those close to him, and his heart said to put them first.

Armed servants opened the double doors before he reached them, bowing as he strode past. Even without his father's title, Tobias had status there. As the Gold King's maker, he was in and out of the building several times a week. Despite his sour mood, he gave them a friendly nod as he passed. They probably didn't enjoy groveling any more than he did. Perhaps because of that status, or because he was civil, they never searched him for a weapon. The Webley hid under his coat once more.

Inside, the black marble walls of the cavernous foyer ate the wan sunlight. More armed guards stood at strategic points, their expressions shuttered in deliberate neutrality. These Tobias also knew by sight and passed without stopping, earning slight bows from a few. The deference soothed his mood, and his step sounded gratifyingly loud in the empty space—rifle shots wrapped in shoe leather.

Keating's offices were on the second floor, up a grand sweep of stairs. Here the decor changed from stark grandeur to bureaucratic opulence. Gaslights flared in amber globes, casting a sulfurous glow over dark green walls. Bleak Highland landscapes—with many portraits of hairy cows—only added to the gloomy atmosphere.

The door to the Gold King's suite was ajar, his secretary absent. All the guards, it seemed, were stationed on the ground floor, because there was no one to announce Tobias's arrival. Impatient, he barged through to Keating's office. He'd barely made it to the doorway when a voice assailed him.

"Ah, Roth, there you are," the Scarlet King said jovially.

He was lounging in Keating's favorite leather armchair, legs crossed and a lit cheroot in one hand. "How pleasant to see you. How fare your lovely sisters?"

Surprise made Tobias pull up sharply. He reached for his gun before he knew what he was doing. "Where's Keating?"

Reading held up a gloved hand, the cheroot trapped between two fingers. Smoke curled lazily in the gaslight, somehow as insolent as the Scarlet King's smile. "I wouldn't pull that if I were you. I might misinterpret your intentions."

"Where's Keating? I thought he was waiting for me. Why are you in his private office?" And where was the secretary who was supposed to be guarding the door? Tobias's fingers lingered on the butt of the gun, twitching with tension.

"He is not here," Reading said very distinctly. "I arranged a small ruse to bring you here because I felt it was time that you and I had another private word."

"I gave you my answer. What could we possibly have to say to one another?"

Reading gave him a caustic look. "I know Keating well enough to be certain he pulls your strings as much as he does anyone else's. That is his nature, rather like that tiresome fable about the scorpion and the frog. Please, sit." He indicated another chair.

Tobias sat and waited. "What do you want now?"

"When we talked before, you made a brave show of loyalty, and I respect that. I see your worth, Mr. Roth. But to be perfectly honest, I also saw that you were no happier in your situation than I am in my alliance. As peculiar as it may sound, seeing that despair in your eyes gave me hope. It is time we made common cause."

Tobias was nonplussed. "I refused you and all but threw you and your drunken hangers-on out of my father's party and now you want to be friends?"

Reading laughed. "No, Mr. Roth, not friends. I don't make friends. Call it collaborators of convenience, if you must put a label on it."

"I think not."

"Fair enough. Let me prove myself to you."

He watched curiously as the Scarlet King pulled a portfolio into his lap. It had been sitting beside the chair. Now he could see that it was made of fine Spanish leather, the lock a complicated affair that looked like two clasping hands made from chased silver. Reading took a key from his watch chain and inserted it between the hands. The tiny fingers opened with a faint click, and suddenly the two hands were open, palms up. He lifted the cover and extracted a sheaf of documents. They looked stark white against the gray of his fine kid gloves.

"What is that?" Tobias asked.

An amused smile curled Reading's lips. "I'm sure you've spent rather a long time with your nose inside that rogue airship. I came across these plans and thought they might be of interest."

Curious, Tobias took them from Reading's hand. They were indeed the plans, detailing every measurement in neatly labeled pencil. Tobias began thumbing through the stack of pages, pulling off his right-hand glove to flip the pages faster.

Reading watched with detached fascination, his blue eyes almost sleepy. "Even from the plans it is not clear who deployed the thing, but I can tell you its origins. I paid a fair price for those scribbles."

"Spicer Industries," Tobias said, his thumb stroking the edge of the page. "Their man of business purchased the logic device from Italy. I have the paperwork, but even if I didn't, the evidence is plain to see. It employs the same principles as a machine for mathematical calculation in the Green Queen's offices—"

"Ah, yes, darling Jane's little engine," the Scarlet King interrupted, clearly annoyed that Tobias had already solved the puzzle. "Crashing bore once she gets on about it. And I think you'll find the steering has features in common with those carts that rush the post around the underground rails."

"I know. But why did the Green Queen do it?" Tobias

looked up from the plans. "Of all of you on the Steam Council, why her?"

"Why does Jane Spicer do anything? Damned if I know. Becoming a widow and assuming the mantle of the Green Queen was the most exciting thing to ever happen to that vile woman. All she's ever cared about is her bank and her army of clerks, lawyers, and insurance men. Only she would fail to see the humor in making her vehicle of attack a blood-sucking bug."

Mind reeling, Tobias passed the papers back to Reading, who tucked them back into their leather case. "But why are you telling this to me, and not claiming the credit of discovery for yourself? Surely my assistance can't be worth that much."

The Scarlet King's eyes grew cold. "It's not. I might have forgiven you for treating me like a common lackey at your father's party—I am perfectly serious about the good we could do for each other—but if my offer is not tempting enough for you, well, there's not much I can do about that."

"*You* forgive *me*?" Tobias raised his eyebrows. "For objecting to your behavior?"

The Scarlet King rose from his chair, his spine military-straight. "Your betters know to show respect. I'm not some brewer's son you can toss into the street. Not anymore."

Rising as well, Tobias looked him in the eye. He saw a man not that many years older than he was—clever, good-looking, and strong—but for the first time, he also saw the uncertainty of someone who had scrabbled his way to social heights no one had thought possible. One who didn't think about the responsibility that came with power. "There's more to wearing big boots than demanding obedience."

Reading backhanded him across the face. Caught by surprise, Tobias only managed to lessen the blow, not dodge it completely. "Bloody hell, Reading!"

"I don't forgive you. If you had accepted my offer, I might

have spared you. And you should have. I've given you Jane Spicer. I couldn't have delivered the old bag any more neatly than if I'd put her on a platter with an apple in her mouth."

That was a picture Tobias could have lived without. "Spare me how?"

Reading clicked the portfolio shut. "No doubt you'll tell Keating about the plans?"

"I already intended to." His words sounded calm, telling nothing of the struggle he'd had to make that decision.

"Fine. Jane took the first shot at him, but like so many of her plans, it just didn't stick. Now that he knows it's Green that started the fight, he'll be obligated to follow up." Reading gave a greasy smile. "Don't think we haven't anticipated that."

Tobias was utterly gobsmacked, too stunned to speak. A warning hung in the air, like a cry echoing in the jungle. And then a flutter of excitement started low in his belly. It wasn't hope or pleasure, just the knowledge that something unexpected had just happened. "You're *trying* to start this war! You're not Keating's ally. You've double-crossed him!"

"Why not?" Reading asked. "He's been plotting against the rest of us for years."

"And you're sacrificing Green to do it."

"Why not? Would you want to put up with that woman?" He put on his top hat and started toward the door. Tobias followed him toward the front office, doing his best to put the different pieces of the conversation together. The Scarlet King paused and donned a long, stylish coat of dove gray. It fell in thick folds, too heavy for the weather, but it was the last stare in Bond Street fashion.

Tobias stood in the doorway between the two rooms, not sure what to do. He was a maker, not a schemer like Keating or the Scarlet King. He didn't know what the next move should be. "If you're trying to provoke Keating by selling out Green, why try to lure me to your side?" *And whom haven't you betrayed in this scenario? This is worse than a Jacobean play.*

"I came with two plans." Reading smiled, teeth white beneath his mustache. "Option one, you treated me with respect. Then together, we might have decided the best use for this information about Green. Option two, you did not. You will tell Keating what you found out. Either way, I win."

"Either way, I would tell Keating, so I don't see what the benefit to me would be of licking your boots."

"Whether you know it or not, you're one of Keating's greatest assets."

Something in the way the Scarlet King spoke reminded him of Bucky's words. The longer he stayed with Keating, the greater the distance from his old life. Keating kept him close for a reason. *Surely I'm not that brilliant, am I?*

Then Scarlet went on. "Because you are valuable, if you're not on my side, I can't let Keating keep you. A sad inevitability, to be sure." He raised the portfolio. "Always go with Italian when it comes to contact poisons. They've made an art of undetectable death. I knew you would fall for the plans like a kitten chasing a string. Too bad you took your glove off, Mr. Roth."

He's poisoned me. Tobias grabbed the customized Webley from beneath his coat, the cool weight pleasing in his hand. Metal he understood, the cause and effect of gear and spring. It was like holding a piece of rationality in the midst of chaos. Suddenly, he had power again.

Still, he knew the fit of bravado wouldn't last forever. He met Reading's eyes and held them, remembering how the man had undressed Imogen with his gaze. How he'd come far too close to Poppy. Tobias allowed his hate to seep out in his expression.

Reading smirked. "Did you know the secret of these red waistcoats? There is very fine chain mail inside them, a very particular steel alloy that I've developed. No bullet will penetrate it. My hat and coat are similarly protected, so you'll have to be a very good shot to get me between the eyes, even at this distance. You don't look the type, and I don't think that Webley is up for fancy shooting.

Put away your gun, Mr. Roth, it's melodramatic even for you."

The Scarlet King clearly hadn't noticed the Webley was customized—hard to see since Tobias had done the job with a view to minimal size and weight. Tobias thumbed a switch and the gun made a faint click, switching over to the aether setting, but the Scarlet King didn't even blink.

"What did you poison me with?" Tobias's heart was thundering, but the emotion seemed distant. He should at least be sad or angry about being murdered, but he wasn't. Clearly, he was losing his mind. Or maybe he was coming to his senses. He couldn't rid the Empire of the entire Steam Council, but he could get rid of one viper.

"If you'd been a better friend, I might have told you. But since you weren't I'll simply tell you there is no antidote, so don't waste your time on useless questions."

"If there was, would you tell me?"

"No."

"How long does it take?"

Reading's blue eyes were cold and reptilian. "Ah, that's the interesting thing about it. A day. A month. Dosage is so unpredictable in cases like this."

Tobias couldn't think of anything else to ask. So he pulled the trigger. The one thing Reading hadn't calculated on was that he was a crack shot, and hitting him at this distance was a toddle.

The aether blast hit with a vicious smack. Reading's skull and brains splashed across the office like a thick, viscous rain. The body toppled backward into the door, sliding down to leave a wide red slash of blood.

Tobias watched with detachment, vaguely aware that there had been a loud noise in the room. The air stank of spent aether and shredded flesh.

And then in slow, inexorable increments, horror combed chill, dead fingers up Tobias's nape as he slowly realized what had happened. *I just killed a member of the Steam Council.*

Tobias wondered what that would mean for the Empire, and then decided he didn't want to know. If there hadn't been a war before, there would certainly be one now. *And I did it.*

What it meant for him was easy to discern. He was in this so deep he was never getting out. Maybe it was just as well he was going to die.

That last thought opened the floodgates of panic.

CHAPTER TWENTY-SEVEN

London, October 2, 1889

HILLIARD HOUSE

6:35p.m. Wednesday

ALICE ROTH MOUNTED THE BROAD STAIRS OF HILLIARD House with her head high and her heart in her throat. This wasn't a social call. She'd been summoned—and by her father, which was worrisome. Why was her father demanding she come here, to Lord and Lady Bancroft's house?

Furthermore, the tone of his note had been sharp, and that had raised her ire. It was beyond annoying that her father could snap his fingers and she—a married woman, a mother, the wife of a steam baron's maker—didn't have the courage to tell him to go polish his gears. But Jasper Keating wasn't a man one disobeyed lightly, and though she had always loved her father, she'd seen a side of him in the last year that made her afraid.

The door opened before she'd even reached the top step, a footman bowing her in. "Mrs. Roth."

Even after months of marriage, the name still made her blink. "Would you please let the family know that I have arrived?"

"At once, madam."

Madam sounds so old. Alice fidgeted, smoothing the trim on her smart green dress. She had just returned from walking with her son and his nursemaid before she was summoned. At least she had been dressed to go out. *But what is this about? And where is Tobias?* Her hands were growing damp inside her gloves.

She heard a young voice cry in disgust, and then feet pounded up the curving oak stairway that loomed just out of Alice's sight. *Poppy.* She smiled to herself. The girl brought a touch of drama to every occasion. Then Bigelow, the butler, appeared and intoned, "This way, madam."

If Bigelow himself has come to fetch me, this is a grand occasion indeed. She suspected her father's hand in it. He liked a touch of staging to set a serious mood. Alice followed, keyed up to the point that the tip of her nose had gone numb. But she was too well trained to let it show. The doors of the small drawing room stood open, and she entered without breaking stride, putting on her brightest smile.

It was a beautiful room, with a tall bay window and a grand piano in one corner where Imogen used to sit and play. The furniture had been recovered with one of those bold Kelmscott designs—big pink flowers on a green and wine background.

The first person she saw was her mother-in-law. "Good evening, Lady Bancroft."

The older woman rose, taking her hands. She looked tired and drawn. "Alice, my dear, I am so delighted to see you. But where is our grandson?"

"Down for a nap with his nurse."

"That's all very interesting," came her father's voice from behind her, "but please sit down, Alice. There is business to discuss."

She knew that tone of voice, though it was softer with her than it would have been with anyone else. He was in a dour frame of mind. Alice turned to where he was enthroned in a large wing chair and curtsied. "Father."

Alice made one last curtsy, this time to Lord Bancroft. He half rose and gave her a cold bow. She wasn't his favorite person, but then the feeling was mutual. "It is not my opinion," Lord Bancroft said dryly, "that including the young Mrs. Roth in this discussion is wise. We require objective viewpoints, and it is not reasonable to ask a new wife to decide such pressing family matters."

Alice found a seat and realized it was just the four of them. *Family matters?* "What happened? Where is my husband?"

"There has been an accident, my dear," said Lady Bancroft in a faint voice.

They all looked at one another in a way that said that had been an understatement. Alice bounced out of her chair again, heart skittering with alarm. "Where is he?"

"Sit down, Alice," said her father curtly. "We need to make some decisions."

But Lady Bancroft said "Upstairs" at the same time, raising her hand to catch Alice's and keep her there.

She was already out the door, racing up the staircase, past the longcase clock and up to the bedrooms. Something had happened. Was he shot? Downed by some dread illness? Had this bizarre family of his finally driven him foaming mad? She hoped Poppy was there, because they had been allies in the past. If anyone would tell Alice what was going on, it would be her.

But the hallway was empty. Imogen's door was shut, her sister-in-law no doubt still in her unending sleep. Then she heard a noise—the rattle of drawer pulls and the scrape of wood on wood. Her steps quickened again, and she was at Tobias's old bedroom door.

Alice stopped, her skirts swinging with the sudden cessation of movement. She could hear Tobias moving. She knew his breathing, the way he'd stop to think halfway through a motion. *What's going on? Why aren't you downstairs with the others?*

Her chest squeezed with tension. The door was open a crack, and she pushed until it drifted open on silent hinges. And there he was, rummaging in his dresser, a large leather satchel open on the bed. He was packing.

"Tobias?" she cried, bewildered. "What are you doing?"

He stopped, his hands full of folded shirts and stockings— castoffs he'd left behind when he'd moved from his parents' house—and stared at her. His mouth was slightly open, as if he'd been about to speak but forgotten his words.

"Well?" she asked a little tartly.

"Alice," he finally said, and tossed what he'd been holding into the satchel. "Oh, Alice, I'm so sorry."

She would have preferred open arms and hot kisses. "What's going on?" she demanded, but this time kept her voice soft.

"I have to go."

"Where?"

"Dartmoor."

Exasperation rasped through her. "Dartmoor? What in the name of little brass teapots is in *Dartmoor*?" She took a deep breath, her momentary fear bubbling out in words. "What is Father thinking? First it was that bug and now this. You've hardly been home all week, and now I'll have to cancel dinner with the Whitlocks."

He turned away, snapping the bag shut. "I didn't know I would have to go until this afternoon. If I could stay, I would." He looked up, his gray eyes solemn. "Believe me when I say that. I would much rather be with you and Jeremy."

"Then stay. I'll speak to Father."

He held up a hand. "It's best I get out of town for a while. And Holmes has asked for his niece to join him on a case, so I'm to escort her. There's a murder investigation on the moors involving a cursed dog or some such blither."

That was too much. "Evelina Cooper?" *The woman you actually love instead of me?*

"Yes." Tobias made a helpless gesture. "I have to take her."

"You're not her jail guard!"

"I am now."

"But why you? Why not someone else?" Alice counted herself a good sport, but this was pushing things. She sat down on the edge of the bed, rattled by the bizarre conversation.

"You know your father," Tobias said tightly.

She did. *He's playing games.* "I said I'll speak to him."

His face had gone pale, with a flush high on his cheekbones. "No, don't. He's right. I have to leave London for a while. That's what they're deciding downstairs, but I already know the answer. Whatever else might happen, it's better I distance myself for the time being."

A suspicion worse than jealousy was beginning to crawl through her, dragging all her anxiety back to the fore. "Tell me what happened."

Tobias circled around to sit next to her. He took a deep breath and then let it out roughly, as if he had been pushed beyond the bounds of endurance. Alice leaned close, all too aware of the line of his shoulders, the curve of muscle beneath his sleeve. Her body tensed with sudden nervousness. So often their time together was like walking a high ledge, exhilarating and terrifying because a slip could be fatal. But every step toward a real understanding was a risk she couldn't refuse. They'd been obliged to marry, but there was still a chance to make something real if neither one of them lost their nerve.

And there had never been any question about their physical desire. She could feel his warmth like a magnetic pull, the scent of him reminding her that she'd been a woman before she'd been Mama or Mrs. Roth.

But he stared straight ahead instead of at her. "I don't know how to talk about what happened."

She jerked her chin up. "Be blunt. You know that I deal with that better than a lot of dancing about."

For a moment, he looked amused. "Yes, you do."

"Then out with it."

He took a ragged breath. "All right. I shot the Scarlet King. Your father's Yellowbacks got rid of the body, but it would be better if I were out of London until the investigation is over."

"William Reading is dead?" Alice was dumbstruck, and then her mind lurched forward, grasping everything he'd said. "You're right, you need to go!"

That seemed to surprise him. "You need to understand—"

She held up a hand, stopping his words. Horror was rising inside her, a jittering, chill menace that threatened to shake her to pieces any moment now. But as Keating's child, she'd learned about the savage landscape of the Steam Council long ago. She wasn't as sheltered as her father thought.

Now she willed herself to iron, ready to fight instead of crumble. "I do understand. He was a vile man. I knew William Reading when he was a clerk in the Green Queen's counting house."

"A clerk?" Tobias said in surprise, finally angling toward her.

"You don't believe all that military nonsense he put on?" Alice scoffed. She could see the horror beneath Tobias's mask, and wanted to brush it away. "He knew military *contracts*. He never marched a day in his life."

Tobias dragged his hand down his face. "I still killed him."

His eyes were pits of rage and guilt. Alice had always loathed the Scarlet King, but her anger tripled because he'd put that look on her husband's handsome features. She slipped her arms around Tobias, pulling him close. *Dear God, I'm comforting a killer,* she thought. And then, *What does this mean for my son?*

In truth, it meant that Jeremy wouldn't grow up in a world with William Reading in it. That was a good thing, whatever else came of this. Alice closed her eyes, feeling wet heat escape onto her cheeks. And then Tobias pulled her tight, his breath ragged. The strength of his embrace crushed her small frame and when his mouth sought hers, his kiss was fierce. "I'm sorry," he whispered. "And thank you."

He released her enough to study her face. Their embrace had loosened a strand of her hair, and he pushed it behind her ear. It was a tender gesture, one she would have trapped in her memory and treasured, but she caught sight of his hand.

"What is that?" she asked, catching his cuff and drawing the injury back into view. His fingers looked swollen, the tips reddened.

"Ah," he said, with a tight twist of his lips. "It's nothing. A chemical burn."

Alice let his hand go and he hid it away behind him, as if the sight had offended her—which it hadn't. But something in his manner left a hollow place in her chest. "Get a doctor to look at that."

"I will," he promised, cupping her cheek with his good hand. "You know, the problem with you coming here like this is that it makes going all the harder."

She touched his face, tracing the clean lines of his cheekbone and jaw. He was the most handsome man she'd ever known—far more striking than she'd ever be. "Do you have to go right away?"

He kissed her ear, the angle of her jaw, the pulse in her throat. "If I hesitate, I might never leave. And it's too dangerous for you if I remain. There are men watching the town house in Cavendish Square. I didn't even dare go home to our place."

Our place. Alice bit the inside of her lips to keep them from trembling. *There is something he's still not saying.*

"Reading wasn't a popular man." She kept her voice reasonable, like a child trying to sound brave in the dark. "The investigation won't go on long before they give up. You'll be home soon," she said. And then wished she hadn't. Something in Tobias's face denied it. "You will come back. Promise me."

The tense line of his mouth wavered. "I promise."

She wanted to believe that with all her heart. *He means it. Of course he does.*

CHAPTER TWENTY-EIGHT

London, October 2, 1889

HILLIARD HOUSE

6:45 p.m. Wednesday

POPPY FLOUNCED TO HER ROOM IN A MUTINOUS SULK AND slammed the door. The pictures jiggled where they hung from the picture rail and an old stuffed rabbit toppled from its perch on the rocking chair. Then she threw herself onto her fluffy yellow bed with a growl of rage. *How dare they send me to my room! I'm a young lady, not a child.*

Her chin trembled, so she bit her bottom lip to stop it. Then she grabbed her pillow, squeezing it because she needed something to hold on to. It smelled like licorice and the sweet perfume she liked, and that calmed her a little.

All she'd been able to figure out before Lord Bancroft exiled her upstairs was that Tobias was in trouble. Extreme trouble—bad enough that he had to go away to a part of the country where no one would go looking. Of course, no one would tell her why. If the Gold King had his way, her brother would leave without even saying good-bye.

But Tobias can't go. We need him here. What if he hadn't been there the night the Scarlet King and his bird had come to the party, and when the Scarlet King had caught her just outside her father's study? That whisky breath of Reading's didn't bear thinking about, and the thought of what he might have got up to next frightened her down to her shoe buckles. She'd turn to Tobias a hundred times over before going to her parents. Her father never had time for his children, and her mother wished she were somebody else.

Poppy rolled to a sitting position, tossing the pillow aside. The feather mattress was soft, the bed frame high, and that made sitting straight nearly impossible, so she ended up in an uncomfortable slouch, her feet not quite touching the floor. That made her feel six years old, so she squirmed off the bed and went to sit in the old rocking chair in the corner.

Much better—she needed to be straight and firm and clearheaded. Something momentous was going on and she had to figure out what it was. More than that, she needed to decide if there was a thing she could do about it. She'd never been a delicate miss and now was definitely not the time to resort to smelling salts and the fainting couch.

What on earth had Tobias done? It couldn't be *evil,* because though Tobias was sometimes an idiot, he wasn't wicked. And he wouldn't leave home without seeing her. *Whatever happened, it made Mr. Keating nervous and angry, but underneath that was another look, like he'd just won at cards. Is that good or bad?*

The longcase clock on the landing struck the hour, the bong making her start because it just didn't sound right anymore. Her foul mood was fraying at the edges—no less bitter, but the sharpness of it was strained by an anxious knot inside. *First Im and Evelina and now my brother gone from the house. I'm going to be alone.* She felt like the last chicken in the yard, and the stew pot was creeping closer.

Then she heard a faint *scritch-scritch* at the door. Poppy stopped rocking her chair, and she heard it again. She stood and softly crossed the floor, pulling open the door. There was no one there. She frowned into the empty space until she felt something cold brush her leg—cold enough to feel right through her stockings.

She gasped and sprang back, doing an inelegant, one-footed hop. And then she spied the mouse. "You!"

The mouse sat up on its haunches, looking up at her with sharp black eyes. Poppy glowered back, her hands on her waist. Evelina had given the mechanical mouse and bird to Imogen, and they were supposed to be simple novelty toys—but Poppy knew better. She'd seen the little menace scooting all over the house, its etched steel fur almost invisible in the shadows.

But since Imogen fell ill, the things had been stiff and still as—well—toys. Poppy had even picked them up and shaken them to see if they were broken inside, beginning to doubt what she'd seen. Her mother wasn't *entirely* wrong when she said Poppy had a hectic imagination.

But now here the mouse was, back to its old self. "You are a shameful playactor!"

The mouse put its forepaws on its middle, mimicking her pose.

"Why did you pretend you weren't alive? You made a right fool out of me!"

It started cleaning its fine wire whiskers, obviously unconcerned by her outrage.

Poppy huffed a sigh, thinking she didn't have time for mice while Tobias was in trouble—though the notion that there was still one marvelous thing at Hilliard House made her feel much, much better. Lots of people were terrified of magic but she was curious. And the mouse wasn't exactly terrifying.

"How might I help you, Mr. Mouse?"

It dropped to all fours and skittered from the room on silent paws. The thing never seemed to make noise unless it wanted to. Poppy leaned out of her doorway, remembering she'd been told to stay put, and looked around to see where the mouse had gone. She caught a glimpse of its tail snaking into Imogen's room. Surely her father wouldn't object if she looked in on her ailing sister. Not even he was that much of a stickler for obedience. She decided to take the risk and slipped out of her bedroom, closing the door behind her, and tiptoed down the hall.

Imogen's room was the same as ever, the blue tones cool and serene in the afternoon light. Imogen was exactly where she always was, looking like a fairy-tale princess in her bower. As usual, there was a nurse in Imogen's room—but it wasn't the one she was used to seeing. Poppy froze, disliking strangers near Imogen.

"I don't know you," Poppy snapped, fear and anger flaring. "Where is Nurse May?"

The woman turned. She was wearing a dark gray dress and white apron, and her gray hair was pulled back beneath a white cap, a few frizzy wisps escaping to frame her face. She smiled reassuringly, then bent to let the mouse run into her hand. "You must be Poppy," she said. "My name is Nurse Barnes."

Poppy frowned, watching her stroke the mouse's back with her finger as she straightened. "Why are you here? Are you a real nurse?"

"Nurse May required a day off, and a mutual friend arranged it so that I could take her place. I believe you know Dr. Watson? And Mr. Holmes?"

"Mr. Holmes? Yes, I asked him for help, but . . ." Poppy squinted at the woman, distrust now warring with excitement. "He was going to send someone, um, someone else." She didn't want to say Madam Thalassa because there was no telling who might be listening. After all, Jasper Keating was in the house, and he always brought minions.

The woman smiled. "My friends know me by one name and my clients by another. Miss Barnes is what my friends call me, but I do have another name."

Poppy nearly staggered as the thought sunk home. *This is Madam Thalassa? But Keating is here!* Of all the times for a magic user to come to her house! *This is dangerous.* Poppy bit her lip. *But better than any book.* This was real, and it was happening right here and now!

Holy hat ribbons! Mr. Holmes kept his promise! Poppy stepped closer, pulling Imogen's door shut behind her. "How do you do, Miss Barnes, I'm very pleased that you could come."

"It was the least I could do, Miss Roth. Mr. Holmes doesn't ask for help without a good reason."

"And I appreciate that with all my heart, but this isn't the best day to call, with the Gold King in the drawing room downstairs."

The woman gave a dismissive look in the direction of the door. "He wouldn't know magic if a flock of fairies were taking a bath in his whisky glass. I have a demanding schedule, and had to come when I could."

"But aren't you worried about getting caught?"

Miss Barnes narrowed her eyes. "I'm not the nervous type."

The mechanical bird, bright with jeweled feathers, flew to Miss Barnes's shoulder and settled there with an odd mechanical chirp. Poppy watched, so fascinated she almost forgot everything else. She'd never actually seen the bird fly before. "How did you make them work?"

The woman smiled, dumping the mouse into Poppy's hand. The little creature padded about on velvet-tipped paws, its cold little body plump and round against Poppy's fingers. She was utterly charmed.

"I didn't do anything," Miss Barnes explained. "Mouse and Bird were just waiting for someone who could speak with them. They've been helping your sister as much as they could, but now they need assistance."

Poppy was mystified. *Speak with them?* "But how *do* they work?" Springs and gears could not explain everything she'd seen them do.

She gave an enigmatic smile. "It was the creature's choice to come to you for your aid."

"My aid?"

Miss Barnes—or Madam Thalassa—moved to the head of Imogen's bed and placed her hand on the young woman's pale forehead. "From what Miss Cooper was able to tell me, your sister suffered a severe shock. Her soul separated from her body and has drifted. She needs to find her way back home."

Someone walked down the hall and they fell silent, waiting until the footsteps passed. Poppy's fingers were cold and clammy, as if all her blood had been sucked up by her whirling brain. There was too much to take in all of a sudden—and not all of it as wonderful as the mouse.

Imogen wandered away? How was that possible? And Miss Barnes had spoken to Evelina—who was locked away someplace and not allowed even to write a letter. How had she managed that? Poppy's mind was beginning to feel like melting ice cream. "I don't understand very much of this."

The woman nodded. "What you need to know is that Mouse and Bird will try to bring your sister back, but it's not an easy journey. And there is interference."

"Anna?" Poppy asked under her breath.

"Perhaps."

Poppy looked doubtfully at Mouse. "Are they really big enough to help?"

Bird gave an indignant chirp. Miss Barnes made a shushing gesture. "They have the right kind of strength for this job. But they need to be anchored to someone here. Someone who is going to stay by Imogen's side."

Poppy thought about that, searching for some frame of reference. "Like on a quest, there's always one knight who has to stay behind to watch the horses while the others sneak into the castle."

"Exactly."

"I can do that," Poppy said quickly. "I'm not going anywhere."

"That's what Mouse thought. He said you are very loyal."

Poppy eyed the creature. It stood on its hind legs and looked up at her, whiskers tickling her thumb. "You're cheeky," Poppy said. "But I'm glad you're going to help."

"But you may need to be more than loyal, Miss Roth. You might need to be brave."

"Why?"

"If I open a door, things may begin to happen. You might need to guard that door."

"How can I? I'm not magical."

"Magic doesn't always happen with spells. And you may need to get reinforcements."

Poppy was growing nervous and a little impatient. "Whatever needs to be done, I'll do it."

"Good. Then I think it's best we get started," Miss Barnes said briskly.

Poppy wondered what would happen next, but held her tongue. She could hear doors slamming and people moving around, and she locked the bedroom door just to be safe.

The last thing they needed was Lady Bancroft sailing in while the infamous Madam Thalassa was conjuring a passage to a magic land.

With an efficiency that suggested Miss Barnes was in fact a real nurse, she began clearing space on the dressing table, dislodging the bottles of perfume, necklaces, and powder boxes no one could bring themselves to put away. In danger of being tidied, Bird flew over to where Poppy stood and landed on her arm, digging sharp claws clear through her sleeve. The creature was much more ornate than Mouse, though it had been patched in a few places by a clumsier hand. It chirped and picked at the lace of her cuff, cocking its head as if waiting to see what she would do.

"Don't be a pest," Poppy scolded.

Bird opened its beak wide, waggling a bright red tongue. Poppy was sure that was the same as a rude noise.

"Bring them over here," Miss Barnes directed.

Much had happened while Poppy had been distracted. The dressing table was bare except for a circle drawn in a very fine white powder, and a small candle burned at every point of the compass.

"What is all this for?" Poppy asked.

"The candles provide a beacon. It's hard to navigate the spirit realms."

"What's the white dust?"

"Quartz. It contains the properties of both light and earth, and they will need both illumination and stability."

Mouse jumped from Poppy's hand to the dressing table, then Bird. They hunkered down in the middle of the circle, suddenly looking worried. "Are they going to be safe?" Poppy asked.

"Safer than your sister," Miss Barnes said in a voice that made Poppy twice as uneasy. "Now we need to anchor them to you. That way you'll be able to help them find their way home."

"What do I need to do?"

And then they froze again while someone with a heavier tread walked down the hall. Poppy thought she recognized her father's footsteps, and she looked at the dressing table in panic, her pulse so violent that she could feel it in her mouth. How quickly could they snuff out the candles and hide the evidence of the spell?

But Miss Barnes looked much calmer. "Hold out your hand."

Poppy did, and to her horror Miss Barnes picked up a tiny white-handled knife. "I'm going to prick your finger. Is that all right?"

Poppy caught her breath, but nodded. This sort of thing happened in fairy tales all the time. The only proper response was to be brave. And she was, although she felt a little sick when Miss Barnes held her finger first over Mouse and then over Bird, letting the bright drops fall onto their sleek metal backs.

Then Miss Barnes began to chant in a hushed voice:

> *Blood of faith and blood of fire,*
> *Hear the cry of danger dire;*
> *Fly to realms unseen or heard*
> *With the power of my word;*
> *Seek the one who there is lost*
> *And bring her home at any cost.*

As Miss Barnes spoke, a feeling grew inside the room that Poppy couldn't quite describe. It felt like the pressure right before a sneeze or a yawn, tingling behind her eyes. And then it seemed to pop. A clean smell like peppermint wafted through the air. It made Poppy slightly dizzy.

"Aether," Miss Barnes said, taking her shoulder. "It will pass in a moment."

But Poppy was staring at the dressing table in consternation. Mouse and Bird sat very still, but they were right where they had been a moment ago. "What went wrong? They didn't go anyplace."

"Oh, but they did," Miss Barnes smiled. "These are just toys. The devas inside them are gone." She gave Bird a slight push. The tiny metal statue fell over with a clunk, making Poppy wince. "They will go do their part. What you need to do is watch you sister closely for any signs of change.

And trust your instincts. You'll know what to do when the time comes."

Poppy wasn't so sure about that. "Like what?"

"Every case is different. Imagine being lost far away from home. Your guides might find you, and you come straight back, or there might be some adventures before the end. It's impossible to know. All you can do is be ready, and try to anticipate your sister's needs."

Poppy was always game for an adventure, but this was her sister's life. "Isn't there supposed to be a knight or a hero involved in these situations? Someone qualified?"

Miss Barnes shrugged. "Not necessarily. A hero is never a bad thing, but they're not the only option." Then the woman made a shooing gesture. "I need to clean up, and you had best go back to your room."

"Will Mouse and Bird come back?"

"That's up to them."

That was too vague for Poppy's comfort. She cast a last look at her sister's smooth, serene profile, thanked Miss Barnes—Madam Thalassa—and left. She scampered back to her own room, closed her door as silently as she could, and let out a huge breath. And then wondered what was going to happen. She was almost as worried for the two little toys as for her sister, because whether they volunteered or not, they hadn't looked at all happy about being sent to who-knew-where.

She crouched by the doorway, listening until she heard Imogen's door close again. Then she ran to her window and watched until she saw Miss Barnes's straight-backed form leave through the side gate the servants used and march down the street, disappearing quickly into the falling darkness. Relief robbed Poppy's limbs of strength, and she slumped onto her window seat. *She did a spell right under the Gold King's nose and got away with it.* Even Poppy knew that was insanely risky—and she was more grateful than she could say. She'd make sure everything went right from here. She would do it anyway for her sister, but it was also the best way to honor the medium's kindness.

And then a movement caught Poppy's attention. She saw another form leave through the servants' entrance, wrapped in a billowing coat and carrying a satchel. *Tobias!* She hadn't known that he was actually in the house. She'd assumed he'd gone to his own place.

A lump caught in Poppy's throat. That bag was the one he used whenever he packed in a hurry. He was leaving without saying good-bye. He'd never done that before. *This has to be worse than I thought.*

Foreboding stilled her thoughts, as if she couldn't bear to keep going. She raised her hands to the glass, blotting out the image of her brother walking away and leaving her without a word of explanation.

Then Poppy heard a woman crying, and realized it had to be Alice.

Unknown

IMOGEN SAT HIGH in the workings of the clock, balanced on the metal rail that formed part of the wheel of the zodiac. Her feet dangled over a lot of nothingness and a cushion would have been nice, but it had rapidly become her favorite spot. She had a good view of everything and there were no moving parts that required her to duck.

She squinted, sure she saw a glimmer of yellowish light slipping between the gears. One hand on a crossbar above her, she leaned over, straining for a better view. And then it was gone—except a strange minty smell drifted her way. *That's odd.*

Below, the clock bonged, shaking her teeth in her head. If she went deaf in the spirit world, would her physical body lose hearing, too? Of course, that was assuming she got back into her physical body before her twin. And *that* was a sufficiently revolting thought to guarantee she would fight until the end of days. Anger flamed through her at the thought of Anna getting anywhere near her family. Near Bucky.

Imogen snatched her thoughts back from him. Whenever she thought about Bucky, she started to cry, and she wasn't naive enough to think that Anna wouldn't turn her weakness into a weapon. She hitched herself higher onto her perch, refusing to let her emotions show. There was every chance Anna was spying on her. After all, she had delighted in it as a child.

A squawking noise rose suddenly, ricocheting around the cavernous, gear-filled space. Imogen scrambled to her feet. She was so used to the monotonous grind and tick of clockwork, the discordant noise seemed to boom through the space. Then came a scrabbling noise and a screech. Imogen crawled along the rail, trying to see past the knot of workings that blocked her sight.

She had almost reached the end of the path when a gigantic steel mouse—at least as big as a cat—bounded into view, black velvet paws clinging to the rail. Imogen stopped and stared, mesmerized by the many-jointed tail snaking to and fro in an agitated sweep. Long wire whiskers quivered, giving off a faint hum as they moved.

Imogen's heart pattered with excitement, for she recognized this extraordinary creature. "You're Evelina's Mouse!"

I am.

She nearly fell off the rail. "I can hear you!" It wasn't with her ears, but with her mind. "How can I hear you?"

We are more alike here. It scampered forward a few steps until it was touchably close, though it was across one of those heart-stopping gaps that dropped down the length of the pendulum. She reached out, brushing her fingers to the cool, sleek tip of Mouse's ear.

"I'm so happy to see a friend," she said, her throat filling with emotion. Suddenly everything seemed different. Mouse wasn't just a friend, it was a creature made for this sort of bizarre world.

We have a problem.

The bubble of hope Imogen had been nursing burst, leaving her empty. She nearly broke into tears. "What is that?"

The creature sat up, black eyes glittering in the dim light. *Your sister caught Bird.*

CHAPTER TWENTY-NINE

London, October 2, 1889

HILLIARD HOUSE

7:45p.m. Wednesday

"THE BEST THING FOR THE BOY IS TO LEAVE." BANCROFT filled his voice with a confidence he wasn't sure he believed. "Keating will handle the fuss, the police will go through the motions, and after a decent interval Tobias will come home. There are too many other things to worry about. The Blue King is acting up. Cholera's broken out again. The Stock Exchange is down."

His wife was sitting in the same chair she'd occupied when Alice had first arrived. Her hands were clasped in her lap, squashing the dainty square of lace that she'd been using to dab her eyes. "I can't believe my boy shot and killed a man! How did this happen?"

Presumably with a gun. But sarcasm would be less than kind when applied to his wife, especially where the children were concerned.

"Adele," he said softly, "he did what was necessary."

He had no idea what had actually occurred, but he knew Tobias. His son was not violent, and everyone knew that William Reading had been overdue for murder. Something had provoked that shot. Bancroft could see it clearly, even if his wife could not.

"Necessary? How is any of this necessary?" Adele stood so suddenly, Bancroft fell back. "What is happening to my children?"

His stomach twisted like a basket of snakes. One child was dead, one unconscious, and now a third was on the run. The fourth—Poppy—was so different that he barely understood her. Bancroft closed his eyes to his home life for a perfectly sound reason—there was too much he couldn't fix, and his attempts in the past had nearly damned them all. It was better to look forward, praying that his future success would bring enough money and prestige to redeem all losses. "I'm sorry, Adele."

She looked so lost, Bancroft's heart wavered. She was still beautiful, carrying herself with grace despite her distress. He took her hands in his, gently cupping the delicate fingers. "Look forward. That's all we can do. Alice and Jeremy will need you to watch over them until Tobias returns."

His wife regarded him with tear-starred eyes. "Poor Alice. She was so distraught, her father had to take her home."

That's because the little red-haired vixen is smart. He still hadn't forgiven the chit for snooping through his private papers, but he gave credit where it was due. She was clever enough to know Reading's death meant war—and whether Tobias would be hailed as a hero or a villain depended on the tale the public chose to believe.

By killing the Scarlet King, Tobias had upset the balance in the Steam Council. If Bancroft guessed right, the remaining members would scramble for supremacy. That meant war, with privation, death, and woe—and Tobias would go down as a devil. But that moment of confusion also represented the Baskervilles' best chance, which could bring a new world order snatching prosperity from the jaws of chaos—enter Tobias the Initiator, with harp and halo. It was all a matter of adjusting history once the dust had settled.

"We will get through this," he said in his best comforting tone. "We always do."

But rather than accept his words, she gave him a scathing look. "Do you expect me to be content with that?"

He dropped her hands, now wary. "What would you have me say?"

"Do you realize that he would never have been at risk if he had not been working for the Gold King?"

"There is hardly a direct line of cause and effect between the two," he said somewhat defensively. He walked to the sideboard to pour a whisky, and then remembered he no longer drank. *Damn.*

"But there is," she said in a calm, quiet voice she rarely used but he knew better than to challenge. She only ever used it in private, but it had been coming out more often since the debacle that had ended with their thankfully short-lived Disconnection.

He turned to face his wife with his most dignified expression in place. "How so, my dear? I did not arrange for Tobias's job with the Gold King."

"But it's your fault he's there." In the dim lamplight, with her back straight and eyes flashing, she might have been twenty years younger. "You are far too clever to need me to recount every step down into this pit of folly, and I would not sully my tongue with the retelling of it. Suffice it to say that where your ambition leads, we are all forced to follow."

"You enjoy the fruits of that ambition." He made a gesture that encompassed Hilliard House. "Your father is an earl, and it was my responsibility to keep you in style."

"Don't lay this at my door. I was happy to be an ambassador's wife," she said in that same dangerous tone. "I played the gracious hostess, even when it required that I welcome killers and madmen at my table. I smiled pleasantly while men I knew kept torture rooms pressed their slobbering lips to my hand. I even looked the other way while you conducted diplomacy of a different kind in your private bedchambers."

Bancroft flinched at that. How had she known?

"But leave my babies out of your machinations. I only have one left to me, and Poppy is too innocent for your games." Her voice cracked with a sound so painful that Bancroft felt it in his gut.

He felt a tingling anger rise through his body, as if he were surrounded by a magnetic coil. When he spoke, each word came out crisp and exact. "This is not my fault!"

And yet she went on. "You allowed Tobias to bear the brunt of your useless animosity toward Keating, and now see what has happened. If you do anything to jeopardize Poppy or Jeremy, I will strangle you in your sleep!"

"Don't be ridiculous," he snapped.

But she had gathered steam. "Can you honestly tell me that you wouldn't sell either of them to a slave trader if it got you a position that had the prime minister's ear?"

"That fool?" *The queen's ear, perhaps.*

"Don't be coy." She sounded weary, as if her last outburst had taken the remainder of her strength. "I'm going to my room."

"Adele!" The note of resignation in her voice stung like vitriol. It was like her cool recital of his failings—hard to wrestle with because of its complete lack of passion. *That rather describes our entire marriage.* But the cynical voice inside him faltered. "I'm worried about Tobias, too."

She paused, her body angled slightly away from him, shutting him out. "I thought you said there was no need for concern."

"That doesn't mean I don't feel it. I'm his father. He's too"—Bancroft searched for the right word—"good. No, a purist. He refuses to play the game."

That brought her gray-eyed gaze to his face. "I know. He drives me to distraction. But that's not what he was made for."

And then she turned and left, leaving him standing alone in the room, fidgeting with the coins in his pockets. The argument had left him shaken. *I shouldn't have told her I was worried.* That wasn't the sort of thing the man of the house was supposed to say—but it was true. *I can't think about this. There's too much at stake to take my eyes off the mark.*

Bancroft left the drawing room and went up to his study. He opened the door, allowing the scent of tobacco and old leather to waft over him as he walked in. Not so long ago, he'd done the same thing to find Tobias sitting at his desk. The memory of his son wrenched him unexpectedly. *He'd damned well better be fine!*

Bancroft shut the door behind him, taking a deep breath and letting it out a bit at a time. Solitude and silence settled over him, slowing the pounding of his heart. The privacy of the room held half its value to him. The other half was the memory of all the plots, feints, and victories he'd orchestrated from behind his desk. There had been failures, too—his investment in Harter Engine Company, for starters—but he'd won his share of hands. Here, in this room, he was in control.

Calmer, he sat down at the desk and shuffled a stack of papers to one side, squaring the edges with an authoritative *thump*. The volatile state of the Empire screamed for prudent diversification, and over the last few days, he'd been transferring assets out of London banks and into accounts he held in France and the United States. He knew it was a smart move, and that certainty released the tense knot forming at the back of his neck.

But relief didn't last. Beneath the financial papers was the note he'd received at Duquesne's. Annoyed, Bancroft picked it up, tempted to toss it into the dustbin. Nothing more had come of it, and he had enough complications to wrangle without cryptic threats.

Then he paused, remembering the difficulties he'd had dealing with the Chinese traders. He wondered again about Harriman and the goldsmiths. The episode felt like ancient history, even though it had not been two years past. No doubt he was worrying for nothing. He hadn't personally met any of the Chinese workers, outside of Han Zuiweng. Engaging and directing the help had been Harriman's job. By rights, no one involved with hiring the Chinese should even know Bancroft's name.

He turned over the note, studying the Chinese character on the reverse side. Again, he thought it looked familiar, although that might have been his imagination. Bancroft shrugged his shoulders, shaking off the sensation that he was being watched. *Nonsense.* The only other pair of eyes in the room belonged to the stuffed tiger's head fixed to the wall above his desk. *Figure this out and get it out of your brain. You can't afford the distraction.*

He opened his desk drawer and pulled out a file of correspondence he'd received from merchants in the coal trade. Leafing through the thin stack of pages, he wasn't sure what he hoped to find. When he'd taken on the task of finding a source of coal for the rebels, he'd done much of the legwork in person. In part, he'd become personally involved because of the delicacy of the mission. One didn't simply march up to the sales desk asking for contraband supplies for a group of traitors. Bancroft had needed all his ambassadorial skills, building personal relationships with the merchants who came and went among the ever-shifting population in the Limehouse area.

But there had been a few letters, most in English. His idle flipping began to take on purpose, and he turned the pages faster. The ones that interested him were the few that had come on paper stock with the company crest printed at the top. He pulled them aside one by one until he found the one he wanted—a letterhead with ornate Chinese dragons down the margins. The note itself had been a polite but brief apology from a merchant who was closing down his operation to return to his own country.

Bancroft shoved the note with the hand-drawn character closer to the letter. There it was: a match to the character that formed part of the design. Even though he couldn't read the script, Bancroft had long ago trained himself to remember shapes and ornamentation. In the diplomatic business, remembering the details of a piece of jewelry or the crest on the side of a coach could be key. After a while, it became habit.

But now that he'd made the connection, what did it mean? Had the note from Duquesne's come from someone connected to the merchant company? He picked up the letter, reading it over again. It was still the same bland apology as before, so he turned his attention to the letterhead itself— and the two fierce dragons descending to the underworld, smoke pouring from their nostrils. He'd thought them picturesque but irrelevant before, and yet now he began to wonder. Han, the Chinese foreman, had commanded some sort of magical serpent guardian.

Spurred by a fresh idea, Bancroft returned to the file and kept flipping pages until he found a second paper. It had been a list of companies in the Limehouse area that he might want to contact. He'd got it from the tax rolls. These were the official company names gathered by the local authorities, and they sometimes differed from what the traders put on their signs. Bancroft found the listing with the same address as his dragon letterhead. It was for the Mercantile Fellowship of the Black Dragons of the Hidden Sea. There were two contacts listed, and with a ping of surprise, he recognized one of the names. It wasn't the signatory of the letter, but instead a Mr. Fish.

Bancroft sat back in his chair. *Mr. Fish?* He knew the name from the minutes the Steam Council published in the *Bugle*. He knew the minutes were just official drivel meant to project the image of public-spirited men of business—and probably reporting about 5 percent of what actually occurred—but the list of attendees was probably correct. The oddity of the name—who called himself Fish?—had made it stick in his mind though he had only seen it on two occasions, for the Black Kingdom sent a different representative to the council almost every time.

That raised brand-new questions. Did the Mercantile Fellowship of the Black Dragons of the Hidden Sea have a connection with the Black Kingdom underneath London? Since the Chinese were supposed to be unaligned with any member of the Steam Council, that gave Bancroft pause. Had he stumbled across a little-known alliance?

But worse was the possibility that he'd drawn the attention of the underground world. Nobody knew much about it, and those who did were too afraid to speak of what they knew. Black ruled more than the utility infrastructure that passed beneath the streets—and the other barons had paid dearly for permission to install most of that anyhow. Silence Gasworks, the company that provided Black's steam and gas, produced just enough for the underground's use. No, Black's true power lay elsewhere, ruled over by a presence— no one knew precisely who or what—that seemed to be far older than the Steam Council.

There were certainly places the daylight traveler could go beneath the earth—the carefully negotiated territories of the underground rail lines, for instance—but it was folly to

step outside those carefully demarcated boundaries. Few
who strayed into the labyrinth of Black's subterranean passages ever came back.

Bancroft's fingers twitched, then started to shake.

So what did the Black Kingdom want with him?

CHAPTER THIRTY

BASKERVILLE HALL WAS ONE OF THOSE NIGHTMARE PROPER-
ties that argued for a box of matches and a barrel or two
of oil. Watson had first thought so upon arrival and now,
standing outside and staring up at the grim edifice, he was
ready to assist the would-be arsonist. The beds alone were a
felony.

The hall had probably been the last word when it was
built—Watson guessed the original parts of the house dated
to Good Queen Bess or maybe even her father. But nothing
in it had been updated since. The furniture and finishes
were oily black with age. The house itself was square and
dark, made gloomier still by the fact that someone had
bricked over many of the windows, probably during an era
when windows were taxed. The only people who could have
been happy there were Gothic novelists, maniacs—more or
less the same thing—or perhaps moles.

And when one tried to escape the dank chill of the house,
the main attraction was a path—about twenty feet across,
counting the lawn—flanked by impenetrable twelve-foot
yew hedges. And, to complete the effect, the only way in or
out of the walk was a wicket gate that led onto the bleak,
wandering vastness of the moor. And there, amid the rolling
sea of wild gorse and prehistoric ruins, were bogs waiting to
suck down unsuspecting ramblers and the occasional pony.

It was at that place, near the moor gate, where Sir Charles had died. The man had been found face down, his arms splayed and clutching the ground, and his face contorted with fear. There had been no physical injuries to speak of, beyond heart failure. The consensus at the hall was that the old gentleman had been frightened to death. Maybe he'd finally noticed where he'd been living.

Holmes, who had been peering at the ground where the body had been discovered, came up beside Watson. "I found nothing but the footprints of a dog."

"Well, you were looking for a legendary agent of death. Besides the mildew in my bedding, that is. Perhaps it was the ghostly Hound of the Baskervilles enacting an ancient curse."

Holmes looked amused, but it was fleeting. "Very good. See what you can do with that in your literary exploits. I've convinced the Gold King that Evelina's presence is mandatory to the investigation, but we have yet to give substance to the tale. Make it convincing."

Watson was getting just a little testy. He had set out to chronicle Holmes's cases, not spin tall tales. "One thing I wish to question from the start. Speaking as a medical man, I don't understand how heart failure translates to murder."

Holmes grew serious. "Sir Charles clearly died of terror. Perhaps not a usual weapon, but effective nonetheless."

Watson considered that. "Despite the man's appearance at the moment of death, how can we prove such a thing? What kind of clues, much less evidence, can we hope to find to convict this bogeyman?"

Holmes hunched slightly, as if to fend off the question. "We shall work the same as we always do, my good doctor. No detail will escape our notice."

Watson was doubtful. "And Evelina?"

"The Gold King is sending Tobias Roth with her, which may prove a nuisance."

"He shot you not so long ago."

"Thank you for reminding me." Holmes gave a short laugh. "Perhaps you should be the one to keep him distracted. I propose that we—by which I mean you—find a means of sedating the young man, relieve him of the key to her manacles, and get her to safety. Once she is gone, it will be no great matter to lead him off in a false direction as he searches to recapture her. He must leave before the rest of the Baskerville council arrives. And just to complicate matters, Miss Barnes and her friends are installed in the town, waiting for Evelina to join them. They are devoted to the Baskerville cause, and yet not all of the council are friendly to magic users. We have done what we can to ensure the two groups do not mix, for the last thing we need now is a spat between our allies."

"That's a lot of stage management," Watson said uneasily. "A lot of players to keep out of each other's way."

Holmes made a face. "Very true. And it would be bad enough if Evelina had come with an ordinary Yellowback, but Roth will make this harder. He is smart, and anything he sees will find its way back to the Gold King."

"Is it worth the risk to attempt this all at the same time?"

"When else would we have these circumstances? If we can free my niece, then take down the laboratories, we shall have struck two blows against the Gold King. With some victories behind us, swaying others to the Baskerville cause will be easier."

Watson heard the call to action in his friend's voice and felt his blood stir. "What made you join in this Baskerville affair?"

"My brother, Mycroft, believes he recruited me." Holmes gave him a serious look. "But any doubts I had about the cause vanished the moment the steam barons pushed the makers underground. No nation can survive when the free play of thought is outside the law."

It was a sobering observation. "How did the Baskervilles become involved in the rebellion? I've seen their home. It looks ordinary enough."

The detective looked down the length of the yew walk toward the house. "Prince Albert was a planner. Even after he had suppressed the steam barons, he could see they would not remain obedient to the Crown and so he set up safeguards. If only he had lived a little longer, he would have strengthened those plans, but he did not. So we are left to work with an imperfect solution—but at least he pointed the way. And he made Sir Charles the keeper of his plan."

Watson shook his head. "That's not an explanation. That's not even a hint."

Holmes laughed, his mood suddenly light. "Work with it, Doctor; you have all the pieces you need."

He'd said that to Watson on far too many cases, leaving him stumbling behind in the dark. "Holmes, I *loathe* it when you say that!"

"And I enjoy watching you puzzle it out. It is most entertaining." Holmes turned and walked toward the house.

After a moment of stewing frustration, Watson followed. A steam-assisted carriage, looking rather like a smoking horse-drawn tea caddy, had pulled up in front of Baskerville Hall, and both Holmes and Watson hurried to greet the newcomers. The doctor blinked in the gloom as they entered the front hall, but quickly spotted Evelina Cooper and Tobias Roth, accompanied by a lady's maid no doubt meant in part as chaperone. Evelina launched herself at a slightly flustered Holmes with a squeal of delight. She looked pale, but as pretty as ever, with the waves of her dark hair pulled up under a black straw hat adorned with a spray of pheasant feathers. *Mary would like that hat,* Watson thought, then remembered his wife was gone.

Evelina turned from greeting her uncle, her lovely blue eyes wide with happiness. "Dr. Watson, I'm so glad you're here! It's been ages."

"Delightful as always to see you, my dear girl." Watson squeezed her hand, feeling suddenly old. One glance said that she wasn't actually a girl anymore. He'd heard a little of her misadventures from Holmes, and that experience showed in her confident manner—and in the shadows behind her eyes. *Perhaps maturity is the knowledge of how much we can survive.*

More greetings were made—congratulations on the birth of Roth's son, condolences on Mary's death. Watson paid little attention, instead studying Tobias Roth. Holmes had said it was his job to keep the young man distracted and, if necessary, drugged. It would have been easier to simply kill him, but no one was prepared for cold-blooded murder when a bit of medical mischief could get the job done.

But unless he was mistaken, something was already amiss with the young man. It was hard to tell when they were still wrapped up against the moor winds, but Roth's color wasn't good. He looked almost green, and the circles under his eyes were the purple of fading bruises. It was obvious, from the way Evelina hovered near him, that she was worried, too. As Baskerville Hall's two servants—a surly caretaker named Barrymore and his surlier wife—moved in to deal with luggage, coats, and fresh linens, Watson took the opportunity to pull Roth aside.

"I have been consulting on your sister's case," he said, and then wondered about the nurse Holmes had asked him to recommend as a substitute at Hilliard House. Watson had never learned the details, but Holmes had hinted that she might uncover a clue as to what was ailing Miss Imogen Roth.

"Ah, yes, I know." The young man gave him a tired smile. "My sister still clings to life, for which we all have to thank your excellent care."

Watson wasn't so sure about that, but he moved on. "Perhaps, if you have time later, you would permit me to discuss a few ideas for treatment. I am wondering if an unwholesome substance might have brought on this latest fit."

They were moving toward the stairs, lagging a little behind the others. Tobias was puffing harder than someone of his age and obvious fitness should have. "What do you mean? That my sister was poisoned somehow?"

Actually, Watson was making it up as he went along, but he nodded. Anything to engage Roth in a long conversation that might involve a drug in his brandy, the theft of a key, and so on—although now Watson felt cautious about administering a sedative to someone whose breathing was already compromised. "Since I have worked with Mr. Holmes, I have acquired quite an extensive knowledge of poisons and their antidotes, and what I do not know I have means of finding out."

For the first time since he'd arrived, a spark came into Roth's eyes. "Yes, indeed, Doctor, we shall have that conversation."

Watson gave his most trustworthy smile, exuding the aura of a serious medical professional. "Come to the library once you are settled. The scenery here isn't much, but Baskerville has a most satisfactory stock of brandy."

CHAPTER THIRTY-ONE

MRS. BARRYMORE, THE HOUSEKEEPER, SHOWED EVELINA TO a small bedchamber that was as spare and old-fashioned as the rest of Baskerville Hall. The only modern convenience she'd detected was the glimpse of a steam-driven lift running up the side of the barn for delivering feed. The steam barons hadn't yet invaded with their gaslights and engines—but she'd seen plenty of their soldiers patrolling the moor.

The sight of her room did little to comfort her. Like everything else in the house, it felt oppressive. Dark beams crisscrossed a low ceiling and heavy leading made a diamond pattern of an old casement window. The only furniture was a sagging bed, a washstand, and a wardrobe large enough to hide a body. Even the student quarters at the college had been luxurious by comparison.

"Thank you," said Evelina, wanting to bring a smile to the dour woman's face. "This is most pleasant."

Her good manners had little effect. "Your maid can have a bed in the attic with the other servants. We will ring the bell when meals are served. Will that be all, miss?"

Evelina hesitated, slightly taken aback by the woman's tone. But she had to remember that the Barrymores had suffered a loss, too. "Were you a long time in Sir Charles's service?"

"Aye, miss."

"I am very sorry for your loss."

The woman's face softened a degree. "Thank you, miss. But there have been so many comings and goings of late that it was no wonder Sir Charles up and died. It was too much for the old man."

"You have that many visitors here?" Evelina could not help being surprised. They were a long way from anywhere.

"Aye, miss. One gentleman after another, it seems, in the last month. But I suppose with a new head of the household, we'll be faced with entertaining more."

"I imagine Mr. Edmond Baskerville will be a pleasant master."

"He is not the heir, miss. Sir Charles took him in as a babe and raised him as one of the family and he turned out as good a young man as you please. But there is a nephew, Mr. Henry Baskerville—Sir Henry now—who will be coming home from Toronto to take up residence at the hall." And she didn't sound particularly pleased about the fact.

So Edmond took Sir Charles's name, but was never formally adopted. That kept things simple where an entailed estate was involved, but it was still an interesting fact, especially where there was suspicion of murder. If Sir Henry was overseas and Edmond was not the heir, that weakened any argument to include them as suspects.

She was leaning toward a killer from Her Majesty's Laboratories, but there was still Edmond's radical politics to consider. She had known the Schoolmaster was one of the rebel leaders, but had never suspected he was *actually* a Baskerville—although technically he wasn't a Baskerville at all. Still, if anyone knew he was a radical, they might go after his family. Evelina chased that thought a moment, mesmerized by the sight of the moor through the wobbly glass of the ancient window.

"Miss?" asked the housekeeper.

"Thank you, Mrs. Barrymore. I can look after myself from here."

"Very good, miss." The housekeeper left, her solid tread receding down the corridor.

Evelina eyed her suitcase, sitting patiently beside the bed, along with a bag that carried, among other things, two of the books on rare elements she'd taken from the college library. She'd read through all of one and most of another on the train. Neither of them were terribly thick volumes.

She had been a long time without a maid to perform little

services such as unpacking, and decided to take advantage of her presence. Feeling delightfully lazy, she turned her attention instead to her toilette, using the comb from her reticule to tame what she could. There weren't enough hairpins in the Empire to combat the frizzing effect of the damp moorland air.

It hadn't been an easy trip down. Tobias had said little the entire way, explaining nothing of why suddenly, when he had been about to divulge a secret that would start a civil war, he was taking her south to investigate the death of a minor baronet. Questioning him had got her nowhere, and that was unusual. Tobias used her as a sounding board. Silence meant something serious had happened, and that had her worried. *But he can't stay mute forever. We've always been too close for that.*

Her fingers stilled, a hairpin in one hand and her comb in the other. Here she was, focused on Tobias Roth one more time, even if she no longer wanted him for a husband or even as a lover. And yet she still cared for him as one of her oldest friends. As long as he was in trouble, she wasn't walking away.

There was a light knock on the door, probably the maid. Evelina looked up from the mirror above the washstand, and nearly dropped her comb in surprise. "Nick!"

He flashed a smile, dark eyes widening with interest as his gaze traveled over her. He'd spent time outdoors and looked much more himself, tanned and confident as he moved. Not that there was much room to move in the tiny room. She was in his arms before she'd drawn another breath, and it felt wonderfully right.

"Hello," he said, the vibration of his voice traveling from his chest to every nerve in her body. A warm, liquid ache made her lean closer, as if contact alone could relieve it.

"Hello," she replied, glad they were in daylight. She could see the mahogany lights in his eyes this way, like sunlight trapped deep inside them. "What are you doing here?"

His grin widened. "I came with the Schoolmaster. We stopped along the way. That news report you showed me about the *Red Jack* was correct. I was able to find Athena!"

His excitement sparked through her, and her heart lifted. "That's wonderful news! Is she here?"

"Under lock and key. I stayed as long as I could in hopes of seeing you, but now I'm off to Cornwall."

"Cornwall?"

His smile faded. "There's a town there where Striker and I were building a second ship. If anything happened, the crew agreed to leave word there for the others. That way we'll know if there were survivors."

Evelina's joy faltered. She'd heard this story before, and felt the same chill in her blood. The chance of finding survivors was not good. She put her hands on his shoulders, the wool of his jacket rough to the touch. "Be careful. I don't like the thought of you traveling alone."

"I won't be half dazed from falling out of the sky. I won't be easy pickings this time."

Evelina frowned. Nick was a creature of the air. Without a ship, he was trapped and vulnerable on the ground. "Does anyone else know that you've found Athena?"

"Three of the Schoolmaster's friends: Edgerton, Penner, and Smythe. They're staying in town."

"I know them. Michael Edgerton and Bucky you can trust. Smythe is a hothead."

"I'm not worried about what they'll do to me. They want an airship, and with Athena I can give them the best."

"I'll be happier when you're back in the air."

He gave her a reassuring squeeze. "Whatever I find in Cornwall, I'll be back with a ship. Any pirate worth his salt has booty stashed here and there, hopefully at a decent rate of interest."

She couldn't help smiling. "You always did keep a few coins at the bottom of your saddlebags."

"Gran Cooper always said to hope for the best and plan for the worst." He kissed her forehead lightly. "And there are people I want to look after. That means looking ahead and making plans. And you're the heart of those plans, Evie."

They were still holding each other, carrying on their conversation with noses almost touching. That was just fine with Evelina—she could have stood there holding Nick all day. But she could feel his energy, forward-moving like a hawk in flight. He wouldn't stay still for long—not when he was on the cusp of regaining what he had lost.

"And now that I've told you my tale, what about yours?" He tapped her bracelet. "How did you get out of the college?"

"Tobias brought me here on the Gold King's orders. I'm here to help Uncle Sherlock with Sir Charles's murder."

A muscle in Nick's jaw thumped with tension. "The Schoolmaster has taken it hard. He loved the old man. But was there really a supernatural connection?"

"I don't know yet. It's rather hard to sort out fact from Dr. Watson's embellishments." As she spoke, uneasiness crept through her. She wanted to tell Nick about Nellie Reynolds and the laboratories, but if she did he would stay to make sure she was safe. That would mean a delay in leaving for Cornwall—which meant more risk. Even if they could trust the Schoolmaster and his friends, there was a chance someone else might find out about Athena and a pirate captain with a rare strain of the Blood. Never mind the usual thieves and villains—they were far too close to Her Majesty's Laboratories. If the attempt to destroy them failed, she didn't want Nick caught in the struggle. Her own feelings aside—and they were legion—the rebellion needed Captain Niccolo and his ship.

He leaned closer. "Is there a chance you can escape for good?"

"Uncle Sherlock is working on that," she said. "He's thinking along the same lines."

"Good." He put a hand on either side of her face. "He's one of the few I'd trust with you."

"I'm sure he'd be honored to hear it," she said dryly.

Nick kissed her forehead again. "I'll be back here with my ship soon. Take a chance if one comes and know I'll be looking for you."

"Is this good-bye?" she asked plaintively.

His smile grew wicked. "We can make it a long good-bye."

Hot guilt surged, accusing her with every secret she was holding back. *I'm as bad as Tobias.* But she buried her chagrin in a kiss, hiding her secrets behind sweet affection. Her heart hurt even worse when Nick returned the kiss with a passion that said he hadn't detected her ruse. *But I'm doing it for him.* She'd thought him dead once and never wanted to suffer that tearing grief again. Nick wanted to protect her from the world. Was it so selfish to protect him back?

He took her lips again, and every other thought melted into mist. His mouth was hot and hungry, his breath warm as it fanned against her skin. She seemed to come apart inside, not sure if she was dropping away or launched into flight. Excitement and desire tingled deep inside, as if the kiss was transforming her very bones.

Nick gave a chuckle, one of those deep, masculine sounds of pleasure that said he knew exactly how he'd conquered her. In response, she nipped his lower lip, drawing another sound, this time of curiosity. She could feel their magic pulling toward each other, churning and eddying like a current where a river meets the sea, but they both held it in check. There would be time enough for dalliance when they were both on his ship and safe in the sky. And Evelina would commit any misdemeanor to make that future come true.

She put a hand on his chest, melting a little more as she felt the beat of his heart, alive and precious. "If you don't leave, I won't let you go."

He sighed, and she felt the rise and fall of his chest. He stepped back, and all at once the room was there again, cool and spare. She shivered, feeling exposed without his arms around her. She bit her lips together, not wanting to cry because he was leaving so soon—or because sudden fear made her want to beg him to stay.

Letting him go wasn't the selfish choice. Holding him back would be. "Good-bye, Nick, and come back quickly."

He sketched an extravagant bow that came straight from his days in the circus ring. "Be safe, Evelina."

She waited until the door closed before she let her tears fall.

CHAPTER THIRTY-TWO

"THE KEY HAS TO BE TURNED EVERY TWELVE HOURS," EVE-lina explained to her uncle as he fussed with her silver bracelets. "Nothing Tobias has will take the bracelets off. And I can't believe Dr. Watson drugged Tobias!"

They stood behind the hall, the vast expanse of the moors stretched out before them. Many described the place as desolate, but she didn't agree. To her, there was a fierce loveliness. The land rolled in an undisciplined patchwork of browns and greens, the fieldstone fences more suggestions than effective walls. Splashes of gold and vibrant red flamed by the creek beds and ditches.

The wildness of earth and broad, sweeping sky didn't bother her in the least. The place was rich with spirits of every kind—both the devas of the natural world, and the echoes of the primitive men who had built the cairns and stone huts that dotted the landscape. They weren't hostile, but they were indifferent to the mortals that huddled into tiny, whitewashed villages. Unlike the tame farmlands closer to the big towns, the moors had business of their own.

Rather like the landscape, Holmes was unmoved by her protest. "Mr. Roth is in excellent care and, from the looks of him, he is overdue for medical treatment. What is the matter with him?"

"He won't say. In fact, Tobias barely spoke at all the whole way here."

"He always was an idiot."

Evelina stiffened, but there would be no changing her uncle's mind on that point. "I wish we could get the bracelets off altogether."

"I will get the Schoolmaster on it as soon as possible. He knows every maker of consequence. One of them will figure it out."

She wondered if there were safety measures that would render the key useless once Tobias discovered the theft—but raising that now wouldn't help anything. Instead, she took the key from Holmes and strung it on her necklace for safekeeping. "What now?"

Her uncle gave her a serious appraisal. "Now you join Miss Barnes and help her destroy Her Majesty's Laboratories. I am surprised that you didn't guess that she and Madam Thalassa were one and the same."

Evelina was still smarting at the deception. "I didn't recognize her without her medium's robes. Those sketches in the newspapers are never any good."

Holmes raised a brow. "She's already held up her end of the bargain and visited Miss Roth in her sickbed. She is guardedly hopeful that her solution will work."

"And you kept your promise to Poppy."

"Indeed I did. And now we move from small promises to larger ones. On to the destruction of the laboratories, and after that, the Steam Council."

The energy in his voice rippled down Evelina's backbone, carrying a power of its own. At Nick's side, she'd spied out the Blue King's army and survived an attack by his soldiers, and she knew just what kind of horror a war would unleash. And yet she knew equally well the price of doing nothing. Nellie Reynolds had shown her that all too clearly.

Still, she was afraid. Everyone she cared about had endured some sort of tragedy in the last few years, and this was only going to increase the danger hovering over her small world. No matter what choice she made, it wouldn't keep her loved ones safe—not all of them, anyhow.

And her instinct said to fight, for all that road frightened her. She closed her eyes, holding the intoxicating beauty of the moors inside herself, storing it against what was coming. Soon enough, she would need all the loveliness she could find. When she opened her eyes again, she was steady enough to smile.

"I've always wanted to work by your side," she said to Holmes, "but this isn't anything like your usual cases."

Holmes raised his eyebrows. "The details change, but every case involves someone who wants what they shouldn't have, a great many lies, and at least one instant when I wished I'd became a baker's apprentice."

"Don't be so sure," Evelina said lightly, remembering her adventure in the Gold King's warehouse. "The last baker I met had a problem with dragons."

And for once—though it was for a very short while—she rendered her uncle speechless.

"THERE WAS A gunpowder factory back there," said Miss Barnes in a low whisper, pointing straight ahead through the dusk. "Do you see that?"

Evelina crouched in the ragged grass, doing her best to avoid the gorse bush poking her with long, needle-sharp spines. They were approaching the laboratory from the moor, rather than the road. Normally she enjoyed a ramble across country, but she'd heard nothing but tales about bogs swallowing up innocent victims, and the ground here was squishy—not to mention that they were sneaking up on armed men. They had waited until twilight, but there wasn't enough cover for her liking—especially not here, where the land sloped downward from a high tor. Evelina might have magical powers, but what she really wanted was a good revolver.

Nevertheless, she looked for the ruined factory. What she saw were the stumps of stone buildings, pale against the heath, one cylindrical tower still stretching into the sky. "What happened there?"

"Some sort of explosion. After that they closed it down

and the laboratories moved. That's what's in the buildings on the other side of the ruins."

Her Majesty's Laboratories looked like nothing so much as a row of cottages with a dairy behind them. Which explained the cows—they were the perfect cover. Rough-coated, white-faced beasts, they dotted the land between where Evelina crouched and the cottages began. She eyed the pasture suspiciously, wondering about the wisdom of sneaking through the long grass.

"Do you know what you are supposed to do?" Miss Barnes asked.

Evelina nodded.

"Best of luck. Remember, you're the only one of us whose power works a little differently. That's why you're going in first. The dampening shields inside the building should not work as effectively on you, but don't take that for granted." The woman squeezed Evelina's hand and crept away, her homely tan-colored coat all but vanishing in the grass.

Left alone, Evelina felt insignificant beneath the vast sweep of sky. The sun was low, outlining fractured clouds with pale fire, but already the moors had assumed a purplish hue. She could see the faint glow of devas—spirits of the land—flickering across the moor. They'd resisted all attempts to communicate, but she hadn't pushed. It was enough to know that they were there, because that meant the moor itself was healthy. Although—she noticed the lights came nowhere near the buildings Miss Barnes had pointed out.

The cows were drifting toward the enclosure, clearly feeling it was time to be milked. Evelina squinted, trying to reconcile what she knew of the place with the pastoral view. This looked more like a source of clotted cream than the infamous laboratories.

The only way to find out for sure was to ask. Evelina stripped off her gloves and pressed her hands to the earth, feeling for the energy of the land. She could touch most places with little effort, but the moors were not shy. The presence of the place rose up to meet her with the force of a blow. She rocked back on her haunches with a gasp, but held on. The vibrancy of the earth and untamed nature churned through her like a fast-running stream, but beneath that was something foul. The land didn't like it, wishing it could flick it off the way a dog shakes its coat dry. All at once, Evelina understood Miss Barnes's plan.

She shifted her power, seeking the other members of the Parapsychological Institute. They came to her inner sight as fuzzy points of light, all bright—although some were green, or white, or a friendly yellow. There were a dozen strewn in a loose circle around the moor. Some, like Leonidas Wood, she recognized. Most she did not—which was both a comfort and a concern. She wanted to know with whom she was working, but she wasn't so sure—after years of hiding her talents—that she was as comfortable with them knowing her. Besides, none had the dark quality of Evelina's power. She was like a crow among a flock of doves.

Evelina let the power go, taking three deep breaths to steady herself before checking the position of the sun. It was time to get started. She abandoned her gorse bush and began skidding down the slope of the hill, wishing her boots had better treads. Her dress was dark, so she kept to the shadows, doing her best to stay invisible. Once the ground leveled out, she began trotting toward the cows. A few of the massive beasts turned and stared, their short curved horns looking particularly sharp. Distracted by the herd, she forgot to watch where she was walking and stepped into a rut, her foot sliding in the mud and wrenching her ankle. She went down on one knee, sliming her skirts. *Oh, brilliant.* She scrambled back to her feet, dirty and limping, but carried on, using a red and white cow for cover.

Now she could see the guards posted at regular intervals, one just within sight of the next. She edged along the side of the long dairy barn, hearing the hiss of steam-operated milking machines and the clatter of milk buckets over the incessant lowing of the cows. There was a boy outside with a stick, urging them inside with shouts and swats, and a black and white collie pup bouncing in circles around his feet. The guards paid no attention to the boy or the cattle, but instead scanned the yard right where Evelina wanted to go.

She caught movement to her left and saw an old, bent man

carrying a bundle of straw across his shoulders. Uncle Sherlock, in one of his disguises. He jerked his head and she changed course, following him deeper into the shadows and finally breaking into a trot. The twilight was deepening. They had to move quickly before they lost all the light.

"There is a door right beside that fellow there," Holmes said as she drew near. "I can pick the lock if we can get past him."

Evelina thought a moment. "Won't the other guards notice he's gone?"

"In this light, all they need to see is someone in uniform holding a gun. I can take his place. The problem will be rendering him unconscious without making a noise."

Evelina bit her lip. "Leave that to me."

Holmes gave her a curious look, but dropped his bundle and pushed an apron into her hands. "You are a dairy maid, I am your grandfather, and I require medical attention."

He thought of everything. Evelina looped the strap of the bib over her head and quickly tied the strings. A moment later, she was helping her staggering elder across the gravel-strewn yard. "Please, please sir, we need a doctor!"

The guard poked at her with the butt of his rife. "Go on, you know you don't get inside. Send one of your own down to the village. You're not our concern."

"But please!" She abandoned Holmes and reached for the guard, putting one hand to the side of the man's head. Then she loosed a quick jolt of power. The man's eyes rolled up, and he fell back against the wall.

"You must tell me someday how you do that," her uncle muttered.

"Maybe." It was a trick she'd learned from Magnus, and not one she was particularly proud of—but like all the sorcerer's lessons, it was useful. That was what had made his instruction in the dark arts so tempting. "He'll be out for at least an hour."

She leaned in, trapping the guard against the wall long enough for Holmes to take the man's cap and rifle. No one would see anything but a girl entreating the soldier a little too enthusiastically. Once they'd lowered the guard to the ground, they took his jacket, too. In the growing dark, Holmes had effectively changed places with him. In another moment, no one would see the extra body at all.

Then he bent and, with a pair of slim tools, set to work on the lock while Evelina searched the guard for a sidearm. She'd just found a knife and a pistol when she heard the telltale click of success. "Good luck," whispered Holmes. "I'm giving you two minutes before I come looking."

"Give me ten," she whispered back.

"Five."

And she was in. The door opened into a stillroom, probably once a kitchen but now it was filled with glass-stoppered jars labeled with specimen numbers and cryptic lettering. The next door was unlocked and led into a corridor. A glance told her that what looked on the outside like a string of adjoined cottages was actually one large structure with a smooth stone floor. The corridor where she stood ran end to end, one side disappearing into the laboratory proper. The nose-wrinkling smell of antiseptics made her skin pebble with dread.

Evelina wrestled her nerves under control. Though the mission was dangerous, her goal was strictly reconnaissance. She was there to find anyone who, like Nellie Reynolds, might be able to escape. And according to the sketch the actress had made, the holding cells were to her left. Evelina hauled in a breath, turning her steps toward the row of tiny doorways.

The dampening fields that Miss Barnes had warned her about descended like a hot, wet cloak. She could feel them weighing down her power, drowning it in a soggy haze. So much for the immunity of dark magic. *No, they work on me just like everyone else.*

She fished in her pocket for the glass vial that Moriarty had given her. She'd read about salt of sorrows on the train. Holding up the vial, she could see the salts were clinging to the sides of the glass, attracted to the ambient energy in the room. *I'm in an active dampening field, all right.* But the interesting thing about antimagic devices was that balancing the magic and its counteragent was key. If the balance was even slightly off, the dampening field would collapse and magic would force its way through.

Based on that principle, Evelina had formed a theory that all she had to do was double up the antimagic charge, and it would cancel itself out. Then her power would be free.

She popped the top off the vial and shook the salt into the palm of her hand, having to pound a little to get it free of the container. When she was done, there was barely a pinch of the compound to work with. Nevertheless, the powerful substance began to itch as soon as it touched her flesh. Carefully, she tucked half the salt under each bracelet, pushing the silver rings up onto her forearms to hold the salt tight against her skin, where the compound could react to her Blood. It was a primitive solution, but if she had calculated correctly, even with her bracelets deactivated, the combined charge of the salt inside the bracelet and beneath it should tip the balance of the energy fields and render them useless. Providing, of course, that her theory was correct.

The effect was immediate, as if someone had pulled a bag over her head, suffocating her. The next sensation was nauseating dizziness, filled with the prickling echoes of pain, like a pale version of the agony that had stopped her at the college gate. The skin where the salt touched began to burn, reacting violently against her Blood. As she began to sweat, Evelina thought she would vomit, but just as suddenly the sensation faded, leaving her head clear and her heart hammering. She sucked in a breath, trying to control the reaction, but then she smiled. The dampening fields weren't working anymore. But in the next moment she realized that was only partially true. Only part of her power had forced its way past the barrier. Her darker magic was alert, active, and it was—for want of a better description—enthusiastic. It approved of being left in charge. It stretched itself like a big cat and began looking about for something to eat. *Dear God, I don't like this.*

But there was nothing to do but get on with the job at hand. Evelina shoved the empty vial into her pocket and inched along, listening for signs of life. The place seemed empty, but surely there had to be nurses or doctors to watch over their experiments. She paused to peer into the window of the first doorway. A single light had been left on, but low. There was a steel table with something on it, but a sheet covered whatever was there. The next table held something that wasn't human, and she wasn't sure it ever had been. It might have once been a dog. She turned away, breathing hard, her hand slippery on the butt of the pistol.

Many of the doors had a card tucked into the corner of the tiny windows. She drew close to one, bending to read it because she didn't really want to touch anything she didn't have to. It read: *Subject 21-14, released 1889-09-27.* She peered inside the window, but the room was dark and empty. *Released a week ago? Released? Where to?* Dozens of the doors said the same thing, only the number of the subject changing. *It doesn't make sense.*

Something in the cell across the corridor lunged against the door with a savage scream, as if it sensed her there. Startled witless, she staggered against the opposite wall, torn between fear of what was behind that door, and what might respond to those cries. *No, no, no, be quiet!*

She looked frantically at the number of doors left to go, and then started moving as fast as she could, not stopping to do more than glance at each one. Tears streamed down her face; she was so hurt by the act of witnessing such pain that she couldn't imagine the nightmare of living through what she saw.

None of the subjects left in the laboratories were escaping. There were bodies, but they were all strapped to hospital beds, unconscious or bandaged or trapped in steel machines she didn't understand. Sometimes the machines seemed to be erupting from the flesh, bolts and ends of steel rods poking through necrotic skin. She saw one woman suspended in a globe of glass, her body eviscerated but for an aether distiller where her heart should have been, her mouth open in an endless scream. The dark power in Evelina stirred, wanting to destroy something that was so obviously wrong.

A hand fell on her shoulder, and she realized she had been hypnotized by the horror. But she did not turn immediately, instead taking her time to grip the gun and wheel in such a way that the muzzle landed against the man's diaphragm. At the same time she raised a hand, releasing a bolt of power to knock him out as she had the guard at the door. She heard him suck in a surprised breath, but he just blinked.

"How unfortunate," she said. *Now I have to shoot him.*

But as the nose of the gun bumped against him, it clicked against metal. Not a button or a breastplate, but something muffled by the cloth of his coat. Surprised, she looked up into a broad, bald-headed face with cold hazel eyes. "Don't try to appeal to my heart," the man said in a dull tone, but beneath that flatness was a void that made her flesh crawl. "They took mine out years ago."

She shrank back, wanting space between them, but then he pushed her so that her head cracked against the wall. Stars made her reel, blocking sight and sound and dragging nausea upward in a rush. Evelina shook her head to clear it, the room reeling as the man bore down on her. Evelina made a shuddering moan, nearly losing her grip on the gun. "Stay away from me."

"No," he said simply, reaching for her.

She dodged, trying to skitter around him so she could run the other way. He laughed and pushed her again, and she smashed against the door with the thing lunging at the other side. For an instant she could feel the vibration as the cell's occupant leaped for her, claws scrabbling on the glass just behind her head. *Claws?* Was this the savage hound Nellie Reynolds had described?

And then the guard grabbed her wrist in a grip meant to crush bone to dust. She cried out, wrenching herself free and squeezing the trigger all at once. The sound of the gunshot ricocheted through the empty hallway. Unexpectedly, he let go and she staggered back, her momentum sending her flying toward the door where she'd entered the building. The man toppled, hitting the floor, and Evelina collapsed against the wall, revolted by what she'd done.

The bullet had entered beneath the soft underside of his chin and blown away the top of his head—and not even a mechanical heart could help that. Skull, brain, and blood splattered the stone floor and the hygienic white of the walls. The creature battering against its cell door began to howl. Evelina retched, splattering the hem of her skirts, while the thing across the way stopped howling and began to snuffle at the crack under the door.

The darkness in her, already alert, uncoiled at the scent of the dying man's energy. It—she—didn't have the power to take life from the living, but when a body surrendered it, she was free to feed. A shudder of expectation went through her, leaving her weak enough that she slumped against the wall. It had been so long since she'd drunk down life. The hunger rose, insistent and oblivious. Her other powers were dampened, unable to resist. Evelina sucked in breath after breath, unable to get enough air.

And then the hunger lunged. A taste that wasn't a taste filled her senses—something spun of honey and champagne and sunlight. Or it should have been, except the man's life tasted stale. Disappointment wrenched her, but she quickly forgot it as the rush of energy hit her, drawing a noise of relief from her throat. It was a primitive, animal response. She'd been so *hungry,* but now she was strong again, strong in a way that she hadn't been since giving up her studies with Magnus.

It all happened in a matter of seconds, though it seemed to go on for a lifetime. A sense of warning opened her eyes and she drew herself up to see the other guards rushing down the hall, drawn by the sound of the shot.

For a fleeting moment, that reptilian hunger wanted them, too, but then Holmes burst through the stillroom door. "Evelina!"

She plunged after him, diving past the shelves of glassware and into the open air. The next instant, the moonlit, crystalline night soared above her. Evelina could feel the power of the other magic users crackle through the air. She stopped running, suddenly caught in the ecstasy of that much magic. She'd always worked alone, or with Nick, but never like this—part of an enormous web driven by a single purpose.

Holmes grabbed her arm and dragged her toward the

dairy barn. Snapped back to herself, she heard the thunder of the guards' heavy boots. A shot fired, alerting the others who were watching the yard. Deep, angry shouts filled the night.

Part of Evelina was aware that this was a problem, that she needed to get to cover so Holmes could use his rifle and protect them both. But the rest of her was still drunk with magic. The guardsmen were nothing; she'd already proven that. She swept her arm, using the ambient power to knock their pursuers flat to the ground. With an oath, Holmes grabbed her by the scruff and dragged her away before the men got up again. Shots whizzed past them, and Holmes turned to fire, but she barely noticed, because the magic of the others had entranced her again.

Evelina flickered in and out of awareness, feeling her feet run and her hands dig into the cold earth as she scrambled across the ruins and up the hill—but her consciousness strained to join the spell. *They're raising the devas. I need to help them.* She wondered what the spirits in these parts would do. Folk magic depended on the devas agreeing to help, but the moors might not be easy to convince.

Whenever she lagged, her uncle pushed her on. Holmes wouldn't let her rest until they'd reached the cairn at the top of the hill. She knew he'd chosen it as a good place to shoot from, but she could feel the ancient power radiating from the stones. It had been a place of worship for the first men who walked these lands, and old magic clung to it still. Holmes shoved her down and she went to her hands and knees, her awareness digging deep into the roots of the rock.

Below, she could see a few dozen devas had answered the call and were flickering over the laboratory buildings. The guards milled about in confusion, unable to pursue Evelina and Holmes, and unable to tell that it was a cloud of tiny spirits that turned them back every time they tried. But that wasn't enough to cleanse the labs from the face of the earth.

And then Evelina understood why they needed the dark magic—and it wasn't just so she could reconnoiter the cells. Dark magic led to death magic, and right then they needed the power of the dead. She dove deep into the land, calling for the presence of those first men who had left behind the cairns and barrows, the stone circles, and the huts that dotted the untamed land. Energy lingered there like the notes of half-remembered song, more a mood than a memory, but her summons roused it from sleep.

And it came, rising like a gray cloud in her mind's eye, sinuous as mist. It was made of voices too far away to hear clearly, snatches of firelight and stories no one recalled. It was what was left of the daily hopes and fears of vanished people. The fog of memory clung close to the land and roiled down the webwork of magic, beyond the gunpowder mill and the guards in the yard to surround the building like a smothering cloak. Evelina rose to her knees to see it shimmering silver in the moonlight, hiding the atrocities in the laboratory like a sheet thrown over one of its victims.

And then her power flexed, a visceral twist of anger, and the cloak squeezed. The other magic users, their power linked to hers by the web, moved with her like the fingers of a giant fist.

The building split with a huge cracking noise, as if a giant egg had smashed. Whatever spells had been guarding it— the magic wrung out of those practitioners too frightened to fight—gave way like wet paper. And then the devas rushed into the breach. In the space between one breath and the next, flames erupted from the roof.

A frantic lowing of cows rose up, but the barn was too far away to catch fire. The living humans—those who could run—fled. Or tried to. The devas of the moors, working by a code only they understood, only let every third man free of the flames. The pitiable creatures in the cells perished, their lives no more than sparks in an updraft, too spent to even stir Evelina's hunger.

Except one. Evelina gasped as something bounded from the flames. It ran on all fours and was larger than a calf, but it moved with the easy glide of a hunter. *Was that the creature behind the door?* Its eyes flashed red in the firelight, throwing sparks into the blackness. It was only visible for an instant, an outline against the flames, and then the magic twisted again. The creature disappeared from view, as if somehow the dark spirits of the moor had swallowed it whole. Evelina shook her head, trying to clear it. Whether the devas had caught the creature or it had escaped was impossible to tell, and Evelina was too exhausted to pursue it right then.

Lying atop the cairn, Holmes watched it all without twitching a muscle. Evelina studied his face. There was much in the spirit realm that he couldn't see, but the resulting destruction was plain. And apparently fascinating. He was watching, cataloguing, and filing away every detail, barely taking time out to breathe.

He dealt in fact, not magic. He'd done his job protecting her, and no doubt he'd helped destroy the laboratories because they contravened his sense of justice. For him, the adventure was—if not simple—at least plain in its objectives and result.

Not so for her. She shifted her gaze from her uncle to the wreckage below. She'd felt the wrench that had cracked the building. Her power still rang with it like a vibrating bell, thrilling her with victory and whispering of what chaos might come next. *More. This is only a taste.*

The thought appalled her, and she couldn't watch another moment. Evelina got to her feet in silence, not wanting to disturb the mesmerized Holmes. She needed to turn away, to put some distance between herself and the destruction she had wrought. She needed control.

"We must locate Madam Thalassa," Holmes said.

Evelina could feel the woman's magic, as bright as her own was dark. "I know exactly where she is."

"She will take you to a safe place. It's been arranged. When the search for you has died down, I will come fetch you." He started to rise.

"In a minute," she said quickly. "Let me rest."

He subsided, returning his attention to the scene below. *She will take me to a safe place?* Evelina wasn't sure there was such a thing. Not until it was possible to run away from herself.

I shot a man. And then I ate him. The notion made her insides swirl dangerously, and she desperately wanted the solace of darkness and open air. She walked a little distance across the stony top of the hill, and then a little more—away from every other presence. It was too dark to go far, but the moon above and the glow of the fire reduced the chances of breaking her neck. She could still see Holmes, the white of his shirt a smudge where he lay. Then she began reeling in her senses, shutting off the connection between herself and the magic, herself and the earth, herself and anything beyond the privacy of her own mind. Evelina wiped her brow on her sleeve, the solitude making her feel a tiny bit better.

I am in control. She repeated it to herself a dozen times, blocking even the rustle of the nighttime insects from her perception. It felt good, like pulling the covers over her head and falling into a deep sleep. The vibrating inside her stopped, the excitement unwinding like a spring slowly robbed of tension. She loosened her bracelets, dusting away the remains of the salt. It was spent now, though her skin was raw where it had touched her.

But then something stirred behind her, just loud enough that it broke through her shield. A sour-smelling hand clamped over her mouth and a knife pricked against her throat, tickling her just below the ear. "Well done, kitten."

She knew the voice all too well. Rage seared white hot, making her struggle until the knife dug in, pricking through skin.

"Oh no, you don't," whispered Magnus. "If you ever had any doubt that you were mine, just think about this night's work. I felt you leave your hiding place like a ripple on a pond, but I would have had to be deaf and blind to miss you here."

Evelina growled from behind his stifling fingers.

"Oh, come now. You'd never have put on such a show unless you wanted me to catch you. Surely you didn't think I would leave you forever?"

He pressed his lips close to her ear. "I'm sure by now you've learned I cannot die."

CHAPTER THIRTY-THREE

Southwest Coast, October 5, 1889

SIABARTHA CASTLE

7:25 a.m. Saturday

WIND WHIPPED THROUGH EVELINA'S HAIR AS SHE RAISED her head above the rim of the basket of Magnus's balloon. Above, the black silk globe rose like a storm cloud, captured in a net of silver rope. Below, the southern coast spread in jagged beauty, the green fingers of land lost among mists of salt and spray. They'd flown through the night and now morning spread with grim purpose beneath a steel-gray sky.

Fear slammed her, making her knuckles white on the wicker rim. It wasn't the height, but the fact that she had no idea where they were going—or how she would ever get back. "Where are we?"

"Tintagel is that way," Magnus remarked with a wave of one gloved hand. "All crashing waves and Arthurian claptrap. The property values on places like that are astronomical and for what? Useless unless you want to attract day trippers."

He raised his voice to be heard over the wind, the quartet of steam-driven propellers, and the rush of the pumps converting aether distillate into the lifting gas that kept the balloon afloat. And somewhere in all that machinery was a navigation system that had kept the craft on course despite the dark. The black balloon was clearly designed for nocturnal journeys—and with Magnus that meant nothing good.

Evelina fell back into a slump at the bottom of the basket

and buried her face in her hands. A new chain rattled where Magnus had strung her bracelets together, turning them into handcuffs. She'd had to turn the key in the bracelets a few hours ago when she'd felt the first tingles of pain that signaled their reactivation. It hadn't been a dignified operation with her hands bound together and the key on a chain around her neck, and in the end Magnus had been obliged to help her—one captor assisting with the bonds of her other.

Vertigo assaulted Evelina, a mix of fatigue and the pure insanity of her predicament. It was too much after what she'd seen the night before. It was too much ever, because it was Magnus.

"Oh, come now, kitten. Surely this is better than returning to the Gold King's thrall. I heard what you did for your pirate, sacrificing your freedom for the *Red Jack*. Very touching, if somewhat pointless."

That made her lift her head to glare. She was about to protest that Nick had lived, despite everything, but stopped herself just in time. Magnus had baited a trap for Nick once; she wasn't going to help him do it again. The longer he believed Nick dead, the better. "I made my choice and you weren't it."

"No," Magnus said with a flash of irritation. "And that poses a logistical problem for me. I was prepared to wait for you to come to your senses, but things became a little more urgent now that Serafina is gone."

Serafina, the insane, murderous star of his automaton ballet. Anna's vessel. Even the memory of her reawakened the pain of her knife sliding through Evelina's body. "Gone? Truly gone? Or is she as hard to kill as you are?"

"Alas, she was completely destroyed, as were all of my creations. Otherwise," Magnus said with a twist of a smile, "I would have far less need of you."

What does that mean? she wondered. *And what does he know about Anna?* But Magnus had busied himself with the pumps, adjusting the dial on the silver canisters lashed upright in the middle of the basket. That was the difficulty of being spirited away by air. Killing one's abductor wasn't a good response, unless one knew how to fly the wretched contraption—which she didn't.

"I see from the burns beneath your bracelets that you were playing with dangerous chemicals. What was it?" he asked in that professorial voice he had used so often as her teacher.

Instinctively, she cradled her hands against her chest and wondered how to respond. Was it better to pretend to be his student again? Or was it time now to make it plain that she was done listening to him? She compromised. "I overbalanced the dampening fields in the laboratories."

"Using an elemental salt, no doubt? Clever, but very dangerous. Most of the available substances are utterly toxic. Next time, use a few drops of your blood to activate it, and don't touch the stuff with your bare skin." He flashed a derisive smile. "And if it's salt of sorrows, don't even breathe near it. If that was what you used, be glad you didn't have more than a pinch."

Somehow, he knew exactly what she'd done. Evelina crouched against the wicker of the basket, misery welling up inside her. Magnus was worse than the bracelets. They only reacted to what she did. The sorcerer detected where she'd been and half the time what she was thinking.

The balloon began to dip, drifting downward. Gripping the woven wicker rim above her, Evelina ventured another peek at the ground. The cold sea wind raked her face, blurring her vision with tears. Magnus was wearing goggles, she was not.

But she could see well enough to feel a swell of panic. Spears of dark rock thrust out of the water, their bases disappearing into a churn of waves. A scatter of whitewashed houses clung to the base of the cliffs, seeming to huddle for shelter from the open water beyond. There was no sheltering cove here, no harbor or breakwater to spare the shore. There was only a finger of barren land thrusting into the sea and at its crest, a castle of bare black stone.

"Was it going for a song?" Evelina asked dryly. "Not many day trippers here, I suspect."

Magnus laughed. Whatever his legion of other faults—

including a gruesome sort of insanity—he did have a sense of humor. "Ah, no, this is an old pied-à-terre from former days. I had been living in the Black Kingdom, but grew tired of endless caves. At least this place has windows. It may be inconvenient and drafty as anything, but it's wonderfully private. We'll be quite cozy here until this nonsense with the Steam Council blows over. We can catch up on your lessons."

Evelina cursed under her breath, yanking in futile frustration at the chain that bound her hands. Magnus's instruction had proven a double-edged sword. He was the only creature she knew who could teach her about her own power, but at the same time he had used her curiosity against her, cursing her with a sorcerer's hunger. The more time she spent around Magnus, the less she could count on remaining Evelina Cooper. That, more than anything else, spurred an overwhelming motivation to get away.

Magnus deftly adjusted a lever that angled the propellers a degree. The balloon shifted slightly west, rotating lazily until it caught the wind. They were close to the castle now. The style of it was ancient—a misshapen tower of dull black stone surrounded by a high wall on three sides. But the most striking feature was the front edge of the tower, for it thrust out over the cliff, leaving a sheer drop to the thrashing ocean below.

The basket cleared the edge of the wall, and Evelina could see the details of a bailey—an enclosed yard where once there might have been stables, blacksmiths, chicken coops, and all the other necessaries that made up a community. Now the auxiliary buildings were deserted, the wood crumbling and bleached gray by the chill salt air. There were a handful of servants standing by to assist with the balloon, but they looked like they wanted to bolt at the first opportunity. *This is the absolute end of the earth.* And from what she could see, it hadn't ended well.

Magnus turned the pumps down another notch, and opened a vent to let the aether escape. The balloon began to subside onto the ground with a graceful sigh. Then he tossed a series of ropes over the edge of the basket and the waiting men caught them, hauling the craft down until Evelina felt the bottom bump the ground.

"There you are, kitten, welcome to Siabartha."

She schooled her face, pretending not to recognize the name. It was a word in the old tongue, and something to do with the netherworld. *Trust Magnus to go for the traditionally sinister.* There was no way she was giving him the satisfaction of seeing her spooked any more than he already had.

She stayed put while Magnus swung his long legs over the edge of the basket, a superstitious dread taking her. She didn't want to set foot in his castle, as if stepping there meant that she could never leave. But he held out his gloved hand, and, bound as she was, she had no choice but to take it and let him help her over the edge. And yet even his touch made her shudder.

"This way," he said gallantly, taking her elbow to escort her toward the castle. "Once you've earned the privilege, you may feel free to roam the grounds as you please. The views are better from the tower, but there is no substitute for a walk in the fresh air."

Evelina looked around at the dingy stone and scruffy grass. The most interesting feature was an old well that looked as if it was still in use. "And outside the walls?"

"Not much to see for a good fifty miles, although there is a certain charm about the place in spring."

"In other words, no need for locks when there is no place to go."

He gave her a tight smile. "For now you will be escorted. The balloon and stables are off limits and you will find them guarded by spells. But when you learn what I wish, you will have the power to leave. I've been patient with you in the past, but now it's time you understand that when you do as you're told, we both get what we want."

I don't do what I'm told. Not by you. "I want to go home."

"And so you shall, when I deem you ready."

That statement horrified her worse than anything else. *Who will I be by then? A mad thing, like your dancing doll?*

He signaled to one of the servants to open the arched,

iron-bound door of the castle. From the way the man dug in his heels, the door was as heavy as it looked. Magnus strode in, grabbing a torch from its holder near the door. Evelina trailed after, agape.

It was a great hall, straight out of *Ivanhoe,* with high beams and a vast oak table dominating the room. Iron chandeliers hung from the ceiling on chains, ancient wax clinging to the black metal. Shields hung against the wall, though a few had toppled to the floor, but the dust was so thick Evelina couldn't see the faded designs painted there.

"It's been a while since I entertained," Magnus said dryly. "It's intolerably cold down here and impossible to heat. We live upstairs."

With that, he led her through the hall and up a long, winding staircase that reminded her of the church tower she'd climbed with Nick. Arrow slits pierced the stone walls at every turn, letting in light and a brisk ocean breeze. It was almost colder here than it had been in the balloon, as if the black stone had soaked up the cold for centuries, never letting any of it go.

Evelina was feeling her muscles by the time Magnus stopped at a landing near the top of the tower. Three doors clustered there. "My rooms, your room, our workroom," he said, indicating each in turn.

Frozen through, Evelina grasped the handle of the door meant to be hers, and tried it. It opened easily, and she looked in. The first thing she saw was a fire. It drew her forward like a magnet and she crouched before it, holding out her frigid hands.

Magnus followed after her. "I hope you like your accommodations."

Evelina cast a glance around the room. It had a certain medieval splendor, with a velvet-draped canopy over the bed, tapestries along the walls, and a scatter of brass-bound chests. At least it looked clean.

"There are fresh clothes in the chests, as well as everything you will require for your studies. There is the workroom, of course, but I thought you might prefer a few things here to practice with. Your meals and hot water will be brought to you."

"Very thoughtful." Thawed enough to tear herself away from the fire's warmth, she rose and held out her hands. "Are you going to keep me bound?"

Magnus flicked his fingers and the chain fell away, clanking at the floor near Evelina's feet. "No need now that we're here."

They studied each other in silence for a moment, the air tense between them. He'd won her trust once, but it wouldn't happen again. And yet they'd shared magic together. That created a familiarity that would never be brushed aside.

"How did you survive the air battle?" she asked.

"I'm very hard to kill."

He'd died once before, that she knew of. That had left him looking older. Now he looked ill, the aquiline face thinner, his olive complexion pasty. And while certain things were the same—he was still the tall, slender, and elegant figure she remembered—not everything remained. Where there had been a few silver hairs at his temples, his dark hair and goatee were now salted with white. His depthless eyes were still intense, but they were lined and circled where the flesh had sunk against his skull. This time, it had been harder to come back. And there was something wrong—she wanted to use the word *unstable*—about his face. It was as if whatever measures he'd taken hadn't quite worked. Worst of all, he didn't smell quite right.

"How do you do it?" she asked, her voice gone hoarse with cold and revulsion. "Death magic?"

"Yes."

Surprise arrowed through her. He'd always danced around the question of his sorcery before. "That's blunt."

"I've given up being coy with you. You saw what Serafina was to me."

Evelina nodded. The mad doll had sucked the life out of her admirers and then fed it to Magnus. It had left the automaton—who was at least in part Anna—hungry, confused, and ultimately homicidal. "She did your hunting for you."

"I thought to free myself of the burden. After you have lived as long as I have, stalking the unwary becomes a chore."

Outrage twisted through her, drawing a strangled sound from her throat. How like Magnus, to reduce everything to its amusement value. "Don't your victims deserve personal attention? Or is that just a bourgeois shopkeeper's view?"

"Such sharp little claws." Then he gave a short, mirthless laugh. "But perhaps you're right. Perhaps the universe in its infinite wisdom is punishing me for my neglect, for in creating Serafina, I made a tactical error. I put too much of myself in her."

He had split off a piece of his own life force to make Serafina live, but she wasn't sure that was what he meant. "How so?"

"Now I discover I seem to have sacrificed much of my ability to feed. Not something I anticipated, let me assure you. And in my weakness I can't breathe life into another such child of my genius. I have restored myself as best I can, but I must solve this conundrum immediately."

"How?" she asked, but the word had barely left her lips before his eyes told her the answer.

"My dear Evelina, that's where you shall play a role. You, my little cat, will learn to bring me my prey."

And like that, her hunger woke, a flare of yellow eyes in the dark privacy of her soul. Eagerness and disgust hit her with a hurricane's force. She remembered the taste of the guard's life sliding inside her. She flinched as if Magnus had slapped her. "Dear God."

"It is a small service, given the immense amount that I've shared with you. That I *will* share with you in our time together."

"No!" She pushed him away with both hands and kicked the chain at her feet into the fire. "You may think you have me, but I will fight you for every inch."

Magnus staggered back a step, the angry flare of his eyes giving the lie to his amused smile. "You need not stay forever. Just long enough to allow me to make a new little helper of my own."

"And what would be left of me by then?" Evelina snarled.

"Your true face," he said. "As long as I've known you, my dear, you've been an event waiting to occur."

And with that, he left her, locking the door with a sound like doom.

CHAPTER THIRTY-FOUR

Cornwall, October 5, 1889

KILLINCAIRN

1:17 p.m. Saturday

NEXT TIME NICK CHOSE A SECRET HIDEOUT, IT WAS GOING TO have more amenities, like a convenient train station—preferably one with a decent alehouse nearby. Unfortunately, locations where one could hide the hangar for a steamspinner tended to be off the beaten path. Far, far off, where not even the customs boats watched for smugglers.

The railway stop closest to the tiny fishing village of Killincairn was at Falmouth, and from there it was horseback all the way south along the coast. Nick had missed horses, but this was a long ride in the pelting autumn rain, and in Cornwall that meant bucketing torrents. Nick's coat was soaked right through. He'd stopped to buy some extra shirts with the money the Schoolmaster had loaned him, but he was fairly sure his bags were sodden, too.

He went back to his daydream about the alehouse, because fantasy was more bearable. His perfect tavern would have that good brown stout he'd had at the place a few miles back, and decent bread and cheese—the sharp, crumbly white stuff that went with hot pickled relish. And there would be an inn, with a warm bed and a real wood fire. Oh, yes, a good night's sleep felt just the thing. Not that he was complaining. At least he was free, even if his backside did hurt because he hadn't ridden for a year.

Evelina would be in that bed.

But he couldn't afford to think of her right then, or he would think of nothing else. She was the key to his happiness, but it was as if that key was hidden inside a Chinese puzzle box. He could hold it, but he couldn't get to it without solving the riddle of how to free her from the complex prison Keating had created for everyone she cared about. And if everyone Evelina loved wasn't free, she wouldn't be, either. Loving that way was her curse and blessing, and therefore Nick's.

Of course, puzzle boxes could be solved two ways—with a clever mind, or with a hammer. Nick was starting to vote for the latter.

Nick pulled the horse up and looked toward the horizon. He was fairly sure he was near the road to Killincairn, but he couldn't see the path. Rain pattered off his hat brim, obscuring the view he might have had if it wasn't all buried in a thick gray mist.

Where the blazes am I? He sat pondering a moment, the rain chattering around him. He felt like the last living man in the Empire. He'd seen no other travelers for miles. No birds peeped, but he could hear the ocean in its constant, restless churn. The air was fresh and salty and Nick sucked it in, feeling every lungful expel another particle of Manufactory Three's soot. The mare shifted restlessly beneath him, and he absently patted its neck. *I should have stayed in the last town and waited out the storm.* But he wasn't able to do the sensible thing. Not when his ship and crew were so close—or at least he hoped they were. The closer he'd got to Killincairn, the greater the magnetic pull to reach it. It strained on him now, as if his breastbone might crack if he didn't keep moving.

Niccolo? He felt the touch of Athena's mind, warm and familiar. Her metal cube was in his saddlebag, no doubt as wet as everything else. She'd been quiet for the last several miles, as if the rain had depressed her, too. *Why have we stopped?*

"I'm looking for the path."

Do you have a map?

Nick felt the twinge of her impatience, but answered reasonably. "It's too wet for a map."

Is there someone you can ask for directions?

Now he was getting irritated. "I'm not lost. I just don't know where I am. There's a difference."

There was a beat of disgusted silence. *Odysseus said the same thing, and look how long it took him to get home.*

Nick tried to think of a smart rejoinder, but he was just too damp and cold. But as he sat hunched on his mount, beneath the smells of horse and sea he caught something else—a sharp odor almost like mint. *Aether.* And the only way aether was detectable at sea level was if something brought it there—like the propulsion system of a steamspinner.

Nick straightened in the saddle, his spirits revived by an urgent excitement. The horse pricked its ears and whuffled a question. "I need to follow that scent," Nick answered. "There's oats in it for you if you find the road."

He wasn't sure it had understood. He had the power to speak to birds, but other animals were hit and miss on an individual basis. Nevertheless, the horse started forward at a determined walk. Nick loosed the reins and let it go. It couldn't do worse than he would in this fog.

At least someone has a sense of direction.

"You're the magical navigation device, not me."

I fly winds, not mud trails. And I would use a map.

"If you were human, you'd require three porters, two maids, and a Spaniel in a diamond collar just to visit the dressmakers."

I've had thousands of years to develop a sense of occasion.

They found the turnoff a quarter mile farther on. The path snaked over hill and dale, winding toward a cliff overlooking the sea. The hangar sat on the cliff's edge, the doors ready to open and launch the ship to fly free over the waves. The last time Nick had seen the steamspinner, it had only been half built and paid for with gold he'd stolen—along with Athena—from Jasper Keating. He was assuming a lot, he told himself sternly, thinking he'd found his ship and his crew. There were other pirates who might have found his hideout and made it their own. A year was a long time in his world. But Nick couldn't hang on to his caution and felt the bloom of hope anyhow.

The ground rose slightly, the veils of mist parting enough to make out the tough green grass and red earth. The ruins of an old tin mine rose like ghosts around him, walls and chimneys tumbling down the hill to the cliff. Nick noticed a dark shape detach itself from a crumbled wall in one enormous flap of wings.

Fair winds, Captain Niccolo, said Gwilliam. *You've come home.*

"Fair winds, Lord Rook," Nick cried, and suddenly everything was all right because a friend had been there to greet him. "You've come a long way from London."

Because you would come as surely as geese fly in autumn.

Fair winds, Gwilliam, said Athena.

The ash rook spread his wings wide, as if in salutation. *The lady of the skies has returned!*

And then giant black birds erupted from all sides, rising into the mist in a rough-voiced swirl of black. Ash rooks were warriors, armed with sharp beaks and talons, and Nick felt his back prickle at the rush of feathers as dozens of the flock whooshed overhead, streaming toward Killincairn.

The mare shied, rearing up, and then Nick was working to stay on his mount. The horse landed, prancing in a tight circle until he got it back under control. When he finally did, and pointed its head the right way again, he saw a lone figure standing at the top of the road, right where it forked— one path toward Killincairn, the other toward the hangar. The figure stood with his feet apart, arms folded, the hood of his long coat pulled over his face. But Nick didn't need to see the man's features; the coat was enough. It was covered with random pieces of metal sewn over every inch of the garment. It was wealth in a world where the steam barons controlled access to anything that might be used to build a power source, and it was protection against damn near everything. Nick knew several of those metal pieces bore the mark where bullets had been stopped cold.

Ah! said Athena. She did not need to say more.

Despite himself, Nick started to laugh and urged the horse

into a trot. It was as if the long months in Manufactory Three suddenly ceased to matter. He'd made it here now, where he was supposed to be. There was something left of his old life he could reclaim.

The figure didn't move a muscle until he was almost on top of him, and then he raised one hand and pushed back his hood. Striker's spiky brown hair lay plastered against his skull, and Nick wondered how long he'd been there if that damned coat was soaked through.

"Where the feckin' hell have you been?" Striker snapped, breathing a little too hard. His second in command narrowed his eyes angrily, glaring at Nick.

"Nice to see you, too," Nick said calmly, doing his best not to grin. It was just so damned good to see his friend's grumpy face. "I knew you were hard to kill."

Striker cut him off, his voice tight. "I made it. So did Digby, Beadle, Poole. Royce, Knaur, and Smith didn't."

That sobered Nick, swift as a knife cut. "Damn it all, Smith was just a boy."

Striker didn't respond, but then he'd probably seen the lad die. "Where were you?"

Nick wiped a trickle of rain that was now leaking through his hat. "When I parted company with the ship, I must have gone down a mile or two from the rest of you. Landed in the wrong place, apparently, because patrols picked me up. Before I knew it, the Scarlet King had me taking the waters in one of his spas."

Striker rolled his eyes, playing along with his sarcasm. "I knew you were just larking about out there while I was stuck finishing your damned ship."

Nick swung out of the saddle, stifling a groan as he moved. He stood facing Striker a moment. The man was still scowling. Taking a gamble, Nick grabbed him anyway in a rough embrace.

Striker tensed, as if not sure what to do, and then started to laugh. It was a rare, fat sound that had every bit as much power as his glare. Nick laughed, too, until he found himself in a bone-crushing bear hug that threatened to crack every rib. He made a muffled wheeze and Striker let him go, pounding him on the shoulder.

"Damn your eyes, it's good to see you, Nick!" Striker looked away for a moment, eyebrows drawn sharply together while he swallowed. Then he took a quick breath and carried on in a voice almost like his own. "You need to see your steamspinner. She's a beauty like no other. Floats like a whisper and is deadly as a falcon."

"I know Athena is eager to see it."

Striker's eyes widened. "She's here?"

Nick patted the saddlebag as he slung it over his shoulder, unable to stop a grin.

"Then let's get to it." Without another word, Striker started leading him down the path toward the hangar. Nick followed with the long-suffering mare.

"The plans worked?" Nick had stolen the drawings for the ship from Dr. Magnus. They had been the inspiration that had launched Nick and Striker on their piratical careers.

"Perfectly. I added more aether pumps so the ship could run without Athena," Striker said.

"And you've flown her?"

"Across oceans," Striker replied, pride shading his words. "Last spring we went to Devil's Island with the Black boys and snatched Captain Roberts out from under the Frenchies' noses. That was something, but took a wee bit longer than expected. There were repairs to be made. Didn't get back into these airstreams until late summer."

Nick's jaw drifted open before he snapped it shut again. "Captain Roberts?" He was a pirate's pirate, a storybook blend of showmanship and guile.

Striker gave a wordless shrug, his eyes rolling skyward. "I couldn't say no to his crew. They missed the bugger. I'm not sure why. Now he keeps popping up like a weed, wanting to share a drink. Just because you rescue someone from certain death, it doesn't mean you want to be friends. We just got rid of him again last week."

"Is he up to something?"

"He's a bloody pirate. What do you think?"

Nick coughed to stifle a laugh. "You've got some tales to

tell me." Devil's Island was a French prison off the coast of South America, believed to be impenetrable. Striker must have worked some magic of his own to manage that rescue.

"There's a tale or two. Spent the last three months picking off supply ships coming in from the Continent and put away a nice little stockpile of spare parts. The air traffic has gone wild."

Nick's stomach tightened. For every one the pirates captured, dozens more made it to their destination to build the barons' armies. It wasn't good news. "Have you done any business with the rebels?" The Schoolmaster hadn't seen Striker, but he wasn't the only possible contact.

"No. Since we returned from the Americas, we've been working the supply routes. We haven't been into London. There've been more patrols since the air battle that destroyed the *Jack*. Not as easy just to slip in and make some deals. I stopped in Truro and ran into old Harvey. He says all the pirates are complaining about the London situation. We'll have to start shipping cargo in by boat, but that takes some organizing."

"I heard about the air patrols," Nick said. Then he noticed Striker was moving with a slight limp. "Hurt yourself?"

"When the *Red Jack* went down. It's the damned weather here. I think my joints are starting to rust."

"Were the others hurt?"

Striker's dark face twisted in a fond grimace, not quite admitting that he liked his crewmates. "Digby had to get a new fiddle, but they're all healthy enough. Poole is one sharp lad."

"You've been in charge?"

"As much as anyone. Call me the keeper of the madhouse."

They were drawing close to the hangar, which looked like an enormous barn. The ash rooks had gathered there, roosting under the eaves like a welcoming committee. "When did they arrive?" Nick asked.

"They turned up outside the *Athena* about a week ago, squawking their heads off. Of course no one knew what they wanted, but eventually we gave in and followed them. They led us back here."

"I crossed paths with Gwilliam in London."

"That fits. He must have guessed you would be on your way back."

As surely as geese fly in autumn. Then Nick saw a small wirehaired dog chasing one of the smaller rooks and yapping at the top of its lungs. The rook was obviously in control, sailing in lazy circles just out of the mutt's reach. The dog didn't put weight on one of its hind legs, so the best it could manage was a determined bounce in the direction of its tormentor. But when the dog saw Striker, it left off at once and dashed toward him with a gamboling run. It bashed into his ankle with tail-churning enthusiasm.

"This is Bacon," Striker said, lifting the mutt under one arm. "He's decided to stay with the crew." The man squinted at Nick, as if defying him to point out how the Striker everyone knew was hardly the cute dog type.

Meanwhile, Bacon looked at Nick with bright black eyes, panting enthusiastically. Hiding his amusement, Nick presented his hand for a sniff. "Welcome aboard."

They'd reached the hangar and Striker pulled open one of the double doors with his dog-free hand. A young lad poked his head out, and Striker gave him orders to take the horse to the inn at Killincairn and see that it was well tended. The boy left with a curious glance at Nick.

"The barmaid's boy," Striker explained. "He likes the engines."

It wasn't dark inside, as Nick had expected, because the bay doors that opened over the sea were drawn back. Striker had designed the doors as overlapping panels that slid back into a circular aperture, the mouth exactly at the edge of the cliff so the pilot could dock the steamspinner directly inside.

"So what do you think?" Striker said, casting a sidelong glance at Nick.

But Nick had lost the power of speech. He began to walk forward, toward the open door and the prow. The ship was enormous, bigger than the *Red Jack,* and she was of an en-

tirely different design. Her shape was a sleek oval, with fins
that swept back like the wings of a stooping hawk. The gondola was snugged tight to the bottom of the balloon, forming a single unit. There was far less chance of an accidental
fall, which made him feel better about letting Bacon on
board. *And a much more comfortable place to bring Evelina.*

They walked in silence for the time it took to reach the
prow. Outside the bay doors, the iron-gray sea churned restlessly, the rain falling in relentless sheets. The wind caught
Nick's wet garments, making him shiver. But he forgot that
the moment he saw the name of the ship painted in graceful
lettering he knew for Digby's work: *Steamspinner Athena.*
They had re-created the same hawk figurehead that had
graced the *Red Jack.* A feeling of grief for his old vessel
mixed with the bittersweet sense that they'd done what they
could to keep it alive.

He felt Athena's emotions, a painful urgency to feel the
ship around her. Someone in the distant past had locked the
air deva inside the metal device that became her prison. It
was only as part of an airship that she could fly again.

"It's better than the plans," Nick said softly. "It's more
than we ever thought it would be."

"True," said Striker. "Like I said, we took her out a few
times, tried out some new crew. It takes a few more hands to
run this beauty. I've been training that boy you saw for an
assistant."

Nick could believe it. "How many does it sleep?"

"Twenty-six, if we want it. We ran with a crew of sixteen,
but we weren't manning all the gunports."

Sixteen was double what they had usually had on the
Jack. "Let's go aboard," Nick said, all eagerness.

Nick climbed the ladder into the belly of the steamspinner, the saddlebag carrying Athena slung over his shoulder.
He could feel the deva's mounting excitement as he as-
cended, doubling his own sense of awe. As he came through
the hatch and craned his neck to see all the way up to the top
of the balloon, he felt no bigger than a mouse. Although he
had known from the plans the exact measurements of the

vessel, it was only now, from this inside view, that he grasped just how enormous it was. Almost speechless, Nick fell into step with Striker, who gave him the penny tour.

"The engines are running because we're distilling aether," Striker explained, raising his voice to be heard over the rumble of the equipment. "Our supplies are down after the last voyage."

Unlike other dirigibles, steamspinners were of rigid construction, the inside of the balloon a honeycomb of gas pockets. Two walkways ran its length—one inside the keel, which traversed the domain of steam engines, propellers, and weapons lockers—and one to the axial corridor that accessed the aether systems. At several points, ladders ran between the two corridors. Up there, an unearthly lime-colored fog surrounded the four double-helix shapes of a complex glass apparatus. This was the system that separated aether from the surrounding atmosphere, converting it into a distillate that could be stored or pumped directly into the ship's balloon. From where Nick stood below, he could see the weird green light spearing down the vent shafts, giving the gloom of the walkways an underwater mood.

This is very fine, said Athena. *I can feel the power like a thunderstorm in waiting.*

Electric lights—a rarity in the gaslit world of the steam barons—hung from wires strung above the walkways. Both levels contained a series of gunports for aether cannons. In addition, there were trapdoors in the bottom of the balloon for bombing enemy sites below. Nick calculated the ship was capable of obliterating a small city entirely on its own. The thought sobered him more than he cared to admit. It was a beautiful vessel, but a deadly one—and he was its captain.

He walked forward with Striker, who had brought Bacon along. The dog scampered ahead with a curious, three-legged gait, stopping to sniff this and that as it waited for the slower men.

"This is the hatch into the gondola," Striker announced, opening an oak door and stepping through.

The engine noise dimmed the moment the door closed,

though it could still be heard like a distant heartbeat. A long corridor stretched ahead, doorways on either side. "Crew quarters?" Nick asked.

"Crew quarters here," Striker replied. "Mess hall and kitchen ahead."

Nick could feel Athena's impatience rising to a fever pitch. He waved at the saddlebag. "Let's go straight to the bridge. I assume accommodations were made?"

Striker gave a nod. "Absolutely."

So far they hadn't seen many crew members, but now several looked up as they passed. All were strangers, which Nick found disorienting. The *Red Jack*'s crew had been very small and closely bound, almost to the point of claustrophobia. A few greeted Striker, but he just waved and kept moving.

Are we nearly there? Athena asked, sounding querulous from inside the saddlebag.

In a minute, Nick replied silently, shifting the bag to a more comfortable spot on his shoulder.

Bacon bounced ahead, tail wagging like some canine propulsion system. From the mess, they passed through a map room and Nick caught a glimpse of the bridge ahead. Even from here he could see that tall windows wrapped around the entire prow of the gondola, the panoramic ocean view out the hangar doors utterly breathtaking. Athena must have caught the image, because if the deva in the metal cube could have eagerly hopped up and down, she would have.

Finally the map room gave way to the bridge. Here, all the readouts of the vessel's complex infrastructure were available at a glance. Beneath and between the tall windows was a jungle of brass and copper pipes, pressure gauges, dials, valves, and knobs. He recognized some of the equipment— one cluster to his right was surely for the helmsman. There was only one crew member there, taking a reading from a large brass dial on the wall. Striker sent him out with a jerk of his thumb, and they were alone.

And in the center of the bridge was the only chair—the captain's chair, carved from mahogany and set on a swivel so the occupant could see all parts of the bridge. It was *his* chair. His first instinct was to claim it, but a captain's first responsibility was always the ship.

He saw at a glance the spot he was looking for. A rib of steel ran between the two panes of glass right at the nose of the gondola. There was an ornate piece of brass, etched with scrollwork, screwed to the steel rib at about the height of a man's head. Striker stepped forward, pulling a screwdriver from somewhere inside his coat, and removed the brass plate in moments. Behind it was an empty space about two feet square lined in dark blue velvet. Nick unbuckled the saddlebag and took Athena out. He had washed her and scrubbed the rust away, lightly oiling the metal and wrapping her in a square of turquoise silk. He placed her, silk and all, on the velvet, securing her in place with fine leather straps anchored into her private chamber. Then Striker replaced the brass panel, tightening the screws before stepping back with a look of satisfaction on his dark face.

"Now the ship is finished," he said.

Nick felt the change almost at once as Athena's consciousness flowed from the metal cube to embrace the whole of the steamspinner. It was as if the entire ship took a breath and shook itself awake. The hum of the engines changed, the lights dimmed and then grew brighter, and the entire ship— it was hard to put a word to it—*glowed*. Not brightly, and not so much that he'd have noticed unless he'd seen the ship a moment ago. But he had witnessed the change, and he could tell there was a luster on every surface that hadn't been there before. The crew must have felt it, too, for suddenly the low conversation floating from the distant mess grew brighter, as if they were suddenly filled with hope.

Nick put a hand on the brass plate. *Welcome home, my lady.* He felt her touch, almost like a kiss on the cheek, and she was gone, no doubt to explore every cupboard and cannon in her new vessel. In no time at all she'd be back, demanding to fly.

CHAPTER THIRTY-FIVE

A TALL, LANKY MAN WITH RED HAIR AND WIRE-RIMMED glasses skidded to a halt in the doorway. It was the helmsman, the residue of shock still on his face as he looked at Nick. Digby had been one of the *Red Jack*'s crew, and a friend. The man's eyes grew bright with moisture, but he blinked and drew himself up, offering an awkward salute. "It's a good thing you're back, sir. We have a visitor."

"A visitor?" Nick looked around the bridge, where he'd been listening to Striker explain the instrument panels. He wasn't ready for visitors. Hours had passed since he'd returned, but they had gone by in a blink.

"Who is it?" Striker asked, and then his face fell. "Bollocks, now what does he want?"

A man pushed past Digby, and Nick knew him at once. *Roberts*. There weren't *that* many pirate captains hunting the skies—especially ones who made themselves at home on other people's ships. Often permanently, and with their unlucky host at sword point.

"You might have warned me," Nick muttered.

"I told you he keeps dropping by," Striker grumbled. "I still don't trust him."

Nick folded his arms, telling himself not to make assumptions—but the man was a wolverine in a tailcoat. Even if Striker had plucked him off an island prison, and even if by some freak of circumstance he really did want to be friendly, showing weakness could be a fatal mistake. "Captain Roberts," Nick said cautiously.

Roberts was a tall, big-boned man, but he had lost weight since Nick had seen him last—probably during his time on

Devil's Island. There were shadows under his craggy cheek-bones and his ruddy complexion now looked fevered. He was dressed in a dandy's clothes, but they'd seen better days, hanging limp and greasy around his frame. Nick could smell the brandy on him from where he stood.

"Ah, Captain Niccolo." Roberts ambled across the bridge, pausing in front of the chair. "Back from the dead, I see," Roberts mused, the burr of a Scots brogue rounding the words. "Where the hell were you, lad?"

"In a prison," Nick said, trying to keep the chitchat brief. "I escaped."

The man made to sit down in the captain's chair. Nick pulled the knife from his belt and threw it in one smooth motion. The blade flashed through the air and clunked into the arm of the chair, pinning the man's sleeve. "That's my seat," Nick said smoothly, "if it's all the same to you."

Roberts looked up from the knife that quivered a bare inch from his flesh. The man's dark eyes narrowed with anger for a heartbeat before he broke into a great, booming roar of mirth. "Ah, Niccolo, for a dead man, you are mighty fast!" Then with a grunt, he tugged the knife from his sleeve.

"Let's start again. Hello, Captain, what are you doing on my ship?" Nick asked, struggling to keep his voice calm.

"It's a bit of a tale. I was on Devil's Island until Mr. Striker here brought this marvelous ship to set me free."

"So I heard."

"Aye, and I'm a grateful man. That island is bloody awful, let me tell you. As hot as hell and not a drop of spirits to drink." Roberts began to sit down again, thought better of it, and leaned on the back of the chair instead. His long, lank brown hair swung forward over his shoulders. "I owe your crew a favor, Nicky my lad, for helping my boys break me out of the Frenchies' prison. It was a bloody miracle and each one of your crew is an angel born and bred."

Striker shifted his weight, his coat clanking as he moved. "We were along for the exercise. It was your old crew that wouldn't rest until you were back."

Nick began to relax—not much, but enough to take his

hand off the second knife he had hidden up his sleeve. "And that is why you're here? To acknowledge this debt?"

Roberts broke into a devilish smile. "Nay, lad, I've done that time and again already until Mr. Striker is ready to bar the door. This time I came to ask another boon." He held up a hand before Nick could protest, and Nick saw the flash of a gem-studded ring. Roberts had never been shy about showing off his loot. "Let me explain. I have my own ship, the *Dawn Star,* three hours' ride up the coast. It was, uh, being underutilized by a Portuguese trader I met in Barbados, where Mr. Striker here was good enough to leave me and my boys after we left Devil's Island behind." Roberts gave a regretful shrug. "There were a few glasses of rum and a game of cards and suddenly the ship was mine. You know how it goes."

In other words, Roberts had cheated the Portuguese captain of his ship. There was a reason every honest seaman dreaded his name. "The favor?" Nick prompted.

Roberts pulled out a flask, took a swig, and smacked his lips. Despite the costly ring, there was grime worked deep into the creases of his fingers, as if he hadn't washed in weeks. "Right to the point you are. Well, as I said, I have my own ship again, and I'm thinking to myself, ah, Roberts, what's next? What are you going to do with your last few years in the great blue sky?"

He leaned forward, gripping the chair. "And then I say to myself, what about this whisper I heard that there's a pardon for every pirate that sides with the rebels against the Steam Council?"

Striker looked at Nick, head cocked. He hadn't heard this yet.

Roberts went on. "It sounds like a crock of nonsense, but then I think, the *Red Jack* did business with those rebel boys—they all said so at the Saracen's Head, back before you went away, Nicky boy. So yes, thinks I, *that* crew would know the truth of it, and those kind souls would steer me right. And so I'm here, but from your face it's news to you, Mr. Striker. Is my errand a waste of time and aether?"

"It's new information," said Nick cautiously. "The pardons would come only under certain conditions." He was making this up, but he was sure the queen wouldn't hand them out willy-nilly.

The pirate regarded him steadily, all business now. "I want that pardon, lad. After the island, the savor has gone out of this life. Pillage for its own sake has paled. Perhaps I'm just tired, but I want to bounce my grandbabies on my knee and look back at the good old days with a wistful sigh."

Nick tried to picture Roberts in his dotage, and failed. Nevertheless, the Schoolmaster wanted ships. "I don't know what the work would be. More than just running supplies. Maybe defense against the Scarlet King's dirigibles. Could be against foreign allies attacking the coast."

Roberts stood up straight, his feet planted apart, as if riding a heaving deck. "And I'm more than ready to show them the business end of my cannons, but those cursed Baskervilles are as hard to find as cockroaches at high noon. How do I treat with them?"

"I can deliver your terms to the Baskervilles," said Nick. "Standard negotiation rates."

Roberts's eyebrows curled in suspicion. "Two percent of plunder?"

"Three." Nick wasn't going to get greedy—the rebels needed an air fleet more than he needed gold—but not bargaining would have undervalued the pirate's offer. "Subject to the acceptance of looting as part of the agreement."

"Fair as an April morn," said Roberts. "And I won't be the only one to think so. Our pirate brothers have a bone to pick with the steam barons. In the time you've been gone, conditions have gone down the crapper. Fuel is costly. Parts are hard to come by. The Violet Queen wants to shut down our pleasure ships because they're not authorized brothels. As if the Steam Council has any business where we take our pleasures! She even wants to tax our rum. Now I know that men in our line of work like to go our own way, but it's time we banded together. And since the men of the *Jack* knew the rebels, and I knew the men of the *Jack,* I was chosen as the one to speak."

The captain fished inside his filthy coat and extracted a

soft leather case. From it, he drew a fistful of papers that he thrust at Nick. "Take these to your Baskervilles. Same terms as mine. I trust you to see us right, my boy, because you of all of us play a fair game. It's damned convenient you're not dead."

Nick shuffled through the pages, a light-headed sensation overtaking him. There were dozens of papers, each one representing a pirate ship and its crew, each one outlining a request for pardon in return for service.

He started to chuckle out loud. This wasn't a few disgruntled thieves. This was an armada.

Dartmoor, October 5, 1889

BASKERVILLE HALL

3:17 p.m. Saturday

TOBIAS POUNDED ON the door of his room, awkward because he was using his left hand. He'd fallen asleep sometime yesterday and had just come to, pausing just long enough to dress before mounting an angry assault on the door. Disorientation swamped him. He recalled the journey down from London with Evelina and coming to Baskerville Hall. After that, things got fuzzy.

But he knew two things: he was missing the key to Evelina's bracelets, and the damned door was locked. Everything else flowed from there.

He raised his fist to pound again, but the door flew open. It was Dr. Watson. "Mr. Roth," he said sharply. "Calm yourself!"

"What's going on?" Tobias snapped.

"You fell asleep," the doctor said, a little more softly. "You were ill and exhausted. We put you to bed."

The exhausted part had been true—the last weeks had been nightmarish, to say the least. Although Tobias would never admit it, he felt better for the rest. "We were drinking in the library," he remembered. "Did you put something in that brandy, Doctor? And where is Evelina?"

The name hung in the air, unnaturally resonant.

"We had begun to talk about contact poisons," Watson continued as if he hadn't spoken. He walked forward, forcing Tobias back into the room. Although the doctor was the shorter man, his confident bonhomie made one automatically obey. "I grew curious, so I took the liberty of making an examination once you were asleep."

Instinctively, Tobias looked at his right hand. His fingers weren't swollen anymore, but the tips had bruised. *Is that normal? What does that mean?* The poison had burrowed into his imagination, a lethal and unpredictable fairy that had him at the mercy of its caprice. But after serving the Gold King, that almost felt normal.

"Your gesture gives you away," said Watson. "You knew precisely what you were asking when you raised the subject of poisoning by touch. It's a variety I've encountered before, by the way. Where did you come in contact with it?"

"Papers," Tobias answered curtly. "I touched papers coated with the substance, and I was told there is no cure."

"Which was why I imagine you left London without a word," Watson added. "Evelina knew nothing of your condition. Very noble, trying to spare your family the pain of watching your illness progress."

Since that had been exactly what he'd been thinking, Tobias didn't even flinch. "I thought I could put Evelina into her uncle's care toward the end."

"Very sensible," said the doctor.

Tobias turned away, bracing his hands on the windowsill and looking out at the rolling moors. "How much time do I have?"

Watson hesitated. "How do you feel? Nausea? Numbness?"

"Not bad, actually. Better than before."

"There is a—not an antidote, but another drug that slows the action of the poison. You appear to have responded well."

That made Tobias turn around. "You treated me?"

"I'm a doctor," Watson said. "Are you refusing my care?"

"I'm the Gold King's maker. Evelina's jailor. Why would you lift a finger to help me?"

"Dear God, you're a young man in trouble, not the arch villain of a melodrama. From the first moment I ever met you, you've been reeling on the brink. Take the medicine. I don't know precisely how long it will work, but you should have an extra month of reasonable health. That will at least give you the time to put your affairs in order."

Another month. Combined with the time he had left anyway, that might make six weeks. Or eight. It was too little and too much. Too little to fix anything and more than he had nerve for. All the walls he'd built around his panic ripped open, spilling terror like entrails.

"I killed the Scarlet King," Tobias blurted out, not knowing that he was going to say it. "The reason Keating agreed to let me come here is to escape any possibility of scandal." He was aware of Holmes materializing in the doorway, but he didn't care. "My wife and son are in London. They're the ones Keating cares about."

"And your job is to go quietly to the grave, is that it?" Holmes asked. "Was it the Scarlet King who killed you?"

It sounded like a question for a séance, and Tobias laughed. It sounded hysterical. "Yes."

"You're in good company. The crown prince died last night of the same affliction."

"What?" Tobias wheeled to face the detective. "The prince is dead?"

"Discoveries are coming thick and fast." Holmes exchanged a look with Watson. "Intriguing news on all sides, it seems."

"Besides the prince?"

"There will be a riot for the evening papers. Not only is His Royal Highness deceased, Her Majesty's Laboratories are burned, and the body of the Scarlet King was discovered bobbing face down more or less where the Gray King was found last year."

"They found Reading!" Tobias exclaimed.

Watson looked grim. "It is fairly certain that any usable evidence will have been destroyed by the water."

"Of course, Keating has quietly annexed all of Scarlet's interests beginning with his air fleet," Holmes went on.

"The Steam Council will no doubt object with predictable results. It seems, Mr. Roth, that you may well have pulled the trigger that fires off a civil war."

"I know," Tobias murmured under his breath. *Well, don't say I never did anything with my life.* But it had been easy to be a fatalist before he had been a father. Now he would have given anything, everything for more time with his son, and he would pay twice that to know Jeremy and Alice stayed safe.

"The incident with Her Majesty's Laboratories is of particular interest. All those connected with its destruction have vanished," said Holmes. "Including my niece." The way Holmes said it made it clear Evelina's disappearance had been planned in advance.

"Really?" Tobias replied. "And that has nothing to do with why I was locked in this room?"

Holmes looked almost apologetic. "I suppose you will wish to mount a search, Mr. Roth?"

"No, let her go."

"Will not the Gold King take that as a dereliction of duty?" Dr. Watson asked.

But Tobias was already staggering under the weight of what Holmes and the doctor had told him. He sat down on the edge of his bed. *Six weeks. Maybe eight.* "No doubt he will, but I don't have much time and Evelina has suffered enough at his hands. The least I can do is let her go."

"You will hear no objection from me," said Holmes, "although I fear Mr. Keating will hardly let you return home. Not with the Scarlet King's murder still under investigation."

Holmes was, of course, completely correct. Tobias cursed softly. The crown prince was dead, war was upon them, and all the choices Tobias had made looked wrong. It was time to stop betting on the steam baron least likely to harm the ones he loved. Playing it safe had already cost him his life. Now it was time to fight.

Tobias shook his head slowly. "I'm not proposing to crawl home like a sick dog to curl up and die. I have a wife and child. I have sisters. They need protection." And he had friends. Bucky had urged him to join the resistance—and Bucky had a workshop crammed with a maker's tools. "There is one thing I can do with the time I have left that will help them all."

"What is that?" Watson asked.

"I know Keating's war machines like no one else does. I know exactly what they can and can't do, and I know how to make them dance to my tune. I put an end to one steam baron. I can finish the rest."

Dartmoor, October 6, 1889
TAVERN AT THE EAST DART

1:30p.m. Sunday

THE SCHOOLMASTER'S GATHERING of generals took place not at Baskerville Hall, but in a small tavern some distance away.

"Where the bleeding hell is this place?" Striker muttered. "We're in the middle of feckin' nowhere."

"We're there." Nick pointed to a faded inn sign announcing the East Dart. "I think the Dart refers to the river."

The landscape was indescribably beautiful in the bright sunshine, the sound of the rushing water a counterpoint to a flock of tiny cheeping birds. Ahead, a half-timbered inn squatted beneath a canopy of turning leaves.

"Tell me there's beer." Striker eyed his surroundings suspiciously, as if the birds and flowers were about to turn on him.

"Hard to say. It's Sunday." And if laws serving beer on the Lord's day might vary, local customs varied more.

His friend grunted in disgust. "I know London isn't everything for a man of the world like yourself, but at least I could count on a decent bit o' bacon and a good pint."

"At least the place looks open," Nick reassured him, and pushed through the dark wood door. "Just ask for something local."

Striker strolled up to the bar, rolling his shoulders under the weight of his heavy coat. They'd fallen back into the rhythm of their friendship within seconds, but Nick knew Striker wasn't letting him go far without a watchdog. There was no question of Nick vanishing twice.

However, he would have to content himself with a station outside the council room door. Nick had been told to go to the back room, so he carried on through the taproom, nodding to the barkeep to his right and taking a quick inventory of the faces sitting near the fire. They looked like locals out for friendly conversation, but he catalogued them anyhow just in case.

Some of the faces he expected to see were in the back room. There he saw the Schoolmaster as well as Edgerton, Penner, and Smythe, in addition to a handful of others he didn't know. He'd half expected Sherlock or Mycroft Holmes, but both were absent.

The Schoolmaster rose to greet him, his face splitting into a grin. "Captain Niccolo. So your journey to Cornwall was a success. That is good news."

"I found my ship and most of my crew. Even the ash rooks." Nick couldn't help smiling back. Athena had been entranced with her new vessel, and the crew had been entranced with the way she could make it fly.

"Please, have a seat. Those of you who do not know the captain have heard of him, I am sure. We owe him a great deal for the intelligence he's provided on the enemy's weaponry."

Nick felt the eyes of the others on him, but he'd been a showman too long for that to bother him. He sat down with as much casual sangfroid as he could summon. "You are welcome to what I could find."

"Captain, allow me to introduce these gentlemen. Edgerton, Smythe, and Penner you've met. This is Lord Elford, General Fortman, and Sir Simon Yates. They are by no means all of my advisors, but they are the most directly involved with the deployment of ground forces. We've just been reviewing the strength we have to draw on, and where the enemy is situated. It seems the majority of the Scarlet King's forces are in the north or else due east of here."

"My regiment is one that Scarlet bought wholesale for his

private use," Smythe put in. He was wearing the blue uniform of his cavalry unit, and looked far more at ease in it than the civilian clothes he'd worn before. "Scarlet left our command structure alone when he took over, but now the top officers are all being replaced by the Gold King's men. Something's happened at the highest level. No one knows what, but our lads have had enough. We swore an oath to the queen, not some boilermaker—and certainly not a string of 'em. We're not a box of spoons to be passed from hand to hand. Most of the regiments the barons took over feel the same. It's not right and they're ready to take a stand."

"As noble as that is," said General Fortman—probably a retired general, back in the traces for queen and country— "that only represents a small percentage of the steam barons' total forces."

Smythe wasn't daunted. "We may be small, but we're close in. We're yours when you need a precise blow straight to the heart."

Nick knew Evelina didn't like Smythe, but he couldn't fault the man's courage. What he was proposing could easily become a suicide mission. From the expression on the other men's faces, they knew that, too.

Edgerton spoke up next. He talked about weapons, production, and distribution of the scattered makers and the forces they had gathered. Penner put in the occasional remark that indicated he was heavily involved in research. They were young, but the others listened with attention.

"That's all very well and good," said Fortman. "This will be more a battle of engines than of troops. However, we need *some* troops besides what Smythe has proposed—men who are more than mobs."

The Schoolmaster answered. "They have been gathering in London over the last months. Mycroft Holmes put the word out through his cronies. He found an entire network of retired commanders connected through their clubs and country house parties who were more than pleased to call their old units together."

"We know that," replied Lord Elford. "But those men are

in London, not with the machines coming in from the countryside. The rural forces need support."

"What they need," Edgerton countered, "is power. We can invent what we like, but unless we have fuel to run it, we have nothing. We've tried power storage devices, but distribution is a problem."

Nick sat up straight. "Your air fleet can help with both those problems. Defense and distribution."

They all gave him a curious look. "Your steamspinner is no doubt an amazing ship, but she isn't quite a fleet," said the Schoolmaster.

Nick drew out the papers Captain Roberts had given him and pushed them across the table. "These men are willing to help. For a price of a pardon, certainly, but you won't find more experienced fighters."

The Schoolmaster picked up the papers and flipped through them. He pushed the green-tinted glasses up on his head. "Damn it all, these are the pirates!"

"They are," said Nick. "You put the word out and they heard you. They don't like the Steam Council any more than the rest of us. The sky patrols are bad for smuggling."

The Schoolmaster's expression was caught between laughter and tears. "Of course."

"Can they be trusted?" asked Sir Simon Yates, every inch the aging dandy with his monocle and carefully tied cravat.

It was a reasonable question, and Nick didn't mind answering it. "Some more than others. I can tell you who would be suited best to what task, but you can trust them all to fight. There are no cowards there."

"That is excellent," Edgerton replied. "Two of our problems solved, at least in part."

"But can we make enough storage cells?" the Schoolmaster asked.

Both Penner and Edgerton shook their heads. "We're moving mountains to fill the need," Edgerton said. "But we could use that supply of coal."

Nick frowned. If they ever needed Evelina and her ability to mix magic and mechanics, it was now. She had created Mouse and Bird by coaxing devas to take up residence in the clockwork toys, and more or less brought them to life without the need for any kind of fuel. Centuries ago, Athena had been created in a similar way. Nick didn't have the skill himself, but he knew enough to see the possibilities. "Have you thought of working with magic users?"

An uneasy rustle went around the table. The Schoolmaster looked at him curiously. "The use of magic in warfare is not something this council has been able to agree on, but there are some besides yourself with talent in the Baskerville fold. Did you not hear about the destruction of Her Majesty's Laboratories last night?"

"No." Nick had been on the road, and then in the air.

"The building and most of the workers were destroyed by an attack coordinated by the Parapsychological Institute."

As the words soaked in, Nick experienced an odd moment of displacement, as if his reality had shifted. The laboratories hung over the head of everyone with a drop of the Blood. To find out they were gone was . . .

"Of course," said the Schoolmaster. "Holmes knows more of the details."

"What did he have to do with it?" Nick asked, and then it became clear. *Evelina! That's why she was here!* And, he realized with a wrench, she hadn't told him anything about this.

But his rising anger was forestalled by the look in the Schoolmaster's eye. "Holmes was present," the Schoolmaster said. "I will receive his account of the event when I return to Baskerville Hall tonight. But for now I'm sure you'll be interested to know that it was arranged for Miss Cooper to go with the members of the institute when the deed was done. Their representative sent a runner with news that the mission was a success, and not one of our number was injured."

"Where are the representatives of the institute now?" Sir Simon asked.

"In hiding," the Schoolmaster replied.

Evelina is free! A rush of hot joy spilled through Nick, making it nearly impossible to remain in his seat. She might be in hiding with the other magic users, but she was out of the Gold King's clutches. He closed his eyes, a wave of impatience and energy lending him hope.

The Schoolmaster carried on. "Gentlemen, we've already struck a decisive blow against the Steam Council with the destruction of one of their favorite weapons of oppression. It has a literal value, but also a symbolic one. And we've done it just in time, because now is the critical moment when the citizens of the Empire must choose their leader."

He paused, his gaze traveling around the table and touching on each man there. "I have a piece of news that changes the game entirely. A telegram arrived this morning. By now you have all heard that the last of my brothers, the Prince of Wales, is dead."

His brother? Nick stared, as stunned as if someone had knocked him on the head. He wasn't the only one—Penner, Smythe, and Yates were also wide-eyed with confusion.

The Schoolmaster pulled a telegram from his pocket and held it up. "But there is more you may not know. The word from Mycroft Holmes is that Palace physicians have confirmed that the crown prince died of poison, and not from typhoid as the newspapers report."

A general babble erupted around the table.

"Just a moment," Nick said, his voice rising above the others. *"Athena called you* vasiliàs."

"Yes," said the Schoolmaster, his face pale. He pulled off his tinted glasses, abandoning them on the paper-strewn table. "Athena was correct. I'm the last living prince, and now I'm taking back my throne."

CHAPTER THIRTY-SIX

5:12 p.m. Sunday

PANIC ONLY TOOK A DAMSEL IN DISTRESS SO FAR, AND EVE-lina was impatient to be on her way. She wasted no time in investigating every crack and corner of her room—a process that took the remainder of her first day in Magnus's castle aerie. She repeated the entire process the second day, just to be sure she had missed nothing.

The door was locked with a heavy iron affair that belonged in a dungeon. Evelina wasn't sure she could lift the key that opened it, much less pick the wretched thing. Access to the chimney was blocked with an iron grate. The casement window was not locked, but looked over a sheer drop to the crashing waves below.

The floor and walls were all solid, unless one counted a few chinks in the mortar large enough for rats. The tapestries hid no secret doors or listening holes, and, though faded, appeared to have been recently cleaned. Lifting the carpet—a threadbare affair of Persian design—revealed nothing, either, outside of a hidden pile of dirt one of the maids had sought to disguise.

Defeated, she sank to her knees on the carpet before the fire. Her fingers traced the geometric pattern of the border, wishing its symmetry would help her think. Weariness pawed at her, seeking to smother her in a gray fog of despair. She drew her knees up and wrapped her arms around them, hugging herself. At least she had basic creature comforts—fresh clothes, a warm room, and adequate food. She had the key to her bracelets so that every twelve hours she could fend off their pain. The wood fire—so rare in the steam barons' London—gave off the comforting scent of well-seasoned pine. Magnus's plans depended on her continued health—but those were about the only positives. *It was bad enough being Keating's prisoner, but at least he let me attend the college.* There would be no smuggled notes to her uncle here, and the only lessons would be of Magnus's devising.

Evelina closed her eyes and propped her forehead on her knees. She'd spent the night crying and was wrung out, her emotions worn thin as a garment sent too often through the wash. Now was the time for a clever plan—except she had no idea where to begin. *Do I really not know? Or does some slippery part of me not want to know? How do I trust my own impulses now that Magnus has already given me a taste of power?*

There had to be a test, some objective measure that her uncle Sherlock might design, but he wasn't there to guide her. She could feel the hunger coiled inside her, quiet for the moment, but alert to any opportunity to hunt.

She'd wondered what would happen without the restraint of her bracelets. Now it seemed she would find out. Twelve hours was almost up again, and the silver bracelets were tingling, ready to be deactivated one more time. Evelina drew out her necklace with the tiny key Dr. Watson had filched from Tobias and turned the key in each of the locks.

But instead of fading away, the sensation coursing up her arms increased. Panic surged through her. The key wasn't working anymore. There must be a limit as to how many times the bracelets could be stalled, or maybe there was another trick she didn't know. The tingling had become prickling, and that had swelled to a stabbing that reached from wrist to elbow. The key slipped from clumsy fingers, falling useless to the carpet. Evelina staggered to her feet, tripping on her hems because her hands were too numb to lift her skirts. *I don't know what to do!*

It was the last coherent thought she had before pain dynamited through her. As if smashing a barrier, it no longer seared through her arms; it made her entire body an open wound. Evelina shrieked, the sound ringing against the high stone walls. Then sight and sound attenuated, as if the searing sensation in every nerve stretched them out of focus. She had no idea if she was still screaming. She was gasping for air, trying to move away from the agony, but direction had ceased to have meaning.

And then the smell of the room changed to a choking smoke. Hard hands grabbed her, dragging her from her feet to the floor. She was aware of something heavy smothering her and she beat at it feebly, her arms no longer obeying her commands. Dimly, she realized it was the blanket from her bed and someone was using it to put out whatever was burning.

"Did you mean to set yourself on fire?" Magnus barked harshly. "Fashion be praised, at least there were layers of petticoats between your skin and the smoldering fabric."

Had she blundered into the fireplace? Evelina struggled to focus, but the world around her was a vague shadow beyond a searing wall of hurt. She tried to lift her hands and wasn't sure she succeeded. Her mouth worked, chewing at the words before she could get them out. "Get these off."

She felt his hand, cold as death, through the biting agony. He lifted her wrist, cursed, and dropped it again. A few heartbeats later, she realized he was gone. She surrendered, her limbs going boneless. There was nothing more she could do.

And then he was back, busying himself with tools. He spoke a handful of words she didn't understand, and the right bracelet sprang open. He tossed it aside and began working on the left. "Buck up, my girl; this is the last of Keating's hold on you."

But Evelina remained sprawled on the floor, barely twitching as he worked. The pain didn't stop immediately, and when it did begin to recede it left her like a drowned body washed up on shore. Magnus picked her up and deposited her on the bed.

"I apologize for not noticing the condition of the operating spell before now. I should have seen it winding down, but there was rather a lot going on."

And it was a sign of how much he had lost. The old Magnus would have spotted it in seconds. Evelina blinked, the first motion that didn't make her nerves squeal. She realized that she could think again.

"Thank you." She still wanted to stab Magnus through the heart, but she was prepared to give credit where it was due.

He turned, his dark eyes guarded. "You're welcome. Those bracelets are a vile contrivance."

Then why didn't you take them off before? But there was no point in asking—this was Magnus. "I had hoped somehow they'd break when the laboratories burned down." Her voice was thready, and she coughed. That still hurt.

"I'm afraid they don't work like that. There is a controlling mechanism operated by sympathetic magic. It probably sits on Mr. Keating's shelf. No doubt it just put out a piercing alarm to indicate that you have slipped his leash." Magnus propped her up with another pillow, but the motion made her dizzy. She lay back, closing her eyes in hopes the world would stop spinning.

"Let me get you some sherry," Magnus said with a note of concern.

Evelina gave a weak smile and opened her eyes. Then she cursed softly. Now that she was sitting up, she could see the ruin of her dress. She'd been lucky he'd pulled her out of the fire.

He chuckled. "There are more clothes in those trunks."

"I liked this dress."

"Consider it a fair trade for disposing of your unwanted jewelry." As if by magic—which was entirely likely—one of the taciturn servants appeared with a bottle on a tray, and Magnus poured out a measure, handing it to her.

Her hands were just steady enough to take a sip, but the smooth, sweet burn of it made her take another. It was very good quality, no doubt stored in the castle cellars for a very long time. She immediately began to feel better.

Magnus picked up the remains of the bracelets, opened

the casement window, and hurled them into the gathering dark. "Good riddance."

She could tell he was putting on a bit of a show, but she was still grateful to have the bracelets off. "Will there be any lasting effects from those?"

"Outside of a dislike for silver bangles, I think not." Standing with the mullioned window behind him, his features lost in the soft, firelit shadows, he looked like himself again. "I think we shall resume your lessons tomorrow, now that your collar and leash are off."

Evelina finished the drink and set the glass aside. "I think not."

"No?" Magnus asked, his voice silky.

She pretended a poise she didn't feel. "I don't want your instruction. I don't deny that you taught me well, but your lessons come with a steep price."

"Your innocence, perhaps?" he asked, the sarcasm plain. "By all means, let's preserve that. No doubt the teachings of the Wollaston Academy for Young Ladies have served you better."

"That is hardly a fair comparison."

"But isn't that what you mean?" Magnus made a sweeping gesture with his hand. "Ladies turn the other cheek. But what is the etiquette for a war that threatens to extinguish your very species, not to mention whatever friends and family you call your own? If I sent you home to London, would the Gold King merely pat you on the hand and apologize for nearly exploding your skull with agony?"

Evelina bit her tongue, because he had a point. She'd thought to take vengeance on Keating once, but had let him take her captive to save Nick. She'd based her tactics on a fair bargain, and the Gold King had played her false.

Magnus lowered his voice. "You *need* what I have to show you, because you're not going to survive out there any other way."

"But is it worth it?" Sudden tears ached behind her eyes. "Every time I learned something from you . . ."

"Every time?" Magnus smiled.

"Many times that I learned something from you, my

magic grew a little bit darker. And hungrier. I don't want to be a sorcerer, and I don't want to know about death magic."

"Your objections are noted, though I should make it clear that I didn't bring you here at knifepoint for you to learn to crochet. This is your path, Evelina. You're a fighter, and power is your natural weapon."

He was right. Magnus usually was in these arguments—and yet it still might be better to lose than to win on his terms.

"There is the chance," he added, folding his arms and taking a swaggering step forward, "that if you learn what I have to teach you, you might best me at my own game. I told you once that you might be my equal."

Evelina jerked with surprise—and some revulsion—at the idea. Now that she was feeling well enough to move, she swung her feet off the bed. Lying there felt too vulnerable. "I know better than to think you would let me win."

"But the notion intrigues you, does it not? All that dislike you have for me, and finally there is an outlet, something positive you can do about the Magnus problem." His smile would have done Mephistopheles proud.

"You must think I'm an idiot," she shot back, getting to her feet.

And then she noticed a shadowy shape lurking behind Magnus. She started, feeling her eyes going wide. It wasn't quite solid, showing the diamond leading of the mullioned window through its body, but she still could see details of its waistcoat buttons. It had too many limbs, though she couldn't quite tell—and didn't want to know—where that extra one attached. Its head bubbled and sagged like melted wax and sightless eyes watched her with empty pits. "What's that?"

Magnus glanced over his shoulder with obvious unconcern. "That's right, you can see them, can't you? Every castle requires a garrison. These don't require feeding in the conventional sense and yet they do an excellent job of carrying out orders. I brought them along when I moved from the Black Kingdom. They have them by the bucketful down there. I think it's the faulty drains."

Evelina swallowed, fear jagged in her throat. Mouse had called those creatures the Others—the opposite of whatever kind of spirit the devas were. "I've only ever seen them after using dark magic."

"Perhaps they are simply stronger here." Magnus gave a shrug, and then another knife-edged smile. "All the more reason to stay safely tucked in bed at night. Unless—and this is merely a suggestion, of course—you bestir yourself to find a way to defend yourself against such creatures?"

He reached over, making a crushing gesture, and the thing melted into a splotch of dark shadow at his feet. Magnus's hand trembled, as if the thing didn't go easily. Evelina winced, wondering which one of them it had hurt worse.

Magnus looked up, triumphant. "Maybe *that* is a challenge you can believe in, since you think besting me is so far beyond your reach."

She made an inarticulate growl of rage. He'd clearly revealed the thing right when he wanted her to see it.

"There is the spirit, my kitten." Magnus started for the door, the darkness trailing him along the floor like a tremulous shadow. "I can work with that."

Her sherry glass smashed against the door as he closed it.

CHAPTER THIRTY-SEVEN

Unknown

ANNA HAD BIRD. IT HAD TAKEN A WHILE TO FIGURE OUT where she had constructed her prison, but Imogen and Mouse had found it.

It was below, near the part of the clock where the bizarre, multicolored tubes of bubbling liquid filtered messages from the aether. They rose like glass pillars all around Imogen, each tube lit from within and shedding a soft light over the surrounding clockwork. The tubes were held within a velvet-lined rack, so for once Imogen had something soft to sit on or, in this case, lie on.

She was stretched out on her stomach looking down and across empty space to another structure that supported a pump. Bird was there, too, looking frightened despite the fact it was the first lark on record that was the size of a large turkey. But the cause of Bird's distress was clear, because Anna stood there, too.

"It's very strange," she whispered to Mouse. "Watching her is like looking at myself."

Whatever you see, that's not what she is, Mouse replied from its spot near her elbow. *She's putting on a show to rattle your nerve.*

It was working. Imogen clenched her teeth to keep from raging or screaming or weeping as Anna—wearing Imogen's face and clothes—used a long bit of wire to poke at Bird through the bars of its prison, grinning as if she wanted nothing more than to pluck and roast the clockwork lark for her dinner. The petty cruelty was bad enough, but that wasn't what bothered Imogen the most. It was that Anna made her face look so evil. *Am I seeing a piece of something that lives inside me?* And then she revisited the fact that Anna had been responsible for the Whitechapel murders. If she had Bird captive, it would only be a matter of time before something very bad happened to the poor beast.

Imogen squeezed her eyes shut, wishing herself anyplace else. It was too much. She had been stuck in the clock forever, and every step forward she made—figuring out where she was, or confronting Anna, or finding Bird—was accompanied by the discovery of another problem.

But giving up means that Anna wins. And then her twin would wake up in her body, loved and trusted by her family. Who knew what damage Anna could do in Imogen's name?

Imogen forced herself to open her eyes and wriggle forward another inch to see if a slightly different angle improved matters. It didn't. Bird was clearly visible, but she still had no idea how to get to the creature.

The clockwork lark had been confined within the upright frame of the pump that fed air through the tubes of bubbling liquid. Even if Imogen could have jumped or flown across empty space to the platform holding the apparatus, and even if she could have reached between the bars and dragged Bird back through the too-small gap, there was still no chance of success.

"How did she get Bird in there, anyhow?"

Mouse didn't answer, but crept closer to the edge of the rack, tail snaking to and fro. Imogen sensed the creature's worry.

The biggest obstacle was the mechanism of the pump itself. It was a length of brass that rocked up and down to operate a bellows, each steam-powered plunge of beam and counterweight forcing air bubbles through the shimmering tubes. The rush of the bellows sounded like rasping lungs, inhaling and exhaling in wheezing harmony with the rest of the clock. But with each gasp, the metal cage around Bird moved with a sweep of clanking, bone-breaking brass and steel. Anna snatched her wire back with each swing of the pump's arm, but then laughed as time after time the clock-work nearly smashed Bird's snapping beak.

Rage clawed at Imogen, and she dug her fingers into the thick velvet covering the rack of tubes. Bird had been the lookout when she'd crept through her bedroom window to visit Bucky; the clown who flew away with her hair ribbons; the faithful friend who had come here—to this insane place—to help her. "What do we do?" she asked Mouse. "Can we stop the pump at least?"

She didn't think that would do anything drastic to the clock. The purpose of the bubbles, she guessed, was to infuse air into the aether so that it could be scanned for information, and then the choice bits of news coded onto one of the clock's cryptic cards.

The mechanism is magic. We can't stop it, but we can break the spell that put Bird behind those bars.

"How?"

Destroy your sister, Mouse replied. *I'm sorry, but that is the only answer I know.*

Imogen buried her face in her hands. Her skin was hot with her emotions. "I destroyed her once before. It didn't work."

You destroyed her vessel. She is not in a vessel now.

Frustration made her pragmatic. "So what are the rules of this place? Can I hurt her?"

Mouse's whiskers twitched, tickling her arm. *As long as your sister is wearing a face, she is vulnerable.*

Imogen thought about that. Although Anna had been a presence throughout Imogen's life, she had always appeared as an unseen force in Imogen's dreams. Furthermore, since Anna had died as a child, she had never possessed the woman's body she was wearing now. She must have had to manufacture what Imogen was seeing now. "How does wearing a face work?"

All her essence is occupied giving herself shape. The longer a mortal has been without a physical body, the more energy it takes to maintain a face.

"So if I hurt the body she's made for herself, I truly weaken her?"

Correct. Mouse curled its tail over Imogen in a comforting gesture. *I know it is not a pleasant thing to contemplate, but she can hurt you the same way.*

Which meant Mouse and Bird were most likely vulnerable, too. Imogen chewed her thumbnail, her thoughts skittering anxiously.

Anna had given up teasing Bird with the wire and was moving away from the pump, leaping lightly from one foothold to the next across the cavernous gaps. Imogen began to think about moving to a more secure spot, although it would be hard to leave Bird stuck there in a prison too confining even to fluff its feathers.

"I remember one winter Anna learned how to make snowballs. She threw them at me until I learned to make them, too. After I hit her once, she hid."

Do you think striking back will convince her to let you go?

"No, I think if Anna figures out that I might actually hurt her, she'll stop taunting me and hide. The only way I can get a clean strike is if she doesn't think I'll do it. I have to surprise her." Imogen scanned the scene below, wondering what sort of attack was possible. "But how? I don't know magic, and I don't know how to fight."

You use what you have.

"All we have is a lot of clockwork. Maybe Evelina or Tobias could make an aether gun out of spare gears or something but . . ." An idea struck her silent for several beats. What she had was imagination, and a lot of faith in her friends. "Mouse, would you recognize the mechanism that types out those cards? I need to send a message."

London, October 8, 1889

HILLIARD HOUSE

11:17 a.m. Tuesday

"SOMETHING IS WRONG," Poppy said to her mother. "Imogen looks unhappy."

They were in her big sister's room. Lady Bancroft visited

every day, usually right before the midday meal, and would sit with a vaguely shocked look on her pale face. Today, though, she looked almost resigned. She hadn't taken Tobias's departure well. Nevertheless, what she said next startled Poppy.

"I suppose it is only a matter of time."

Poppy glanced at her sister, who was beautiful as always. But now a single line of tension faintly creased her brow. It was the first change of expression they'd seen, which both reassured Poppy and made her uneasy. "She doesn't look sicker, she looks worried."

Lady Bancroft shot her a glance bright with a mix of grief and indignation. "Really, Poppy. It is quite inappropriate to make up such things now."

Poppy opened her mouth to reply and then closed it again. There was absolutely no point in trying to explain magic doorways and talking mice to her mother.

"I must go check on luncheon." Lady Bancroft rose. "Your father's been keeping early hours lately to accommodate all the work he's taken on. It's quite provoking."

"Are we eating soon?"

"Shortly. Mr. Penner is speaking to your father at the moment."

That caught Poppy's interest. "Oh?"

"I can't imagine why he's visiting with your father, but I suppose I must ask him to stay. I would appreciate it if you would let me know when he leaves the study."

Bucky wouldn't join them for a meal. That would be painful for all concerned, when Lord Bancroft blamed him for luring Imogen to elope—not that anyone ever lured Imogen somewhere she didn't want to go. But it was true that she had been on her way to join Bucky when Magnus had grabbed her, and Poppy knew Bucky had never forgiven himself. She could see it in the way he walked and heard it in his voice, and it bruised Poppy's heart.

But Bucky would stop to sit by Imogen's bed for a while. He was there every few days, keeping a quiet vigil, as unobtrusive as a ghost. Poppy reached over and squeezed her sister's hand. "He still cares for you," she said in a whisper.

And with that, she slipped out of the room and down the stairs to her father's study to watch for Bucky. She walked slowly, wondering what was happening to Imogen, and whether Mouse and Bird had reached her safely. It was too bad she couldn't have gone through whatever doorway the medium had made, or maybe Bucky should have gone, riding that big black horse of his, like some knight from a storybook. Bucky had always been kind and funny and a terrible prankster. It said a lot about him that instead of making guns like his father, he'd opened a toy factory on Threadneedle Street.

As Poppy reached the landing, the clock made a sickly bong. She turned to glance at it, alarmed. It had never made a sound like that before—and then it spat out a card. Poppy eyed the clock suspiciously, remembering how the cook's cat yowled before it spat up a hairball. She gave the clock a pat, hoping it would be all right, and bent to pick up the card before continuing down the stairs. As she folded it and put it into her pocket, she remembered with some satisfaction that Mr. Holmes had sent her the key to the cipher, as well as a copy of his monograph on the subject.

She arrived at the study door and listened a moment, trying to figure out if the conversation sounded like it was winding down. She caught the words "coal" and "airship," but not much else before it broke off into the usual good-bye noises. Then a chair scraped and she backed away, careful not to look as if she had been listening at the keyhole.

The door to the study opened and Bucky emerged. "Mr. Penner," she said, giving a polite curtsy.

"Miss Penelope," he replied, bowing very correctly, but with a spark of his old mischief in his brown eyes. He'd glued her shoes together once when she'd fallen asleep, and then laughed as she tripped and fell on her nose. Mind you, that was a great many years ago, before he'd fallen in love with her sister. That seemed to have improved him all around.

"My mother wishes to speak to you," Poppy said very correctly. "She is in the small dining room." There was no need to tell Bucky where that was. As Tobias's school friend, he'd stayed at Hilliard House many a holiday, especially since his own family lived all the way up in Yorkshire.

"Thank you, Poppy." Bucky bowed again, letting a little of the formality drop. "How are you?"

"Well, thank you," she said in a not-very-convincing tone. "And you?"

"I've learned to fly small dirigibles," he said. "It's bound to come in useful, if only for scaring pigeons."

She bit her lip. "Do you know Tobias is gone?"

"I know he left, yes." His expression grew serious.

Bucky was Tobias's best friend and was utterly trustworthy. The next words tumbled out before Poppy could stop them. "I miss him. He didn't even say good-bye and that worries me. I think something horrible happened."

Bucky leaned very close, speaking softly into her ear. "He's safe. He's at the toy factory. *Don't tell anyone.* His life may depend on it."

Poppy caught her breath, relieved and surprised, but she was getting used to knowing life-and-death secrets and she gathered herself quickly. She gave a solemn nod. "Thank you."

Bucky's mouth quirked, almost smiling. "I'll go find your mother," he said with a final squeeze of her hand.

As he left, Poppy peered around the corner of her father's doorway. Lord Bancroft was bent over his desk, his head in one hand, reading a piece of correspondence. He didn't look happy about it.

Poppy waited while he finished reading the page, glancing up at the stuffed tiger's head above his desk. The tiger and her father had a certain resemblance—down one fang, but still feisty enough to put on a good snarl. Her father stuffed the page into a file folder. She noticed an unusual decoration on the page that looked like dragons. "Yes?" he snapped. "Whatever it is, Poppy, it will have to wait."

"The meal is almost ready," she said quickly, and then made herself scarce before he could snap at her. She ran back up the stairs to her bedroom to tidy up before she had to present herself in the dining room.

But of course, the moment she pulled the card out of her

pocket, she had to have another look at Mr. Holmes's letter, which meant opening the monograph to the page on this kind of cipher, which meant pulling out some notepaper to work on and spreading it all out on her bed so that she could look at it all properly. Poppy flopped onto her stomach, chewing the end of her pencil and not even noticing how badly she was crushing the skirts of her dress. Even with the key, the puzzle of the cipher was intriguing—it made her brain tingle like something minty was being poured through the top of her head. It was far, far better than any of the stupid problems her schoolteachers had made her do.

She barely noticed when Dora, the upstairs maid, began pounding on the door. "I'll be down in a moment," she called through the door, figuring out the last three letters of the message.

Then she bounced off the bed, hardly believing what she was reading. She gathered up the papers, burst out of her room, and ran down the hall to Imogen's bedchamber.

As she had hoped, Bucky was there, one of the other maids sitting quietly in the corner for the sake of propriety. Even so, it was unusual for a man to visit the sickroom of any female who was not a close relation, but Bucky was an old friend of the family and he had been her fiancé.

The sight of him sitting by the bed with his head bowed stopped Poppy in her tracks. His hat dangled from one hand, and the other held Imogen's as tenderly as if they were sitting on a park bench watching the swans. But the look on his face was weary and sad. Poppy turned away, certain she was intruding on a private moment. It suddenly struck her that she wanted a Bucky of her own someday—not exactly the same, but one who would love her this much.

"Poppy?" Bucky looked up, his earlier manners pared down by grief.

She nodded to the maid, who left them. Poppy pushed the door as far closed as she could without *technically* being in a closed room with an unmarried man.

"What is it?" Bucky asked, looking suspicious and not in the mood for pranks.

"I need to tell you something," she began, unsure how to

proceed. "I'm going to give you some bare facts and I swear these are absolutely true."

"Very well," Bucky said, frowning.

"Did you know the clock on the landing was made by Dr. Magnus?"

"Yes, Tobias told me that."

She was starting to grow nervous, certain he wouldn't believe her. Bucky had a good imagination, but what she had to tell him was hardly credible, unless you knew everything. "Do you also know that it prints cards in a cipher?"

"Y-e-e-e-s," he said, drawing out the word. "I've seen them many times. I used to all but live here during school holidays, if you remember."

"Mr. Holmes gave me the key to the cipher," she said, her words speeding up as she rushed to the end, "and I worked out the message of the card the clock printed when you were in the study with Father."

Bucky waited. When she didn't speak—her tongue was momentarily frozen—he made an impatient circle with his hand. "What did it say?"

She fussed a moment with the corner of Imogen's blanket, then laid everything out across the foot of the bed. "Here is the card, and Mr. Holmes's letter with the key, and his book, and the answer. Check my work if you must. I'm not making this up."

Bucky rose slowly, leaving his hat behind on the chair. The room was silent but for Imogen's soft breathing and the distant bellow of Lord Bancroft calling Poppy to the table. She ignored her father. This was more important.

Bucky's hand went to his mouth as he read, and then he picked up the paper with Poppy's answer. As she had anticipated, he looked utterly poleaxed. "I don't understand."

"It's all there. I can do a dance for you, try and convince you what I think, but you'll assume I'm just playing a game. Then you'll either grow angry or indulgent, and neither one of those helps us at all. So, you need to decide what this means for yourself."

He walked closer to the head of the bed, his eyes on Imogen's face as he spoke to Poppy. "Do you mind very much if

I take the cipher and the card away and work through the message? Just to be sure?"

"No," Poppy said. "I expected you would."

"Thank you." He shot her a glance, his eyes kind. "But tell me what you think this means. I promise not to judge what you say."

She fidgeted, not wanting to choose the wrong words. For all the times Bucky had come to see Imogen, she'd never talked to him this way. She knew she was on delicate ground. "How much do you know about the night of the air battle?"

He looked at Imogen's still face, and Poppy felt the full weight of his distress. His features barely shifted, but the set of his eyes and mouth were all at once a dozen years older. "I was at the theater with Evelina and Holmes."

"Did Tobias ever tell you what happened aboard the *Helios*?"

He nodded. "Yes, and he told me her last words. Your brother believes she meant Anna."

She couldn't tell from his voice what he thought of that. "Do you think he's right?"

"Before the battle, Imogen was having very bad nightmares." He looked down at his hands, as if not sure how much he should say.

"I remember," Poppy said, not sure what to think. "A lot of them were the Whitechapel murders."

It took him a while to reply, as if he was choosing his words with care. "She thought there was something not quite normal going on. She thought she knew things about the cases she shouldn't have."

Intriguing. "Did you believe her?"

He sighed. "Who am I to say? Just because I don't understand magic doesn't mean it's not there. Dr. Magnus was a sorcerer, for pity's sake."

"Someone talented in that way paid a visit to look at Imogen," she ventured.

"Who?" Bucky asked a little sharply. "You know that could be dangerous. They might not be honest, or you might be caught. Then what would happen?"

"What this person said was that Imogen's soul was lost and couldn't get home. I think that's what happened when she fainted. Something pulled her soul away, and maybe it was Anna."

Poppy heard the emotion in her own voice and made herself sit back and take a long breath. Nothing good would happen if she got so agitated she slipped back into the role of the strange little sister.

Bucky rose to stand by Imogen, his hand resting on the edge of the pillow. "Dear God."

To her horror, Poppy was starting to cry. *Oh, no, this is going to make me sound hysterical!* But she was already too far in to quit now, and there was only one more thing she had left to say. She took a ragged breath and finished. "She's in trouble, Bucky. You fought a duel for her. You can do this." Then Poppy tensed, waiting for him to stomp from the room as he called her a disturbed little girl.

Instead, he furrowed his brow. "How would I even get to her?" His hands began to shake, and Poppy understood the conversation was finally penetrating his practiced calm. He was a man of logic—the type who could master dirigibles and weapons—but he was also a toy maker filled with imagination. He was starting to believe, and it was breaking him apart.

She swallowed hard, not sure if she was helping her sister or simply causing him pain. "I don't know. Maybe it's not my role to know. The message wasn't for me, anyway."

It read: *Bucky help me Imogen*.

Chapter Thirty-eight

**MEMBERSHIP OF THE STEAM COUNCIL,
OCTOBER 1889**

LISTED IN ORDER OF SIZE AND IMPORTANCE OF TERRITORY:
MR. JASPER KEATING,
KEATING UTILITIES, GOLD DISTRICT
MR. ROBERT "KING COAL" BLOUNT,
OLD BLUE GAS AND RAIL, BLUE DISTRICT
MRS. JANE SPICER, SPICER INDUSTRIES, GREEN DISTRICT
MR. WILLIAM READING,
READING AND BARTELSMAN, SCARLET DISTRICT
MRS. VALERIE CUTTER,
CUTTER AND LAMB COMPANY, VIOLET DISTRICT

ALSO:
SILENCE GASWORKS,
BLACK KINGDOM, SIZE AND REPRESENTATION UNKNOWN

London, October 8, 1889
STEAM MAKERS' GUILD HALL

2:40 p.m. Tuesday

JASPER KEATING PAUSED JUST BEFORE THE SPOT WHERE THE Scarlet King had bled all over his office carpet. The body had been removed, the carpet changed, but still he could not help that hitch in his step. *Bloody fool got what he deserved.* And yet . . .

His foot hung in midair a moment, but he forced it to step down and thus resumed his course through the office. A little squeamishness was understandable; not even Keating could deny the gruesomeness of finding his reception room splattered with brains. But this superstitious dread of crossing his own floor had to end. Being so off balance wasn't like him at all.

Frowning, he picked up his jacket from the back of his chair and pushed his arms into the sleeves. Everything hinged on which story he told the world about Scarlet's death. How much should he say about Roth's involvement? Was it worth his while to keep his maker's name out of the press? Should he take the credit himself? Or was blaming a man who was about to be dead anyway the cleanest solution? *Timing is everything.*

Timing and an eye for opportunity. Alice was about to be a young, pretty, rich widow with a titled son and another alliance to make. Keating could use that, and a dose of mourning would force her to remember who was in charge. He was more than a little annoyed with his daughter. She had become far too attached to Roth when Keating required her loyalty for himself, and this premature change of cast would put her in her place.

Of course, Alice didn't know about the poison yet. Roth had hoped to spare her, and Keating had agreed. He couldn't afford hysterics right now, although he would miss the touch of drama. *Damnation.*

As Keating finished buttoning his jacket, his gaze fell on a wooden box the size of a carpet slipper. It sat on the shelf behind his desk, right at elbow height. Irritation made him tug at his cuffs, straightening them with a decisive snap. There was only one thing worse than finding out your maker shot his poisoner all over your office carpet, and that was discovering that same maker was a turncoat. Both Roth and the Cooper girl had vanished.

With a leaden feeling in his belly, Keating reached toward the box, his fingers twitching. Nothing he saw beneath the lid would make him happy, so he stopped, rubbing his thumb against his fingertips. *Don't bother. You already know the answer.* But knowing wasn't the same as being certain, so he picked up the box and set it on his desk. It was heavy, the polished rosewood finish hiding the heavy mechanism within.

Evelina's bracelets were only one half of the containment device that imprisoned her. This was the rest. He unlatched the lid and raised it with a faint click. Beneath it was a series of round dials showing direction, distance, and time. Keating looked at the position of the needles and swore.

Roth had unlocked the bracelets to allow Evelina to leave the university grounds, but that didn't disable the tracking mechanism. Unfortunately, the device used her dormitory rooms as the central point from which her location was calculated. Setting the tracking mechanism was a cumbersome business requiring the services of Her Majesty's Laboratories. Baskerville Hall, just over two hundred miles to the southwest, had been within its range, if only just. Keating hadn't seen the need to reset the whole mechanism for a trip scheduled to last only days. Now he wished he had, because all the indicators on the device were in the neutral position, unable to read a thing.

Bile soured Keating's mouth. Evelina was out of range of his device's reach. Tobias Roth had vanished. Her Majesty's Laboratories were destroyed and there were rumors that Madam Thalassa and her followers had done it. It didn't take a genius to figure out that Evelina had played a role in the sabotage and then escaped—and that meant she had the key to the bracelets.

Keating polished a fingerprint off the convex face of one of the dials, his knuckles brushing the green felt inside the lid. Then his temper overcame him and he slammed the lid shut with a bang. Roth was an idiot or a traitor, and Holmes had been no help at all. He'd claimed to be fully occupied chasing a giant, murderous hound over the moor.

This much he knew: Evelina's disappearance had happened overnight. Keating had sent out a search party of his best men, but they'd turned up nothing, and that was no surprise. He had gone to bed one night knowing just where she was, and by the time his streetkeeper had checked the device the next morning, she was beyond the limits of its

reach. *I was duped.* And he would bet his last shilling
Holmes was in on it. Holmes, Roth, and perhaps even those
fools at the university.

Of course, the restraints had an automatic safeguard
against just such events. This latest model didn't depend on
the bracelets being within range, but upon the number of
times the key was turned. The key would soon stop
working—if it hadn't already—and she would die in agony.
A just punishment, if the waste of a promising operative. *So
much for lenience. I should have burned her long ago.*

Fuming, Keating left his suite of offices, slammed the
door closed, locked it, and stalked down the corridor of the
Steam Makers' Guild Hall. He glanced over his shoulder,
missing Roth's presence, and then cursed himself for doing
it. *Damn Roth.* Still, it had been good to have a future viscount on staff; it gave his entourage presence. *And damn
Scarlet,* he thought grimly. Reading had cost Keating a
valuable asset. Good makers didn't fall out of trees. Now,
sadly, the only future left for Roth was to die quickly off-
stage and with the least fuss possible. *And maybe he deserves it.*

Anger throbbing in his gut, Keating reached the stairs and
began to descend, wondering how much of all this to reveal
in the meeting that would begin—he checked his watch—
mere minutes from now.

He continued, turning left toward the meeting rooms. He
saw the Blue King up ahead, with three of his ragged Blue
Boys guiding the steam-powered chair he rode in. Although
his territory comprised the poorest parts of the East End,
where starvation was commonplace, he was enormously,
grotesquely fat.

Behind the chair, carrying a portfolio under one arm, was
Mr. Juniper, the Blue King's elegant man of business. The
fellow paused, bowing slightly in Keating's direction. The
gesture rankled, reminding Keating of one other unpleasant
discovery he'd made in the last week—Juniper's true name
was Moriarty, and he was a mathematics professor at the
very same college where Evelina had been attending. Could
he have played a role in her escape?

Keating slowed his pace, not wanting to confront King Coal's entourage right away. For the first time the Gold King could recall, he was actually nervous. There was an unusual amount that could go wrong today.

A dainty gloved hand fell on his arm. "Mr. Keating, a word if you please."

He tensed when he realized that it was Mrs. Valerie Cutter, better known as the Violet Queen. She had a small geographical territory, but her true kingdom was the brothels and a few of the London periodicals—though some hinted at a significant spy network. Information was her specialty, and thus she was not a woman to brush off. Keating stopped. "How may I help you, madam?"

Mrs. Cutter was dressed in a deep magenta costume decorated in long fringe that no doubt cost dearly but put Keating in mind of a lampshade. She was in her midforties, dark haired, and still handsome except for the cold glitter in her eyes. "We are in tumultuous times, Mr. Keating."

He cast a glance at the monumental steam clock mounted above the entrance to the council chamber. "Not only tumultuous, but fleeting. I am all ears for whatever you have to say, but keep in mind that we are in danger of being late."

She gave him a coy smile that still managed to be annoyed. "Then I will come directly to my point. You need a friend."

"Do I?"

"Don't be foolish, darling. We've all heard about the laboratories."

A bad taste formed at the back of his mouth. "And what do I have to do with that?"

"Nothing, officially, but everyone knows you took an interest in the place. Having it blow up like that looks bad. Some even say it was magic."

"It was the boiler," he said with a stiff smile.

"Something came to the boil, that much is certain." She snapped open her fan, covering her smiling lips.

He'd had enough of the exchange. "Are you volunteering to be my friend, Mrs. Cutter?"

"I find myself casting about for a safe harbor. The last one appears to have been shot."

Keating had been half expecting this, since Scarlet and Violet had always been close. "I have mooring points available for such a delightful craft as yours, but such things require negotiation."

"Trust me when I say you won't regret my offer. I know what evidence Scarlet had on Green. I got it for him. My network is second to none. I can get you whatever you want on whomever you please." As she spoke, her words dropped to a huskier range, losing at least half their polish. It was a bit like listening to a voice undress.

"And all you want is the shelter of my armies?"

She cast her gaze downward, thick lashes dusting her cheekbones. "I'm the only baron without regiments of my own. I wouldn't mind a few of those German airships that Scarlet had his eye on, if you can see your way to throwing them into the bargain."

And what, pray tell, would a whore do with airships? Still, he would rather have an alliance than not. Of any of them, Violet was the weakest and the one he trusted least. With the fewest obvious weapons, she would aim for the throat at once, not bothering with a warning blow.

He raised her hand to his lips. "Why don't we commit to an agreement in principle and work out the finer points after today's council?"

"Do you promise that we will both survive it?"

"It goes without saying that will depend on both of us. Together, perhaps we may."

She slipped her hand through his arm, awarding him a practiced smile. "I would feel much better with a friend at the table."

"As would I," he said, knowing that all he had gained was a slight delay before her knife sank into his spine.

He escorted her through the double doors to the council chamber. Their aides were already assembled and talking loudly among themselves. Those with status—like Mr. Juniper/Moriarty and like Roth once upon a time—stood directly behind the chairs of the principals, forming a ring of spectators around the table. The hubbub collided with the sound of glassware as servants placed glasses and pitchers of water on the table.

He saw Violet to her seat and then circled to his own. Green was once again playing the role of chair, which had the disadvantage of forcing them to listen to her grating voice; it was enough to make one's ears bleed. Keating sometimes wondered if she had talked the late Mr. Spicer into his grave.

He glanced around the table, noting that the Black Kingdom—better known as the underground realms beneath the London streets—had sent three people this time. A nursemaid in her apron and starched cap sat between a girl of about twelve and a boy of about eight. They were dressed very correctly, the girl in a pinafore and the boy in short pants, but all was black and white without a stitch of color. All three were utterly unsmiling, with eyes slightly too large for their faces.

Normally, Keating would have objected to seeing children at the table, but this was the Black Kingdom. No one knew who ran it and no one really wanted to know. There was an aura of something *wrong* about everyone who appeared from down there. Keating wouldn't have been surprised if any one of the three had extracted a live rat from a pocket and eaten it whole and squirming.

The Green Queen banged her knuckles on the table to bring them to order. "Gentlemen! And ladies. Order, please!"

Her voice sliced through the room, mowing down conversation like so much hay. She then began the recitation of several points of order, which Keating tuned out. His attention went back to the rest of the table, wondering who was in league with whom. There was rumor that Blue had made a pact with the Black Kingdom, but wasn't sure that was true or even possible. Nevertheless, of all the steam barons, the Blue King—better known as King Coal—gave him pause. Thanks to Evelina Cooper, he knew that before the air battle Dr. Magnus had been Blue's maker.

Then the Green Queen's words broke into his thoughts. "Let us take a moment to remember those absent today."

"Yes, let us," Keating interjected. "William Reading is no longer in his chair, regaling us with his unique sense of humor." *Or his lethal poisons.* "However, despite what the newspapers would have us believe, his death is hardly a mystery."

And then he heard the sound that he had been waiting for—the deep rumble of an engine. His stomach uncoiled as one element of uncertainty resolved itself in accordance with his plans.

Gr-r-r-r-r-r-r-R-R-R-R-R-R.

As the motor grew louder, they all looked up at the model of the dirigible hanging from the ceiling, but the engine they heard was actually flying low over the rooftops. Keating pulled out his pocket watch. *On time down to the second.* He started to feel downright cocky.

"What do you mean, not a mystery?" asked the Blue King in his high, reedy wheeze.

Keating made a gesture and one of his aides produced William Reading's portfolio, as well as a pair of gloves. Keating pulled the extra gloves over his own and snapped open the portfolio, removing the plans for the brass abomination and spreading them across the table. "Pray, do not touch these unless you are adequately gloved. There is a deadly poison on these pages."

The few who had been leaning forward with interest drew back at that, but everyone obviously recognized what the pages were. Moriarty bent closer, his eyebrows raised as he peered over the Blue King's shoulder.

"Did Reading give you these?" asked the Green Queen, her square, unlovely face flushing a mottled red.

"Yes," Keating said. Did it matter that Scarlet hadn't precisely *meant* to give them up? "Though I think the more interesting point was how he came by them."

He gave Valerie Cutter a significant look. In the last few days, he'd dug out the secrets of her involvement in the matter of the Clock Tower, and he was putting her on the spot. Now was the moment where he found out what her alliance was worth—would she stand with him, or not? She fidgeted for a moment, toying with the fringe on her sleeve, and then replied with a dainty sigh. "He received them through one of my intermediaries."

"And your intermediary got them from?" Keating prompted.

"Green's maker, Mr. Blind."

King Coal wheeled his chair to get a better view of Green, his look incredulous. "You put the bug in Big Ben? That hardly seems your style."

"Oh, I don't know," said Mrs. Cutter, a hint of claws in her tone. "Mrs. Spicer runs the financial district, after all. Clerks, bankers, lawyers, insurance men—those folks are good at putting a stick in the spokes when they take a notion."

Jane Spicer rose from her seat, ramrod-straight beneath the stiff silks of her bottle-green dress. Then she fixed Keating in her sights and raised a finger, pointing like the accuser from a Shakespearean tragedy. "No one ever stood up to him. I had to make a statement."

No, you didn't. Keating's gut clenched, knowing everything depended on the next two minutes. Either he was going to get rid of this harpy, or they would all turn on him together. "You, Mrs. Spicer, wanted my territory in the City of Westminster. If you think destroying a national monument—"

"You seized Scarlet's territories without so much as a by-your-leave!" she snapped.

"Did you have first refusal on a piece of it?" Keating asked coolly. "I'm sure you have a solicitor who could call upon mine."

"You took it right out from under the rest of us."

"Isn't winner take all the point of commerce? I'm sure some of the smaller counting houses had the same complaint when you swept in."

He'd barely finished speaking when the first bomb dropped. The rumble of the explosion rattled the drinking glasses on the table. A puff of dust fell from the model dirigible, indicating that it was time to clean.

"What was that?" wheezed the Blue King, visibly anxious.

"Most likely the Imperial Bank," Keating replied. "Your headquarters are upstairs, aren't they, Jane?"

Mrs. Spicer's cheeks went from red to white. "Curse you, Keating!"

The nursemaid from the Black Kingdom rose, and silence fell. The representatives of the underground rarely spoke, but when they did the rest listened. "Destroy what you must, but do not disturb what lies below. If your weapons shake the earth, you threaten to wake our king." She spoke with a cut-glass accent more befitting a duchess than a servant, but it was her words that caught Keating's attention. "You wouldn't like him much when he is awake."

"Wake your king?" he repeated. "I doubt anyone in this room has the slightest notion what you are talking about."

"He sleeps," she said, the tilt of her head reminding him of a bird hunting a worm. "Do not wreck yourself upon his anger. He will demand recompense."

"And what would he do?" the Blue King asked, sounding caught between incredulity and something close to fear.

The nursemaid turned to him, eyes impassive. "Whatever you dread most."

"What is your name?" the Violet Queen demanded. "Who are you to threaten us like this?"

"The daylight world banished its nightmares long ago." The nursemaid put one hand on each of the children, caressing their hair. "Leave us be, and we are an uneasy dream you will soon forget. But disturb us . . ." The rest of her statement hung unspoken.

The ground shook with a second explosion, and it broke the spell of the nursemaid's warning, replacing a vague threat with something much more immediate. The Green Queen wheeled on Keating. "What are you doing?"

He bared his teeth in a not-quite smile. "Retaliating for what you did to me—only I'm better at it. Withdraw your troops from Scarlet's borders."

"I don't bow to threats. Surely you know that by now."

Another explosion followed, this one closer. A glass fell over, swamping Scarlet's poisonous papers. People shuffled out of the downstream path.

Blue laughed, sounding like leaky bellows. "That's not a threat, Mrs. Spicer. And I'd tell your troops to worry about your own territories. It sounds like there won't be much left at this rate."

Keating gave Blue an acknowledging nod. Green tossed her agenda to the floor. "This meeting is adjourned."

There was a beat of silence. The children from the Black Kingdom watched the poisoned water trickle past them, their faces impassive. Keating tore his gaze from them and back to Jane Spicer.

"There are formalities to be observed. You defaced the Palace of Westminster," Keating reminded her. "I'm sure the queen would like a word."

Green scoffed. "I'm sure she'd like a word with you about those streets of hers you're bombing."

But then the double doors opened and Keating's own soldiers filed in, their gold uniforms almost tastelessly bright. The Green Queen's aides—pinched-looking men who looked like they hunched over ledgers from dawn to dusk—stood quickly aside.

"Surely you jest, Keating!" There was a flash of bewilderment on Mrs. Spicer's plain face. He'd seen it before, in this very room, when they had ousted Gray. That time, she had been quite happy to take Gray's property and let him go to the devil. *This moment of ignominy will come to each of us, sooner or later, until one of us has won.*

But the moment the soldiers touched her, she came back to life. "I left instructions!" she barked, struggling as her wrists were lashed behind her back. "If I don't return, my people will know what to do."

If you don't return, your people will be popping champagne corks.

She'd lost the iron control that kept her spine so straight and was thrashing wildly, kicking out at her captors. "Unhand me! I have wealth. I can pay you."

"I'm sure Her Majesty's private service will be interested

in the details, Mrs. Spicer. Be sure to answer their questions regarding your income promptly and without omission." Keating kept his face in a superior sneer, but he didn't relax until he saw her marched from the room.

Then he looked around at Blue, Violet, and the unsettling delegation from Black. *We're the only ones left. Once events begin to move, they don't dally.*

Another boom shook the earth. He'd given orders to flatten as much of Green's territory as possible, sparing his own bank, of course. He gave the table a light rap with his knuckles. "Any other items of business we want to discuss?"

King Coal gave him a withering look. "Not now, Mr. Keating."

"Then shall we discuss terms?"

Blue laughed, exchanging a glance with Moriarty. "You're blowing up London. I have a lot of terms for you, none of them polite." He reversed his chair away from the table, and his Blue Boys assembled behind it. "I'll see you at the barricades."

This wasn't how Keating had wanted it to end. There should have been a treaty—one he could break at his leisure. "You're inviting the Baskervilles to do their worst."

"I'm tired of wondering what they'll do. Maybe it's time we broke a few eggs, Mr. Keating. Let's see what kind of a pudding we have at the end of the day."

Keating sneered. "And no doubt you'll eat it, whatever it is."

King Coal chuckled. "Put what you like on my plate, Mr. Keating. I have a prodigiously strong stomach. Perhaps I'll eat you alive."

He wheeled out of the room, leaving the Gold King alone with Mrs. Cutter and the alarming children. *Damnation.* He turned to the nursemaid. "I imagine there will be a great deal of panic on the streets. Would you like an escort to your homes?"

"Thank you, sir, but no," the maid replied in her cultured accent. "We're used to fending for ourselves."

Then the boy smiled, showing a row of sharply filed teeth.

Keating caught his breath, a primitive response making him push back his chair. *Are they even human?*

Which was the only reason that when Moriarty ducked back into the doorway and fired his weapon, the bullet slammed into Keating's shoulder instead of his heart.

The war was on.

CHAPTER THIRTY-NINE

"MOTHERS ARE OBLIVIOUS CREATURES," POPPY PROCLAIMED. Poppy had come to visit Alice for the afternoon and they'd taken Jeremy for a walk, leaving his nurse behind. It had seemed like a delightful idea—they both needed some cheering up, and Alice was one of her favorite people. Poppy wasn't sure how well it was working, though. She kept thinking about the coded message—wondering how Bucky was getting on with it—which led her to what Bucky had said about Tobias, and that kept ending up with her wondering how long she could go without telling Alice her husband was nearby. Poppy would have felt better if she could have *done* something instead of stewing with anxiety, but she hadn't had a single good idea. She bit her lip, trying to concentrate on how cute the baby was, and not how guilty she felt.

"We quickly develop the ability to ignore what is not essential." Alice picked up Jeremy, who was fussing and—Poppy had to acknowledge it—slimy with drool. "I learned quickly not to wear silk in the nursery so that I could put cuddling my son first." She then made adoring noises until Jeremy giggled.

Poppy smiled at a pair of older ladies, who were all but staring at the striking red-haired woman and her perfect child. They didn't notice her, so she returned to the task of pushing the perambulator. It was one of the clockwork models, so it trundled along practically on its own, ticking gently as the spring wound down. It was one of the newer models, so they'd only had to stop and wind the crank once.

The day was dry, if not sunny, and cool enough to make a brisk walk pleasant. Still, it was a long journey around the park near Cavendish Square—about twice the circumference of the world when one had an infant in tow. By the end Poppy had been tempted to weigh Jeremy to see if the quantity of liquid emerging from the baby in various forms corresponded in any way to what went in, or if he was somehow pulling all that fluid from the aether. Alice took it utterly in stride, mopping up her infant with a doting calm.

Some of the fussing was surely because, having discovered that he could squirm from one place to another, Jeremy was already plotting his next adventure. Being carted about like luggage was beneath his dignity—at least for the next dozen yards. After that, he began to content himself with a speculative gumming of his blanket. The state of blissful silence lasted until they arrived back at Alice's door.

Poppy gathered their shopping while Alice sent one of the footmen out to wrangle the perambulator. Jeremy was starting to nod off, face squashed against his mother's shoulder, and Alice mounted the stairs to the nursery, not even bothering to shed her wraps.

Poppy let Alice go ahead, the fresh air making her yawn. She stowed the packages of embroidery thread and adventure novels that she'd bought—all of them took place in exotic lands and one even had headhunters!—and took off her coat. Then she trotted upstairs, hearing the faint clatter of the housemaids in the kitchen, she hoped making tea.

Alice was just tucking Jeremy into his nest of blankets when Poppy slipped into the room. Alice bent over to kiss her son, a loose strand of her fox-red hair sliding over her brow. "He misses his father," Alice said.

"How can you tell?" Poppy asked dubiously—but still with a pang of guilt and worry.

"I just can."

There was no point in arguing, and after Madam Thalassa

and Mouse and Bird, Poppy wasn't sure what to doubt anymore. "I'm sure Tobias wishes he were home."

Alice gave a half smile, her eyes full of complexities. "Thank you for coming today. I was very glad of the company."

Poppy bent over the cradle, wanting to tickle the sleeping baby but knowing better. "I was glad to. I like having someone to visit on my own."

Making a considering sound, Alice turned to adjust the curtains. "It was hard, you know, coming into your family. You and your friends are all so close knit. I didn't have brothers and sisters, so it's been a bit hard knowing how to make a place for myself."

That surprised Poppy. "I think we all just barged our way in."

"Even Evelina?"

"She's always been around," Poppy said, and then wished she hadn't. Alice had tensed—but Poppy soon realized that sudden hunch of the shoulders had nothing to do with what she had said. Thunder was rolling through the air.

"Come look at this," Alice said, the curtains pushed back in one hand. The gray afternoon light washed over her, making a strong contrast to the dim room.

Poppy came up beside her, wary of the tension in her voice. "What is it?"

"Look at that dirigible." Alice pointed to the skyline. "Isn't that the *Helios*?"

"Yes." The shape of it was seared into Poppy's brain, a souvenir from the night of the air battle. "I wonder what it's doing right over London? It's flying awfully low."

And then its belly opened, and tiny black shapes spilled out. "Damnation!" Alice cried, grabbing Poppy's arm so hard pain shot through it.

"What?" But Poppy found out in the next instant. The windows rattled as a distant boom shook the entire world, as if a giant boot had just stomped the earth. *Not thunder at all.* Three more rumbles followed in quick time, and Poppy grabbed for Alice—but she had whirled away, snatching Jeremy from the cradle and clutching him close.

Mrs. Polwarren, the wet nurse, flew into the room, the baby gown she had been mending still in her hand. "Ma'am, what is it?" she demanded in a querulous voice. "What is going on?"

Whatever it was, Poppy couldn't make sense of it. She scrambled back to the window, trying to see more, but there were trees and buildings in the way. What she could see was dirigibles appearing in twos and threes in the northern skies, their balloons a bloody red. *The Scarlet King's air fleet.*

But the Scarlet King was dead. Someone else was raining down destruction. *Who? Why?* She started to shiver even as she craned her neck to see the airships fly over like swift, silent birds of prey. This was a nightmare. It was completely illogical and awful. She fixed her glare on the dirigibles, willing them back to where they came from. *There are people down here. What did they do to deserve this?*

Then Alice was at her elbow, still holding the baby as Mrs. Polwarren rustled in the drawers behind them. Alice spoke quietly. "I told her to pack a bag in case we have to leave in a hurry."

Suddenly Poppy wanted to be home so badly her stomach twisted. Im was there, and her mother. "And go where?"

"I don't know," Alice said, her blue eyes suddenly bright with tears. "Someplace safe for Jeremy. I wish Tobias were here!"

She looked so terrified, every bit as bad as Poppy felt. She leaned in close, dropping her voice to nothing. "He is; he's at Bucky's toy factory."

Surprise bloomed on Alice's face. "What?"

Poppy held a finger to her lips, and Alice gave a short, sharp nod. The next moment, a fresh barrage of rumbles growled low and distant. Mrs. Polwarren knocked a picture over on the dresser, making everyone jump. Jeremy started to cry.

Poppy's nerves howled in sympathy. *I have to get home.* She felt like a small animal needing to bolt for her burrow, and she would feel even better if Alice and the baby came along. She laced her fingers together, squeezing hard to stop the convulsive trembling in her hands. "I can't see anything from here. I'm going up to the attic."

"No, it's too dangerous!" Alice protested, but Poppy was already rushing for the stairs. There was no more danger up there than anywhere else in the house if an airship dropped one of its explosives.

What she wanted wasn't just the attic, but the tiny iron balcony that ran outside the window of the maids' chambers. Poppy hurried through the small room with its sloping walls, stepping carefully around the sewing machine with its pile of mending to get to the window. The balcony was just big enough for a few potted plants and it had the view Poppy wanted. She pushed up the sash and stepped outside, easing her feet between the clay pots filled with geraniums.

The first thing she saw was people milling below, looking up and pointing. A few noticed her and started pointing her way instead.

"What do you see?" a man called up from below.

Poppy shaded her eyes. It wasn't sunny, but the gray sky still held a glare. And now to the east the gray was joined by roiling black smoke. "They're all going toward the Tower," she said.

"Whitechapel?" he called back.

"Closer, I think." At least it wasn't in the direction of Hilliard House. Maybe that was a selfish thought, but she wasn't about to apologize. *I want to go home!*

Poppy began to feel queasy and gripped the window frame behind her. The balcony didn't have a railing to speak of beyond a lip of black iron curlicues as high as her bootlaces. Fear and vertigo were mixing in her stomach in a most unpleasant way.

But all thoughts vanished when a heavy shadow crept over her, blotting out the light. All noise on the street below stopped. Poppy lifted her face slowly, more than her hands shaking now. The huge belly of an airship was right above the house. She could see the flat wooden bottom of the gondola, close enough that she could make out the edges of the bomb bay doors. Her teeth chattered, and she felt as if it would squash her as mindlessly as a boot sole snuffed out an ant. But that wasn't the right comparison. That flat, threatening expanse above her was more like a face—featureless, pitiless, and wondering if perhaps she *ought* to be crushed.

A primitive instinct made Poppy crouch, her skirts pooling over the flowerpots. She could hear the growl of the propellers as the gigantic ship sailed overhead. The blood-red balloon told her it was more of Scarlet's forces—one of a trio hanging over the nearby rooftops. "Go, go, go," she whispered, urging it to pass by, now too scared to even wonder why the airships were there. She just wanted them gone.

The streets below were emptying as the gawkers ran for cover. Her curiosity crumpling, Poppy began to climb back inside the attic window, but not before she saw a black victoria pull up in front of the house. She paused long enough to untangle her skirts from the flowers, and glanced down to see Jasper Keating jump from the carriage and stumble to the front door. Something about the way he moved didn't look right.

Poppy gave the airships one last baleful look and closed the window. She didn't like the Gold King, but maybe Keating was there to take them someplace safe—or at least he might take her home. She clattered down the attic stairs, but slowed when she got to the carpeted hall that ran past the bedrooms. She could hear the nurse singing to Jeremy, trying to hush the baby as he made small, uneasy noises.

Instinct told her to move quietly as she descended to the drawing room. Perhaps it was the same sense of self-preservation that told her when her parents were arguing, because she could hear the Gold King's raised voice as she drew near.

"The laboratories are destroyed," Keating barked.

"I know," Alice replied. "I read the newspaper."

Poppy paused just outside the door, which was slightly ajar. She'd heard about the business with the secret labs as well, and had been hugely interested in the few news reports she'd been able to read. *But why are they arguing about this when someone is bombing London?* Surely the immediate threat of destruction was more important?

And yet nothing tempted her to interrupt the conversation. The air in the drawing room nearly glittered with tension. Poppy could see both speakers, but at an oblique angle. Alice was standing with her back to the tall window, the daylight embracing her like a cloak. She clasped her hands in front of her, standing close to her father.

Keating's black suit looked rumpled and his temper was in even worse condition. "They were all party to it!" he fumed.

"Who?" asked Alice.

"The Baskervilles. Holmes."

Poppy tilted her head, pushing the hair away from her ear to listen. Now the servants were hurrying to and fro upstairs, probably packing, and their heavy tread was making it harder to eavesdrop.

Alice's voice fell to a pleading tone. "You're not making sense, Father. Sir Charles is dead, and Mr. Holmes is investigating his murder."

Keating was pacing, moving in and out of Poppy's line of sight. By the way he was moving, she could tell he'd been hurt. He was holding his arm at a strange angle, and then she realized that it was in a hastily tied sling. "I know that, girl. But Holmes requested that niece of his, and I sent her there with your husband."

"I still don't understand the problem."

"It's plain," he snapped. "The Cooper girl disappeared the night the laboratories burned, and the survivors claim it was magic that brought them down. Madam Thalassa was seen in the neighborhood."

Poppy gasped, creeping a step closer. *Madam Thalassa?* And Mr. Holmes was in the area as well. Had they been working together?

"Are you saying Evelina Cooper played a role in the destruction of Her Majesty's Laboratories?" Alice asked incredulously.

"Don't underestimate her."

Poppy was too close now, but she couldn't bring herself to back away. She *had* to hear this. And she was beginning to worry, because Keating was waving a finger just under Alice's nose. "And your precious husband let her go."

"Impossible!" Alice protested, her voice rising again with anger. "Why would he disobey you?"

"The Cooper girl couldn't have escaped without his aid. She was wearing restraints and he had the key. And she had to have an accomplice because these restraints have the means to tell me where she's gone. She left so fast, so secretly, and went so far she had to have someone waiting to take her away."

"Where is she?" Alice sounded incredulous.

"So far away that she's beyond the range of my device. But she was heading west when I lost her. And it's all Roth's doing."

"But . . ." Alice trailed off, and Poppy caught her breath, suddenly terrified that she would give away the fact that Tobias was in town. All the more because it was plain that Tobias wasn't looking for Evelina. Whether he'd been responsible for her escape or not, he had let her go—and Alice would realize that.

But instead, the red-haired woman rounded on her father. "Have you stopped to think that the reason Tobias has his reservations about you might be because you threatened his family and bullied him into working for you?"

"Forced him to marry you, you mean?" he said with oily sarcasm.

Poppy gasped, clasping a hand over her mouth to stop the sound. *How can he say that to his own daughter?* If she were Alice, she'd be mortified.

But Alice was braver than that, unclasping her hands and pulling herself straight. "We've made a home."

"Yes, I can see that," said Keating quietly. "I would be proud of you if it was anyone else."

"The marriage was your idea. There was a time when I would rather have crawled home in defeat, but you wouldn't hear of it. So I stayed and made it work."

Oblivious, Keating paced in a tight circle, his coat furling behind him, and then suddenly stopped to lean with his good arm braced against the wall. "I thought he'd come to heel. God knows there is enough money and power to tempt him, but I see what he's thinking behind those fine manners. And so I don't trust him."

Alice said nothing.

"And I don't trust you. Both of you know too much for me to leave you like threads waiting to unravel. I need to tie you off in a sturdy knot."

Alice stiffened. "What does that mean?"

What *did* that mean? Poppy suddenly sensed danger in the air like something she could taste. The fear she'd felt on the balcony quickened again, but this time it was more immediate. *I don't know what to do,* she thought desperately. These were deeper waters than she'd ever experienced before.

"Tobias knows far too much about my army. He built the damn thing," Keating growled, leaning in so his face was just inches from his daughter's. "And there aren't many ways of guaranteeing his silence."

"Guaranteeing his silence?" Alice repeated incredulously.

Keating's voice turned to ice. "I had to rethink my position about your little family, Alice. It's amazing what passes through one's mind while a medic is digging a bullet from one's flesh. This afternoon changed everything. I concluded I need to be more careful about my enemies right now."

"Since when am I your enemy, Father?"

A cry of surprise came from upstairs. *The nurse.* Poppy spun and rushed toward the stairs. Right then she realized what the Gold King meant. Three of his Yellowbacks were hurrying down the stairs in their long black coats. They must have gone upstairs using the servants' staircase, because Poppy hadn't seen them enter. *But that's what I heard. Those weren't servants thundering overhead.*

She'd almost recovered from her surprise when the next shock came. Behind the first two Yellowbacks was the much smaller figure of Mrs. Polwarren, holding Jeremy cradled in her arms. The third had his weapon drawn and pointed at the pale-faced figures of the other servants who stood clustered on the landing above.

"What are you doing?" Poppy cried, terrified but dumbfounded all the same.

Jeremy sent up an angry wail. Alice rushed from the drawing room, but Keating caught her midstride. He cried out in pain, but the sudden stop jerked Alice off her feet so roughly that she dangled for a moment in her father's hand. "What is the meaning of this?" she all but shrieked.

None of this had stopped the progress of the Yellowbacks. Baby wailing, they carried on down the stairs, their hard faces set. The sound of Jeremy's distress made her too furious to give in without a fight. Poppy rushed to get between them and the door, throwing herself before it so hard that she felt the dig of the knob in her back. *I'm a viscount's daughter. They can't do anything to me.*

But the Yellowbacks simply shoved her aside as if she were no more than a bothersome cat. Poppy slipped and fell on the slick tile, banging into the wall. Her elbow sang with agony, making her eyes water. "Stop!" she snarled, scrambling back to her feet.

But there were two more Yellowbacks emerging from the back of the house. They were carrying enormous aether rifles, and one of them trained his weapon on Poppy. Suddenly, she wasn't so confident that her father's name protected her.

Alice hadn't stopped screaming at her father. "Why are you taking my baby?"

Keating had endured enough. He shoved her away and then cradled his injured arm. "It's the one thing I know will keep you and your precious husband in check."

"But it's not safe!" Poppy protested. "Someone is attacking London."

Keating rounded on her, his face ashen. He looked haggard, his eyes wild and sunken deep into his face. "That's me dropping the bombs, you stupid chit."

He swept out, following his men, and the last two guards followed him. Alice lurched after, but Poppy rushed to her side, grabbing her before the Yellowbacks interfered. She was terrified that they might just shoot.

"Let me go!" Alice tried to free herself, but Poppy just clung more tightly.

Tears leaked from under Poppy's lashes. "No, they'll hurt you and then no one will be there to save Jeremy."

She heard the baby wailing all the way to the victoria, and the sound dragged her heart bruised and aching after. Within seconds, a whip snapped and wheels scraped on the cobbles. Soon Jeremy's voice was drowned by the sound of clopping hooves.

Alice slumped against the wall, weeping. "Why is he doing this to me? He's my father!"

Shame and rage seared Poppy. Now that the guns were out of sight, she was trembling so hard that her legs were almost useless. A cold sweat just added to the shivering. *I should have been able to do something.* It would have been better if she'd had a gun of her own. "We'll get him back."

Alice's eyes were wild. "How?"

"We'll get Tobias. Mr. Keating might think he's got you trapped, but Tobias is clever. He'll figure out a way to beat him at his own game."

But Poppy gulped as she said the words, even though they seemed to give Alice hope. If Tobias was at Bucky's toy factory, he was in the midst of the war zone. So how were they going to get there?

Chapter Forty

"WAIT!" POPPY TORE AFTER ALICE, WHO WAS RUNNING DOWN the street into the flames. "Alice, wait!"

How do I get her to stop? Alice's beautiful red hair had escaped its pins and was streaming about her shoulders, her hat lost somewhere a block behind. Fortunately, her stays and bustle were more securely attached, slowing her down enough so that Poppy could catch up to her.

Poppy grabbed Alice's arm, feeling the slim bones beneath. "It's not safe!"

That was stating the obvious. Threadneedle Street was in the area where the dirigibles had finally finished dropping their explosives only an hour or so ago, and parts of it were on fire. It had been next to impossible to even draw close to the area by hackney—they'd had to go on foot forever, Alice periodically breaking into a stumbling run.

Poppy was certain they should turn around. There was plenty of light from the fires, but it was dark out and the streetlights had all been smashed. And besides, Poppy was terrified. On top of everything else—the bombs, the kidnapping, and everything else that had gone on today—this street was right where Imogen had been kidnapped. Nothing good happened here, especially not now.

It was one thing to see the bombs from a distance, and quite another to see the destruction up close. Fires bloomed everywhere, sometimes so close that Poppy could feel the heat. Buildings stood gaping like skulls with their teeth smashed in and some were simply rubble. Soldiers and police were beginning to move in, but it was clear the attack had taken everyone utterly by surprise.

And that didn't begin to cover the human cost. A lot of people had worked on those streets, and a lot of them never would again. Poppy gripped Alice as hard as she could as they moved forward. She needed to feel someone solid and whole next to her. She tried not to look at the dead man sprawled across their path, but steered her sister-in-law around him. *I can't help him now. All I can do is get Alice to Bucky's before she goes crazy.*

And then Poppy's foot brushed against something. She glanced down to see blood and cloth and knew it wasn't attached to where it should have been. *Oh, Lord.* She took quick, shallow breaths, doing her best not to vomit, and ended up choking on the smoke instead.

The building across the street was on fire, so they were forced to hug the opposite side and hurry by as fast as they could. At least it distracted Poppy from the blood on the ground.

"Where is it?" Alice asked. "The factory should be here, shouldn't it?"

Poppy looked around, trying to orient herself. She'd been there twice before, but nothing looked the same. "It was on this side," she said, waving her right hand.

Alice grabbed her wrist and hurried on. "Is that it?" she cried pointing.

Poppy saw the red and green sign dangling by one end. "Yes!"

Alice let her go and began running again, leaving Poppy behind once more. She caught up as Alice began pounding on the door, ignoring the knocker altogether. Bucky opened it to stare at them in alarm. "Ladies! Come in at once. What on earth are you doing out at a time like this?"

"Ah, Mr. Penner," Poppy said dryly, "your manners intact despite the complete collapse of civilization."

"And Miss Roth, always in the thick of things." His brown eyes brimmed with questions.

"Where's Tobias?" Alice demanded.

"How did you know—" Bucky began, casting Poppy a hard look.

"Is he here?" Alice cut him off.

"Yes, I am." Tobias came out of the back, Lord Bancroft a step behind him, and suddenly the tiny front room of the factory—already packed with toys on every surface—was too crowded. But at least her father was holding a lantern. The steady light made everything better.

Now Poppy could see that Bucky had recently converted his front offices to a miniature fairground complete with striped tents and dancing clockwork horses. Then Poppy noticed that the window must have shattered, because the miniature circus was covered with broken glass and flakes of gray soot. Her throat closed with a sudden stab of pain for the little circus animals. This wasn't their fight.

Tobias came forward, holding out his hands. He looked awful, like he'd had a terrible fever. "Alice, Poppy, what are you doing here?"

Alice opened her mouth, looked at Poppy, then back at her husband. Her eyes were wild with panic. "Father said he did all this!"

Lord Bancroft frowned, but for once it was sympathetic. "I'm afraid it's true. He destroyed this district as an act of retaliation against Spicer Industries. It seems the Green Queen was responsible for the damage to the Palace of Westminster."

Poppy's stomach roiled with anger and disbelief, and suddenly she was too hot. She leaned against the wall to stop her head from spinning.

Alice made a sound like someone had punched her in the stomach. "Papa took Jeremy!"

Tobias drew in a quick breath, his already pale face draining to white. "What?"

But Alice was crying too hard to answer. Tobias held her, murmuring shushing noises that only seemed to make things worse. Poppy's father shot her a look of inquiry.

"Mr. Keating came to the house in Cavendish Square," Poppy answered, her voice ragged. She could feel the tears crawling up her throat, but they were met by a hot anger that kept them at bay. "He took Jeremy and Mrs. Polwarren as insurance."

"Against what?" Bucky asked, sounding bewildered.

"To keep Tobias and Alice loyal because Tobias knows too much about his army. I think Keating's afraid because someone shot him."

"Who?" demanded Lord Bancroft. "How badly is he hurt?"

Not badly enough, Poppy thought. "It's just his shoulder."

Alice pushed away from her husband, her face twisted with pain as she looked into his eyes. "The Blue King's men shot Father. But that's not the only reason he's taking action. Her Majesty's Laboratories burned down. You were gone and Evelina Cooper is missing." She stopped speaking and swallowed hard. "He thinks you helped her escape."

By then, Tobias had gone very still. "Me? He took Jeremy because of *my* actions?"

Alice took a painful-sounding breath, wrapping her arms around her ribs. "Yes, he's taken Jeremy and his nurse because he believes you have betrayed him and you will again."

"Damn him!" Tobias was swelling with anger, his pale face flushing a hectic, mottled red. "Where is Jeremy now?"

"I don't know, Tobias," Alice cried. "What are you going to do?"

SPEECHLESS, TOBIAS STARED at his wife, her soot-smudged features drawn into a mask of grief. She looked up at him, her blue eyes bright in the lantern's glow. "How do we get our son back?" she asked, her voice sunk to barely more than a whisper.

She'd been one of those papa's girls right until Keating had sold her into a loveless marriage. The shock of this second betrayal had to be even more profound. She only needed one thing from her husband now—reassurance that he would stand by her and make things right. Yet it was the one thing he couldn't give her—at least, not for long.

Tobias felt a strange numbness in his chest, the residue of grief. He'd exhausted all emotion in the last few days, and what was left was a primitive roughness. She'd come to *him*. After all he'd done—after all he'd done to her, in those early days of their marriage—she trusted *him* with the one thing that mattered most to a mother. It was a sacred trust he didn't deserve, and it went without saying that he would tear London apart stone by stone to get to his son.

Something shambled to life inside that was stronger than hatred or even outrage at his own doom. It had the feral will of a curse. "I will get him back for you. Whatever it takes."

"How?" She was looking into him—not *at* him—and speaking directly to the naked, raw will he'd somehow found.

He glanced around the room, seeing the faces of the others. Poppy was slumped against the wall, Bucky's hand on her shoulder, her face stricken. *She shouldn't be seeing any of this.* He turned to his father. "I'm going to have this conversation in the back."

Bancroft nodded, for once not arguing.

Tobias led Alice to a small room that had a threadbare sofa, table, and a litter of dirty cups. The smell of fresh wood and turpentine vied with the strong scent of cheap black tea. Alice sank onto the sofa, heedless of the sawdust coating every inch of it. "What do we do?" she asked.

"We fight."

She'd stopped crying, but her face was still smudged with tears. "How?"

"Keating is on the defensive. That means he's worried, and that can only happen if he's vulnerable. We may not see a weakness in his forces, but he knows it's there."

Alice's eyes narrowed. "What are you doing in London? What happened in Dartmoor?"

Tobias sat next to her, careful to sit on her right so that he could take her hand with his left. The hand that had touched the poison had become weak and painful inside its glove.

"Evelina is free and the laboratories were a vile abomination. I wasn't behind it, but I'm not unhappy that they were destroyed."

"But Father is." Alice's eyes flashed. "Until he feels safe . . ."

"Alice," Tobias began, knowing he was at the edge of a precipice. "Your father isn't going to be safe. The Blue Boys simply pulled the trigger first, but after today there will be others who want to settle accounts. I came back to London because I believe your father and the rest of the steam barons must be stopped."

"Then he's right about you," she said, her voice barely above a whisper. "You're not loyal."

"No, I'm not."

"He's my father," she said softly, tears glittering in her lashes.

"He . . ." Tobias faltered, and then recovered himself. "You see what he's done. You came here through those fires. What kind of a man takes his own grandson? And what sort of a world is he making for Jeremy?"

"Yes, I know," she cried, her fingers convulsing in his. "I'm not a fool. He's my father and he has stolen my boy. I don't know how to act or what to think. I just want Jeremy. He's only a baby!"

Blood and thunder. Tobias pulled her into his arms, the numbness inside him cracking open again to let fresh anger rise up, raw and terrible. "You know your father better than anyone. He has properties all over London, but we will find them and search them one by one until we get our son."

"But he has properties all over the Empire," Alice protested.

"He won't be far from the war. Keating needs Jeremy close by to keep us in line."

Alice pushed him away, giving him another searching gaze. "You've turned rebel."

"Maybe." Tobias's thoughts went sideways. In the past, he'd tried to be a better man for Evelina. He'd used her as a touchstone and measure, and he'd liked who he'd been at her side. But now opinion and measurement didn't matter—everything was simple because Alice and Jeremy needed him. "I'm going to do what needs to be done. If that means calling myself a rebel, so be it."

"You went to work for my father to protect your family," she said softly. "What if the rebels lose?"

"You are my family, and I have to believe doing the right thing will be its own protection. I've tried to play by your father's rules and he still took our son. It's time I changed the game. We'll get our son back. You're going to help me do it. And we'll win in the end because you and I are going to make a plan that won't let the Gold King stop us."

She gave a slow nod, and he could see her shifting her view of the world as he watched. They remained just so, their hands linked, long enough for him to kiss her gently on the lips. He felt the relief of confession, or maybe it was that he no longer had to pretend to her or anyone else where his sympathies lay. He hadn't given her the full truth, but it was more than they'd shared before.

"I'm so glad you're home," she said.

CHAPTER FORTY-ONE

Unknown

IMOGEN STARTED AWAKE, UTTERLY DISORIENTED. THE ROOM was dark and oddly familiar, but she couldn't place where she was. Was she back in the salon?

Don't panic, said Mouse.

"Fine. Then tell me where I am." At least she remembered who she was and where she'd been before falling asleep with her head cushioned against Mouse's etched steel fur. She'd retreated to the top of the clock with Mouse so they could make plans. Nestled in among the ticking, turning wheels, they'd started considering their next moves—but she'd been exhausted. "Did I fall asleep?"

You are asleep.

"Then why am I talking to you?" She sat up, realizing Mouse wasn't anywhere in sight. "Where are you?"

Right where you left me. You're dreaming.

"Dreaming?" If she was dreaming, then she really was asleep. "Is it safe to sleep?"

I'll wake you if I need to. But maybe right now you should have a look around.

Groggy, Imogen put a hand to her forehead. Fatigue had almost come as a surprise. Though Imogen had been sickly all her life, here she was climbing and running as if she'd never had so much as a sniffle. However, sending the ciphered message had been grueling, almost as if she'd been asked to do algebra and climb a mountain at the same time. "Why do I feel so awful?"

Let's see. You had your soul ripped from your body,

you're trapped in a sorcerer's alternate reality, and you're being hunted to the death by the malevolent shade of your dead twin. Not to mention using previously untapped parapsychological strengths to send coded messages into reality. A bit of a lie-down was in order.

Imogen bristled at the sarcastic tone, then realized the rush of temper had cleared her head. "Why do I need to look around?"

You're about to learn a new trick—one that not every spirit can manage, but I'll tell you what to do.

"All right," Imogen said uneasily.

Dreams are what happen when your spirit wanders into another place—it might be a real place, or one that you've created for just that moment. But you're already a wandering spirit. The only way you can dream while you're in this place is through someone else.

"How?"

Everyone is connected to those close to them. That is how Evelina found you, and how you knew there was a séance. Those who know how to look for it can see the weave of connections on the spirit plane. All you need to do is find the thread you want and follow the spiderweb into someone's dream.

That sounded like a fine theory, but she still couldn't visualize how it worked. "And yet I'm already in a different place, so how did I get here?"

Sometimes a living soul wants to see someone so badly they call that person right across the spirit plane. Find out whose dream you're in.

"Someone dragged me here?"

Not a kind way of putting it, but essentially correct.

She shuddered, remembering the horrible nightmares she'd shared with Anna for so many years. The only thing that had kept her sister out of her dreams was laudanum. The invasion had felt like such a monstrous violation— sleep was one of the few places a person could be truly private. The last thing Imogen wanted to do was haunt someone else.

A feather of uneasiness brushing through her, she rose.

She'd been asleep on an old worn sofa. A dirty teacup sat on the floor beside it, along with a notebook and pen. Imogen looked around, realizing she was in the back room of Bucky's toy factory.

Bucky? Knowing it was him made everything different. With a rush of anticipation, she slipped through the door. The great, cavernous workshop loomed, machines and workbenches lost in a wilderness of shadows. There were shelves of toys in various states of assembly—mostly wood and clockwork, but some with soft bodies and luxurious fur. She saw a small army of ducklings with their wings outstretched, bills opened as if to quack. The next row down, ranks of tiny leopards were drying their spots. But there weren't as many toys as she remembered seeing the other time she had visited, and she felt a pang of disappointment.

In the darkness beyond, near the bay doors that opened to the outside, something enormous loomed. She couldn't quite make it out, but she wondered if whatever it was had consumed all of Bucky's time. *Of course, this is only a dream and what I see might not be real. I mustn't forget that.*

And then she began wandering through the dark warehouse. It had the shifty feel of a dream, as if the furniture and rooms weren't quite right. Even stranger, it was pitch black, but she could see perfectly well. But then a sudden bloom of candlelight drew her like a moth.

Bucky was slumped over a table with his head cradled on his arms. Imogen stopped, her hands clasped against her middle. It felt like it had been years since she'd seen him, and she drank in the sight of his sleeping face as if it were the only cool water in the desert. *I love him so much.*

It wasn't just that he was an educated, pleasant, well-off or good-looking young man. He was all those things, but he was also the one who'd put her happiness before everything else. Plus, he'd known her from the time she'd been a skinny girl in braids. If he knew her that well and still liked her— that said much.

However, she'd had no idea until that moment that he snored. "I suppose no one is perfect," she muttered, drawing near. The candle had burned low, giving off the smell of hot wax. The glow flickered across the worn wood of the table and spilled over his broad, capable hands. Bucky was in his waistcoat and shirtsleeves, his coat tossed carelessly over the back of his chair. Imogen reached out, her fingertips almost, but not quite, brushing the waves of his hair. It was a true brown, the highlights just hinting at auburn. She could just see one sleeping eye and the straight blade of his nose. She wondered if she could get away with kissing him before he woke up. After all, what was the fun of a dream without a dash of fantasy?

"Did you call me into your dreams?" she whispered. Was it just chance? Or did the fact that she'd been longing for him—and for his help—influence what had happened?

She peered over his shoulder at the papers scattered on the desk and saw it was a pencil and paper with a graph filled with alphabets and a lot of crossings-out. Imogen frowned, trying to make sense of the jumbled letters. Then she recognized the card from the clock and realized with mounting horror that it was her message—except that the clock had spelled it out in cipher.

Frustration stung. It looked like her message had been deciphered but now he was trying to find some alternate meaning for her words. And why not? The terse message she'd managed to scrape together hardly made sense. *Damn and blast!* Any scruples she had about haunting him vanished.

She put out a hand to shake his shoulder and paused a beat, wondering if her fingers would pass right through him, but she touched the smooth, cool cloth of his shirt and the hard muscle beneath. "Bucky!"

He sat bolt upright, blinking. "Huh?" His brown eyes looked almost black in the candlelight. When he saw her, they went wide. "Imogen!"

She nodded, her heart beating wildly. "Yes, it's me. I'm in your dream."

"You always were," he said, getting to his feet and holding out his hands to her.

"How are you?" she asked, perhaps a little stupidly but

she'd never contacted anyone in a dream before—at least not anyone she actually wanted to see.

"I've had a very strange day," he replied. "This is going to be the only good part, but why are you here?"

"Why wouldn't I be with you whenever I could?" She wanted to fall into his arms. She could feel his embrace already, that strong, steady warmth healing her from the bones outward. But first she had to make sure he understood. "The message from the clock is real. I need your help if I'm going to make it home."

His eyes suddenly lost their unfocussed look, replaced by the sharp intelligence she knew so well. But he still took her hands, engulfing them in his as he drew her close and pressed his lips to her brow. His touch was like a lifeline, saving her when she hadn't even known she was drowning.

"What do you need?" he murmured. "Just ask, and it's yours."

She caught his scent—male and redolent of freshly cut wood. His presence was making it desperately hard to concentrate. And he kept looking at her as if she had descended from the heavens on a glittering cloud, her bedraggled dress a gown of moonbeams. Suddenly shy, she babbled an answer, barely aware if she was making sense.

His expression turned thoughtful. "Are you sure?"

"I don't have any other weapons," Imogen replied, aware that the room seemed to be fading around them, so that they were the only solid things there.

"Then I have what you need," he said, releasing her hands. "Wait here."

And he walked into the darkness of the workshop. Alone and slightly disoriented, Imogen clasped her hands. They felt lonely without his answering grip, like half a set.

Hurry, said Mouse, startling her. She'd forgotten all about him. *We don't have much time before we need to move.*

"Bucky?" she called plaintively.

And then he was suddenly there again, holding an object in both hands. It was the size of a pineapple and covered in many overlapping plates of silver metal. "Be careful with this."

She took it from him, the weight surprising her. In the way of dreams part of her understood everything it could do while the rest of her could not. "Thank you. I think you just saved my life."

"Then open your eyes so you can save mine," he whispered, leaning over. This time he kissed her on the lips, cradling her face as if she were a flower. The living warmth of his breath thawed her, returning color to her soul. She'd been lost and starving for touch, and his touch most of all.

"Don't let me go," she pleaded. "Let me stay with you here!"

His gaze met hers, and she saw his heartbreak there. "If only I could," he whispered.

Imogen trembled as he kissed her again, and she tasted him thoroughly and long, but eventually the pressure of his mouth on hers began to fade. She became aware of the ache of fatigue, the heavy, incessant ticking of machinery, and a heavy weight on her stomach.

"No!" she cried softly as her eyes opened and she found herself back in the clock.

I feel as if I have been caught between the pages of a penny romance. There was enough sticky sweetness there to ice a dozen tea buns.

Imogen narrowed her eyes. "If you don't like my dreams, stay out of them."

At least your steely jawed hero has some useful talents.

"Of course he does," she said automatically as Mouse shifted, making her sit up.

It was then she looked down to see what was sitting on her stomach. Her fingers ran over the chill metal of the silver plates. A wave of triumph made her laugh out loud and she scrambled to her feet.

The bomb Bucky had given her was still in her hands.

CHAPTER FORTY-TWO

London, October 9, 1889

THE VIOLET QUEEN'S RESIDENCE

2:15p.m. Wednesday

"YOU ASSUMED RESPONSIBILITY FOR MRS. LOREN'S HOUSE of pleasure, did you not?" said the Violet Queen to Miss Hyacinth, motioning for her to take a chair in the over-stuffed, overbaubled purple velvet parlor. The decor was at once titillating and inappropriately amusing. Purple might have been the color of sin in the Empire—Hyacinth had dyed her own hair the lightest shade of lilac—but this sitting room was too much. All in all, the place was a bit like the inside of a grape.

"That is so, madam," Hyacinth replied with excruciating politeness, settling on the edge of a chaise longue. She was wearing a dark blue corded silk that spread like an ink stain across the plush fabric.

"Which is why I asked that you come to see me." The Violet Queen resumed her own seat, nearly sitting on a peach-colored Pomeranian, which yapped querulously at the descending bustle. "It's customary to pay a courtesy call, my dear, just for the sake of being good neighbors. We are in the same line of work after all. Better yet, Mrs. Loren should have brought you around for an introduction. But there you are. Times just aren't what they once were."

Hyacinth smiled apologetically at the so-called Queen of Whores. *Indeed. Once upon a time, my parents' footmen would have tossed you down the front steps in the unlikely event that you set foot on our property.*

And then, of course, there was the fact that a piece of the metropolis had been blasted to smithereens. Not here, well north of Russell Square, and not in Whitechapel, where Hyacinth kept her establishment, but right around where the ill-fated Green Queen had counted her coin. The morning had brought a queer mood to the city, as if everyone was holding his breath for what came next. Hyacinth expected business would be hopping. Danger brought out the need for pleasure.

"I apologize for my tardiness in paying my courtesies, madam. Unfortunately, there was much to do and learn. I must say that I'm surprised you thought to keep this appointment, with everything else going on."

"Our business doesn't stop for war." The Violet Queen tilted her head slightly. She had once been a beautiful woman, but time had reduced her valuation. Lines bracketed her mouth, and no amount of powder could substitute for the flawless sheen of youth. But her dark hair was still glossy and elegantly dressed, and her dark rose gown was the latest in French couture. Hyacinth filed away the details for future reference. It was good to know a whore could age so well. If she lived long enough, she might need the pointers.

"But never mind all that," said the Violet Queen. The woman pulled the dog into her lap, stroking its puff of fur. "You are here now, and we can catch up our acquaintance. I have it on good authority that revenues have gone up in your establishment. You are to be congratulated."

"My clientele sets a high premium on novelty," Hyacinth replied. "There had been a shortage of fresh ideas in the establishment before I arrived."

The Violet Queen narrowed her eyes. "And where would you have got such ideas, Miss Hyacinth?"

"I was always good with a riding crop."

"And you have no qualms about applying it to human flesh?"

"None. In fact, I have laid in quite the selection of aids. I had, um, acquaintances who were quick to instruct me once they realized I had an aptitude for such work."

"And I take it word has spread of your particular talents?"

"Indeed it has." Hyacinth allowed satisfaction to creep into her voice. "It is quite gratifying to see one's efforts rewarded, especially at the higher levels of Society. It seems a good beginning to a satisfying enterprise."

"And your business grows?"

"It has trebled, madam."

The Violet Queen dumped the dog from her lap, her manner suddenly cool. "Such fiendish ways, and a young beauty to boot. I was once such as you, winning favor. Showers of jewels one day, a journey to Paris the next."

She's jealous. Best watch my step.

"I understand the Duke of Morton has become one of your clients."

"That is not for me to say," Hyacinth demurred.

"Don't be coy," the Violet Queen snapped. "I warmed his bed for years. Don't forget we deal in information just as readily as pleasure."

So it seems. But Hyacinth just gave a respectful nod.

"Tell me," the older woman went on airily, though her voice was as hard and thin as blown glass. "Since you fancy the darker arts of our profession, do you enjoy receiving like treatment?"

"Only from experienced hands," Hyacinth replied, an edge creeping into her own words. No matter her profession, some things were personal. "Too many who pick up a whip have no sense of finesse. Flogging is not merely clubbing someone to death with strips of leather. That is not only ineffectual but embarrassing in the extreme."

That surprised a laugh from the Violet Queen. "I think I may come to like you, Miss Hyacinth. It is hard not to appreciate a connoisseur—especially one who looks fair to earning me a profit."

"A profit, madam?" Hyacinth sat up straight. She'd guessed this was more than a social summons, but she hadn't seen this coming.

The dog, clearly sensitive to the charged atmosphere,

began to whine and run in circles. The Violet Queen hushed it with a sharp word.

"We shall get to that point, but before we do, tell me something of yourself," said the woman. This time, her tone brooked no argument. "I know a little, Miss Asterley-Henderson."

Hyacinth flinched inside. She hated hearing her old name, hated remembering the position she'd lost, but she'd be damned before she showed that to this old tabby. Yet that stab of regret was followed by an icy trickle of fear. Her true identity was her Achilles' heel.

She folded her hands in her lap, eyes demurely downcast. "Then you are aware that I was previously known as the Honorable Violet Isadora Asterley-Henderson. My father was a viscount." And she'd had a dowry that could have bought a decent slice of Mayfair.

"Your given name is Violet?" asked the Violet Queen.

I state my personal tragedy—the loss of rank, family, honor, virtue—and this is what she fastens on? "I changed it, of course," she said hastily. "To bear the name Violet in this occupation would be presumptuous."

"I should think so," the queen of whores said tartly. "I assume you received a decent education?"

"At the Wollaston Academy for Young Ladies." *And what does that have to do with anything?*

The Violet Queen's lip curled in feline satisfaction. Hyacinth was clearly under the velvet of her paw, but the claws could come out at any moment. "Ah, yes, where you dabbled in black magic, exposing your family to the law. Not a highly intelligent move, I must say. It would be best for you if you considered that lesson learned."

The door to the purple cave suddenly opened, making Hyacinth jump. A finely boned serving man glided in with a silver tray. A quick assessment told Hyacinth he was likely a pleasure boy who had aged out of his role. He set down the tray, waited for the Violet Queen's dismissal, bowed, and left.

Hyacinth stared at the tray of glasses, cups, and pastries, trapped between her current reality and her history at Wollaston. Remembering was like vitriol on her soul. There had been a young man, and he had died, and she had wanted him back. All it had taken was a spell. How was she supposed to know that he would return as the shambling dead? The only one who'd tried to help Hyacinth out of that disaster had been Evelina Cooper, but there was only so much even she had been able to do. *She helped me put Tom back into his grave, but she couldn't save me from my own folly.*

The spell had been a terrible mistake, one born of unspeakable grief. Her family had paid. She'd paid. The school had been shut down, the headmistress ruined for failing to stop illegal acts within its walls. And now this hag was dragging it all up again.

"I believe you were the only member of your family spared execution by fire, and that only on account of your youth. You were supposed to spend your remaining days in Her Majesty's Laboratories, I believe." She paused, her cat's smile widening to show small, white teeth. "Would you care for some cordial? You've gone a trifle pale, Miss Hyacinth."

"I learned a lesson about magic, madam." Hyacinth's stomach was a painful knot and nervous sweat soaked her chemise where it was trapped beneath her stays.

"And one about obedience as well, I hope."

"More than one, in fact. My obedience, and the enforcement thereof, was why my captors granted me leniency. That was where I discovered I had a talent for persuasion, and they were the ones who showed me the use of my tools. As I mentioned before, they were quite the enthusiasts once I convinced them I was an apt pupil."

The Violet Queen poured out a tiny glass of syrupy liquid and passed it to Hyacinth. She accepted it, her fingers quivering slightly within her pale silk gloves. "Necessity is an efficient schoolmistress," said the older woman. "That is how we all come to this business, I'm afraid. I am willing to let the past stay in the past, but it is best to put our cards on the table right away."

"You hold the trump," Hyacinth said, setting aside the glass. She wasn't about to trust anything she hadn't seen the Violet Queen drink first.

"Correction. I hold *all* the cards, and it's best you don't forget that fact, young lady." The Violet Queen's eyes turned flinty. "You are operating a business within my area of influence. I was fortunate enough to wed a member of the Steam Council, but I ruled the pleasure houses of London long before I was wife or widow. And my heart is still in that work, even if I no longer give the clients my personal time."

"Duly noted, madam." *In other words, the clients prefer lamb to mutton.*

"I require regular reports on your customers. Who they are and what they say. Which way their preferences run. And I require the usual portion of your earnings for a house of your standing. Do you understand?"

I understand extortion when I see it. "Of course, madam. And do you say this to every new procuress in London?" *Which I know you do not, or I would have heard about it.*

"Only those worth my time. As I said, you are turning a profit, and I want half."

"What?" Hyacinth was on her feet.

"Manners, Miss Asterley-Henderson," chided the Violet Queen, clearly enjoying herself. "You might have tupped your way out of prison before you ever reached Her Majesty's Laboratories, but I can send you back with a single telegram. The laboratories might have burned, but there are those who will find a place for you in their private facilities nonetheless. I just have to ask. I have that kind of power. You do not."

Hyacinth was speechless with fury, heat rushing to her face. She jerked in a breath, but nothing would come out.

"You're a pretty thing, and you know it. Just think what vivisection would do to your looks. And I doubt even you would enjoy the experience. Perhaps you will have to work your household a little harder to meet my terms, but I am sure keeping your skin will make the long hours worthwhile."

"Very well," Hyacinth spat, but she wasn't sure what she was agreeing to. The only thing she was certain of was that it wasn't to the Violet Queen's terms. She'd clawed her way up from ruin to run her own house, and could see no reason why she should bow to this woman. And she was *Violet* Asterley-Henderson, no matter what people called her just because this old baggage had usurped her real name.

"Good. I will send inspectors to ensure you comply. Sit down, Miss Asterley-Henderson."

Hyacinth clenched her teeth, but she obeyed.

"And now that we have settled that detail, there are so many more pleasant things to discuss." The Violet Queen bestowed a sweet smile that didn't reach beyond her lips.

Hyacinth's eye fell on the decanter of cordial—it would hide the taste of poison so excellently well—and a single thought filled her mind to the exclusion of all else. *I should be the Violet Queen.*

CHAPTER FORTY-THREE

Unknown

IMOGEN DIDN'T LIKE BEING SEPARATED FROM MOUSE, BUT someone had to keep watch over Anna while she fixed Bucky's bomb in place. The trick was to have it ready in a spot where she was sure Anna would go, and that was near Bird.

It wasn't as simple as setting a timer and running away to hide. This was, after all, one of Bucky's creations. The bomb was meant for precision work, and that meant setting it off in the right spot at exactly the right moment. Unfortunately, Imogen had reservations about anything more mechanically complex than a pair of scissors.

In this world of stark clockwork, there weren't many places to hide a device. The clock didn't even have consistent floors, just platforms and walkways over the gaping chasm below. The only way to make sure Anna was in the path of the bomb was to drop it on her unexpectedly. Or—remembering Bucky's childhood prank involving a rather nasty-looking frog—to lower it from above until she was certain that the device would hit its mark, and *then* drop it. That would at least compensate for the fact that she had abysmal aim.

A long, thin chain hadn't been hard to find, but a good place to lie in wait had been. There was a metal grid above the area where Bird was imprisoned, but it was very high up and the crossing beams were narrow. Imogen would be all but invisible up there, but she was far from certain she'd be able to balance over yawning nothingness while holding a bomb.

Nevertheless, while Mouse kept watch on Anna, she climbed up to the top and crouched at the edge of the lattice, gathering her courage until the moment came. The only light came from the many tubes of colored liquid that bubbled quietly to themselves. She tried to guess how badly the shifting, murky glow would hinder her ability to accurately drop the device on Anna's head.

Bird was still in its cage, hemmed in by the moving, clanking parts. Fear radiated from the creature's stiff form like heat from a stove. "We're going to get you out," she whispered from her perch above. "We're not leaving you behind."

And here I was getting used to the decor. Bird cocked its head, looking her way with one bright, jeweled eye. *It's amazing what minimalist charm one can conjure with wing nuts and a bit of aether.*

"It's the least I can do, after you put your life on the line to come here." Imogen began examining the oval shape of the bomb, locating the loop where she would fasten the chain. It was surprising how quickly she'd begun to think in terms of building things. Maybe having makers around all her life had been good for something besides leaving grease all over the furniture. "Besides, I've never rescued anyone before. It'll be a novelty."

A lovely sentiment. But I'd be more concerned about a beau who sends explosive devices. It rather pushes the boundaries of etiquette. Flowers are a much more standard gift.

Flowers had been one of Bucky's first gifts, and the memory made her smile. "He gave me what I needed, no questions asked."

He let you into his dreams. He was willing to trust you. That's rare in someone with no magical blood.

Imogen paused, the chain in her hand. "We love each other. A lot of people say they're in love, but we really are." And it hadn't come all at once, the way it did in her mother's novels. It had grown unremarked for years, like a sapling in a neglected corner of the garden, only discovered once it bloomed.

Bird didn't reply. At first she thought it was because of what she'd said, but then she realized Anna was below. Mouse was there, too, silent and still as the shadows. A sudden, suffocating panic overtook her, making the chain slip through cold, sweaty hands. Anna was *right there* and Imogen had to act; everything had just been talk until now. She'd shot Anna once before when her twin had been in the body of Serafina, but that had been in the heat of the moment with no time to think. Now she was plotting her murder and had to make every move with a deliberate intent to kill—and it wasn't sitting well in her stomach.

"Well, little bird," Anna said in a conversational tone. "My sister has always had a weak spot for her pets. I wonder if she cares enough for a piece of clockwork to come out of the shadows and play this game face to face."

With the strange magic of the clock, Anna suddenly had Bird outside the makeshift cage. Imogen blinked, trying to understand how she'd pulled the creature through the narrow bars. Anna held Bird's feet in one hand, letting it dangle upside down. In the clock world, the creature was the size of a turkey, its wings beating frantically to get free. Sparkles of light refracted from the jewels along Bird's wingtips, making a swirling net of rainbows until Anna hauled it to a nearby plinth. Then she pulled out a pair of pliers.

Catching her lip between her teeth, Imogen gathered up the bomb in one hand and the loops of chain in the other, and began walking the latticework beams to reach the spot directly over Anna's head. Her body wanted to shake in fear because the pathway was barely as wide as her feet, but she promised herself she could tremble all she wished later. Right now she had to be as sure and graceful as a dancer.

And so far, Anna seemed oblivious to the fact that she was there. She had Bird on its back, one hand on its belly, and was considering her prize from one angle and then another. "To be honest, I rather hope my sister will prove stub-

born. There has been very little entertainment in this place
since I came."

Imogen cast a sidelong glance at Mouse, who was hiding
in the vast rack of glass tubing. She could tell by the set of
the creature's ears and whiskers that it was intent, but there
was no easy way for it to reach Bird. The outcome was up to
her.

Leaning forward, Anna probed Bird's eye with her tool.
"You know there is a song about plucking larks, don't you,
little *alouette*?"

Imogen made it easily enough from her hiding place
along the narrow beam, but then she had to make a right
angle, stepping from one level to another about a foot below.
It would have been nothing if there had been a rail to hold,
but she had to force herself to concentrate completely on her
feet.

Bird's cries filled her head like the shattering of glass.
Imogen wavered, but instantly tightened every muscle to
keep herself straight and strong. It was a trick Evelina had
taught her at school when they scrambled over logs and
across streams on girlish adventures. Who would have
guessed she'd be betting her life on those lessons now?

"There we go!" Anna held one of Bird's emerald eyes to
the light, turning it to and fro to admire the glitter. "Paste,
of course, but still a pretty bit of glass."

Mouse was on its feet, no doubt as appalled as Imogen.
Bird's agonized wail ripped through her like a blade. Devas
didn't have bodies according to Evelina, but here Bird's
flesh was vulnerable. Had the devas even truly understood
physical pain before coming here? The idea made Imogen
light-headed. Bird could die by inches if Anna willed it—
and there was no doubt she had the appetite. As Serafina she
had been the Whitechapel murderer, tearing woman after
woman to shreds.

"There are no shops in the clock, of course, and nowhere
to get such pretty baubles," Anna went on. "And I like pretty
things. My sister, of course, has no end of lovely clothes,
while I'm forced to grab at what I can." She dropped the
emerald onto the plinth and leaned over the struggling bird.

"I'd love to make some emerald earbobs, but of course that means I'll need two."

The memory of her dreams—Anna's memories—rose up like bile, all but blotting out Imogen's sense of sight. Imogen forced herself to the present, to putting one foot before the other and calculating exactly how far to go before she was in place. *Six steps.* The air up here above the tubes of aether was warm enough that she was starting to perspire. *Five steps.* She'd taken off her shoes for a better grip, and the hard, ridged metal of the beams was hurting her feet. *Four, three.* She was in luck—there was a crisscross of beams right where she needed it, giving her a tiny bit more room to put her feet. *Two, one.* Imogen was in place.

Anna leaned over, intent on her prize. "Hold still, little Bird."

Bird's scream cut Imogen in two. Any qualms she'd had about her plan vanished. Imogen pulled the pin on Bucky's bomb and swiftly lowered it, feeding the chain smoothly so the weight didn't make it sway. She was perhaps twenty feet above her sister, and the task was dropping the device quickly enough before detonation. Free fall was too fast, and she didn't have enough chain to go all the way. The question would be when to let go, and time was turning to toffee—each second stretching impossibly far.

Bird gave an unearthly shriek and Imogen flinched so hard she let go. The bomb dropped too soon, plummeting with a clatter. The chain snaked afterward, hitting the platform with a sound like icy rain. Anna looked down, saw the thing, then looked up to spot Imogen frozen above in horror.

"You stupid girl," she snarled.

"Surprise!" Imogen whispered under her breath.

The bomb went off. It was Bucky's device, so it wasn't just a simple explosion. The shell cracked, releasing a bolt that shot upward at a deadly angle. It angled through Anna's body from the front of the right hip through the back of her left shoulder, sprouting wickedly curved hooks that held the bolt in place. The other end of the bolt was tethered with a steel chain to the bomb itself, and that locked with steel claws into the floor. Anna was immobilized, and Bird launched into the air, finally free.

Stunned, Imogen could do no more than look down at the impaled body of her twin. Anna whimpered faintly, the pliers dropped forgotten beside her. Blood and ripped flesh spattered the floor and surrounding metalwork like dark, living oil. Imogen's stomach gave a dangerous flip, and she straightened, looking away. Her head felt stuffed with cotton, and she was unable to think.

Step by agonized step, she retreated from the beams, gathered her shoes, and worked her way down to where her sister lay. One-eyed and awkward, Bird had made it to roost beside Mouse, who was grooming each of Bird's feathers with careful paws in a gentle ritual of comfort. The first thing Imogen did when she made it to the platform where Anna sprawled was gather up the green gem that Anna had dropped on the plinth and place it carefully inside her pocket. Then she picked up the pliers, thrusting them into the waistband of her skirt. She didn't trust Anna even now.

Her sister's lips peeled back from her teeth. There was blood in her mouth, turning the grimace to a bloodstained horror. "Happy?"

The statement snapped Imogen completely back to herself. "Damn you, Anna, I take no pleasure in this." Imogen touched her sister's face. It was cool, as if lack of blood was already robbing the skin of heat.

Anna flinched away from the touch. "You haven't won yet."

Imogen closed her eyes, shutting out Anna's—her own—pain-racked face. "Please give in. I've won."

"No, you haven't." Anna gripped her hand, digging sharp nails into Imogen's flesh. "Your lover can't kill me by proxy. It had to be by your own hand."

"Why?" Imogen demanded.

"You're not savage enough to live. If you were a real killer, you'd be strangling me right now."

Imogen flung off Anna's hand and sprang to her feet. "I'm done with you!"

"You're not." The spear had skewered her twin and it obviously had hurt her, but in the real world Anna would have been dead. Here—Imogen couldn't tell what was happening. Anna gave that bloody smile again, her features rippling like water stirred by wind. Imogen remembered Mouse's words. *She's having trouble keeping a face.*

Anna gave a cough, spitting out gouts of blood. "But I will grant you that was a good match."

And with that, Anna and the bomb vanished like smoke. *And now that she's figured out that I'm willing to hurt her, she'll be harder than ever to catch.*

CHAPTER FORTY-FOUR

Word of a fracture among the leading members of the Steam Makers' Guild, known to most as the Steam Council, has spread throughout world markets. The arrest of Mrs. Jane Spicer, the owner of Spicer Industries, for the outrage committed on the Palace of Westminster has done nothing to calm this unrest. It might be said that trading at the London Stock Exchange would be in free fall, except that it is uncertain if any traders, or any place where those traders traditionally gather to do business, remain.

—*The Bugle*

In an unanticipated move, all roads leading to and from the metropolis have been blockaded by the Gold King's forces. Food, of course, is an issue, but also the supply of coal, gas, and other fuels to and from the city. Likewise, the industrial plants providing steam heat, gas, and any form of electricity have been shut down voluntarily or by force. Since it has long been the policy of the Steam Council to prevent the construction of private means of generating power, or indeed the sale of materials necessary to do so, the withdrawal of all trade in fuels will be felt throughout the city. Rationing of existing supplies is already being implemented. It is believed that this move is designed to force the populace to surrender the whereabouts of the rebels. The advent of colder weather is sure to play a role in the outcome of this tactic.

—*The Bugle*

London, October 10, 1889

2:10 p.m. Thursday

THE SOUND OF THE RAILS BENEATH THE UNDERGROUND train filled Bancroft's brain, taking room he needed for more useful thoughts. He squirmed against the seats, wondering who else's backside had been there. Riding on public conveyances—even first-class ones—was an indignity he did not lightly endure. However, right now it was a damned sight safer than wandering the streets.

Nevertheless, some of the routes had been damaged in the bombing. A tunnel had caved in with at least one train still in it. Bancroft had read the death toll, but just as quickly tried to forget it. The only way to survive politics or war was to never look back.

The man in the seat facing Bancroft sneezed, but fortunately the fellow was reading the newspaper. It spared Bancroft the sight, if not the sound, of snuffling and honking into a handkerchief. The article on the page facing Bancroft was about the recent cholera outbreak caused by a sudden spike in the cost of clean water. Epidemics didn't belong in an empire with so many resources. It was a symptom of pure greed, and for that reason alone, the Steam Council had to go. He just wished they'd hurry up about it.

Everything was poised exactly as they needed it to be: Green and Scarlet were defeated or absorbed by other barons, Keating and King Coal were snarling at one another like curs, and Violet—well, no one much cared what Violet did when it came to armed combat. All they needed was Gold and Blue to polish each other off, and the rebels would sail in and win the day.

The question was who would make the next move. Keating had bombed Green on the eighth. Two days had passed since. Two days of anxiety, two days of speeches, two days of frantic preparation. And two days of searching for Jeremy with no success. Bancroft had long nurtured a grudge against Alice, but in these last days his enmity had withered. The poor girl was beside herself, and Bancroft found himself torn between searching for his grandson and doing his duty as a Baskerville. In the last few days, neither activity had met with much success.

Speculation about the delay had set the political hive buzzing. Bancroft had assumed Keating would make an immediate stab for Blue territory, but rumor had it that Tobias's absence had caused problems. No one else understood Keating's war machines the same way, and there had been unexpected delays pulling the Gold army together.

In Bancroft's estimation, it was a textbook blunder. By dropping the bombs before he was absolutely ready to press his advantage, Keating had given the Blue King a gift-wrapped opportunity to marshal his own forces. That single mistake might just have cost Keating the war.

And it gave the rebels a chance, too. That meant Bancroft was in a race against time to find a source of coal. And that led him inexorably back to the East End warehouses to try his luck once more.

He exited the train and all but ran for the stairs to the surface. Trapped within the tunnel, the smoke and steam of the underground rail lines was choking. The overall effect was like smoking a cigar soaked in steaming piss.

Daylight made him squint as he emerged onto the street. He got his bearings and turned left, head down against a brisk wind off the water. It was a shabby neighborhood, with far more caps and coveralls than top coats and hats. He wanted to do his business and head home as soon as possible since there was a chance the trains could stop running at any time.

The street was crowded with newspaper boys, barrowmen, and idiots on soap boxes. Blue Boys swaggered in the streets, but always in groups of at least three.

"Get the *Prattler*! Latest edition!"

"Eels! Get your fresh eels! Good in a pie!"

"Long live Prince Edmond!" someone shouted from a window overhead.

It wasn't the first time Bancroft had heard the cry. And while he kept his thoughts from his face, his heart surged with excitement. Who knew the young man was a prince? And he'd come to Duquesne's to thank Bancroft personally for his help—and most wondrous of all, Bancroft had actually liked him!

Here at long last was a master worthy of all his energy and ambition and, more important, an excellent chance for rewards. If the prince needed coal, Bancroft was damned well going to get it, regardless of the cost.

And he had reached the row of warehouses that had been his destination. His first thought had been to investigate a small Dutch firm he had overlooked on his first round of inquiries, but a sign down the side street caught his eye. It had no words—or at least none in English. There were three Chinese characters and a serpent painted in black on red. Bancroft recognized the sign for the Mercantile Fellowship of the Black Dragons of the Hidden Sea.

Annoyance swept over him. The Black Dragons had coal but wouldn't sell it. They'd sent him threatening notes and now they were lurking down side alleys when he was trying to do business. The worst part of it was that he didn't *actually* know what they had against him. All he had were a lot of nasty guesses.

That should have been enough to make him back away, but today—when he was nursing a kernel of hope for his future—it wasn't. A bell on the door chimed as he entered. The tiny space carried the faint, sweetish pungency of incense. There was a narrow counter and reams of posters tacked to the walls, all in Chinese, but no one was there.

"Hello?" Bancroft called out.

There was a rustling and the ratty silk curtain that made up the back wall swung aside. An elderly Chinese man appeared and bowed. "Pardon me, if you have waited long." The words were delivered in accented but perfectly clear English.

"May I speak to the proprietor?" asked Bancroft.

"I am he." The man bowed again. "Han Lo, at your service."

"Are you the same Black Dragons that hold a larger warehouse at the docks?" Those were the men with whom Bancroft had dealt before.

"We are. I am but a more modest piece of the whole."

Bancroft strolled up to the counter, doing his best to look relaxed. "Your friends weren't able to help me, but perhaps you can."

"Perhaps," said the old man. "But I am sometimes obliged to ask more. Economies of scale, you understand."

"I don't have a problem with that," Bancroft replied, feeling optimistic for the first time in a long while.

"Then by all means." Han Lo held the curtain aside, inviting Bancroft into the back.

For the first time, Bancroft noticed the sleeves on the man's jacket. They were wide, edged in a thick border of black silk, and covered with tiny black dragons stitched on a field of gold. The luxurious sheen of the cloth was at odds with the shabby office.

With a whisper of misgivings, Bancroft followed the man into the back rooms. He half expected a den of Oriental splendor, but the room was disappointingly ordinary. A central table was covered with ledgers, as if Bancroft had interrupted a bookkeeping session.

"Please, sit," Han Lo said. "May I offer you refreshment?"

"No, thank you," Bancroft replied. "I mean no discourtesy, but my time is short."

"No doubt. Conflict makes men hasty."

There was mild rebuke in the man's tone, but Bancroft ignored it. "I need coal. Lots of it."

"I am well aware of what you need, Lord Bancroft, and why."

Halfway into his seat, Bancroft froze. "You know my name?"

"Yes," the man said smoothly. "You have come to our attention in the past."

Bancroft wanted to ask how, but that would have revealed his anxiety. As it was, his heart thumped so loudly his ears sang. He could see the face of the Chinese foreman he'd shot, his brains splattering the earth as his skull exploded. He wondered if Han Zuiweng had been any relation to Han Lo.

Bancroft settled into the chair with as much casual ease as he could muster. "Then you must know that my inquiries are serious."

"We do."

A lacquered door opened, revealing the figure of a pretty young girl about Poppy's age. Bancroft glimpsed a stairway behind her—probably to living quarters above. She said something in an Oriental tongue and Han Lo replied. She bowed and disappeared, shutting the door behind her.

"My daughter asking if we wanted tea," he said with a smile. "I told her we were content for now. Forgive the interruption."

"Of course," Bancroft replied smoothly.

The older man nodded, then seemed to gather himself. "First I must ask, my lord, why you think that I will sell to you when others will not?"

"Since I have never understood their refusal, I cannot say."

"Ah." Han Lo considered. "Do you understand who the Black Dragons are?"

"You are merchants."

"We are one of the mercantile arms of the kingdom underground. The Black Kingdom has not been consulted in this coming conflict and we are conscious that backing one or the other faction may impact our own position."

This was the closest that Bancroft had ever come to real information about the Black Kingdom, and he leaned forward with curiosity. "I thought you had an understanding with the Blue Kingdom."

"Only insofar as the Blue King stored some of his weaponry underground for a price. A considerable price. That does not prevent us from making a deal elsewhere if we so choose."

"Then your reluctance to do business with me is based on the fact that I represent the rebels?"

There was a pause. "Yes."

Then it wasn't personal. Relief made Bancroft's limbs feel rubbery. At the same time, ambassadorial instincts came awake. "Perhaps I can represent your interests to the prince."

Han Lo smiled, steepling his fingers. Bancroft noticed the nails were long and coated in gold. "Perhaps you can. But we are already cautious. The rain of explosives has crushed some of our tunnels. Your dead fall into the waterways and foul our underground spaces. Worst of all, our king awakes."

"He awakes?" Bancroft was lost.

"He has been asleep for a century. When he is awake, he grows hungry and the darkness stirs."

"And what does that mean?" The conversation was sending a chill up Bancroft's spine, although he desperately wanted to believe the old man was speaking in metaphors.

"Let me say simply that the Black Kingdom is the receptacle of all things the daylight world abhors. Centuries ago, before the Empire and before gunpowder came west, your king demanded that magic users cleanse the land of black sorcery. And so everything that dwelled in the dark—the revenants and beast-men, necromancers and shades—were banished beneath the earth by powerful spells."

Bancroft gaped, unsure how to respond. He knew all too well that sorcery was real, but he'd never heard any of this before. "Are you telling me there are monsters imprisoned beneath the streets?"

"It is not so simple as that. Spells fade and the Black Kingdom wanes. Our king no longer desires to rule. It is custom more than force that keeps the dark gates closed."

"And your king *sleeps*?"

"Just so. The kingdom is not so much ruled as maintained through the administration of men like myself. It is in everyone's interest that we succeed."

Bancroft had to ask. "And if you don't succeed?"

"If the Black Kingdom fails, all those horrors would have no place to go but aboveground." Han Lo gave a faint smile, but it wasn't a happy one. "Trust me on this, Lord Bancroft. What is below the earth should stay there. It should not stir."

Frustration heated Bancroft's face. He wasn't sure what to believe, and this tale of buried horrors and sleeping monarchs had no bearing on his very real problems in the here and now. He shoved Han Lo's story aside. "Sell me the coal I require, and I will do my utmost to supply the kingdom with whatever it needs to remain in good health. And asleep, if necessary."

Han Lo's eyebrows quirked. "Do you give us your word on this?"

A thread of caution tugged in Bancroft's gut. "If it is within my power to achieve, yes."

"Then consider our bargain made." Han Lo held out his hand. "And the scales will be balanced."

Bancroft took it, feeling the papery dryness of the man's skin. "I am not certain what scales you mean, but I'm glad we could do business."

The old man rose to show Bancroft out. "Indeed, my lord, justice is the nature of the Black Kingdom. Unlike the other members of the Steam Council, the Black Kingdom is ancient and has its counterparts throughout the world. In my own language it is called the Kingdom of Ashes, in others the Kingdom of Alchemy. Though mortal, my family has served the underground for time immemorial."

Mortal? Bancroft's mind reeled as they passed through the curtain to the front of the shop. After their conversation, the tiny space seemed even more tawdry and cramped than before. *Ashes? Alchemy?* "Where does the alchemy come in?"

"The transformative nature of the underground journey. Some liken it to a rebirth, others to a chemical reaction. All is destroyed and reborn in harmony, assuming whatever state is necessary to achieve balance."

"That is a very philosophical view." The only thing Bancroft had ever heard was that those caught wandering in the underground vanished, never to be seen again—transformative, yes, but not necessarily harmonious.

"It is also a historical one. Chemistry, law, and the realms of spirit and dreams were once its area of influence. Now most regard the Black Kingdom as the dustbin of the world's immortal community."

Bancroft had listened to enough. He just wanted to leave. "With a new heir to the throne, your lot will no doubt improve," he said heartily.

"Which throne would that be, Lord Bancroft?" Han Lo

smiled. "There are more kingdoms than your daylight empires."

For a moment, Bancroft was lost for words. "I'll send a man around with instructions on quantity and distribution."

"Good day, Lord Bancroft." Han Lo bowed low and with a hint of mockery. "And good luck."

Dartmoor, October 10, 1889
TAVERN AT THE EAST DART

4:35 p.m. Thursday

"I COULDN'T HELP but overhear that you fine gentlemen are staying at Baskerville Hall, where poor Sir Charles was frightened to death by a dog." So said the barkeep of the public house by the East Dart River. He was a young, dark-haired fellow with a quick, sly smile.

"You must have read the account in the papers," replied Watson, who in accordance with Holmes's original plan was author of the report. As Holmes had said, there were stories about a savage dog roaming Dartmoor and there had been plenty of material to embellish. In particular, he was proud of the history he'd invented for the infamous Baskerville ancestors and their curse. With a little work—and perhaps a love interest for the heir?—it might even make a decent novel.

"I've seen the creature you speak of. Rumor has it that they made it in those laboratories and it got out from time to time."

"Indeed?" Holmes replied as he began packing his pipe. "I have managed to remain happily innocent of all of Dartmoor's canine peculiarities until now."

Watson frowned, his stomach cold at the thought of what had gone on in those labs. Holmes had given him an account of their destruction—or at least a partial one—but he'd gone to look at the wreckage himself. There had been corpses there that would give him nightmares to his grave.

The afternoon shadows were growing long, making a stark contrast to the slanting autumn sun that streamed in the open door. And that brilliant passage of day into evening would be over soon.

Watson pushed his glass toward the barkeep. "Another, if you please."

The young man gave him that quick smile. "Ah, Doctor, you must try the scrumpy. It just begs to be drunk, it does. We make it local."

"Scrumpy?"

Holmes blew out a string of smoke circles. "Oh, yes, Watson, you must."

"You as well, Mr. Holmes?" asked the barkeep.

"Oh, no," said Holmes. "I've taken a fancy to this brown ale, but you, Doctor, go ahead."

Watson lifted the fresh mug to his lips, and then wished he would die. "Faugh!" He spat and slammed down the mug, slopping some of the cloudy yellow substance over the side. An indescribable miasma assaulted his tongue that brought to mind the specimen library of his student days, the rows upon rows of jars filled with every permutation of tissue, tumor, bile, and excrescence pickled for his educational benefit in what looked and smelled like the vile putrescence in his mug. "What is in that?"

Holmes gave the mug a cool glance. "They tell me it has something to do with apples, but in my opinion the data is inconclusive."

"Good God." Watson wiped his mouth with his pocket handkerchief and gagged slightly. The barkeep had vanished, no doubt to indulge his hilarity in the back room.

Then the Schoolmaster walked in the door, wearing his usual green-tinted spectacles and long striped scarf. He carried a battered leather shoulder bag and a heavy walking stick. He spotted the barely touched mug and flashed a grin. "Been trying the local delicacies, Doctor?"

"For my sins." He still felt odd talking to this young prince in hiding. For practical reasons, Prince Edmond insisted on being treated as the Schoolmaster, with no ceremony or titles, but it grated on someone who'd been trained since boyhood to revere the Throne.

Holmes, however, was on his feet, clearly impatient. "Do you return alone?"

"Yes," the Schoolmaster replied. "Come into the back and I'll tell you all."

They followed him into the private room and he closed the door, standing against it. Watson thought, for a fleeting moment, just how young the Schoolmaster looked, but then he seemed to recover.

"My business in Bath went precisely as planned," said the Schoolmaster.

"I'm relieved to hear it," said Holmes. "How can we assist you now?"

A variety of emotions flickered across the man's face. "I'm about to begin an undertaking, for good or ill, that in some measure will figure in history. I would do so with as little doubt as it is humanly possible to achieve."

"Doubt about your cause?" Watson asked, concerned.

"No." The Schoolmaster gave a wry smile. "Not that. But there have been casualties I would lay to rest."

"Ah," said Holmes.

"Ah?" Watson was skilled at interpreting Holmesian monosyllables, but this one eluded him.

The Schoolmaster waved toward the table and chairs. "First, I must ask. Are you any closer to solving Sir Charles's death?"

Watson sat down opposite the Schoolmaster, Holmes at the head of the table.

"Yes, at least in part," Holmes replied. "As you know, there was every sign that his heart had failed due to an extreme fright."

"Which the good doctor has attributed in his official account to a family curse in the form of a giant hound," the Schoolmaster replied dryly. "How enormously Gothic."

"In any event," Holmes went on, "his death bore marked similarities to two others you have asked me to investigate."

"Who were they?" Watson asked.

"A year ago we had two individuals in custody at Loch Ness, a Mr. Elias Jones and Mr. Bingham," the Schoolmaster said. "They both perished before we were quite done extracting information from them."

Watson blinked, speaking before he could stop himself. "You tortured them?"

The Schoolmaster frowned. "No. That was never our method of operation, but still two healthy men died unexpectedly. At the time we suspected there was a turncoat in our midst, but an exhaustive review of everyone's quarters, whereabouts, history—none of it turned up a thing."

"And their deaths were caused by a very particular substance," Holmes replied. "They were poisoned in a manner that induced heart failure, but I would postulate that the noxious formula also possessed a psychoactive property, as both the prisoners and Sir Charles retained the marks of severe terror above and beyond what one normally sees stamped on the features of such victims."

"Are you saying that Sir Charles died by the same hand as our prisoners?" The Schoolmaster fell back in his chair, his expression incredulous.

The detective's face was serious. "I am saying that circumstances point to the fact that at the time of the prisoners' deaths, someone was in our midst and pursuing his own agenda. Someone who did not desire the prisoners to reveal everything that they knew to us. And someone who then wished to determine what Sir Charles could tell. After all, Sir Charles had all your secrets."

Dr. Watson followed this exchange carefully, trying to remember Holmes's account of the bombing at Baker Street and all that followed. "Was there someone in particular who was in both places at the right time?"

"That would not be necessary," said Holmes. "All that would be required would be someone able to pull the right strings." Holmes turned to the Schoolmaster. "Do you recall accompanying me to the Blue King's court when I was searching for my niece?"

"Of course."

"At that time, King Coal suspected there was a traitor in his establishment. He wanted me to take that case, but circumstances changed and I never pursued it. However, the matter remained in my mind."

"Are you saying that his turncoat and ours are the same?" asked Watson.

"At the time, I thought it odd that both Jones and Bingham were double agents, playing Blue and Gold off against one another. Even more strange that orders were issuing from the Blue court that were not authorized by King Coal. At first I suspected the hand of my brother, Mycroft, but there were some things that happened I believe he simply would not do. Most significantly, while he might question Sir Charles, he would never kill him."

The Schoolmaster had that fixed expression so many got when trying to follow one of Holmes's chains of logic. "So your suspicions lean to a member of the Blue Court?"

"Yes, and for two reasons. One is the nature of the poison used. Sir Charles and the others weren't given a drug to keep them silent, it was to loosen their tongues."

Both Watson and the Schoolmaster jerked to attention. "There are drugs that lower inhibitions in that fashion," Watson said, "but they're not always reliable."

"And the most efficacious of those drugs are not available to the honest physician, but . . ." Holmes trailed off, waving a hand carelessly. "They are excellent for extracting information. The subject remembers nothing of the incident, and if the dosage is correct, they die. Perfect if someone wanted to empty the brains of our two turncoats, and then stop their hearts."

"And Sir Charles?" Watson asked.

"He already had a weak heart. I do not think he was meant to die, but the strain on him was too much. Either he suffered a recurrence of the psychoactive effects of the drug, or perhaps he did see something that frightened him, as the local rumors would have it. Either way, it was too much."

"You said there were two reasons you believe the killer is the same," the Schoolmaster prompted, his expression grim.

"The other is more oblique," Holmes continued. "I think King Coal made the connection between Edmond Baskerville and the Schoolmaster long ago. One of his key advisors picked up the thread—I believe independently of his master—and deployed his own scoundrels to learn the truth of that and who knows what other secrets of the rebels, the Gold King, and anyone else. We are dealing with a villain intent on building his own empire."

"A villain who then came after Sir Charles?"

"But only after Mycroft came here first. The Steam Council has been watching my brother for some time. When he visited Sir Charles recently, the unusual break from his routine was noted. And then the killer struck."

The Schoolmaster's face had gone pale. "Who? Whose hand did these things?"

"We may never know who delivered the poison to Jones and Bingham, but I am convinced they received their orders from the same gentleman who visited Sir Charles on the twenty-ninth of September. I questioned your housekeeper, Mrs. Barrymore, on the matter of your guardian's visitors. Sir Charles had an unusually full schedule of late, but it seems he took the time for tea with a professor of Camelin University who was very interested in the local fauna. Butterflies, to be precise."

The news sent Watson spinning. "Camelin University is where Evelina—"

"Indeed," snapped Holmes. "And the notion that she has been resident near this individual turns my veins to ice."

"Who is it?" demanded the Schoolmaster.

"His name is Moriarty, but he goes by the name of Juniper."

"The Blue King's man of business?" the Schoolmaster exclaimed.

Holmes's lip curled into a snarl. "The more I learn about this individual, the more threads there seem to be to his web. We must have a care with this one, gentlemen. He is not the kind we take to trial, because for all the investigation I have done, there is not one scrap of hard evidence." He slammed his hand on the table. "I can prove nothing."

The Schoolmaster pulled off his green-tinted glasses. His blue eyes were icy. "I am tired of hearing that we cannot prove such crimes. I've heard it all my life as prince and princess died of dubious causes, and court officials wrung their hands and said there was never enough evidence to point to the Steam Council. Perhaps the law as it stands cannot prosecute these wretches, but soon *I* will be the law. We will catch this Moriarty, and then you can ask him whatever you please."

They sat in silence a moment, the mood crackling with tension. Then the Schoolmaster stirred. "Well, if we are going to catch him, we have a war to win. And to do that, we must reach London, which is no longer an easy task. The southern armies are already starting north, but advance scouts report the roads are blocked by the Yellowbacks. They were handing out these pamphlets."

He reached into his leather bag, withdrew a handful of leaflets and paper, and tossed them onto the table. Watson picked up the topmost handbill.

LOYAL ENGLISHMEN UNITE!

The citizens of London are under attack from the REBEL MENACE.

Traitors have rallied under the banner of the VILE PRETENDER hiding under the name of the Schoolmaster, also known as Edmond Baskerville. This man is to be shot on sight for VARIOUS AND HEINOUS CRIMES including the death of his own father, Sir Charles Baskerville, as well as theft, printing libelous documents, frequenting houses of ill repute, and passing forged pound notes as well as intimate and unspeakable acts.

All roads to and from London have been closed until this dangerous miscreant has been apprehended. If seen, contact the constabulary at once.

Watson threw it down in disgust. The fact that they were calling Edmond a pretender meant that somehow the secret of his birth had been discovered. "This is preposterous. They make you sound like Bonny Prince Charlie come to take back the throne."

"But that's it, you see, Dr. Watson. Most of it's nonsense,

but somehow the author of these pamphlets stumbled upon the secret of my birth. That's been kept hidden for more than thirty years."

"But is that not precisely what Moriarty would have gleaned from Sir Charles?" Holmes didn't look up from his perusal of the newspaper that had been at the bottom of the Schoolmaster's pile.

The Schoolmaster covered his face with his hand. "In some ways I thank God Sir Charles did not live to find out that he had broken his silence. That would have been a crueler kind of murder."

CHAPTER FORTY-FIVE

Unknown

IMOGEN WASTED NO TIME WITH GOOD MANNERS. SHE dragged Evelina's covers off. "Wake up!"

Evelina sat bolt upright, her eyes wide and round. "Im! What are you doing here? Does Magnus have you, too?"

Imogen put her hands on her hips. "Don't be daft, I'm in your dream. I must have tried half a dozen times to get here."

"I'm so glad to see you!" Evelina scrambled to her feet, throwing her arms around Imogen.

After so long in the clock, the touch of another human made Imogen gasp with relief. She returned the embrace, fighting back the ache in her throat. The comfort of her friend's embrace felt so good, but not everything was right. Evelina felt tense, her muscles braced.

Imogen looked around as she released her friend, taking in the old stone walls. "Where is this place?" She strode to the window, looking out at the sea and down at the drop to the rocks below. "Are you really here or have you been reading Mrs. Radcliffe again?" She turned, her eyes searching the high ceiling and iron-bound door. She half expected an ogre to come bounding in demanding someone to eat.

Evelina's forehead furrowed. "I'm really here. It's Siabartha Castle. I've been kidnapped."

"Kidnapped!"

"It was Magnus, of course. Where are you? I tried to reach you."

Imogen flopped down onto the bed and heaved a sigh. "In

Magnus's stupid clock. Anna dragged me there and now I have to kill her if I want to get out."

Evelina sat down beside her, grasping her hand. "If you've walked into my dream, we probably don't have much time. Anna might interfere."

"I don't know about that. I smacked her a good one." Imogen tried not to sound too pleased.

Her friend stared. "That's a side of you I haven't seen."

Imogen squeezed her fingers. "You're stuck here with Magnus. What do you need, Evelina?"

Evelina didn't hesitate. "If you can get to somebody at home, let them know where I am."

"Done."

"And what do you need?" Evelina asked. "You came here for a reason."

Imogen rubbed her face with both hands. "I keep trying to kill Anna but it doesn't work. She says I'm not done with her."

"Then you aren't."

"I don't understand!" Imogen cried in frustration. They were in a dream, but she still felt mortified by the bizarre conversation. *I'm talking about killing my sister!* Even with Evelina, it was too much.

But her friend took her by the shoulders, shaking her slightly. "Listen. It's not that complicated. You've been sick all your life, so you're used to the idea of coping with your own weakness. You're a good daughter and a good friend, so you're used to the idea of being patient. You obey the rules. You endure. That's your strength. But it's going to get you killed. You have to prove you want to live even more than she does."

"Then what do I do? Mouse and Bird are there with me."

"Excellent!"

"No—disastrous. She caught Bird and tore out his eye."

Evelina's face went white. "What? She did *what*?"

"I got him free, but . . ."

"How?" Evelina demanded.

"With a bomb that shot a long dart right through her, but she got away."

"You attacked her?"

"Of course! She was hurting Bird."

"You defended Bird, but you didn't kill her." Evelina's eyes were serious. "The spirit world looks metaphorical, but it's extremely literal. If you don't kill her with your own two hands, it won't count. And you have to do it because you want to live. Defending friends is wonderful, but you need to do this for yourself."

Imogen bit her lip, thinking of that moment when she could have leaned down and strangled Anna as she lay bleeding. "Why does it need to be that brutal?"

"Because it's exactly the type of thing you don't do well. Forgive me for saying it; you have acres of courage, but not that kind. Anna has set up a game that she's certain you won't win."

Imogen stared down at her hands. They were dirty, the nails torn. Her hands hadn't looked like this since Anna was alive. "How do you know all this? Is this something all magic users know?"

Evelina smiled. "I know you, and I know what you've said about your twin. It's not the wisdom of the ages." She rose from the bed and knelt by one of the trunks stacked against the wall. She lifted the lid and rummaged inside. "I had a conversation with Tobias not that long ago. He was dealing with a dark side of his work he didn't like, either."

"What does that mean?"

"Maybe nothing. Or it means we all have pieces of ourselves to face. Here." Evelina handed Imogen a white-handled knife. "My Gran Cooper gave me this. Next time you have a chance, do your worst."

Imogen started to reach for it, but then pulled her hand back. "I hate her for making me do this."

"Just remember that she's already dead. You're putting a ghost to rest."

Imogen studied Evelina's expression, trying to decide if she meant what she said. "It's getting harder every time I try to end it."

"That's exactly what she wants. Go on." Evelina jogged the knife in the air. "Don't hesitate."

Imogen took it, clutching the ivory handle like a lifeline. The bomb had been easier, because it was less intimate—and that meant Evelina was absolutely right. "I'll do it for myself, and I'll do it with my own hands, but I'm going to hate it."

"That's allowed. You're still you."

Imogen hesitated, knowing she was done but not wanting to leave her friend just yet. "If I put Bird's eye back in, will he be able to see?"

Evelina held out her hand, and a small box covered with colorful print shimmered into existence. She handed it to Imogen.

"How did you do that?" Imogen squeaked, reading the label. It was a kit for resin-based glue.

Evelina smiled, and for the first time she looked like her old self. "It's my dream. I can bloody well do what I like."

Southwest Coast, October 11, 1889
SIABARTHA CASTLE

5:05p.m. Friday

FOR ALL HIS talk about lessons, Magnus kept to himself much of the time, shutting Evelina into the workroom from early morning until late afternoon to read the ancient books that lined the shelves. Some of the tomes she recognized from his study at the Magnetorium Theatre, which answered the question of where that library had gone when he'd left Whitechapel.

The room was bright and spacious, perhaps once a lady's solar, and was set up with worktables, magical implements, and alchemical supplies that reminded her more than a little of the laboratory at Camelin, if it had been antique and built for sorcerers. Sadly, none of the paraphernalia appeared to hold the key to her escape—and after days of confinement, and days without the dampening effect of her bracelets, Evelina was restless. She searched high and low for salt of sorrows or any other poison she might drop into Magnus's wine, but there was nothing that would not immediately taste foul. If she'd been there of her own free will—not locked into the classroom and rather less in danger of turning into a soul-sucking fiend—she would have been an eager student. As it was, she spent a lot of time pondering how to get away.

Nevertheless, the afternoon found her curled into a chair with a book and a modest glass of sherry, which had become her one vice in the godforsaken place. She barely looked up when Magnus entered, but she sensed him pause and note which book she was perusing. "The separation of the soul from the body?" he commented. "That is rather an advanced topic, don't you think?"

This was their routine. He would always interrupt her studies at the end of the day and question her on what she'd read. "I thought this would be acceptable reading since I had finished the work you set for me." Evelina marked the page with her finger.

"Ah, indeed." He sat in the other chair. "It is a fascinating topic. There is a theory that wandering souls are the source of those shadowy figures you dislike so much."

"The Others?"

"They are sometimes called that."

She frowned. "You said they were the opposite counterpart of devas."

"And they are. But who is to say where they originate? I have met those who claim the Others wander the earth looking for a vacant body to leap into. I've never observed it myself, but it is not my area of study."

"Was the Other I saw in my room the other night real, or an illusion?"

"You doubt your own eyes?"

"You're a mesmerist. You can make me see whatever you like. And you're enough of a showman that you made your living making folks pay for those lies."

Magnus clapped his hands together, rubbing them in a mockery of glee. "Ha! Such a compliment you pay me. But let me assure you that this place is guarded by those you call Others."

It was an answer, but not. Evelina shuddered a little, retreating to her original topic. "I have a friend who has fallen into a deep sleep and will not wake. Imogen Roth."

Magnus's eyebrows rose. "Ah, yes, Serafina's twin. I thought Miss Roth had escaped the *Wyvern*."

Fresh hatred seeped through Evelina. The sorcerer bore much of the blame for Imogen's plight. "She did, but collapsed when it fell from the sky."

"Interesting" was all he said.

Evelina's temper bubbled. "Is she in danger?"

"Undoubtedly, but I would think squatting spirits to be the least hazard in the netherworld. Her sister's spirit was the very devil, as you well know."

"Can I help Imogen?"

"Perhaps." He waved a lazy hand at a slim black book. "What was your opinion of that little volume?"

Magnus refilled her glass and poured some wine for himself. Evelina wanted to scream with impatience, but knew she would make more headway by playing along. This sociable moment, too, was part of their daily routine. It jarred because it was false, and because it was not. She was his prisoner, already his victim, but the communion between them held a grain of truth. He had taught her things no one else could.

The afternoon light caught his face, and she could see that where he had been pale before, he was now corpselike. *For someone who obviously has so little time, he's being extremely patient with me.* That made her more, rather than less, nervous.

"The Latin was a slog," she admitted.

He tutted and sipped his wine. "Perish the intellectual laziness of the young."

Evelina couldn't help a smile. "You haven't had a good intellectual debate since Erasmus, I suppose."

He crooked an eyebrow. "Mind your manners, kitten."

"I read the book. It is a primer for little sorcerers."

"It lays out the rules of their system of magic. Even if you have no ambitions in that direction, it is best to understand how it works."

"It was very well organized," she conceded, deciding it

was the only compliment she could stomach. "Clear, concise, well indexed. The section on how to harness death in all its permutations, with subheadings on what to kill and how to kill, it would have done Mrs. Beeton's cookbooks proud."

There was even a separate appendix on the course of potions necessary to awaken the power to drink life from the living—which sounded like a nasty, smelly brew indeed. *And I expect he'll want me to ingest that if I'm to be his next Serafina.* She was definitely sticking to food and drink she recognized.

"Then tomorrow," he said, "I recommend the next volume. It sets the record straight on the correct use of resurrection spells. Something of a lost art these days, and so important. Correct procedure is the difference between healing and the shambling dead."

Magnus was wearing gloves, but last night she'd caught a glimpse of his blackening nails. *Is there a bit of shambling in your future, Doctor?* She cleared her throat to force down her rising gorge. "Let me guess. The amount of life force available is a key factor in a successful resurrection."

The look he gave her might have frozen the sherry in her glass. "Indeed. Perhaps we should break for a rest before dinner. We can resume the practical side of your instruction after that." And he took out the heavy key that would lock her in her bedroom, which was the signal for her to put away her books.

But Evelina wasn't done. "What about my friend? I dreamed of her last night."

"That's not unusual. Often wandering spirits have a way of pestering us. My advice to you would be to put her out of your mind. She has no value to your future."

"She's my friend!"

"Friend." Magnus said the word as if he had forgotten its meaning. "Let me put it this way: nine times out of ten these ghosts have their own reason for never returning home. There is something in them, some darkness or some failure of willpower they cannot face, much less conquer. In the end, it's easier to give up on fighting for their lives. All the sorcery in the world can't change that, kitten. Now rest."

But the last thing Evelina intended was a nap. If Magnus had dangled the promise of Imogen's cure, it might have made a difference, but his indifference was just one more reason to get free of him. What good was power if you couldn't help the ones you love?

Magnus had given her a seemingly inescapable chamber, but she wasn't done searching it yet. She emptied two of the brass-bound trunks and heaved them on top of a third, making a precarious stair so that she could investigate the ceiling. The construction was primitive, just a heavy lattice of beams overlaid with the floor above. Since they were at the top of the tower and she rarely heard anyone walking above, she assumed it was an attic.

The clock in the workroom struck the half hour, and she was always summoned to dinner precisely at seven—the one meal she and Magnus ate together. Since her free time was so limited, she'd had to work her way around the room a bit each day. At first, she found nothing—not even cobwebs. But as she teetered on the stack of trunks beside her bed, she noticed a scattering of dust on the top of the red brocade canopy. She would have thought nothing of it except that the room had been scrupulously cleaned. And then she noticed a thin strip of daylight above. With the handle of the fireplace poker, she gave the underside of the attic floorboards an experimental poke. One shifted slightly, enough to tell her that the end closest to the wall wasn't tightly nailed down. Pushing it loose would be easy, and from there she could begin to pry up its neighbors. Her insides squeezed with excitement. *It's not much, but it's something!*

Then a noise made her stop and listen, and crane her head toward the door. *Footfalls.* Magnus was early. A rush of hot panic flooded Evelina and she scrambled down, replacing the poker and dismantling her makeshift ladder. She had the first and smallest trunk back in place by the time the key was in the lock. The second was larger, requiring her to bump it onto the floor and drag it against the wall just as the door rattled open. Evelina jumped away from it at the last second, breathing hard and with the contents of two trunks strewn across her bed.

"Tidying?" Magnus inquired, eying the chaos. "Quite a noisy occupation."

"I am moving my things around," Evelina said, trying to hide the fact that she was still puffing. "Trunks are hardly the same thing as a proper chest of drawers."

Magnus looked nonplussed. "Perhaps we can find you something more to your liking. In the meanwhile, perhaps you could join me for a practical demonstration before we sit down to eat. Bring your wrap."

He led her up the stairs to the level above—it was indeed used for no more than storage—and then up a final flight of steps. A door in the tower opened onto a parapet that stretched across the entire castle, interrupted only by the tops of the other, smaller towers. A battlement provided some shelter from the constant wind, but the air was still bitter as the sun dipped toward the horizon. Evelina pulled her shawl close, teeth clenched so they would not chatter.

Magnus walked toward a piece of ornate wrought-iron scrollwork that was mounted on the west side of the battlement, rusted bolts piercing the stone. It stretched between two of the merlons, forming an ornate grill. "One of the themes of magic is illusion. We are all guilty of it, some of us even gifted, but the truly powerful are those who have the gift—or curse—of seeing through such spells."

He pulled an object from the pocket of his dark tailcoat and held it out. It was a plain, flat stone, entirely unremarkable except that there was a hole at its center. Evelina nodded, suddenly more willing to endure the cold. "My grandmother gave me one very like that, except that someone has painted it."

"I recall the piece. Painting the stones is quite common among the folk practitioners. If one finds a good seeing stone, it becomes an object worthy of celebration." He placed the stone into a holder at the center of the grill, so that the hole was at the exact middle of the ironwork. "The way these work is to catch the light at the precise moment of dusk or dawn. For an hour, or two, or twelve after that—

much depends on the stone and the user—that eye will have the gift of true sight."

"It is that simple to use?" Evelina exclaimed.

"There is nothing simple about the truth, my dear. But yes, the mechanics are no more complex than that." He swept his arm toward the grill, an echo of his theatrical past. "Step forward and look, if you dare."

Evelina approached the grill, which was made for Magnus and too tall for her comfort. The first thing she saw was the blaze of the fading sun on the water, shocks of pink and orange mirrored on the sea and sky. Then she stood on her toes, stretching up to peer through the stone with her left eye. The magic struck her like a firm tap that echoed from head to toe. The view of the sea itself didn't change, and she watched as the silver-blue edges of the water faded to a deep indigo. She backed away with a final shiver. "I'm more than ready to go inside."

"Very good then," Magnus said, collecting the stone and leading her down to the workroom, where their dinner would be spread out.

She looked around curiously, half expecting to see that the dinner was rotten or the books nothing but old leaves, as from the pages of a fairy tale. But everything inside the castle looked the same, even Magnus. He looked haggard, but had not sprouted horns or a second head.

They sat down to eat. The cold had pricked Evelina's appetite and she gratefully selected a warm roll and broke it apart. "So what precisely was the point of that exercise?" she asked.

Magnus toyed with his spoon. Dinner was a fish stew, as it seemed to be every other dinner, and they were both growing a little weary of it. But he also looked apprehensive. "What do you think is the truth?"

That I want to go home. That I'm afraid of you and myself. "Should it be that subjective?"

Magnus didn't answer, so she bit into the bread and chewed. But the moment she began to eat, she realized the demonstration had affected her nerves badly. Magnus never did anything without a point, so why all this talk of truth?

Was there something hideous that should be revealed? She couldn't keep herself from glancing into the corners, looking for the Others. She'd caught glimpses of them often enough, usually in the corridors or creeping around the bailey, but they rarely approached the rooms she lived and worked in.

Magnus finally summoned up a reply. "I think the truth should be obvious. I am a sorcerer and, willing or not, you are my student."

"And you're a master of illusion," she said sharply. "And you're a mesmerist. I've seen you hypnotize an entire theater into believing a lie."

"Just so," he replied, putting down his spoon. "You're growing closer to the answer, kitten."

"What are you hiding?" Evelina jumped up and began a circuit of the room, looking at everything.

"Nothing. I'm attempting to teach you to see through deception."

She stopped dead in front of the sherry decanter. Rather than the clear amber she'd seen before, now it looked like liquefied decay. She snatched the crystal stopper away and reeled back from the smell. "Bloody hell, what's in there?"

"You read the recipe earlier today," Magnus replied, blotting his lips with his napkin.

She dropped the stopper from nerveless fingers. "That potion in the appendix. The one that enables a person to feed from the living." She rapidly calculated the number of days, the number of doses. She'd had more than enough to do the job. "You tricked me into drinking it! You left my bracelets on just to set the stage to give me the first dose!"

Magnus gave a short laugh. "Trust me, this was kinder. I wish I'd thought it was a top-drawer liquor when I was a student. The taste is indescribably bad."

Evelina rounded on him, rage making her feel eight feet tall. "This is the way you confess to what you've done? By turning it into a practical demonstration?"

"What I've done?" He rose from his chair in a single swift move. His dark eyes were bright with anger of his own. "You simper and you snap and I let you. I bestow my knowledge freely, all the while putting up with your puling conscience. I endure you, Evelina, but make no mistake. You will do as I say."

"You've made a monster of me!"

"Then that is who you are. There is nothing I can make you into that does not already dwell in your soul." He raised a finger, pointing it into her face. "This is your lesson in truth, kitten. *You are my thrall.*"

Evelina drew up short. It had been a long time since she'd felt his wrath, but it made her own feel stronger. She narrowed her eyes, no longer caring what he did. He'd already destroyed her. "Be careful what you make of me, Doctor."

She turned and walked back to her bedroom, then sat unmoving at the edge of the bed. It was still strewn with the contents of her trunks, but she ignored that entirely. A minute or two later, she heard the key fasten the lock.

The sound made her feel better. If Magnus was turning her into an implement of his will, there was no way she could ever let herself go home.

CHAPTER FORTY-SIX

"DARK MOTHER OF BASILISKS, WHAT IS THAT?" NICK GROWLED. He shoved the tankard back toward his helmsman, rising from the scrubbed wooden table in the mess area of the ship.

"Scrumpy," Digby replied, his wide smile showing crooked teeth. He was tall, red-haired, and perpetually good-natured, even toward vile substances masquerading as drinkable liquids. "Striker brought a fair supply on board."

"As an incendiary weapon?"

"No, he said it was a right proper drink for pirates. And I rather like it."

"You can have my share." Nick gave up and started toward the fore of the steamspinner.

"Right you are, sir," Digby said cheerfully, draining Nick's mug in a single draft.

As he walked away, Nick waited for the sound of his body falling in a toxic heap, but apparently airmen were manly men well able to survive the rigors of scrumpy.

From the mess, he walked forward to the bridge, still amazed by the view from the arc of huge windows. With deep satisfaction, Nick regarded the brilliant greens and golds of Somerset unrolling below. He had survived the Scarlet King's hell. Now Scarlet was dead, and Nick had this amazing ship, his crew, and Athena. The only other thing he wanted for himself was Evelina.

He had been on the *Athena* when Her Majesty's Laboratories had been destroyed, or he would have whisked her away then. As it was, she had escaped with Madam Thalassa's crew. Holmes was learning her exact location now, then Nick would pick her up, and all would be right in his world. If His Princeliness the Schoolmaster came out on top, there was even a chance of a pardon.

You are whistling, Niccolo, said Athena.

"I'm happy."

But you are not musical. And there is a rook awaiting you below.

The mention of the birds sobered him. Gwilliam had reported disappearances from his flock—scouts who went out and did not return. Then they had found the savaged body of a rook dropped in pieces against the starboard portholes. The birds had little idea what was stalking them, but it always seemed to happen when there were enemy airships nearby. Evidently, the steam barons had a new weapon.

Nick retraced his steps through the mess, the crew quarters, and out the door that took him from the gondola to the main workings of the ship. This was Striker's kingdom. He could hear the crash-banging of crates being moved in the storerooms as his second in command tidied away the bolts, grease, and other parts necessary to keep the ship running in top form. It was a bit like witnessing a clockwork badger stocking his burrow for the winter.

Nick's destination was a small doorway on the port side of the ship. It led into a small, narrow chamber with no furnishings other than roosts. There were three round portholes as well as a narrow hatch that opened straight into the clouds. Here was where the ash rooks could come and go at will.

He put his head inside the roosting area. "Do you have a message for me?"

A young rook with a simple chain around his neck flew down from his perch and dropped a note at Nick's feet. *Fair winds, Captain, I come from the place of brick and water below.*

"Greetings, Talfryn." As they had nearly reached Bath, Nick assumed the message must be from the Schoolmaster's headquarters just outside the city. He bent to retrieve the message.

Will there be battle soon?

Without answering, Nick unfolded the paper, which had been somewhat mashed by its trip in the rook's strong beak.

Captain,

I beg your indulgence, but I trust you will understand the contents of this message better than most. I received a telegram from the younger Miss Roth this morning with a very strange piece of information. She woke up with a firm conviction that her elder sister, who has been ill and insensible for months, visited her in a dream and gave her instructions to advise me that Evelina Cooper is being held captive by the sorcerer Magnus at Castle Siabartha. As you can well imagine, this is not within my usual area of expertise.

However, I extend these three facts for your consideration. First, it has come to my attention that there were indeed several sightings of an unmarked black air vessel between Dartmoor and the coast north of Tintagel immediately following the destruction of Her Majesty's Laboratories.

Second, there is indeed a Castle Siabartha on that coast.

Third, my initial assumption was that Evelina left the moor on the night of the laboratories' destruction with Madam Thalassa. There was another set of footprints near the location where I last saw her, but it had rained so heavily before dawn that any information they might have provided was badly obscured. And, to be frank, I thought I knew the reason for her silent departure. She was visibly upset at the time, and until now I believed she left quietly in an effort to keep her troubled state of mind to herself. *This delicacy of feeling is, as I'm sure you know, part of her nature. Nevertheless, I have since confirmed to my great consternation that I was in error, and there is a strong probability that she was coerced and kidnapped.*

In brief, I believe Miss Roth's information should not be discounted, however irregularly she has obtained it.

Captain, I am well aware that in this time of conflict, you and your ship will be pushed to the limit. However, I beg you to investigate. The coordinates for the castle are listed below.

—*S. Holmes*

Nick read the message, and then read it again. *Evelina is gone.* It was like being thrown in Manufactory Three all over again, with the rage and helplessness that dragged with it.

A remote castle on the coast? Magnus? Nick's mind veered sharply away. *I saw Magnus fall. He has to be dead.* But he'd thought that before and been wrong.

He looked down at Talfryn. "Tell Gwilliam to prepare for a siege."

Southwest Coast, October 12, 1889
SIABARTHA CASTLE

4:10 p.m. Saturday

THRALL? IN YOUR fantasies, you moth-eaten charlatan.
When she'd left Whitechapel, Evelina had been horrified by the price Magnus's lessons had made her pay. And yet, there'd been a lingering corner of regret for all she would never learn.

After last night, any lingering disappointment had just gone up in a ball of flame. She wanted out before he did something else to her. *Where am I going to go?*

Part of her wanted to be locked away somewhere, back at the college or maybe in a dungeon where she couldn't hurt a soul—at least until she knew she could control this new curse. And part of her was terrified of confinement. In a way she didn't quite understand, she wasn't entirely civilized anymore.

And Magnus's behavior wasn't helping. He'd left her locked in her room all day. There had been no hot water to wash, and no food. She'd ended up drinking the last of the wash water left in the pitcher from yesterday. If he'd meant this treatment to tame her mood, it had produced the opposite effect.

The dark power shifted inside. It was restless and watchful, waiting for her least command. It felt eager for an opportunity to stretch, perhaps to hunt—but that was the one thing she wouldn't allow. She knew from that slim little volume that first taste of fresh life was the beginning of a whole new darkness.

Even the notion of it made her power twitch with anticipation. Evelina gave it a mental smack on the nose. *If you want to be useful, find me a way out of here.*

But the only option continued to be that loose board. She stepped back from the bed to get a better angle, and peered up to the high, shadowy ceiling. The problem was going to be getting up there with the bed in the way. The bedframe was massive, a four-poster affair far too heavy for her to drag aside. Then again, she'd been raised in the circus, hadn't she?

Evelina hadn't bothered to put her clothes back into her trunks. She'd simply shoved them aside to lie down for last night's fit of brooding. That made the empty trunks easy to lift now, so she piled them up in a tower next to her bed. Grabbing the poker again, she climbed the makeshift ladder, going slowly to keep the tottering stack from a sudden shift. From there, she tested the strength of the oak rails holding up the canopy. Carefully, she swung a leg over the closest rail, leaning forward to avoid knocking her head on the beams above. She scooted forward, one arm wrapped around the finial of the bedpost. Even padded by the bed curtains, the position was desperately uncomfortable, and the fact that her right leg was hampered by the canopy didn't help. But the only way to improve matters was to get the job over with, so she prodded the loose board with the fireplace poker and got to work as quietly as she could.

It quickly became apparent that there was no one upstairs, because it was a splintering, puffing, grunting sort of job guaranteed to attract attention. The boards were wide but it took time to get the first one detached all the way, and then more to figure out how to use that to her advantage. The old square spikes holding the boards down were sturdy. It took using the poker like a pry bar, plus a trickle of earth magic, to work enough boards free so she could push her shoulders through the gap. From there, she braced her elbows on the attic floor, got her feet on the canopy rail, and pushed.

Evelina landed on the attic floor, gasping like a landed fish. One palm was bleeding from catching it on a splinter, but she welcomed the pain. It was proof she was doing something instead of waiting like a lamb for Sunday dinner.

When she'd caught her breath, she rolled away from the loose boards and stood up, then tamped them back into place with her foot. If Magnus came looking for her, she'd need every moment. Picking up the poker, she glanced around the attic, wondering where to go next. Magnus had said the balloon and the stables would be guarded with spells, so she would simply have to walk. Maybe it would take her a week to reach the next village. If that was her only option, so be it.

Evelina was all too aware that Magnus was starving her, probably waiting until she was good and hungry in every possible sense before giving her someone to eat. And then, if he used her like he had Serafina, he'd wrest that energy from her, leaving only scraps. It had driven the doll mad. Evelina might last longer, but eventually she, too, would be a ravenous, mindless feeding machine, her only purpose to keep her master plump with stolen lives.

She had to find a way out of the castle, but the only way in or out of the attic room was the main staircase. That would take her past Magnus's quarters—too risky. Instead, she mounted the stairs to the battlements, hoping to find another way down.

Cautiously, she peered out the door. From the sky, she could tell she'd spent a long time getting out of her room. The last streaks of sun shot through the clouds, looking as if something had cracked the firmament and blood had leaked through. She cursed the fact that she hadn't brought a lantern.

There was no one there. She closed the door behind her and began an immediate search for an alternate route down to the bailey.

The merlons rose along the edge of the roof like broad, sullen figures. Evelina felt an instinctive urge to shrink away, as if they might reach out and grab her shoulder. Nonetheless, she forced herself to creep along through their concealing shadows, wary that a guard might yet appear and surprise her. Somewhere above, the sea wind moaned through a chink in the stone, a counterpoint to the lashing sea below.

Of course, it was in the shadows that the Others hid. A squat figure sprang from nothing, one moment not there, the next mere inches away. She cried out in disgust and scrambled back, raising the poker like a club.

Even that close, it was hard to make out, as if it defied her eyes to make sense of what it was. The head seemed to be collapsed onto the shoulders as if it had rotted from the inside. Only twin pits remained where the eyes should have been.

She wished she'd learned how to crush them like Magnus did, but she was stuck with the tools she had. She took a two-handed swipe with the poker, but the weapon passed right through it.

Cold iron doesn't hurt us.

The voice spoke directly to her mind, exactly the same way devas did. But it wasn't the same kind of voice. It *hurt*—not in terms of physical pain, but she felt her heart tear as the cruel, dry whisper ripped through her.

Evelina dropped the poker, and it clanged on the stone. "Get away from me."

She'd never encountered one of the Others this close before. They'd always stayed just out of reach, lurking in corners. It grabbed her arm, maybe with a hand or a tail—she couldn't be sure. Cold shot through her—a pain that struck the gut and radiated clear to her jaw.

You don't get to leave.

She wrenched away, seeming to surprise it, and slammed it with her boot. It staggered back with an angry shriek. *If you can hurt me,* she thought, *I can hurt you back.*

And then it opened a slash in its head that was lined with a double row of jagged, pointed teeth. A dark, shadowy tongue lashed out, longer than it had any business being, and the thing hissed with the sound of a shovel scraping on Evelina's grave.

She bolted. And as if losing her nerve was the signal for mayhem, the parapet swarmed with Others. At first she thought there were just many of them, but then she realized it was a boiling sea of shadow rearing up in waves of grotesque limbs and sightless eyes, as if they'd melted together and heaved as one. Hands and mouths and things that had no name shot from the mass to trap her legs, to pull her under and devour her. Evelina screamed in sheer disbelief. Such things did not belong in a rational world. But this was Magnus's world.

The only part of the roof free of Others was the end with the iron grill where Magnus had used his seeing stone. She made for that, stumbling when something caught her foot, but she kicked loose and surged forward, grabbing up her skirts so she could go faster. But it was a roof, and it ended. She banged against the merlon beside the grill, catching herself with her hands. For a moment, all she knew was the terror of prey. *Oh, damnation!*

She whirled around, only to see the hideous tide rushing at her. Without thinking, she jumped to the ledge of the crenel, backing against the grill. She felt the back of her legs against the iron, but inched further away as the first Other separated itself from the clot of its fellows and loomed toward her, somehow growing taller and thinner as it came so that it could grope upward, the shadowy hands—with far too many fingers—all but touching her face.

Evelina shrank away, arching her back, and then was dimly aware of a chiming sound, like metal grating on stone. She had a brief memory of the grill's rusted bolts, and then she was sailing backward, somersaulting through space toward the foaming surf.

CHAPTER FORTY-SEVEN

IT WAS THE NEXT MORNING, AND EVELINA KNEW COLD.

Her perception had narrowed down to a spark sheltered deep inside herself, the merest pinprick of life. Cold was the only concept she could find a word for. The was no question of moving. She couldn't feel individual things like arms and legs. They were useless to her now.

That wasn't the worst outcome. There was none of that thing called pain, just a growing darkness that told her the pinpoint of her life force was about to be snuffed out. Then she wouldn't even have to worry about the chill.

She was fairly sure she'd drowned, but there were other things wrong, too. The waves had been harsh, tossing her against rocks before they finally vomited her up here. Her legs had never bent at that angle before now.

She wasn't sure how long she lay there. Long enough the sound of the water grew less and something many-legged tracked across her body. Gulls began to gather in the faint gray of the dawn, crying like the disappointed dead.

Then she heard feet crunching across the stones, the rhythmic step of a man stuck in the track of his routine. "Lor' what's this, then?" And the steps turned into a jog, stones crunching louder with each heavy slap of a boot.

A hand, rough and cold, touched her throat. "Miss? *Miss?*"

Another hand pulled the wet curtain of her hair away from her face and the sun hit her eyes. The spark flared, alert. From beneath her lashes she could see a face was near hers, lined and forested with a thick gray stubble. Breath smelled of strong tea with a drop of the good stuff to keep out the morning cold. The face turned, an ear close to her lips to catch any faint sigh of life. Evelina wasn't sure if he would feel anything or not.

The face turned back, wrinkled with sorrow. Within the weathered face, his blue eyes were surprisingly bright, like a flash of sun on a pale blue sea. The hand left her throat and pulled off a shapeless black cap. "I'm that sorry, miss. A bad end for a pretty girl."

The words sang with the lilt of the countryside, and she thought as last rites went it could be worse. At least it was heartfelt.

She wasn't expecting it when the dark power struck, swift as a cobra. It lanced up from deep inside, arrowing through her too quickly for conscious thought. Suddenly she was sitting and her lips were on his, tasting that tea and smuggler's brandy, and devouring the man's life with savage, thirsty gulps. Life coated her mouth and throat, soothing like honey until it hit, sweet and burning, in her core. She felt the healing strength of it stretch out through salt-logged lungs and crushed bones, stitching her torn body anew. But more than that, it rippled through her veins with heady pleasure, drawing her up to her knees so that her mouth could get a firmer fix. Her mind was staggered with it, blinded, so she was as helpless as her prey as she sucked and drank, shuddering with the intensity, the shattering fullness of so much power ringing through her. She was gorged, and then almost sick with it until, finally sated, she fell away with a sigh. Only then did she let the man go.

Evelina rocked back on her heels, reeling as if drunk. Ideas were slow to arrive. The gulls had flown away. The sun was warm on her face even if the rest of her was water-logged. She wasn't cold anymore, and all her limbs worked as they should. She closed her eyes and opened them, bringing the world into painful focus.

Where am I? She turned her head slowly, the world sloshing a little as she did it. Her back was to the ocean and Magnus's tower was far to her left. To her right was a lone cottage and a dock thrusting into the water, a boat tied at the end. A fishing vessel, she thought, and then she remembered the man.

With a gasp, she looked back at him, alarm and guilt confusing the part of her that had deemed him prey. *I survived. Now I should just run.* But she stayed.

He'd fallen on his side when she'd let him go. Evelina crawled over to him, her mind still squabbling about what she should do. In a reversal of roles, she reached for his throat to feel for a pulse.

He sat up with a cry, grabbing for her wrist. His grip was weak—she'd taken all his strength. "Devil!"

"I see you're all right." Her voice sounded strange to her own ears, cool and detached.

"You came from the castle," he hissed, fumbling with his free hand inside the neck of his threadbare shirt.

"Have you had problems with the castle before?" she asked, still in that distant way. *I'm in shock,* she thought.

"The Lord Magus set his fiends on us in my grandsire's time." He held out a silver medal stamped with the image of Saint Peter, patron of fishermen.

"Magus. Magnus," she muttered. The same Symeon the Mage, perhaps, from the ancient writings? Just how old was the sorcerer? She found herself staring at the medal the man thrust toward her, and felt a twinge of temper. Saint Peter didn't bother her, but the fact that he was waving the medal at her did.

She pulled away easily, rising to her feet. The fisherman rose and scrambled backward, putting some distance between them. "Please," he said. "Take me but spare my wife."

Evelina's jaw dropped, but then the full realization of what she'd done broke through. The man was pale and breathing hard, unsteady on his feet and trembling as if he had a violent fever. She'd clearly hurt him—might have done some permanent damage. If he'd been anything but the tough fisher stock, she could well have drained him dry. *But I was nearly dead.* What she'd done was pure instinct, as reflexive as fighting for air.

The why of it didn't matter. This was how Magnus kept coming back, and back, and back. He'd done it so long he couldn't let go even when he'd gone off like old cheese.

She put a hand to her mouth, sick—but it wasn't the kind

of sickness a simple spasm of her gut could fix. She had passed some point of no return, the darkness in her now stronger than the rest. "I'm so sorry. I didn't mean to do it."

The man took another step back, still brandishing the medal. "The demon has you in his thrall. Heaven save your soul but please don't come back here."

"I won't." She hoped that was true. She had no idea what she might do. Evelina began backing away, hoping that meant this poor man would escape her. *He called me a thrall. Just like Magnus did.* And then she turned and began to run. She'd lost her shoes, but her feet flew over the rocks and sand as if they barely touched them. Her limbs moved with an ease they hadn't had since she was a child, her hair streaming behind her in a wild dark mass. She ran and ran, barely touched by fatigue, leaping up the rocky tumbles of the cliffs as if they were no more than the shallow steps to a ballroom floor. As she ran, the sun broke fully into the sky, spilling orange and pink flames across the rippling sea.

One thought filled her mind. *I'm no man's thrall.* And as she thought it, her feet turned toward Siabartha Castle. She had tried to run to avoid activating these powers, but that had happened anyhow. Escape hadn't solved a thing.

And she needed a solution. She'd finally got a stitch in her side by the time she'd reached the wall of the castle. Her clothes were dry, though they were stiff and stained with salt. Her skin and scalp itched. Otherwise, she felt strong, almost invincible. She hated what that stood for. *I'm not like him. I'm not!*

She arrived at the castle gates. She tried the postern first, but it was locked. Then she tugged fruitlessly at the enormous main entrance. Apparently her extraordinary stamina didn't extend to tearing doors off their hinges.

"Magnus!" she bellowed at the top of her lungs. The word faded too soon, answered only by the keening of a gull. "Magnus!"

And then she saw him, leaning out of the window of the gatehouse tower. "Gone for a wander, kitten?"

"And I'm back," she snapped. *Back to stop you, once and*

for all. Most miraculous of all, she thought she knew how it would happen.

He gestured to the smaller postern gate, and she heard it unlock. *Always a showman,* she thought darkly, and flung through the door. He caught up with her as she strode across the bailey.

"What happened to you?" he asked.

"Your pets chased me off the roof. I went for a swim." He caught her arm and she wheeled on him. "Take your hands off me!"

She half expected retaliation, half desired it, but his look grew speculative instead. "You've had an adventure," he murmured, and his dark eyes glistened with hunger. "Tell me."

"I stink of fish. I need a bath." She turned and started walking. Magnus followed two steps behind.

"Fish or fisherman?" he asked.

She didn't reply, for once having the upper hand. She kept going, her shoulders squared, praying he wouldn't outwit her just this once. It was all she could do to keep her hands steady as he unlocked her bedroom door, letting her enter.

It looked clean and neat. Someone had rearranged her trunks and put her things away. *He knows how I got out.* A moment of panic seized her as Magnus stood between her and the door. She could end up a prisoner again. She hadn't thought through every detail. She was flying on rage and a gambler's confidence. Finally, she couldn't stand it any longer and turned back to him.

He gave her a gentle smile. "I left that loose board. I was curious to see how long it would take you to find it."

Shock made her flinch, and then anger drove her forward a step. But she clenched her fists, forcing herself to be still. Was he telling the truth? Did it matter? "I trust I met expectations?"

"That depends." He took a step toward her, then another. "What did kitten bring me?"

She was going to gag if he called her that one more time. But she stayed mute, gritting her teeth to stave off the revulsion she felt as he drew closer. He smelled wrong—a putrid, gangrenous stench that set every particle in her straining to get away. As he bent close to her, she could see how the flesh wasn't quite adhering to his bones anymore. She'd seen the walking dead once they'd begun to go off. Magnus was well on his way.

She closed her eyes, bracing herself, and then pressed her tongue to the roof of her mouth to stop the impulse to vomit. Even though she knew it was coming, the touch of his lips on hers sent a deep shudder through her core. And then she felt the tug of his power on hers, prying the life she had stolen from her grasp. *No,* she thought. *This is mine!*

Her dark power sprang to life, snarling, but his roared. Whatever she was, Magnus was a thousand times older and more cunning. She clutched her prize hard, but he twisted it from her grasp, reeling it in as easily as if she had no more strength than a babe.

Fury made her writhe and she wrenched it back, surprising him for an instant, but then he stopped being gentle. His power slammed against hers, tossing her back. *I've beaten you before,* she thought frantically, but it was only once, and it was quite a different kind of fight.

But she only needed once. *Come on,* she thought to her power. *Where are your fangs now? You struck out this morning, fast and hard. Do it now!* Locked in a desperate struggle, she tried to think of what she'd done to the fisherman, how it had felt. It was no use. What had happened by reflex wouldn't come on command.

And it was hard to fight when all she wanted to do was squirm away. Magnus was just so *revolting*—and she didn't really want to have to see this through. But that was the one thing that had been different with the fisherman. Her magic had taken command, and it hadn't hesitated.

She couldn't flinch now. And so she threw herself into the moment, summoning all her magic, all her desire, all her anger. She leaned into the embrace, grasping Magnus's face in her hands and pulling him close. She kissed him like he was her long-lost husband back from the wars.

Once she had committed to the act, it took only a moment to learn that she was the stronger. His strength was spent;

hers was brand-new. And so she pulled the stolen life back into herself—and then she kept going, drinking what was left of Magnus down. It tasted bitter and black, like the sandy dregs of cold, strong coffee gone to tar.

She faltered when he began to struggle, but then some predatory instinct took over as she dragged out the remnants of his strength, feeling the terrible deeds he had done brush against her soul. There was remorse and pain and loneliness in him, as well as the pride and madness she had come to know. And when she had felt the last shudder pass through him, she tasted his death. Then she finally released him, staggering back as vertigo rushed through her.

Magnus dropped to the floor in a boneless heap, already dead. Evelina wiped her mouth with a salt-encrusted sleeve. He wasn't getting up again. She'd made sure there wasn't one drop left.

CHAPTER FORTY-EIGHT

Southwest Coast, October 13, 1889

SIABARTHA CASTLE

3:10 p.m. Sunday

THE *ATHENA* ARROWED TOWARD THE COORDINATES HOLMES had provided. They'd been delayed by a skirmish and a bit of a chase with some of the Scarlet King's dirigibles. It would have been fun, except for the urgency to reach Evelina. Now Nick stood at the front of the ship, watching out the large windows. Digby, his russet head bent in concentration, studied a series of brass gauges and adjusted the huge ship's wheel a degree.

The ash rooks had flocked around the ship and paced it now, their vast wings occasionally blocking his view of the coast. More had joined them since they had reached the ocean—Nick suspected this part of the Empire was their native territory—and now they spread like spilled ink across the clouds, metal flashing from the helmets and neck chains that marked their status as warriors.

More had joined them, but when they had veered close to the area where they'd sighted the red dirigibles, three more rooks had been killed. Gwilliam was growing reluctant to deploy scouts, and that would be a problem once they returned to enemy territory.

"Anything?" Striker said, coming up beside him.

"The castle should be dead ahead," Nick replied.

No sooner had he spoken than the flock split in two, birds

veering right and left to give the ship a clear view. Nick saw a claw of rock thrust into a thrashing sea and the black castle rising above it like the figurehead on the prow of a ship. Dread rose from the place, as much a palpable mist as the ocean spray. Nick's chest tightened as he leaned against the window, trying to gain a better view, even as every fiber in his body yearned to turn away.

Magnus. Nick knew what the sorcerer could do, and felt the creep of fear along his bones. But Nick would crack the place like an egg before letting Evelina spend another hour behind those stygian walls.

Striker looked down and gave a huff of disgust. "Nice place."

"I'm going in to get her."

"Of course you are."

Digby cleared his throat. "Captain, there aren't many places to take a ship this size down, and anchoring in this wind adds a complication, even with Her Ladyship's assistance." He nodded respectfully toward the panel where Athena was housed.

Such good manners, the deva said approvingly.

"What about the roof?" Nick asked, disliking the idea the moment he said it.

"Maybe," Digby said. "It will be a bit of tricky flying to get close to those towers."

I shall inhale.

Striker stabbed a finger at the glass, a scowl on his dark-skinned face. "That's all well and good, but where are his defenses?"

It was a good question. Nick hovered between caution and a deep desire to get in and out before dark. The roof would be fast, and there was no evidence of guards or weapons up there. In fact, the castle looked utterly deserted. Was that good or bad, or did they just have the wrong place?

He made a decision. "We'll give a roof approach one try, but back off the moment the ship is in danger. I'd rather walk a mile if I have to."

Striker gave a derisive snort. "If someone lives in a castle like this, if you don't take him by surprise, you don't take him at all."

"You can't sneak up on someone in a steamspinner," Digby pointed out. "It's not that kind of ship."

"I rest my case," Striker said darkly, stomping from the bridge with his coat swinging behind him. "I'm going to the weapons locker."

The *Athena* slowed, and they drifted closer, the deva's uncanny ability to hover under her own power giving the enormous vessel a precision that would otherwise be impossible. One thing Nick noticed was that steering the new, larger vessel required more teamwork between the helmsman and the air spirit. The engines quieted as they made the final approach, the crenelated battlements sweeping into view.

The ash rooks circled, almost but never quite in the way. But then they shot out from under the ship, sweeping upward in a chorus of croaking so loud that Nick could hear it through the glass.

"What is it?" he asked.

There is something below, Athena replied. *The ashes of souls.*

Nick had no idea what that meant, but Evelina was down there with it. "How do I get through?"

Only darkness will allow you to see them. Look into the darkness and refuse to fear what you see.

That sounded more than usually vague, even for a deva. "Any practical advice?"

Take Mr. Striker's special blue weapons.

By the time the ship was in position, gray clouds were rolling in from the water and making an early dusk. Striker groaned when the ladder unfurled from the ship's hatch— he had never been a fan of heights, and was even less so after the wreck of the *Jack*—but he made no move to back out of the mission. Nick descended first, his gaze sweeping the rooftop for anything suspicious. Above, Striker crouched, weapons drawn for covering fire. The rooks clung to the rigging of the ship like a ragged cloak, loath to leave its shelter. When Nick's feet touched stone, he drew his own weapons, covering Striker while the other man made a laborious descent. The guns were of Striker's own design, shaped like a gourd that had mated with a cannon. Nick thumbed the switch that activated the weapon's charge, and it hummed slightly as a crackle of blue light snaked around the barrel in a continuous double helix.

Striker landed with a grunt, and the ladder began to ascend. The crew was on standby, waiting for the signal to send reinforcements.

"What now?" Striker asked.

Nick pointed to the door in the top of the tower. They started forward, their boots scuffing on the stone. Nick could see nothing unusual, but he could feel something there. It wasn't even as literal as eyes watching from the shadows. It was a scent, or a mood, or a taste in the air that was wrong, as ephemeral as the tension in a room after a fight.

Striker reached for the door handle, but hesitated, swore at nothing in particular, and then yanked it open. "I hate this damned place."

Refusing to look afraid, Nick went through the door first. It took a moment for his eyes to adjust, and he pulled out his chemical light. Striker did the same. But then his eye caught something just as Striker twisted the brass tube and began the chemical reaction that gave off a thick, greenish glow. "Wait," Nick said urgently. "Turn that off."

Without argument, Striker snapped the shutter closed. Nick squinted, trying to make out what he thought he'd seen in the near darkness. Not much met his searching gaze—just boxes and crates stacked on the wooden floor and a spiral stair leading downward. Even castles, it seemed, needed rooms for miscellaneous storage.

And then he saw it. At first he thought it was a shadow, but it shouldn't have been there. To his eyes, it looked simian—the limbs out of proportion, the head low and jutting, the eyes sunken pits of black. There might have been six limbs, or three, or perhaps more than one head, but the one overriding fact was the menace that rolled off it like smoke. "Black Mother of Basilisks," he swore softly.

"What?" Striker snapped, clearly unhappy. "I'm just an ordinary bloke. I don't see a thing."

"I believe I've found the sorcerer's guard dog." But the moment he said it, he realized there was more than one. He saw them wherever the room was darkest. He watched one move, vanishing as it flowed across a feeble ray of sunlight, only to reappear on the other side. Light didn't hurt them; it cloaked them. "There's a whole pack," he amended.

"Where?"

One sprang at Striker. It thumped into him, baring needle-sharp fangs. The man roared in disgust and alarm, firing the magnetic gun. The blue charge slammed into the thing, exploding it into black droplets that faded before they reached the floor. *Athena said to take the magnetic weapons.* The electric charge scrambled whatever the things were made of.

That made the others creep backward, pressing themselves to the walls. Nick heard, more in his mind than with his ears, a soft muttering eddy around the room.

"You saw that one?" Nick asked.

Striker was breathing hard, but the gun was steady in his hand. "Just as it was about to bite my face off. What the hell was it?"

"Some sort of shadow creatures. I can't see them unless they're in near darkness. I think they have to become solid to attack, which means they're visible for that one instant."

"Did I kill it?"

"I'd say yes."

"That's all I need to know."

They began moving toward the stairs, Nick first and Striker moving backward, the muzzle of his weapon in a constant sweep from side to side. The staircase was a tight spiral only wide enough for one, so Striker was forced to turn sideways to cover their backs as they began their descent. Nick's heart pounded, nerves wound to the breaking point, but the shadow creatures didn't seem willing to risk another attack. They were a third of the way down the stairs when he realized their mistake.

The stairway was made from the same slick black rock as the rest of the tower, the curving stairs slim triangles just wide enough for a man's foot. Oval slits let in gray afternoon light that hung uncertainly in the gloom. It took them a moment to realize that the stairway was filling with a thin mist.

"Nick?" Striker asked in a tight voice as the mist rolled down, engulfing them both.

They kept going another moment, stair by stair, while Nick thought. "They know they're vulnerable when they attack, so they don't want to be caught. We can't fight a mist."

"But then why . . . ?"

His question was answered before it was finished. In the next heartbeat, the mist divided into individual forms and became solid. The stairwell was full of the creatures, blocking them in from above and below. Shooting them in such close quarters should have been easy, but they were already too close. Nick was pinned, his back pressed against Striker's, his arms too confined to properly take aim. He fired a random shot, but the creatures dodged out of the way. They began to open their misshapen mouths, revealing teeth that belonged to some horror from the ocean deeps.

Nick had brushed against Magnus's sorcery as well as the Black Kingdom and its minions. He knew these were phantoms of dark magic, and their teeth were inches from his face.

Behind him, Striker stumbled, the man's weight lurching against Nick. He pitched forward, barely catching himself against the wall. And then with a cry, Striker slammed into him again, sending his feet skidding off the narrow steps. They were being herded, half by the force of the massed spectral bodies, and half by their own terror.

Look into the darkness and refuse to fear what you see.

"Great bloody help that is," he snarled, falling to his knees. Pain shot through his legs and hips as bone hit rock. And then he was sliding, cradling the gun as best he could as the slither became a tumble that seemed to go on forever.

Dizzy, he eventually rolled to a stop in a large, open

space. Every bone and joint yowled in pain, promising a nightmare of bruises. Had he lost consciousness? Had he broken anything? Then he felt himself floating upward, and he snapped fully alert.

He was lying supine, suspended above the ground, with a cloud of contorted, melted heads fastening on his flesh, their fish-teeth digging in deep. Pain seared through him as if a thousand needles made of ice were pricking into his flesh. Somewhere else in the room, Striker bellowed with rage.

Nick's reaction was instant. He dug inside for his magic, flailing it wildly into the mob of hungry mouths. It flared, hot and white, scorching the front ranks. The mob recoiled as one, and Nick fell. The stone floor slammed into his spine, leaving him stunned long enough for the mob to regroup. He rolled onto all fours, looking around for his weapon. It was there, a dozen feet away. Nick felt the weight of the mob on his back, crushing him down. He lashed out again, using his air magic as he would the magnetic weapon—light and spark against the dark and cold. They fell back a second time, but not as far as on the first. The nasty beggars were quick to learn.

Nick dove for the weapon, leaping as much as running to outdistance the shadowy, mistlike horde. His hands closed on the gun, praying it still worked after the tumble down the stairs. He was sure the only reason he'd survived was because they wanted him fresh and squirming.

His weapon was dead. With a curse, he switched the thing off and on, and then gave a cry of relief when he heard the telltale hum. The things swooped in, leaving him just enough time to take aim. And then he began firing.

He began with the mob in front of his face, then quickly located his friend. He shot near enough to Striker that the creatures let him go, and winced when he heard the thump and scrape of his body hitting the floor. After that, it was a massacre. Black splatters flew into the air, burst after burst. The room had once been a banqueting hall since fallen into ruin. Nick added to the destruction as his shots crashed into the derelict furnishings, but he refused to stop until the last creature was added to the rain of slimy mist slowly settling over the table and floor. He wasn't interested in a repeat visit from the needle-toothed horrors.

When his weapon finally clicked empty, he stopped. Nick trembled with spent adrenaline, his teeth clenched until his skull ached with it. Every object stood out with crystal clarity, as if his senses were overwound. He rose slowly, then crossed the room to where Striker was picking himself up.

"Bloody hell," Striker cursed, twisting his neck experimentally. "Remind me not to piss you off."

Nick's face heated, but he didn't reply as he hauled his friend to his feet. "Now that the opening act is over, maybe we can get down to business."

Striker gave him a bleak look, mirroring Nick's own thoughts. What were the chances that Evelina was alive with those creatures roaming the halls? Nevertheless, they began searching, working up the main tower room by room. While they had technically passed that way already, Nick remembered no details from his roll down the stairs. He found his hat, slightly crushed, and Striker's battered old flask, but mostly empty rooms. Only when they had nearly made it back to the top did they begin to see signs of recent habitation. And then they came to three doors. The first was a workroom, filled with old books. The second was an empty bedroom Nick guessed belonged to Magnus since there were a gentleman's dark clothes strewn upon the bed. When they reached the third door, Nick thought he heard a sound. He held up a hand, signaling Striker to wait, and gripped the old iron handle.

When he opened the door, the first thing he saw was Evelina sitting on the edge of the bed. He opened his mouth to cry out, but then he saw more. She was still and silent, giving no sign that she'd heard the firefight right downstairs. There was the state of her clothes, caked in filth. The hunched anguish in her body. The dead thing on the floor.

"Evelina," he said in the soft, careful voice of the sickroom. He had no idea of what had happened, but he could sense her fragility from across the room.

She looked up with the quick, frightened eyes of a captured bird. He'd expected relief—joy even—but what he saw there rocked him backward. She was terrified. Her eyes flicked to the thing on the floor.

"Who?" he asked, thinking the dry husk of a corpse looked like something dragged from an ancient tomb.

"Magnus. He's really, truly dead."

Nick felt Striker behind him and turned.

"You go ahead," said Striker. "I'll keep watch."

With a nod, Nick stepped into the bedroom and closed the door. His mouth went dry for a moment, sensing trouble on a monumental scale. "What happened?"

Evelina looked up at him, her mouth working. "I killed him. I used his own magic against him."

"Good."

Her eyes, always a deep, rich blue, seemed to grow yet darker. "You have no idea what you're saying."

"Then tell me."

"He tricked me. He made me . . . he made me like him." She looked down at the corpse with fierce loathing. "So I drank his life. Every drop."

Nick blinked, not quite understanding at first, but then putting it together from what she'd said about Magnus and his doll. Horror reared up, throwing him back to the fight downstairs. Except now there was no weapon, no way to blow the evil to smithereens. Helplessness rolled over him, leaving his body weak and aching.

His first instinct was to tell her it would all be fine, that he'd find a way to fix everything—but he knew better. First, there was no way of knowing what could be fixed. Second, she always knew when he lied.

Evelina rose from her position on the bed, her eyes wide in her heart-shaped face. Those eyes filled, star-bright with tears. "I'm sorry, Nick. I'm not who I was."

He gave a slow nod. "I can see that." The darkness was in her, flowed from her like the fire of a dark gemstone. It was beautiful, but dangerous. *Whatever was in Magnus is in her now.*

There was a corner of him that wanted to recoil, but instead Nick began to approach, circling around the flaking remains of the sorcerer. Another corner of him wanted to philosophize, to list all the reasons she would never be like the thing on the floor, but he kept that babbling voice to himself. Words weren't what either of them needed right now.

"He took off the bracelets," she said suddenly. "That made the hunger worse."

"That makes sense," Nick said with deliberate calm. "All that iron in the manufactory kept my magic from working. We'll get you some new bracelets, if that's what you want."

"Yes. No. I don't think they would be enough anymore. It's too strong." Now they were just a few feet apart. She was breathing hard, reminding him again of a captive bird. "I'm afraid to touch you, Nick."

"I'm not just anybody." He raised one hand, extending it palm out. "You and I have always been together."

"I killed *Magnus,*" she repeated.

"Good," he said again, and kept his hand right where it had been.

He saw her fingers twitch, wanting to respond, but her fear was fighting his invitation. He felt the flutter in his own gut, the sense that his own strength was about to be tested. And then she quickly raised her own hand and pressed her palm to his. Her magic had always been of earth, of the green and growing fields, the rich soil and sun-warmed rocks. Now Nick felt the force of her magic like a bolt, dark and terrifying as an abyss. She was all that she had been, but there was utter darkness, too.

He felt that darkness lick at his power, wondering if he would be good to eat. A fine shiver crawled over his flesh, but he knew how to respond. After all, he'd grown up around lions and tigers and had seen them tamed often enough.

Nick unfurled his magic—not to hurt as he'd done with the shadow creatures, but with the slow, insistent radiance of sun and air. His magic pressed against hers, blazing to a corona of light. There had always been a silver sheen when they touched, but this was a starburst of silver. He heard

Evelina catch her breath, every bit as awed as he was by the potency of the wild magic they could call.

"You have something Magnus never had," Nick said, putting all his reassurance into his voice.

She met his eyes, looking just as she had with one foot out of girlhood, testing what it was to be a woman. "What is that?"

Nick gave his best, his most piratical smile. "Me."

CHAPTER FORTY-NINE

London, October 13, 1889

HILLIARD HOUSE

11:55p.m. Sunday

A FAINT BREATH OF WIND FLUTTERED THE LACE CURTAIN. IT was slight enough that Bancroft, adrift between wakefulness and sleep, wondered if it was just a trick of the gold-washed light from the street outside. Then the clock on the landing bonged. He blinked, and told himself he had better get some rest. It was hard since he had sworn off strong drink. His mind never quite shut down.

The nervous chatter in his brain was worse now than ever, however much he shied away from any thoughts of Tobias or Imogen. The search for his grandson continued, and with it the anxious despair of his family. They'd tried letters, telegrams, and delegations to the Gold King with no effect. He'd vanished, and Jeremy along with him. Bancroft had called on his allies to help, but those he could interest in the plight of a single baby didn't have any more access than he did. And everyone was far more interested in the war.

Skirmishes had broken out between the Gold and Blue forces, but they had yet to progress to full-on battle. Bancroft's guess was that neither side was as ready as they'd imagined. What had begun with a bang had fizzled to a whimper as one side or the other attempted to negotiate. The proposals were utterly insincere overtures—tactics meant to put the other off his guard—but still they dragged on. It was like waiting for a boil to burst.

Bancroft tossed, plumped his pillow, and heaved a sigh as his mind skipped to yet another topic. He'd spent the evening in the offices of the Whitlock Bank—one of the few still standing after the Gold King's attack on the Green territories—transferring funds to Han Lo for the coal. There was plenty of coal in the city now for whatever attacks the rebels planned. Unfortunately, the supplies were in London and most of the rebels were in the south. Han Lo had promised some assistance—Bancroft wasn't certain how far the Black Kingdom's influence stretched—but the rest Bancroft would have to get through the blockades. He had no idea how—yet. He needed a miracle but he *had* managed to get the coal, so that meant he hadn't lost his capacity to work wonders.

He closed his eyes and imagined possible rewards for all his care: a ministerial appointment, accolades in the press, maybe a handshake from the future king. He had gambled heavily on the Baskerville affair, risked much and paid more, but dreaming of all he might win took the sting from his efforts.

He had just about sailed into peaceful oblivion, when he heard a light footfall. This time he sat up, the covers falling to his waist. He glanced first at the connecting door to his wife's bedchamber, but it was closed. Then he wondered if it was his youngest daughter up to no good. "Poppy?"

A knife flashed, and the next moment he was pinned against his pillow. Bancroft heaved in a gasp, shrinking into the softness, his skin twitching to get away from the blade. Automatically, his hand shot toward the bedside table where he kept a gun, but the knife dug in.

"Greetings, my lord."

A black outline blotted out the square of light from the window. Bancroft's mind whirred, grasping for facts, but there was little to work with. The only thing that he could determine was that the figure was small.

"What do you want?" he asked.

"Remembrance." The word was precisely spoken, but with a curious accent. Chinese, he thought, though more pronounced than that of Han Lo. "I had a brother who came to these shores."

Bancroft waited, deciding that the voice sounded female. "How can I help you?"

The knife jerked, making him gasp.

"I do not need your help!"

"Then tell me who you are."

"Hush!"

The blade turned, the point spinning against this flesh. A terrified sound worked its way from his throat. His gaze flickered to his wife's door, praying that she remained asleep.

"Do you know what happened to Mr. Harriman?" said the voice in a whisper like dry, dead leaves.

Harriman, Keating's cousin, had been Bancroft's partner in the forgery scheme—the one that had ended with so many Chinese bodies in the underground rivers. If Bancroft had entertained any doubts, now he was sure he was in trouble. "He died in prison."

"How poorly that describes his fate," the voice mocked.

"I don't know the details. It didn't matter to me."

"It should." The knife turned slowly, snagging in his flesh. "He died one cut at a time. It didn't matter if his keepers locked him away. The knife came each night and took a little bit of him away."

"Good God!"

"Not good if you were Harriman. Every dawn would find less. An ear, a finger, a toe. Eventually the easy pieces were gone and the rest had to be done in strips."

Bancroft had had enough. He reached up to grab the knife hand, but a hard blow slapped him on the wrist, making his fingers turn to rubber.

"If one is frugal, there is enough flesh on a man to last a year before he dies. But Mr. Harriman did not live through the summer. He stopped sleeping, too afraid to shut his eyes for fear of what he would lose next. A man cannot go on forever like that."

Bancroft's flesh pebbled in disgust. "What did Harriman do to deserve such an end?"

The knife pricked hard enough to draw blood. "You do not remember?"

Bancroft's heart was pounding now, but the fear was clearing his head. "Harriman was versatile. He did many things."

The knife jabbed again.

"All right, all right." Bancroft had been the brains, but Harriman was the actual perpetrator of the forgery scheme. "He hired goldsmiths from China. A dozen workers in all."

"A dozen workers and my brother, the one you called Han Zuiweng," the figure said, the words little more than an angry hiss.

Bancroft shuddered at the name.

"Harriman confessed that he paid my brother to kill the others, but he swore that it was you who killed my brother."

Of all the moments for Harriman to start telling the truth.
"It was Harriman."

"He swore it was you. Who should I believe?"

"Do you trust the word of the man who accused your brother of murder?" With glacial slowness, Bancroft edged his hand toward the night table.

The knife flashed viciously, biting into flesh. Bancroft began to cry out, but the knife was back at his throat, a hand across his mouth and nose, all but cutting off his air. The move had been almost superhuman in its quickness.

"Silence! Just because my grandfather was courteous to you, that does not mean I shall extend the same favor."

So this was the little flower of a girl he had seen peeking through the doorway? His heart pounded double-time. He could smell a woman's scent on the slim hand that gripped him like a vise. The unfamiliar mix of the feminine and the deadly coiled his guts with terror. "You sent the note at Duquesne's?"

"Not I, but one of my kin. After we had sated our wrath with Harriman's flesh, we had let you slip from our minds until you came knocking on our door, waving your coin. Our thirst for vengeance was suddenly reawakened. You see, our mother trained us—brothers and sisters—for a special kind of work. She also trained us to look after each other."

The hand left Bancroft's mouth, and he gasped. He felt

blood, hot and sticky, trickling over his hand. "What do you want?"

"Reparations must be made, my lord. I want reparation for my brother's death. That is the custom of the Kingdom of Ashes, and you have rung the bell at our gates."

"He was a killer!" Bancroft gritted his teeth, pain and fear heating his temper.

The woman's voice was implacable. "He was my brother. If it makes you less confused, call him my brother knife, for we were made to be two blades shining on midnight silk."

"Harriman was your blood money."

She gave a huff of contempt. "He was not worth a jug of cheap wine. When the time is right, the underground will name its price."

And suddenly the figure had withdrawn to stand by the lace curtain, so fast she had moved before his eyes could follow. "Do not think to escape. Harriman tried it, and discovered that he had nothing with which to run."

And the figure slipped through the window, a drop of ink that left no stain. Bancroft fell back to the bed, and then plowed his fist into the pillow, speechless with rage.

One might ask what we know of this Prince Edmond. He is said to be an affable country lad with a ready smile and a fondness for witty conversation. And somewhere between pints of ale, he's managed to assemble an army of makers without the Steam Council's notice. We say give the bloke a try—the Empire could use a bit of pluck.

—*The London Prattler*

London, October 14, 1889

PENNER TOY AND GAMES

1:30 p.m. Monday

"WILL YOU CONTINUE to help Alice? Regardless of what happens?" Tobias asked, worried by his father's haggard appearance, but worried even more that he would say no. "It's not her fault who her father is."

They were once more in the back of Bucky's factory, but it was largely deserted. Bucky and his most loyal workers were out giving the news to the locals that the prince's armies were only a day outside the city. Those not already involved in the skirmishes to the north and east of the city were to stand ready to rally. Tobias coughed, his lungs wet and aching.

"Of course." Bancroft waved a hand. It was a curt, frustrated gesture. "Jeremy is my grandson. I'll make sure he gets home to his family and that includes his mother."

And then his father looked at him, his face a hard mask. He knew about the poison, but in typical fashion they'd talked around it far more than about it. "How are you feeling?"

Horrible. The drugs that Dr. Watson had given him might have been helping but it hardly felt like it. The numbness that had begun in his fingers was spreading upward. His entire right hand was clumsy now, but that was only the half of it. He felt like every organ, every joint was preparing to collapse. "It's not too bad."

His father held his eyes, acknowledging and perhaps regretting all the missed opportunities for closeness between them. It would have been the perfect moment for a statement of affection, but that bridge had burned too long ago.

Tobias reached out as far as he was able. "I'm glad we're on the same side in this affair."

But talking about what passed between father and son was much harder than focusing on a concrete problem. Bancroft nodded and promptly changed the subject. "How are you coming with the devices?"

After the disaster with the malfunctioning aether distillation unit, Tobias had ordered all the Gold King's war machines equipped with an override on all their major systems. These could be remotely activated and some even reprogrammed from remote, handheld units. "I remember the specifications for almost everything. But I've had to rely on Bucky's workmen to construct them." His hand had lost all its dexterity. The pain of it went beyond inconvenience—as a maker, his clever fingers had defined him. "I don't know if they'll finish in time."

"They will," Bancroft said in that tone that had enforced treaties and ended careers. "I'll make sure it happens."

"Thank you." Tobias swallowed, hating the fact that he was too weak to hunt for his son and remained confined in the factory. He'd tried to split his time and strength between searching for Jeremy and working on the devices, but he couldn't hide his weakness from his wife anymore. "And thank you for helping Alice. The longer we search with no results, the more she's suffering."

"Keating is too smart a fox for the obvious. No doubt he has houses even Alice doesn't know about. Where does he keep his property records?"

"In his main residence. There will be no chance of simply strolling through the door. He may be in hiding with his hostages, but the servants will be there."

"I'm sure Alice still has a key." Bancroft gave a wry smile. "She broke into my safe, after all. This should be easy."

Tobias balked. "I don't like putting her in danger. God knows what Keating would do if his men caught her snooping."

"Give the girl a chance. It's her father and her child. She knows that landscape far better than you or I."

And yet Tobias could still picture her delicately freckled face white with fear as one of her father's hulking Yellowbacks thrust an aether rifle in her stomach. His gut went cold. "Don't tell me how to care for my wife."

"Why not? Once upon a time you seemed to need the instruction."

Tobias felt the barb twist, stirring up his own self-recriminations. He rose slowly from his seat. "Must you turn this into one of our futile sniping matches?"

"Damnation, Tobias!" Suddenly his father's face was gray with grief and fury. He rose, too, and gripped his son's shoulder, squeezing so hard that despite himself, Tobias flinched. Bancroft wore the look of a drowning man.

A beat passed between them. A suffocating, crippling moment pregnant with defeat. Tobias groped for something to say, but failed. They'd forgotten how to speak anything but angry words to each other.

And then whatever bound them together cracked under the monumental weight of their sorrow and regrets. With a stifled curse, Bancroft turned and left the room, all but breaking into a run.

CHAPTER FIFTY

Where, oh, where has the Gold King gone?
The wretched old villain has left with the dawn
With a scuttle of coal and a lamp full of oil
He's left our good queen in the darkness to toil
  —Drinking song, reprinted in *The London Prattler*

London, October 14, 1889
MISS HYACINTH'S HOUSE OF PLEASURE

2:15 p.m. Monday

HYACINTH STOMPED DOWN THE STAIRS OF HER PLEASURE house, fingering the whip at her belt. She played at punishment for a living, but at the moment she wanted to lash out in earnest. "Where is Mr. Tunbridge?" she demanded, each word a jagged shard of flint. She stopped at the third stair from the bottom, using the height to glare around her drawing room.

It was all but empty. Only Gareth, the useless young lout, lounged on the sofa. He was half pet, half dogsbody, and spent most of his free time eating her food. He was also one of the few she wouldn't automatically savage when the mood was on her. He rose now, his eyes cautious. "Were you expecting him?"

"Of course I am. It is Tuesday, and it is two o'clock. He always comes for his beating at two."

"A man of regular habits, then?"

"Like clockwork," she said, biting off every syllable. "But

he is not here. And neither was Monsieur Dubois, nor yet again Lady Christopher. They are my top-drawer clients, so what is going on?" She looked around the empty drawing room, experiencing a moment of panic. "Where are any of my clients?"

Gareth gave a short, solemn nod. "I don't know about t'others, but I had a word with the Frenchie."

"With Dubois?" Hyacinth folded her arms across the elaborate bow adorning the front of her bodice. Her outfit was a startling pink striped with cream, the front of her skirts cut away to display her elaborately embroidered black stockings. Men liked fantasy, and she looked good in it.

Gareth nodded.

"What," she asked, "could possibly be more enticing than me?"

"The Violet Queen offered to do him personal, like." Gareth shrugged. "No one's going to tell her to shove off."

Confusion made her sway on her ridiculously high heels, and she put a hand on the stair rail. "What would that old carcass want with Dubois?" Hyacinth wrinkled her nose. "She doesn't even have to work anymore."

"Didn't you go see her the other day?"

"Yes. She was all good manners and second-best tea." But still, the woman had to be up to something. "Is that all Dubois said?"

Gareth shrugged.

"Damn it all." She turned and clattered back up the stairs. She strode to her private chambers, where she should have found a plump, pale body strapped to her chevalet—a tilting frame vulgarly known as a Berkley Horse—waiting for the first kiss of pain. She gave it a savage snap of her whip, as if the smooth wood could feel the burn of her displeasure.

Then she stood glaring at the rack of switches, whips, and cat-o'-nine-tails she'd mounted on her wall. There were more extensive collections out there, but she fancied herself an artist who had no need of an excess of tools. *So then where are my regulars?*

"Forgive me, Miss Hyacinth, but I overheard," said a soft voice from the doorway. It was Tigress, a new girl the Violet

Queen had sent over and most likely there to spy on Hyacinth's activities. "I know my former mistress. You have the essence of what she wants."

Hyacinth's head snapped up. "What does that mean?"

The girl bowed. She was slender and dark-eyed, her black hair long and straight. A fool might have called her delicate, but Hyacinth could see the lean muscle beneath the girl's tawny skin.

"You interest her," said Tigress. "Perhaps she wishes to understand your success."

"So she takes all my customers?" Hyacinth asked indignantly.

"Forgive me if I am mistaken." The girl bowed again, retreating. "Perhaps it is not the queen, but just the war that keeps your customers away."

"I don't believe that."

But Tigress was already gone.

Irritation soaked Hyacinth's mood, coupled with alarm. The Violet Queen had been anxious to bring Hyacinth to heel, but there had to be more than an urge to discipline an underling at work. After all, if a business failed, the Violet Queen could take none of the profit. And in Hyacinth's book, the only thing stronger than money was irrational, overwhelming emotion—not exactly the response one wanted to inspire in a steam baron.

Perhaps she wishes to understand my success? Unlikely. The woman had been in the business for years, and had made it to the top. She knew what made it successful. It was something else—something more primal. Something that looked too much like what the Violet Queen had lost.

Hyacinth wanted another talk with the old baggage, and she wanted it now.

HYACINTH CHANGED INTO a more sedate ensemble—this one at least covered her ankles, if it left rather a lot of visible décolletage—and decided to take Gareth and Tigress with her. There were no cabs on the rubble-strewn streets, so they had to walk the distance to the Violet Queen's house. Hyacinth had never lacked confidence, but there were times when numbers gave one a feeling of security, and crossing London had just become one of them. Police and soldiers were out in force, but they were sorely outnumbered. Looters circled the carcasses of the banks like hungry dogs, and mercenaries—the Gold King's Yellowbacks or King Coal's Blue Boys—fended them off or joined them, depending on the odds at the time.

"How much farther?" Gareth asked nervously, listening to distant rifle shots. Tigress lifted her head as if mildly interested in the noise, but said nothing.

"It's just up ahead." Hyacinth kept her voice even, even if her heart was pounding hard enough to make her light-headed. They'd seen a lot of Blue Boys in the last few blocks, and they were far enough out of Whitechapel to catch the attention of rival crews. The last thing she wanted was to get caught in the middle of a fight.

"What exactly do you hope to accomplish, Miss H?" he asked. "You can't just give the Queen of Whores a talking to."

"She took what's mine. She took what I laid my skin and sweat down to have. The last girl who did that to me . . ." Hyacinth trailed off. It had been a lot of years since anyone had crossed her quite that way. "It was Sarah Makepeace, who took my paint box at school. I waited until we were at archery and then taught her a lesson." But even that hadn't been the same. The paint box had been a gift. She'd cultivated her customers, and that made them more truly hers than any ordinary possession.

They turned a corner and the large, elegant house came into view. Hyacinth's two-story, in need of paint and a proper gardener, was a hovel in comparison. This place had four levels, an enormous porch, and an acre of stained glass. The grounds were no less stately, with a rose garden flanked in ornate iron benches.

Gareth gave a low whistle. "Where do the customers go?" Hyacinth was about to say this was the Violet Queen's residence, not her whorehouse, but Tigress spoke up. "The pleasure rooms are in the back. You see, there are no windows. Discretion is complete."

Hyacinth cleared her throat. "I should go in alone. Sit out here and wait for me."

Tigress bowed and Gareth folded his arms unhappily. Ignoring them both, Hyacinth mounted the broad porch with its scrollwork ornamentation and reached for the bell. But then, almost of its own accord, her hand drifted to the bright brass of the doorknob and turned it.

The door opened easily and she stepped inside. The front hall, with its potted palms and black-and-white tiles, was as elegant as upon her last visit, but something was different. *There are no servants.* A footman should have reacted the moment she came up the porch. Now that she was inside, she should have heard a maid or the butler or even just a tweenie bustling about. Hyacinth narrowed her eyes. Something was going on—if the servants had run away, they would have picked the place clean, and there was still a valuable china vase on the hall table.

Now very curious, Hyacinth began drifting through the house, aiming for the intimate sitting room where she'd met with the Violet Queen. That led her down a short hallway punctuated by portraits of reclining nudes, perhaps the chief attractions of the establishment. One might have been a younger version of the proprietress herself.

Hyacinth felt the tickle on her neck that said someone was watching her. Turning slowly, she saw nothing, but heard an eerie clicking. Nerves brought gooseflesh to her arms and she suddenly wished she'd brought a gun. There was a hideous, slavering, huffing sound that made her stiffen.

And then the Pomeranian trotted into view, a menacing puff of cinnamon fur. Hyacinth heaved an irritated breath. It gave a single yap in response. *Brilliant.* If there was anyone in the house, this creature would give her away.

"Hush!" She crouched and it skittered aside on ridiculously tiny paws. "Oh, don't be like that." Hyacinth generally liked dogs better than people, but she didn't have the patience to deal with this now. She grabbed the thing, gloves sinking deep into the silky coat, and shoved it back into the room it had come from, shutting the door. There was a whine and a scratch, but then it was quiet.

She kept on, and in another few steps she heard voices— a man and a woman. Instinctively, she shrank against the wainscoting, inching toward the sitting room. The paneled doors were shut, but she could hear just enough to recognize that the female was the Violet Queen, speaking quickly. The male voice gave one-word replies—not enough to decide if it was familiar.

Tight with anticipation, she bent close to the door, her ear pressed to the crack.

"You can't win this, Keating. No one is with you after what you did."

Finally, the man gave a complete sentence. "That's quite a different tune than the one you sang a week ago."

Jasper Keating? So that was the mystery man! And that explained why the servants must have been banished to another part of the house. The Gold King wouldn't risk having his business overheard.

Hyacinth reached for the doorknob and turned it all the way, making sure there was nothing to catch as she pushed the door open a crack. All of a sudden, the voices were much more distinct.

"You hadn't blasted half of London then." The Violet Queen's voice was harsh. "If you want allies, leave them a bit of ground to stand on. You make enemies when you destroy their livelihoods."

Hyacinth put one eye to the crack in the door. The pair was standing at an angle, the Violet Queen almost with her back to Hyacinth. Mrs. Cutter was wearing a deep indigo costume, the short jacket stitched heavily with glass beads that glittered with every motion. Keating was close to the mantelpiece, one hand on its pale marble shelf, the other in a sling. His features, usually the picture of distinguished elegance, looked hollow with shadows.

"I didn't hurt anything of yours," snapped Keating.

"Of course you did. I live here."

"Men will always come to your door, Mrs. Cutter."

She made a disgusted noise. "Courtesans require more than a back alley shag. We are the demimonde, and that relies on prosperity. You are the great financier. What do you think happens when you block the roads, stop trade, and crush half the banks?"

"I hold all the cards."

"You hold the cards to Armageddon. Enjoy your hand."

Bristling with anger, Keating took two steps toward Mrs. Cutter. "I'll take Green's territory just as I did Scarlet's."

"No, you won't."

"You plan to stop me? You barely have territory. You don't have an army. You don't even have a maker."

Hyacinth bit her lip, utterly enthralled. *There has to be something here I can use to my advantage.*

The Violet Queen raised her chin, the picture of hauteur. "I may be a whore, but there are only so many ways I will agree to be fucked, Mr. Keating." And she reached beneath the short jacket of her costume and pulled a pearl-handled Derringer from the small of her back.

It was small, hopelessly old-fashioned after seeing so many of the makers' fancy guns. Still, the sight of it caught Hyacinth by surprise, and she gasped. It wasn't loud, but it was enough to distract the woman for a fraction of time. With his uninjured hand, Keating pulled out a slender rod—more of a wand than a proper gun—and fired. A ball of blue light crackled through the air, but the Violet Queen was quick. She ducked out of the way in time for the shot to sizzle against the door Hyacinth still held. The next instant, a chunk of the heavy paneled wood exploded into splinters, raining sharp points down on Hyacinth's head. She shoved the door away, accidentally catching the other woman in the face as she turned to run. Mrs. Cutter's eyes flew wide as she saw Hyacinth standing there, clearly seeing another enemy. It was that look in her eyes, guilty and afraid, that startled Hyacinth. *She's done something that she knows has turned me against her.*

By then, Keating had caught up. He thrust his strange weapon against the Violet Queen's temple. "How dare you!"

The woman swore and spun around, clawing at his face. Red lines sprang up on Keating's cheek, but he barely flinched. Instead, he fired. The Violet Queen flew backward, over the back of the sofa, and slammed into the wall. She fell to the floor, her neck twisted almost completely around. The room filled with the stench of burning cloth and flesh.

Appalled, Hyacinth staggered back into the corridor, trembling starting in her knees and working upward through the rest of her. "Bloody hell."

Keating noticed her, giving her a sharp look. "Who are you?"

"Miss Hyacinth," she said automatically. "Governess of one of her houses."

"I hope you found this instructive," he said with a curl of his lip.

Bastard. She was still shaking, her skin in a slick, cold sweat—but she knew how to play this game. She'd been the tyrant of the Wollaston Academy for Young Ladies, and head-hunting savages didn't hold a candle to a crowd of bored debutantes. "I found it liberating," she said in her best boarding-school drawl. "Madam had been poaching my clients for herself. I'd come to settle accounts, but you've done so admirably, sir." *Though really, this was rather more than I'd planned.* She swallowed hard, hoping she wouldn't vomit.

He was studying her now, cradling his injured arm as if the sudden activity had hurt him. "You have admirable nerve."

"A professional asset." Her gloves were damp, clinging unpleasantly to her palms, but she forced herself to look him in the eye. "And I only saw as much as you say I saw."

He put the strange-looking gun away. "I'd rather that wasn't a necessary consideration. It's always unpleasant when a friend lets one down."

And it gives your enemies ideas. She knew that from the schoolyard, too. If the popular girls turned on one of their own, it was only a matter of minutes before the unfortunate victim became the school pariah. And this is where she saw her opportunity. "You are the ally of the Violet Queen.

There is nothing to say that position needs to be held by Mrs. Cutter. Her network of informants, her houses and clients, are all still there."

"What are you saying?" Now he looked almost amused.

Hyacinth edged up to the body, attempting to look more steady than she felt. Her mind whirred frantically, calculating odds, reading every nuance of his expression. She knew how to survive, and much of that depended on reading her marks. "I'm educated and I understand this business. I can help you. I can even cover this up for a few days."

"I don't know you."

Oh, but you do, now that I think about it. It was your judge and jury that murdered my family and made me a whore. But the smile she gave him was conspiratorial. "A few days, Mr. Keating. Check on me as often as you like, but I will keep the information flowing for you. And I saw what you did to someone who crossed you. I may be a tart, but I'm not a fool."

"All other considerations aside," he said coldly, "there will be fierce competition to fill this sudden vacancy at the top. If I grant you this position, how do you propose to keep it?"

That almost made her smile. "Your support will of course be an important factor, but I also have my own means, and my own staff. Not to mention my own tools of the trade. I know how to *maintain discipline.*" She lingered slightly— just slightly—on the last words.

He caught his breath, the pupils of his eyes expanding, and she knew she had him. *It's always the dominating ones that secretly want it.*

"I'll be back tomorrow," he said. "I don't want to hear a word that anything here is different. Not a whisper about Mrs. Cutter. I'll send Yellowbacks to watch you."

And she had no illusions that he'd let her live one second longer than it suited him. She gave a low curtsy. "I'll be waiting."

Keating left.

I'll be waiting and we'll see what sort of a reception we can arrange, Yellowbacks or no. Hyacinth rose and waited a moment, looking around the room but avoiding the sight of the dead woman on the floor. The place still wasn't as lush as the home she'd grown up in, but it was a sight better than Whitechapel. *A step in the right direction, at least.*

She went to the door and called in Tigress and Gareth, then gave them a series of orders beginning with the quiet removal of the body. Such things weren't unheard of in their line of work, although thankfully not all that common.

Then she found an unopened bottle of wine, uncorked it, and poured herself a glass. She bet the Violet Queen had a nice bedchamber, and nice clothes, and perhaps a nice little safe with lots of jewels. She could see herself holding court in the demimonde, young and beautiful, courted by rich men, pretty men, and titled men. But she would keep her heart for the Pomeranian. The dog at least would be likely to love her back.

Hyacinth finished the glass of wine, wondering if she should reclaim her real name of Violet, or if that would just be too confusing.

And then she went to the back of the house, opening doors until she found the one she wanted. As expected, there was a plump, pale body strapped to a chevalet much nicer than the one in her old house. "Hello, Mr. Tunbridge. You were quite a naughty boy, sneaking out to come here instead of to our usual appointment."

The man strapped to the table made an inarticulate sound—that special mix of anticipation and fear—as she opened the doors to a very lovely mahogany cabinet. Floggers of all kinds hung on gleaming brass hooks. She picked one out, testing its flexibility.

"I believe we shall have to clear the air between us, don't you?"

CHAPTER FIFTY-ONE

"WHAT WENT ON DOWN THERE?" STRIKER DEMANDED, catching Nick's arm as he tried to walk past him in the *Athena*'s narrow corridor. Striker's dusky skin was scraped off in some patches and bruising in others, and it looked like it hurt.

"I found Evelina and I brought her back," Nick replied tersely.

"I'd expect more celebration," Striker said dryly. "She hasn't stirred from your quarters. Normally, I'd say that was a good thing when a pirate catches a wench, but this isn't like that."

"She needs time."

Striker's eyes narrowed. "I saw the body. You didn't do that. Did she?"

Nick grabbed the front of Striker's jacket, pulling him close. "And what of it?"

The man held up his palms. "I had your back, remember? I just want to know what I'm dealing with. This big ship could get small enough if there's danger on board."

Nick swore and let him go. "Evelina's no danger to us."

Striker folded his arms, his bulk nearly filling the corridor. "Your wench was with the sorcerer and it doesn't look like it went well for him."

"I wouldn't call her a wench to her face. Or mine."

"Then what is she, Captain?"

"She has the Blood like me." Nick scrubbed his hands over his face. He had slept a few hours after they'd got back to the *Athena,* but it had been the collapse of exhaustion and not true rest. "She's my responsibility."

Striker's silence was eloquent.

"Get used to her," Nick growled. "We'll need her talents before this is over."

Striker grunted. "If she wants to fight for us, then that's all right."

"Good," Nick said with finality.

Striker shot him a look that bordered on amusement. "We're an hour outside of Bath. Maybe this time we'll actually get to dock." With that he turned and limped toward the navigation room.

Nick stood in the corridor, the narrow doors of the crew quarters looking clean and neat in a way that still surprised him. The *Red Jack* had been a fine ship, but old. This had the scrubbed look of a debutante.

The thought catapulted him into a memory of seeing Evie before her first ball, her dress white as whipped cream and just as tempting. Of course, he'd been gawping at her through the iron bars of a gate. He'd wanted her with all his flesh and soul. He still did. Nick strode to the last door, a shade larger than the rest, and went into his quarters.

Evelina was on the bed, curled into the corner of the room with her knees tucked under her chin. It was dim, the only light coming from a modest porthole above the side of the bed. A tray of food sat on the desk, untouched. Nick's gaze swept the tiny room and concluded she hadn't stirred from that spot since he'd left her. Sadness, tinged with a pinch of frustration, stiffened his shoulders.

Something in the way she held herself reminded him of a spooked horse. He didn't know exactly what had gone on at Magnus's castle, but it had shattered any ideas Evie'd had about a benign universe. Rebuilding them would be long and hard, and he would have to be patient. And yet, he couldn't help a surge of pleasure at seeing her there, in his room and on his ship. He was on the right side of the gate this time.

"You should come out and see the rest of the *Athena*," he suggested mildly.

"I saw it coming in. It's lovely." Her voice was soft, as if made from the subdued light. It was also just as gray.

With an inward sigh, he crossed the room and sat down beside her, his back to the wall. He put an arm around her and pulled her close. "I'm sorry, Evie girl."

She let out a shuddering breath, leaning into him like a tired child. "I was foolish not to tell you about the laboratories, but I wanted you to find your ship."

He kissed the top of her head. "Stop making choices for me. It never ends well." Twice she'd even parted from him, thinking it would be for his own good. But they always ended up back together, where they belonged.

"I'm a soul-eating monster," she said dismally.

"With cold feet."

He felt her mood shift, resisting his attempt at levity. "You say you can stop me from turning into another Magnus, or worse."

"All in a day's work." He wasn't sure how, but it wasn't the kind of thing one could plan in detail, anyway.

"He'd lived for thousands of years, stealing the life from others," she murmured. "And it makes sense. If there was a way to stay alive, how could he stop himself from taking it?"

"Do you want to stay alive forever?" Nick asked, working to keep his voice calm. "It's the sort of thing we all think we want."

"No," she said flatly. "The worst thing about Magnus is that I think he might have been a decent man once. Maybe even great. There were traces of who he'd been, relics like the arrowheads in a farmer's fields, but the rest had been eaten away. And he was utterly alone."

Nick thought about what he had seen of Magnus's home in London. He'd been impressed by the huge library, the experimental equipment, and most of all the wealth. But there hadn't been a single servant. "Why didn't he have minions or lackeys or even a butler?"

"He had some at the castle, but not many. He had too

many secrets, I think. Or maybe one of his pets drained them dry and they died."

She was shaking, a fine tremor that wouldn't stop. He pulled her closer, warming her with his body. "I won't let you do that."

She lifted her head. "Promise me."

"I promise."

But that wasn't good enough. She pulled herself up to sit facing him, one hand on his chest. "If it looks like I'm going to start killing people just to keep on living, you have to stop me, even if it's the last thing you want to do." She caught his gaze and held it, keeping him pinned with the fear in her eyes.

"I can't imagine you doing that," he said, and that was true. Still, cold was creeping through him, solidifying like frost in his veins. *By the Dark Mother, she's asking me to kill her.* It was more than he had bargained for, but she needed to know he could make that hard choice if she lost her way. Love wasn't just about flowers and kisses.

She shook her head, leaning forward in her urgency. "Not now. But in ten years or twenty."

"It won't come to that. Not with me here. I won't let you go that far."

Tears trembled in her eyelashes. "I may need you to re-mind me who I am right now, this day. I can't forget that I love my friends and my family, even if I am a little afraid of Grandmamma Holmes. I can't forget how much I hated choir, but that I loved geology."

Nick grasped the hand she had pressed against him. It had gone chill with panic. "But we all change and grow with time, Evie. I can't keep you under glass like a museum piece."

Tears were standing in her eyes. "You can keep me from losing sight of what counts. Like the fact that I love you more than I can say."

"Oh, I'll remind you of that, Evie." Nick felt an ache squeeze his heart. It was heavy as iron, but strangely light as well, as if he'd come to the end of a grueling journey. Every-thing he had ever done had led to this moment. He had her trust, not just when it came to her life, but with her very soul.

His put his other hand over hers, clasping it tight. "And if it makes you feel better, I promise you that I will do whatever needs to be done. Trust me on this. I love you, and I will not let you fall."

She bowed her head, her long hair tumbling forward like silk over his hands. The silver fire glowed softly between them, an echo of their desire for one another, but it seemed wrong to stir those embers now. There were many kinds of healing, and right now was the time for hard truths.

"I have one condition," Nick said.

Evelina raised her tear-stained face. "What?"

"It's time you ate something and came out of this tiny dark room. There's a whole world out there waiting for you."

"How can I even think of it?" She pulled away sharply. Clearly, he'd made the suggestion too soon.

"What else are you going to do?" Nick asked, using the same practical, steady voice he used with his men when they were under fire. "You're being forced to face a piece of yourself that you fear. You have to find a way to use it to make you strong."

A strange look came over Evelina's face.

"What?" he asked, fearing he'd struck the wrong tone.

"I had this same conversation with Imogen in a dream." She looked up at him, her expression drawn. "Except it was about Anna, and I gave her very different advice."

Unsure what she meant, Nick picked his next words very carefully. "I can be your safeguard, but in the end you have to find a way to master this power."

She looked away. "How?"

"Make it your ally. Make it your weapon." He squeezed her hands in his.

"My weapon? What kind of advice is that?"

"I'm a pirate. I know something about darkness and choices."

She gave him a long look, taking in everything he'd said. "And here I am struggling to stay on the path of goodness and light."

"I know you're capable of anything."

"Anything?" she said dryly. "Such as?"

He shrugged. "I was hoping you'd come along and redeem me from my wicked ways. This business of redemption is a two-way street, you know."

Evelina sank back against the pillows, her gentle curves reminding him why he had marched into a haunted castle to play the hero. "Saving you might take some time."

And finally, she smiled.

AS SHE STEPPED onto the bridge some hours later, Evelina felt exposed and vulnerable, like an egg that had lost its shell. Nick was right to coax her back into the light and air. The bright, brisk atmosphere of the ship was the opposite of Magnus's gloomy castle, and the sheer normality of it kept her magic quiet. She played with Bacon until the little dog got lured away by the smells from the mess, and then she busied herself with all the novel equipment on the bridge. But the noise and press of so much active, eager energy was almost too much after the solitude of Siabartha. The greatest comfort was Athena's presence, feminine and warm. Evelina had never been able to speak to the air deva, but it was something to know she was there, especially since Nick had gone down to the city below with Striker.

Evelina found a spot by the high windows and tried to stay out of the way. Bath spread out over the green earth, looking serene from this vantage point. She had been there a few times with Ploughman's Circus, and remembered the warm color of the stone and the beauty of the River Avon. She could see the arcs of terraced homes and the roof of the cathedral. It was as small and perfect as a diorama—and it looked about as unreal. If not for the tiny moving specks that were people and carriages, she might have thought it all a toy.

"How long will we be here?" she asked Digby, who was working at the station closest to where she stood. He was one of the few whose name she knew, and the easiest to talk to.

The tall, red-haired crewman shook his head. "I'm not

sure, miss. We've been loading cargo long enough that they should be almost done. Then it's picking up a few passengers, and we're away."

"Where to?"

"Wherever the cargo needs to go." Digby gave her a sly smile. "It seems pirates have become the new Royal Mail."

She didn't have time to ask for a better explanation, because another crowd of men entered the room, Nick among them. A purely feminine panic brushed her when she saw Michael Edgerton, an old friend of Tobias's. Some of her chagrin was the sensation of the past and present colliding. The rest was sheer vanity. The last time she'd spoken to the man had been at a ball. Now—ragged and reeling from her struggle with Magnus—she wasn't exactly at her best.

Edgerton spotted her, his eyes flaring slightly with surprise. He was still tall and thin, although he had filled out some in the last year. As he shifted, she saw someone else she knew—the Schoolmaster, now Prince Edmond, who was deep in conversation with Nick. The last time she'd seen the Schoolmaster, he'd been handcuffing a man on her uncle's floor.

Curiosity got the better of her. There didn't seem to be any formality around the rebel heir, so she drifted their way to join the conversation.

"The city was known to the Romans as Aquae Sulis, or the waters sacred to the god Sulis," Edgerton was saying. "The hot springs have been known for centuries, but rarely exploited for their geothermal power. The steam barons have overlooked it. Nevertheless, we would need time to build facilities with more capacity. As it is, we have neither the power nor the power storage cells to do more."

"It's the best answer we have with no coal. Bancroft has worked miracles for us, but getting the coal out of London has proven a challenge," said the Schoolmaster.

"Where does that leave us?" asked Nick.

"If we get this cargo to our northern makers, we can mobilize our forces there."

So we're carrying batteries. Evelina considered it an interesting solution, but a limited one. Not enough to win against the forces of Keating or the Blue King.

"Will this many cells even get them to London?" Nick asked doubtfully.

Edgerton and the Schoolmaster exchanged glances. They'd obviously worked together long enough to read each other well, because a decision was made without words.

"In part," said the Schoolmaster. "There is a question of which of our northern forces to mobilize. There isn't enough power for them all."

"We were counting on them to hold the north flank," Edgerton said quietly. "To be utterly frank, this presents a problem."

Nick met Evelina's eyes and inhaled, as if he were going to take that moment to pull her into the conversation. She turned instead, staring out the window without seeing a thing. She was aware of the tension all around her, the collection of large personalities a power source all their own. But she could also feel her newly bolstered magic simmering inside her. If she'd felt like a peeled egg earlier, now she was just the shell, caught between those inner and outer pressures. She wasn't ready to deal with this. She wanted a dark room, silence, and solitude.

But she knew the answer to their problem, and she had the means to make it work. She'd wanted to reconcile the two halves of her being for so long—magic and logic, the world of spirit and the world of machines. She'd created Mouse and Bird years ago, solving the riddle of how to harness the power of devas to make living clockwork. She'd gone to the university to understand the dual nature of her heritage, but perhaps that wasn't something that could be solved by study. Maybe that duality was just something she *was,* and a union would be forged just by recognizing what she could do. And her newfound power gave her the means to make it happen on a grand scale.

It all flashed through her mind in moments, leaving her with the sensation that her stomach was dropping through the bottom of the *Athena*'s hull. The situation reminded her of a card in her Gran Cooper's fortune-telling deck that showed a man walking off a cliff: *the Fool*. It was supposed to represent a trust in fate she just didn't feel. But the prince would lose without her help.

Evelina turned. "Gentlemen, I have a solution."

Edgerton and the Schoolmaster looked up in surprise. Nick folded his arms, looking like the cat who'd got the cream.

CHAPTER FIFTY-TWO

"ARE WE NEARLY THERE?" THE SOFT FEMALE VOICE CAUGHT the Schoolmaster's attention. He was alone in the mess, drinking a cup of tea thick enough to stand on—in his opinion, the only kind of brew worth drinking.

"I'm not the one to ask," he replied, eying Miss Cooper. "They let me think I'm in charge, but I'm really the idiot passenger with the upside-down map."

It was cool on the ship, and she wore an airman's jacket over her dress, her long, dark hair spilling in waves over her shoulders. The jacket was far too large and the sight of her sleeves drowning her dainty hands was oddly charming. So were the big blue eyes in her heart-shaped face, but he knew better than to act on that attraction—and not just because of his birth or Captain Niccolo's knives. He could feel the power this young woman commanded like a magnetic charge. She wasn't to be trifled with—especially when she'd offered him the ability to run machines on magic. That was the power every one of the steam barons coveted as if it were the Grail.

The Schoolmaster was grateful, but he was also a little nervous. Nothing miraculous ever came without a price and, to be utterly frank, there was a fragility to Miss Cooper. All he knew was that she'd been through a great ordeal.

He didn't want to be responsible for her collapse. Overtaxing her wasn't gentlemanly, and with her powers might be bloody dangerous.

She came to stand beside him at the window. "I've only ridden in tiny ships before this, and they didn't fly nearly so high. The views are mesmerizing."

"Mm," he said, telling himself there was no possibility that he was actually afraid of her. He watched as she fingered a figurine on a chain around her neck. It was one of the souvenirs the street hawkers sold in Bath—a tiny pewter owl copied from the remains of the old Roman spa. "Is that a memento from the captain?"

She flushed a delicate shade of rose. "Yes."

The Schoolmaster hid a smile. That part of her—the girlish part—he had no problems with. "The owls are sacred to Minerva—or Athena, if you prefer the Greek. There are plenty of ancient shrines to her in the old ruins."

A shy smile followed the blush. "Perhaps then it is a good luck charm, considering our ship."

He clasped his hands behind his back. "How did you get involved in this adventure, Miss Cooper?"

She was silent long enough he assumed she wouldn't answer, but then she gave a short, low laugh. "I had two grandmothers, my lord. One was a fortune-teller with a circus and the other a tyrant for good behavior and a respectable marriage. I've spent my life trying to please them both."

"So you plunged headlong into a civil war?"

She lifted a shoulder. "With the two sides of my family being so different, I've been in one all my life. And I'm hoping for a better empire."

The Schoolmaster swallowed. He'd heard that note of expectation a thousand times already, and he could feel each hope adding to an ocean of responsibility. "You blew up the Dartmoor laboratories. I think you've made your criteria for improvement clear."

She cast him a wary glance. "I prefer a society that lets me live unmutilated."

A mild shock passed through him at her words. *She is as*

uneasy about me as I am of her. It didn't make him feel any better.

Edgerton and Captain Niccolo came into the room. Edgerton spoke first. "Look down, sir."

The Schoolmaster drew closer to the window, peering through the patchy cloud. Dawn was just breaking, pinking a steely sky. At first all he saw were indeterminate shapes that might have been carts, sheep, or haystacks dotting the fields below. But as he looked longer, the growing light revealed edges of steel and brass. Soon he saw the ground was covered in a procession of wagons, some pulled by heavy draft horses, some powered by steam. In the bed of each were one or two devices. There were various types of guns and cannons, and others that were not so easy to recognize from the air.

"By the coordinates, it's the lowland army," Edgerton replied, his face serious. He pointed to the rear of the force, where a particularly heavy vehicle rolled on a kind of movable train track. Smaller vehicles ran alongside the main one, taking up track the larger one had crossed and setting it down in front in a perpetual cycle. "There's the coal supply."

"That's it?" Captain Niccolo exclaimed from where he stood beside Miss Cooper.

Edgerton nodded. "That's all that's left. They're hoping to capture additional supplies along the way. It's a desperate gamble."

The Schoolmaster rested his forehead against the window, silently cursing. He'd heard the northern armies were short of supplies, but seeing their condition brought it home. Desperation made people do foolish things, including him. He had anticipated the shortage of fuel, but he had counted on having more time to solve the problem. He'd encouraged the makers to go ahead and build their battle machines. But that time had never materialized, and now—because no one could deny the urge to fight for their freedom, not even for lack of coal—the men below stood an excellent chance of being captured and slaughtered once their engines died. He needed a miracle.

He sighed and turned to the young lady with the dark shimmering power, praying that she was his answer. "Miss Cooper?"

EVELINA CLUTCHED THE owl in one hand and Nick's hand with the other. When she had made Mouse and Bird, there had been a ritual with amber and blood and the words her Gran had taught her. But she'd raised the devas on the moor without formal tools, and she needed that freedom again.

The pewter owl, warm from her grasp, dug into her palm. It would serve as a focus—a simple object that would be her touchstone within the physical world. Nick's fingers wrapped firmly around hers, the wild magic skimming along their flesh in a continuous current. She was the conduit between those poles—magic and reality—and would twist the energy coursing between them to her purpose.

Evelina's eyes unfocused as she drifted inward, searching for the power she needed. With the bracelets on, the process had been like rummaging for whatever she could find. Now it was like running her fingers over the treasures of a jewel box, judiciously selecting the piece best suited to the occasion. Her hunger stirred, but she forced herself to look past those darker magics. What she needed now belonged to a different path, to the herbwives and folkways of the olden times. Magnus's power would serve only as an amplifier.

She cast her mind toward the earth below. It had been lush not long ago, but now was scarred with smoke and ash. Her consciousness turned toward the remnants of the grass and trees, flitting through them with the speed and grace of a swallow. There were devas there, clustered in the safety of the green places.

There were many versions of the summons that would bring them to her hand, but she chose a simple rhyme.

> *I summon you by Will*
> *To perform a task for me.*
> *If you do it well,*
> *I'll reward you willingly.*

With Blood I give you strength
And with Tears I pay your fee;
With Words I give you wisdom
And my leave to fly home free.

She felt their attention stir, pricked to life by the touch of wild magic and then called by the ancient spell. In her mind's eye, Evelina could see them—a cloud of colored orbs drifting like falling petals. Each one should have had its own tree or stream to live in, but that wilderness was gone. As her consciousness swept past, they spun and eddied in agitation.

The collective of their thoughts coalesced. *What do you want from us?*

Evelina smiled to herself. *Do you wish to fight the men who took your home?*

The devas swirled faster, rising like a sparkling funnel, the song of their excitement the pained howl of the Earth.

THE SCHOOLMASTER LOOKED down in disbelief as a cloud of light appeared and then vanished in a wash over the army below. Then he blinked, unsure whether or not he had actually seen it. Perhaps it had been a trick of the dawn light.

But then a sigh seemed to pass from Evelina Cooper, and the scene below shimmered at the same instant. And then, to his gaping astonishment, the devices drawn by the carts came to life. The guns swiveled, legs extended, wheels rolled—and the machines bumped off the carts to trundle forward on their own. And it wasn't a disorderly mob of rampaging machines, but rather a quiet and businesslike maneuver respectful of the human shepherds in their midst. Yet the machines had a defined notion of where they were going, just slightly off the path they had been following heretofore.

The Schoolmaster's body tightened, every nerve screaming that what he saw wasn't supposed to be happening. He had seen magic before, but not on this scale. And it might have been what he'd hoped for, but nothing had prepared him for a self-propelled aether cannon, barrel jauntily swinging in march time toward the rising sun. "Where the fardling hell are they going?"

"Wherever you like," said Miss Cooper softly. "As long as they can make one stop along the way."

"Where?" He put one hand against the frame of the glass, leaning casually while he tried not to pass out.

The captain answered in a tone of bloody satisfaction. "Manufactory Three. There used to be a forest there. The devas would like to clear the way for it to grow back. It won't take them long."

The prince felt the ship change course, following the stream of marching machines. "Lovely. Um, do you suppose they could invade London when they're done?"

"Absolutely," said Miss Cooper with a dangerous smile. "And there are plenty more where those came from."

Chapter Fifty-three

PEOPLE ARRIVED IN ONES AND TWOS IN THE CRISP EARLY hours of the morning. Despite the bombing, there were still buildings standing behind the toy factory, and there was still an alleyway where folk could congregate out of sight of the main road. Not that there were many passersby that morning to see the growing crowd. The air along Threadneedle Street stank of ash and aether, like cigar butts drowned in mint liqueur.

Tobias leaned against the back wall of the factory, falling into conversation with the arrivals as Bucky handed out tin mugs of tea. It was bitter and dark—not at all the drawing room beverage Lady Bancroft would have served—but it went perfectly with the heavy bread one of the local bakers brought around in enormous wicker baskets.

The baker had come like the rest, gathering in the alley behind the factory in response to Lord Bancroft's summons. "If you don't mind my saying, it's past time to put an end to this, Mr. Roth," the big man said. His name was Moore, and though he wore no apron there was still flour clinging to his clothes. He seemed not to notice it. "First they tell me I have to buy coal instead of burning good wood as before and then the bread never tastes right. And then we go to central heat at twice the price, and all the lights have to be gas. And then the Gold King or the Green Queen or whoever puts their lights on my street wants a piece of my profits. Well, sir, there won't be any this month. The banks are all gone and no one in these parts"—he waved a huge hand at the burned-out streets—"is going to be buying cinnamon pastries for some days to come."

Tobias swallowed his mouthful of bread, wishing there were a few of those pastries looking for a good home. Lately, his appetite came and went, sometimes fading under a wash of nausea. Last night, he had felt particularly bad. But the thick, fragrant bread was going down easily. Moore had talent with salt and flour that said his business was well worth fighting for—but he also had mentioned a family, and that made Tobias balk. "If we march on the Gold King, we'll be facing the Yellowbacks. Some of us won't make it through."

The baker smiled in a way that made Tobias's muscles twitch. "I was a sergeant in the Forty-fifth, sir. I'm good with a rifle. And there's no shortage of guns and ammunition laid by. We've been waiting for this day, Mr. Roth. We just never knew we'd be opening the door for a prince."

"We?"

"London, Mr. Roth. The bakers and shopkeepers and guttersnipes, West and East both—we're the city."

"Did you meet him, sir?" The speaker was a small man who looked like he might have been one of the Green Queen's clerks, or perhaps a ferret bespelled into human form. "Have you met Prince Edmond?"

Tobias met the small man's eyes. "I have. He was, um . . ." he hesitated, searching for the right adjective. Engaging? A bit new to the whole prince business? A tiny bit frightening behind that grin? But Tobias knew these people needed something to hang on to while they offered up their lives in hope of something better. "He was very fair to me. He is a man of honor."

The little man nodded, as if that was exactly what he'd wanted to hear. "Fair is what we want. All a man wants in life is a chance to show what he's worth."

Tobias wondered what the fellow's story was, but there

wasn't time and a dozen more had shown up in the alley behind the warehouse while they were speaking. His gut was reconsidering breakfast. Part of it was the alley, which was beginning to stink as the sun warmed it. The rest was Scarlet's poison. Tobias reached into his pocket, taking out the small tin of medication Dr. Watson had given him. He pressed the catch and the lid popped open. There were a dozen pills left—a better indication than anything else of how long the doctor had estimated that they would continue to help him. One-handed, he fumbled out two of the little white spheres and put the rest away.

The noise level was growing as yet more voices were added to the excited babble. Not all of them looked to be from the immediate neighborhood. This area was relatively prosperous, and some of the newcomers looked like the ragged denizens of London's rookeries. The air was growing charged with expectation and Tobias began to be nervous. Windows were opening in the clutch of buildings that still stood behind the factory. Heads were poking out to see what was going on.

"What made you change your mind and fight for our side, Mr. Roth?" asked Moore.

There were a lot of answers, including the fact that he had never really been on Keating's side. Not really. But again he picked something they would easily understand. "The Gold King took my infant son. He's holding Jeremy so that I won't cross him."

The two men recoiled in shock. "That's pure evil," the baker said, the words a curse.

"It won't work," Tobias answered with more calm than he felt.

It wasn't going to work because he knew Keating wouldn't kill an heir with a title until he absolutely had to. Jeremy was everything the Gold King wanted—a living embodiment of old tradition and new wealth who would be groomed to steer Keating's businesses into a glorious future. No, Keating wouldn't kill his grandson as long as Tobias was dancing in his crosshairs, playing the enraged but ineffectual buffoon. His job was to make himself a highly visible target that would hold Keating's attention while others used the knowledge he had about the Gold King's armaments. In other words, Tobias was the sacrificial decoy.

And he would probably die—but he'd gladly lay down his life for Jeremy because that was what fathers did. It would be a gift compared to a shivering, puking end courtesy of the Scarlet King's poison. But he was worried about these men. "I might be leading you straight into the Gold King's armies. I'm not a general."

"We don't need a general," Moore said. "We know our business and we've planned this for a long time. What we want is someone to lead the way."

Church bells began to toll the hour, a voice answered far away, and then again to the west. It was the city calling to itself, an individual and collective spirit. Tobias squinted up at the sun, the warmth on his face like a blessing. "It's time to get started," he said, finally ready to say the words. They tasted of defiance, but they left the lemony sweetness of freedom behind.

And then a handful of men and women pushed open the enormous doors at the back of the factory. This was where the lumber and other supplies were delivered, but what came out was extraordinary. And big. The head of it scraped the top of the doorway, and a train could have driven through those doors. Tobias stared open-mouthed, flashing back to that defining moment when the Society for the Proliferation of Impertinent Events had built the mechanical squid that destroyed the opera house. But that was a primitive ancestor to what he saw now. *Bloody hell!*

Bucky was the son of the North's most prominent gun maker, but he was also a toy maker. And it showed. This was a lethal engine of destruction disguised as an amusement.

The gigantic caterpillar had a dozen jointed sections that swayed side to side as it steamed forward, an engine churning in each segment. It was brightly painted in yellows and greens, a happy smile on its round face. A pair of legs emerged from each joint, each foot tipped with a bright red boot.

Bucky rode at the controls behind the head. He leaned

down, smiling widely for the first time in as long as Tobias could remember. "Do you like it?"

"Festive" was all Tobias could think of to say.

"I told the Yellowback inspectors that I was making it for the amusement park." Bucky waved to the ladder that ran up the side of the machine. "Come on up. There are plenty of seats."

Tobias complied, finding the first two sections were in fact fitted with seats covered in brown leather—eight in all. The back sections were piled with weaponry, food, and what looked like the making of barricades. Three men, including the baker, scrambled up and began tossing rifles to the crowd below. And that crowd was becoming a mob as more and more people arrived, many in the uniforms of a dozen different military units. The baker began shouting orders, and men fell into line.

Tobias took the seat beside Bucky. "Can I run this with one hand?" He could still use his right arm, but his hand was useless.

"Absolutely." Bucky pressed a bright red button on the toy's head, and the legs began to move. The motion began with the back legs and slowly rippled forward, each pair of legs lifting and setting down, pushing forward and then lifting again in waves. It reminded Tobias of the oars on a boat, rhythmic and graceful. The caterpillar sped across the ground, each red boot making a thump on the hard-packed earth. Bucky pushed a blue button to stop the machine, and then pointed to a long wooden lever mounted between the two seats. "That will steer it. The gun controls are on the other side."

Tobias recognized the array of switches and levers from Bucky's other projects. There would be plenty of projectiles when he needed them. "I'll need a gunner, then."

"Corporal Yelland will assist. He was trained as a sharp-shooter."

Tobias turned to see the ferret-faced clerk behind him. The man gave a short nod. "I'm as accurate with a bullet as I am with my sums."

"Excellent," Tobias said, his spirits lifting despite everything. He could do this. He had managed the rescue party that had brought Imogen back to the *Helios*. He commanded a small army of craftsmen every day. He was no soldier, but he knew how to point people in the right direction and look confident while doing it.

"The controls are far easier than the ones on the squid," Bucky said, rising from the seat. "You won't have any trouble with them."

They stood facing each other. They all had their roles to play, and Bucky's wasn't on the caterpillar. This was farewell.

Wordlessly, Bucky held out a hand. His left one. Tobias gripped it, grateful he hadn't had to fumble with his numb fingers. His friend's grip was firm and warm, familiar as an old coat. Time stopped as memories slammed into Tobias, so vivid they left him light-headed. They'd been friends so long—school, cricket, clubs, women, SPIE—and the chance that they'd see each other again was next to nothing.

"I'm glad you're with us," Bucky said evenly. "It's about bloody time."

"Look after Jeremy and Alice. Look after my sisters." There was a lot more he wanted to say, but his chest was beginning to ache, and he couldn't afford grief.

"You know I will." Bucky inhaled, the sound of it uneven. "Good luck, Roth. London has your back. And may you get what you need from this."

What I need? All Tobias had ever wanted was a workshop and the freedom to indulge his imagination. But nothing had ever been that simple. He squeezed Bucky's hand tight one last time, and then let it go. His friend left quickly, his motions those of a man holding too much inside.

Tobias swallowed hard, the world around him blurring with sadness. But he heard Corporal Yelland slide into the seat to his right, and the presence of a stranger forced him to gather his wits. He turned, and was shocked to see that the alley was full, and the alleys beyond that, and all the distant streets winding to the horizon. London had turned out in force.

His mouth went utterly dry. *Blood and thunder!* Not even

his father had been asked to deal with this kind of mob. But Tobias wasn't his father. *He* knew what it was to put in an honest day's work in the sweat and noise of a workshop. *He* wasn't there for ambition, but because he was so angry that the pit of his gut boiled like the steam engines beneath his feet. He was one of them.

"Friends," he said, raising his good hand into the air for silence, "we have work to do!"

The crowd roared like an ocean, and Tobias smiled. The rebellion wasn't just a handful of spies or noblemen passing notes in the back rooms of their clubs. It went down to the very grime in the gutters.

The steam barons had no clue what was coming.

CHAPTER FIFTY-FOUR

London, October 16, 1889
HILLIARD HOUSE

7:35 a.m. Wednesday

POPPY TRULY DIDN'T KNOW WHAT TO DO NEXT. THEY'D spent another day yesterday hunting for Jeremy. She'd put Alice to bed at Hilliard House after Lord Bancroft had administered a hefty glass of brandy and—after another bout of weeping—she'd fallen into a stupefied sleep. Poppy, on the other hand, had stared at the ceiling until murky waves of exhaustion had finally claimed her just as the first birdsong chimed in the pearl-gray sky.

She couldn't have slept more than a few hours before Alice was shaking her awake. "Poppy, wake up!"

"Alice?" Poppy groaned, more grumpy than she meant to be but really, she'd hardly napped. She pushed a tangle of hair out of her face, realizing she hadn't bothered to brush it out the night before. It felt like something had nested in it, and she really wished she had taken the time to clean her teeth.

Alice sat on the edge of the bed. She looked haunted, the bones of her face too prominent under pale skin. Even the glorious waves of her fiery hair were subdued in the cold morning light. "I think we're going about finding Jeremy the wrong way," she said in a steady voice nothing like last night's sobs.

Poppy blinked, pushing herself up on her elbows. Alice had her attention. Gone were the hysterics of the night before, and the Gold King's daughter had taken charge. "All right, then. What are we doing wrong?"

"If Father is using Jeremy as a means of keeping us in line, he has to be able to prove our baby is still alive." There was a slight hitch in Alice's voice that said she wasn't as calm as she was putting on. "That means keeping him close."

"I suppose that means a place he thinks will be safe from attack."

"Deep in Gold territory," Alice agreed. "Preferably someplace he owns."

Poppy struggled to sit up properly. "Isn't that where we've been looking?" And holy hat ribbons, did Jasper Keating own a lot of properties. She felt like she'd tramped through half of London in the last week.

"We've looked at all his factories and private residences. They're all places that he knows I know." Alice slumped forward, her elbows on her knees. "I've been stupid to even suggest such places."

"Don't be daft, you're doing wonderfully well," Poppy reassured her, stifling a yawn. "But where else is your father going to put Jeremy?"

Alice turned pasty pale. "Think about it. What would happen if, say, the Blue King trampled through London and found Keating's grandson?"

Poppy didn't like that scenario at all. "What do you mean?"

Alice pushed on. "He'd hide him in plain sight. Just look at Prince Edmond. The newspapers said he was adopted by Sir Charles Baskerville and nobody noticed that he was at all different. He went to school with the other boys, played on their rugby teams, and did whatever normal boys do."

"Maybe," Poppy said softly. "But remember Mr. Keating took the wet nurse, so she would have to be inconspicuous as well." Then she succumbed to another yawn.

"There are two possible places." Alice waved a finger, her eyes bright. "First, my father established a foundling hospital in Soho."

Poppy clapped her hands. "That's perfect: deep in Gold territory, and with plenty of nurses and babies."

"Let's start there, then!" Alice said urgently.

Despite herself, Poppy glanced at the window. She could hear the distant boom of something exploding. The skirmishing between Gold and Blue forces was getting worse, and word had it the rebels were just outside the city. There was no point in asking if it was safe to walk the streets because it clearly wasn't. And that was all the more reason Alice had to find her son. Fear twisted in Poppy's stomach, but she wasn't about to desert Alice now. She wasn't that kind of girl.

"I need tea," she said. "And *then* I'll follow you into the jaws of hell."

Alice grabbed her in a desperate hug. "You're the best."

"Remember this when I ask to borrow one of your Worth gowns."

THERE HADN'T BEEN any cabs for hire—the chance of being bombed had kept them all at home—but there had been a steam tram still running from Mayfair toward the intersection of Oxford and Regent streets. It had been a matter of minutes to get there from Hilliard House.

Soho wasn't the nicest part of town. Poppy had been through the area plenty of times, but never on foot. At least half of it looked starved for money, the houses cramped and ragged from lack of repair. There were lots of theaters, taverns, and coffeehouses, but most ranged from shabby to mildly dangerous. And there were any number of places with purple doors, and even Poppy knew that meant they were houses of dodgy repute. She'd never seen a brothel before, but after walking past the third one, the novelty wore off. There were plenty of other things to worry about, like getting shot by enemy soldiers or what her mother would say when she discovered Poppy was missing. *Best not to think about it.*

And best not to think about the men she saw here and there, watching as two well-dressed women scurried past.

Instead, she stayed glued to Alice's side as they hastened down Marlborough Street, not letting her out of sight. In her present mood, Alice was moving with a careless desperation that spelled trouble. A single glimpse of an infant was likely to send her bursting through brick walls to snatch it from some innocent nursemaid's hands.

But that was far from her only concern. Although there were no signs of damage here, there weren't as many people on the street as there should have been. It felt as if London was holding its breath, waiting for the next assault.

"There's Poland Street," Alice said, pointing to the sign at the corner of a soot-stained brick apartment block. "It should be right down there."

They were about to turn when Poppy caught her arm. "Wait!"

Alice let out a cry. Yellow flags hung from a dozen windows, fluttering in a halfhearted breeze. The signal was one Keating had borrowed from maritime conventions and instituted in his territories. *Quarantine.*

Alice began pelting down the street, her skirts flying out behind her. Poppy bolted after, running hard to catch up. "What are you doing? Have you lost your wits?"

"Maybe." Alice stopped abruptly in front of a shabby-looking door, and Poppy nearly crashed into her. She was about to make some scathing remark about running headlong into contagion when she read the sign above the door: Beatrice Keating Memorial Foundling Hospital.

"Who was Beatrice?" Poppy asked.

"My grandmother," Alice replied absently.

It was hard to imagine the Gold King having a mother, much less one he wanted to honor. But the matter quickly faded to unimportance when Poppy saw more yellow flags hanging from the windows above. The hospital was infected. *Oh, no.*

"What if it's a trick?" Alice said hoarsely. "What if he's made them say there is disease so that I won't go in and find my son?"

What kind of a father is he that she can even think that?

Poppy wondered, but she knew the answer. He was a steam baron. "You can't go in."

"I have to know."

"What if you do, and then you find Jeremy later, and then you make him sick because you're coming down with some fatal disease?"

Alice fell silent. *Good.* Poppy put a hand to her head, wishing her brain would work faster. "Let me think."

"Let's at least knock on the door," Alice suggested. "Surely we can ask some questions."

"All right." Poppy crouched, scrabbled in the dirt for some pebbles, and stood, trying to ignore the dirt clinging to her gloves. She tossed a pebble at the window, then another. Both smacked with a satisfying clack against the glass. It didn't take long before the sash next to Poppy's target slid up.

The woman who leaned out was terrifying—square, stern, and looking as if she was in severe want of ears to wash. "What is the meaning of this?"

Poppy heard the distant spatter of what might have been gunshot. Her entire body went cold and she searched frantically in the direction of the noise—but she couldn't see that far with all the buildings in the way. A wail of terror sounded deep inside her, but she bottled it up as tightly as she could manage.

"Well?" the woman demanded.

Poppy glanced at Alice, but the young woman looked about to cry. It was up to her. "Have you received any babies in the past eight days? A boy about seven months old."

The gunshot sound repeated, and she began shifting from foot to foot, anxious to be gone. The shots had been closer this time. And somewhere inside the building a baby started to cry—a weak, frail squalling like the mew of a kitten. Poppy took Alice's arm, and felt her tremble.

"There is cholera here," said the woman severely. "No one enters or leaves, not for two weeks. Now leave before you come down with it yourself."

The window slammed shut, leaving Poppy and Alice standing in the dusty street. A sound came out of Poppy's mouth, somewhere between a curse and a cry of frustration. It matched the feeling bubbling along her nerves. They'd achieved exactly nothing.

Not sure what else to do, Poppy grasped Alice's hand and led her away, taking the shortest road she could find back to Regent Street. They moved quickly, all too aware of the growing sounds of fighting to the east.

"I think she's telling the truth," Poppy said.

"I do, too," Alice said in a wavering voice. "Look over there."

Between the buildings, Poppy could see men digging in a yard. There were three of them, and it was going to be a very large hole. "What are they doing?"

Alice swallowed hard, and the next words were stronger. "It's going to be a lime pit. They shouldn't be digging it this close to the houses. Papa's going to be furious."

A lime pit was for burying masses of bodies, which meant the cholera was real. Her stomach skittered with chill terror and she ran a few steps, as if a yard or two would make any kind of difference.

Alice caught up, her eyes wide. "What now?"

"Does your father own any other foundling hospitals?"

"No. Charity work isn't a large part of his business."

That Poppy could believe. The streets around them were growing steadily worse, without even the pretense of respectability. "So where else can he hide a baby?" Poppy saw the broader, brighter expanse of Regent Street ahead and nearly broke into a run. "You said there were two possible places."

"There are a thousand places," Alice said, despair creeping into her voice. "I can't keep dragging you across London like this. Not without a better chance of success and a lot less danger."

"Don't worry about me," Poppy said, almost automatically.

"But I have to."

"I can worry about myself well enough."

"Poppy, think. We're only theorizing about what Father has done. We have no facts." Alice looked guilty and miserable. No doubt her heart was dragging her forward, but her common sense was reining her back. "You need to go home. I'll keep looking."

Gunfire cracked again. A flock of enormous black birds flew overhead, croaking like doom. Both women looked up, momentarily startled, but the birds passed by.

"But your theories are good," Poppy protested, refusing to give up. There was no way she would let Alice go on without her. "We're looking for your father's property, or at least within his territory. He needs to hide a baby and a nurse someplace they won't be noticed. Where is the other place you came up with? Does he have a home for unwed mothers?"

"No, but he has a rooming house in Covent Garden where a lot of actresses live." Alice's cheeks flushed and she looked away. "He thinks I don't know about it, but he used to keep a mistress there."

"Then we try that," said Poppy. "It can't hurt, and it has to be nicer than this place."

"Are you sure about that?" Alice said sharply. "Be sensible. Covent Garden is due east." But Alice's words didn't match the look in her eyes. She was pleading to go.

East was right into the gunfire. Poppy grimaced, wishing she could give in to the terrified wailing insider her—but she just couldn't. "But what if we're right, and Jeremy is there?"

CHAPTER FIFTY-FIVE

THE CATERPILLAR CRAWLED DOWN THREADNEEDLE STREET, surrounded by a human sea. The air smelled of river and ash and the press of lost humanity, as if the Styx had emptied onto the London streets and this was the new land of the dead. And the throng only grew, gathering more and more bodies as they progressed. Volunteers arrived out of alleyways and taverns, or were simply swept up like flotsam from the curbs. They marched or ambled; some brought weapons and others beer. Moore and the other professionals kept order, but there was hardly any need. All were unified by a cheer distilled from reckless despair.

From atop the caterpillar, Tobias could see the devastation left from the bombs and the subsequent conflagration. It might have been a week ago, but the scars were still fresh. Blackened smears of ash were all that remained of shops and homes. Where the Bank of Empire had once stood, a choking black smoke rose from a crater the size of a battleship. All around, shards of stone thrust into the air, snaggletoothed remains of the Green Queen's stately countinghouses.

"I worked there," Corporal Yelland said, pointing to a particular heap of rubble. He had to raise his voice over the babble of the crowd, so it came out half as a yell. "Fifteen years perched on a stool, tallying debits and credits."

He was far from the only one whose livelihood had vanished overnight. Tobias wondered where all those workers would go—and how they would survive. "Were you there when it started?"

"I'd gone home for a few minutes to see to my old Da," Yelland replied. "Saved my life. He's with my sister now, in her house further west." He paused. "My home's a pile of kindling today."

"Your house and work gone in one night?" Tobias's chest tightened.

"I was one of the lucky ones. I didn't lose anyone, not even my cat." Yelland gave a grim smile. "That means I can keep a level head getting the job done, eh, guv'nor?" And he patted the butt of the rifle propped next to him. It wasn't one of the many Moore had handed out, but his own, fitted with a clockwork loader and an aetherscope for measuring the direction and velocity of the wind.

"If only everyone's head was as level as yours," Tobias replied. "But then, we wouldn't be here if that were true."

Tobias stood behind the lever that turned the caterpillar left or right, gripping it with his left hand. The machine was easy enough to steer, the sectioned tail following smoothly after. Still, it required concentration. Too many people were crowded close to make a sudden move. Perhaps that was why Yelland spotted the Blue King's army first.

"Look, guv'nor!"

He looked, and then blinked. The dome of St. Paul's Cathedral floated like a meringue over the skyline, but from either side of the precinct came a mob of Blue Boys, azure sashes tied over one shoulder like a sword belt. The sash was their only uniform, the rest of the Blue Boys' attire left to chance, the only requisite to personify trouble on two legs. But Tobias wasn't fooled—they might look disorganized, but the Blue King's forces had always been thorough killers. And their number had to be equal to the rebels gathered around the caterpillar. *Damnation!*

"How did they get here?" Tobias snapped, his stomach dropping to his knees. The Blue King's territory was east and south of there. By rights, the Blue Boys should be nipping at their heels, not threatening their flank.

He hadn't expected an answer, but Yelland gave one anyway as he poked buttons on the weapons panel. "The Blue King negotiated for Blackfriars Bridge, back when he took the Gray King's head. That gave him guaranteed passage over the river."

"Bugger." It was all Tobias had time to say before the rebels and Blue Boys surged toward one another like crashing streams, forcing the caterpillar to a halt. Where once the machine had been at the vanguard of the procession, now it was somewhere in the middle, mired as wave after wave of angry rebels stormed toward their foe. The sheer force of the stampede rocked the caterpillar from side to side, making Tobias grab for the back of his seat.

Suddenly the potential of war became reality—and then it became death. Rifles fired on both sides, the sound weirdly like applause. Men fell, blood, brains, and limbs spraying London's soil. Outrage skewered Tobias. "Give me a weapon!" he snarled.

Yelland was already there. At the push of a button, the smiling caterpillar's antennae rose and tilted forward, a scope popping up. Tobias bent to peer through it, the margin where the rebels met the Blue Boys near the steps of St. Paul's zooming into view.

A bullet whined past his ear, proving the enemies had shooters of their own. Tobias started, alarm turning every nerve ending into a pinprick of heat. He crouched, making himself smaller as Yelland raised his rifle and returned fire. Tobias heard a distant scream.

Releasing a shaky breath, Tobias returned his attention to his scope. Firing and hitting something wouldn't be a problem. But getting a clean shot at the enemy would be as the two forces began to swirl together. Tobias swore, his fingers shaking as he adjusted the aim of the antenna.

"Never mind, sir," Yelland said. "You'll know when to take your shot."

Tobias was about to protest when a rumble of engines caught his ear. He raised his head from the scope and spotted movement to the west of the church. There were half a dozen machines coming their way, the likes of which Tobias had never seen. They were the size of an old-fashioned coach and powered by steam, with wheels as high as Tobias was tall. In the front were three appendages like fat fingers made of sectioned steel. He stared for a moment, wondering what on earth they were for.

The machines fanned out, forcing their way into the crowd. The three steel fingers began striking the earth in steady succession, one-two-three, one-two-three. Vibrations shook the steel plates beneath Tobias's feet, sending up a faint rattle from the caterpillar's gears. At first he wondered if they were just meant to frighten the enemy, but as the pounders moved forward, he saw the destruction in their wake.

"Dear God," he breathed, momentarily frozen. A red trail followed them like the path of a scythe through wheat. Those steel fingers weren't meant simply to pound earth. They were meant to crush living flesh. Bile rose, souring Tobias's mouth and burning his throat.

Horror snapped him back to himself, firing a new sense of purpose. *Shoot the operators,* he decided, bending once again to the scope. But soon he saw there was no one driving, and a new fear twisted in his gut. Magnus had been the Blue King's maker. *These are driven by sorcery!*

Yelland fired, the careful aim of his bullet useless against the machine. The crowds were parting before them now, all too aware of what the pounding steel could do. It was a wise plan, except that it allowed the machines to move all the faster, and they were heading right for the heart of the rebel forces—including the caterpillar. Tobias fired the mounted antenna rifle. A blob of magnetized aether zipped through the air, bursting on the front panel of the nearest machine.

"Good shot, sir," Yelland said, barely pausing in his campaign to pick off Blue Boys as fast as the clockwork loader would permit. There hadn't been any more bullets hitting the caterpillar, and Tobias guessed this was the cause. No one wanted to become Yelland's target.

Tobias pulled the lever to reload the antenna and grunted, considering the results of his last effort. The blast had been hard enough to make the thing rock on its wheels, but the only result was that one of the pounding fingers hung limp. The other two continued to crush without pause. *This won't work.* He watched the things, his mind all but rotating the machines in midair, searching for flaws in the design. All machines had them—it was just a matter of seeing what was in front of him. He fired another shot, watching as the machine rocked again. Watching for the center of gravity, which was too high for stability. *Come at them at the right height and the right angle, and they'll topple over like a discarded toy.* Tobias felt himself smiling, and he was fairly sure it was an evil grin.

"Moore!" he bellowed, looking around below. The sergeant had been nearby, controlling the troops close to the caterpillar. "Moore!"

"Sir!" came a brisk voice from the crowd below. The baker's face appeared, sweaty and streaked with dirt and sweat.

Tobias took a deep breath, wondering how best to explain what he wanted. "Do you know how to tip a cow?"

LORD BANCROFT CURLED his lip in distaste, but said nothing as he watched Bucky Penner work. They were in the back of the toy factory, the thin sunlight from the high, narrow windows augmented by an oil lamp suspended over the workbench. He'd spent more time around tools in the last few days than he had in a dozen years, and it brought back black memories. Plus, Bancroft hated the fact that he'd been forced to cooperate with the man who'd done his best to steal Imogen—an escapade that ended in an illness that would probably kill her.

"How many are there left to do?" Bancroft asked in an unfriendly voice.

Penner fitted another piece into the device without looking up. "This is going to take me hours, my lord, and watching me isn't making it go any faster."

Bancroft narrowed his eyes at the comment. Penner was finishing the handheld switches that would seize control of the Gold King's massive machines. There were dozens of them, each attuned to a different unit, and all required the last few components to be inserted and the housing assembled. Tobias had originally created the design as a safeguard in case the weapons were seized by the enemy. Now—if Penner finished his work in time—the Gold King's machines could be turned against their commanders. "We don't have hours."

Wordlessly, the man picked up a plate and began screwing it onto the back of the device, his movements swift and dexterous. Bancroft had to admit that Penner had talent. He'd seen it in him when he'd still been a lad in short pants, getting into scrapes with Tobias. Bancroft encouraged the friendship, even though the Penners were nothing more than newly rich social upstarts. Bucky had seemed a steadying influence on his highly strung boy. A good lad all around—until he'd forgotten his place and started making eyes at Imogen.

But as much as he disapproved of Penner, it was difficult to stand and watch with nothing to do. "Wouldn't the Alldevice Number Two have better grip?"

Penner straightened, pushing the magnifying goggles he'd been wearing to the top of his head, where they looked like stumpy horns. "Respectfully, my lord, would you like to help? We might actually make it in time if two people worked on this."

The toymaker's tone was even, but the words still hit him like a slap. *Lords don't do, they supervise.* But it was far more than that. His will to create had been wrapped up with Anna's death and Magnus's black magic, and he'd mentally hidden the whole tangle from the rational part of his mind. *I made a mechanical doll and let Magnus trap my daughter's soul inside.* And when Tobias had tried to tell him Anna had escaped to terrorize the East End, he'd refused to listen. There was only so much a man should be expected to take. But long ago, he'd sworn never to touch a rack of tools again, and he'd held to that promise.

Bucky Penner was standing there, a questioning look on his face. "I can't do this alone, and Tobias is counting on us to get these to the prince."

Tobias. It would have been nice to believe that he could reclaim his love of building again. After all, it was something he could share with his son. But he would never hold a tool without thinking of the screams of his dead daughter. And soon the scent of a workshop—bitter with oil and sharp with the smell of hot metal—would remind him of his dead son, too.

Grief—more real and deep than he ever thought possible— tore him in its claws, ripping right through his breastbone. *I'm sorry, my boy.* And yet his eyes stayed dry. Lord Bancroft had banished tears right along with any joy he took in working with his hands—and filled those rents in his soul with ambition.

Wordlessly, he took the screwdriver from Penner's hand. It felt clumsy and unfamiliar, but he knew his skill would quickly revive. A furtive happiness stirred, but he stepped on it. This deviation from his personal rules was for the good of the Empire, not for him. "Move over," he snarled.

Penner had the gall to smile. "I hear you were quite a talent as a maker, my lord."

Bancroft braced his hands on the workbench, for the first time risking a mental glance backward. "I was. I used to live for the time I spent away from my daily work. No one bothered me when I had a tool in my hands."

He wasn't sure why he'd spoken—perhaps it was simply an acknowledgment to himself that he would be forced to work beside Penner, not just to finish the damned devices but to cross enemy lines and put them in the hands of the prince. And they had to do it within hours.

"I understand," Penner replied, clearing a second spot at the workbench. "I do my best thinking here."

Bancroft stepped up to the bench, picked out a few tools, and remembered those hours of quiet self-reflection he'd enjoyed so long ago. A queasy sense of unease assailed him. *The past is quicksand.*

And then he picked up one of the devices Tobias had begun, and his breath hitched at the sight of his son's elegant handiwork. *I'm so sorry, my boy.* However bad the past was, the future looked even more strewn with regrets.

He picked up a component and began screwing it on, because he didn't know what else to do. If he was lucky, he wouldn't start to think.

CHAPTER FIFTY-SIX

EVELINA STOOD ON THE BRIDGE, PEERING DOWN THROUGH Nick's spyglass at the land below. Nick was on the other side of the room, talking to a crewman she didn't know. She'd overheard that something was going on with the ash rooks, but she hadn't caught the specifics.

She was tired, her senses flattened from doing too much magic. The *Athena* had visited two other of the maker's armies before joining the column moving toward London from the south, and in both places Evelina had called on the devas to mobilize the machines. As before, they had taken care of the manufactories first, tearing them brick from brick with the relentless drive of nature itself, returning all to earth and stream.

The forces in the south would not require the same kind of help. Prince Edmond's march from Bath had begun as a relatively small force, but many had joined along the way. Above sailed those pirates—including Captain Roberts— who had not dispersed to watch the coasts for foreign invasion. Below marched makers and their creations, some with steam-driven wagons and others riding whatever invention they contributed to the cause. There were many men who had trained in secret for this uprising, and there were folk who had simply shown up, weapon in hand. This was truly the people's army.

The swelling numbers were heartening, but they slowed the column down. The group would have fragmented—some speeding ahead and leaving the rest behind—had not the makers brought several of those steam trains that Evelina had seen earlier with the self-laying tracks. Those now trundled in the middle of the pack, sandwiched between those trained to march.

The *Athena* hovered over the long tail of humanity, Evelina sweeping the circle of the spyglass along its length. The prince stood a few feet away, doing his own reconnaissance through the telescope mounted at the foremost point of the bridge. He had been down with the troops most of the morning, but had returned to the ship with its superior vantage point to plan their next move.

"What is that at the back of the column?" she asked. "It looks like a frisky cow."

"It's not," he replied. "I'm not sure what it is, but the men are frightened to death of it."

Evelina squinted, but Nick's spyglass had its limits. All she could see was a black shape loping twenty yards behind the last clump of men. "How long has it been there? Since Bath?"

"Since Dartmoor." The Schoolmaster—she still hadn't grown used to thinking of him as anything else—lifted his face from the eyepiece of the telescope. "It first appeared the morning after the destruction of the laboratories."

She thought of the monstrous animal she'd seen bound from the flames and reflexively drew back from the windows. "If that is the case, beware of it."

He shrugged. "So far it has done nothing but follow us."

Nick strode onto the bridge, with Striker behind him. They had news; it was written plainly across their tense features. Bacon scrambled from his basket by the door, but promptly sat at attention, eyes wide, when the atmosphere in the room turned grave. "It's not going to be as simple as we think to enter the city."

"We go up King's Road and through the barricades," the Schoolmaster said stubbornly. "There are too many of us to hold back. That will take us right to Westminster."

"This is going to be won in the air," Nick replied. His

face was flushed, the color high on his cheekbones. "The ash rooks bring word of the Gold King's dirigibles coming in from Hampstead. It makes sense; there is an airfield on the heath."

Evelina saw the panic flicker behind the Schoolmaster's eyes, but he quickly submerged it. "Who are the best tacticians?" he asked.

"Me and Roberts."

"Then coordinate with him and give me options. If there's no time for options, do what needs to be done."

"My pleasure." Nick reached for his spyglass and Evelina handed it over.

"What can I do?" she asked.

"Come with me," Nick said.

They left Striker on the bridge, discussing something with the Schoolmaster. Nick led her through the hatch that opened between the gondola and the main body of the ship. She could hear the engines churning, the minty smell of the aether cloying and thick. She'd been on the *Athena* long enough to know that meant they were filling their fuel reserves. Nick finally stopped when they got to the sheltered roost they'd built for the rooks, but he didn't open the door to it quite yet. He stood with his head bowed, dark brows drawn together.

"What is it?" Evelina asked, touching his sleeve. She could feel his muscles beneath it, tight as a drawn bow.

"I lost my ship and half my crew the last time we fought," he said quietly. "This ship and you on it is everything I want. All I could think of before was revenge for Manufactory Three, but suddenly that seems less important."

"You always were practical." Evelina ran her hand down his sleeve until she found his hand. The moment she touched his fingers, he gripped her hard, turning her until she faced him.

"You're damned right I am," he murmured, brushing a loose strand of hair from her face. "I don't deal in thrones and ancestors. I deal in weapons and wind, and if I'm very lucky I get to hold the woman I love when I fall into bed at night. And I don't ask for more."

Evelina's heart ached and she leaned in to him, needing to feel the reassurance of his body against hers. "Nick . . ."

He put a finger over her lips to silence her. His gaze roved over her face as if to fix her features in his mind. "There will be hell to pay if they try to take what's mine."

She pulled his finger from her lips. "No one can take me from you."

"But they've tried."

She couldn't argue with that.

"Men fight for different reasons. I believe in all the fine talk of secret heirs and the right of the common man to thrive, but in the end I fight for us, Evelina."

He kissed her then, his mouth hot and possessive. His hands slid down her back, his touch both gentle and hard as he traced the curves of waist and hip. Evelina reveled in his strength, rocking her hips forward and raking her fingers through his thick dark hair. She felt the surge of power between them, but they held it back. This stolen scrap of time was just for them.

They broke the kiss but stayed just like that, nose to nose, warm breath mixing between them. She tingled from head to foot, as if she might ignite from sheer, giddy desire.

"When we get through this," he said softly, "you and I are going to go someplace quiet, where there is nothing but sun and sand and warm night breezes. We are going to sleep in each other's arms until we're thoroughly bored with doing nothing."

That sounded like heaven, but right then it also sounded as impossible as a flight to the stars. Evelina didn't say any of that, but kissed him again instead, letting her lips linger against his. He was about to gather up his courage, ignore what happened to the *Red Jack,* and fight for their future. This was a battle, and there was no telling if they would ever touch again.

"I love you," she said. "What do you need me to do?"

And suddenly the moment was over. "I need you to help with the rooks."

* * *

AFTER A FAR less pleasant, but very immediate, conversation, Nick left Evelina and ran back to the bridge. He could feel Athena turning north, preparing to face London and the threat ahead. It was time to shut down all the parts of himself extraneous to battle, to summon his magic, and to think only of victory.

But as he raced to make up the time he'd spent on that last kiss, it was impossible to shut down his joy. *She said she loved me.* The first time she'd ever said it was wonderful, but this was better. It had sounded so natural, so easy, so part of who they were. After so many years, he truly knew he'd won his heart's desire. What more could a man possibly want?

With a whoop, he leapt into the air, spinning with his old acrobatic flair, and fairly bounced through the hatch to the gondola. Digby was in the corridor between the cabins, and gave him a curious look. Nick forced himself to slow to a brisk walk.

You had best keep your mind on the task at hand, Athena chided, but he could feel her pleasure, too. *Beneath all those knives, you are a romantic fool.*

"Only about some things."

Indeed, you do well to let her know you love her, especially when the girl is filled with doubt about so much. You are overdue for a longer conversation about your future.

His mood darkened. He'd never been as good with words as with more immediate means of communication—such as a bullet, or his lips. "We've always done better grabbing the moment."

I'm sure that's not all you wish to grab.

"What would you know? You're not even flesh and blood."

I'm not that ethereal. You simply know too little of our kind.

That caused a hitch in Nick's step, and he was about to start in with some probing questions when he felt something shift in Athena's mind. If she had been human, it would have been a gasp. Heart leaping, he broke into a run, pushing his way through to the bridge.

The very edge of the horizon was dotted with ships, but

even as he watched, they were growing bigger. Memories of the *Red Jack* thrust up, spearing him with white-hot panic. Suddenly, Nick couldn't move. His face went numb, as if he'd drunk far too much. *I can't do this again.*

But the spell was broken as Striker turned from where he was watching at the window. "Roberts is there." He stabbed a finger toward the east. "Lucas, Pinkwell, Laforge." He poked the air three more times. "Five of us, and a million of them."

With another inward curse, Nick counted. There weren't a million enemy ships, but there were more than a dozen. He refused to despair. Any pirate ship was worth at least two. Plus they had the ash rooks, clustered close to the *Athena* in a thick cloud. He felt the Schoolmaster hovering, waiting for a verdict. "Three to one," Nick said, forcing himself to sound careless. "Not good, but we've come through worse."

"Roberts's ship is signaling," Striker said. "I'm no good at reading it."

Striker had never learned to read at all, which made piecing together the letters of the message a meaningless task. Nick crossed the rest of the way to the tall glass panels and leaned to get a better view of the *Dawn Star.*

It was an old-style ship, the buxom figure of Aurora riding proudly at the prow. A young lad raised his signal flags and began his message once more. Nick nodded to himself. Reading the signals was one of the first skills he'd picked up when he'd taken to the air. "He keeps repeating *Morrigan Bay* over and over."

"Morrigan Bay is in the Caribbean," the Schoolmaster offered. He was clearly curious but trying to stay out of the way. Nick approved.

"Ah," Striker said. "Then I know what Roberts wants."

So did Nick. The raid on Morrigan Bay was one of those tavern favorites that pirates loved to tell when the rum ran freely and the candles guttered. "Then you'd best get to the engines."

"Aye, Captain," Striker said with a feral grin as he swept from the deck, his coat furling behind him.

"What's going on?" asked the Schoolmaster. "What does Morrigan Bay mean?"

"It's a tactic. You can only do it when the clouds are right and you have the proper ship. One that can fly like a feather." Nick turned to the bosun. "Poole, signal acknowledgment to the *Dawn Star*. Digby," he said, glancing at the tall, red-haired airman, "take us up."

"Aye, sir."

Digby saluted, but Athena was already lifting the ship high into the clouds. Through the window, Nick could see the ash rooks fall away like drifting petals, not able to follow the sudden vertical lift. The motion of the ship beneath their feet made the Schoolmaster grab for the wall. Suddenly, the windows were blocked with white mist, and then just as quickly the bridge flooded with brilliant sun. Below, a cushion of cloud swirled like a bowl of whipped cream.

"How can you see the enemy?" the Schoolmaster asked, both hands against the glass as he peered down.

"We will, when it's time." Anxiety chewed Nick like a rat caught in his gut. He paced the bridge, passing his chair three times but never sitting down. In fact, the captain's job seemed to involve very little relaxation. He returned to the window, looked out, and tried to estimate where they were. He was lost until he saw a break in the clouds and caught a glimpse of the ships ahead, bright red balloons like cherries ripe for picking.

The *Athena*'s engines slowed. *What now?*

Nick was already in motion, glad of something to do. A table sat to one side of the bridge, and on it sat a large polished basin half filled with water, a green glass bottle next to it, sealed with a cork. Nick pulled the cork and poured out a generous measure of rum, carefully floating it on the water. Then with a word, he set it alight. Flames rose, blue and wild, but he gentled them, letting the devas of the high winds soak into the fire. It would burn as long as he needed it. *Show me,* he commanded, flexing his will.

The fire shimmered, and all the ships came into view, tiny miniatures in three dimensions suspended over the silver basin. At the very top, a tiny replica of the *Athena* bobbled in the waves of heat. *I'm getting good at this,* Nick thought.

"Blood and thunder," the Schoolmaster said, circling around the table to see the display on all sides. "How does that work?"

"With a great deal of concentration," Nick said.

"More magic."

"Yes."

"I'm not complaining."

In the moments since he'd brought them into view, the pirate ships had spread out. Laforge's ship, the *Belle,* was light and quick. She was running out a long steel rod that Captain Laforge called the *aiguille,* or needle, designed for midair skirmishes. The other two were opening their cannon bays and holding position.

Then he heard the prince and Digby curse under their breath and he was forced to agree. The enemy, which had been flying a wedge, was breaking apart. If they kept coming, the pirate ships would be swarmed in a matter of minutes.

"Why don't they move?" the Schoolmaster demanded, looking as if he wanted to poke the tiny ships with his finger to get them going.

"Scarlet's ships don't even know we're here, even though we're sitting above their heads," Nick replied.

"And the other pirates?"

"They're waiting for us," Nick replied.

"To do what?"

"This."

Almost silently, Athena released the first shower of explosives. The miniature ship in the fire did the same, and after a long, agonizing count, three red dirigibles directly below them burst into flame. It would have been better if there had been more, but three was still good.

They saw the explosion in the fire a moment before the roar of the bombs shook the ship, making the fiery water in the bowl lap the sides. "Almost two to one now," the Schoolmaster said. "That was a brilliant move!"

"We grab the chances when they come along." It was almost the same thing Nick had said about Evelina, but it was just as true. He knew they'd gone about as far as any plan would go before it came apart at the seams.

He was right.

CHAPTER FIFTY-SEVEN

I LOVE HIM.

Evelina had gone over the fact a dozen times before she opened the hatch that led to the rooks' perch, but she didn't deny herself the pleasure of one more repetition. He'd known just when to kiss her. Whatever came next, he'd given her the courage to face it, because he'd held her in his arms.

Even better, he'd given her a problem to solve. A black mass of feathers lay on the deck of the roost, as if the rook had crawled into the corner to die. It was panting, beak open, wings sprawled to the sides. Pity pulled a noise from deep inside her. She couldn't speak to the creatures the way Nick could, so she crooned gently as she stroked the bird's feathers, trying to assess its injuries.

The rook wore a helmet and breastplate, and that might have been what had kept it from being killed outright. Nevertheless, the breastplate was still bloody, as if punched through with steel claws. But what on earth was big enough to fight a rook? They weren't small birds, more the size of a small goose than a crow. But that was precisely the task Nick had set her: to find out what new enemy was silently stalking the ship and attacking their allies. The rooks had often made a difference between victory and defeat, and the loss of any one of their flock was a blow to the crew.

She gathered the bird into her lap, letting it absorb her warmth as she released a thread of healing magic. What came back to her was a flood of images, but little she could interpret. The birds saw differently, and her brain couldn't sort through the information the way Nick's could. But she did learn that this was Saria, Gwilliam's mate.

"I'll have you back to him as soon as I can," she murmured, and Saria opened one shrewd black eye.

Healing magic had been one of the first lessons Magnus had taught Evelina and it came to her easily. When Saria was strong enough, Evelina turned the bird over and removed her armor. The rooks hunted their own meat, but Nick kept water in their roost. Using her handkerchief, Evelina dribbled some into Saria's beak. The bird drank it down greedily and soon hunched in her lap, allowing Evelina to wash her wounds.

As she worked, a number of the smaller, younger birds crowded into the roost. These were the ones with no armor, too inexperienced to fight, and Evelina guessed the battle must be near. She crouched in the corner of the roost, bracing herself and cradling Saria, so when the *Athena* suddenly rocketed into the sky, her ears popped but both of them were entirely safe.

The battle has started. If there was an enemy, they would show themselves now. Wanting both hands free, she wrapped Saria in her shawl and tucked her in a safe corner. Then Evelina crawled to the opening the rooks used to fly free, keeping low to avoid the pull of the wind. She heard the rattle of the bay doors open and the bullet-shaped bombs drop like scat. She scuttled away from the opening, gripping the heavy poles the rooks used to roost. Light flared from beneath, and a cascade of guttural roars shook the ship. The rooks croaked, flapping and rustling. Heavy wings smacked her arms and she ducked her head, waiting until the birds calmed. The stink of rook and aether was joined by a choking stench of smoke.

Slowly, she raised her head, only to be met with a row of beaked faces. "I think that's done."

One of the youngsters squawked. It sounded like good sense, so she nodded, allowing her shoulders to come down from around her ears. But no sooner had she relaxed than the *Athena* went into a dive. The clouds rushed up toward them, filling the tiny roost with an icy, damp mist. The ship angled slightly, and her feet began to slide. She heard the cannons fire on the far side of the ship, the sound weirdly muffled where she clung.

By the Dark Mother! she thought desperately, but the ship leveled out and the clear skies were back. The first thing she saw was the *Belle* ramming the long swordfish needle on its prow into the red balloon of an enemy ship. It didn't just puncture, it sheared through the dirigible's balloon. The vessel collapsed, seeming to fold toward its damaged side as the prow tilted upward at a sickening angle. This wasn't a case where a good crew could still land a deflating ship. This was a wreck, the wounded craft already circling, ready to spiral and drop like a stone.

Sickened, Evelina looked away. The smoke in the air was burning her nose and throat, but she felt secure enough to loose her death grip on the perches and inch toward the opening to the sky. She dropped to her stomach, peering around the corner of the door into nothingness. Wind whipped the strands of her hair back, clawing her nose and eyes like a living hand.

Oh, God. The enemy ship was falling now, the balloon no more than a lopsided blob of red. She thought she might hear screams from the enemy vessel—or maybe that was just the wind. But she knew it would haunt her nightmares.

As Evelina looked down, she saw the *Dawn Star* and four more of the red dirigibles. More rooks flew beneath them, harrying some airmen who had crawled onto one of the red ships to repair a serious gash. Beneath them was London.

The falling ship crashed. She closed her eyes, but she'd already seen too much to forget the spray of splinters flying into the air. When she opened them, the *Belle* was already searching out its next victim.

Athena banked the ship, but gently this time, and Evelina shifted her weight to compensate. They were circling around the battle zone, and she saw the *Dawn Star* fire on another red ship. The volley was answered with a sound like the pop of a paper sack. Before she could determine whether the blow landed, her sight was blanked by a rush of black wings.

A rook dived over her head, clearly ducking to safety. What came after it blinded her in a flash of sunlight on metal.

She reared back, raising her arms to ward off the thing. It was a shining metal bird, flame licking from its beak. Blood stained its talons. It hovered outside the doorway for three wing beats, and the rooks sent up a frantic ruckus of rage and dismay. Then the brass creature fell away, swooping down on a new victim.

With an outraged scramble, Evelina took up her position again, stomach pressed to the deck and her head all but hanging over the edge as she scanned the skies. Down here the sun was filtered through the clouds, but it was still bright enough to flash on several pairs of metal wings. They seemed to circle around one of the ships that had belonged to the Scarlet King. *A new weapon, designed especially to counter the rooks.*

Dark magic unfurled inside Evelina, waiting as if in question. There was a flurry of black feathers as the metal raptor tore a rook asunder. The other birds screamed, flapping around the attacker, but there was nothing they could do against brass and steel. With a terrible shriek of its own, the metal bird shot out of the flock and toward the open sky, its wings opened wide as if in triumph. Then it breathed a tongue of flame, catching its pursuers as they reeled around it. Evelina unleashed her anger, throwing up a barrier right in the thing's path. The bird shattered, bright shards fountaining skyward like a roman candle.

"Got you!" Evelina slammed the deck with her palm as the rooks croaked their jubilation. The brass bird hadn't been a living thing, but it still felt like victory. Someone on the enemy ships had to be sending and controlling the killing machines, and she'd just destroyed their weapon. Triumph sweet on her tongue, she started hunting around for others. The sky was chaos, filling with flame and ash to the point where it was impossible to see the earth below. And the noise was constant now, as if a dozen giants were hammering at the heavens. She caught a sudden flash of light in her peripheral vision. There was a resounding boom as an aether cannon discharged nearby, and with cold horror she realized it was aimed at the belly of the *Athena*.

Inside her mind, Evelina heard a cry of terror from the ship's deva, who suddenly understood the threat. The vessel lurched, struggling to shrink away, and Evelina reacted without thinking. Pulling all of her power, she thrust against the spinning ball of blue-green fire, trying to contain it just as she had the explosion in the laboratory. She felt the shield form, shimmering and bright, and leaned in with all her strength to brace it.

It might have worked had it been an ordinary explosive, but magnetized aether was concentrated energy. Her magic slammed against it with all the effectiveness of a damp towel trying to stop a bullet. Evelina screamed with the shock of impact and the dizzying lurch as her barricade was swept aside.

But Magnus's dark power had its own cunning, and it had fused to her need to protect. It couldn't block a ball of pure energy, but it could absorb it. Time stopped as Evelina felt the rush of sparking blue fire like tendrils snaking through her veins, a million pinpricks firing within her in places that she couldn't even name. It was as if every fiber, every nerve was suddenly glutted with energy and still swelling. She scrambled to the back of the roost, some primal impulse willing her away from the assault. She grabbed the rail the rooks perched on, muscles needing to strain against *something* in response to the sensation. Sight and sound deserted her. All that was left was painful blue fire, boring into her as if it meant to wear her skin.

And then her magic ran out of time. The blast hit the belly of the steamspinner's rigid balloon. She had absorbed the deadly magnetic power, but the concussive force of the blast was still effective. Some part of Evelina was aware of the jolt and clung on to the rail. There was a crack and a tearing that she felt more than heard. All around her the rooks exploded into frantic flapping as the ship shuddered and lurched. Evelina struggled to breathe, as if some of the energy that her magic had absorbed was detonating, too.

She snapped awake at the sound of a rook croaking in her

ear. The ship was listing and she was sliding toward the sky, her limbs like soggy bread. Waving the bird aside, Evelina scrambled to her knees, grabbing for a handhold. She could only have been unconscious for a moment, but the loss made her frantic. The fact that the constant din of battle had stopped clawed into her mind. Scrambling until she could look out, she clung to the sides of the opening to the empty air and peered below.

What she saw stunned her. She gave an odd little hiccup of dismay as sheer terror stiffened her limbs. There were only four of the red ships left, but she saw none of the other pirates. And all four of the Scarlet King's ships were right there, a ways off but in a narrow arc, clearly focused on the wounded *Athena*. Seconds ticked by like an ominous drumroll as Evelina groped for her magic and couldn't find it. It had swooned right along with her, gorged on magnetized aether.

Ash fell, coating her hands and tangling in her dark hair. Tears started down Evelina's cheeks, the salt stinging a scrape she hadn't noticed. The only thing she could think of was that she wished she were near Nick, but she was too horror-stricken to move. It was as if her engines had died right along with the ship's.

And then the enemy vessel farthest to her left fired a hot harpoon right at the *Athena*'s side. It rose, flame furling around it like some exotic bird. Then each ship followed, launching its long iron weapon in sequence until the sky was bright with a flaming arch of death. They were far enough away that it would take the harpoons an endless, painful minute to find their mark. Enough time for a nimble ship to escape, but the *Athena* was all but dead in the sky. Swearing, Evelina strained, flailing for some scrap of power to throw up a shield—but there was nothing. They were going to die—Nick, Striker, the prince—and the steam barons would win.

The guns of the *Athena* boomed, and she felt the recoil ripple through the drifting ship. The blast caught the foremost harpoon, knocking it from the sky, but the other three kept coming. Evelina closed her eyes, helplessly willing the flames away.

And yet as she forced herself to open them again, the *Dawn Star* appeared, dropping out of the sky with a falcon's grace. Evelina gasped, her throat aching with a rush of gratitude. Captain Roberts must have been hiding somewhere in the clouds, waiting for the right moment to ambush the remaining ships. He couldn't save them, but he could still turn the tide of the fight.

The *Dawn Star*'s guns boomed, and one of the red ships shuddered, the prow of the gondola seeming to inhale a moment and then burst apart in a shower of wood and metal. Evelina felt the pulse of the lives aboard as they flared out, a faint warmth fluttering against her power.

As if kissed out of sleep by a lover, her dark magic awakened to taste the deaths. Revulsion rippled through Evelina, but there wasn't time to think. As Roberts wheeled to fire again, she targeted the harpoons, spinning them around. The long iron shafts seemed to wobble in confusion, one of them dropping altogether, but the other two sped back toward the red ships. From somewhere inside the *Athena,* Evelina heard a cheer, and she couldn't help a grin.

The three remaining red dirigibles scattered. The *Dawn Star*'s next shot clipped the long tail of one, sending it into a spin with the sheer force of the blow. With that much damage, the ship might make a decent landing, but it wouldn't be maneuverable enough to fight. With a roar, the *Athena* fired again, and a second ship exploded, caught squarely in the center. They were down to one opponent.

The last of the Scarlet King's dirigibles fired, and the *Dawn Star* was suddenly limned with brightness. Evelina watched, her breath caught in her throat, as the ship was suddenly snared in a web of arcing blue energy—the same as what she had absorbed from the blast that had hit the *Athena*. She could hear the crackle of it, like the snapping of giant sheets in the wind, or what she'd read about the aurora borealis in the far and frozen north. It resonated inside her, sending that needling energy through her once more.

A hydrogen ship would explode from that dancing blue

fire, but one that ran on distilled aether simply burned. Flames began to leak from the portholes of the *Dawn Star* like a dozen fiery wounds. Tiny specks leaped from the ship, and Evelina fully understood what had happened to Nick the year before.

Outrage coiled, a hissing, violent thing. For a moment, she couldn't see, but then she focused with needle-sharp intensity at the vessel that had fired the shot. The *Dawn Star,* the ship that had come to their rescue, was a comet of flames hurtling earthward—and now the attacker was turning its broadside to them.

All the magnetic fire Evelina had taken in coalesced into a single upsurge of rage, and she thrust it forward. It ripped from her as if her insides were yanked through her breastbone, skin and skeleton flying apart. She screamed with the pain, but with rage as well. She'd made plenty of shields, but never used magic like a spear. But the dark power knew exactly what to do.

The last of the Scarlet King's ships was there one moment and gone the next, a fine, powdery dust raining down from the empty sky.

CHAPTER FIFTY-EIGHT

THEY WERE ALREADY CALLING IT THE BATTLE OF ST. PAUL'S. Tobias was glad to let the men and women trooping after the caterpillar rejoice in their victory, but their march westward through London felt like a journey into a mire he wasn't sure they'd survive. Tipping those pounding machines had been costly—many had been crushed, and many more had fallen to the Blue Boys.

Plus, it had been a stroke of luck. They couldn't count on all the steam barons' weaponry being vulnerable to a schoolboy imagination any more than he could count on the coal supply for the caterpillar lasting all the way to wherever the Gold King was holding his son. They had been fighting their way west for hours, Moore and the other soldiers were holding the Blue Boys off their tail—but so far the rebels had only made it past the law courts of the Temple, right to the point where the Waterloo Bridge reached the north side of the Thames.

The crowd thickened and bulged, like water hitting a clogged drain. The roar of guns and voices was deafening, almost a touchable wave of pressure against his face. Tobias guided the caterpillar to a stop, unable to go further without stepping on someone. Yelland got to his feet, shaded his eyes, and swore.

"What?" Tobias demanded. Talking was more a matter of lip reading, but they bent close to each other to catch what sound they could. "Why can't we move?"

"It's the Gold King's army fighting the prince's men coming up from the south," said the sharpshooter. "And there's an air battle up there."

Tobias had seen the smoke in the sky, but hadn't had the leisure to wonder what had caused it. Now when he looked, he could see the balloons between the billows of cloud and smoke. From where he was, they looked no bigger than apple seeds, the colors lost to distance and the angle of the sun.

The army in front of them was a more immediate problem. "There are thousands."

"Mercenaries," Yelland spat. "And they're sweeping the population ahead of them. The Blue Boys in particular."

"Doesn't the crowd get in their way?"

"Of course it does, but then they hold all the empty streets. And they know the rebels won't fire on civilians."

Tobias understood. Until the prince's armies arrived with everything the rogue makers had devised, the rebels had fewer fancy weapons than the barons. The steam barons' war machines could fire over a sea of civilians, but the rebels risked shooting innocents. The rebel army's hands were tied.

"Listen," said Tobias, his voice cracking with the strain to be heard. "I made a lot of the Gold King's weapons. I can disable them, but I didn't have time to make the devices that can do it."

Yelland shot him a look. "And?"

"My friend was finishing them this morning. He's going to carry them to the prince's army." Tobias looked at the sea of humanity surrounding them. Even if Bucky could fight through the crowd of rebel supporters, he would have to cross enemy lines first. That was going to be more dangerous than they'd assumed. "It would be very useful if we could get a few of those devices for ourselves."

"Are you talking about Mr. Penner?"

"Yes."

"He needs an escort," Yelland said flatly.

"He thought he could slip by unnoticed if he went alone. And he's good with a gun."

"He needs an escort," Yelland repeated.

Tobias gave the man a long look. "The plan was that if he could make it down Threadneedle to Mansion House, he could use the underground tunnels of the District Railway.

The trains won't be running in all this"—Tobias waved a hand at the chaos around them—"but it's a lot faster even if he runs all the way."

Tobias would have gone that way himself, if he'd been a well man, but he didn't have the strength to run or the ability to shoot anymore. The poison had taken too much. He was far more useful as a decoy.

"Bloody dangerous if he gets trapped down there. The steam barons will post guards." Yelland looked at the position of the sun. "I'm guessing it's not too late. We should send men down to watch for him. There's an entrance at the Temple."

"Do it," Tobias said. He wasn't technically in charge of the soldiers, but the fact that he led the procession gave him authority.

Yelland reached down to grab someone's collar and issue orders while Tobias squinted at the mass of armed men ahead. The air stank of panic, blood, and the smoky, minty stench of aether weapons. His skin itched with sweat and he thought briefly how much he wanted something to drink, but the thought faded the moment he grasped what he was looking at.

The Gold King's army was ahead, the Blue King behind and to the north, where Covent Garden sounded like a war zone. The Thames was to their south. They were boxed in.

And Jeremy was somewhere ahead, on the other side of the Yellowbacks. He'd had no idea Keating's army was so vast. He'd made pieces of it, but never seen it all at once. With a sinking sensation, he recognized the fruits of his own genius trundling toward them. There were the wheeled domes of steel and brass, equipped with gunports on top, the knobs of the aether devices looking like shiny hats. He would have been proud if the bloody things weren't opening fire.

Men were grabbing objects from everywhere—chairs, crates, broken carriages, and dead bodies—and piling the mass across the road. The barricade offered some protection and would slow down anything with wheels. A handful of Moore's soldiers crouched behind the makeshift wall and braced their rifles in a ready position.

Someone waved a Union Jack. "Down with the Steam Council!"

Tobias took up the cry, raising his fist in the air, then ducked when a bullet whizzed by. Yelland returned the compliment, and the bullets stopped.

The domed devices were every bit as dangerous as Tobias had made them. They were manned from inside, combining the best of human intelligence with mechanical durability. Even more worrisome were the small clockwork explosives that could scurry about like mice. He'd been particularly pleased with the cleverness of the concept, but now he saw a swarm flowing toward the Blue Boys. It was war, and the Blue King was his enemy, but how many lives would be lost, Tobias wondered, because he'd had a clever idea one afternoon?

The only mercy was that the rebels weren't the primary target of either army; Blue and Gold were most intent on killing one another. Bombs struck, fountaining flesh and masonry into the air. The merciless noise intensified and Tobias's body tightened until every muscle ached. Primal instinct begged to flee, but he was trapped and all they could do was fight to the end.

He aimed one of the mounted aether guns that formed the caterpillar's antennae and searched for a target. A brass-plated dome came into sight. It seemed wrong to destroy one of his own creations, but he fired anyhow, aiming for the spot where he knew the aether distiller hid behind the metal plates. He was rewarded with a bright, hideous flash as the thing went in a glory of fire. Someone screamed, "Vive la révolution!" as if suddenly they were in Robespierre's France.

The moment Yelland understood the device's weakness, he began aiming at its cousins. Unfortunately, ordinary bullets couldn't penetrate the shell. Even worse, the devices began firing back in double time.

It took him a moment to realize that the rebels weren't the target. Tobias swung the gun around, using its sight to get a better view of the battlefield. He nearly staggered back when he was suddenly confronted with the hideous, sweat-slicked visage of King Coal himself. Tobias raised his head to see where the Blue King was and made an inarticulate moan of dismay.

So far they had only seen half the Blue army. The other half was rolling across the Waterloo Bridge, the weight making the old pilings shake. They were huge monsters of steel—every one a gigantic engine trapped in a spherical metal cage as tall as a house. Each cage rolled forward like a ball, the engine inside suspended upright as its latticework superstructure crawled ahead. Twin channels had been left free of the crisscrossing steel bars of the globe, accommodating huge magnetic aether cannons jutting from the core of the engine. Tobias counted. There had to be two dozen of the things surrounded by ranks of armed Blue Boys. At the front of the column, the foremost of the rolling spheres was occupied by the Blue King, who peered out from the thing's cockpit like a malevolent frog. Directly beside him marched Moriarty in steel and leather armor.

The sight rendered Tobias dizzy with disbelief—if he'd been trapped before, now he was all but pinned in place. And they were coming straight at his left flank.

What else could go wrong?

EVELINA WAS HUDDLED under Nick's arm, but the joy and relief of their reunion had been short-lived. Striker was hunched over the aether distillers, as close to tears as Evelina had ever seen the man. "All three of them are blasted to pieces, and we're down to fumes in the engines. Athena can hold the ship together for a bit, but we're going to sink without more aether."

"How long?" Nick asked in a leaden voice.

"Not long."

Evelina blinked unsteadily. She had just come inside from the roost, and the interior of the ship was murky, robbed of the green underwater glow of the distillers. But she could see well enough to grasp the damage to the *Athena*. Part of the rigid honeycomb inside the balloon had been torn, allowing about a third of the gas to escape. In addition, the tall glass distillers had cracked and would need to be replaced.

"Our best chance is to boil up some of this stuff." Striker kicked a sack at his feet.

"What is it?" Evelina asked.

"It's a powdered form of aether."

Evelina slipped from Nick's grasp and bent over the bag. She picked up a few grains that had escaped onto the floor, rolling them between her thumb and forefinger. She gaped, realizing that it was precisely the same stuff she'd used in her chemistry experiments at school. "I wouldn't suggest boiling it," she said in a small voice, realizing that she'd never actually completed the assignments without flames or explosion. "I could help you if you like."

"The instructions are on the bag," Striker grumbled, leaning against the walls to cradle his head. "I can't remember the formula right now."

He'd taken a bad blow when the ship had been hit. He was still on his feet, but Evelina suspected he'd been struck harder than he was letting on. Combined with the fact that he couldn't read, he wasn't the best candidate for mixing up a highly combustible stew.

"How much do we need?" Nick asked.

"A few barrels should do it," Striker said. "Enough to fill the pumps a few times over."

A few barrels? Professor Bickerton's face filled Evelina's mind, and she suddenly began to giggle. She put a hand over her mouth to silence it. Nick and Striker wouldn't understand.

I wanted the freedom to conduct experiments on my own. Who knew all I had to do was blow up an air fleet to get it?

"All right," she said more calmly, hoping she remembered everything she'd learned at Camelin. "The first thing we'll need is the exact proportion of water and alcohol."

"What kind of alcohol?" Nick asked. "A lot of the stores were destroyed in the blast."

Evelina began to dread where this was going. "What do you have?"

Striker grinned. "We've got the scrumpy. I'd say that was getting pretty close to pure."

CHAPTER FIFTY-NINE

"STOP!" POPPY COMMANDED, PULLING HARD ON ALICE'S arm.

The red-haired woman obeyed, quickly jerking around. "What is it?"

A shabby man hurrying in the opposite direction bumped against her, but Alice ignored him. The street was crowded with rushing people—most of them moving east while they forged west. Poppy dropped to one knee and began tying her bootlace, which had been flapping loose for the last hundred yards.

They had walked for ages because even the steam trams had stopped now, and Covent Garden was a lot farther than she had assumed. As Poppy knelt, somewhere in the back of her mind she could hear Lady Bancroft nagging her for soiling her skirts, but she was beyond caring. Poppy's shoulders screamed with knots of tension, and her feet ached and pinched in the silly, ladylike boots her mother insisted she wear. The next time she went on a rescue mission, she would utterly refuse to wear heels.

There had best not be a next time. The air hummed with expectation, and none of it good. The farther west they went, the more gunfire they could hear. Some of it popped like dry logs on the fire, but there were a few bangs that sounded big and close. Poppy and Alice had wavered between scurrying down hidden alleys and melting into whatever crowds they could find on the main streets. It was impossible to guess which was safer. If Poppy hadn't been so certain that Alice's logic was sound and that *surely* they could find and rescue Jeremy, she would have turned tail and bolted home.

"Hurry," Alice begged. .

"It'll be faster if I don't trip and break my nose," Poppy grumbled as she knelt on the hard cobbles, but she didn't blame Alice for complaining. Nerves were making her fingers clumsy, and she flinched as a pair of steam cycles rattled by, their metal wheels loud on the street. Somewhere a woman was sobbing, the sound making Poppy's stomach muscles jump. She was already feeling queasy from the stink of ash and explosives thick in the air.

A shadow blotted out the thin sunlight. The gray of the sky was growing thicker, and for a moment she assumed it was just more cloud, but then animal instinct made her look up. Her mouth fell open, a sound of surprise escaping her. It was a small, zephyr-class airship, but it was an intense blue that made it look like a gap in the moody clouds. Poppy's fingers finished the knot, powered only by the force of habit. The rest of her was mesmerized by the sight. "That's got to be one of King Coal's ships."

"What's it doing . . ." Alice trailed off, her voice fading before she could even make it a question. There was only one reason the Blue King would be flying a ship so low over Gold territory that it could almost touch the rooftops—it was there to do damage. Her face, already wan, grew paler.

"How did it get past the Yellowbacks?" Poppy rose and gripped Alice's arm again, needing her close.

How did another steam baron get this deep into the Gold King's territory? She'd always assumed Keating was much stronger than any of the others, but perhaps that wasn't true. *Jeremy is Keating's grandson. If the Blue Boys find him first, something horrible will happen.* Her scalp crawled with apprehension as she watched the airship move ahead until it hovered over the heart of the neighborhood.

A trapdoor in the belly of the blue ship's gondola opened. Black shapes dropped out of it, some large and long, some small and round. They curled and spun as they fell, reminding Poppy of nothing so much as thin slices of carrot, or those long beans Cook served with slivered almonds. Other bystanders saw it, too, and the noise level in the street went up another notch. She braced, expecting to hear a violent explosion, but no sound came, and the zephyr slowly rose back into the sky.

"What were those?" Alice wondered aloud, wavering as if not sure whether to run forward or back.

"I don't know, but if the Blue King's army is this close, I don't think we have much time."

Alice's mouth set. "Then let's go!"

They ran forward, hand in hand. The odd thing about being frightened for so long was that eventually the fear gelled, like custard left out too long. Once that happened, Poppy could step over it—and she had to. They'd come too far not to push on.

Alice pulled her to the left and they darted down one of the narrow, winding streets that made up much of Covent Garden. Poppy glimpsed the front of the Theatre Royal on Drury Lane where she had been to see a play not two weeks past, but now Yellowbacks were ranged in front of it, weapons drawn. At the sight of them, Alice veered down another street. They might have been her father's troops rather than the Blue Boys, but clearly Alice wasn't taking any chances.

No sooner had they turned the corner than there was a belching cough of sound several streets away. That was followed by a whooshing, ripping noise that made Poppy look up. A blaze of light speared through the air, and she realized it was flame clinging to the metal of a giant arrow. She'd seen these in the air battle over London—it was a hot harpoon. Her gaze skipped forward, skimming past the forest of chimneys to see the zephyr desperately banking to get out of its path. It was not quite directly overhead, but she had to crane her neck to see it. She skidded to a stop, transfixed. The street around her faded as she stared in appalled anticipation.

The ship couldn't fly fast enough. From where they stood, the impact of the harpoon was noiseless. What came next was not. Even she knew that zephyrs were not aether ships, but used cheaper hydrogen instead. That meant it was doomed.

The flame from the harpoon hit the gas in seconds. A wave of pressure thrust both women backward, knocking Alice from her feet. The explosion seemed to peel the scalp from Poppy's head, more feeling than sound. It vibrated in her bones with a sudden clap that made her heart jump. Light flashed white-hot, leaving a burning image on the back of her eyelids.

Reflex made Poppy shield her face—a lucky thing. A chunk of the old chimney above tumbled free, smashing apart as it bounced off the roof and fell. Shards of masonry flew up, stinging her arms. As Poppy brushed them away, she saw burning timbers tumbling from the air, which had turned a sooty black. She wondered how long it would be before those planks of flaming wood started a blaze. She wondered how many had died. Her stomach gave a dangerous lurch.

"Poppy!"

She looked down, realizing that she had been standing there gawping for who knew how long. Dazed, she noticed Alice was still on the ground, a cut bleeding into one eye. Fresh panic sent her scrambling to Alice's side. "Are you all right?"

Alice awkwardly found her feet and fished for her hand-kerchief. She pressed the cloth to her head. "A piece of brick hit me. It's nothing. We have to go."

Poppy grabbed her arm when she stumbled. "Not so fast."

Alice braced one hand against the wall, her eyes wide with shock. Ash was falling from the sky like filthy snow, leaving smuts on their clothes. "Which way did we come from?"

Poppy pointed back past the debris from the smashed chimney. "Are you sure you're well?"

"I won't be well until I have Jeremy again." Alice bit her lip, crushing the handkerchief in her fingers. Her voice was distant but bitter all the same. "The place we want is called the Beryl Lane Manor. It's right behind Bow Street. Once I walked by it every day, looking for my father's carriage. I was such a little fool that I wondered why he would go to such a place."

Poppy bit her lip, unsure what to say. But any words she might have found were buried beneath the roar of a cannon, and then the answering rattle of gunshots.

"Come on." Alice lurched toward the sound, catching Poppy in her forward momentum.

Every instinct told Poppy she'd been a fool to insist they come here. They should have gone home after Soho rather than waltzing into the battle zone, but a moment later she saw the sign for Beryl. *It's only a minute more.* And she knew there was no way Alice was going to leave without trying to find her son.

Beryl Lane was barely wide enough for three people to walk abreast, the old cobbles undulating like waves frozen into stone. They were about to turn down the narrow space when the sound of running feet made them draw back. Black-coated Yellowbacks came tearing in their direction. Poppy and Alice squashed themselves against the bricks. Poppy felt the rush of air against her face as they passed, the hem of their coats brushing hers. The men paid them no heed, but galloped ahead to where the lane emptied into a square. Then the leaders fell to their knees, raising their weapons, while the men in back aimed over their heads. Something was coming this way.

Alice ran, heading in the direction from where the Yellowbacks had come. Poppy trailed after, casting anxious glances over her shoulder. They didn't go far. The old house sat in a bend of the street, jutting like a peninsula into the cobbles. From the look of it, there had never been a manor involved, though it showed signs of once housing a tavern. One look around told Poppy that no carriages—let alone the Gold King's—waited nearby. Alice was already mounting the steps to go inside when a heavy woman—the kind who had lived hard but not necessarily well—came rushing out with a carpetbag stuffed with clothes.

"Out of my way, love!" said the woman, pushing Alice aside.

Poppy got squarely in her path. "A moment of your time, *love.*" She snatched the carpetbag out of the woman's hand. The woman cried out, but Poppy already had both hands in the bag. That was enough to tell her what she wanted to know.

"What are you doing?" the woman snarled.

"I'm looking for a baby."

The owner of the bag looked startled and then incredulous. "Well, I don't have one!"

"Ma'am," Alice clutched the woman's sleeve with both her hands, her expression pleading. Poppy could see all the strain of the last week in Alice's face. The color had left her lips, making her look deathly ill. Dried blood trailed down one side of her face. The only brightness about Alice was the fire of her hair, which was falling loose from its pins. "Ma'am, please, I'm looking for my son."

The woman stopped, her face softening a degree. "And he's supposed to be here?"

Alice swayed slightly, but took a deep breath. "The Gold King or his men would have brought him, most likely with his nurse."

"No one has come here." The woman shook her head. "Everyone who can is leaving, and I suggest you do the same." With that she pulled away, grabbing her bag and hurrying as fast as her short, thick legs would go.

Alice let out a despairing cry. "He has to be here!"

But Poppy didn't think the woman had lied. She held Alice a moment, giving her what comfort she could—and needing some of that comfort herself—but her mind was racing. "We need to go."

But then the soldiers at the end of the alley began firing round after round. It was a steady barrage—some rifles and some aether weapons—so fast that the individual shots melted into a steady noise. However, it only lasted seconds before the men fell back, yelling with terror.

Poppy screamed, too. A huge snake reared up in the entrance to the lane, head higher than the Yellowbacks, body a thick rope of glistening black scales. Its mouth opened in a warning hiss, swordlike fangs unfolding from its jaws. The hood of its neck flared, half the width of the lane. It swooped down, striking one of the Yellowbacks with a blow so hard Poppy heard bones crack. And then it unhinged its huge jaws and began gulping the man headfirst with convulsive swallows. The other Yellowbacks rained bullets on the monster, but they plinked off harmlessly.

"Poppy!" Alice cried.

But she couldn't take her eyes off the thing, her entire body turning cold with horror. She was fascinated, caught like a rabbit. A soldier with a magnetic aether weapon opened fire, but the blast sizzled harmlessly around the snake in a coruscating blue haze. Whatever the thing was, it was not made of flesh and blood, but magic and steel. *This fell from that zephyr. There were hundreds of them!* Suddenly, every inch of her skin was crawling.

"Poppy!" Alice shook her. "Run!"

Poppy snapped out of her daze as the snake started on its second course. "Run," she repeated with an enthusiastic nod, and then set action to words. Running felt wonderful.

Alice led the way, hurrying east. They burst into the square where the market should have been, but it was in disarray. The square was usually bustling with vendors selling fruits, vegetables, flowers, and whatever else a person could want. Now it looked as if the wares had been set up for the day, but then chaos had taken over. Produce was strewn everywhere, and the sharp scent of crushed fruit permeated the air. A handful of people were dodging through the square trying to get to the other side, some of them with weapons drawn. Poppy skirted around a table, her feet rolling dangerously on a scatter of apples. She stooped to retrieve a walking stick that someone had dropped and gripped it like a club.

A snake as long as Poppy's arm fell from the building above, landing on the cobbles a few yards to their left. It coiled and wound, moving in a weird sideways crawl that ate the distance between them. Alice jerked Poppy away, but she was saved only because the thing struck at a man who tried to push past them. He fell with a cry, immediately paralyzed by the bite. Poppy spun, shocked, but Alice hauled her forward.

There were more serpents oozing out of the windows

above. One dropped, landing nose-first, and its head shattered in an explosion of gears—but the tail kept thrashing. A man shot it with his pistol, the force of the bullet making it flip in the air. But then a serpent shot from beneath a bushel of onions, slithering up the gunman's leg.

Cold metal brushed Poppy's leg and she shrieked, slashing out with her stick. It connected with something, but she was bolting too fast to see more. Poppy's feet were heavy and numb, but panic forced her onward. She could hear herself gasping, her ribs struggling against her stays. Alice looked no better, tears streaking her ashen face, but both kept moving. There wasn't a choice—until a knot of people milling in panic up ahead told Poppy the west side of the market was no escape. The crowd swirled and eddied like water hitting a dam.

"More snakes," Alice gasped, pointing. "Straight ahead and north." She was trembling in panic, her raspy breath starting to catch in terrified hiccups.

Poppy clung to her own self-control. "Then we go toward the river. We have to get away from the buildings."

Alice gave a sharp nod and they turned left as soon as they could, fighting through the press of bodies. Others had the same idea and it would have been hard to change direction if they'd wanted to. The surge carried them forward, Poppy's feet barely touching the earth at some points, but she clung to Alice's hand.

The squash of the crowd got slightly better the moment they emerged onto the Strand. At that moment Poppy realized that the snakes hadn't been working randomly. Thousands of people were being forced out of the market and toward the Thames, where the Blue Boys waited.

It might have been a massacre, but the Blue King's army weren't the only ones there, and the press of civilians pouring out of Covent Garden was the least of their worries. The Yellowbacks had opened fire on the Blue. There was an enormous steamspinner coming in from the west, heading toward the gardens along the embankment, and it was firing on the Blue King and the Gold. And there was another force straight ahead, led by a giant, smiling caterpillar. She recognized the man at its helm.

Poppy's heart leapt, and she began yelling at the top of her lungs and waving her stick in the air, not caring if nobody could hear her over the din. "Tobias!"

CHAPTER SIXTY

THE *ATHENA* WAS DROPPING FAST. IT WAS A SUBTLE THING, but Evelina could feel the deck sinking beneath her feet, almost as if she wasn't firmly connected to the floor. And the ship wasn't holding her own against the wind anymore, either; the crosscurrents of air made her shudder and bounce.

Evelina stole a nervous glance through the porthole, and the sight made her recoil in astonishment. The ground was a lot closer now, looking a lot less like a living map. They were over the outskirts of London, streets and houses sliding by beneath. *We're too close too fast,* Evelina thought grimly.

A sound like a gunshot emerged from the pump, making everyone jump. Striker thumped the side of the pump again and adjusted some valves. "Bubbles in the aether," he said.

Evelina peered nervously at the lime-green concoction, which seemed to be effervescing. She'd mixed the aether without blowing anything up, but she was still holding her breath that it wouldn't explode. A large bubble of gas formed and popped, and the ship shuddered again, reminding Evelina of a hiccup. "It's not supposed to do that, is it?"

"Huh," Striker said, an odd expression on his face. "Looks like green beer."

More bangs and pops emerged from the pump, but the ship began to stabilize. Evelina felt the rapid descent slow and then reverse, new lift floating them upward. Striker met her eyes, and they shared a moment of relief.

Evelina went to find Nick, holding on to the handrail of the walkway because the steamspinner seemed to be listing slightly from side to side, her responses sluggish. She guessed the hole in the *Athena*'s side had done something to her stability.

When Evelina reached the bridge, there was only a handful of people there; everyone else was busy readying arms or repairing damage. Digby and another man seemed in charge of guiding the ship down—a task she knew would be touch and go. Nick and the Schoolmaster were at the very front, the prince pointing out something on the ground.

As Evelina drew near, she could see the green sweep of Hyde Park to the left and the grounds of Buckingham Palace coming up on the right—but nothing looked the way it was supposed to. Armed men were everywhere, but that was only the beginning. The war machines of the makers pushed forward, from Steamers armored like armadillos to many-legged trebuchets, from shambling siege towers to a gigantic drill on steam-powered wheels. Evelina caught a closer glimpse of the enormous dog that had followed them from the laboratories. Though she couldn't hear, it seemed to sit up on its haunches and howl as the steamspinner flew overhead.

"They look like an undisciplined rabble compared to the Gold King's army," said the Schoolmaster. "But no one is truly powerless when they have an idea, a pint of bitter, and a screwdriver."

The ship lurched, and Evelina stumbled. Nick turned just in time to catch her. "Athena!" he snapped, and then winced as the ship said something back.

"What's wrong?" Evelina asked, grabbing the wall as the ship clumsily righted herself.

"She's drunk!" Digby snapped from his position at the helm. "The bloody ship is soused as a sailor. That's not supposed to happen."

"We used the scrumpy to mix the aether," Evelina explained sheepishly. "She's literally running on fumes."

Digby gave her an incredulous look.

Another hiccup shuddered through the vessel. "It's giving me a headache," Nick said under his breath. He looked as if he already had the hangover while his ship enjoyed the party.

The Schoolmaster was facing the window, but his shoulders shook with laughter.

"You're not helping, Your Highness," Nick said sourly.

There was another hiccup and the engines sputtered.

"Losing altitude again, Captain," Digby said, his voice tense.

The steamspinner dropped lower, coming in to land with a dangerous bob and weave. Evelina gripped Nick's arm, dizzied by the sudden nearness of the roofs and spires as they rushed toward the ground. He clasped her hand, pulling her around to face him.

"You look afraid," he said, his dark eyes questioning.

"I got your ship drunk. That can't be wise."

He smiled at that, albeit a bit painfully. "Perhaps. But you saved us, and more than once. I know that was your magic that turned those hot harpoons, Evelina. We didn't lose a single crewman, thanks to you."

She managed a smile. "For whatever good I did today, you're welcome." But she thought of everything she hadn't done. Captain Roberts was dead and the ship badly damaged. It seemed no matter how much power one had, it was never enough.

The *Athena* bumped slightly as it settled to the earth. The next instant, three armies rushed the steamspinner. Only the desire to capture such a magnificent, magical ship in one piece had kept the cannons from blowing her out of the sky, and now the race was on to seize her as a prize of war. But the first of the Gold King's troops had barely reached the Embankment Gardens when the regiments that the steam barons had purchased turned on their masters. The cavalry led by Captain Smythe was the first. They cleared a circle around the *Athena,* driving the enemy back to establish a protected zone clear to the river on one side and all the way to the Strand on the other.

As soon as it was even marginally safe, Evelina left the ship, needing to feel green under her feet. Nick was of the air, but she needed good earth. But as she stepped away from the ladder, to stand in the shadow of the *Athena*'s belly, it took a moment to orient herself. The ship had swallowed a huge portion of the gardens, and the stink and noise of battle stripped away any sense that they were in a park. The constant booming of weapons rolled like restless thunder behind a steady roar of voices. Screams of pain, outrage, and loss swirled around them. Evelina's magic shifted restlessly, agitated by the tension snapping through the air—and the death. The dark power within her scented prey and rose eagerly, hunger knifing through her.

Nick came up beside her, shading his eyes to see the battle. "What do you think?" His voice was sharp with concern.

Evelina blinked, called back to herself. "I think the rebels are fighting bravely, but I'm no soldier. I can't tell who is winning."

"Are you strong enough to do that trick of yours with the devas?" he asked with a lift of one eyebrow. "I think the steam barons' armies could use some unexpected retooling."

For a beat she didn't understand what he meant, her exhausted brain slow to respond. But then she found herself grinning—with both love and an appreciation of his guile. She'd animated the prince's machines; there was no reason not to do the same with the others. "Captain Niccolo, you are a devious man."

"Always, but only as a force for good."

She opened her mind to the surrounding landscape, and was dragged into the alternate landscape of war. Where smoke swirled in the sky, so did a dozen species of passion—the counterpoint to the constant cries and screams. The billows of emotion didn't have a color, but her mind's eye translated it as shifting shades of red and orange, snapping sheets of tortured energy rolling against the gray pall of smoke and destruction. Where the red waves gathered to a peak, crackles of blue fire fountained to white. She had seen such fires once before, the first time Magnus had taught her to use a wand. They were lives, escaping as the body that tethered them died.

Time had no meaning in that state, but it felt as if she stared for a long time in horrified fascination. *So many!*

And then her dark power rose inexorably to feed—an impulse far beyond her control. It lunged, and she was suddenly immersed in a sensation that was both hot and cold, as if every nerve was overwhelmed with sensation. And it was delicious—a taste and smell that was intoxicating and yet had nothing to do with her external senses at all. It was like absorbing starlight, or bathing in the sound of rain. Most of all, it was ending starvation. After using so much magic to protect the ship, she had been drained without knowing it.

Cautiously, she took Nick's hand, preparing to call their shared magic. For a seasick moment, she wasn't sure it would work—perhaps her magic had grown too dark to summon that pure, brilliant light, or perhaps Nick would push her away in disgust now that he had witnessed her replenish her powers. Slowly, she looked up to see Nick watching her, his dark eyes carefully neutral.

"So that is how death magic works," he said softly.

Cold seeped through her. With one word of disgust, he could blast her world apart as completely as any aether weapon. She began to shiver. "Are you appalled?"

"No. You saved my ship and crew. It would be churlish to complain now." He kept his features still, making his thoughts impossible to read.

Evelina's heart lurched, afraid of the worst. "Nick!"

Quickly, he squeezed her hand. "Evelina, I told you to make this power your weapon and your ally, and you're doing it." But the lines around his mouth were tense.

She swallowed hard. "It's another thing to see it, isn't it? You were raised by Gran Cooper, too. You can't help being horrified."

He shook his head, and his stiff expression melted into one of contrition. "Not horrified. Sobered, because now I see the edge you must dance. I don't think I completely understood what you were going through. And I'm sorry if I treated anything with less weight than I should have."

"Don't be," said Evelina, finally breathing again. "If you'd coddled me any more than you did, I think I would have crumbled altogether."

At that, he finally stirred, taking both her hands and raising them to his lips. His dark eyes met hers for a long, languorous beat. Nick was Nick, always on her side, and the silver fire of wild magic burned bright between them even in the full light of day. Evelina squeezed her eyes shut, her entire body aching with relief and gratitude.

When she opened them again, his lips curled into a smile that mixed mischief, pride, and a vulnerable softness she rarely saw in him. For an instant she glimpsed the family man he might become. And then it was gone, and the captain was back. "You don't crumble, Evelina."

No, she just melted whenever he looked at her. She cleared her throat. "I think you were saying something about needing the devas again."

When she opened her consciousness again—more gradually this time—she felt the familiar rush of spirits eager to join with the wild magic she and Nick shared. She caught them—this time dispensing even with the short verse she had used before. She made her offer wordlessly—more with mental images than anything else. The devas of earth and tree grasped her meaning at once. Too many of the city's gardens had been swept away to make room for commerce, forgetting what was owed to health and spirit. They were willing to fight for their place in the metropolis.

They flowed into the machines, eager to turn the battle against the barons. But the nature spirits weren't plentiful enough to subvert two entire armies, and Evelina searched further, drawing on Nick's strength and the deep well of dark power. When it was firmly in her grasp, she delved deep into the earth and sky around them.

There were other kinds of spirits there, ones that barely had names—but the battle had stirred them to consciousness. At first Evelina thought them earth devas, but they were more than that, and less.

Who are you? she asked.

At first, they didn't know how to answer.

Where do you come from? asked Nick, who seemed to be able to speak to these creatures as easily as she could. *Where do you live?*

Here, they said, and suddenly Evelina's mind was filled with images of alleyways and iron gates, churchyards and cellars. There was the song of bells and the splash of fountains, the hidden waterways and the whisper of wind in the high places. *We are London.* And then came angry images of the ramshackle rookeries and sickness, and she understood that these city spirits were every bit as furious with the steam barons as the country devas.

She felt Nick's intake of breath at the same moment as hers. These devas were something new, something neither Gran nor Magnus had spoken of. And yet it made perfect sense. When a city grew old enough, it began to have devas of its own. These were babies compared to the devas of Dartmoor, but they were there and willing to help. Best of all, there were thousands of them.

The dark power rose like a tide, lifting them all. Evelina felt the mass union of magic and machine almost as an audible click in her mind. It wasn't so much a spell as opening a door between possibilities, permission asked and received.

The devas poured into the war machines of the steam barons, destroying them from the inside out—or turning them on each other. When the foot soldiers saw the artillery developing a mind of its own, many threw down their weapons and ran.

Evelina laughed, but it came out more like a gasp. The magic had left her ringing like a bell, joyous and somber at once. She reached up to realize that her face was wet with tears.

"That should keep them busy," Nick said under his breath, still grasping her hand.

Too soon, the intimacy of the spell was broken. The prince joined Nick and Evelina, a number of airmen ranged around him like a guard. He was tense, the muscles of his jaw jumping. "I need a report. What's going on out there? What is that caterpillar doing?"

Nick answered. "The air devas say the forces with the caterpillar are holding the King Coal's rolling spheres on Waterloo Bridge."

"How? They can't be anywhere near as strong."

"Through sheer cheek and a handful of sharpshooters, from the sound of it."

A cluster of men broke through the fighting and ran forward. Nick and the other airmen drew weapons, closing ranks before the prince, but Evelina cried out in pleasure as soon as she saw who it was. It was half a dozen of the cavalrymen in their blue coats, a lieutenant in the lead, and in their midst walked two figures in civilian clothes. She'd never thought she'd be glad to see Lord Bancroft, but there he was with Bucky Penner. Both men were bruised and dirty, but wore triumphant smiles as they bowed low before the prince.

There was little time for more than the barest formality. Both men nodded a surprised acknowledgment to her, but Bucky quickly unslung a sack from his shoulder and knelt before the prince, Lord Bancroft at his side.

"Your Highness," said Bancroft. "Here are devices that will disable the Gold King's war machines. We brought them to you through the underground, but you should know that from this point west, the tunnels are filled with enemy soldiers."

"How did you get through?"

Bancroft blinked, as if not quite sure how he was still alive. "The men who are in company with my son found us. Not all of our rescuers made it back."

"Your son?" the prince asked.

"The one on the caterpillar."

Tobias? Surprised and yet not, Evelina craned her neck, trying to see over the crowd, but she couldn't see him.

"I thank you for your efforts, gentlemen," said the prince, but he looked at Evelina. "Will these devices conflict in any way with what you have done?"

"No," she said. "The devas will override the war machines, no matter who commands them."

Bucky looked at her with fresh interest, but the prince was already issuing orders. "These need to get to Edgerton and the army to the west. Lieutenant, take a party and see Lord Bancroft and Mr. Penner get through to them safely."

The lieutenant gave a smart salute and gathered his charges, but her attention was drawn away. Several things were happening at once at the near edge of the battle.

Tobias must have had some of those devices, because all at once several of the Gold King's battle engines were using their cannons to clear a path for his caterpillar. This had two effects. The rebel army to the west began pushing toward him, but a ripple passed through the Gold King's lines as a group she hadn't seen before crashed through.

"Who are they?" Evelina demanded, but no one had time to answer her. Smythe's cavalry scattered like rain before the onslaught, horses whinnying in terror. Within seconds, she knew why.

Here were some of the missing inmates of Her Majesty's Laboratories, gathered into a fighting force the likes of which no one had ever seen. They carried no weapons, and rags hung from their gaunt frames, as dirty and bedraggled as the matted ropes of their hair and beards. Like Nellie Reynolds, many were part machine, but where she had kept her personality, these had been turned into something else. Evelina's guess was that their magic had been ripped from them, or twisted somehow to damage their minds, because there was nothing human left behind. Fearless, they arrowed forward at unnatural speed, snarling with savage, catlike teeth bared.

There were more than a dozen, but just as many guns opened fire. Half went down at once, but half still sprinted toward the prince—and such fast targets were difficult. A second volley took more down, but two still came. One was male—his head and one arm seeming to be the only part left that was flesh. The other was a woman, her left leg and right arm made from a framework of shining steel. Nick aimed and shot the man full in the face, sending him spinning backward, but the woman lunged, clawed hands already reaching for the prince.

They hadn't come all this way for this to happen. Panicked, Evelina thrust her power forward, willing the tragedy to just *stop*.

And it did. Time froze.

Panic morphed into bewilderment. Evelina stared around her. Everything was as immobile as if it had been cast in bronze. The half-woman's long gray hair streamed behind her, the ropey muscle of her calf straining as she launched from the grass, and yet she did not move. The prince's expression was a mask of wide-eyed revulsion, one arm raised to block her attack. Nick was there beside her, caught in the midst of his weapon's recoil as his target fell backward, suspended at an impossible angle in the air.

Evelina's scalp crawled. She'd never done anything like *this* before! She took a deep breath, relishing how quiet it was with the din of battle stopped. Except it wasn't silent. Something else besides her was moving around.

She turned toward the noise. It was the giant dog, standing just inside the ring of frozen battle. It really was the size of a small calf, with the huge, square head of a mastiff. The coat was brindled brown and black with a white chest and two massive white paws on its front legs. It might have just been a big dog except for its glowing red eyes and the blue-green slobber dripping from its jaw. *A dog that drools aether?* Evelina thought. What had the scientists at the laboratories done to the poor creature?

And yet here it was, oblivious to her magic. It started to lollop toward her, a deep baying cry escaping from its chest. Evelina backed away, unsure how to stop it but knowing she must. She gathered her magic—or tried to—but it seemed as immobilized as the scene. She fumbled, her abilities blunted by having used so much power only minutes ago. Had she even cast the freezing spell, or had it been the hound?

The creature sprang for the prince. Evelina leapt to stop it by sheer strength, but her fingers slipped from the sleek fur, the muscled body far too powerful to even flinch at her assault. But it didn't grab the Schoolmaster in its massive jaws; it savaged his attacker instead. Those huge white paws slammed into the half-human's sides, bearing her to the ground before snapping her neck with a single, sickening crunch.

Evelina gasped, and the hound turned its head, red eyes like a whirling mass of clouds turned ruby by a spectacular sunset. There was something ancient about them and very uncanine, and something that told her she wasn't the only magician in the war.

"I saw you at the laboratories," she said.

An image formed in her mind that made her skin crawl. This was indeed the dog Nellie Reynolds had described— part hound, part clockwork, and part aether engine. But through the magic unleashed during the wreck of the laboratories, the beast had become host to Dartmoor's spirits— and they were just figuring out the potential of the hound's internal workings.

"Is this trick of stopping time your magic or something built inside of you?" she asked.

Both, it replied.

The hound's deep voice startled her tired magic to attention.

"Why did you follow us?" she asked.

Events have been set in motion. The dragon awakes. Magic walks. Crowns rise and fall. No one can stop the wheel from turning now.

The creature's words chilled her to the core. Her power rose, tingling and ready for a fight, but the creature gave an acknowledging *whuff* and bounded away. As soon as it had vanished from sight, the racket of the battle resumed with the force of a thunderclap. Nick's victim fell. The prince gave a surprised cry, blinking as he saw the woman dead on the ground. Evelina slumped into a crouch, her head spinning.

"What the bleeding hell happened?" Nick demanded.

What indeed? Evelina reeled from the suddenness of what she'd just seen. What had Dr. Watson been writing— something about a hound that haunted the Baskerville family?

She thought he'd made it up, but she would bet her last shilling she'd just seen the object of the good doctor's latest tale.

CHAPTER SIXTY-ONE

THE NEXT MOMENT, THE AIRMEN LEAPED INTO ACTION, breaking Evelina's thoughts.

"Get the prince back inside the ship!" Nick commanded, and his crew sprang to obey.

"No!" said the Schoolmaster. "Others have fought on my behalf long enough." He unslung the modified rifle he had over his shoulder. "I can't command what I will not do myself."

"Pardon, my lord, but you need to stay alive long enough to actually win the day," Nick broke in, waving a hand. "Otherwise, this has been a colossal waste of time."

The prince bridled. They might have argued longer, but a roar of cannon made the ground shudder and drowned out anything else they had to say.

Evelina ran for the ladder that led back inside the *Athena*, but instead of crawling back inside she used it to work her way onto the ship's backswept wing. A handful of rooks were already there, and they hopped aside to make room for her. Her skirts started to tangle around her ankles as she climbed, but she kicked them aside, no longer worried about the rips and mud along her hems. She finally got to her feet, shading her eyes against the falling angle of the sun. She could sense Athena, who was lost in a swirling, hazy doze despite the chaos all around.

"What do you see?" Nick called up from the ground.

"The battle's shifting," she replied, but another boom ate her words.

It didn't take long to figure out what was going on. The caterpillar and its surrounding mob had lifted the barricades and were pushing in their direction, assisted by Smythe's cavalry. The sudden gap between the Gold and Blue forces had an instant effect as the two opposing forces rushed to fill the breach. Evelina noticed at once the difference between the steam baron's armies—a vast wave of thugs and mercenaries—and the small number of professional regiments still loyal to the Crown. The Yellowbacks and Blue Boys were serious fighters, but the regiments were disciplined soldiers fighting for their home. It was unfortunate they were badly outnumbered.

A handful of the Gold King's machines—there were a few still functional—began blasting their way toward the Blue King's rolling spheres. It would have been an equal match, as far as Evelina could tell, but neither side had counted on the prince's southern army.

Keating's Yellowbacks had largely ignored the ragtag mob of makers, retired soldiers, and malcontents—right until they drove a wedge through the back of Keating's main line, splitting it. One half was forced north into Covent Garden, the other straight into the Blue Boys.

Nick landed lightly beside Evelina. "I can't hear a thing you're saying from down there." But then he followed the line of her pointing finger, and fell silent.

The Gold King's main force had been split, but it had one last card to play. From her vantage point she was just high enough from the ground to see the small, light dirigibles rise from the northwest. They were a pale green, telling Evelina that they had been commandeered from the Green Queen's holdings. Though they were small, they were non-explosive aether ships and that was a good thing, for a long chain dangled from each, and at the end of the chain was a round cage filled with flames. Evelina recognized it as the same wicked, clinging fire used in hot harpoons. The ships began unleashing the blaze over the ranks of the Blue Boys.

King Coal's army broke like a puddle exploding from beneath a stomping boot. Panic raged through the tightly packed ranks as the southern portion of the Gold Army surged forward and the two armies became one seething mass of men and machines. The Blue King's wheeled spheres ground forward through the mob, meeting the Gold King's mobile cannons like two species of Titans battling with thunderbolts.

One of the Blue King's spheres exploded in a shower of flame and shrapnel. The noise sent the rooks into a hysterical flurry. When the smoke cleared, Evelina could see flames erupting from several of the buildings nearby. She wondered how much of London would be on fire before this was done.

Nick grabbed her arm and pointed. Two of the professional regiments surrounding the prince began working east. "Look."

"What are they doing?" asked Evelina.

"Pushing back the Blue Boys, from the looks of things." Nick let out a joyous laugh. "They're making a safe passage for Roth and his merry men."

Sure enough, she could see the head of the caterpillar bobbing above the crowd that was streaming past its rippling rows of red-booted feet. Evelina let out a whoop as the running mob shouted Prince Edmond's name. And then suddenly the prince was on the wing with Evelina and Nick, waving his striped muffler in the air.

"Welcome, friends!" he cried, and the rebels screamed their approval. Another war machine exploded in the distance, melding with their roar until the sound seemed to reverberate like thunder. "That's the spirit. Let's give them a taste of our steam!"

Hats, scarves, and someone's lacy knickers flew into the air in approval of the handsome young prince. "They never do that for me anymore," Nick complained. "Not since I gave up the circus."

"It's all a question of venue," Evelina replied. "Would you really want to see Striker's unmentionables?"

Nick made a face. "That thought's going to give me nightmares."

At that moment, General Fortman and a group of other men arrived. The prince gave a bark of satisfied laughter and immediately climbed back to the ground. At the same time, a handful of the newcomers—these looked like former soldiers—pushed through to the front. "We have a prisoner!" one of them announced. "One you're going to want to question."

"Beg your pardon, Your Highness, we need to coordinate our plan," Fortman countered.

The prince turned to address Nick and Evelina. "Please see what the prisoner has to say while I tend to this." With that, he strode off.

Nick signaled to the soldiers to bring their charge forward. Two more appeared, dragging a man between them. "Dark Mother of Basilisks," Nick growled. "It's Juniper."

Nick swung back to the ground, dropping lightly before he strode easily toward the man. Sudden vertigo seized Evelina and she crouched, waiting out the shock that sent her head spinning. The prisoner was looking up at her, his face a pale circle below. She recognized the lean visage of Professor Moriarty. The Ladies' College seemed far away now, like a story from a book, and yet all her emotions about the place were just as keen. He'd been the only faculty member who had even tried to understand her, and now—just as he'd predicted—they were on opposite sides.

Evelina gathered herself, quickly scrambling for the ladder. When she reached the ground, Nick was walking toward her. "He wants to speak to you," he said, curiosity shading his voice. "He seems to think you can help him."

"I'm not sure how," Evelina replied as they approached a sheltered spot near the *Athena* where there were far fewer people milling about.

The two men holding Moriarty had forced him to kneel in the muddy grass. One still gripped his hair, tilting his head back slightly so that he regarded her through slitted eyes. His hands were lashed behind him so tightly that his shoulders twisted backward. The sight of it made Evelina's stomach hurt.

"How did you make out with the salt of sorrows?" Moriarty asked as she drew near.

Of all the things he might have said, she wasn't expecting that. All her ambivalent feelings about the man came flood-

ing back. "Did you know that I would try to use it to over-
load the mechanism of the bracelets?"

His mouth twitched, but it didn't make it all the way to a
smile. "I never know precisely what people will do. There
seemed a high probability you would figure out a way to get
the bracelets off if you got out of Camelin."

"The salts didn't help with that, Professor, although they
did assist with destroying Her Majesty's Laboratories." She
wondered if he knew the chemical compound would make
her ill. It was hard to tell.

The guard let go of his hair and Moriarty wrenched himself
away. "Then my little gift did give you an advantage."

That was true, and Evelina didn't like it. "Why did you ask
for me, Professor?"

"Remember that I arranged for you to get out of captivity.
You might, uh," he rolled his eyes toward his guards, "think
about returning the favor."

She remembered his words: *Shall we bargain, Miss Cooper? My influence on your behalf for a future consideration?* Anger hissed through her blood. "I don't have the
authority here to grant you favors, Professor."

Moriarty gave an ingratiating smile. "But you can convince Prince Edmond that I am a man of honor. I keep the
promises I make. Think back, and you'll see I'm telling the
truth."

"Are you intending to make a promise now?" Nick asked
dryly. "It doesn't seem to me that you have much to offer at
the moment."

"A good portion of the Blue Boys owe their allegiance
directly to me. Let me go and I will turn the tide of battle for
you."

"To you, eh?" Nick returned. "And what did they do to
find themselves in that position?"

Evelina remembered Moriarty's description of his
network—the favors owed and debts gathered. "I think the
battle is already turning. Perhaps the prince doesn't need
your help."

"Brave words, but not well founded. We've kept the bulk

of our forces under the earth. There's another third of our force the rebels haven't even seen."

"The Blue King kept his army in the Black Kingdom?" Nick asked.

"The army rented space under the streets, no more than that."

"And you would turn your coat for queen and country?" asked Nick.

"I value my life."

"What's to keep you from turning it again?"

"The prince needs my loyalty for today. By midnight this war will be decided. And to be honest, I tire of serving King Coal. This is my chance to escape from his service once and for all."

Nick looked to Evelina. "You know this man. What do you think?"

Evelina considered. The dark power was tasting Moriarty's promises, rolling them around like candy on its tongue. They tasted like truth, but in a dangerous way. "I owe him a service, so I am discharging that service by speaking on his behalf. I believe what he has just said is completely true. He will fight for Edmond."

"But?"

"Just that. By destroying King Coal, he serves himself. He does not do this for the Crown."

"What a charming ally." Nick paused, eyes narrowed. "What surety can you offer?"

One of the Gold King's rolling cannons boomed close enough to hurt Evelina's ears.

"Only my own character," Moriarty returned. "As Miss Cooper so delicately puts it, our interests coincide. This is a three-way battle. I can give the rebels an edge."

"I believe in you about as far as I could hurl my airship. But I do believe in Miss Cooper's instincts." Nick gave a curt nod and turned to the guards. "Get him ready to present to the prince."

They looked doubtful, but they cut his bonds while Nick went to make his report to Edmond. Moriarty rose stiffly and made a bow. "You will not regret this choice. All obligations between us are fulfilled, Miss Cooper. But no doubt we will do business again."

Evelina sincerely hoped not.

And then Moriarty pointed toward the top of one of the rolling spheres. It was just visible from where they stood, the muzzles of its twin cannons pointing above the battle. It was turning back toward Waterloo Bridge.

"Do you want extra surety of my good faith?" asked the professor. "Then there you are. *That* machine holds King Coal, and he's abandoning his Blue Boys to the tender mercies of Gold's army. He thought he had the stomach for battle, but it appears he has lost his appetite for once. Fancy that."

Evelina gave him a sharp look. "Are you telling the truth?"

He looked mildly offended. "Absolutely."

She set off at a run to find Nick and Prince Edmond. The chance to capture one of the steam barons was too tempting an opportunity to pass up. She didn't have to go far, because the two men were already headed her way.

"Where is Moriarty?" Prince Edmond demanded. "He killed Sir Charles Baskerville!"

Evelina recoiled in shock. "He just pointed out the war machine the Blue King is riding in."

Prince Edmond's eyes widened as if he'd just stepped into a magnetic coil. "King Coal?"

They broke into a run, but when they reached the spot where Moriarty was being held prisoner, the two guards were lifeless on the ground and the professor had vanished. Nick bent over the guards. "Their necks are broken."

"I have to catch him," Edmond said at once. "If there's a search party, I have to be the one to lead it."

"And who will chase the Blue King?" Evelina asked. "Moriarty will be impossible to find. The Blue King isn't."

Nick looked up. "You don't have infinite resources to waste seeking individuals in the middle of a battle. At least none who aren't steam barons."

"And he knows that," Edmond said bitterly. "Moriarty knows I can't afford a personal vendetta when he's thrown a bigger prize my way."

Nick and Evelina waited while Edmond cursed under his breath.

"Fine. King Coal it is." Then the prince was suddenly in motion, striding into the surrounding throng. "Get me some men! Get me weapons and a horse!"

Nick gave her a worried look. "I should go with him. Striker can stay with the *Athena*."

Evelina grabbed his arm. The Blue King's forces were using weapons Magnus designed and no one understood that magic better than she did. "I'm going, too."

Meeting her eyes, Nick gave a slow nod. She could see he wanted to protect her, but he also relied on her strength. "Bring a pistol," was all he said.

THEY WERE ON a battlefield crammed with machines, but the cavalry unit led the charge toward the Blue King. Nick, Evelina, and the prince were mounted in their midst. She had no difficulty riding astride, and the horse was better trained for war than she was. The hardest part was getting to the bridge through the crush.

She was taking part in a land battle, yet it was hard to say exactly what it was like. The airship had given her a good view of everything, but here she was but one ant in a swarm. There was too much noise and smoke to pick out much detail. In fact, Evelina couldn't see farther ahead than the horse and rider in front, and often they were slowed to a walk until finally the group cut south to circle the worst of the crush.

Adding to the chaos was a furor about mechanical snakes escaping from Covent Garden. According to a rebel messenger, the fires breaking out all around the area were driving them into the open, but not before the creatures cut a swath through the Gold King's retreating forces. It took the large-wheeled war machines to crush the seemingly indestructible serpents, because even aether weapons had little effect. The only advantage they had was that rooks could find the snakes no matter where they hid.

At one point, the prince's party passed close to the caterpillar, which had finally reached the edge of the gardens where the steamspinner had landed. With a thrill of excitement, Evelina thought she caught a glimpse of Tobias and possibly Alice over to her left, but they were too far away to hail.

The prince's party reached the Savoy Chapel at the north end of the bridge where dozens more of the Gold King's machines must have fallen under the control of the rebels. There was an eerie lurch in the battle as one by one they stopped cold, releasing a puff of steam, limbs and cannons drooping. *That means Lord Bancroft and Bucky made it safely through to the prince's main army!*

Evelina laughed at the sagging machines, but then one of the smaller units whirled like a dervish, flailing dangerously through its own troops before it finally toppled over. "Look out!" someone cried as its casing burst in a blast of steam, and a scream of pain split the air and made Evelina's horse flatten its ears. Her first instinct was to leap off the horse and help the wounded, but then the prince broke into a gallop. At long last the crowd gave way, and the pursuit was on.

In no time at all, the prince was in the lead, Nick and Evelina hard on his heels. A thrill built inside her, and she leaned forward over her horse's neck, the wind in her teeth as she grinned. The bridge had finally cleared, and the Blue King's sphere was rolling madly ahead, far faster than Evelina would have expected.

Her first response would have been to use magic, but her power was too exhausted after calling the devas to trust in its accuracy. In turn, she'd wondered why he didn't just turn and blast them to pieces, but now she saw a deep fissure had opened in the housing of the engine inside the machine. The recoil of another volley would probably crack it in two. No wonder the king was holding fire. As to why he had turned tail and run rather than surround himself with his Blue Boys—she could only guess that somehow he'd learned of Moriarty's deception.

Although—the thought occurred to Evelina with the sick, cold, squishy feel of being handed something nasty at the fish market—it did seem odd that someone as wily as the Blue King would allow himself to be dangled like bait.

CHAPTER SIXTY-TWO

KING COAL WAS NOT AS EASY TO CATCH AS THEY'D EX-
pected, even though most of the fighting was on the north
side of the Thames and they were following the south bank.
What they saw here was mostly the aftermath of explosives
dropped from the few dirigibles not destroyed by that morning's air battle. There were piles of rubble and the blackened
remains of fires, but no ground troops.

But there were grenades. Whenever they got close, the
machine would launch an explosive, forcing them to fall
back. Then the rolling war machine would drop out of sight
despite its size, and they would waste time hunting to pick
up the Blue King's erratic trail. The chase moved steadily
east, and Evelina guessed their quarry meant to go to ground
deep in his own territory near the docks.

The horses were growing winded as the sunset painted
the sky. She saw lights along the northward curve of the
river that said they'd passed the Tower. This was King
Coal's territory, and they were running out of time to catch
him.

The prince reined in. The riders were blowing almost as
hard as their mounts. "We've lost him again," he snarled,
every word a curse. "If we go much further, we'll fall into
the Surrey Canal. Where's he gone?"

One of the cavalrymen jumped down to check his horse's
shoe. The others shifted uneasily, some dismounting and
others surveying the twisting lanes around them. The neighborhood looked old but well kept. "Where are we?" Evelina
asked.

"Rotherhithe," said one of the cavalry.

The prince swore. "When I went with Holmes to see the Blue King last year, his headquarters were across the river. Why did he come this way?"

"No armies in the way," Nick answered. "And it's no trouble getting back across. The tunnel under the river runs right from here to Wapping across the water. Almost to his front door."

"Of course!" Edmond grabbed his reins, urging his mount forward once more. "Then that's where he's gone. To the tunnel!"

Nick and Evelina were right behind him, but the sudden departure caught the others by surprise and they lagged a few seconds behind. So when the Blue King's magnetic aether cannon took its shot, it caught the soldiers full on.

It was too close and too sudden for Evelina to react. The roaring flash—barely a dozen yards away—scattered the horses. Evelina's mount reared and she fell, her scream cut off in a brutal *whoosh* as she fell hard. She rolled away from the churning hooves as the horse whirled and bolted, feeling the graze of an iron shoe nonetheless. She scrambled to her hands and knees, body screaming from the abuse.

Immediately, she looked for Nick. He was leaping down from his own horse, letting it gallop away, and drawing his weapon. The prince was picking himself up off the ground. A quick glance told her there was nothing left of their cavalry escort, or the shed that had stood to their left. A sound of horror ripped from her throat. Smoking embers and a bad smell turned the narrow street into a snippet of hell. Evelina's gorge rose, and even her magic was flattened to stunned silence. She hadn't known the men personally, but they were more than random strangers.

Shock thawed to anger, but survival forced her to think. The shot had come from across the road and somewhere behind Nick's position. She was far more vulnerable where she was than in the shelter of the buildings across the way.

She risked dashing across the cobbles to join the others, never so grateful to feel the warmth of Nick's arms as she crouched against the brick. "What now?" she whispered.

"We find him," the prince said grimly. "He's in the street behind us."

They drew their weapons, Evelina carrying a Webley much like the one that Jasper Keating had given her once long ago. Slipping between buildings, they circled toward the machine from behind, Nick in the lead.

"What the hell happened?" he muttered under his breath. Evelina and the prince crowded forward to peer around the corner.

The sphere seemed to be in pieces. Even in the darkness, Evelina could tell the engine had failed, steam pouring from cracks in the housing. The front of the sphere seemed to have fallen away, but as they edged closer it became clear that what they saw was a large open hatch. The machine was empty, its occupant gone.

The prince made a face. "Where's that tunnel?"

THE PASSAGE UNDER the Thames, designed by Marc and Isambard Kingdom Brunel, had been the engineering marvel of the age when it had opened as a pedestrian subway forty-five years ago, but it had since become part of the East London Railway's underground lines. Two arched tunnels greeted them, one for trains going north, the other south. The northbound entrance was blocked by a fall of stone— no doubt the result of an air attack—so there was no choice but to take the other. Evelina might have been worried about the prospect of meeting a train, but there was little chance of anything coming from the north side of the river with the battle going on.

Evelina's first instinct on entering the tunnel was to flee the claustrophobic shadows. Gaslights flickered at distant intervals, giving just enough light to avoid utter blackness. Glad as she was for the meager illumination, it seemed a waste of power. "The trains don't need light, so why are there gas lines down here?"

Prince Edmond answered, "These tunnels aren't just for the trains. The citizens of the Black Kingdom use them as well."

They were speaking in hushed tones, as there was something in the air that demanded caution. Nick bent to examine the ground. There was just enough space to walk comfortably beside the tracks, but Evelina wondered how easy passage would really be for the Blue King in his steam-driven chair.

"These ashes are still warm and they're not from a train," Nick said. "Someone came through here not long ago."

"Are there wheel tracks?" Evelina looked down the tunnel. Arches rimmed it, giving the appearance of a gigantic segmented worm. Every so often side passages appeared beneath stone archways, no doubt for use of the underground residents.

"Yes, and boot prints. He's not alone."

The prince patted the bulging pockets of his long coat. "I have restraints, weapons, and water. We'll catch up to them. That chair of his doesn't move all that fast."

Nick rose, dusting the ash from his fingers. "I look forward to it."

They set off, but it wasn't the straightforward journey Evelina expected. They hadn't gone that far before they found the tunnel blocked, not by a collapse, but by barricades made of rubble and rusted iron. As the lightest of the three of them, Evelina tried to climb the eighteen-foot pile of detritus to see what was beyond, but it was too unstable.

"We know King Coal didn't come this way," Nick said. "He must have gone into the side tunnels."

"That's Black territory," said Evelina. "Even if no one catches us in there, it would be too easy to get lost."

"Maybe not." The prince rummaged inside his pocket. "What about this device the Scarlet King's men were testing at Manufactory Three?"

Nick stiffened at the name of the place, but Evelina leaned forward for a closer look. It was an octagon of black metal just a little larger than a man's hand. The cover was hinged at the bottom and latched at the top, and the prince opened it carefully.

"It's easiest to view by looking at the mirror inside the cover," the prince explained, sounding much more like a true schoolmaster right then. "The map is drawn backward so that someone wearing the device as part of their gear can open the cover and read it from the mirror."

"What does it do?" asked Evelina.

"It's an elaborate kind of compass," said the prince. "You tell it your destination, and it points you there."

"I never figured out how to tell it where I wanted to go," said Nick.

"I did," said the prince. "I needed to do something to keep busy on the *Athena*, at least until people started shooting at us." He popped the back off the device and began fiddling with the gears.

Curious, Evelina had to hold her hands behind her back to keep from snatching it away for a better look. When the prince finally surrendered it, she could see a series of red arrows pointing to a tiny spot on the painted map of London.

"There are two painted faces for the compass," said the prince. "One for London and one for England. I switched it to the London map. It's too small to see a lot of detail, but I told it we were aiming for Wapping across the river. The arrows will tell us which way to go."

Evelina saw a series of red arrows, all swiveled to point at a single location on the map. She turned to face another direction, and the arrows swayed to keep their points fixed firmly north. "Amazing." She desperately wanted to take it apart and examine the insides.

While they were setting the device, Nick had been checking the passages, peering carefully at the ground. "This is the way Blue went."

Soon they were following after, carefully watching for signs of the underground inhabitants. She dreaded encountering more of the shadowy Others like the ones Magnus had kept at his castle. She had even less appetite for encountering Wraiths—the Black Kingdom's equivalents of the Blue Boys or Yellowbacks. She'd seen them once before and had no desire for a repeat.

Barely speaking, they walked down the side tunnel for some minutes. It branched, and branched again, but they used the device to keep on in the right direction. She could feel Nick growing more and more restless. She didn't like the place, but she could tolerate the feel of the earth around her. By the way he kept glancing up with a frown, the weight of earth and water above them didn't agree at all with a magician of the air.

But something about the underground felt familiar to her. She remembered Magnus saying that he had studied in the Black Kingdom for a time, and she recognized a flavor that he had carried in his magic, almost the way a cook will pick up a spice during his travels. The source of that essence was somewhere deep in the earth and it was a magnet to her dark magic. She knew it for the root of power, the same pure essence that she had touched to call the devas of London to her hand. It was the commonality between the folkways of Gran Cooper and Magnus's sorcery. Somewhere in the Black Kingdom was the origin of everything she was. The touch of it pulsed inside her like a second heartbeat. It lulled her into a dreamlike state, pushing out every other thought.

The prince shuffled to a stop. "I'm losing my sense of direction down here. Where are we?"

Shaking herself awake, Evelina opened the octagon and saw at once that the needles were pointing every which way. "Damnation!" Dismay rolled through her as she snapped the case shut. "If we turn around now, we can still retrace our steps."

A female voice came from the darkness ahead of them. "Equipment doesn't work well down here. There's too much ambient power for anything magnetized to work properly. Of course, we're the exception."

Evelina's breath caught as half a dozen of the half-human victims of Her Majesty's Laboratories emerged from the shadows ahead. They looked every bit as ragged as the band that had attacked the prince before. All had at least two metal limbs, and one had half a metal face. The leader pushed a few steps ahead of the others, the faint gaslight gleaming on the sculpted strands of metal that made up her forearm. "You do realize, of course, that you're trespassing?

And once you're in the Black Kingdom, you don't leave until questioned."

There was a scuff behind her and Evelina wheeled around, heart hammering. There were another five of the creatures behind them, weapons raised. Even if she tried, she couldn't raise a spell in time to attack before they fired. They were trapped.

The prince lifted his hat, sketching a polite bow to the woman, whose body seemed to be as much metal as it was flesh. "Then, madam," he said as easily as if she had announced that tea was in the drawing room, "I expect we shall have the honor of accepting your invitation."

CHAPTER SIXTY-THREE

5:05 p.m. Wednesday

TOBIAS CLAMBERED ABOARD THE SMALL, FLEET DIRIGIBLE that had brought his father and Bucky to the caterpillar. Alice and Poppy were just settling into their seats. Tobias sat beside Alice, grasping her cold hand in his good one. He'd barely been able to stop touching her since Yelland had hauled the two women onto the caterpillar. In that one heart-stopping moment he'd grasped how close he'd come to losing them in the madness sweeping the city.

"What the blazes were you doing in the middle of the fight?" Lord Bancroft exploded, his gaze riveted on Poppy.

"We were looking for Jeremy," she said stoutly. "Circumstances changed along the way. There were snakes."

The door slammed shut and the craft lifted. It had set down in the relatively safe zone near the *Athena,* but there was no wisdom in lingering.

"When I get you home . . ." Bancroft growled.

"You can't keep me from helping." Poppy gave her father a mutinous look. "I'm getting the knack for defying danger."

Alice flinched. It might have been a stifled laugh, or it might have been chagrin. Tobias had heard most of their tale from Alice, who looked utterly exhausted. He didn't feel much better, but fondness for his sister made him smile. "It doesn't matter. We're getting them out of the battle."

His father muttered something under his breath, but the sound of the propellers drowned out his words. Bucky looked back from the pilot's seat. "That's the thing. We weren't expecting to find the ladies."

"What do you mean?" Tobias asked.

Lord Bancroft answered. "We commandeered the aircraft. The Gold King's forces have split and Keating's gone north. We came to give the news to the prince but he's gone after Blue."

"Have you found my father?" Alice asked, her voice tight.

"We think we know where he's gone," Bancroft replied. "And I would very much like to confirm our information."

Tobias could hear the eagerness in his father's voice. Gift wrapping Jasper Keating for the new heir to the throne was one of those rare moves that would make a duke out of a viscount.

"He's put my baby in danger," Alice said, the pain in her words wrenching Tobias's guts. "Please don't hold back because of me."

The dirigible turned, and Tobias caught a glimpse of the wreckage below. His breath nearly stopped. Fire and smoke billowed up from Covent Garden. Blue-white flame bloomed from an aether cannon, ripping through a line of the Gold King's machines. The resulting explosion blew a hole in the Royal Opera House. Then several city blocks northwest of there were flattened, mere crumbs of stone left behind. Two of the rolling spheres from the Blue King's army sat abandoned in the midst of the scene, giving testament as to what had levelled the landscape.

He didn't quite believe what he saw. These were the streets he'd haunted all his life—the places he'd drank and loved and played. Gone. Destroyed. Lost. It was as if all those memories had been ripped from him and trampled. A wave of hatred turned him cold.

Bands of men ran through the ruined streets—mostly rebels and Yellowbacks—sometimes fighting, but more often trying to catch up with the rest of their forces. Bodies and pieces of machinery remained behind, like silt from a receding flood.

"I don't see many Blues here," Tobias said. He could hear Poppy crying softly as she looked out the opposite window, and he thought he might lose his mind. He couldn't stand the thought of her distress.

"There was a split in their ranks," his father replied. "Their command fell apart after the Blue King ran. After that it was easy to push them back east."

"Rumor says there was a turncoat among them," Bucky added. "Blue's own man of business corrupted the troops."

Tobias didn't answer, distracted again by the spectacle out the porthole. It was going to take years, if not decades, to repair the damage from this single day. The dirigible passed over a thick mass of fighting, rebels pushing Yellowbacks north. "Isn't Keating down there in the midst of all that?"

"No," said Alice. "He would stay one step ahead."

"There's what's left of Russell Square," said Tobias. "We're near the Violet Queen's house."

"That's where our informant says Keating's gone. It makes sense. He publicly allied himself with her," Bancroft said, "and she's just the right distance out of the fray."

They touched down on the rooftop of the Grand Caliphate Hotel, a comfortable stroll from the British Museum. The hotel had evidently been abandoned as the battle moved north, but its large, flat roof—one of the first redesigned for the convenience of guests arriving by air—was still accessible. Bucky stayed behind in charge of Poppy and the ship. The others availed themselves of the steam-powered lift to the streets.

Yellowbacks, with their long black coats and outlandish weapons, patrolled the surrounding area looking for anyone remotely resembling a rebel.

Tobias wished Alice would have remained with Poppy, but she had the best chance of talking sense into Keating if they got him in irons. So he offered her his arm and they strode quickly toward the Violet Queen's extravagant home, with Bancroft on Alice's other side. All three of them looked dirty and rumpled, but for once no one was likely to report it in the gossip pages.

They'd nearly reached the corner of the lawn when he saw

a scatter of Steamers parked along the road—a fair collection even for a wealthy neighborhood. Then with some surprise he spotted Michael Edgerton slouching against one of the lamp standards, smoking a cigarette as coolly as if there was no war tearing apart the city.

Tobias's stomach tightened as his old friend turned around, offering a smile. "I wouldn't go any closer," Edgerton said pleasantly. If anyone overheard without quite paying attention, it would have sounded like a cheerful greeting. "My men are already in place. Keating is in there."

Bancroft sucked in air, and Tobias knew what it meant. They'd had Keating's location correct, but others had arrived there first. As he looked around, he saw the dark-clad figures, all but hidden in the shadows.

"By the by," Edgerton said amiably, "good work out there today, Roth. I knew you had it in you."

"But . . ." Alice began, but Tobias put a hand over hers. He could feel distress radiating from her like body heat, but he knew Edgerton. They could count on his help.

"Keating has our boy," he said. "We need him to tell us where he's being held."

"We intend to take him alive," Edgerton said confidently. "These men won't make mistakes."

He'd no sooner said it than the crack of gunfire sounded from the house, then an explosion. The front corner of the house blew outward, a cloud of smoke and dust billowing out with volcanic force. Tobias pushed Alice behind him, his one thought to get her behind cover. The rebels charged the front lawn. Guns leaped from beneath tailcoats. Then the Yellowbacks opened fire.

Alice screamed in shock as one of the rebels flew backward, chest imploding as one of the fearsome rifles blasted through him. Blood and bone splattered the street. Tobias thrust Alice inside the nearest Steamer, wanting steel around her. "Lie down!"

He fumbled for his own weapon, using his left hand. His father scrambled to his side. "Where did Edgerton go?"

Tobias scanned the scene. There was no sign of his friend. "Damned if I know."

Then just as quickly Edgerton was back. "They think Keating's gone, headed south. He got out when the wall blew."

"Damnation!" Tobias cursed. So much for Edgerton's men not making mistakes.

"Go after him!" his father ordered. "I'll stay here. If they're wrong, I've got it covered."

Tobias scrambled for the Steamer as more rebels bore down on the house. The engine of the vehicle was already hot, so Tobias released the brake, jumped the curb, and sped the puffing vehicle through the park across the street, barely managing the job with just one hand.

The jolting brought Alice out of her crouch in the back-seat. "Where are we going?"

"Your father's fled south."

She swore under her breath—something Tobias had rarely heard her do. "He's been ambushed. I know him. He's going to hide in earnest. It's going to be next to impossible to get him into the open again."

"Not if we can catch him first. Where would he go?"

She was silent for a few seconds as she climbed awkwardly into the front seat. "How many men does he have with him?" she asked.

"I don't know. Maybe none."

"He might go to Hilliard House," she said, her voice shaking. "He could take hostages there."

Tobias bumped the vehicle back onto proper road and dialed up the steam. The vehicle shot forward. When he spoke, his voice was tense but reasonable. "I don't think so. He'll try to run to his own men first. This was a nasty surprise, but it's hardly an endgame. Gold still has a good chance of winning this war."

"Then he'll go underground," Alice said with a sudden lift of her head. "Some of his properties have a way out beneath the streets."

Tobias blinked in surprise. "Really?"

"Only he knew about it. I don't think he even told his streetkeepers. The only reason I know is because I used to follow him sometimes."

Tobias looked at her in surprise. She had a way of making him do that. "Do you think he took Jeremy down there?"

"Not for long—they're nothing but tunnels," Alice replied. "They're a way to move around, not to stay. But he could make it back to his army unseen."

"Are you sure?" asked Tobias. "We've already looked at all his properties. He's not there, and the rebels have spies on all of them. There aren't many places he could go, even inside his own territory."

"But there was Uncle Harriman's old warehouse. Almost no one knows it's even there."

"Where's that?" Tobias asked.

"A little way off Bond Street," Alice said, and then quirked a smile utterly lacking in mirth. "You may not have been there, but surely you remember it. There was a goldsmithing workshop beneath it for a while."

THEY LEFT THE Steamer on Bond Street—although it was hard to believe it was the same street he knew. Every one of the businesses was closed and many of the windows were boarded over. A Yellowback with a rifle turned to look as they walked away from the vehicle. Tobias held his breath, but nothing happened. He took Alice's hand. "Where do we go now?"

She led him down a narrow side alley that led to a number of storage buildings. He'd walked past that section of Bond Street a thousand times, with the bakery and the draper's shop, but he'd never realized any of this was behind the tidy storefronts.

Alice approached a run-down wood structure with a rusted automaton parked outside the door. They went first to a side door, but when she rattled the handle, it was secure. "How are you at picking locks?" she asked.

He couldn't hold back a smile. "You've been too much in Poppy's company."

She looked up at him, her face set and determined. "I wish I had her bold spirit to see me through this."

Her mouth set, she marched around to the front where the

automaton stood motionless. If there was any doubt that it was defunct, the amount of bird dung on its head said the boilers had been inactive for a long time. Alice shot it a contemptuous look as she approached to examine the wide double doors.

"I think you're blessed with more than enough spirit," Tobias said, and then his breath caught as a wave of pain ran through him. He tried to hide it, but he wasn't quick enough.

"Tobias?" Alice asked softly. "What's wrong?"

"A bilious attack. Nothing more."

"This is more than a stomachache. You're ill. You've been ill since you went to Dartmoor."

Dread filled him. He didn't want to tell Alice what was wrong. She had too much to shoulder already. "Let's worry about Jeremy first."

Alice tilted her head up to him, the light turning her hair to molten fire. Fine wisps of it curled around her ears, drawing the eye to the fine arch of her cheekbones. He was transfixed by the light dusting of freckles he found there. She was as exquisite as a fine porcelain vase, every line in perfect proportion.

Her brow furrowed. "I'm worried about you, too."

"Alice," he said, sounding plaintive in his own ears. "Please. This isn't the time."

"It never is with you." She pressed her lips together, then thrust out her hand. "Give me your gun."

Chagrined, he surrendered it. Then she took careful aim at the lock of the warehouse door, and fired. The padlock jumped and then fell in pieces to the ground.

"My father was finally right about something," Tobias said after a pause.

"What?" she asked, freeing the last scraps of metal from the hasp.

"I should never underestimate you."

CHAPTER SIXTY-FOUR

INSIDE THE WAREHOUSE, THERE WAS NOTHING BUT EMPTY crates and half-forgotten secrets. The trapdoor beneath the floor creaked open with the smell of mildew and old blood, and Tobias was faced with his first view of the world beneath the streets. A narrow flight of steps led down to a derelict workshop, where worktables and equipment lay under a blanket of dust. He raised the old candle-lantern he'd taken from a table upstairs and held it high, letting the feeble beam beat against the murk. *So this is where it all happened—the forgery scheme to steal the gold from Keating's artifacts.* There had been six perpetrators, including Keating's cousin and the owner of this warehouse, John Harriman. But Bancroft had been the mastermind, and so he was the one the Gold King had blamed.

When Holmes had uncovered the crime, events had fallen like dominoes. Keating had been prepared to ruin Bancroft and his family, which had led to Tobias agreeing to work for the Gold King, which had led to him standing here. It felt as if he'd closed an insidious loop.

The memory of Holmes brought Tobias back to the present, and he thought to look down. The blanket of dust had proved a perfect medium to capture a single set of footprints leading straight ahead. *So he came in the first door we tried, got in with a key, and came down here. He'll have no idea that he's being followed.*

"Look." Alice had followed him down the stairs and now she pointed to the far shadows. Tobias could just make out the faint gleam of old cages, decorated with brass scrollwork like some forgotten menagerie. "I heard they kept the goldsmiths locked away down here. In the end, they were killed and thrown into the river."

Her voice was soft in the still shadows, raising the fine hairs down his neck. There had been thirteen bodies in the end, and those had only been the ones involved in this part of the crime. There had been the maidservant, Grace, and more. He wanted to love his father, but so much made it difficult. "Let's go."

One side of the underground room opened up into a cavern, and they walked toward it, huddled in the lantern light like children from a folktale wandering into the woods. Tension wound up Tobias's spine. He knew little of the Black Kingdom, but he knew enough to be sure that this was their domain. His eyes flicked from shadow to shadow, knowing that what he wanted—or perhaps feared—to see was just beyond the faint bloom of the candle's glow.

"How does your father cross beneath the streets? This isn't his territory," he asked quietly.

"Perhaps he obtained permission."

It wasn't the most satisfying of answers, and he couldn't help looking around for he knew not what. The dark was oppressive, for all the rough rock of the cavern ceiling stretched high above. "If your father knew about this place, how could Harriman hide the goldsmiths down here?"

"But he didn't," Alice frowned. "It was only after, when they gave this place a proper search, that he discovered this passage."

The cavern they were in reached another, vaster hole. The ground was strewn with pebbles, making walking relatively easy, but there was more than one way to go. After a moment of decision, Alice turned right.

"Maybe there is a clue that he came this way?" Tobias began searching the ground and wishing Holmes were there. The detective would find a mote of dust disturbed, or a thumbprint, or—Tobias squinted at a pebble wondering if it looked recently scuffed. He flicked it with his boot and noticed the underside was a paler hue. *That's odd.* He brought the light closer. "Is there water nearby?"

"There is a river. Once Father said it was the Tyburn, I think. I'm afraid I wasn't paying much attention at the time."

Tobias set down the lantern, touching the earth. Having only one working hand made the simplest actions awkward. "The ground is damp here, but this pebble was wet-side up. Something turned it over very recently."

"Then that proves Father came this way."

The admiration in her voice made him ridiculously proud. He didn't bother to point out the stone might have been disturbed by someone else. "Where does this lead?"

"There's a building near Manchester Square."

He rose, feeling pain in every joint. If this was the effect of the poison with Dr. Watson's remedy to counteract it, he didn't want to contemplate the alternative. "Then let's go."

They set off, seeing more signs of the river as they went—a patch of dark water moving within the caverns, and sometimes he could hear the rush of it slipping over stone. There were signs of human habitation as well—brick vaults marking an entrance or exit to the world above. A few were recent, but most were centuries old. Many had been sealed off, some neatly, some with a hodgepodge of brick and stone obviously mortared in haste. Those doorways made Tobias uneasy. What was down here that they had wanted so desperately to contain?

In a few places, the cavern narrowed to passages so thin that they had to pass one at a time. Many of these seemed to angle downward, but after the last such passage, the caverns lost all traces of human engineering. To Tobias, they looked almost like sea caves he'd seen once near Torquay, with stone dribbling from the ceilings in long points like teeth.

Alice's feet slowed, then stopped. "I don't remember this."

Tobias leaned against the cavern wall, conserving his strength. *If we're lost down here, there will be no finding our way out.* Anger bubbled up, but he quashed it. Alice's face was pinched with concentration, her eyes flicking to each landmark in turn. *She will solve this before I do.* He busied himself with fumbling in his pocket for one of their spare candles, lighting it, and squishing it down in place of the one guttering in the lantern. Fresh light bloomed, widening their range of visibility.

"There should be a bridge," she said, pointing. "Ah, look, there it is. We came to this part of the tunnel a little early, that's all."

Relief pushed back his paranoia. "Clever Alice."

Dark smudges shadowed her eyes, but she managed a smile. The sweetness of it brought an ache to his chest, knowing how much it cost her. She had reined herself in with iron self-control, but she was still a mother who had lost her child—and that didn't begin to touch the question of her father, or the war. Her strength staggered him.

He stood, leaving the lantern at his feet. He brushed her cheek with his fingertips. "You amaze me."

Her lips parted, as if in reply, but he kissed her before she could speak. The taste sang through him, muddling in his senses with the still, heavy darkness and the distant sound of water. He deepened the embrace, exploring the sweet warmth of her. He had never embraced the magical, but the moment was ripe with significance, as if they had been stripped down to the bare essentials of themselves.

"Do you think there will be anything left of London when we get back to the sun?" she whispered, as if the question were too dreadful to be spoken aloud.

He wished he could keep her there, and trade the world above for a bed with her in it and all the time to prove himself the husband he'd always wanted to be. But he made himself smile instead. "That depends. I'll probably be out of a job, at any rate."

She wound her arms around his neck. "I want to see what you can do without my father breathing down your neck."

His heart quickened, awakening the pain in his stomach again, but he swallowed it down and let himself dream for an instant, turning the pages of the future like a storybook. "I might be a disaster and land us in poverty. I'm not particularly practical."

She narrowed her eyes. "Leave the money to me. I know my way around a patent application. I'm not entirely ignorant of my father's business, even if *he* doesn't know it."

You would have been the perfect wife. But he stepped back, out of her arms, because otherwise he would shatter. "Then let's cross that bridge and get this little task out of the way."

The look she gave him promised much, but he tried not to see that promise, picking up the lantern and letting her lead the way. His head was spinning slightly, emotion combining with the close atmosphere.

They approached the bridge, and his heart lurched. It was a slab of stone about four feet wide, with no railings. Both edges sloped down, giving it a slight ridge all the way across, though there was plenty of room to walk. It was the chasm underneath that gave Tobias pause. It was around twenty feet across and—at least as far as his eye could perceive—a bottomless rip in the earth.

"Are you sure this is the way?" he asked.

Alice gave a slight, unhappy laugh. "One doesn't forget something like this. The only way to cross it is to just start walking and not look down."

If Keating had crossed, he would do no less. "Then lead on, my lady."

She did, her slight form confident as she began the crossing. But Tobias had gone about six steps when another fit of wet, desperate coughing hit him. Eyes blurred with tears, he pulled out his pocket handkerchief and fought for air, forcing himself not to move his feet as he doubled over. He felt Alice's touch. *No, you should be halfway across by now. Don't risk coming back for me!* But of course, he couldn't speak a word.

"Tobias?" she asked gently once he had finally quieted.

"Just go," he gasped. "I'm all right." And he hid the bloodstains on the handkerchief.

This time, her expression was accusing. But she turned and went, which was what he wanted. He followed after, drained by the fit. It was a mental effort to put one foot before the other, but slowly they progressed across the yawning gap below. When they were three-quarters of the way across, he saw movement on the other side of the bridge.

Tired as he was, at first he thought it was just a trick of his eyes.

He was wrong. It was torchlight. His first impression was of a band of ragged, dark figures with hoods drawn over their faces. Dread shot through him. He'd never seen these creatures, but he'd heard of them. *Wraiths*. They were the soldiers of the Black Kingdom, and they carried an aura of something fearful, like the knowledge of injury just before the strike of pain. Around their knees swarmed a crowd of something—eyeless faces, twisted limbs, and headless things melted into a shadowy pool.

They'd attracted the wrong kind of attention. "Alice!" he said, hoping to warn her.

She saw them the moment he spoke. The sight of the spectral figures startled her enough that she scampered back a few paces, and in doing that she lost her footing on the sloping bridge. She fell backward, skidded, and began to slide toward the edge.

Tobias lunged for her, throwing himself down to stop her fall. He clung to her, all too aware of her heart fluttering beneath his chest. Her gaze met his, wide with alarm, and a protective warmth surged through him, clogging his throat until speech was impossible. He was aware of everything— the hard, sandy surface of the rock beneath them, the soft tickle of her hair against his skin.

"I have you," he said. *As long as there is breath in my body, I'll keep you safe.* "I love you."

And then he felt the pressure of a gun barrel against the back of his head.

CHAPTER SIXTY-FIVE

EVELINA, NICK, AND PRINCE EDMOND WALKED WITH THEIR escorts in silence. The creatures kept their weapons drawn, moving with a whisper of mechanical joints that made Evelina's skin crawl. Her unease was compounded as the air grew stale. She could feel the tunnel dipping, and the sense of the magnetic power of the place increased.

"May I ask how it is that you came to be down here?" the prince finally asked the group's leader. She seemed to be the only one willing to talk.

"Those of us who wished it were made welcome in the underground. At least," she gave an odd shrug that didn't quite move the way it should, "those of us who are mostly sane. All of us sacrificed pieces of our flesh in the laboratories, but some of us gave more."

"Why weren't you in the battle aboveground?" the prince asked.

She turned pale eyes on him. They might have been blue, but in the poor light they looked almost without color at all. "That was the intention of our so-called masters, but there were too many opportunities to escape."

"You could have fought the steam barons."

"Your rebels do not care for us any more than the rest." She held up the hand that was still made of flesh. "Perhaps you yourself do not recoil from our kind, or perhaps you simply cover your disgust well. But not everything changes because of one battle. Win or lose, we are condemned to hide."

The prince looked about to argue, so Evelina jumped in. "I thought the laboratories were there to discover what made magic work. And yet what I saw there looked like experimentation of all kinds." She'd meant to smooth over the conversation, but a low snarl rippled through the entire group.

The woman waved them to silence. "It is a fair question. The barons learned enough to destroy our abilities, but never to replicate them. Lack of progress prompted them to try other things. After all, they had a steady supply of subjects for their testing." She gave Evelina a curious look. "When were you there?"

"I was there the night it was destroyed."

"Ah, you were with Madam Thalassa?"

"Yes."

"That was a blow well struck." The woman's look of satisfaction made her look younger. Once upon a time she might have even been pretty, but suffering had stripped any softness from her features.

The conversation dwindled as the tunnel gave way to a cavern lined with brick. Barrels were stacked against the wall and Evelina thought perhaps it might have once been part of a merchant's cellar. The party came to a stop.

"This is as far as we go," said the woman. "Our job is to patrol the tunnel and bring any who stray beneath the streets to this way station."

"Did you see the Blue King?" Nick spoke for the first time since they'd been captured. His voice sounded strained, and Evelina remembered this wasn't the first time he'd been taken prisoner.

"We do not share information," their captor said. "What you learn from the underground is Lord Fawkes's decision."

"Lord Fawkes?" asked the prince.

The skin on Evelina's back began to creep and she turned. There stood a Wraith with two of the Others cringing at his feet like whipped curs. An aura of fear surrounded him as it did all the Wraiths, making her grow short of breath. It wasn't something she could see or smell, but it writhed around him all the same, turning her stomach to a tight, icy ball.

"I am Fawkes," said the figure in a cultured accent. The voice was the only clue Evelina had about the man. He was tall, dressed in a tailcoat and top hat, but the hat was draped in a black veil that hid his face. The torch he held revealed nothing. "Follow."

The word had the force of a compulsion. Evelina gripped Nick's hand, reluctant to leave the half humans behind. At least she knew they had once been men and women. She wasn't sure about their new guide. She'd always assumed the term "Wraith" was a term of affiliation like "Yellowback," but now she wondered if it might refer to a species.

All conversation ceased as they carried on, the top-hatted Wraith in the lead. The two Others followed behind, more than ensuring that no one tried to leave the procession. Here most signs of the world aboveground dwindled. Vast caverns opened up, revealing dark streams and lakes that never saw daylight. The scent of magic hung everywhere, giving a faint glow to the surface of the rock and sometimes manifesting in fantastic vegetation that had no business growing underground. Strange and disturbing birds clung to the branches, singing like the echo of heartbreak.

But the landscape wasn't the strangest thing there. Evelina caught glimpses of figures darting through the darkness—some humanlike, some not—and felt the presence of ten times that number hiding just out of sight. Her magic reared up, ready to fight as she caught the scent of their predatory interest. It occurred to her that no one had asked for their weapons. Perhaps for these creatures, anything short of an aether cannon simply didn't matter.

It was hard to say how long they'd walked, but Evelina was about ready to drop when they reached a narrow passage in the rock. Lord Fawkes stood aside, signaling for them to proceed.

Nick balked. "What's on the other side of this?"

"Your destination," Fawkes said without emotion. "I shall be right behind you."

Nick looked at Evelina, then pulled her tight, giving her a hard kiss that left her lips hot and aching. Then wordlessly, he pushed through the gap in the stone, turning so his shoulders would pass. She followed, and Prince Edmond after her. The passage was only about eight feet long, but it opened into a vast cavern large enough for the *Athena* to dock twice over. Torches burned along the walls and more wraiths stood at intervals between the flaming lights, their features hidden with hoods and veils. Some of the figures were dressed like Fawkes, in relatively modern clothes. More looked as if they wore the costumes of a bygone age. All had Others crouched like guard dogs at their feet. In the center of the cavern sat a metal throne in the shape of a hand, but the clawed fingers that formed the back said no human had served as its model.

Something was curled around the throne. At first Evelina thought it was simply part of the surrounding stone, but the light caught a gleam as the thing shifted. Nick's breathing quickened and she felt him move to get between her and the uncoiling ropes of muscle and rippling black skin. Evelina caught his shoulder. "Wait," she whispered. "I need to see."

And there wasn't much Nick could have done to protect her as the dragon reared up. Red eyes glittered, but they were bright with an intelligence every bit as old as Athena. Pale horns coiled from the black head, long whiskers trailing from a mouth filled with ivory fangs. The thing wasn't tall, standing only the height of a man, but it was at least twenty feet from nose to tail.

Prince Edmond turned pale. "What . . ."

"Do not speak in the presence of our king!" Lord Fawkes ordered. Then his voice dropped. "Unfortunately, the noise of your war has awakened him. That was not a wise thing."

"The Black King is a dragon?" Edmond breathed.

"Indeed," the Wraith intoned with a touch of sarcasm. "That escapes the notice of so many."

The dragon was clearly the conduit of the ancient power she'd been feeling. How, she could not say, but she suddenly understood that the Black Kingdom was the door through which magic manifested in the land, and the dragon had soaked in that power for thousands of years. Evelina felt it like the brush of fingertips as the serpent glided through the cavern, oddly graceful on its six short legs.

She'd met a fire drake before, but it had been a kind of deva, more an elemental than a literal reptile. There was no mistaking the solidity of this creature, miraculous though it was. She could see a ridge of bony plates along its back, and old, white scars where something had once done battle with it. She could feel the primal hunger for life radiating from it and knew that in some way, through Magnus, she shared its appetites.

But while it moved gracefully, she detected a hitch in its movements that spoke of age and pain. For a moment, it reminded her of Magnus, long past his time. The beast stopped to sniff at each of the Wraiths as it passed, a forked tongue flicking out to taste the air. As it worked their way, Evelina instinctively pressed into Nick's chest, protective and seeking protection.

Edmond inched closer, too. "What's it going to do?"

"Not quite sure yet," Nick said, stiff with tension. He had an arm around Evelina tight enough to ache, but she wasn't about to make him stop.

The dragon stopped, huge head reaching forward to tongue at the prince. *This is the one who would be king above the ground?*

Both Nick and Evelina jumped, hearing the voice in their heads. It sounded like sandpaper and fur—silky and rough at once, and very deep.

"It is, sire," Lord Fawkes replied.

The prince looked confused, but held utterly still as the red tongue flickered close to him. His jaw muscles worked, his expression less afraid than angry. But when the dragon stopped tasting the air before him, the prince bowed, making a perfect courtier's leg. "Fair greetings to the king below the earth."

The dragon snuffed, pawing the earth with one taloned paw. Evelina wondered if that was the equivalent of a laugh. *The princeling has courage and manners. That is well, for as much good as that does him.* The dragon moved stiffly on, stopping at Nick and Evelina next. *A lord of the air and a queen of many kingdoms. My realm grows rich with royalty today.*

The Black King finally turned to Lord Fawkes. *These I would keep for a little while. You have other prisoners, do you not?*

"I do, my king."

Then bring them out. I am weary of waiting for a meal.

A meal? Evelina and Nick exchanged panicked looks. A sound of anticipation rustled through the Wraiths that said they were eager, too. Evelina stiffened and Nick pulled her yet closer, moving to be shoulder to shoulder with the prince. She'd always heard people who wandered too far into the underground never came out. Some might have been recruits like the half humans who had caught them in the tunnel, but the rest, it seemed, might well have ended up dinner. Cold, sweaty fear started to work its way up her spine.

She reached for her magic, wanting it at her fingertips, but the moment she did so, the dragon's head swiveled her way. *Do you truly think yourself a match for me, little mouse?*

Evelina bridled. At least Magnus had compared her to a kitten. She drew on her dark magic, spooling it into her core, ready to strike. And then she regretted her defiance.

The weight of the Black King's power crashed down on her with the brutal indifference of an avalanche. Old and in pain, perhaps, but it still had strength she hadn't even dreamed of. The smack of power was only a warning, but darkness swirled up as if she were about to swoon. Leaning into Nick, Evelina slowly released her magic, letting it slip free until the dragon looked away. As the world righted itself, she set her jaw, refusing to give in just yet. She'd come to count on her power, but a direct assault was foolish. It would take more than brute force to get past such an old and wily foe. They would have to wait and watch for clues to its weakness.

Wraiths vanished through a crude doorway to her left, presumably to check the larder. Evelina caught her breath when they returned with the first prisoners—a mature woman holding an infant. The woman was mute, but the baby was whimpering softly. Nick swore under his breath.

The next made them all murmur in surprise. It was Jasper Keating, his silver head held high, his jaw thrust forward as if ready to fight. The last was King Coal, ranting as he was pushed forward by three trembling Blue Boys. "No. No! I will *not* comply. Whatever it is you think you can accomplish, you great lizard, it will come to nothing! I will bury you down here. I will seal you up like a potted ham until you rot!"

"Will you be quiet!" snapped Keating.

The Blue King smacked the arm of his chair. "Don't order me about, you pomaded idiot. In case you hadn't noticed, this isn't Grosvenor Square."

The dragon shuffled forward, tongue flicking at each of the prisoners in turn. The woman and babe interested it little. Its attention lingered longer on Keating, but when he reached King Coal the dragon's tail gave a flick. And then it snapped, jaws plucking the fat man from the chair.

Evelina barely saw the sudden motion. Then she gasped. They might have chased the Blue King through London, and he might have killed most of their company, but instinct made all three of them lurch forward.

Fawkes thrust out an arm. "I wouldn't interrupt his meal." His voice slammed her to a stop. It seemed to reach deep into Evelina, freezing her limbs. All of a sudden, it wasn't possible to move, not even to reach for her power. "My advice is for your own good, of course."

Keating and the woman holding the baby were pulled aside, but the three servants of the Blue King were herded forward from behind the mechanized chair. And then the Wraiths surged forward with an excited murmur, closing in like a pack of hyenas, clearly waiting for their king to eat his fill so they could feast.

The Black King dropped his prize to the ground and trapped King Coal beneath his claws. Then he tore away a chunk of flesh, tossing it down his gullet like a bird with a fish. Evelina caught a glimpse of red gore and yellow fat and turned to bury her face in Nick's shoulder, too shocked even to feel sick. *He's not even dead yet.* The screams and wet, slippery sounds twisted inside her, cracking open a whole new layer of horror.

Make it stop! The plea was almost wordless, any sound lost beneath the chaos of carnage.

But Nick somehow heard her. "Evelina." He took her face

in both hands, tipping it up so that the most natural thing was to meet his gaze. His eyes were dark and liquid in the shifting light. "Look at me. My love is the only thing in this room, and it's all yours. Think about that. Only that."

Her breath shuddered in, shuddered out. She wanted to be deaf, or perhaps able to crawl out of her skin and flee—anything to not be there. But Nick's eyes held her, giving her refuge, a lifeline that held her secure from the horror.

He lowered his head, giving her his lips. His kiss was warm and raw, salty with the sweat and smoke of battle. His hands slipped to her waist, his touch fierce with need. All the yearning they shared welled up, and suddenly she was airborne a thousand miles from this place. Her heart unfolded, her chest suddenly free. She tasted the heat of his breath, living and real and nothing to do with darkness. Nick had power, but this was the spell he had over her.

"We're going to get out of here," he whispered.

Her soul leaped to believe.

But in the next moment, they heard a gibbering howl swirl up from the Wraiths. Evelina turned at Nick's indrawn breath. They had brought fresh prisoners.

CHAPTER SIXTY-SIX

TOBIAS STEPPED INTO THE PRESENCE CHAMBER AT THE heart of the Black Kingdom. His eyes took in a handful of details—the fresh kill on the floor, the sharp-toothed Wraiths lapping at the blood, their deathly white faces finally exposed as they fed. Beyond them were the red glowing eyes of a monster, enough to make any man weak with terror. But he had gone to a place far beyond fright—and he'd gone there long before this moment.

For now he knew precisely what the Black Kingdom was. From the bridge, he and Alice had been bound and marched through the underground wilderness until they'd come to a waterway. There, they'd been thrown onto a flat-bottomed boat that had brought them here, the Wraiths using long poles to guide the craft through the sluggish black water. From the boat, he'd seen creatures no mortal was meant to discover—tentacled, eyeless things in the water, half-human creatures hanging upside down from the roofs of the great caverns, man-wolves and white-skinned women with fangs. This was the kingdom of nightmare, and death seemed the only means of waking up.

He'd held Alice as best he could, his heart breaking as her composure finally shattered into tears. All he had asked of Fate was that she survive and go free, but he was far from sure now that his wish would be granted. He would have to fight for her and, hell, he didn't have a lot to lose.

She was behind him now, head bowed in stupefied silence. Tobias took another step forward, racking pain making him feel oddly disembodied, as if he were really floating just above the ground. The dragon lifted its head, tongue flicking out to mop up a smear of blood from its snout. *Dragon?* He nearly burst into a hysterical laugh. After all the bullets, bombs, and magnetic aether he'd survived that day—not to forget the Scarlet King's poison—and he was about to die by dragon. No one could ever accuse him of taking the conventional path to a gruesome death.

"Tobias!"

He looked over to see Evelina, Captain Niccolo, and— dear God—the man they were calling Prince Edmond. "What are you doing here?"

The instant he spoke, a baby began to cry. The sound, all too familiar, speared through him. "Jeremy!"

Oblivious to the guards, Alice sprang from behind him and raced to her child and Mrs. Polwarren. He moved to follow, but a magnetic aether rifle poked him in the chest. "Stay where you are," the Wraith said.

But Tobias barely heard, the implications of Jeremy's presence crashing home. The dragon was watching Alice sob over her child. Tobias couldn't read lizard faces, but he thought he caught a glint of speculation in those red eyes. Too many people he loved were in the room, and in peril. He glanced around, afraid to see more.

Then Tobias noticed Keating. "You evil bastard," he snarled with a vehemence that surprised even him.

But the Gold King looked too shaken to care. "Don't waste your breath on me, boy. That *thing* just ate the Blue King and three of his men."

Inexorably, Tobias's eyes returned to the stain on the floor. There were bits in the gore—inedible buckles and scraps of bone—but the only thing he recognized was the steam-driven chair shoved into the shadows. King Coal had been a huge man, and for any creature to eat him and three others beggared the imagination. Tobias had a fleeting thought about greasy food and indigestion, but it vanished as the monster rose and began moving his way. "What is it? Why isn't anyone killing it?"

"Because it's the Black King," Keating returned, his voice grim.

The dragon's tongue flicked his way. With what seemed

like prudence, Tobias fell to one knee and bowed his head. The tongue flicked again, this time touching his face.

Death sits upon you, said a voice in his head.

Tobias looked up sharply. "What's going on?"

Yes, you hear me. The Black King's eyes gave a lazy blink. *You are close enough to the realm of spirit for me to speak with you.*

Rage shot through Tobias. "No!"

Why deny it?

Because he never wanted anything to do with magic. Because he wanted to be home in his bed with Alice, making up for everything he'd never got right. But the clock that measured his life was winding down, every tick weaker than the last. He felt Alice's eyes on him, questioning. Loving. Hot tears burned in his eyes, but he refused to let them fall. This creature hadn't earned the right to see his weakness.

A rueful chuckle rippled through his mind. *Do you know what it is to be old, Mr. Roth?*

"No, Your Majesty." *And I never will.* He furtively glanced about the room, which was largely unfurnished but for the throne on its dais. Though Tobias had seen gaslights elsewhere, this room was still caught in a time before industry. Torches were thrust into sconces along the walls. The Wraiths had ended their feeding frenzy and stood motionless in a regular circle around the perimeter, puddles of squirming shadows about their feet.

Old age is when some ambitious peddler of coal lands in your home and proclaims himself your master. He thinks it is the shiny, steaming toys he owns that makes him king. Blue King. Gold King. Scarlet King. What do they know of kingship?

Tobias bowed his head again. "Your Majesty, are you not also a member of the Steam Council?" Then he recalled that the Black Kingdom was always represented by proxy. Now he knew why.

I was here long before the first machines. My only requirement was that I be left in peace, but your war shook me from my sleep. So I had the tunnels blocked and my servants deployed to bring the remaining barons my way. If they cannot solve their differences, I will do it for them.

A wave of pain made Tobias giddy. "Devouring the opposition is a tactic I honestly hadn't considered."

The dragon gave an amused blink. *Why are you here?*

"The Gold King stole my child."

So it seems, but your search is over now.

It was, but not the way he would ever have imagined it, with his wife and child in even more peril than before. He cursed himself for letting Alice accompany him, even though he well knew that wasn't his decision to make. Misery and fury claimed him, bringing on another heaving, wet cough. "All I want is for my family and friends to go free," he gasped at the end of it.

We don't always get what we want, Mr. Roth.

Bitterness made him foolish. "What could you possibly want that you don't have?"

Tobias felt, rather than saw, the Wraiths and their pets drawing closer. Anxious, he began to rise, the sickness in his body suddenly roiling to the fore. Pain shot up from his gut, leaving him sweating and breathless. Blind terror jumped along his nerves as the Wraiths seized him, hard hands crushing flesh against bone. He heard Alice and Evelina cry out, but the sound was distant. The burning eyes of the Black King consumed his mind.

What do I want? I am a creature of another age, Mr. Roth. I am the last of my kind. No one else walked beneath the new sun, when fire was a marvel and men lived like a lesser kind of wolf. No one remembers the songs or the sorrows of that age. I have changed with the endless roll and churn of time, but after so long, the will frays like old silk. I have been the object of fear and veneration. The race of Man has worshipped me, and they have reviled me. I have been dishonored, tricked and cast down to these depths. I no longer wish for anything new, so I sleep. But sleep is forever interrupted by the antics of children. I want forgetfulness. I want abdication. Death is the only true peace, and it is one I am denied.

"Death is not as pleasant a prospect as it sounds," Tobias growled.

You do not value it.

"I'm not ready." Pain made his voice sharp.

Few ever are, Mr. Roth.

"I would fight for those I love."

What would you trade for your wife and child?

"Let the other prisoners go and you can have what you want of me."

And if what I want is to taste your death?

Fresh terror made him flinch against the Wraiths' iron grip. He heard the dragon's words, but they made no sense. A thousand questions battered against his fading will until, with his last scrap of strength, he pushed the confusion away.

He was instantly calmed. The details didn't matter. Saving his family did. If surrender was his final card to play, his last weapon to save them, so be it. "Then consider my death yours."

Very well, Tobias Roth. Are you prepared?

Agony racked him, bowing his back until he heard bones crack. *Why not?* He could no longer speak, but he somehow felt the Black King understand his thought.

One of the Wraiths pulled out a long and evil-looking knife, but it was as nothing next to the dragon's talons.

EVELINA'S GORGE ROSE. She was certain she would pass out and clung to Nick with clammy fingers. Her mind couldn't grasp what she was seeing, and wouldn't accept that there was nothing she could do.

"Remove the others!" said Lord Fawkes, sweeping a hand toward the archway. "The king is at work."

The Wraiths surged forward. Alice screamed again, the baby's wails multiplied by his mother's terror. Evelina plunged toward Tobias.

"Evelina, wait!" Nick leapt after her, grabbing her elbow. "You're going to get yourself killed!"

He was probably right, yet she refused to turn away. She'd

felt Tobias's illness at Baskerville Hall, but had not fully understood it at the time. Now she could sense his death hovering, too near for any healing magic to help him—but loss and grief insisted she be there at his side. "Tobias!"

"Silence!" Lord Fawkes demanded. "Get back with the rest."

But Evelina wasn't moving, so neither was Nick. She could just see into the tight circle around Tobias. The Black King was so close that his breath stirred his hair, and one wickedly curved claw was pressed to the hollow of his throat. Tobias cried out in agony, twisting against the pain as his flesh succumbed to the Scarlet King's poison. He was dying. The only question was whether the dragon or the toxins would get to him first.

"Evelina!" Nick said again, grabbing her elbow. "What are you thinking? Because if you're seriously planning to take on the entire Black Kingdom, I need to know."

"I need to stop this!" She needed Tobias alive. She needed everyone out of there safely. But the dark magic she felt coursing through the dragon was enormous—too much for her to fight. She had to use her wits, not spells. "My lord king," she cried out, "if you have superior magic, do you not have superior powers to heal?"

I do, but why would I do such a thing? Do not look for mercy from me.

"Why not show mercy? What about building alliances? Working with the rest of the Empire? What about governing your realm?" She heard the Wraiths stirring, but she couldn't tell if that was good or bad.

My realm? This is the pit where all the outcasts are flung, away from the sun and the sight of Man. Once I ruled empires. Now I am the steward of the dung heap. There was no missing the sourness in his tone. *I was tricked into this realm by your ancestors, little mouse. Do not mistake me for a friend.*

"But you're the conduit of all the magic here. You have immense power."

I am but the lightning rod the power uses to enter this

world. That is why I have lived so long. The power of the underground needs a king to be its avatar.

Evelina licked her lips. As long as the dragon was talking, Tobias lived. She seized on another question. "What would happen if you weren't here?"

My power would shatter and the Black Kingdom would fall. Those who dwell beneath the streets would be free to roam in the world above.

Evelina quailed. The creatures would be loosed upon London? That wouldn't end well. "But—"

Remove her! the Black King commanded. *I will have peace while I eat.*

Lord Fawkes was suddenly in her way, forcing her back at knifepoint. "The king demands silence."

Ignoring Fawkes's weapon, Nick stepped between them, putting a hand against the Wraith's chest. "Would you care to think about where you're pointing that blade?"

Taking advantage of the distraction, Evelina pushed past Fawkes and thrust herself nearer to the dragon, reaching for the creature's aura of power. She had a half-formed notion that she might be able to steal its stronger magic and use it as her own. But then the dragon's claws plunged home, and Tobias gave a final roar of agony. As she felt his life flutter, Evelina screamed her fury.

Sight, sound—all sensation from the physical plane left her. What remained was the shifting vision of power in her mind's eye. The dark fog of the Black King's magic consumed Tobias's life, swallowing it down like mist blotting out a star. *Stop it!* she raged, thrusting her power at the beast. It bounced off like pebbles against a mountain.

You interfere, came the Black King's voice. It was the booming of the ocean in sea caves, as old and worn as the rock itself.

I have the right. He is dear to me.

For the first time, she felt the tug of curiosity in the beast. *Who are you?*

While the Black King had taken her measure before, this time it was more than a cursory flick of the tongue. His mind drilled into hers with the force of one of the Gold

King's war machines. *I am Evelina Cooper. I have put magic into machines. I destroyed Her Majesty's Laboratories and the sorcerer Magnus. I have fought against the Steam Council.*

And this gives you the right to raise your magic against me? The dragon sounded amused, but sleepy now, as if a full stomach took the edge off its concentration. *You are just a beginner.*

There was barely a spark remaining of Tobias's life. Evelina grabbed that sliver of light and held on. The dragon was consuming not just his body, but also the essence that held the spice and sweetness of his death. She couldn't let that happen. Nothing would remain of his soul, not even scraps enough to haunt her.

Tears burned Evelina's face. Whatever had happened between them, she still loved Tobias—no longer as the man she would marry, but now as an old and comfortable tenderness. They'd come so far together, and Evelina yearned to see him happy. To lose him now would be a defeat her universe could not abide. But all that was left of him was a guttering flame.

Then Evelina was roughly hauled away as the Wraiths circled their master. Bound to Tobias, she felt the slice of flesh from bone as his mortal flesh was destroyed. The huge fangs of the Black King bit deep, then the sharp knives and needlelike teeth of the Wraiths. Bones broke with white-hot torment, and the flame of life sputtered, but Evelina would not surrender. Screams ripped from her as she thrashed against the Wraiths, agony blowing past whatever controlling magic they possessed.

Desperate, she wove her dark power into a binding, winding it protectively around the scrap of Tobias's life, feeding magic to the embers of him like tiny bits of kindling. Weaker than the Black King's, her own power was subtle enough to sustain life, but not enough to rebuild it. For that, she reached deep into the dragon, to the magic that filled the Black Kingdom like smoke, and fed it into her spell.

But the dragon wasn't willing to share its power. It slammed back against her, buffeting against her with the force of a gale. Evelina braced herself, shielding Tobias as she pulled more and more from the beast to protect the flickering scrap of life. It was power such as she'd never seen—such as she was sure Magnus would have taken for himself—but she didn't need it. Tobias did.

How did you find your way through my defenses? Snarling, the dragon stopped feeding and turned its attention to her. She didn't know the exact answer, but before the creature could react, she lunged for the center of its magic, yanking free great chunks of it and packing it around Tobias's life force.

Stop! the dragon thundered, smashing her down. It was a blow meant to pulverize, but she let the force take her, offering no resistance. Still, it crushed her consciousness to the point of agonizing pain.

No! Summoning what strength she still possessed, her power surged forward, ignoring the danger to seize upon the core of the dragon's essence. *You* must *help my friend!*

But the beast was having none of it, and crashed into her again, twisting violently against her magic's hold. Something tore, and for an instant she wasn't sure which one of them it was, but a blinding flash exploded in her mind, leaving a sensation of searing heat.

She was snapped back to reality by a roar such as she had never heard. It filled the cavern, the sound kneading against the stone walls like something thick and elastic. She covered her ears, dropping to her knees and curling into a ball until her bones stopped vibrating. Blinking stupidly, she uncoiled one degree at a time. The memory of pain had left her rubber-limbed and weak, even if it was not her own.

She pushed herself up on an elbow and saw Nick face-down on the ground. Shocked back to herself, she scrambled over to him. "Nick?"

Keating's voice slid out of the shadows. "Lord Fawkes knocked him down. Your pirate is a good fighter, but no match for a Wraith. Nonetheless I do not think he is badly hurt."

Since Nick's pulse and breathing were fine, she decided that Keating was telling the truth. "Weren't you locked up?"

"The Wraiths never made it that far before they were tempted back to the spectacle out here. They left us to fend for ourselves against the inmates of this pit."

"Where's Edmond?"

"The fool prince is guarding my daughter, thinking I'm going to collect you and Captain Niccolo so that we can all escape together. I'll bet you a shilling which one of us will survive to rule the Empire."

"So why aren't you running?"

"Your pirate has something of mine. We're overdue for a chat about stolen property."

"Athena!" Evelina sucked in her breath, trying to steady herself to face this new threat.

Keating gave a derisive snort. "Indeed. I suppose I should thank him for revealing what it can do."

She rose slowly, glancing at the Black King's bulk. The great serpent had fallen to its side, shudders running through it. Wraiths were scattered on the floor, still as death. Blood seeped in a pool near its head.

"I wouldn't look too closely. There's not much left of my son-in-law."

A sound escaped Evelina's throat, remembering the slice of fang in flesh. "Did he . . ."

"Bedtime snack." Keating's voice was hoarse with disgust. "It put them to sleep. All that poison is bound to give the lizard nightmares."

But it wasn't poisoned nightmares the beast was having. She'd somehow hurt it, and the Wraiths along with it. She guessed the vampirelike creatures were tied to the dragon through shared magic, and whatever damage she'd done to the Black King had shocked them, too.

Keating stepped forward, holding one of the Wraith's weapons. Evelina quickly stepped between him and Nick.

The Gold King's yellow eyes were both angry and amused. "How did you get away from Dartmoor?"

"Magnus. In the end, I killed him," she said bluntly. There was no time to waste on a battle of words. Besides protecting Nick, she needed to save Tobias—if there was enough left of him to save. The flicker of his life was cupped in her magic like an egg in a nest, but it wouldn't survive long. She could feel it fading already, dragged away piece by piece into the source of the dark magic as she wasted time on the Gold King. Anxiety made her heart race, leaving her slightly breathless.

Keating made a noise of distaste. "Good riddance to the sorcerer, but that leaves you. We had an agreement, but it's clear you can't be trusted."

"Me?" But she stopped there. Enumerating the ways Keating had betrayed her loved ones would take all night—and right now she simply needed him to be quiet and go away.

"You."

He raised the weapon—or started to. Impatient, Evelina raised a shield, slamming it into him with the force of a frying pan. He flew backward, a blast of blue fire shooting toward the ceiling. She almost enjoyed his look of surprise, but it didn't last. Staggering, he caught himself and took aim again.

But by then Evelina had rushed him. There was no time for bargaining and finesse. She was fighting for people she loved. She grabbed Keating's coat with both hands, pulled him close, and unleashed the dark hunger. It rose on a wave of anger, smoky and hot, and she made no effort to hold it back. Keating had no idea what to do. He was lost the moment she touched him.

There was no resistance, not like there had been with Magnus, and no uncertainty. This was retribution. It was for the thousands of lives broken for want of clean water, or heat, or medicine. It was for the *Red Jack* and the thousands of dead she had seen that day. It was for Nellie Reynolds and all the lives lost in Her Majesty's Laboratories. It was for Nick, and Tobias, and Jeremy, and Alice. And it was for her.

She took no pleasure as Keating fell dead to the ground at her feet, but the world seemed a fraction cleaner. And then she turned and threw up.

There wasn't much in her stomach, but it still seemed to take forever to vent her revulsion. Some of it was simply the thought of any iota of Keating inside her, but more of it was that she'd done too much magic that day. Overfilled and overstretched, her power spilled over, tipping and splashing like an imaginary cup. Every nerve in her body jumped, sending more bolts of pain and nausea through her gut. Flashes of light speared her vision, dazzling her until she didn't know if she knelt or stood or had collapsed utterly to the floor. When she reeled forward, she felt the brush of Keating's sleeve against her hand and she shrank back, repelled by even the dead shell of his being.

And then, horribly, she lost her grip on Tobias. She grabbed for that last glitter of light, but it was like darting to catch a glass before it fell. Her magic brushed it, but she was too late. A piece of her heart went with him as he sank into the darkness, pulled down by the primal magic she'd tried to use to save him. A final stab of sorrow doubled her over.

"I'm sorry," she whispered. She had power, but it hadn't been enough. The Black King's estimation of her as a mouse was completely true.

When the spasms finally stopped, Nick was stirring. She was empty, scraped hollow as an eggshell and just as vulnerable. Thought and emotion had deserted her. Wiping her mouth on her sleeve, she rocked back on her heels, trembling and cold. When she had enough control over her limbs, she went to Nick's side and helped him to sit.

"Keating?" he asked.

"Dead."

He squeezed his eyes shut and gave a slow nod, holding his head. "About damned time."

Evelina wrapped her arms around Nick, pulling him as close as she could. She needed his warmth and the rough brush of his cheek as never before. Tears leaked from her eyes.

"Hey," Nick whispered. "What's wrong?"

"I couldn't save him."

He stroked her hair. "I'm sorry. But you tried above and beyond what anyone else could have."

She gave a shuddering sob, but swallowed back her tears. There would be time enough to weep later, but they were still in a dangerous place. Tobias's face, and smile, and the sound of his cries flickered beneath the surface of her mind like a river beneath ice, threatening to crack her apart.

Nick got to his feet, pulling her up with him. "What's wrong with the king and his Wraiths?"

"We fought." Her numbed magic groped to read the dragon's life force, feeling like a limb that had gone to sleep. She was just able to touch the Wraiths' auras. They were weak, but alive. The Black King was another story. The dragon had yearned for death, and it had got its wish. Immortal did not mean invincible, especially when its will to live had worn away. "We fought, and we both lost."

Nick's eyes widened, but his only response was to slide an arm around her. They could both feel the magic of the place already weakening. "We need to leave," he said.

For an instant, she remembered what the dragon had said about the underground needing a king to keep its denizens in check—but she was too tired to hold onto the warning. It slipped away from her, carried off in the torrent of her sorrow.

"What about Tobias? We can't just leave him here." She was starting to sob, horror giving way to grief.

Nick pulled her close. "Think of it this way. He has an entire kingdom for his grave."

CHAPTER SIXTY-SEVEN

Unknown

IMOGEN FINISHED REPAIRING BIRD'S EYE, WIPING THE LAST smudge of glue from the creature's brass hide. Bird blinked, cocking its head this way and that, then bobbing up and down with pleasure.

"Can you see?" Imogen asked.

Good as new.

"Hurrah!"

But I'd like to know why it is that every time I go on one of these adventures, I'm the one who requires reassembly?

Perhaps it is a commentary on your intelligence, proficiency, or skill level? Mouse suggested.

I don't take criticism from a rat.

Nor I from a creature that tastes best dredged in flour and submerged in a vat of boiling oil.

"Gentlemen, please!" Imogen cried. She was glad they were back to normal, but their bickering was growing tiresome.

You're quite right, said Mouse. *We need to discuss next moves.*

They'd seen no sign of Anna for what felt like days—although it was hard to tell exactly how long it had been since she'd rescued Bird. There had been enough time to visit Evelina, and then later slip into Poppy's dreams. That had been—interesting. Her little sister's sleep had been so restless, it was all Imogen could do to deliver her message about Evelina before Poppy bolted upright in bed, sending Imogen reeling back to the clock. That was a far cry from the Poppy she knew who required nothing short of wild horses to part her from her pillow. Why was she so on edge?

The only way Imogen would find out was by going home, and for that she would have to draw Anna out. "Nothing is going to happen unless she thinks she can catch me alone."

Do you want us to hide? Bird asked.

"No," Imogen said slowly, hating what she was going to say next. "I need you to go home. I have to finish this myself."

London, October 16, 1889

HILLIARD HOUSE

9:05 p.m. Wednesday

POPPY WATCHED AS Bucky finished screwing the tiny mechanical door to the side of Magnus's clock. It was made from whatever he could find at Hilliard House, because getting back to his workshop after delivering Poppy and Lord Bancroft wasn't an option, especially with the fighting coming so close.

By that night, the battle had clearly turned in the prince's favor, but communication had become sketchy. Some said the prince had disappeared. Others that he was in the palace. Still more had seen him in Cavendish Square, near Tobias's home. The last report made her the most curious. There had been no sign of Keating, Tobias, Alice, or Jeremy and Mrs. Polwarren.

Poppy was more than happy to have Bucky there. Tobias had said plenty of times how he was good in a fight, and she figured her big brother would know. Plus, she needed Bucky to make the door. It might have seemed a strange request after all that had happened that day, but he hadn't given it a second thought. It was for Imogen, after all.

Bucky stepped back from the clock. "There. Is that how you wanted it?"

"Show me how it works."

He pushed a button on the frame of the door. It popped open, showing an opening cut through the side of the clock.

"Brilliant," said Poppy. Madam Thalassa had told her to guard the door, but she'd found it a difficult thing to visualize. Having a lot of imagination was all very fine, but she'd kept changing the door from an ordinary front door to a castle gate to the bronze masterpiece she'd seen in a book of Italian cathedrals. If Poppy's participation *actually* mattered—and it wasn't just Madam Thalassa making her *feel* as if she were helping—she needed to settle on one door and stick with it. After all, how was Imogen supposed to find something that kept changing?

Bucky looked down at her, his eyes tired and sad. "Did I tell you I dreamed of her?"

Poppy nodded. "You gave her what she needed. And now you're doing it again."

"How do I know it wasn't just me wanting her back so hard I invented it?" His voice sounded lost.

Poppy's heart squeezed. He'd been with her father, dodging the enemy and risking his hide to get Tobias's equipment to the rebels. Bucky was smart and brave, but when it came to Imogen he was as fragile as spun glass. "Because when she came to my dream I wrote to Mr. Holmes, and he found Evelina because of what Imogen said. It's real, Mr. Penner, and you've made her a door to get home."

He looked down, nodding. "I'm going to go sit with her for a while."

Poppy touched his arm as he left, feeling oddly maternal. She watched as he went down the hall and turned into Imogen's doorway. The house was deathly quiet, everyone subdued and waiting for news, good or bad, of the prince and his army. Behind her, the clock ticked like the countdown to doom. She sank to the floor, not caring if her mother caught her like that. After everything that happened, dirty hems were of no interest. She fished in her pockets, pulling out the metal forms of Mouse and Bird and warming them in her hands. She'd had the feeling all day that it was time for their adventure to be done.

Resting her head against the clock, she felt the deep *tock-tock* resonate through her skull. She imagined the open door and wondered what it would look like from the other side if she were small enough to walk through it. The view down the stairs would be rather odd, given that Bucky had put the door about five feet up. The first step out would be extreme, but disembodied spirits would probably manage . . .

And then her imagination was inside the clock, with all its moving gears, and she felt a malevolent breath on her neck. It rippled over her scalp, leaving a tingling at the tips of her ears. She wished she had a sword, or an aether weapon, or anything besides her own weak hands to fight with. She backed up until she was braced in the doorway, ready to jump herself if need be. Mouse and Bird rushed her way and she reached out to help them. They had to get home safely— that was her role to play—but more than that, more than the nightmare of getting trapped inside the clock, she was terri- fied of what might get out. Once again, she felt the dribble of cold terror down her back.

"Hurry!" she screamed, poised to fling herself into ac- tion.

And jolted back to herself, wondering if she had really cried out. Her heart hammered as if she'd just woken from a nightmare and she had that same disoriented feeling of being inside her body and yet not. Poppy shook herself, set- ting the toys down and wiping her clammy palms on her skirts. The clock ticked calmly behind her and no one was pounding through the house, so she suspected that she hadn't actually screamed.

Thank heavens for that. Everyone was hysterical enough as it was.

Poppy heaved a sigh, thinking about her mother weeping, the servants fainting, and whatever else might have oc- curred. War, mayhem, and mediums aside, she really did live too much in her fantasies. Maybe it was time to get at least a little bit serious about life.

And then Bird opened its wings in a flash of crystal and brass, and launched into the air. Mouse sprang into motion, clambering over Poppy's ankle, and scampered down the hall toward Imogen's room.

Poppy sprang to her feet, hiked up her skirts, and ran. Serious was for people who didn't have adventures.

THE CLOCK FELT unspeakably hostile without Mouse and Bird, but Imogen was done waiting. She wandered aimlessly through it, so used to the precipitous drops by now that she hopped from walkway to platform with barely a look down. She took risks, leaving herself exposed in the hopes that it would tempt Anna to jump from behind a gear with murderous intent. This insane adventure had to simply *end*.

Perhaps her impatience was an excuse for Anna to draw things out longer, because nothing changed. Time dragged on as meaninglessly as before.

Annoyed, Imogen flopped on the velvet-covered rack that housed the tubes of aether. She closed her eyes, letting the incessant ticking of the clock hypnotize her into a stupor. "I want to go home, Anna," she said dully, doubting her sibling was even nearby to hear. "Why don't we get this over with?"

As she lay there, eyes closed, the ticking pounding in her brain, she became aware of a sound that didn't belong with the others. *Tick, tick, tick,* skrick, *tick,* skrick . . .

Imogen's eyes snapped open. A pair of feet dangled just above her. She scrambled to her feet, stumbling back for a better look. Anna—dressed just like her, of course—was hanging from the beam above, a rough rope twisted around her neck. The face was mottled a ghastly hue, the tongue protruding. Imogen cried out in disgust. "What is this?"

The corpse started to laugh, the distorted features leering down. "Isn't this what you're begging for, sister?"

"Yes," Imogen snapped. "I'm *done* with you."

"Oh, poor, frustrated Im. Are you sure I can't be redeemed? Forgiven? Absorbed back into your soul like some missing piece that's wandered off?"

Imogen didn't respond.

"Isn't it all about enduring?" Anna taunted. "You'll fight back, but never like you mean to make it stick. You're the peacemaker, the good girl, the one who sees the good in everyone."

Imogen wasn't sure that was true anymore, but she was too tired of the whole business to argue. "Whatever you say, Anna."

"Not even a wee little protest? Some show of spirit? You're no entertainment today."

The dead body vanished, and Imogen groaned. Was that how it was going to be now? Just brief episodes of mockery?

She slumped back to the velvet, her head on her knees. Maybe she could escape into another of Bucky's dreams. Maybe she could make it last awhile, and just rest in his arms. It would be easier than grinding through this non-sense. *No. You can't escape. You have to see this through if it means taking the clock apart gear by gear to corner her.* A tear slid out from under her lashes. She felt like a trapped animal slowly turning vicious, and she didn't like knowing that much anger was inside her, but she could feel it rising like a storm-swollen river and was more than a little afraid of what it would do.

A cold wind pulled at her clothes, making her shudder. Imogen lifted her head in surprise, then gasped in shock. The clock was gone, and she was sitting on cold stone steps, looking out at an alpine winter view. It looked like their old home in Austria, which had been a castle perched on a mountainside just like this. Imogen looked up, not wanting to be right—but she was. The black stone edifice was all too familiar, and the topmost tower was where Anna had been locked up and died.

Imogen got to her feet, her shoes slipping on the icy steps. "This is an illusion, Anna! I refuse to be entertaining for you."

And yet . . . Imogen gazed out at the landscape, feeling its power. Her childhood home had been beautiful, even if it was the fertile ground where the seeds for all their tragedies had been sown. Maybe it was fitting that things ended there. At least she didn't have to listen to the wretched ticking.

She turned to ascend, but lost her footing on the ice and stumbled down a few steps. Grabbing the stone handrail, Imogen began to climb more carefully, wondering what horrors Anna had for her inside. She'd always wondered whether the place had a dungeon.

When she reached the top of the stairs, the double doors of the castle swung wide. Imogen approached the threshold, already lost in memories of the place. They'd had a huge, shaggy black dog, and between banquets Papa had turned the great hall into his workshop, with sawdust littering the flagstones. There had been happy times here and there.

But Anna had ignored all their true history. As Imogen crossed the threshold, she beheld a brocaded fantasy of banners and tapestries and still, silent pages with long trumpets raised to their lips.

Anna's voice came from behind her. "Do you like it? You always were the good little princess, whereas I was the interesting one."

Imogen spun. Anna was wearing a tall, pointed hennin with a cloth-of-gold veil, her gown of peacock silk embroidered with silver stars. Her gray eyes were as flat as ever.

"What do you want, Anna?" Imogen snarled, her voice barely like her own. "It's bad enough this isn't real, but it's not even a ghost of our past."

As soon as she spoke, the image collapsed, leaving nothing but a heap of silks on the floor. Unnerved, Imogen took a few steps forward and kicked the cloth on the floor. She half expected something nasty to run out—spiders or snakes—but nothing.

Imogen considered. Anna's anger was over her death, so there was only one logical place for this to play out. Without wasting another moment, she began looking for the door to the highest tower in the castle, where Magnus had trapped Anna's soul.

Unfortunately, the castle wasn't quite as she remembered it. It was oddly disproportionate, with the doorknobs too high up as if from a child's perspective. She found the first set of stairs going up, but had a hard time with the second, as if Anna hadn't been sure where they were supposed to be. The next two floors were like a treasure hunt, each one lined with a series of doors leading to empty rooms. *These were*

*the servants' quarters. Anna would barely remember these
at all.*

But eventually she found the low, humped doorway that
led to the tower stairs. They would originally have been
used by soldiers defending the mountain pass below, but Dr.
Magnus had claimed the tower for his own during the time
he'd stayed with the Roth family. Later, her parents had
made it Anna's sickroom until she died. Imogen had fuzzy
memories of this tower, but Anna had provided minute detail, from initials scratched into the stone by long-dead lov-
ers, to a dead spider in the corner of the winding stairs.
Imogen wondered how much was fact, and how much was
Anna's imagination.

At the top of the stairs she found an arched wooden door
into the tower room. She grasped the old iron ring and
pushed. It swung open with a sepulchral creak, showing an
empty room with whitewashed walls. The stone floor was
painted with symbols, and Imogen remembered her father's
tale of how he'd found Magnus with Anna's twisted body,
and the crude automaton where he'd imprisoned her essence
in lonely darkness.

Pity wrung Imogen. For all that the seeds of Anna's insanity had begun in the cradle, what had happened to her
hadn't been fair. But it didn't make Imogen's will to live any
less.

She stepped across the threshold, the knife Evelina had
given her in her hand. The round room was ringed with
pointed windows, chill sunlight spilling through with diamond brilliance. It was cold enough that Imogen could see
her breath, and she began to shiver, but fear kept her focused.

There was a door on the far side that hadn't been there
before. By Imogen's reckoning, it would have led to thin air.

"That's the way home," said Anna. She was sitting in a
plain wooden chair against the wall to Imogen's right. She
hadn't been there a moment before.

"And what happens if I walk through it?"

"If you try, I kill you."

"Or I kill you," Imogen returned.

"I don't think so. I was the one who should have lived."

Imogen had lost by hesitating before, so this time she took the first step. Anna rose from the chair, and then—she wasn't Anna anymore.

Mouse had said the longer a soul lacked a body, the harder it was to maintain a face. Now Imogen knew what the creature meant. The closest words she could come up with was that Anna melted and a *thing* took her place. It crouched like a dog, three legs on one side and two on the other. It shuffled side to side as if seeking shadows to hide from the sunlight, fading into translucence where the light was brightest. In fact, it looked as if it were made of shadows, with a melted head and two pits for eyes.

Imogen's first instinct was to scream and run, but desperation made her slash with the knife. It was an ungainly, awkward slice, but then she'd never fought like this before. The thing dodged, scuttling to the side in an unnatural crab-walk. It made a sound that was half a wail, half a savage snarl.

Imogen swore under her breath. The thing that was Anna was so hideous, Imogen couldn't figure out if it had an expression, much less what it looked like. Drool dripped from it, as if it was starving.

Maybe it was. The thing lunged, the shapeless gash of a mouth opened wide to show needle-sharp teeth. But Imogen was ready, and raised the knife, letting the misshapen thing skewer itself upon the point. The Anna-thing howled, struggling backward. The knife slid out with a slurp, something wet oozing over Imogen's knuckles. The substance— whatever it was—burned her with cold.

Imogen staggered back, her back bumping the embrasure of a window. It was a bad position, because there was no glass and the shutters were wide open. A fall would easily snap her neck. Something in the posture of the Anna-thing said she had come to the same conclusion. Imogen scooted to the side, her eyes glued to the remains of her twin.

When Anna lunged the next time, Imogen feinted to the side, slashing under one of the thing's limbs at what might have been ribs. It howled, lashing out with a clawed hand to rip open Imogen's back. White-hot fire ripped down her shoulders, sending her to her knees. Anna pounced, mouth gaping, but Imogen rolled away in the nick of time. After a lifetime of sickness, pain didn't slow her down.

Both sisters scrambled upright at the same time. "Let's end this," Imogen muttered, and this time she went on the attack.

Anna clearly wasn't expecting it. The knife slid smoothly into the creature's throat, burying itself to the hilt and growing icy to the touch. A terrified wheeze escaped Anna, and for the first time, Imogen saw the flicker of real emotion. It was pure, abject terror.

For the barest second, Imogen balked. But backing away meant surrendering all that she was. She *had* been the lucky one, but she had paid with nightmares and illness, never quite living for all that she had survived. But the evil dreams had been Anna invading her sleep, and without that drain on her soul, there was every chance she could live in good health.

"I have too much to live for." And Imogen ripped the knife free.

Anna screamed. So did Imogen. A sensation like a blanket of ice smashed into her as the other half of her twin's soul tore free. Agony blinded her as she fell to the hard floor, the knife still clutched in her hand. Anna was down, too, flailing and scrabbling at her throat as black ooze poured out. Imogen got to her hands and knees, crawling across Magnus's scrawled symbols, knowing she had to get home, but even more aware that she couldn't leave until Anna was finally dead.

The monstrous thing thrashed, the pits of its eyes growing even darker. Imogen rose to her knees, raised the knife in both hands, and thrust downward with all her strength. The blade scraped on bone, but slid to find the heart. There was a rending sound, and Anna stilled.

"Be at peace, sister," Imogen said softly.

She knelt there for a long time, at first solemn, and then too exhausted to move. A corner of her knew that she would never be the same. The shadow of what she'd just done would never leave her.

Most of her knew she would be a thousand times stronger. As Anna's tortured form dissolved, the room slowly faded back to the clock's interior. Only the mysterious door that had stood in the tower room's outer wall remained.

And she ached to go home. Imogen picked up Evelina's knife from the floor, thrusting it through the sash of her gown. The ticking had returned, driving Imogen to her feet. She was going to return to Hilliard House and push this blasted clock down the stairs.

Imogen opened the door homeward and stepped through.

And then she fell. At first it was hard to say if she fell down, or even if it was head or feet first, or if she spun in a whirlpool or just dropped like a stone. It was just blackness and falling and she wondered if she would ever reach the end. Leaving the clock was only that. She had yet to find her body. Panic began to squeeze her and she tried to cry out . . . but then she knew she wasn't alone—and for once that thought didn't fill her with dismay. Anna was gone.

Strong arms caught her and she automatically grabbed for balance. She was suddenly aware of broad shoulders and a muscular chest, and the warm, comfortable feeling of home.

"Hello," said Bucky. "I've come to take you home."

They were the best words she'd ever heard.

IMOGEN OPENED HER eyes to see Bucky asleep and snoring slightly, his head propped up on one hand, the other hand clutching hers. She felt slightly drugged, as if she'd forgotten how to move, or she would have done something about Mouse and Bird, who were chasing each other across the bed.

Ouch, stop catching my tail, you disgusting chicken.

As if you haven't caught my feathers in your nasty little rodent teeth.

She could still hear them! Mouse tackled Bird and they rolled over and over, tumbling over her knees.

"Thank you," she said softly.

"Hm?" Bucky came awake, blinking. And then he looked down, and met her eyes.

And grinned. It was the sweetest smile.

"Still waiting to marry me?" she asked, her voice scratchy with disuse.

He leaned down and gave her a kiss that any fairy-tale princess might have envied. Neither of them noticed Poppy as she peeked inside the door, and then quickly backed out again.

CHAPTER SIXTY-EIGHT

BANCROFT GLARED AT THE CAT SITTING ON HIS DESK. THE ragged yellow thing belonged to the cook, but keeping it in the kitchen was like catching smoke in a butterfly net and every so often it found its way here to deposit hair and paw prints across his private papers.

"Shoo," he said, waving a hand.

The cat rolled onto its back and admired the tiger's head on the wall as if it were its own reflection. Bancroft subsided into the leather armchair by the fire, too disheartened to argue, and put his head in his hands.

He should have been celebrating. The Baskervilles had won. There would be a procession and fireworks and speeches tomorrow. It would be a chance for the populace to admire their long-lost heir—and more to the point, it was time for Bancroft to collect his prize. Somewhere under the cat's filthy paws was an invitation to be part of Prince Edmond's household. If he played his cards right, the future held more. This was everything for which Bancroft had risked reputation, fortune, and life since the day he had left Austria and returned home.

And it tasted like ash. Oh, Adele had extended her congratulations, but he might have been the neighbor reporting that his bitch had whelped. Her mind was on other things and, to be honest, so was his. Everywhere he turned, everyone he spoke to had something more immediate to attend to than his elevation to the prince's retinue.

Imogen had returned to them, but with such a strange tale that he wondered if she was right in the head. The doctors proclaimed her in perfect health, but none of them could tell him if she had gone mad. Either she had, and it was a matter of time before she broke down utterly, or her twin really had dragged her inside Magnus's clock.

He wasn't sure which outcome he dreaded more, but he and Penner had dismantled the clock and burned it. The one positive outcome he could point to was that he seemed not to mind Bucky Penner half so much anymore, and the young man would marry Imogen as soon as it could be decently arranged.

And that would be as soon as they were out of mourning for Tobias. Bancroft leaned his head back against the thick padding of the chair, fighting the ache in his throat. It seemed like only yesterday that his son had stood in this very room, attempting to hide his idiot escapade with that mechanical squid he'd ridden into the opera. As if his own father hadn't known—but there were times when a parent had to pretend to be deaf and blind because that was the only way a child found his way. Not that Tobias ever had the least idea where he was going. But according to Alice, and the prince, and even Evelina Cooper, who had cried and cried when she had told the tale, he'd given his life so that they could go free. In the end, his son had been the hero Bancroft himself could never be.

His son had died in the Black Kingdom. There was another letter on the desk and under the cat and of a very different nature from the first. The Mercantile Fellowship of the Black Dragons of the Hidden Sea had written, and the letter was signed by Han Lo. All it said was, *The scales are balanced, the alchemy is done. That which dwells beneath the streets shall remain below. The kingdom remains in health.*

They were all phrases from the conversation they'd had about the coal. Han Lo had talked about the nature of the kingdom—alchemy, justice, and a lot of other drivel Bancroft had flushed from his mind the moment he'd walked out the door. But now he wished he'd paid attention. The Cooper girl had blathered something about the Black King's death releasing all manner of monsters aboveground, but Han Lo's letter seemed to contradict that. All Bancroft remembered was promising to do his utmost to supply the kingdom with whatever it needed to remain in good health. What could Tobias's death have achieved?

Unless it was simple revenge, as Han Lo's girl had threatened. Tobias for Han Zuiweng. A son for a son. That he could understand. Or perhaps he was inventing shadows where none walked.

The cat jumped down from the desk with a thump and trotted to the chair, yellow eyes watching him with far more personality than a cat should have. It bumped against his knee and Bancroft, glad the door to the study was closed and no one could see, reached down to scratch its ears.

Dragons, Han Lo, magic—it was all dust to him. The real truth sat like lead in Bancroft's stomach. Tobias was gone and all the court favor in the Empire couldn't bring him back. A moralist would point out that he'd paid too high a price for ambition.

And for once that moralist would be right.

London, October 26, 1889

BUCKINGHAM PALACE

2:30pm Saturday

"CAN YOU SEE anything?" Imogen demanded.

Evelina clung to the lamppost and teetered. She was standing with one foot on its blocky base, doing her best to see over the ocean of top hats and coiffures. It wasn't a ladylike stance, but the holiday atmosphere made it easy to forget good behavior. "I see them coming!"

She hopped down beside her friend. Imogen, like many of the women there, was dressed in black. Under normal circumstances, those in deepest mourning shunned the public eye, and right now many still did. Alice wasn't anywhere in sight. But these were hardly conventional times, and others had turned their grief to a defiant hope for the future. The streets around Buckingham Palace were jammed with crowds, all wanting a look at the new heir to the throne as he made his first winding procession through the London streets.

Peace finally reigned, and the city was slowly getting back to the regular business of living. Evelina had been terrified of the Black King's prediction that his death would mean packs of Wraiths—and who knew what else—roaming the streets, but none of that had happened. Nor had there been any magical disturbances once the war was over. There had been a few days of *something*—but that soon went away. Thankfully, the dragon had been wrong, and the magic of the kingdom had obviously somehow stabilized despite their terrible fight. It was safe to celebrate.

Imogen and Evelina had found places near the front of the pack, but there was still one row of people ahead of them—all of them tall. Fortunately, the day was cool and a little cloudy. With all the wool coats and fur collars hemming them in, it was a little bit like being stuffed into the back of a closet.

"You should be in that carriage with the prince," Imogen said, poking Evelina in the ribs. "I can't believe you declined his offer to be in the procession."

"I'll be at the banquet. That's quite enough." Evelina turned to her friend, her soul expanding with happiness to see Imogen awake and glowing with health. "I'm like Uncle Sherlock. I'd rather dispense with the accolades and get on with the next problem."

The truth was that she wanted to spend time with Imogen. She'd missed her friend deeply ever since they'd been separated more than a year and a half ago, and being at her side was worth all the applause in the world. And it only seemed right to share this moment with her friend; the last trip they'd taken to the palace was as debutantes to be presented to the queen. Coming here together, their grand adventures done, was closing a circle.

The thought brought Evelina a stab of melancholy. She'd danced with Tobias the night after her presentation. *So much has changed.* He should have been there, with Alice and Jeremy, rejoicing with the rest of them.

But her pensive mood receded a little when Imogen rose up on her toes, craning her neck. "Is that them?"

Evelina hopped back onto the lamppost, narrowly avoiding the elbow of another bystander. A woman was selling hot cider from a steam-driven cart, and the tangy scent of it hung heavy in the air. Evelina was tempted to wave the woman down when a flash of scarlet caught her eye. She looked up to see Prince Edmond's triumphal procession gradually coming closer. "Yes, it is!"

At first all she saw were mounted guardsmen in their bright-red coats, and then the four black horses pulling the carriage, the brass of their harnesses polished bright as gold. But as they drew closer, they turned the corner and Evelina saw the prince waving from the open carriage just yards away. Edgerton, Smythe, and Mycroft were seated with him, proving how firmly Edmond was standing by his old friends. Flanking the carriage were a number of other riders, including Nick on a large gray stallion. Evelina smiled, thinking how much he must have enjoyed a chance to ride that magnificent steed.

"I don't think Captain Niccolo is having any reservations," Imogen said slyly. "I think he rather likes the attention. And he does look fine in a uniform."

Evelina flushed at her friend's teasing look. "He deserves his share of applause."

And he did look particularly handsome in the uniform of the prince's household. The public was clearly besotted with the dashing pirate rogues who had come to their rescue, and roared with approval whenever Nick raised his hat to the people. There was already talk of a statue to the brave Captain Roberts.

Queen Victoria had insisted on a ride in the *Athena,* which had been repaired and restored to good humor. Today the elderly monarch would be waiting at Buckingham Palace for the speech and banquet part of the proceedings. By all reports she found her youngest son an agreeable if unconventional young man and had set about grooming him for the position of heir to the throne. The fact that Edmond had the former prince consort's interest in science and economics had raised him in her estimation.

Evelina saw Edmond lean forward to say something to one of the outriders, who then shouted a command she couldn't make out. The horses came to a halt with a snort. The crowd hailed their excitement, pushing forward. Evelina jumped down again, grasping Imogen's hand so they didn't lose each other in the milling sea of people. But good fortune was finally with her as the two men in front parted just enough to grant her a clear view.

Prince Edmond stood, raising his hands for quiet. Like a single beast, the crowd fell into an eager silence. He looked around a moment, and for the first time Evelina noticed that he wasn't wearing the tinted glasses. The change was subtle but significant, as if she could finally see him properly. He spotted her in the crowd and gave her a quick grin, but then settled his features into a serious expression.

"I know all of you have sacrificed," he said, parting his hands to embrace the sea of people. "All have struggled. Many have suffered irreparable losses."

Imogen gave a pained sound. Somehow Edmond heard it, because his bright blue gaze fixed on her with a look of honest sympathy. "It is with the greatest humility that I stand here today, because we have all paid this price. This, you and I share."

Evelina thought of the empty cavern that was Tobias's grave. He had struggled to avoid the war, hated the fact that he had built so many lethal machines. Had giving his life to save his loved ones balanced the scales for that brief moment before everything went dark? Evelina felt her throat closing with tears again, and bit her lip to keep it from trembling. *If only I had been able to save him!*

Edmond dropped his arms, giving a slight shrug. "I know you as I know myself. I didn't grow up in a palace. I've eaten at your tables and slept beneath your roofs, and I know what it means if the price of bread rises or the price of wool falls." He nodded, and then his voice began to grow stronger. "I know the shackles you threw off and I know why you did it. And I share in your pride in overcoming those impossible odds. Triumph belongs to us all!"

The crowd cheered in approval and a striped scarf landed on the prince's head, tossed by an enthusiast. He peeled it off and waved it like a flag. The scarf had become something of his unofficial symbol, and half the people there wore one.

"I know what you want me to do," said Edmond in a clear, carrying voice. "You want me to find a way to prosperity, but you want me to find the right way, the way of justice and foresight. You want today's dreams to sink deep roots so that in twice ten thousand tomorrows, our great-grandchildren can hold their heads high in pride."

He wound the scarf around his neck with a flourish. "Your wish is my command, because I serve every one of you. And I ask you—the heroes of this battle—to continue to serve, not just for glory or gain, but for the love of home and Empire."

Imogen blinked rapidly, as if chasing away tears. "I hope Father takes that part to heart," she murmured in Evelina's ear.

Evelina looked around, wondering where Lord Bancroft was. He'd been offered a post in the prince's administration, but hadn't accepted yet. After striving so long for just such a position, his hesitation showed how much the last few weeks had shaken even him. Evelina put an arm around her friend, glad to be able to offer at least the comfort of touch.

It was then she noticed that Nick was looking straight at her. He sat easily on the gray stallion, wearing the bright uniform with its gold and silver braid as if he had been born to it. But it was his eyes that arrested her, dark and smoking with possessive hunger. The look ignited her as quickly as match to tinder. Evelina dragged her gaze away, her cheeks blazing despite the cool air. She swallowed hard, her mouth suddenly dry as paper.

Edmond was still talking, his words muddling together in her distracted mind. She forced herself to pay attention. A handsome pair of eyes shouldn't rob her memories of one of the Empire's great moments—at least not for more than a few thudding heartbeats!

"And when I say that we must love the Empire, I mean *all* the Empire, for while the throne is the embodiment of human invention, heart, and wisdom, it is but one half of a timeless equation. The other half is the soul of the land itself."

Edmond paused, seeming to gather himself. "And when I say the land, many of you say magic, and that invokes the specter of the Steam Council's greatest injustice. Those with designs to plunder the fields and woods, the wild places and even the farmlands have long pursued a campaign of fear and superstition. They have taken what is natural and given it a demon's face, bid us shun it, and threatened any who would call it friend."

A low murmur ran though the crowd, but Edmond raised a hand again for silence.

"And yet the land forgave us. There is not one among you who does not know how the devas rose and defended us against our common enemy. It is past time we extend our hands in gratitude and partnership, and make room for all—city, country, factory, and field. We have been shown what the devas can do, what machine and magic can accomplish together."

Evelina's heart lifted. She had released the devas from their bonds, but many had stayed to help build and restore the factories in a way that wouldn't destroy the land.

"The spirits offer us limitless power we can all enjoy. Power does not belong to a select few, or to those with gold, but to every citizen whether they are human or not. In partnership, we can raise the Empire to untold heights of achievement and prosperity!"

The people all around her began shouting approval, pumping their fists and flinging hats and scarves into the air. Evelina and Imogen cheered with the rest, pleased with their new prince, relieved to be delivered once and for all from the steam barons, and determined that so much sacrifice would never be wasted. Evelina's cheeks were wet, but she wasn't sure when she'd started to cry. She clapped and shouted and hugged Imogen, and then hugged the lady behind her even though they were complete strangers.

Euphoria swept her, and with it came the realization that finally she was in a world that accepted—no, *needed*—the balance of magic and machine she'd been trying to achieve all her life. There would be no more burnings, no more laboratories, and no more hiding. At long last, there would be harmony.

She met Nick's eyes again and he gave a slow, sensual grin, as if he knew just what she was thinking. Once they'd had to live apart because the combination of their magic might have betrayed them as magic users, but now their powers were welcomed. The incredible beauty of the silver fire they made together was private, but it, too, would have a place free from danger. She and Nick finally had a secure future.

Even the darkness in her magic had its place. She had deeply feared that power, but experience had taught her its true nature. Evelina had needed its strength to fight, but she'd always used it to protect the ones she loved. She had failed against the dragon, but it wasn't because she'd lacked courage or selflessness—those tests she'd passed. And they'd revealed that the darkness was her weapon, not her master.

Light-headed with elation, Evelina danced where she stood, reaching skyward as if she might suddenly start to fly. Imogen grabbed her, sharing in her bounding joy. "I don't think I've ever seen you this happy!" Imogen shouted above the din.

Evelina threw back her head, laughing up to the sun. "I've been holding my breath for so long! Hiding. And now it's over!"

But the celebration abruptly ended when a great baying rang through the streets, as deep and haunting as an ancient bell. The cheering crowd fell silent, the only sound a collective gasp of terror.

"Damnation, what was that?" a man behind her muttered.

And then to the north the people began to move, a shuffle in the packed mass becoming a wedge of clear space. An electric prickle announced the presence of magic, and the silence around her rippled with anxious whispers.

Then she saw the massive red-eyed hound padding through the empty avenue between the people, heading straight for the prince with a determined but unhurried step. But it stopped beside Evelina a moment. The dog regarded her steadily, and once more she recognized the ancient power within it; the spirit of the moors had found a vessel in the laboratory's prized creation.

She heard Imogen's intake of breath, and put a hand on her friend's arm. She wasn't sure what the dog would do if someone startled it with a scream.

So we meet once again, sister, it said. This time, there was mischief in its expression, almost as if it enjoyed watching the humans squirm.

"Why are you here?" Evelina asked it, startled that it had called her sister. Yet it was true that those of the Blood, like her and Nick, owed much to the spirit realm. If nothing else, their magic was related.

To greet the one who would be king, as he has acknowledged us. We have waited many a year to breathe the air of a just reign.

Evelina could smell the grassy wilderness of the moors as the words sounded in her head. Suddenly she was back there under that vast, open sky. "You protected him in the battle."

The land owes fealty to its king. Besides, he grew up in our neighborhood. With that, the hound trotted forward, its shoulder brushing her hand as it passed. The fur was as warm and soft as any dog, but left a tingle of magic behind.

Imogen crowded close to look, her earring brushing Evelina's cheek. "What *is* that thing?"

"I think it's like Mouse and Bird."

"Really?" Imogen sounded unconvinced. "It's a little bit larger."

"But strangely, less grumpy."

"That's not hard," Imogen grumbled, but Evelina smiled. The two devas had bonded with her friend and refused to leave Hilliard House. Their devotion pleased Evelina no end, since she knew they would look after one another long into the future.

Several of the outriders, Nick included, drew their weapons as the hound approached, but Edmond held up a hand to stop them. Evelina could see by the set of his shoulders that the prince was tense, but he still opened the carriage door and jumped down, landing a few feet away from the dog.

The hound sat at his feet, not with the subservience of a true dog with its master, but more as one equal greeting another. The prince removed his top hat and gave a respectful bow.

Imogen leaned close to whisper. "Doesn't the hound of the Baskervilles terrify the family members to death? Or did Dr. Watson make that up?"

The story had originally been a ruse to get Evelina to the moors so that she could go free. In an odd, convoluted way, it had worked far more profoundly than anyone could have predicted. "Stories sometimes develop a life of their own," she replied softly, watching the terrifying creature give a wag of its tail. Like her dark magic, its power could protect as well as destroy. "And sometimes the things that terrify you turn out to be your best friend."

A murmur went up as the hound lifted a massive paw. With a bemused expression, Prince Edmond shook it.

CHAPTER SIXTY-NINE

London, October 26, 1889

PORTMORE HOTEL

9:10 p.m. Saturday

THE GRATEFUL PRINCE HAD GIVEN NICK TWO THINGS: THE entire crew of the *Athena* was pardoned of its piratical past, and Nick was granted the best rooms at the Portmore Hotel until he decided where he wanted to call home. Officially Evelina was staying at Baker Street, but she'd been at the hotel just as much as at her uncle's. Holmes had been patient about playing chaperone, but tonight he'd given up and gone down to the common room for a pint, leaving the couple to their own devices. Evelina was grateful.

Nick looked at home lounging on the sofa of the hotel suite's parlor, but then, like a cat, he looked at home everywhere. Evelina stood at the window, studying him as he read an official-looking document. He'd shed his coat and his olive skin looked dark against the white of his shirt.

He raised his eyes, and they were bright with amusement. "His Princeliness has seen fit to solve the bureaucratic difficulty of my surname. Or lack thereof."

"Excuse me?" Evelina scoffed. "Isn't Captain Niccolo, Terror of the Skies, good enough?"

"He has officially declared me to be Nicholas Baskerville."

"That has a nice ring." She sat down on the sofa next to him, trying not to think of Dr. Watson's hound. "And it implies that he considers you to be family."

"As long as I don't get stuck in that bloody great hall of theirs," he grumbled, but she could tell he was pleased.

It turned out that Nick had a stack of papers from the hands of the prince's new secretarial staff. Evelina tapped the top sheet. "What's this one?"

"An official appointment. It's for both of us. He wants us to talk it over and let him know whether it suits us."

"An official appointment?" She frowned, propping herself up on her elbow. "What is it?"

"I would rather you'd been there when he explained it," Nick said apologetically.

"It's all right. I was with Imogen all afternoon, and that's exactly where I needed to be."

He nodded. "It seems that Edmond sees trouble ahead."

"Where from?"

"The Steam Council had allies and they aren't pleased with the new order. He wants someone he trusts to look into this and that."

"This and that?" Evelina asked dryly.

"The sort of enemies that might require a steamspinner packed with clever pirates and one very mighty sorceress to solve."

Evelina looked away. As intriguing as the offer sounded, her failure to save Tobias still stung. "I feel less than mighty."

"After all you did?" Nick asked gently. "You blew the bollocks off half the dirigibles in the Empire."

She gave a short, bitter laugh. "At first I worried about being too strong and becoming a monster. And now I'm crushed because I wasn't powerful enough to save a good friend. I should have saved Tobias, Nick. I should have . . ."

"Played with life and death?" Nick sat back, visibly working through his answer. "What more could you have done? All this means is that you're still completely human. You don't have every answer, Evelina. And if you still have something to learn, you have a reason to get out of bed in the morning."

She bit her lip, releasing an unhappy breath. He was right,

of course—but that didn't take the ache away. "Do you mind that I miss him?"

"I'd worry more if you didn't." He put a finger under her chin and kissed her forehead.

Tobias had possessed every advantage, and Nick nothing. The fact that he could be generous said a lot about who Nick was. "I love you."

He gave the prince's document a flick. "Fancy trying your hand at espionage?"

She settled back, leaning her head on his shoulder. "Are you sure you want to give up being a pirate?"

"It would be no fun without the steam barons, and Edmond's a nice enough bloke."

"All right, then."

Even though she didn't look up, she could feel Nick's grin. She'd guessed he wanted to do it. It was the sort of thing he was made for. She straightened up just enough that they were face-to-face. His dark eyes looked liquid in the low light, and Evelina felt that familiar melting sensation she got when she was with him. Any moment now, she would dissolve into a puddle just from wanting him so much.

"But none of it means anything unless you're with me," he said, picking up yet another piece of paper and dangling it in front of her face.

She took it and held it up to read. "A special license. For marriage. For us!"

"We will marry, you and I," he said with a sly grin.

Evelina's heart stopped. Suddenly, it felt as if she had no limbs, no body at all. The only part of her that remained was her stuttering, astonished pulse. She supposed it was natural, with more missions in their future, but somewhere along the way she'd lost all notion of something so normal as becoming a wife.

"Will we, Captain Niccolo?" Her voice was barely above a whisper. She wasn't even sure if the words were a challenge or squeak of surprise. "Shouldn't that be framed as a question?"

His eyebrows quirked mischievously. "We'll do it properly, in the eyes of the law, the Church, and any other rules they can dream up. Then everyone will know we belong together."

Evelina reeled. She wanted to marry him—of course she did! But there was the dark magic, and Magnus, and . . . Her thoughts trailed off. Nick's energy was growing sharp as he waited for her to say something. Nick, who saw everything she was but still wanted her. More than that, he wanted her *because* of everything she was. He would keep her true to herself, but he would never hold her back.

"Well?" he asked, the word barely more than a movement of air.

Evelina closed her eyes. *He wants me to be his wife.* The sheer rightness of it melted her like chocolate—the dark, sweet, rich perfection of the moment made her sway with all the giddy girlishness she would have felt had Nick prostrated himself in full dress uniform on a ballroom floor. But a pirate was a pirate, and he had asked for her hand and her partnership on their next mission in the same breath. That made it real, part of his life and not some fantasy from the pages of a book—and that gave a pinch of spice to all that sweetness.

"Marry me, Evelina," he asked giving her his best and most scorching gaze. "Please."

She couldn't bear to make him wait, however much she would have liked time to savor the moment.

"I will," she said firmly. "I will be your wife."

She heard his breath escape in a relieved huff. Had he really thought she would refuse him? *Ridiculous man.*

As he leaned in for a kiss, Evelina cradled the special license against her chest, suddenly anxious in case it was creased. "Careful with that."

"You know I'm careful as a surgeon and just as precise." And he kissed her urgently, pulling her close until she heard crinkling paper.

"Wait!" she squeaked, trying to rescue the license from getting squashed between them.

He lifted his head. "What?"

She gave him a crooked smile. "When shall we marry?"

Nick chuckled, a sound that rumbled from his chest through

her body in pleasant and interesting ways. "How soon can you find a dress?"

London, October 27, 1889
CAVENDISH SQUARE

2:35 a.m. Sunday

THE DOOR TO the bedroom opened and Tobias slipped in silently, his shadow a tall grotesque playing along the wall. The curtain was open, and moonlight flooded the bedroom, falling softly on the cradle where Jeremy slept. He considered shutting out the light to make sure it didn't wake his son, but then he wouldn't have been able to see as well. He wasn't one of the Wraiths, who could navigate in perfect blackness.

He gazed down at the boy, losing himself in relief. There wasn't a mark on the baby's perfectly smooth skin. Wherever Keating had hidden Jeremy and his nurse, the child had suffered no physical harm. That was something to be thankful for—as was the fact that the Gold King would never trouble them again.

Tobias reached down with his left hand and tucked the blanket close under his son's chin. Peace seemed to radiate from the tiny form. That boneless, absolute rest was something Tobias would never feel again. *Sleep well and dream fair, little man.*

He heard the footfall in the doorway too late.

"What . . . ?" It was Alice's voice. He froze, suddenly uncertain what to do. It was the middle of the night, long after she should have been asleep. This wasn't going according to plan.

His wife stood in the nursery door, clad only in her nightdress. She looked tiny and childlike, too young to be mother to the boy sleeping in the cradle. Tobias drew back a step, knowing he had no business being there. As far as the world above the streets was concerned, she was a widow. It was kinder if they all went on thinking it.

"Tobias!" Alice whispered, but it sounded loud in the darkened room.

He stepped away from the cradle, afraid that if he answered he would wake Jeremy. "Hush."

She tilted her face up to him, the moonlight reflecting bright in her tear-filled eyes. Dazzled, Tobias searched for what to say.

"Am I dreaming?" she asked.

No, but I'm having a nightmare.

"I saw you dead!" she said more firmly, and Jeremy stirred in his sleep.

He put a finger over her lips, feeling their petal-soft warmth. Her breath feathered over his skin. She retreated into the hallway, walking backward, never taking her eyes from him. He followed and closed the nursery door behind him. At once, he stepped into the shadows, instinct making him hide.

Her eyes were wide, and with a wrench of his heart, he saw fear there. But Alice raised her chin, hands closing into fists. "How is it even possible that you're here?" She was no longer whispering, but her voice was low and angry. "Why didn't you send a message that you were still alive?"

A message? His brain rocked slightly. It sounded so . . . normal. "We can't argue outside Mrs. Polwarren's door."

"She quit." Alice bit the words off, her chin trembling.

The detail raked at him. Already things were happening in his home that he had no idea about—yet another piece of himself sliding away.

"Tobias, please!"

"I died," he said, the words blunt and brutal.

She flinched. "But you're here."

He remained silent a moment, sifting through events he didn't fully comprehend. In her struggle to save him, Evelina had bound him to the Black Kingdom, and that power had called his name when it needed another king. But how could he explain that to Alice? "The Wraiths found me and put me back together as best they could. I had no choice about it."

No choice, and a lot of horror. Things he tried to forget as he was reassembled, bit by bit in painful and intimate ways. But he gave the simple explanation, the one Alice required. She didn't need to know how the poison had done its work, or the dragon's teeth, and what couldn't be reconstituted from blood and dirt and dragon. Even magic—the magic he hated—could only do so much. And the fact that he was more magic than human had bound him to the underground in ways beyond number.

The Wraiths were his now. He was the Black Kingdom's master, but still it leashed him. He was too new yet to wander far, and it was already tugging at him, impatient for his return. But thank the dark powers that his wife didn't see that. And that at first glance, he looked the same. She had already suffered too much. Perhaps he could convince her this was a dream after all.

"My father is dead," Alice murmured. "Jeremy is all I have now."

That was all she said, but he heard the anger and sorrow. Keating had deserved what he got at Evelina's hands, but that would never stop his daughter from grieving his loss—strained though their love had been. *My poor Alice.*

A tendril of hair curled over her cheek, and Tobias reached out to brush it away. His right arm moved smoothly, but the faint whirr of gears gave it away, stopping just short of her face. He saw her look of surprise, and then . . . her recoil stabbed him to the core.

Alice started to tremble, her gaze sliding to the fingers hovering near her face. Her eyes widened as the truth soaked in. "Tobias?"

Not all of him was as it had been. And in that moment, he hated Evelina for condemning him to this. "I should have stayed dead." He closed his eyes, his heart too full and aching to bear the sight of his wife. He wanted her with all the fervent need of a man for his woman, but there was so much more to it than that. He had found out too late what she meant to him.

He forced his eyes open, and maybe she saw the truth there, because she reached out—but he stepped beyond her grasp. If he was going to survive this, he had to harden his heart. Otherwise, Alice would break it with her gentle touch. "I'm not what I was. That doesn't mean I don't love you, and that doesn't mean that I won't watch over you and our son."

She drew herself up. "Don't be ridiculous. Don't ask me to forget you."

There was no chance he would forget her. His need for Alice had only been intensified by his ordeal. Every sense was new and more than humanly sharp. The smell and sight of his wife might have been familiar, but it was as if he had never truly noticed her fragility or the sweetness of her scent.

But wanting and having were not the same. He wasn't what he had been—and it would be folly to forget that for even an instant. Without another word, he turned away from her, descending the stairs with the silence of a shadow.

"Tobias?" Alice cried.

Defiance flared in him. This was his house. He should have been able to stay. Part of him had been that dragon in the depths, and it didn't take denial well. Whatever he was— maker, man, or monster—the Schoolmaster wasn't the only new Royal in London and he meant to take back what was his. But then more of him knew that wouldn't be simple, because everything was different now. He was different.

And so much around him needed to change, because London's underground citizens were weary of languishing beneath the streets. There were possibilities in that discontent.

One day soon Tobias would return to the daylight world, but it would be on his own terms. When he had healed enough. When he was powerful enough. And he wouldn't come alone.

"I am the Black King," he said, his voice rough. "No one forgets me."

CHAPTER SEVENTY

HOLMES STOOD ALONE IN THE BAKER STREET STUDY. WAT-
son had already gone up the stairs to his bedroom, nearly
stupefied with fatigue. War and cholera had taxed London's
hospitals to the breaking point, a bizarre counterpoint to the
wild celebration of Prince Edmond's victorious return. The
horror and ecstasy were both real and both valid, and they
were also both hell on one's constitution.

Outside, half the streetlights were still broken, but the few
that were lit showed the fog curling through the streets on
cat feet. With meditative weariness he filled his pipe with
shag tobacco, then lit it, puffing smoke in meditative gusts
to create his own indoor London Particular.

Despite the hour, there was a light step on the stairs, and
he hurried to open the study door. "Evelina."

She stood with her head slightly bowed. "Uncle Sherlock?"

He'd anticipated this visit. A wave of sadness tugged at
him, and he turned away, sweeping his hand toward the
room. "Pray, come in. No doubt you have come to tell me
that you are running away with pirates."

She entered, every footfall hesitant. She was plainly
dressed now, her hair tied back with a velvet ribbon. It made
her look younger. "We are married. It's not quite the same
thing."

"I do seem to recall a ceremony." He should, since he'd given her away. "And now you begin work for the prince?"

"It's as good a way as any to see the world." She gave a sly smile. "You'd probably enjoy it."

He'd already had to stifle that particular stab of envy. *That is youth, leaving the rest of us behind.* He waved an arm in mock drama. "Send me postcards."

"Uncle!"

"A sentient ship and a dozen scallywags are sure to find some adventure." Holmes fell into his basket chair, stretching out his legs. Everything in the room was comfortable and familiar—his racks of chemicals, the chaos of his desk, Watson's walking stick leaning against the door.

And Evelina. He hadn't intended to enjoy his role of guardian, but he'd grown used to seeing her there, and he wasn't sure he was ready to give her up. "You are quite resigned to leaving college?"

Embarrassment reddened her cheeks. "I'm afraid they expelled me."

"Ah." He shrugged. "Too many explosions will do that."

She shuddered faintly. "Among other transgressions. I believe there were assignments long overdue. At least I won't have to write that essay about Tacitus."

"And thus your academic career ends in tatters. I can't say that I'm sorry to see you leave that place. No one has heard from Professor Moriarty, but I imagine that it is only a matter of time before he shows himself once more." Holmes searched for words, not liking any he found. Time was slipping through his fingers. Hadn't she just been presented to the queen? "When will you be back?"

She arched an eyebrow. "I'm not sure. For Imogen's wedding, certainly. I trust you'll make time for a visit then?"

He hid a smile behind his pipe. "I might allow myself to be imposed upon, providing that I am not in the middle of a case. However, I think you owe your grandmother a visit. She is beside herself that you married in such haste and has naturally put the worst interpretation on the matter."

"Really!"

"Perhaps I should introduce your Niccolo to your grandmamma?" Holmes said with malicious intent. "Arrange for a pleasant luncheon?"

"Don't you dare!" Her eyes widened in mock horror. "No man deserves that! The last time she grew upset over lunch she threatened you with a pickle fork."

"Make it tea, then, with no cutlery." He allowed himself a chuckle, but stopped as her expression grew serious. "What is it?"

She twisted her hands in her lap, a restless gesture he knew well. "Uncle, whenever you and I have these discussions, there are always unanswered questions. Are there any threads left dangling this time?"

If she was asking that, then things hadn't changed as much as he'd thought. Suddenly, everything seemed better. "Of course there are, my girl. Loose threads are the very essence of life."

She made an encouraging gesture. "Anything specific?"

Holmes considered. Despite his yearning to keep her close, there was nothing he wanted to share. For now, their roads led away from one another. "You, my dear, are about to leave on the adventure of your life. Go, and be joyful. Leave the dangling threads for me."

Evelina's mouth quirked. "Thank you."

"Whatever for?"

"If I tried to list it all I would be here until dawn."

"Then please do not attempt it," he said briskly, dodging an uncharacteristic urge to wax sentimental. "I have to finish this pipe and ponder a small matter that has caught my attention."

Quick as always to read his mood, Evelina rose. She stood on her toes and kissed his cheek.

"Go, my girl," he said irritably.

With her customary grace, Evelina quietly turned and left before the ache in his throat could betray him.

A cab had been waiting for her. He guessed this was her last stop before boarding the airship, and she would be gone by morning. For an instant he thought about his sister, Marianne, and wondered what she would have made of her extraordinary girl.

And then Holmes lit his pipe once more. The smoke curled around him as he let his mind drift, sliding over new problems with a connoisseur's sure touch. The dragon had died and the underworld was restless. In the last few days, rumors of a new king had sprouted up like the first breath of spring—one that was young and filled with new ideas. It was startling news, and the fact that Holmes had learned it at all was significant. The Black Kingdom had always kept its distance from the world aboveground. Few knew exactly what dwelt below.

He had a disturbing notion that wouldn't be the case anymore.